S0-ACL-325

STORY

The Fiction of the Forties

STORY

The Fiction of the Forties

AS EDITED BY

WHIT BURNETT & HALLIE BURNETT

EDITORS OF *Story*

NEW YORK · 1949

E. P. DUTTON & CO., INC.

FIRST EDITION

A Story Press Book

CONTENTS

ACKNOWLEDGMENTS

THE EDITORS OF *Story* WISH TO EXPRESS THEIR GRATITUDE FOR THE courteous permission of the publishers to whom *Story* assigned copyrights, to the authors and to the literary agents whose cooperation have made this book possible. All of the material originally appeared in issues of *Story*, many of the stories being the first printed work of their authors. Copyright acknowledgment is made as follows:

Archibald, J. William: *CONVERSATION BY THE SEA*. Reprinted by permission of the editors of *Story*, the author and the author's agent, David Lloyd. Copyright by Story Magazine, Inc., 1945.

Bunin, Ivan: *THE CALLING CARDS*. Reprinted by permission of the editors of *Story* and the author. Copyright by Story Magazine, Inc., 1948.

Burnett, Hallie Southgate: *THE LITTLE TROUT*. Reprinted by permission of the editors of *Story* and the author. Copyright by Story Magazine, Inc., 1943.

Burnett, Whit: *DESPERATE SCENERY*. Reprinted by permission of the editors of *Story* and the author. Copyright by Story Magazine, Inc., 1944.

Caldwell, Erskine: *THE WINDFALL*. Reprinted by permission of the editors of *Story* and the author through Maxim Lieber. Copyright by Story Magazine, Inc., 1942.

Callaghan, Morley: *VERY SPECIAL SHOES*. Reprinted by permission of the editors of *Story* and the author through Harold Matson. Copyright by Story Magazine, Inc., 1943.

Capote, Truman: *MY SIDE OF THE MATTER*. Reprinted by permission of the editors of *Story*, the author and Random House through Saxe Commins. Copyright by Story Magazine, Inc., 1945; copyright by Random House, 1948.

Coleman, Richard: *THE INFAMOUS MANSION*. Reprinted by permission of the editors of *Story* and the author through Alan Collins of Curtis Brown, Ltd. Copyright by Story Magazine, Inc., 1947.

Conner, Rearden: *THE TWO CRANES*. Reprinted by permission of the editors of *Story* and the author. Copyright by Story Magazine, Inc., 1948.

Cross, Joseph: *EXCHANGE OF MEN*. Reprinted by permission of the editors of *Story* and the author through Margot Johnson of A. & S. Lyons, Inc. Copyright by Story Magazine, Inc., 1946.

D'Agostino, Guido: *THE DREAM OF ANGELO ZARA*. Reprinted by permission of the editors of *Story* and the author. Copyright by Story Magazine, Inc., 1942.

Denny, Alma: *SCHMUEL SAVES THE SCHULE*. Reprinted by permission of the editors of *Story* and the author. Copyright by Story Magazine, Inc., 1947.

Dinelli, Mel: *THE MAN*. Reprinted from *Story*, May-June 1945, by permission of the editors of *Story* and the author. Copyright by Story Magazine, Inc., 1945.

Domino, Ruth: *THE WONDERFUL WHITE PAPER*. Reprinted by permission of the editors of *Story* and the author through the Nicholas Freydberg Agency. Copyright by Story Magazine, Inc., 1943.

Farnham, Alice: *THE SONG THE SOLDIERS SANG*. Reprinted by permission of the editors of *Story* and the author through Harry Altshuler. Copyright by Story Magazine, Inc., 1944.

Faulkner, William: *MY GRANDMOTHER MILLARD AND GENERAL BEDFORD FORREST AND THE BATTLE OF HARRYKIN CREEK*. Reprinted by permission of the editors of *Story* and the author through Harold Ober. Copyright by Story Magazine, Inc., 1943.

Fifield, William: *THE LIFE OF THE HUNTED*. Reprinted by permission of the editors of *Story* and the author. Copyright by Story Magazine, Inc., 1946.

Foff, Arthur: *SAWDUST*. Reprinted by permission of the editors of *Story* and the author. Copyright by Story Magazine, Inc., 1947.

Gizycka, Felicia: *BEAUTIFUL SUMMER IN NEWPORT.* Reprinted by permission of the editors of *Story* and the author through McIntosh and Otis, Inc. Copyright by Story Magazine, Inc., 1947.

Goodwin, John B. L.: *THE COCOON.* Reprinted by permission of the editors of *Story* and the author through Mavis McIntosh of A. & S. Lyons, Inc. Copyright by Story Magazine, Inc., 1946.

Graves, Wallace: *TATTOO.* Reprinted by permission of the editors of *Story* and the author. Copyright by Story Magazine, Inc., 1944.

Gross, Edwin A.: *THE RETURN.* Reprinted by permission of the editors of *Story* and the author. Copyright by Story Magazine, Inc., 1945.

Gustafsson, Evelyn: *THE OPEN-MINDED PAGLEIGHS.* Reprinted by permission of the editors of *Story* and the author. Copyright by Story Magazine, Inc., 1947.

Hewlett, John: *THE RUSSIAN GESTURE.* Reprinted by permission of the editors of *Story* and the author. Copyright by Story Magazine, Inc., 1945.

Hughes, Langston: *ON THE WAY HOME.* Reprinted by permission of the editors of *Story* and the author through Maxim Lieber. Copyright by Story Magazine, Inc., 1946.

Kauffmann, Stanley: *FULVOUS YELLOW.* Reprinted by permission of the editors of *Story* and the author through Mary Pritchett-Barbara Brandt. Copyright by Story Magazine, Inc., 1948.

Langdon, John: *THE GIRLS OF TONGATABU.* Reprinted by permission of the editors of *Story* and the author. Copyright by Story Magazine, Inc., 1944.

Lewiton, Mina: *THE CHRISTMAS STAR.* Reprinted by permission of the editors of *Story* and the author. Copyright by Story Magazine, Inc., 1945.

McCleary, Dorothy: *TAKING OUT UNCLE MONTAGUE.* Reprinted by permission of the editors of *Story* and the author. Copyright by Story Magazine, Inc., 1945.

McCune, Helen: *SEEDLING.* Reprinted by permission of the editors of *Story* and the author through Faustina Orner Associates. Copyright by Story Magazine, Inc., 1947.

Mailer, Norman K.: *THE GREATEST THING IN THE WORLD.* Reprinted by permission of the editors of *Story* from *Story*, Nov.-Dec. 1941, and by permission of Charles Rembar, attorney for the author. Copyright by Story Magazine, Inc., 1941.

March, William: *I BROKE MY BACK ON A ROSEBUD.* Reprinted by permission of the editors of *Story* and the author through Harold Ober. Copyright by Story Magazine, Inc., 1944.

Modesto, John: *PATCHES ON MY PANTS.* Reprinted by permission of the editors of *Story* and the author. Copyright by Story Magazine, Inc., 1948.

Molnar, Ferenc: *MR. NAB.* Reprinted by permission of the editors of *Story*, the author and his agent, Franz J. Horch. Copyright by Story Magazine, Inc., 1942.

Murtagh, Leo Dillon: *THE APOTHEOSIS OF FRANCIS JAMES O'DONOVAN.* Reprinted by permission of the editors of *Story* and the author. Copyright by Story Magazine, Inc., 1944.

Norton, Mary: *PAUL'S TALE.* Reprinted by permission of the editors of *Story* and the author through Harold Ober. Copyright by Story Magazine, Inc., 1945.

O'Flaherty, Liam: *TWO LOVELY BEASTS.* Reprinted by permission of the editors of *Story*, the author and his agent, Jacques Chambrun. Copyright by Story Magazine, Inc., 1947.

Payne, Robert: *THE GREEN PALMS.* Reprinted by permission of the editors of *Story* and the author through Mary Pritchett-Barbara Brandt. Copyright by Story Magazine, Inc., 1947.

Phillips, James Atlee: *THE DELEGATE FROM EVERYWHERE.* Reprinted by permission of *Story* and the author through Willis Kingsley Wing. Copyright by Story Magazine, Inc., 1945.

Prokosch, Frederic: *THE FLAMINGOS.* Reprinted by permission of the editors of *Story* and the author through William Morris Agency. Copyright by Story Magazine, Inc., 1946.

Ross, Fred E.: *THE UNBOWED HEAD.* Reprinted by permission of the editors of *Story* and the author. Copyright by Story Magazine, Inc., 1947.

Salinger, J. D.: *THE LONG DEBUT OF LOIS TAGGETT.* Reprinted by permission of the editors of *Story* and the author through Harold Ober. Copyright by Story Magazine, Inc., 1942.

Selman, Jerome: *A SWORD FOR SERENA.* Reprinted by permission of the editors of *Story* and the author. Copyright by Story Magazine, Inc., 1945.

Shandeling, A. E.: *RETURN OF THE GRIFFINS.* Reprinted by permission of the editors of *Story* and the author. Copyright by Story Magazine, Inc., 1948.

Stuart, Jesse: *THE CHAMPION.* Reprinted by permission of the editors of *Story* and the author. Copyright by Story Magazine, Inc., 1941.

Thompson, Freda: *BLUE BIRD.* Reprinted by permission of the editors of *Story* and the author. Copyright by Story Magazine, Inc., 1945.

Umland, Rudolph: *HOW BEAUTIFUL THE SUN ON THE MOUNTAINS.* Reprinted by permission of the editors of *Story* and the author. Copyright by Story Magazine, Inc., 1944.

Urquhart, Fred: *DIRTY MINNIE.* Reprinted by permission of the editors of *Story* and the author. Copyright by Story Magazine, Inc., 1943.

Vatsek, Joan: *The VIGIL OF BROTHER FERNANDO.* Reprinted by permission of the editors of *Story* and the author. Copyright by Story Magazine, Inc., 1943.

Vining, Donald: *THE OLD DOG.* Reprinted by permission of the editors of *Story* and the author. Copyright by Story Magazine, Inc., 1945.

Williams, Tennessee: *THE IMPORTANT THING.* This story, from *Story* Nov.-Dec. 1945, was reprinted in Jay Laughlin's New Directions collection of short stories by Tennessee Williams entitled *One Arm* and it is included with the kind permission of Mr. Laughlin, the author and the author's agent, Audrey Wood of Liebling-Wood. The volume *One Arm* was copyright by New Directions in 1948.

FOREWORD

In these days, when the roundup of writers for anthologies, treasuries and annuals—prize and non-prize, regional, universal, animal, mineral or vegetable—has been undertaken by everyone from retired army officers and college teachers to the propinquous wives and mothers-in-law of publishers, it is a wise anthology that knows its own father.

This book is an exception. It was sired by an institution. All its stories came from one magazine. The magazine is *Story*, which since 1931, in one place or another, has been almost alone in its dogged devotion to the discovery and launching of writers with a good, if not thoroughly conventional, story to tell.

Story: The Fiction of the Forties originated in one periodical. But it came together from many sources. Its blood lines go back. Its place names range the world. Its characteristics are varied. It is a book of many differences, all engaging. Its separate parts are individual, original. They were handmade. They were not fashioned to a formula of somebody else's. They were not even, in most cases, made for commerce, but for the love of it. And the whole is a book of stories told by storytellers. It is a thick book. And, the editors feel, it is a good book. It ought to be. For there was plenty of material to choose from.

Into the offices of *Story*, the magazine, the postman for years, rain or shine, has brought an average of 1,000 short stories a month, mostly from these United States, but also from other parts of the English-writing world and from every continent. This book represents a culling from the stories actually printed in the last nine years, a mere 600 stories or so out of more than 120,000 submitted and read manuscripts. So, in the fifty-one here a considerable culling has taken place.

We might have culled differently. One anthology from *Story* some years ago was composed of only its longest stories, giving currency to an old word used in a new way, "novella." We might have made an interesting book simply of "unknown" authors, or of *Story* discoveries now grown to fame. Or we might have picked a book entirely of well-known authors who have appeared in the magazine. Either would have been a highly readable volume. One collection from *Story*, although it never achieved a terrific sales rating, started a movement. It took its title from Lord Dunsany's story in its pages, "Two Bottles of Relish." It was a book of fantasy, the first in the field, but it got lost in some of the best bookshops among the cookbooks. Another collection out of *Story*, which sold for twenty-five cents as a Pocket Book, reached almost a million. So . . . it just goes to show you. . . .

In a foreword to a book of short stories, particularly one written by various authors at about the same time, it is the fashion to pontificate. And it would be in tradition to point out to the academy that in *Story: The Fiction of the Forties* you are holding in your hands a book which casts a meaning on our times and shows a deep, a meaningful "trend." That here are all the bright eager writers carving out never-before-seen trails, making highly vital experiments, showing life as it has never been shown before, reaching into the depths to search their souls, and casting powerful light on politics and social meanings. Unfortunately this would be largely poppycock, of the kind doled out each year by those authorities looking primarily for special points in writing and overlooking, usually, the essential of the short story, and that is its story.

Story has put a kind of premium on originality. It does not hold against experiments, or style, or the divine fire. But it has never been a refuge of cliques, literary or political, or an upholder of preciosity. It has been an inlet for writers from everywhere who have been attracted to the short story as the shape in which they wish to write, and by shape we do not mean that worm of continuity which gets you to follow it through the advertising. The stories in this book are mostly narratives, about people, going through an experience, real or imagined, of sufficient interest or meaning to have caused the author to want to tell us about it. If there is any trend in this book it is simply the trend that has existed since the earlier Christians first began to use the parable; it is a trend which would indicate that today a lot of writers still write short stories—war, postwar or recession —and that a lot of these authors, at least those found in *Story*, are Americans—although you should not ignore the Irish—and that a lot of these stories are fine ones, or funny ones, or wry ones, or terrific ones.

From our reading, the trouble we find with most stories of the arty type is that they are not stories, but states of mind, usually the author's—and not very original states at that; and the commercial pieces are not about people but about cardboard figures who talk a lot, and they don't undergo any experience except the motion picture one of attempting to solve their love life, which, while important, is not all there is to living, especially in fiction.

In these fifty-one stories, every author has told his own story in his own way, not the editors'. There is no such thing as a *Story* "slant." In spite of the egotism of the elder of the editors, he is a tolerant cuss with authors. He held Herr Bemelmans' weirdly humorous hand in his first days of print and he let Saroyan write Saroyan on plain yellow paper single-spaced. He believes an author's story is an author's story, not the editors, and what editing takes place should take place with that most in mind. He has consistently let his authors have their heads. No story here has gone back eight times to fix up the ending to suit the boss, or the public, or the business office. Each of these stories came from a writer. Let the reader come to him.

For years a kind of snobbish feud has been waged between the plot and substance schools. De Maupassant, say, or Chekhov. *Story* holds with both. We have used Chekhovian "moods" articulated into stories, and the De Maupassantian stress on narrative has never here been sneered at. As far as possible we have avoided strictly defining our notion of a short story, even through eight long years of explaining things at Columbia. We have gone after quality: material, writers, stories. Material, of course, should be nothing but the best—and a full yard wide—good, fresh, original. The writer should simply be a genius. And the story a masterpiece.

Practically, though, it all comes down to something much less grandiose, whether editing for a magazine or culling from the magazine for a book for those who couldn't get it on the newsstands. If a manuscript comes in that interests us, one of the two of us reads the whole darned thing, even where it has been skillfully glued at the edges to reveal, upon its return to the sender, that the careless editors must have stopped on page three. If it is interesting, that's something. Then we begin testing it as we go for honesty, whether the author is convincing us of his story's inherent truth. And somewhere along here we feel, or fail to feel, its artistry. This latter is not the easiest element in a story to detect, but when it's there you know it, just as you know it when it's not. It is really much simpler if it's there. The pianist Godowsky had it. His furniture men hadn't, though they strained very hard. Indeed, like bad writers, they were proud of their efforts. "All day long," they said, "we move pianos. Feel our muscles." He felt them. "I just sit," Godowsky said, "but when I play *I* move audiences."

It may be noticed, by critical and discerning readers—may their tribe increase—that short stories, at least of the kind that appear in *Story*, are written most frequently by youngish persons. At least that has been our editorial experience. The short story is a little akin to poetry and its short quick impact is often like that of the lyric, and it is largely those with senses fresh who are open to the reception of such impression which, when reflected upon, make this kind of story. After forty a man is married, has four kids, and is either writing novels or working in a machine shop or a college. Thus, this, like other collections from the magazine, is full of the fairly young. There will be noted an absence of the familiar names which were not so familiar when they were first launched some years ago in *Story*. William Saroyan, Ludwig Bemelmans, Mary O'Hara, Richard Wright, Gladys Schmitt, and dozens of others. They have been anthologized; they have had their crowns, of vine leaves and of gold. Let the new ones have a chance. Here are the first published stories of Tennessee Williams, Norman Mailer, Truman Capote, J. D. Salinger, Fred Urquhart, A. E. Shandeling, Richard Coleman, Arthur Foff, Fred E. Ross, and many others. They have been writing, with many others, the fiction of the forties, in the short story form, and they will be the "known" authors, with many others, of the fifties. By their side are authors established, like Faulkner, Bunin, O'Flaherty, Caldwell, Molnar, March, Callaghan, Hughes, Prokosch, Payne, and others.

It will perhaps be surprising that almost one-third of the book is some kind of humor, wry, ironic, satiric, but humor. And although for six of these ten years there were three editors, two of whom were women, it will perhaps be surprising that there are so many stories that pull no punches, which, indeed, are a far cry from woman-editing and all its squeamishness. Perhaps this was because both these editors, Hallie Southgate Burnett and Eleanor Gilchrist, were first of all writers themselves. And when women are writers, not writing for the women's magazines, is there anything tougher-minded? It was sometimes hard to find a nice soft female touch in an issue.

It is needless to point out special stories. This is the book. Norman Mailer, discovered in the wilds of Harvard, one of *Story's* fifteen annual college prize writers, wants it pointed out, however, that his first published story is an early Mailer, and since it was published when he was eighteen, it precedes *The Naked and the Dead*, his big-selling novel. Truman Capote was also discovered by Hallie Burnett, in the mail from Park Avenue. There are discoveries from San Francisco, trailing a cloud of griffins, and others from England, and elsewhere. They all come out of the last decade of *Story*, from the period when, all angels departed, the magazine was tossed into the lap of Whit Burnett to foot the bills and pay the printer. For nine years the bills have been footed and the printers paid. But in 1948, due to no fault of the editors, the magazine suffered a body blow to its financial structure and had to suspend publication for the first time in eighteen years.

This book, then, is a scroll at the end of a page, not, we hope, the last page of *Story*. But it marks a printer's white line space for a breather. The need for a magazine like *Story*, which has been called "the most distinguished short story magazine in the world," * is greater now than it was in the thirties. The trail to the maker of better mousetraps, called attention to by the friendly Lewis Gannett, is just as well trodden now as then. But whether Hallie Burnett and I can, unaided, continue to carry the burden of a national magazine as we have for the last nine years, for the pleasure (or work) of editing the new fiction writers of our day—that is the question.

But if we stop it, what shall we tell the postman—who has followed us out of the high-rent district of Manhattan to the banks of the millpond in this old house in Setauket? And what shall we tell the thousand authors a month for the next ten years?

—by WHIT BURNETT, Labor Day, 1949,
at Setauket, L. I., N. Y., and dedicated
to his coeditor,
H. B.
without whose work on the magazine
since 1942 there would have been no
Story.

* Edward J. O'Brien, editor of *The Best Short Stories*.

STORY

The Fiction of the Forties

THE OPEN-MINDED PAGLEIGHS

by EVELYN GUSTAFSSON

THE FIRST TIME MISS MYNTON CALLED ON THE YOUNG PAGleighs was shortly after their marriage, in the late twenties. She went, not only because she was curious about the young people, but also because Alice had written to ask her to look them up. Miss Mynton and Alice had been friends since Vassar.

"You know I don't often get away," Alice wrote from Brookline. "But you're near New York. And I should like to know how the children are getting on. Naturally they're provided for. I believe there's been a trust fund in the Pagleigh family for some generations. And my niece Betty you already know. The two of them were just barely old enough to be married, so you can imagine how the family feels about their going off to New York! They're quite lively; I expect to miss them. If you find it convenient, I should be glad to hear from time to time how they are, and what they're thinking about."

It was a pleasant mission, Miss Mynton thought, as she rode in from Westchester, one day in 1929. She wouldn't have admitted to Alice that she was beginning to feel out of things. Miss Mynton, for too many years now, had been playing maiden aunt to children not as young as the Pagleighs.

When her shopping was finished, she took a cab and went to the brownstone house in the East Thirties where Betty and Michael Pagleigh had been lucky enough to find a flat. Miss Mynton felt perfectly at home with the sound old Biedermeier. Only the odd-looking pictures over the drawing-room fireplace puzzled her a little. She wondered if it was something Betty had done in college.

As Alice had hinted, the Pagleighs were nice children. Miss Mynton thought them better suited to New York than to Boston. For one thing, they didn't seem to notice her age. They poured her a cocktail as a matter of course and offered her a cigarette.

"The liquor's all right," Michael assured her, smiling. "Strictly off the boat."

He was slim and very properly tailored. Miss Mynton thought his face looked intelligent; he had high cheekbones, and his hair was dark and curly over a high square forehead. Betty was attractive, too. She was just as tall as Michael; and though her skirts were short and her hair even shorter, she wasn't awkward. She seemed to Miss Mynton to be one of those graceful, competent, semi-maternal girls that some illustrator—she couldn't remember his name—had made fashionable that year. Both of the children were good looking and eager in a way that appealed to Miss Mynton.

She didn't quite know how to carry out her errand. One could hardly begin by asking, "Have you read any good books lately?" But Michael made it easy for her.

"That Laurencin—" he nodded at Miss Mynton, who was looking at the picture over the fireplace, "—our apologies," he said. "We expect to rip it down. We're dickering for a real live Picasso—he's gone way beyond the others, you know."

"The others?" Miss Mynton repeated, innocently.

Betty smiled apologetically, and leaned forward to hand Miss Mynton an ash tray. "You know," she explained. "The postimpressionists. All that old nonsense—futurism, fauvism, vorticism, dadaism—we're quite over them all. Oh, I suppose one can still look at Bracque and Orozco and Derain. But if we can't get the Picasso, we'll probably go surrealist and buy a Dali."

"Buy a dolly?" Miss Mynton asked. She got them to spell it out, so she could memorize it for Alice.

Michael got up from his chair and walked over to the fireplace, where he stood looking critically at the Laurencin. "Oh, we've changed our minds about a lot of things," he said, and grinned engagingly. "Take music . . ."

Miss Mynton murmured something about having come into town during the winter to hear Die Walküre. The children smiled. They were perfectly polite about it, but they hinted that opera was one of the things they'd changed their minds about.

By music, the Pagleighs meant Milhaud, Antheil, Satie, Hindemith, Mompou, and Scriabin. Debussy was out of the running; Ravel's "Bolero" had crucified him; Damrosch was a scream; and Gershwin was under suspicion.

Miss Mynton asked them to spell all the names, and then she wrote them on the back of her shopping list. "I promised Alice to tell her everything," she said, laughing apologetically. Secretly she planned to look up the names in the White Plains library.

Betty sat down on a hassock near Miss Mynton and tried to make the whole thing clear. "You see, we've got to get accustomed to new idioms," she explained. She raised her eyes and looked at Miss Mynton in a way that implied, not that she was giving instructions, but that she was generously sharing her knowledge.

Miss Mynton knew the names of most of the writers that the Pagleighs talked about, at least by hearsay; but she had to ask them to spell out Jammes, Rimbaud, Wyndham Lewis, Paul Valéry, and Jean Cocteau.

"All foreigners," she said doubtfully, as she finished her list.

"That's right," Michael agreed. He came away from the fireplace and sat down beside Miss Mynton, speaking in a quick, eager way. "But it needn't go on like that," he said. "We have great hopes for America, too. As a matter of fact, the future is right over here."

Betty looked up from under her lashes in the same diffident way as before. "That's why we're not living abroad," she said. "Even though we could save money."

"The primitive turn of modern art is suited to the vigorous morning air of American culture," Michael said suddenly. He stood up, smiling, and moved his arms in an expressive, un-Bostonian way. "Why, we're only beginning," he went on. "It's a magnificent, fabulous age. Consider the American idiom, Brooklynese, the new architecture, the modern highways, the flood of American invention, the contagious feeling of motion and flow! Even, if you please, our corporations. Say what you like, corporations get things done!"

Miss Mynton nodded. She was comforted by the idea that America was going ahead. Her own U. S. Steel was probably safe.

She left them, finally, and went home to report to Alice. "Don't worry about the Pagleighs," she wrote. "They're sensible, remarkably cheerful, and well informed. Above all, they're open-minded. I shall go to see them again; and I expect to profit by it." She carefully appended to the letter a list of all the names that the Pagleighs had given her.

It was the first in a series of lists that Miss Mynton made. Her visits to the Pagleighs weren't too frequent. Urgent personal matters, including the astonishing behavior of U. S. Steel, took most of her attention for several years. But she remembered a time halfway between '34 and '35, when she went to see the Pagleighs again.

They seemed as young as ever; but everything else about them was changed. They lived in a Village studio, and were almost carefully shabby. Of course, the furniture was Swedish modern, and the glass vases were unmistakably Orrefors; but it wasn't until the modern cabinet in one corner turned out to be a specially designed wrapping for a Capehart, that Miss Mynton gave up worrying about the Pagleighs' finances.

Betty and Michael put on records of Russian music. They played Prokofiev, Shostakovitch and Russian folk songs, including one which they identified as the "Internationale." There was a Modigliani on the wall; Michael explained about Modigliani and his struggles against bourgeois ideas. The word "bourgeois" was evidently a term of execration. It stood for nearly everything the Pagleighs had admired in 1929. Now they went to documentary films, the Theatre Union, and the government theatre. They read Malraux and Silone, and a good deal of political economy and psychology. They admired Harold Laski, John Strachey, Auden, Spender, and C. Day Lewis. They were irritated by the French rationalist Julien Benda, who was "sabotaging social progress." Miss Mynton listened to the whole recital carefully, making notes, partly for Alice, and partly for herself.

"This is no time for frivolity," Michael said. "History is on the march." He said that he and Betty were sick to death of Hooverism, American business, cartels, war, and munition makers. He said the time had come for "group action."

"Mike marched in the May Day parade," Betty said, her eyes shining with pride. "And we've both been in a picket line. By the way, won't you sign our petition against war?"

Miss Mynton signed a statement that she would not bear arms in another war. She didn't smile. Just then she didn't think it at all funny at her age to be relinquishing her right to use a musket. The Pagleighs were too manifestly sincere.

Miss Mynton wrote to Alice that night; and afterward, time seemed to go fast, probably because so much was happening abroad. It was 1938 before she went to see the Pagleighs again, and she found them as charming and as youthful as before. They had moved again, this time to an uptown penthouse. Their furniture was neo-functional, Betty said; but to Miss Mynton it looked a bit like drawings of internal organs in a work of anatomy.

The Pagleighs had discovered the non-objectivists, and had pictures by Kandinsky, Miro, and Klee. On the whole, they were still serious. They were worried about Spain. Things looked bad all over; but Michael envisioned a future which might still be miraculously saved by the Swedish co-operative and Danish Adult Education. Both children were deep in the study of housing. They considered Le Corbusier a little old-fashioned. Their books were by authors who once more were new to Miss Mynton: Rilke, Capek, Kafka, Ortega y Gasset, and Louis Ferdinand Céline. They were playing records of Gustav Mahler, Hector Villa-Lobos, and oddly enough, Bach fugues.

"They're really grown up," Miss Mynton wrote to Alice, afterward. "Only imagine, after all that modern music, I found them playing the great fugues. Do you remember when we were a little foolish about Alfred Noyes, and, later, Amy Lowell, and still later Rupert Brooke? How far away all that seems now!"

Not long thereafter the Pagleighs acquired a new enthusiasm, one Miss Mynton could scarcely begrudge them, for this time she shared it. There was a war on; Miss Mynton was quite busy with it in her own way, up in Westchester. But by 1943 she managed another visit to the Pagleighs. And this time they lived in the same place, and had not even changed their furniture. The significant additions to the household consisted of tin hats, first-aid kits, a sand bucket, and a huge ax that stood in the foyer.

They spoke earnestly of alerts and blitzes. They knew just what to do if they should happen on a man with one leg blown off. Michael had been rejected by the Army, but he was a block leader; and Betty was taking a Nurse's Aide course at the Red Cross. They had the highest respect for the Roosevelts and Churchill, for Norman Corwin, Russia, the Writers' War Board, and freedom. They said that Sweden's middle way had been bound to end in something like fascism; so that you had to expect what was happening there now. They had a healthy scorn for traitors, like Wyndham Lewis and Ezra Pound. They were reading an old copy of de Tocqueville, and a new one of Julien Benda whose latest work on democracy seemed to be definitive. Miss Mynton wrote down the name of the book, along with the others, intending to get a copy, though she never did.

Up to now she had not seen the Pagleighs so vigorous and purposeful. She got almost emotional, trying to set it down later, in a letter to Alice. "It is exactly as I said," Miss Mynton wrote. "Those delightful children have grown up, and they now know where they are, and just where they are going."

Three years later, in 1946, Miss Mynton called on the Pagleighs again. She made the point of taking the time to come in from Westchester for the purpose. She was eager to know what was going on. World affairs had become confusing, even to Westchester; but Miss Mynton felt certain that the Pagleighs would set her right.

She was quite unprepared for the interview which followed. Of course the children were on their way to forty, now, and that might have accounted for the changes in their faces. But everything seemed wrong. It wasn't that the Pagleighs had slowed down, exactly, or even that they had lost interest. Miss Mynton found them surrounded by their usual collection of new things. There were prints and photographs of the works of Rouault, and Matila Glyka, and André Beaudin, lying about. There was a profusion of magazines, among them *New Directions*, *The Partisan Review*, *La Nouvelle Revue Française*, *Verve*, *L'Arche*, *La Pensée*, and *Horizon*. There wasn't much order in the living room; for the first time, books, papers, and phonograph records covered the furniture. Nothing seemed to be put away in place. Miss Mynton picked up books and put them down again. She read a new set of names. Camus, Sartre, Goodman, Patchen, Miller, Connolly. Among the records, Miss Mynton noted Leonard Bernstein's "Fancy Free" and President Roosevelt's speeches.

"I don't know what's to become of us," Michael said. He was leaning against the modern mantelpiece, and his whole body curved like a parenthesis mark. He shook his head. "What can we look forward to?" he demanded. "Better throw the whole thing up and go abroad. Denmark isn't a bad place. God knows you can't expect anything from the British, now."

"Yet England contrives to look socialist to a number of American conservatives," Betty reminded him. "Even that loathsome Churchill—if *he* doesn't like the British government, it must have some good in it."

She looked tired. Miss Mynton decided that Betty had begun to neglect herself. The girl was sitting on the functional love seat, with her forehead on her hand. She began rolling her head from side to side, as if she had a headache, and hoped to massage it away.

"England has been beastly about Palestine, and Spain," Michael announced. He put down his glass, poured himself a second cocktail, then remembered Miss Mynton and apologized.

"No, thanks," Miss Mynton said. She was genuinely puzzled. Without thinking why, she entered the discussion. "Let's straighten this out first," she suggested. "You must have reached some conclusions."

There was no reply for a moment, and then Betty groaned. "Spain!" desperately. "Who hasn't been beastly about Spain?" she inquired.

Michael sighed. "I don't know," he said, wearily. "If it's a question of the church—"

"Consider the Existentialists," Betty said. " 'God is an absence at the back of the sky.' "

"That reminds me of 'a person of quality in the clouds,' " Miss Mynton said. "Isn't that Swift?"

Michael ran his hand backward over his hair until it reached his collar, and then he rubbed his neck thoughtfully. "And yet, the Existentialists appeal to Sören Kierkegaarde, who was deeply religious," he observed. "After all, Russia approves of the church, now."

Miss Mynton had heard a lot of talk in Westchester. "I don't know," she said. "Is it really true that Russia is a threat to democracy?"

Betty sat up. "What is the difference between control by the state, or control by capital?" she asked sharply.

"And neither represents freedom," Michael added. "By the way, Wyndham Lewis has turned pro-Stalinite. Did you know that? And Trotsky carries on from beyond the grave."

Miss Mynton tried to remember the last word she'd had from them on Wyndham Lewis. Michael kicked a magazine on the floor. "Take this fellow Gesell," he said. "Do you know him? Wants to tax idle capital. We've been weighing him against Marx on one side and Hayek on the other. It's enough to send you howling back to Adam Smith."

For a few minutes they went on weighing: balancing Streit against Straight, and Reves against Lerner. Then Betty leaned back in her functional love seat, and groaned. "Oh, my. *Where is love?*" she asked, in a voice that implied she had decided to give it up.

"A lot of people think it's in the gay child hearts of the Germans," Michael replied, darkly. "Betty was quoting Patchen," he told Miss Mynton.

Miss Mynton said "Oh." She had noticed Michael's quotation from Rupert Brooke.

" 'What is needed is a folly of man,' " Betty said, in the same tone.

Michael identified that, too. "Camus. 'The Stranger,' " he said. "Camus is down on fear."

"Like Roosevelt," Miss Mynton began, but Betty interrupted her. "At least we've got Henry Miller really speaking out against our bourgeois stupidity," she said.

"I *think* that's been done before," Miss Mynton put in gently.

"And will be again," Michael agreed. He threw up his arms helplessly. "But where do we go from here?"

"They were asking that one in 1918, Michael," Miss Mynton told him. "It's time somebody found an answer. And out of all this stuff—" She pointed, not only at the papers and the books that were strewn around, but also to the now considerable collection of books, on shelves halfway around the room.

Michael thrust his hands deep into his trousers pockets. Still leaning against the mantel, he turned slowly, so that he faced the room. He stared down at the floor as he drew deeply on his cigarette, and blew out a cloud of smoke.

"That's just the trouble!" he said. His mouth twitched, and his voice was husky with despair. "Who the hell are we to follow?" he demanded. "These days everybody's going a different way!"

TWO LOVELY BEASTS

by LIAM O'FLAHERTY

THE DERRANES WERE HAVING BREAKFAST WHEN A NEIGHBOR called Kate Higgins came running into their kitchen. She squatted on the floor by the wall to the right of the door, threw her apron over her face, and began to wail at the top of her voice in most heart-rending fashion.

"God between us and harm!" said Mrs. Derrane, as she came over from the table. "What happened to you?"

She put an arm about the shoulders of the wailing neighbor and added tenderly, "Tell us what happened, so that we can share your sorrow."

Colm Derrane came over with his mouth full of food. He had a mug of tea in his hand. The six children followed him. They all stood in a half circle about Kate Higgins, who continued to wail incontinently.

"Speak up in God's name," Colm said, after swallowing what he had been munching. "Speak to us so that we can help you, woman."

It was some time before Kate desisted from her lamentation. Then she suddenly removed her apron from before her face and looked fiercely at Colm through wild blue eyes that showed no sign of tears. She was a skinny little woman, with a pale face that was deeply lined with worry. Her husband had died a few months previously, leaving her with a large family that she was struggling to rear on next to nothing.

"Will you buy a calf?" she said to Colm in an angry tone.

"A calf?" said Colm in surprise. "I didn't know your cow had . . ."

"She dropped it a little while ago," the woman interrupted. "Then she died herself. Lord save us, she lay down and stretched herself out flat on the grass and shook her legs and that was all there was to it. She's as dead as a doornail. There isn't a spark left in her. It must have been poison that she dragged up out of the ground with her teeth, while she was mad with the calf sickness."

The whole Derrane family received this news in open-mouthed silence. It was a calamity that affected every household in the village. Each family had but a single cow. By traditional law, those who had milk were bound to share it with those who had none. So that the death of one cow, no matter to whom she belonged, was a calamity that affected all.

"Bloody woe!" Colm said at length. "Bloody mortal woe! That's a terrible blow and you after losing your husband only the other day. There you are now with a houseful of weak children and no cow. Ah! Bloody woe!"

"No use talking, Colm," Kate Higgins said fiercely. "Buy the calf from me. I'm asking you to do it for the love of God. He must get suck quickly or else he'll die of hunger. He'll stretch out there on the grass beside his mother and die, unless he gets suck. Buy him from me."

Colm and his wife looked at one another in perplexity. Their faces were racked with pity for their neighbor.

"Bloody woe!" Colm kept muttering under his breath.

There was no sign of pity in the faces of the children. They moved back to the table slowly after a few moments of open-mouthed consternation. They kept glancing over their shoulders at Kate Higgins with aversion. They hated her, now that they understood her calamity threatened to diminish their milk supply.

"I'm asking you for the love of God," Kate Higgins continued in a tone that had become quite savage. "The price will help me buy a new cow. I must have a cow for the children. The doctor said they must have plenty of milk, the two youngest of them especially. They are ailing, the poor creatures. Your cow has a fine udder, God bless her. She calved only a few days ago. She won't feel my fellow at her teats in addition to her own. She'll be well able for the two of them, God bless her. She will, faith, and she'll leave plenty of milk for yourselves into the bargain. Praise be to God, I never saw such a fine big udder as she has."

Colm was on the point of speaking when his wife interrupted him.

"You know how it is with us," Mrs. Derrane said. "We are giving milk to three houses already. Their cows aren't due to calve for more than three weeks yet. We'll have to help you as well, now that your cow is gone. So how could we fed a second calf? It would be against the law of God and of the people. We couldn't leave neighbors without milk in order to fill a calf's belly."

Kate Higgins jumped to her feet and put her clenched fists against her lean hips.

"The calf will die unless you buy him," she cried ferociously. "There is nobody else to take him but you people. Nobody else has a cow after calving. The price would help me buy another cow. I must have a cow for the children. The doctor said . . ."

"That's enough, woman," Colm interrupted. "I'll put him on our cow for a couple of days. In the meantime, maybe you could get someone in another village to buy him."

Kate Higgins grew calm at once on hearing this offer. Tears came into her wild blue eyes. "God spare your health, Colm," she said gently. "I was afraid he'd die of hunger before he could get suck. That would be the end of me altogether. I'd have nothing at all left if he died on me, stretched out on the grass beside his mother. When you have a few pounds, it's easier to borrow more than if you have none at all. God spare the two of you."

Colm went with her to the field where they were already skinning the dead cow. He took the red bull calf in his arms to the paddock where his own cow was grazing. She consented to give the stranger suck after some persuasion.

"He's lovely, sure enough," Colm said, as he looked with admiration at the wine-dark hide of the sucking calf. "I thought my own calf this year looked like a champion, but he's only in the halfpenny place compared to this one."

"He'll be a champion all right," Kate Higgins said. "He has the breed in him. Why wouldn't he? Nothing would do my husband, Lord have mercy on him, but to spend ten royal shillings for the use of the government bull. Nothing less would satisfy him, faith. He wasn't much to look at, poor man, but he always liked to have the best of everything."

She suddenly rushed over to Colm and put her lips close to his ear. Now her wild blue eyes were full of cunning.

"You should buy him, Colm," she whispered. "Buy him and put him with your own calf. Then you'll have the makings of the two finest yearlings that were ever raised in this townland. You'll be the richest man in the village. You'll be talked about and envied from one end of the parish to the other."

Colm turned his back to her and took off his cap. He was quite young and yet his skull had already begun to go bald along the crown. He was a big, awkward fellow with pigeon toes and arms that were exceptionally long, like those of an ape. He was noted in the district for his strength, his immense energy, and his eagerness for work.

"Arrah! How could I buy him from you?" he said in a low voice. "How could I feed him and so many people depending on the milk?"

Then he turned toward her suddenly and raised his voice to a shout, as if he were arguing with some wild thought in his own mind. "I have only twenty acres of land," he cried angrily. "The whole of it is practically barren. You wouldn't find more than a few inches of soil in the deepest part of it. You wouldn't find a foot of ground in all I possess where you could bury a spade to the haft. Bloody woe! Woman, I tell you I haven't one good single half acre. There is hardly enough grass for my cow, not to mention my unfortunate horse. You could count the bones right through my poor horse's hide. I'm hard put every year to find grass for my yearling. Woman alive, sure there isn't a man in this village that could feed two yearlings. It would be madness for me to try it."

"The English have started fighting the Germans a second time," Kate Higgins whispered. "They won't stop until they have dragged the whole world again into the war with them. The fight will last for years and years, same as it did before. There will be a big price for everything fit to eat. A man that would have two lovely beasts for sale . . ."

"Stop tempting me with your foolish talk, woman," Colm interrupted.

"Your cow could easily feed the two calves," Kate continued. "She could do it without any bother at all. She'd have plenty, beside, for yourselves and the neighbors. You needn't worry about grass, either. There's always plenty of grass for rent in the village of Pusach. You'll have plenty of money to spare for buying any extra grass you'll need, because there is going to be a great price for potatoes and fish. Man alive, there will be lashings of money, same as before. During the other big war, you remember, they were even buying rotten dogfish. I declare to my God they were. They paid famine prices for the rotten dogfish that the storms threw up on the beach beyond there."

Colm turned away from her again and lowered his voice to a whisper.

"It would be madness for me to try it," he said. "Nobody ever tried to raise two yearlings in this village. We all have the same amount of rocky land, twenty acres a head."

"You're different from everybody else, Colm," Kate said, raising her voice and speaking very rapidly. "The others only do what they have to do. They do barely enough to keep themselves and their families alive. You go out of your way looking for work. You never turn aside from an opportunity to earn an extra shilling. You are at it night and day. The spunk is in you. There is no end to your strength. Oh! Indeed, it's well known that there is no holding you, when there is a job of work to be done. You spit on your hands and away you go like a wild stallion. God bless you, there is the strength of ten men in your body and you're not afraid to use it. You deserve to prosper on account of your willingness. You deserve to be rich and famous. All you need is courage."

"Nobody ever tried it," Colm whispered hoarsely. "Nobody ever did. It would be madness to try it."

Kate Higgins stepped back from him and threw out her arms in a dramatic gesture.

"Let you be the first, then," she shouted. "There's nothing

stopping you but a want of courage. Let you be the first. Let you show them how to do it, Colm."

Colm also raised his voice to a shout as he answered her fiercely.

"Stop your foolish talk, woman," he said. "He can suck on my cow for a couple of days, but I promise you no more."

Kate walked away from him hurriedly, gesticulating with both arms.

"Two lovely beasts!" she shouted back at him, when she was at a distance. "Think of that now. There's nothing standing in your way but a want of courage."

"Not another word out of you now," Colm shouted after her at the top of his voice. "What you're saying is against the law of God."

Even so, he could hardly sleep a wink that night through thinking of what the woman had said. In the morning he broached the idea of buying the calf during conversation with his wife.

"That's a lovely calf Kate Higgins has," he said. "It's a pity we can't buy it."

"Buy it?" said his wife. "Yerrah! How could we do that?"

"There is going to be a great price for beasts on account of the war," Colm continued. "With the English and the Germans at it again . . ."

"Have sense, man," his wife said. "Unless you've taken leave of your gumption, you know well it's impossible for us to buy that calf. Not even if we had grass for it, which we haven't."

"All the same," Colm said, "that young fellow makes my mouth water. I never saw such a young champion."

"Yerrah! How could we leave the neighbors without milk?" his wife said.

"I'm only talking, that's all," Colm said. "There is no harm in talk."

"Well! Say no more about it," his wife said. "People might hear you and be scandalized."

"You never saw such a color as that calf has," Colm said as he went out of the house. "He's so red that he's almost black."

Kate Higgins came to him again that day, while he was smashing rocks with a sledge hammer in the corner of a little field that he was trying to make arable. She began to pester him once more. He threw down the sledge hammer and ran over to the fence against which she leaned.

"Why don't you leave me alone?" he shouted at her. "Go to some other village and find a buyer for him."

"I've inquired everywhere," Kate Higgins said. "It's no use, Colm. Unless you buy him, I'll have to give him to the butcher at Kilmacalla. The few shillings that I'll get for his flesh and his hide won't be much. However, they'll be better than nothing."

"I promised to let him suck for a couple of days," Colm shouted. "I can promise you no more. I can't let the neighbors go without the milk that is due to them."

"It will be a mortal sin to slaughter such a lovely young fellow," Kate said as she walked away hurriedly. "What else can I do, though? I must get a pound or two, by hook or by crook. Then I can borrow more. I have to make up the price of a new cow one way or another. The doctor said that the young ones must have plenty of milk. Otherwise they'll die. So he said. He did, faith."

After the woman had gone, Colm went to the paddock for another look at the young bull calf that had a wine-dark hide.

"It would be a mortal sin surely to slaughter such a lovely creature," he said aloud. "He'll be every inch a champion if he lives."

Then his heart began to beat wildly as he watched the two calves cavort together with their tails in the air. He became intoxicated by the idea of possessing them both.

"Two lovely beasts!" he whispered.

He went for a walk to the cliff top instead of returning to his sledge hammer. He stood on the brink of the highest cliff and looked down into the sea.

"Two lovely beasts!" he whispered again.

Then a frenzied look came into his pale blue eyes. He took off his cap and threw it on the ground behind him.

"Sure I have the courage," he muttered fiercely.

He spread his legs, leaned forward slightly and held out his hands in front of his hips, with the palms upturned and the fingers slightly crooked. He began to tremble.

"I have plenty of courage," he muttered.

The skin on the upper part of his forehead and on top of his baldish skull looked very pale above the brick-red color of his bony cheeks. He had a long narrow face, thick lips, and buck teeth. His short nose had a very pointed ridge. His mouse-colored hair stuck out in ugly little bunches above his ears and at the nape of his neck. His shoes were in tatters. His frieze trousers were covered with patches of varying colors. His gray shirt was visible through the numerous holes in his blue woolen sweater.

Yet he looked splendid and even awe-inspiring, in spite of his physical ugliness and his uncouth dress, as he stood poised that way on the brink of the tall cliff above the thundering sea, leaning forward on widespread legs, with his long arms stretched out and his fingers turned slightly inward on his open palms, trembling with a frenzy of desire.

After a while he turned away from the sea and picked up his cap. He felt very tired as he walked homeward with downcast head. His arms swung limply by his sides. He kept glancing furtively from side to side, as if he were conscious of having committed a crime up there on the cliff top and feared pursuit as a consequence. There was a hard look in his pale blue eyes.

Again that night he could not sleep. He lay on his back thinking of the two lovely beasts and how he wanted to possess them. The thought gave him both pleasure and pain. The pleasure was like that derived from the anticipation of venery. The pain came from his conscience.

During the morning of the following day, Kate Higgins came to him again. She was wearing her best clothes.

"I'm on my way to the butcher at Kilmacalla," she said to him.

"All right," Colm said to her. "How much do you want for the calf?"

He was so excited by the decision at which he had arrived that he consented to the price she asked without bargaining.

"Come to the house with me," he said. "I'll hand over the money to you."

"God spare your health," Kate Higgins said. "With that money I can begin at once to look for another cow."

Mrs. Derrane got very angry when her husband came into the kitchen with Kate Higgins and asked her for the family purse.

"Is it to buy that calf?" she said.

"Hand me the purse," Colm repeated.

"Devil a bit of me," his wife said. "It would be against the law of God to put the people's milk into a calf's heathen belly. I won't give it to you."

Colm gripped the front of her bodice with his left hand and shook her. "Hand it over, woman," he said in a low voice.

Her anger passed at once. She was a big muscular woman, almost as strong as her husband and possessed of a stern will. Indeed, she had dominated Colm's simple nature ever since their marriage, until now. Whenever he tried to rebel against her decisions, he had always been easily defeated. He had shouted, broken articles of furniture, and even struck her cruel blows from time to time. She had always merely waited with folded arms and set jaws until his foolish anger had spent itself. Now it was different. He did not shout and she saw something in his pale blue eyes that frightened her.

She went quickly to the great chest and brought him the long cloth purse. "What's come over you?" she said to him, while he was undoing the string. "What are the neighbors going to say about this?"

Colm unrolled the purse and thrust his hand deep down into the long inner pocket. He again looked his wife straight in the eyes. "Shut up, woman," he said quietly. "From now on don't meddle with things that don't concern you. I'm master in this house. Do you hear?"

Again she became frightened by what she saw in his eyes. She turned away from him. "May God forgive you," she said. "I hope you have thought well about this before doing it."

"I've never in my life thought more about anything," Colm said.

Kate Higgins never uttered one word of thanks when she was given the money. She stuffed the notes into the front pocket of her skirt and rushed from the house. "I'll go now," she cried as she hurried down the yard, "to try and get company for these few pounds. Those that have give only to those that have. To those that have not only crumbs are given, same as to a dog."

When Colm went that evening to the meeting place, on the brow of the little hill that faced the village, silence fell among the men who were assembled there. He threw himself on the ground, put his back to a rock and lit his pipe. The others began to discuss the weather in subdued tones after a little while. Then again there was silence.

At length a man named Andy Gorum turned to Colm and said, "We heard you bought the calf from Kate Higgins."

"I did," said Colm.

"Is it to slaughter him you bought him?" Gorum said.

"No," said Colm.

"Do you intend to rear him?" Gorum said.

"I do," said Colm.

Gorum got to his feet slowly and clasped his hands behind the small of his back. He came over and stood in front of Colm. He was an elderly man, very small and thin, with a wrinkled face that was the color of old parchment. His eyes were weak and they had hardly any lashes, like those of a man blind from birth. He was the village leader because of his wisdom.

"I'm sorry you are doing this, Colm," he said. "You are a good man and everybody belonging to you was good, away back through the generations. This is a bad thing you intend to do, though."

"How could it be bad to help a widow?" Colm said.

"You know well it won't help a widow if you rear that calf on the people's milk," Gorum said.

"She begged me and begged me," Colm said, raising his voice. "She kept at me the whole time. How could I refuse her? She said that she had to have the money for another cow. She said her children would die unless . . ."

"You know you are breaking the law," Gorum interrupted. "It's no use trying to talk yourself out of it."

"How could it be against the law to help a widow?" Colm shouted.

"Indeed, it isn't," Gorum said. "We'll all help her, please God, as much as we can. That's how we live here in our village, by helping one another. Our land is poor and the sea is wild. It's hard to live. We only manage to live by sticking together. Otherwise we'd all die. It's too wild and barren here for any one man to stand alone. Whoever tries to stand alone and work only for his own profit becomes an enemy of all."

Colm jumped to his feet. He towered over Gorum.

"Are you calling me an enemy for helping a widow?" he shouted.

"If you put into a calf's belly," Gorum said, "the milk that you owe to your neighbors, everybody will be against you."

"I'll do what I please," Colm shouted. Thereupon he rushed from the meeting place.

"Come back, neighbor," Gorum called after him in a tone of entreaty.

"I have the courage to do what I think is right," Colm shouted.

"We are all fond of you," Gorum said. "We don't want to turn against you. Come back to us and be obedient to the law."

"I'll do what I think is right," Colm shouted, as he crossed the stiles into his yard. "I'll raise those two beasts if it's the last thing I'll do in this world. Let any man that dares try to stop me."

The Derranes became outcasts in the village from that day forward. Nobody spoke to them. Nobody gave them any help. Nobody entered their house. All doors were closed to them.

Even Kate Higgins turned against her benefactors in most shameful fashion. Contrary to her expectations, the hapless woman was unable to borrow any more money, except for a solitary pound that she got from an aunt after lengthy importunities. Neither was she able to find any cow for sale, although she tramped the parish from end to end, over and over again. Her house went to rack and ruin during her continued absence. The ungoverned children burned the furniture to keep themselves warm. They grew so savage and filthy that the neighbor women removed their own children from all contact with them.

Unbalanced by her misfortunes, Kate forsook her peasant frugality and brought tidbits home to her starving brood after each fruitless day of wandering. The poor woman lacked courage to face them empty-handed. In that way she soon spent every penny of the money that she got from Colm and her aunt. There was none of it left after two months. When she had nothing more to give the little ones on her return, as they clutched at her apron with their filthy hands and whined pitifully for food, her mind began to get crazed.

She took to reviling Colm at the top of her voice, in the roadway outside his house, as she shuffled homeward with the fall of night.

"Colm Derrane is sold to the devil," she cried. "He put bad luck on me. I was grateful to him when he bought my calf, thinking he was doing me a favor and that I could borrow more, to put with what he gave me and make up the price of a new cow. Devil a bit of it. There was a curse on his money. People told me it was on account of the war they were unwilling to part with any of their share. They said they were bound to clutch all they had, for fear of disaster. The truth is that they would not lend to a woman that sold a calf to any enemy of the people. Here I am now without a red copper in my skirt, without a cow or a husband and my children ailing. They'll die on me, the poor little creatures, without the milk that the doctor ordered for them. I have no strength to care for them. I'm so tired every evening after my walking, that I can't even pick the lice out of their hair. Ah! the poor little creatures! May God have pity on my orphans!"

Colm paid no more heed to this abuse than he did to the hostility of the people. After his outburst of anger on being told he was to be treated as an outcast, he maintained strict control over his temper. He became dour and silent and indifferent, except when he was in the presence of the two young beasts that he loved. It was only then that he smiled and uttered words of tenderness.

"Oh! You lovely creatures!" he said to them, as he watched them suck at the cow's teats. "Drink up now and be strong. Don't leave a drop of that milk in the udder. I want the two of you to be champions."

He was as ruthless toward his family as he was tender toward the calves. He only brought into the house enough milk to color the tea. He let the calves swallow all the rest. Lest there might be any cheating, he forbade his wife and children to go near the cow under threat of dire punishment.

His wife came to him shortly after the calves were weaned. "I can go without butter," she protested, "although the children tear the heart in me with their whining. They keep asking when there is going to be some. It is too much, though, when I can't get enough buttermilk to make our bread rise. All I ask is enough milk for one churning."

"You can't have it," Colm said coldly. "I can't let the calves go in want, just for the sake of making our bread rise. We can eat it flat just as well. Calves must get a good foundation during the first few months, by having every hole and corner of their bellies well stuffed the whole time. That's how they get bone and muscle and balance and plenty of room. Then it's easy, when the time comes, to pile on the good hard meat. The foundation will be there to carry the load."

His wife kept looking at him in amazement while he spoke. She could not understand how a man, who had formerly been so kind and considerate of his family's needs, could suddenly become so ruthless. She burst into tears after he had finished. "God will punish you for being cruel," she said.

"Silence," said Colm. "Don't take liberties, woman."

Midsummer came. That was the season of abundance for the poor people of that village. The new potatoes were being dug. The young onions were succulent in the house gardens. There was plenty of milk and butter. Great baskets of pollock and rock fish and bream and mackerel were brought each day from the sea. The hens were laying and the spare cockerels from the spring hatchings made broth for the delicate. At suppertime the people gorged themselves on their favorite dish of mashed new potatoes, with butter and scallions and boiled fish and fresh buttermilk. The scallions were chopped fine and mixed with the potatoes. Then a great lump of yellow butter was pressed down into the center of the steaming dish. The table was laid before the open door, so that the people could hear the birds singing in the drowsy twilight and see the red glory of the sunset on the sea while they ate. The men waddled out afterward to the village meeting place, sending clouds of tobacco smoke into the air from their pipes. They lay down on their backs against the rocks and listened to the bird music in raptured content. Now and again one of them joined his voice to those of the birds and gave thanks to God for His gracious bounty.

It was then that Mrs. Derrane rose up in rebellion against her husband. She took the tongs from the hearth one evening and stood in front of him. "I'll stand no more of this, Colm," she said fiercely. "Here we are, living on potatoes and salt while the neighbors are feasting. Everything is put aside for the calves. My curse on the pair of them. You won't even let us eat a bit of fresh fish. By your leave, you made me salt every single fish that you brought into the house this spring, to be sold later on, so that you can have money to buy grass for your beasts. We have to scavenge along the shore, the children and myself, looking for limpets and periwinkles, same as people did during the famine. Lord save us, the lining of our stomachs is torn into shreds from the purging that the limpets give us. We are put to shame, rummaging like seagulls for stinking food, while the people of our village are feasting. There has to be an end to this, or else I'll take the children and follow my face out of the house. You'll have to get rid of that calf you bought. Then we we can live as we did before. We'll be outcasts no longer."

Colm got to his feet and looked at her coldly. "I'm going to raise those two calves," he said solemnly, "even if you and the children and myself have to eat dung while I'm doing it. Let other people fill their bellies in midsummer and remain poor. I want to rise in the world. A man can do that only by saving."

His wife raised the tongs and threatened him with them. "I'll have none of it," she cried. "I'm telling you straight to your face. You have to give in to me or I'll split your skull with these tongs."

"Put down those tongs," Colm said quietly.

"Are you going to get rid of the calf?" said his wife.

"Put them down," said Colm.

"I'll kill you with them," shouted his wife, becoming hysterical.

She struck at him with all her force, but he jumped aside nimbly and evaded the blow. Then he closed with her and quickly locked her arms behind her back. "I'm going to give you a lesson now," he said quietly. "I'm going to chastise you in a way that you'll remember."

He dragged her down to the hearth.

"Call the neighbors," his wife cried to the children. "Run out into the yard and call the people to come and save me from this murderer."

The children ran out into the yard and began to call for help, as Colm took down a dried sally rod that lay stretched on wooden pegs along the chimney place.

"You'll be obedient in future, my good woman," he said. "On my solemn oath you will."

He began to flog her. She tried to bite his legs. Then he put her flat on the ground and laid his foot to her back.

"I'll kill you when I get a chance," she cried. "I'll have your life while you are asleep."

Then she folded her arms beneath her face, gritted her teeth and received his blows in silence. He had to go on beating her for a long time before the sturdy creature surrendered and begged for mercy.

"All right, then," Colm said calmly when she had done so. "Do you promise to be obedient from now on and to make no more trouble about the calf?"

"I promise," his wife said.

"Get up, then, in God's name," Colm said gently, "and call in the children."

His wife looked up at him sideways in amazement. She did not rise. It puzzled her that he was so calm and spoke to her with tenderness, after having beaten her without mercy.

"Get up, woman," he continued. "Don't let us behave like this any more. It gives scandal to the children."

Then he took her tenderly in his arms and raised her to her feet. She ran out into the yard without looking at him.

"Get into the house," she said sternly to the children. "In with you."

She turned to some neighbors, who had come in answer to the children's cries for help. They were standing out in the lane, in doubt as to whether they should enter the yard of a household that were outcast.

"What brought you here?" Mrs. Derrane shouted at them. "It's not for our good that you came. Be off now and mind your own business."

That night in bed, she clasped Colm in her arms and put her cheek against his breast. "I thought it was the devil got into you," she whispered, as tears rolled down her cheeks. "Now I know different. You are trying to raise your family up in the world, while I'm only a hindrance to you and a dead weight around your neck. From now on, though, I'm going to help you. I will, faith!"

Colm took her head between his big rough hands and kissed her on the crown. "God spare your health, darling," he said. "With your help there will be no stopping us."

Seeing their parents happily united again, the children also became imbued with enthusiasm. They willingly consented to make sacrifices for the common effort. Even the youngest boy, barely five years old, had a little job to do every day. The whole family worked like bees in a hive.

The village people soon became so impressed by the turn of events that they began to question the justice of their conduct toward the Derrane family.

"If what he is doing is bad, why does he prosper?" they said to one another. "Isn't it more likely that God is blessing his effort to rise in the world? Maybe it's us that are wicked on account of our laziness?"

At the village meeting place, Andy Gorum strove with all his skill to hold the men steadfast against Colm.

"You'll soon see him come back to us on his knees," Gorum said, "and he begging for mercy. He may seem to prosper now. His two calves are growing powerfully. His wife and children and himself are working night and day. He has a nimble hand in everything worth money. Wait till winter comes, though. Then he won't be able to find grass for his beasts. The butcher of Kilmacalla has bought a herd of black cattle, to fatten them for the fighting English. He has rented all the spare grass in the village of Pusach. Many more big people in the district have bought herds on account of the war. There won't be a single blade of grass left anywhere for a poor man to rent. The big people will have it all clutched. Colm will have to slaughter that dark-skinned calf. I declare to my God, we'll be eating that dark fellow's meat when the Christmas candles are lit."

Gorum's prophecy proved false and Colm was able to find grass owing to the tragedy that again struck the Higgins family. As summer passed, the village people were no longer able to give more than the barest help to the widow and her orphans. Neither did the distraught woman put to the best use what little there was given. Indeed, she now turned on the whole village as she had formerly turned on Colm, denouncing the community at the top of her voice.

"Ah! Woe!" she cried, as she marched back and forth before the houses in her bare feet. "Almighty God was cruel when he left me a widow among people that are worse than the heathen Turks. There I am, with my clutch of delicate creatures, without bite or sup from morning to night. You wouldn't see a good rush of smoke out of my chimney top from Monday to Saturday. All I have to burn on my hearth is cow dung and a few miserable briers. There isn't a hot drop for the children's bellies. Ah! Woe! My curse on the hard hearts of my neighbors!"

There was a spell of cold weather toward the end of September and the two youngest children fell victims to it. They both died in the same week of pneumonia. The second death unhinged the mother's reason. Leaving the child unburied in the house, she wandered away at dead of night, with hardly a stitch of clothes on her starved body. They found her marching along the cliff tops on the evening of the following day and took her to the lunatic asylum. The remaining five children, finding no relatives willing to shelter them, were also lodged in a public institution. It then became apparent that the widow owed money right and left. Her creditors, who were chiefly shopkeepers of Kilmacalla, began to quarrel about disposal of the house and land. The case was brought into the district court.

"Here is my chance," Colm said to his wife. "Here is where I might be able to get grass this winter for my beasts."

On the day the case was to be tried, he put on his best clothes, took the family purse and went to the courthouse at Kilmacalla. After listening to the arguments of the rival lawyers for some time, he got leave to address the magistrate.

"Your honor," he said, "it would be an injustice to the children, if that farm is auctioned now, or divided up among these shopkeepers. It would be taking the bread out of the children's mouths. They have a right to do what they please later on with that land. When they grow up and come out into the world, it's for them to say if the land is to be sold, or given to one of themselves in order to raise a family on it. In the meantime, let me rent it from them, your honor. Year after year I'll pay good rent for it on the nail. Everybody knows me, sir. I'm a man of my word. I never went back on a pennyworth of promises in my natural life. Any man will tell you that, from the parish priest on down. The mother's debts can be paid out of the rent in no time at all. What more would these shop-keepers want, unless they are land-grabbers? In God's name, your honor, you'll be behaving like a Christian if you let me rent it, instead of letting these people slice it out among themselves. God bless you, sir!"

The magistrate finally agreed to Colm's suggestion for settling the dispute.

"Praised be God!" Colm cried on his return home. "I am secure now against the winter. Nothing can stop me from now on. In God's name, the two beasts are as good as raised."

Gorum was furious at this turn of events. He attacked Colm savagely that evening at the meeting place.

"There is a bloody heathen for you!" he cried. "The two little ones are barely dead in their graves, when the blood-sucker that robbed them of their milk puts his two calves grazing on their mother's share. Aye! His two calves are lovely, sure enough. Why wouldn't they be? Didn't they grow fat and strong on the milk that the little dead children should have drunk? Ah! The poor little dead creatures! It's a fine state of affairs truly, with two children dead and two beasts rolling in fat on their share of food. Mother of God! That's a cursed state of affairs for you! Beasts given rich food and children let die of hunger! Damnation has surely fallen on our village when such things are let happen here."

The men jeered at these remarks. They had lost faith in the old man.

"You are envious of Colm," they said to Gorum. "You are jealous of his success and his wisdom. You are no longer a wise man. Hatred has made a windbag of you."

One by one, they entered Colm's house, sat by his hearth and shared their pipes with him. Their wives brought presents to Mrs. Derrane and knitted with her on Sunday after Mass, at the women's hillock. The men came to Colm for advice, just as they had hitherto gone to Gorum. They put Colm in the place of honor at the meeting place.

"God is good to us," Colm said to his wife.

"He is, faith," Mrs. Derrane said. "Praised be His name."

Even so, it became more and more difficult for the family to make ends meet. The rent for the widow's farm put a heavy strain on their purse. The children's enthusiasm vanished during the winter in face of continual hunger. It became almost impossible to make them do a hand's turn.

Mrs. Derrane also forgot her solemn promise of co-operation and began to grumble out loud, when Colm would not allow even an egg for the Christmas dinner.

"Great God!" she said. "There is a limit to everything. We haven't seen fish or meat since spring. You wouldn't let us buy a piece of holly or a colored candle. We are a disgrace to the whole village, with nothing on our table but potatoes and salt for the feast of Our Lord."

"Silence," Colm said. "This is no time of the year to become impudent."

To cap it all, he ordered that the cloth made from that year's wool be sold, instead of turning it into garments for the household.

"Our rags will do us well enough for another year," he said. "In any case, patched clothes are just as warm as new ones."

Everybody in the house got terribly thin and weak. Yet Colm's iron will buoyed them up to such an extent that there was no illness.

"We have only to hold on a little while," he kept saying, "and have courage. Then we'll rise in the world. We'll be rich and famous, from one end of the parish to the other."

He himself looked like a skeleton, for he practically went without food in order that the children might have as much as possible.

"You'll kill yourself," his wife said, when he began to prepare the ground for the spring sowing. "You look like a sick man. For God's sake, let me take money out of the purse and buy a pig's cheek for you."

"Silence, woman," Colm said. "Not a penny must be touched. I have a plan. We'll need all we have and more, to make my new plan work. It's not easy to become rich, I tell you."

The cow relieved the desperate plight of the family by having her calf a month earlier than usual, during the first week of March. The children became gay once more, for they were given plenty of the new milk to drink. There was buttermilk to make the bread rise. There was even beautiful salty yellow butter, fresh from the churn and with pale drops of water glistening on its surface, to spread thickly on the long slices of crusty griddle cake.

The happy children began to whisper excitedly to one another in the evenings about the coming spring fair, when great riches were to come into the house from the sale of the pigs and the yearlings. Over and over again they discussed the toys and trinkets that their mother would buy them in the town on fair day, as a reward for their help in raising the two beasts.

They were continually running to the field where the yearlings were gorging themselves on the luscious young grass.

"They are champions," they cried boastfully, as they stared at the animals over the top of the stone fence. "Nobody ever before saw such lovely beasts."

Colm put an end to the children's dreams a few days before the fair.

"Listen to me, all of you," he told the family one evening after supper. "You have worked hard helping me with the two beasts. They are now fine yearlings, God bless them. We'll all have to work a little harder, though, so as to make them the two best bullocks that were ever seen."

Mrs. Derrane was dumfounded on hearing this news. She dropped onto a stool and fanned her face with her apron.

"Are you out of your mind, Colm?" she said at length. "How could we keep those two beasts another year? How could we keep two bullocks? Won't we have this year's calf, too, growing up and eating on us?"

"I have a plan," Colm said. "We are going to open a shop."

His wife made the sign of the Cross on her forehead and looked at him in horror.

"Why not?" said Colm. "It's only shopkeepers that rise in the world."

"Are you crazy?" his wife said. "Where would we get the money to open a shop?"

"All we need is courage," Colm said. "The few pounds we have saved, together with the price of the pigs, will be enough to open it. I'm telling you, woman, that all we need is courage and willingness. If we all work hard together, night and day . . ."

"God Almighty!" his wife interrupted. "You've gone mad. Those two beasts have gone to your head."

"No, then," said Colm. "That's not true at all. I was never wiser in my life. The war will last for years yet. It's only now the real fury is coming on the fighting nations. Very well, then. While the mad people are fighting and killing each other, let us make money out of them and rise in the world. There is going to be a demand for everything that can be eaten. There will be a price for everything fit to make your mouth water. Food is going to be more precious than gold. So will clothes. In God's name, then, let us open a shop and stock it with goods. Let us go around the parish with our horse and cart, buying up everything the people have to sell, eggs and butter and carigeen moss and fish and wool and hides and potatoes. We'll buy everything that can be parted away. We can pay them for what we buy with shop goods. Do you see? Then we'll sell what we buy from the people over in the town at a profit. Later on, we can buy sheep as well and . . ."

"Arrah! You're stark crazy," his wife interrupted angrily. "Stop talking like that, man alive, in front of the children."

At this moment all the children burst into tears, no longer able to contain their disappointment.

"Stop whinging," Colm shouted, as he leaped to his feet. "Is it crying you are because there will be nothing for you from the fair? Is it for sweets and crackers you are crying and dai-dais? All right, then. I'm telling you now there will be plenty of sweets and dai-dais for you, when we have a shop. There will be sweets every day and dai-dais, too. Do you hear me? Every day in the year will be like a fair day for you."

His uncouth face, worn to the bone by privation and worry, now glowed with the light of ecstasy, as he struggled to wheedle his family into co-operation with his ambition to rise in the world. Such was the power of the idea that possessed him, that the children stopped crying almost at once. They listened with eagerness to his fantastic promises. Their little faces became as radiant as his own.

His wife also became affected, as she saw her dour husband trying to win over the children by means of smiles and gaiety and honeyed words.

"I wouldn't believe it," she said, "only for I see it with my own two eyes."

Tears rolled down her cheeks and her upper lip trembled. "In fifteen years," she muttered, as she rubbed her eyes with a corner of her apron, "I never once saw him dance one of the children on his knee. No, faith, I never once saw him shake a rattle in front of a whinging baby. Yet there he is now, all of a sudden, trying to make a showman of himself. God Almighty! Only for I see it with my own two eyes . . ."

"There will be no end to the riches we'll have when we are shopkeepers," Colm continued. "We can have bacon for breakfast. Yes, indeed, we can eat great big rashers of it every morning in the year, except Fridays. The people of the village will be coming to smell the lovely food that's frying on our pan. Oh! I'm telling you that we can have bellies on us like tourists. We'll hardly be able to carry ourselves, as we walk the road, on account of our fat. We'll have ribbons as well and velvet and a mirror in every room."

His wife and children were won over completely to his side once more. So they all went to work with enthusiasm and the shop was speedily installed. It was an immediate success. People came from a long distance in order to trade with the courageous man, who was trying to raise two bullocks on twenty acres of barren rocks.

"Blood in ounce!" the people said. "He'll never be able to do it, but you have to admire his courage all the same. He'll very likely end up in the asylum with Kate Higgins, but more power to him for trying. He's a credit to the parish."

When Colm went round with his horse and cart, accompanied by one or other of the children, everybody was eager to do business with him. The people sold him whatever they had available and they forbore to drive a hard bargain. He soon had to take the house and barn that belonged to Kate Higgins, in order to store the great mass of his goods. Within a few months he was making trips to the town twice a week and getting high prices for all he had to sell.

Money kept coming into the house so quickly and in such large quantities that his wife became frightened.

"May God keep pride and arrogance out of our hearts," she used to say, as she stuffed the notes into the long cloth purse. "It's dangerous to get rich so quickly."

"Have no fear, woman," Colm said to her. "We denied ourselves and we didn't lose heart when times were bad. So now God is giving us a big hansel as a reward. Be grateful, woman and have no fear."

The promises that he had made to the children were fulfilled. There was full and plenty in the house. The little girls had ribbons to their hair and dai-dais to amuse their leisure. His wife got a velvet dress and a hat with feathers. There was bacon for breakfast.

"He must have touched the magic stone," said the astonished people of the village. "Everything he handles turns into lashings of money."

Andy Gorum alone continued to prophesy that misfortune would fall on Colm for attempting to "stand alone and rise above the people."

"You just wait," Gorum kept shouting on the hill before the village. "God will strike him down when he least expects it. Those two beasts, that are now so lovely, will never reach the fair green alive on their four legs."

This prophecy proved to be just as false as the previous one that Gorum had made. All through the winter and the following spring, Colm and his family lavished the greatest care on the two beasts that had brought them prosperity. So that they were really champions on fair day. The bullock with the wine-dark hide was acknowledged by all to be the finest animal of his age ever seen in the district. He fetched top price.

Tears poured down Colm's cheeks as he walked back from the railway station with his wife, after parting with his beasts.

"Those two lovely beasts brought me luck," he said. "I feel lonely for them now that they are gone. Only for them, I'd never think of rising in the world. Praised be God! He works in strange ways. He strikes one down and raises up another."

"True for you," his wife said. "Praised be His holy name! Who are we, miserable sinners that we are, to question His mysterious ways?"

"Only for that cow dying on Kate Higgins," Colm continued, "we'd always be land slaves, wrestling with starvation to the end of our days and never getting the better of any bout. Look at us now, woman. We're on our way toward riches. God alone knows where we'll stop."

"Enough of that talk now," his wife said. "Don't let arrogance get hold of us. Don't let us be boastful. The people are already becoming envious of us. I can see a begrudging look in the eyes of the neighbors."

"That's true," Colm said. "That's why I'm thinking of opening a shop in the town. It might be better to take ourselves out of the sight of the people that knew us poor."

"A shop in the town?" his wife said. "Don't get too big for your boots, Colm."

"No fear," Colm said. "I know what I'm doing. I'm going to hire a few men and begin buying in earnest. There's money to be picked up by the bushel all over the place. All we need is courage, woman."

"In God's name!" his wife said.

When they were hitching the mare to their new jaunting car for the journey home, Andy Gorum came along with a group of intoxicated men.

"The mills of God grind slow," Gorum shouted, "but they grind sure. The bloodsuckers are taking the food out of our country. They are giving it to the fighting foreigners, while our children die of hunger. We are barefooted and in rags, but they give our wool and our hides to the war people. They are taking all our lovely beasts across the seas to fill the bellies of pagans. The time will soon come, though, when the bloodsuckers that are robbing us will be struck down by the hand of Almighty God. They will roast in Hell for the everlasting ages."

As Colm drove away in his new green jaunting car, quite a number of people whistled after him in hostility and derision. Now that he had risen so far, he had again become an enemy.

His gaunt face looked completely unaware of their jeers. His pale blue eyes stared fixedly straight ahead, cold and resolute and ruthless.

THE IMPORTANT THING

by TENNESSEE WILLIAMS

THEY MET AT THE SPRING DANCE BY THE BAPTIST FEMALE College which Laura was attending that year. The college was in the same town as the state university at which John was completing his sophomore year. He knew only one girl at the college and wasn't able to find her in the ballroom. It was hot and crowded in there and had that feverish, glaring effect which usually prevails at a spring dance given by a sectarian girls' school. The room was lighted by four or five blazing chandeliers and the walls were covered with long mirrors. Between dances the couples stood about stiffly in their unaccustomed formal dress and glanced uneasily at the reflection in the highly polished glass, shifted their weight from foot to foot, nervously twisted or flipped their program cards. None of them seemed to know each other very well. They talked in loud, unnatural voices, shrieked with laughter or stood sullenly quiet. The teachers flitted among them with birdlike alacrity, intently frowning or beaming, introducing, prompting, encouraging. It was not like a social affair. It was more like an important military maneuver.

John walked around the edge of the floor several times and was rather relieved at not finding the one girl he knew. When he arrived at the palm-flanked entrance he turned to go out, but just then his arm was violently plucked by one of the teachers, a middle-aged woman with frowzy gray hair, sharp nose, and large yellow teeth. She looked so wild and Harpy-like that John involuntarily squirmed aside from her grasp.

"Are you alone?" she shrieked in his ear.

The band was thumping out a terrifically loud foxtrot. John rubbed his ear and pointed vaguely toward the door. But she tightened her grasp on his arm and propelled him across the floor by a series of jerks that careened him from one dancing couple to another till they reached a corner where stood an apparently stranded group of young Baptist females beneath the protective fronds of an enormous boxed palm.

The Harpy gave his arm a final twist and John found himself facing a tall, thin girl in a pink taffeta dress who stood slightly apart from her fellow refugees. He caught the name Laura shrieked through the increasing din. He didn't notice the girl's face. He was too furious at being roped in like this even to look at her. They advanced awkwardly toward each other. John slid his arm around her unbelievably slender waist. Through the silk he could feel the hard ridge of her spine. There was no weight to her body. She floated before him so lightly that it was almost like dancing by himself, except that the cord of bone kept moving beneath his warm, sweating fingers and her fine, loose hair plastered itself against his damp cheek.

The foxtrot had reached a crescendo. Cymbals were clashing and drums beating out double time. The girl's lips moved against his throat. Her breath tickled his skin but he couldn't hear a word she was saying. He looked helplessly down at her. Suddenly she broke away from him. She stood slightly off from him, her eyes crinkling with laughter and one hand clutched to her mouth. The music stopped.

"What're you laughing at?" John asked.

"The whole situation," said Laura. "You no more wanted to dance than I did!"

"Didn't you want to?"

"Of course not. When I think of dancing I think of Isadora Duncan who said she wanted to teach the whole world how to dance, but this wasn't what she meant—do you think it was?"

She had a way of looking up that made her face very brilliant and for a few moments obscured the fact that she was by no means pretty. But there was something about her, something which already excited him a little, and so he said, "Let's go outside."

They spent practically all the rest of the evening in the oak grove between the gymnasium and the chapel, strolling around and smoking his cigarettes. While smoking the girl would flatten herself against a tree trunk, for smoking was forbidden on the campus.

"This is the advantage of being a fence pole," she told him. "You can hide behind anything with the slightest diameter."

Everything that she said had a wry, humorous twist, and even when it wasn't humorous she would laugh slightly and John had the impression that she was unusually clever. They went into the empty chapel for a while and sat in a back pew and talked about religion.

"It's all so archaic," Laura said. "It's all a museum piece!"

John had recently become an agnostic himself. They agreed that the Christian religion and the Hebrew, in fact, nearly all religions, were based on a concept of guilt.

"*Mea culpa!*" said John, thinking that she would say, "What's that?" But she didn't. She nodded her head. And he was excited to discover that she, too, was interested in writing. She had won a literary prize in high school and she was now ediitor of the college literary magazine. The teacher who had brought them together was Laura's English instructor.

"She thinks I'm very talented," said Laura. "She wants me to send one of my stories to *Harper's*."

"Why don't you?" asked John.

"Oh, I don't know," said Laura. "I think the main thing is just expressing yourself as honestly as you can. I am not interested in style," she went on, "it's such a waste of time to do things over and get the right cadence and always just the right word. I'd rather just scramble through one thing and then rush into another, until I have said everything that I have to say!"

How extraordinary it was that she and John should feel exactly the same way about this! He confessed that he was himself a writer and that two or three of his stories were coming out in the University's literary magazine—and when Laura heard this she was almost absurdly moved.

"I'd love to see them, I've got to see them!" she cried.

"I'll bring them over," he promised.

"When?"

"As soon as they come out!"

"I don't care how the style is as long as they're honest. They've got to be honest!" she pleaded. "Are they?"

"I hope so," he answered uneasily.

She had taken his arm and was squeezing it in a grip that was almost as tight as a wrestler's, and with every excited inflection in her speech she squeezed it tighter. There was no relaxation in Laura, none of the softness and languor which he found physically interesting in girls. He could not imagine her lying passively still and quietly submitting the way he thought a girl should to a man's embraces.

"What do you think about human relations?" she asked him just at the moment when this disturbing image was in his mind.

"That's a large subject," said John.

"Oh, what a large, large subject! And it is the one I will never be able to cope with!"

"Why?" asked John.

"I'm equal to anything else, but not human relations! I'll always be moving when other people are still, and still when they're moving," said Laura, "and it will be a terrible mess and a mix-up from start to finish!"

"You shouldn't feel that way about it," he told her lamely, astonished at the way her words fitted exactly what he had been thinking.

She looked up at John. "You'll have the same trouble!" she told him. "We'll never be happy but we'll have lots of excitement, and if we hold on to our personal integrity everything won't be lost!"

He wasn't quite sure what Laura was talking about, and personal integrity seemed the vaguest of terms. Was it something like what she meant by "honest" writing?

"Yes, something," said Laura, "but ever so much more difficult, because writing is ideal reality and living is not ideal. . . ."

At the window of the gymnasium they stood for a while and watched the dancers who had reached what appeared to be nearly the point of exhaustion. Faces that had been flushed and perspiring when they had left the room were now quite desperate looking and the men in the jazz band seemed to be playing now out of sheer inability to break an old habit. Some of the paper streamers had come unfastened and fallen upon the floor, others hung limply from the ceiling, and in one corner a small crowd, mostly teachers, were clustered about a girl who had fainted.

"Don't they look silly!" said Laura.

"Who?"

"Dancers—everybody!"

"What isn't silly, in your opinion?" asked John.

"Give me a little while to answer that question!"

"How long shall I give you?"

"I'll tell you right now—The Important Thing isn't silly!"

"What Important Thing?" John asked.

"I don't know yet," said Laura. "Why do you think I'm living, except to discover what The Important Thing is?"

John didn't see her again that spring. Final examinations came soon after the dance, and besides he was not altogether sure that she was the sort of girl he would get along with. She was not good-looking and her intensity which was so charming while he was with her seemed afterward a little fantastic.

Very soon after he returned to school that fall he ran into her on the campus. She was now enrolled as a sophomore in the state university. He barely recognized her. It had been so dark in the oak grove, where they spent most of their time at the spring dance, that he hadn't gotten a very clear impression of her face. She was at once homelier and more attractive than he remembered. Her face was very wide at the top and narrow at the bottom: almost an inverted pyramid. Her eyes were large and rather oblique, hazel brown with startling flecks of blue or green in them. Her nose was long and pointed and the tip covered with freckles. She had a way of smiling and blinking her eyes very rapidly as she talked. She talked so fast and shrilly that he felt a little embarrassed. He noticed a group of girls staring at her and giggling. Fools, he thought, and was angry at himself for having felt embarrassed.

It was noon when they met and she was on her way to the

boardinghouse where she was staying. She hadn't pledged a sorority. She announced the fact with an air of proud defiance that John liked.

"I could see that I wouldn't fit into any of them," she said. "I'd rather be independent, wouldn't you? The trouble with this world is that everybody has to compromise and conform. Oh, I'm sick of it! I won't do it! I shall live my own life just the way that I please!"

John had felt the same way about joining a fraternity and he told her so.

"Ah, we're a couple of barbs!" she shrieked. "Isn't that marvelous? The other girls at the boardinghouse simply detest being called barbs—but I adore it! I think it's really thrilling to be called a barbarian! It makes you feel like you could strip off your clothes and dance naked in the streets if you felt like doing it!"

John felt a warm glow as though he'd been drinking. It was the way he'd felt in the oak grove, talking to her last spring. It seemed suddenly that he had a great deal to say. He became excited and started talking rapidly about a one-act play that he was writing. It was full of involved symbolism and hard to explain. But Laura nodded her head with quick, eager jerks and supplied words wherever he stumbled. She seemed to know intuitively what he was trying to say.

"Oh, I think that's marvelous, marvelous!" she kept repeating.

He was thinking of submitting it to the one-act play contest. His roommate had urged him to do so.

"My goodness, why don't you!" exclaimed Laura.

"Oh, I don't know," John said. "I think the main thing is just expressing oneself, don't you?"

Immediately afterward they both laughed, remembering that Laura had said the same thing about the story her English teacher had wanted her to send to *Harper's*.

"Was it accepted?" John asked.

"No, it came back with a printed card," she admitted ruefully. "But I don't care. I'm writing poetry now. They say that you should write poetry while you're young and feel things keenly."

She laughed and caught John's arm. "I feel things very keenly, don't you?"

They sat down on the front steps of the boardinghouse and talked until the bell tolled for one-o'clock classes. Both of them had missed their lunch.

They saw a great deal of each other after that. They had many interests in common. They were both on the staff of the university's literary magazine and belonged to the Poetry and French clubs. It was the year of the national election and John became twenty-one just in time to vote. Laura spent hours arguing with him about politics and finally convinced him that he must vote for Norman Thomas. Later they both joined the Young Communists' League. John became a very enthusiastic radical. He helped operate a secret printing press and distribute pamphlets about the campus attacking fraternities, political control of the university, academic conservatism, and so forth. He was once called before the dean of men and threatened with expulsion. Laura thought this was terribly thrilling.

"If you get expelled," she promised, "I'll quit school too!"

But it all blew over and they both remained in the university.

All of these things served to draw them closer together. But for some reason they were not altogether at ease with each other. John always had the feeling that something very important was going to happen between them. He could not have explained why he felt that way. Perhaps it was the contagion of Laura's intensity. When he was with her he felt the kind of suppressed excitement a scientist might feel upon the verge of an important discovery. A constant expectation or suspense. Was Laura conscious of the same thing? Sometimes he felt sure that she was. But her enthusiasm was so diffuse that he could never be sure. One thing after another caught her interest. She was like a precocious child just discovering the world, taking nothing in it for granted, receiving each impression with the fresh wonder of a child but an adult's mature understanding. About most things she talked very frankly. But once in a while she would become oddly reticent.

Once he asked her where she came from.

"Kansas," she told him.

"I know, but what place in Kansas?"

He was surprised to see her face coloring. They were in the reference room of the library that evening, studying together at one of the yellow oak tables. She opened her notebook and ignored his question.

"What place?" he insisted, wondering why she flushed.

Abruptly she slammed the notebook shut and faced him with a laugh. "What does it matter what place?"

"I just wanted to know."

"Well, I won't tell you!"

"Why not?"

"Because it doesn't matter where you come from. It only matters where you're going!"

"Where are you going, then?"

"I don't know!"

She leaned back in the straight yellow oak chair and shook with laughter. "How on earth should I know where I'm going?"

The librarian approached them with a warning frown. "Please, not so loud. This room's for study."

"Where are you going?" John repeated under his breath.

Laura hid her face in the notebook and continued laughing.

"Where are you going, where are you going, where are you going!" John whispered. He did it to tease her. She looked so funny with the black leather notebook covering her face, only her braided hair showing and her throat flushed turkey red.

All at once she jumped up from the table and he saw that her face was contorted with crying. She rushed out of the room and he couldn't get her to speak a word to him all the way back to her boardinghouse.

Some time later he found the name of her home town on the envelope of a letter which she'd forgotten to remove from a book of poems she'd loaned him. The envelope was postmarked from Hardwood, Kansas. John grinned. It was a hick town in the northwestern part of the state and probably the deadest spot on earth. . . .

Despising himself for doing so, he opened the letter and read it. It was from Laura's mother and was a classic of its kind. It complained of the money Laura was having to spend on board and books, urged her to spend less time writing nonsense and buckle down to hard work so that she could get a teaching job when she got through with her schooling because times were getting to be very bad. . . . "The ground and the people and the business and everything else is dried up around here," wrote the mother. "I don't know what things are coming to. It must be God's judgment, I guess. Three solid years of drought. Looks like this time God is planning to dry the wickedness out of the world instead of drowning it out!"

That spring John bought a used car for thirty-five dollars and every free afternoon he and Laura drove around the lovely country roads and had picnic lunches which Laura prepared. He was getting use to Laura's odd appearance and her absurd animation, but other people weren't. She had become something of a character on the campus. John was at this time being rushed by a professional fraternity and he was told that some of the fellows thought that Laura was a very queer person for him to be seen around with. Now and again his mind would go back to their first conversation in the oak grove of the Baptist Female College, the talk about human relations and her inability to cope with them, and it appeared to him that she was not even going halfway in attempting to. There was no reason for her to talk so loudly on such eclectic subjects whenever they passed along a crowded corridor of a university building, there was surely no reason for her to be so rude to people she wasn't interested in, walking abruptly away without an excuse when talk turned to things she classified as inane—which was almost everything John's other friends talked about.

Other girls on the campus he could look at and imagine in the future, settled down into average middle-class life, becoming teachers or entering other professions. But when he looked at Laura he could not see her future, he could not imagine her becoming or doing any known thing, or going back to Hardwood, Kansas, or going anywhere else. She did not fit happily or comfortably into the university cosmos, but in what other place or circumstances—he asked himself—could she have found any refuge whatsoever? Perhaps he was no more like other people than she was, but his case was different. He was more adaptable, he demanded a good deal less of people and things. Come up against a barrier, he was of a nature to look for a way around it. But Laura—

Laura had decided that the English department of the university was hopelessly reactionary and the only course she took an interest in, now, was geology. Their favorite spot, that spring, was an abandoned rock quarry where Laura searched for fossils. She danced around the quarry like a bright, attractive little monkey on a wire, her green smock fluttering in the wind and her voice constantly flowing up to him, sometimes shrill with excitement and sometimes muted with intense absorption.

"Don't you ever want to be still?" John asked her.

"Never till I have to!"

John would get tired of waiting and would open the lunch box. She would finally join him on the hilltop, too tired to eat, and would spread her fossils around her and pore delightedly over them while John munched sandwiches of peanut butter and jelly or Swiss cheese on rye. The rest of the afternoon they would spend talking about literature and life, art and civilization. They both had tremendous admiration for the ancient Greeks and the modern Russians. Greece is the world's past, said Laura, and Russia is the future—which John thought a brilliant statement, though it sounded a little familiar as if he had come across it somewhere before in a book.

Their discussions would continue unflaggingly till sundown, but as dusk began to settle they would become a little nervous and constrained, for some reason, and there would be long pauses in their talk, during which it was curiously difficult for them to look at each other. After a while, when it was getting really dark, Laura would abruptly jump up from the grass and brush off her smock. "I guess we'd better be going," she would say. Her voice would sound with the dull, defeated tone of someone who has argued a long time about something very important without making any impression upon the other's mind. John would feel strangely miserable as he followed her down the hill to where they had parked the old roadster. He would also feel that something had been left unsaid or undone, a feeling of incompletion. . . .

It was the last Saturday before the end of the spring term. They were going to spend the whole day out in the country, studying for a final examination in a French course which they were taking together. Laura had prepared sandwiches and deviled eggs. And John, with some trepidation, had purchased a quart of red wine. He put the bottle in the side pocket of the roadster and didn't mention it until after they'd finished eating because he knew Laura didn't like drinking. She had no moral objections, she said, but thought it was a senseless, wasteful practice. She refused to drink any of the wine. "But you may, if you wish," she added with a primness that made John laugh.

They were seated, as usual, on the grassy hill above the rock quarry. It was called Lover's Leap. Laura held the notebook which they had prepared together and was quizzing John. She was leaning against one of the large white boulders scattered about the hilltop and John was stretched at her feet. He held the wine bottle between his knees and drank out of the thermos cup. Laura's constraint at first sight of the bottle wore off. She called him Bacchus.

"I wish I had time to make you a wreath," she said. "You'd look too adorable with a wreath of green leaves!"

"Why don't you be a nymph?" John asked. "Take off your clothes and be a wood nymph! I'll chase you through the birch trees!"

The idea pleased John very much. He laughed loudly. But Laura was embarrassed. She cleared her throat and held the notebook in front of her face, but he could see by the base of her throat that she was blushing. He stopped laughing, feeling somewhat embarrassed himself. He knew what she was thinking. She was thinking what might happen if he should catch her among the birch trees with all her clothes off. . . .

John drank another cupful of wine. He felt very good. He

had removed his jacket and unbuttoned the collar of his shirt and rolled up the sleeves. The sun shone dazzlingly in his eyes, made rainbows in his eyelashes, warmed the bare flesh of his throat and arms. A comfortable glow passed through him. He was newly conscious of the life in his body; flexed his legs, rubbed his stomach, and arched his thighs. He no longer listened to the questions that Laura was asking him out of the notebook. She had to repeat them two or three times before they were clear.

At last she became disgusted and tossed the notebook aside. "I believe you're getting intoxicated!" she told him sharply.

He looked indolently up at her. "Maybe I am! What of it?"

He noticed that she was not very pretty. Especially not when she drew her brows together and squinted her eyes like that. Her face was irregular and bony looking. Rather outlandish, so broad at the top and narrow at the bottom. Long pointed nose and eyes flecked with different colors which were too large for the rest of her and always filled with superfluous brightness. Reminded him of an undersized child he once knew in grammar school. For some reason they called him Peekie and threw rocks at him after school. A timid, ridiculous creature with a high, squeaky voice that everyone mocked. The larger boys caught him after school and asked him the meaning of obscene words or pulled the buttons off his knickers. She was like that. A queer person. But there was something exciting about her just as there'd been something exciting about Peekie that made the larger boys want to amuse themselves with him. There was something about her that he wanted to set his hands on in a rough way—twist and pull and tease! Her skin was the most attractive thing about her. It was very fine and smooth and white. . . .

John's eyes traveled down her body. She wore a black sweater and a black-and-white checked skirt. As he looked at her legs a brisk wind tossed her skirt up and he could see the bare flesh above where the stockings ended. He rolled over on his stomach and placed both hands on her thighs. He'd never touched her so intimately before but somehow it seemed a perfectly natural thing to do. She made a startled movement away from him. Suddenly he thought he knew what the important thing was that was going to happen between them. He caught her by the shoulders and tried to pull her down in the grass, but she fought against him wildly. Neither of them said anything. They just fought together like two wild animals, rolling in the grass and clawing at each other. Laura clawed at John's face and John clawed at Laura's body. They accepted this thing, this desperate battle between them, as though they'd known all along it was coming, as though it had been inevitable from the start. Neither of them spoke a word until they were at last exhausted and lay still on the grass, breathing heavily and looking up at the slowly darkening sky.

John's face was scratched and bleeding in several places. Laura pressed her hands against her stomach and groaned. He had kicked her with his knee trying to make her lie still.

"It's all over now," he said. "I'm not going to hurt you."

But she continued moaning.

The sun had gone down and dusk gathered. There was a big, purplish-red blotch in the western sky that looked like a bruised place.

John got up to his feet and stood silently staring at the angry afterglow. Away off to the left was the university town, beginning to emerge through its leafy clouds with the sparkling animation of a Saturday night in late spring. There would be many gay parties and dances that night. Girls in dresses that seemed to be woven of flowers would whirl about polished dance floors and couples would whisper and laugh behind clumps of ghostly spirea. These were the natural celebrations of youth. He and this girl had been searching for something else. What was it? Again and again later on the search would be made, the effort to find something outside of common experience, digging and rooting among the formless rubble of things for the one lost thing that was altogether lovely—and perhaps every time a repetition of this, violence and ugliness of desire turned to rage. . . .

He spoke aloud to himself. "We didn't have anything—we were fooling ourselves."

He turned from the dark, haunting beauty of the town and

looked down at Laura. She blinked her eyes and drew her breath in sharply. She looked almost ugly, her face covered with sweat and grass stain. She was not like a girl. He wondered that he had never noticed before how anonymous was her gender, for this was the very central fact of her nature. She belonged nowhere, she fitted in no place at all, she had no home, no shell, no place of comfort or refuge, she was a fugitive with no place to run to. Others in her position might make some adjustment. The best of whatever is offered, however not right. But Laura would not accept it, none of the ways and means. The most imperfect part of her was the most pure. And that meant—

"Laura . . ." He held out his hand and put his heart in his eyes. She felt the sudden turning of understanding and took his hand and he pulled her gently to her feet.

For the first time they stood together in the dark without any fear of each other, their hands loosely clasped and returning each other's look with sorrowful understanding, unable to help each other except through knowing, each completely separate and alone—but no longer strangers. . . .

THE MAN

by MEL DINELLI

MRS. GILLIS'S ROOMER, MR. ARMSTRONG, TRIED TO WARN HER that morning before he left on his business trip. They were just finishing breakfast, and he was rather in a hurry. "I don't care what you say," he said seriously, "you're alone here in the house all day. There're no close neighbors, and after all, you know nothing about the man."

Mrs. Gillis smiled. "Good gracious, you'd think I was a pretty young thing of twenty to hear you tell it."

"And another thing," he continued, "it seems strange to me that a young man should be job hunting from door to door in this day and age. Why, there're plenty of jobs to be had."

Mrs. Gillis laughed. "You're a worry wart, Mr. Armstrong. And now that I've found someone to do my heavy work, I'm not going to let you and your silly notions change my mind."

"All the same though," Mr. Armstrong said stubbornly, "I'm not leaving the house this morning till I get a look at the guy."

Mr. Armstrong was late to his appointment that morning; he didn't leave the house until after nine. As he dried the breakfast dishes, he kept looking out the window toward the long driveway.

Mrs. Gillis was still amused. "You're making a mountain out of a molehill—why, there's a phone in the house, isn't there? And I suppose Sarah'd let me down if there was any trouble."

"Sarah's fat and old, and she hasn't a tooth in her head," Mr. Armstrong said sarcastically.

"A growl is more effective than a bite, and besides—" Mrs. Gillis began, but suddenly she noticed Mr. Armstrong was smiling. He'd seen her young man coming up the driveway. And Mrs. Gillis smiled too. Even she had forgotten what a meek, harmless-looking lad he was. Why, he could hardly be called a man at all, she thought, and then Mr. Armstrong laughed. "So that's the critter who's been causing me all this mental anguish," he said.

Mrs. Gillis was pleased at his reaction. "There, you see! You, and your silly notions!"

"Why, the little guy's not strong enough to keep a regular job, I suppose."

"Hush, now!" Mrs. Gillis said quickly. "There you go from one extreme to the other. I won't stand for your making fun of him."

"All right, I can go on my trip now," he said, as he wiped the last of the dishes. "Expect I'll be gone about a week this time."

Suddenly Mrs. Gillis's old dog came out from under the stove; she looked at the door a moment, and then she growled softly.

Mrs. Gillis was surprised. "Well, Sarah," she said, "don't tell me that I'm going to have trouble from you, too, now! What is it, girl?"

The dog whimpered a bit and then she barked weakly. Mrs. Gillis reached down and patted her. "Why, I believe she's been listening to some of your foolish notions, Mr. Armstrong," she said, amused.

There was a knock at the door, and Sarah's barking grew louder. Mr. Armstrong spoke to the dog quietly. "There now, Sarah," he said, "I'm sorry that I made you nervous about him. Why, if you could see the guy—"

"Sh!" Mrs. Gillis said, as she moved toward the door to open it. "He'll hear you!"

"Good morning, lad," Mrs. Gillis said as she opened the door. "I've been expecting you. This is my roomer, Mr. Armstrong—and I don't believe you told me your name."

"I'm Howard Wilton, ma'am," the young man said as he stood there holding his hat in his hand.

"Hello, Howard," Mr. Armstrong said cordially. "I'm glad you've come and I know you'll be a great help to Mrs. Gillis—and you'll be company, too—"

Suddenly Sarah was growling again, and the young man

looked down at her. "I don't believe your dog likes me," he said.

"Of course she does," Mrs. Gillis said quickly. "But she's getting old and peevish like some of my other friends." She looked over Howard's shoulder at Mr. Armstrong.

She finally calmed Sarah down, and then she found a sunny spot for her in the breakfast room.

Mr. Armstrong left, but not before he'd winked at Mrs. Gillis to signify that he'd been a fool to worry over her new hired man.

"Come along now, Howard," Mrs. Gillis said as she started for the kitchen. "I'll show you where to hang your coat."

She led him to a closet storeroom at the back of the house, and she handed him a clothes hanger and a rough, heavy apron which she kept for her cleaning help.

Howard took the apron and then he looked up at Mrs. Gillis. "Is this apron clean?" he asked.

"Why, of course it's clean," she replied, "no one's worn it since it was laundered last."

"There're spots on it," Howard said slowly. "See?" he held out the apron.

"Spots?" Mrs. Gillis took the apron. "Why, that's paint. No dirt in dried paint, son," she said.

"If you don't mind, I'd rather not wear it."

"What will you wear then? You didn't bring other clothes, did you?"

"I'm a neat worker, Mrs. Gillis. You needn't worry about my clothes," he said as he removed his coat.

Mrs. Gillis was silent for a moment. She was on the verge of telling him that she wasn't the slightest worried about his clothes, but when she turned, the light hitting his face from the small storeroom window made him look so strange. She was startled for a moment, and then she thought, you're a silly old woman, and then she smiled.

"Are you laughing at me, Mrs. Gillis?" he asked.

"Why, no, son," she answered kindly. "I was laughing at myself. Come along now, let's get started."

Howard had been at the den floor a short time when Mrs. Gillis heard him walk back to the closet storeroom.

"Can I help you, son?" she called.

"I'm going after my coat," he replied. "I don't like it being out there in the storeroom—it's a breeding place for moths, you know."

"Now, son," Mrs. Gillis smiled, "it takes longer than that for moths to get started."

"Perhaps you won't think it's quite so amusing when I tell you that it's my best and only coat," he said.

"I didn't mean to hurt your feelings, lad. Where would you like to put it—in the kitchen, perhaps?"

"No. The cooking fumes wouldn't be good for it. I'll take it right in the den with me." Then as an afterthought, he added, "That is, if you don't mind, Mrs. Gillis."

"Go right ahead," she said. But her eyes were puzzled as she stared after him.

Suddenly Mrs. Gillis was thankful that there was a phone in the house. He was such a peculiar boy. She wasn't really alarmed. Still, it was good to know that the phone was there and that old Sarah was in the breakfast room asleep.

She went on about her own work that morning. But several times she went into the den to have a look at him. He wasn't doing much, she could see that. He seemed to keep polishing one small square in the corner of the room. Finally she spoke to him. "Is there anything you need, son?" she asked.

But there was no answer. He didn't even bother to look up. He kept running his cloth over the same spot—over and over again.

"Howard," Mrs. Gillis began.

"I won't be spied upon," he said suddenly. "I won't put up with that!"

Mrs. Gillis was really concerned. "See here, lad," she said, "I think we must have gotten off on the wrong foot. I'm not spying on you."

"Then why do you keep popping in like this?" he snapped. And then he was speaking very rapidly, "Would you like me to work faster—would you like me to spill out my life's blood for you here on the floor? Is that what you're after?"

Mrs. Gillis was suddenly afraid. "Howard, lad," she said, "are you well? Are you well enough to work?"

"Of course I'm well. If only you'd quit bothering and questioning and pestering me! Is that too much to ask?"

Mrs. Gillis hesitated a moment before speaking. "Howard, I'm interested in young men. I have two boys of my own—they're in the service. See, that's Bill on the desk there—he's a Marine. And on the table there, that's Dennis. He's in the Infantry, overseas."

Howard looked at her grimly. "So that's why you hate me! I see it all now!" he said.

"Hate you? Why, whatever gave you—"

"Yes, you hate me," he interrupted. "I could tell it the moment I walked into this house this morning!"

"But Howard—"

"You hate me because I'm young and I'm not in the service like your boys."

"It never occurred to me! You must know I was grateful when you came looking for work."

"Grateful!" he sneered. "You resented me. The only reason you have me here is to work my life's blood away. To punish me for not being in the service, just because your sons are in the service and I'm out."

Mrs. Gillis was very gentle when she answered. "Son, you're ill. Let's put the work away now, and I'll make you a cup of tea."

"So you don't want me to do the job, is that it?" he said bitterly. "You're like the Army—there was a job to be done, and they wouldn't let me in—and now you'd like me to stop in the middle of this, would you?"

"I only want you to do whatever will make you feel better," she said quietly.

"Well, leave me alone then!"

"Very well." Mrs. Gillis started to leave, but somehow she could feel his eyes on her. And then she heard him call her, and his voice was low and cold. "Mrs. Gillis!"

"Yes?"

"I'll tell you why I'm not in the Army—if you insist."

"I don't insist at all, Howard."

"If you must know," he said so low she could scarcely hear, "they said there was something wrong with my mind."

Mrs. Gillis closed the door softly behind her. The first thing she thought of when she reached the hall way was the phone. But it was in the den—with him. She ran quickly to the back door, but it was locked; and the key wasn't in its usual place.

A little breathless, she went to the front door. It, too, was locked. She was on the verge of trying the windows, when she suddenly thought of Sarah. She was afraid for her—Sarah hadn't made a sound in hours. Mrs. Gillis had just started for the breakfast room when she heard a crash. It came from the den, and she rushed in to find Howard peacefully polishing away at the same spot. He hadn't moved an inch. He didn't look up at her, and then she saw the phone which had fallen to the floor beside him.

"The phone fell," he said calmly.

As Mrs. Gillis walked over to pick up the phone, she saw that the wires had been jerked out of the wall. She stood looking at the wires a moment and then he spoke to her.

"I suppose you think I ruined your phone," he said.

"The wires—" she began.

"That happened when it fell to the floor," he replied.

"But it couldn't have!"

"That happened when it fell to the floor," he repeated.

Mrs. Gillis started to speak again, "But—"

"I don't suppose you'll be able to use it any more," he said quietly. "Not for a while, anyway."

"No, I don't suppose I will," Mrs. Gillis replied as she looked at him.

She began to feel frantic. All the doors were locked, and the high, old-fashioned windows offered no quick means of escape. And Sarah had disappeared. She called her several times, and she combed the house for her, but she was nowhere to be found. Then she decided to take one last look in the closet storeroom.

"Sarah! Sarah!" And as she entered the closet, she knew that he was behind her, standing in the narrow doorway. A shiver went through her.

"Mrs. Gillis."

"Yes?"

"Are you looking for your dog?"

"Yes. I haven't seen her all morning. She was in the breakfast room."

"Well, she's not there any longer," Howard replied.

"I know. Where is she?" Mrs. Gillis asked timidly.

"Where is she?" Howard repeated after her.

Mrs. Gillis suddenly became excited. "Yes, where *is* she?"

"She's gone," he said flatly.

"Gone?" Mrs. Gillis looked at him. "If you've harmed her—"

"She didn't like me, you know."

"See here," her voice rose, "I've put up with enough! You tell me where my dog is, or—"

"Or what, Mrs. Gillis?"

"I'll—I'll—"

"You'll do what, Mrs. Gillis? What will you do?"

Mrs. Gillis was becoming hysterical. "Sarah! Here, Sarah!" she cried.

"She's gone, Mrs. Gillis. I told you that."

"You've harmed my dog!"

"Have I?"

"You killed her!" Mrs. Gillis began to cry. "Poor Sarah, who'd never hurt a thing."

"She would have hurt me."

"You're bad, Howard—you're wicked! You're a coward!"

"I'm not a coward, Mrs. Gillis. Cowards are afraid to kill."

Mrs. Gillis was sobbing now. "Only a coward would kill a poor old dog."

"If I were a coward, I'd be afraid of you," he said. "And I'm not afraid of you."

"You let me out of here," she said as she attempted to go past him.

But he stood firmly wedged in the doorway. "I have strong hands, Mrs. Gillis. My fingers are like steel."

"I've never harmed you, Howard."

"No, and Sarah didn't either. But she would have, if I hadn't harmed her first."

"Let me out of here," Mrs. Gillis screamed.

"You're getting very noisy," he said. "Perhaps if I locked you in here, you'd calm down a bit."

"Howard! Howard!" She screamed hysterically.

And then he suddenly stepped out of the doorway and he slammed the door shut, and she heard the key turn in the lock. For a moment she had a feeling of unreality. Was this really happening? The dim light from the little square window picked out a limp, lifeless object in the corner among the dusty mops. She knew without looking further what it was—poor Sarah. Sarah, who'd never harmed a soul.

Mrs. Gillis remained in the closet for what seemed hours. And she could hear him moving about the house. Finally he came back and he spoke to her through the door.

"Have you calmed down?" he asked.

"Yes, Howard. Let me out."

"Why?"

"Because it's warm in here. Because I want to get out."

"You were looking for your dog, weren't you?"

"Never mind about that," she said after a slight pause. "Let me out."

"Mrs. Gillis, if I kept you in there, you wouldn't be able to spy on me ever again."

"I won't spy on you, Howard. Let me out."

"Do you know what I've been doing, Mrs. Gillis?"

"No."

"I've been doing your den floors like you asked me to. It was fine being able to work peacefully—knowing that you were someplace where you couldn't bother me."

"I won't bother you, Howard."

"It was very peaceful—nobody to bother me."

"Let me out, Howard."

"Will you promise to do as I tell you?"

"I promise."

"Anything?"

"Yes, anything."

"Very well, then—"

Mrs. Gillis heard the key turn in the lock.

"Now, no tricks," he said.

"No."

"Feel my hands, Mrs. Gillis," and he held them out before him. They were thin hands, and he turned them over slowly, and he looked at them. "Are they nice hands?" he asked.

"Yes," she replied meekly, "they're nice hands."

"You haven't felt them."

Mrs. Gillis knew better than to argue. She forced herself to take hold of one of them. It was icy cold, and the wax had make it sticky.

"Have your sons as nice hands as these?" he asked.

"No, no, they haven't," she replied quickly.

"But they got into the Army, didn't they? I'm just as good as they are, you know."

"Of course you are, Howard. Wouldn't you like some food, lad? You haven't eaten all day, you know."

"Some food would be good," he said quietly.

"Let me fix you some," and she moved slowly past him toward the kitchen. He looked at her, but he seemed preoccupied.

"Mrs. Gillis," he said, "a woman I worked for once said my hands were weak."

"She did?"

"She soon found out, however."

"Here, now, lad, I have some nice cold roast in the icebox."

It was almost as if Howard spoke to himself now. "I taught her a lesson."

"It'll only take me a minute to fix some salad," Mrs. Gillis said.

"Are your sons' hands strong, Mrs. Gillis?"

"Not as strong as yours, Howard. I'll set the table right away," she added eagerly.

"Mrs. Gillis, feel my hands again. They're like steel, you know."

Then Mrs. Gillis heard a car drive into the driveway. She looked out the window, and then Howard saw it too.

"If those are friends of yours," he said sternly, "I'd advise them to go away."

"Now, Howard—"

"I'd tell them to go away," he said, "before anything happens to them."

And then Mrs. Gillis's heart sank—for the car was backing up. Someone had simply pulled up in the driveway in order to back around and turn in the middle of the block.

"They're going," he said.

"Yes, they're going," Mrs. Gillis said.

She finally managed to get some lunch on the table, and Howard sat down beside her. He didn't say much, and he ate very little. Mrs. Gillis tried to appear casual, to engage him in a conversation, anything. "Do you work often, Howard?"

"Not often."

"Do you have any trouble finding jobs?"

"People are anxious to get help these days. Weren't you?"

"Yes, I was, Howard."

He sat a moment without speaking, and then he said, "They're looking for me, Mrs. Gillis."

"Who?"

"I don't know exactly. The people I worked for last, I guess."

"Was that here, in this town?" she asked.

"No. It was in another town. Everyone was looking for me, so I went away. It's horrible to be spied upon, Mrs. Gillis. Do you know what it is to be spied upon?"

"No, no, I don't."

"Would you like to know?"

"No, Howard, I wouldn't."

"Perhaps if you knew what it was like, you'd not spy on me any more," he said.

Then he began to watch her curiously. She rose uneasily to her feet, and she began to clear the dishes, and he followed her. All during the time she washed them, he watched her. Quietly, without saying a word. It took all the self-control she had to keep from crying out. Finally he spoke to her.

"Do you like being spied on, Mrs. Gillis?"

"No, no!" she was suddenly pleading, "Howard, whatever it is you want, take it and go away!"

"There's nothing I want. I only want to stay here with you."

Mrs. Gillis was sobbing, "I can't stand it, Howard! I can't! I'm an old woman. Please go away and leave me alone!"

"I'm not going away, Mrs. Gillis. There's still a job to be done. I'll go away after I've done everything that has to be done."

"Howard, I have some money here in my pocket. I got it upstairs for you. It's a great deal, and I'll give it to you."

"I don't want your money, Mrs. Gillis."

"Then go away," she said frantically.

"That would be foolish. Then you'd tell on me."

"No, I wouldn't. Really, Howard, go away and I'll never tell a soul that you've been here."

"I don't believe you. And I don't trust you. There's only one way of being certain that you won't tell."

He was looking steadily at Mrs. Gillis now, and then they both heard the truck pull up in the driveway. Mrs. Gillis moved to the window and Howard followed her. It was the milk truck.

"Tell him to go away," Howard said in a low voice.

"I can't. I've ordered some extra things," she replied.

"Run into the storeroom until he goes," he demanded.

"I can't, Howard. He knows I'm here, and he'll expect me to pay him."

"You promised to do as I told you!" Howard whispered furiously.

Now they could hear the sound of the milk bottles rattling in the driveway.

Mrs. Gillis spoke rapidly. "Howard, if I tell him to go, he'll think something's wrong—and then you'll get caught for sure."

"All right, Mrs. Gillis. Take whatever you've ordered. But if you pull any tricks, you'll be sorry."

Without another word, he stepped back from sight between the stove and the wall, but he kept within easy reach of her. The milkman knocked as usual at the window over the sink.

"Just a moment," Mrs. Gillis called, as she raised the window.

"Good afternoon, Mrs. Gillis."

"Good afternoon."

"Lovely day, isn't it?"

"Yes, it is."

"I think I have good news for you," the milkman said.

"You have?"

"Yes. Beginning the first, I think we're getting on some badly needed help, and in the future your deliveries will be made in the early morning."

"That's nice."

"I don't believe you ever did like these late deliveries, did you?

"I never really minded." Mrs. Gillis looked uneasily toward the stove.

"If all of our customers were like you, Mrs. Gillis, it wouldn't be such a bad old world. Here you are, one quart of milk, and a pint of half-and-half. Good-by, Mrs. Gillis." As he started to pull the window down, Mrs. Gillis called out suddenly.

"But the extra things—you forgot them!"

The milkman pulled the window up again. "The extra things?" his voice was puzzled.

"Yes, the extra things," she said rapidly. "Now don't tell me you'd forgotten them! The eggs, the butter—"

"I'll get them right away," and he turned down the driveway.

"Mrs. Gillis," said Howard in a hoarse whisper, "I'm going to give you one more chance—when he comes back, you're to get rid of him, do you hear? If you give me away, I'm going to kill you. I'll kill you before he can get inside this house, and I don't care what they do to me."

"I won't give you away, Howard," she said, "I'll only pay him—I have to do that—"

They heard the milkman coming back down the driveway.

"Shut up!" Howard whispered roughly, "and remember!"

"Here you are," said the milkman as he came to the window.

"Thank you."

"Anything else?"

"No—no, that's all."

"Mrs. Gillis," the milkman began, "I was going to say—"

"I'm sorry," she interrupted frantically, "I'm sorry, but I can't stop to talk today. I'm very busy." And she pulled the window down.

Howard stood for a moment behind the stove. His eyes were blazing. Then he spoke without moving.

"You're very clever, aren't you, Mrs. Gillis?"

"What do you mean?" she asked fearfully.

"You thought you were going to put something over on me, didn't you?"

"I sent him away, didn't I?" she asked meekly.

"The *extra* things you ordered! There weren't any!"

"Yes, there were! You saw him! You heard him!"

"He didn't know what you were talking about!" snapped Howard.

There was a sudden rapping on the window. The milkman had returned. He stood outside the window. Howard held his position back of the stove; his knuckles grew white as he clutched his knife.

"This is your last chance," he whispered angrily. "*Get rid of him!*"

"I will, Howard, I will," Mrs. Gillis said. Then she raised the window.

"I'm sorry to bother you again, Mrs. Gillis," said the milkman, "but you forgot the ration points on the butter."

"Yes, the ration points—" she said vaguely. She walked quickly to the cabinet and pulled open a drawer. The ration books were there, and there were knives too. She hesitated for a moment, then she picked up a book and she hurried back to the window. "Here you are."

The milkman took his points and then he handed her the book.

"Sorry I had to bother you, Mrs. Gillis. But you see, I have to account—"

"Yes, yes," she interrupted. "I'm busy—can't you see I'm busy?" She pulled the window down.

"Tell me when he's gone," whispered Howard.

Mrs. Gillis stood by the window and she watched the milkman get into his truck and drive it off.

"So that was your scheme, was it?" said Howard. "So you wanted to give me away?"

"He's gone now, Howard," Mrs. Gillis said.

Howard stepped out from behind the stove. As he moved toward her, she kept stepping back until she was flat against the wall.

"You thought he'd save you, did you?"

"No, no! I sent him away like you asked me."

"Do you know what would have happened to me? Do you?" he shouted.

Mrs. Gillis didn't answer.

"They would have taken me away," he shouted furiously.

"Howard, leave me alone," sobbed Mrs. Gillis.

"I'm going to punish you!"

"No, Howard. I've been punished enough!"

He was standing very close to her now, and he still held his knife.

"Howard! Howard—" she began. But suddenly everything was black for Mrs. Gillis, and she slipped to the floor.

When she came to, she was still on the kitchen floor. Her head throbbed, and she remembered nothing for a moment. Then she remembered everything. But where was he?

She lay there for a moment and she listened. The house was very quiet. She rose to her feet and she made her way slowly to the back door, and tried the knob. But it was still locked.

She tiptoed into the breakfast room, the dining room, the living room. But there was no one. She tried the front door. It, too, was still locked.

She thought of the windows a moment, and decided against

them. If he were still in the house, and surprised her in her attempt—and suddenly she saw the den door. It was closed and she stared at it, expecting it to open at any moment.

Then she heard a sound. A soft, swishing sound—like waves washing up against a hard surface. She stood there for some time listening. It seemed like hours before she could bring herself to move. Then a strong impulse made her walk toward the den door.

Suddenly the hall clock began to strike. Why, it was five o'clock! Mrs. Gillis had been unconscious for longer than she'd thought. Had it all been a dream? Then she heard the swishing sound again, and she moved toward the den door. The knob felt icy cold as she turned it. As the door opened, the swishing sound grew louder.

The room had already turned dark in the late afternoon light, but she could see him now. He stood in the middle of the room. He was pushing the heavy floor polisher over the same spot. Back and forth, back and forth.

She started to close the door, but he looked up and saw her.

"What time is it, Mrs. Gillis?" he asked.

"About five."

"Well, I guess I'll call it a day now." He looked down at the floor proudly. "I've done a nice job, haven't I?"

"Yes, Howard. Very nice," she replied.

"I think I'll be going now."

He picked up his coat which lay on a chair. Then he looked at the floor again. "Doesn't it shine nicely?" he asked.

"Yes, yes, it does!"

"Was it worth five dollars to you?"

"Yes, Howard," said Mrs. Gillis softly.

She hesitated for a moment, and then she reached quickly into her apron pocket, and gave him some money.

As he moved to take it, he looked at his hand. He seemed to study it, then he said, "I have nice hands, haven't I?"

"Yes, Howard," she said quickly. "Here, take the money."

"Thank you." He looked at his hands again. "It's a pity they have to be used to polish floors."

"You've done such a good job," she said breathlessly, "I'm going to give you a few extra dollars."

"Thank you. Will you be needing me tomorrow?"

"No, thank you, Howard."

He went quietly to the front door. Finding it locked, he turned to her with a puzzled look on his face.

"The door's locked, Mrs. Gillis."

"Yes, Howard. Do you have the key?"

"Yes, yes, I have," he said after a pause. "I just remembered." He took a key from his pocket and unlocked the door. Then he turned to her, "Good-by, Mrs. Gillis," he said.

"Good-by, Howard," she replied as he closed the door softly after him.

RETURN OF THE GRIFFINS

by A. E. SHANDELING

GUNAR VRIES, EMISSARY TO THE UNITED NATIONS CONFERENCE in New York from the European Democracy of S——, sat on the edge of his bed in his hotel room, removing his shoes and socks.

He had declined to be present that evening at a party given in his honor by a wealthy expatriate, telephoning his regrets. In his stead he had sent his aide, a handsome young man who, besides being secretary and translator, was also a composer of symphonies; instructing him to confine himself to seduction and to the piano. As for Gunar Vries, he had had his supper sent up and after the tray was removed had locked his door and set himself to his writing: his daily personal letter to his president, in which he imparted observations too detailed to be made by phone, and letters to the members of his family, his wife Alice and his son Theodore at the Technological University. When he had signed his name for the third time, the night was late.

He was removing his second sock when the bed moved. He grasped the blankets to keep from being thrown, believing that an earthquake had struck. But the bottles did not slide from the dresser, no particles of ceiling fell, the chandelier did not sway. Only the bed moved. Then through his lifted knees he saw emerging from beneath the bed the head of an eagle, but three times the size of an eagle's head, and stretching out for a grip of the rug, an eagle's claw. Then followed a lion's body. So the lion had an eagle's head. Or the eagle had a lion's body.

When the creature emerged completely, Gunar saw that it had also two wings, great eagle wings, that now it stretched one at a time across the floor. The wing roots crackled, and the feathers swept across the rug with a swishing, rushing sound. The creature slouched to the center of the room, its forelegs lifting stiffly, like a bird's legs, but in coordination with its hind-legs, which moved in the indolently potent manner of a lion.

Still heavy with sleep, the monster fell over on its side and gently lifting its wing, turned its head under and with closed beak nuzzled along the feathery pocket, in this way nudging itself to wakefulness and woe again. Then lifting its head, swinging it around and up, the creature looked straight at Gunar Vries. The eagle part took prominence—the curved beak, hard as stone, the thick encasing of golden feathers over its head, touched with red at the breast and extending down its forelegs to the very toes. Lion ears protruded through the feathers but were laid sleekly back. Its eyes burned ruby bright in the semi-darkness.

"Change of climate," it explained, "makes me sleepy."

Before he had entered politics, more than twenty years ago, Gunar Vries had been professor of ancient Greek civilization at the University of Afia, capital of S——. His past enabled him to recognize the creature. "Griffin?" he asked. "Is that what you are?" He had several cats on his farm and a trained falcon, and spoke always with tenderness and respect to them, as now he spoke to this great creature.

"Yes," replied the griffin, "and of the pure strain. If you're wondering about the Sphinx and her woman's face, one of us became enamored of a virgin of your species; though I can't see what he saw in her."

The griffin spoke his own language, like no other in the world, and yet a concoction of them all, with archaic Greek like a warrior's chariot rumbling and shining through. It was like everything unspoken that a word cannot be put to and that is comprehended more readily than the spoken among men of different languages.

"You've been away several years," said Gunar, covering his bare feet again with shoes and socks. "What did you do in the time?"

"Took ourselves to the mountains of India," replied the griffin. "Sat in the sun, on the thresholds of our caves, or caught the Arimaspi, one-eyed men who seek gold in the mountains, ate them in a shrugging fashion, already gorged with our prowess. I might ask the same question of you. What didn't you do? By Apollo! Procreated not individuals but nations. Took the lid off a water kettle, and what steams out but ships and cities. Times have changed."

The creature's breath began to fill the room, an overly warm breath, smelling of raw meat, the rich, dark, stinging smell of blood clots and liver.

Gunar Vries had his trousers on and his gray hunting shirt that he wore evenings when alone, but he was cold. He turned the radiator higher. "I presume," he said, standing with his back to the heat, "that you wandered down alone?"

"Only one of the vanguard," replied the creature, preening its breast.

Now Gunar Vries was fully aware of the monsters' significance. They were in their time sacred to Apollo, whose chariot they drew, and as Apollo was the prophetical deity, whose oracle when consulted delivered itself in enigmas, the word griffin, too, meant enigma. And because he was fully aware of this, he preferred not to seem aware.

The emissary rubbed his hands together briskly to make them warm. "What's the occasion?" he inquired.

The feigned innocence did not escape the griffin. The creature picked it apart like picking the tortoise from the shell. A hissing contempt came from its nostrils and partially opened beak. For a moment there seemed to be a geyser in the room.

"Emissary to the UN," it replied, "a conference called to promote the flowering of humanity, and all the time the delegates hard put to it to breathe with the possiblity of atomic dust in the air no more than five years from now. And you want to know the occasion! Can you think of a time when the world faced a greater enigma?"

Gunar Vries was indeed concerned for humanity. It was something he traveled with in addition to his aide and his portfolio. Yet now it seemed to him that it was humanity in the abstract he had been carrying around—the formalities, the rules and regulations, the paperwork of a conference, humanity carefully composed and delivered with dignity. At the griffin's words, humanity suddenly became a third party in the room, and Gunar shivered with life, he shook convulsively as children do in excitement.

The monster slunk around the room, which became small as the cage in which a circus lion is confined. When it came to the desk it turned its head with ponderous grace and ran its eyes over the letters. Gunar Vries stirred indignantly and stepped forward, but on second thought was stricken with shame for his disrespect and stopped still. The griffin turned away, but in the turning managed to drop the nictitating membrane of its eyes, and the perusal became an act of idle curiosity. It padded away languidly, disdainfully, dragging one wing, and the emissary, hearing a strange clicking noise along the floor, looked down and saw for the first time the full length of the creature's talons. At each step they were nicking small holes in the rug.

The creature sat down by the window, and the tasseled end of its tail lifted and fell. There was a feminine restlessness in the way its feathers quivered, and at the same time a great seething of male energy that propelled it forward even as it sat still. "Lift the window for me," it said, "and let me out on the ledge. Isn't there a park across the street?"

The emissary drew up the venetian blind and opened the window. The night entered, cold and fragrant with grass. The lamps in the park were almost pure white, as if encrusted with snow, and shone up through the delicate branches of the trees. People were sitting on the benches, talking and glancing up at the lighted windows of the hotel, where many dignitaries were in residence. Newsboys had built a fire in a refuse can, and taximen and journalists, tired of the plush and statuary of the lobby, were warming their hands around it. An ornate ledge ran along beneath the windows of the top floor, and the griffin leaped onto this.

"It won't be harmed," Gunar Vries told himself. "It's too fabulous. Even an oaf can see." A look of being protected lay in its eyes, a true and natural hauteur from an ancient epoch. He closed the window, and in his mind's eye he saw the creature continuing swiftly along the ledge, tail and wings spread out a bit, a dark and slithering form against the faintly lighted sky.

He went to his desk, took up his pen, and wrote in postscript on the letter to his president, "*My dear friend: This evening I saw one of the first griffins to return. Their coming, though unpredictable, was nevertheless inevitable. They will remain, I gather, until we decide our fate, one way or another.*" Hearing a strange cry in the night, a mingling of lion's roar and eagle's scream and more than both, he wrote further, "*The cry of the griffin in the great cities of the world will become as familiar as the cry of the cock in the country, and even as the cock's cry wakens us from sleep and is portentous of the morning when we shall not be alive to hear it, so the cry of the griffin, on the roofs above traffic, is troublous, calling us, humanity, to a cognizance of our existence and heralding our possible end.*"

When Gunar awoke in the morning it was, as every day, to no other thought but the Conference. Not until he passed the desk on his return from his bath and saw that the three letters had been taken up by his aide for mailing was he reminded of the griffin. He stood still, startled and amused by such a dream. Well, the times evoked it. He had never before worked under such a strain, and the enigma of the times had taken form and substance, emerged in his dream a thing in itself, had become a living creature.

But as he was dressing, the laughter within ceased, and he was overcome by melancholy. It came to him that the griffin might have been other than a dream. His few hours of sleep had been shallow and hot, as if he had slept in a thunderstorm; remembering his sleep, he was almost certain he had not dreamed. If the fabulous being had appeared, it had been an actual one. *But, of course, it had not appeared.* He could negate the event, he could prove it had been a dream by seeing again his letter to his president, the signature constituting the end, without postscript. He walked slowly to the door of the adjoining apartment, already tired as if at the end of the day. How old was he now? Fifty-six? And how long did men live, usually?

"Norbert, young man," he called, rapping at the half-open door, "you've not posted the letters yet? The three letters?"

His aide appeared at the door, opening it wider. "They made the plane at seven-thirty."

"The letter to the president?"

"All three were sealed," said Norbert, "and envelopes addressed. Did you wish to make changes?"

"A whim," he replied. He looked sharply at his aide. Norbert wrote symphonies, the modern kind; his disharmonies were not what they seemed but merged into a complete harmony. Was he not the one to understand the griffin? "If I tell him," thought Gunar, "if I tell him, laughing a little, with gestures, with shudders, why, two believing will make it untrue."

But Norbert seemed more erect than usual this morning, his eyes bluer, his fair hair fairer. He liked parties, and the atmosphere for him was still charged with his virtuosity. The emissary decided that to explain the griffin to him would bring the creature down to the level of a piano recital and the sensual laughter of bare-armed women.

"Come," he said, signaling for Norbert to accompany him.

In the cab Gunar sat in a corner, holding his hat and gloves on his crossed knees, listening to Norbert read foreign newspapers on the UN proceedings. The cab came to a halt as traffic changed, and he gazed into the street. In a basement tailor shop, the name on the window so worn that the dim light within turned the letters translucent and coppery, a tailor sat sewing at his machine while his wife sat by the window, drinking from a cup.

As Gunar took in the shop and its occupants, he saw his second griffin. She—it was a female, as he could tell by the lack of red feathers on her breast—was sliding along the fence before the row of basement shops, the eagle head lifted and stiff with impending alarm.

He grasped Norbert's hand, and the young man laid down his paper. "You see," he said, as if he had tried before to convince his aide, "a female griffin."

Norbert bent across him to look. The griffin slipped down

the stairs into the tailor's shop, pushing the door open with a claw, and for a moment Gunar saw, simultaneously, the eagle's head through the window and the lion's tail waving on the stairs. Persons passing paid no attention, or only slight, as to a cat or a sparrow. The couple did not look up, neither the man from his sewing nor the wife from her cup. Gunar Vries was appalled. They went about their pursuits as before, while this enigma, this beast of life or death, slid along their streets, jangled their business bells.

"But are they so common a sight already?" he asked.

"What are?" Norbert had taken up his reading again, but courteously allowed himself to be engaged in conversation.

"The griffins. A female went into the tailor shop and you made no to-do about it."

"I didn't see one," said Norbert. "I didn't know what to look for. I'm sorry. What is it like?"

Gunar Vries drew into his corner again. "It's not a thing that you look for," he replied.

The delegates to the General Assembly of the United Nations assembled at their quarters at Flushing Meadow. Gunar Vries sat in his place, his aide beside him, taking no part in the conversation before the fall of the gavel. The chairman entered, and following at his heels was a male griffin, larger, older than the one that had slept in Gunar's room. The creature was hoary and unkempt. Its eyes were yellow fire. It seated itself to the right of the chairman and with archaic grace surveyed the persons assembled.

That evening after supper the president replied by telephone. "Gunar, what's this talk of a griffin?" he asked. "It's a beast of classical antiquity, is it not? Well, to what use are you putting it?"

Ernest Gorgas was a fine man, and there was no one Gunar respected more. But how impotent the president's voice, how distant not only in space but in time! Gunar had the peculiar anticipatory feeling of hearing it fade away, as if mankind were running instantly into a post-historic age.

"Gunar," the president continued, his voice grinding into the receiver, louder, adamant, yet deeply kind and respectful, "the plea that you made to the Assembly today for international unity was the most moving I have ever heard. It was more forceful, even, than the American Willkie's *One World*. And the delivery of it—the eloquence, the impassioned tone! Maneuvering it the way you did was uncalled for and yet the most called-for thing in the world. If you are in your way sidestepping praise, being modest, bringing up this tale of a griffin coming to your room with a warning, it's no use. Gunar, my friend, there is no appointment that I have made in my term of office that has given me greater satisfaction."

"Ernest," replied Gunar, "the man who feels that he is not deserving of praise makes no move to sidestep it. He has a deaf place in his ear the size of a pea, and with this he hears praise. No, my friend, a male griffin *was* in my room last evening. Since then I have seen two more. One, slipping along the street, female and playing nervous; the other, a more bestial creature and at the same time looking as if imbued with an omniscient intelligence. It was sitting to the right of the chairman today and commented often, succinctly, too. But though its voice was louder than any there it went unheard. At the conclusion of my speech it came to me and told me that it had heard Demosthenes, and that my eloquence exceeded his. It had been sent alone to take in the American Revolution and had heard Patrick Henry—it said that that gentleman's vigor did not touch mine. I did not take these comparisons as praise but was convinced that the precariousness of our times has never been equalled and that orators are made by the periods in which they live."

A long pause followed. When the president spoke again the subject was changed. He inquired about the discussions underway, Gunar's criticism and forecast of results.

Within another day the rumor had been circulated among the delegates that Gunar Vries, emissary from S——, was suffering from hallucinations. The suspicion was not relayed to newsmen or to anyone outside the circle of official delegates. It was a matter of respect not only for the member, as a distinguished person, and for his family, but for the delegates combined. If one was susceptible to weakness of this kind, it might be construed that all were. The curious thing was that the emissary seemed to be in full command of his intelligence while at the Conference table. No criticism could be cast upon the deft, perspicacious way in which he handled his country's interests. Not only this, he was one of the most energetic in tackling the problems of all humanity.

Gunar Vries was called home on the second day after his speech. Newsmen, inquiring of him the reason for his departure, were told that he believed that his president was in possession of information that could not be discussed by phone or letter or through a messenger. In Gunar's place, to be guided by Norbert through the formalities, there appeared the youngest member of the supreme court of S——, a man not much older than Norbert, but with his own history up to ninety years already in his eyes.

Carrying his portfolio, Gunar Vries returned to S——. He was met at the airport by the president, and together they were driven to the palace. They dined and secluded themselves in the president's study.

"Gunar," said Ernest, as they sat facing each other, "I could not ask for a better emissary. You have used the energy of twelve men. Now, wound up as you are, you will think I am crazy, you will think I am reckless putting your personal health before the welfare of the nation. But I want you to take a rest for awhile. Let someone else, not of your caliber but competent enough, assume your duties. You go to your farm, wear an old hat, go hunting, milk your cows, sow your wheat. We need as many hands as we can get working the land, and as much space yielding. Go home for a while, Gunar."

Gunar Vries had never been so frightened in his life. It was like the fear, only worse, that he had experienced as a boy of seventeen, when he had left his father and come to the city to study, when for the first time he had lived alone. For several days he had been almost unable to breathe. He had thought he would never again see his father or make a friend, he had thought that he was trapped in that one room forever.

"Has any action of mine," Gunar now asked slowly, "met with your disapproval? Have you found that the ability I evidenced as your minister of foreign affairs, have you found that this ability falls short of my responsibility as a delegate to the United Nations?"

Ernest gripped his forehead, half-hid his painful eyes with his hand. "They say that you see griffins."

"But I told you so myself."

"Doesn't it seem peculiar to you?"

"You prefer to quote the ones to whom it seems peculiar? No, my friend, it is the most natural thing in the world."

"But you are the only one who sees them."

"Does that fact make the griffin non-existent?" He felt a sharp derision coming on, took out his handkerchief and blew his nose. He tried to suppress the snort, but could not. It was his opinion of organized disorganization.

"If you take such a derogatory view of the Conference," the president said, "you won't want to return."

"On the contrary," Gunar replied, leaning forward to stuff his handkerchief away in his rear pocket. "They need me. They can't do without me. The time will come, believe me, when everyone there will see that creature sitting to the right of the chairman. And what a creature! What a creature!"

"Gunar." The president hesitated. "Before you go home, perhaps it would be wise for you to consult a psychiatrist. They have not all gone to greener pastures in the United States. There might be still a capable one or two practicing in France or Switzerland."

"I would have no belief in him if he did not see griffins himself," replied Gunar, laughing a little. "But for your sake, to relieve you of anxiety and shame, I shall resign from the UN and from the Ministry. Name someone else to the post."

He wanted to rise from the chair, as a gesture fitting to climax, but found that he could not. His heart was palpitating. Well, he had seen his father again, made a friend, and been in so many rooms he could not remember them all. A boy's loneliness doesn't last, nor does that of a disgraced diplomat. You reach out for people, you have no more enemies. . . .

Gunar traveled home by train that night, and a female griffin was co-occupant of his compartment. When he entered, she was already asleep on the couch, eagle head tucked under her right wing, left wing and left hindleg hanging to the floor. He sat opposite her and watched her in the dimly lit, rocking compartment.

He rode to his farm in the wagon of a neighbor. "You want to surprise Mrs. Vries?" the neighbor asked. The man had found Gunar, portfolio in hand, standing by his wagon, waiting for him to come from the assessor's office.

"No," replied Gunar. "I just came home, that's all."

"You are tired from the Conference?" the neighbor inquired, believing that it was over. He noticed the diplomat's sagging shoulders and sadness, and he halted the horses. "What's the world coming to?" he asked, gently, confidentially, as if Gunar Vries was the one to know.

And Gunar Vries laid his brow in his hand and wept, while the morning sun got in under his overcoat collar and warmed the nape of his neck.

For several days he went about his farm like a man taking a rest. He milked the cows, drove the tractor. There was a deep, still pool in his forest and he went to bathe in it, likening it to his loneliness. If he were drowning in it and cried out, no man would be near enough to help him. But when he left the pool and dressed again, his body was clean and deserving of respect because of its contact with loneliness, and approaching the farm he loved instantly from afar every small figure working.

Then one morning he saw on the roof of the east barn a young male griffin, and he called to it. The creature turned its large golden head slantwise.

"Come," coaxed Gunar, "a lamb? A pan of milk?" And

when the creature eyed him without replying, he added, "A calf?"

The griffin dropped its beak and picked at something between its toes. "But I ate, just a couple of centuries ago. Caught four Arimaspi in a ravine."

Alice begged Gunar to wait until she summoned Theodore, but he said no, that he would probably meet the boy in the city.

"Ah!" he exclaimed, for she had given him an idea. "I intend to speak on the steps of the Technological University anyway. When the scientific students see my griffin, it will be a triumph, believe me."

She went along the road with him, holding his elbow against her side and crying, and he bent his head away, unable to bear her grimaces. The griffin was slinking along the other side of the fence, and in a fit of energy suddenly both flew and ran, beating its wings close to earth, for a good half-mile down the fence. Why couldn't she see a thing like that?

He halted and caressed her, pushing back her short, pale hair. "Do you know that I love you?" he asked.

"Yes," she wept.

"The tour is a minor thing," he said. "I make it simply to return to you. If I don't go, how much longer and of what consequence will our love be?"

When he set out again, alone, the griffin was returning to meet him, loping.

So he came into Afia, capital of S——, with the griffin at his side. He was dressed as for a session of the UN. He wore his favorite suit, tailored in London of a fine Scottish tweed, a white shirt, a dark red silk tie, and he carried a black Homburg and gray suede gloves. He took rooms in a first-rate hotel.

Entering the park around which were grouped the government buildings, he mounted the flagpole base and pleaded with refugees, messengers passing to and fro, and clerks eating their lunches, to recognize his companion. In the evening he let himself be enveloped by the crowds pouring into the operas and symphonies and cinemas. Jostled and stepped upon, he began to recount his experiences, and some persons, with mail order tickets and in no hurry, tarried around him. At midnight, when the streets were being deserted, he returned to his hotel, and the griffin spent the night in the vicinity.

By the second day word had circulated that this man in the streets was actually Gunar Vries, come to tell of the existence of a fabulous beast or bird. The citizens jammed the streets, the fire-escapes, the roofs for blocks around the House of Commerce, and Gunar made his speech on the steps facing the park. Overjoyed as he was with the size of his audience, he spoke with such passion that the griffin, already unnerved by the crowd, its flesh creeping with the emissary's harping upon its existence, suddenly rose straight up into the air, screaming.

"Can't you see it?" Gunar Vries cried, pointing to the griffin beating the air, its beak open and its tongue flickering, its eyes fierier than ever, absorbing the three o'clock sun. After hovering thirty feet above Gunar's head, it continued up and settled on a cornice three stories above him.

The people gazed upward, but lowered their eyes with no change in them. They did not ridicule the speaker, however. They were solemn and attentive, remembering the man he once was. While about them, more griffins, curious as to the throngs, flew in and came to rest on the roofs of distant buildings, their dark forms like statues of themselves against the sky.

Gunar Vries descended the steps, and the people made way for him. He was not disheartened. There was time for other cities and other assemblages. He wanted especially to draw a great crowd in New York, city of the Conference. The griffin flew down and followed at his heels; he heard its wings flapping in descent and then the click of its claws on the stone. A guttural warble was in its throat, a sign of uneasiness.

Two members of the police force stepped through the crowd to Gunar Vries. The force had been reluctant to take action against him for disturbing the peace, considering his prestige, but during the course of his speech they had received instructions from Ernest Gorgas himself: "Quietly, with respect for his person as a private citizen and as a former diplomat, arrest and transport him to quarters in the Hall of Justice. Detain him there until further instructions."

"Gunar Vries," said one, "it's the president's wish."

"If I resist?" he asked.

The other officer touched his elbow, and Gunar told himself, "All their force will be unavailing and will seem afterward like a touch at my elbow." He reached behind him, laid his hand on the griffin, and brought it forward.

"If I mount you," he asked, "can you rise with my weight?"

The griffin nodded, but was perturbed and glazed its eyes. "When you asked me to accompany you, did you also ask that I convey you? It's seldom we convey a mortal."

"That's what it comes to," said Gunar.

The griffin rose reluctantly in the stance of a lion rampant, but the emissary, stepping forward to place his arms around the eagle's neck and seat himself upon the lion's rump, was detained by the officers, who came in under the wing, each taking an elbow and an armpit, and prevailing against him.

Gunar Vries was deposited in the cell reserved for politicians, bankers, celebrated attorneys, actresses, professors. Here were ash trays, a water-cooler and dispenser. The furniture, though old and sagging, was still substantial, with faintly yellowed crocheted stars on the chairbacks. Waiting for him were his attorney and a psychiatrist, a jovial, plump young man.

"If they want bail," said Gunar to his attorney, "then give it to them. I'll be out of the country by morning."

"They're afraid of that," his attorney replied, a man competent as he was handsome. "How would it look, Gunar," he chided, "for a man of your status to misrepresent the country? The other nations will say, 'What choice was this?' They'll have respect for no emissary from S——."

The doctor, with whom he had shaken hands and who had been listening, kindly, alertly, smoking a cigarette, now spoke up. "Mr. Vries, contrary to the expressed wishes of Mr. Ernest Gorgas, I am not going to ask your participation in any analysis. I want a few answers from yourself to clarify, not my point of view as a doctor, but your own, as a man of responsibility. You claim to see griffins, beasts of ancient mythology. Is that true?"

"True," replied Gunar, "both that I claim to and that I see them." He took a cigarette from the silver case the doctor proffered him.

"And why griffins?" asked the doctor.

"Why not?" replied Gunar. "Because that's what they are. They're not snakes, they're not elephants. I'm sorry. I cannot make it as simple as that."

"No, no!" laughed the doctor, lighting Gunar's cigarette. His hand shook, and his small eyes, small mouth, and small mustache all laughed in his round face. "Why have they returned, I mean. Are they, to you, explanatory of our time?"

Well, here was a man after Gunar's own heart, and he would forget, in his appreciation, any ulterior motive the man might have of undermining that which he so eagerly explained.

And so he told of the creature's history and the meaning of its name, and the doctor was absorbed and nodded his head. "Tell me of a time," said Gunar, "when the world faced a greater enigma. We'll either make the earth fruitful as it has never been or we'll exterminate ourselves. We'll either wipe out everything we've built upon, all past epochs, or we'll go on to a greater time than man has ever known. If you look at the situation with your eyes open you'll find that it's quite a creature, a thing with eagle wings and the body of a lion and with eyes of fire."

Gunar ceased, having heard the flapping of wings outside the window as the griffin ascended to the roof. It had followed him, as he had expected.

"Well, it's a pity," sighed the doctor, "that only one man sees them."

The attorney bent forward impatiently. "The president is aware that as a private citizen you may speak as you wish. Nevertheless, he would like your promise, as the promise of a dear friend, that you will make no further speeches in public or in private assembly calling upon the people to recognize the existence of these creatures."

"You tell Ernest," replied Gunar, "that they're bigger than he is."

"Will you commit him?" the attorney asked the doctor.

The doctor had risen, as if he had no more to ask. He shook his head, pressed out his cigarette in the tray. "I prefer," he said, "to commit those persons who cannot see them."

The two men left him to consult by telephone with the president. When they returned they brought with them the guard, as obliging to authority in the release of the emissary as in the confinement of him.

Gunar Vries picked up his hat and gloves. "There is one on the roof now," he said to the doctor, "if you care to see it."

This was an old prison, rigged up now with electricity and hot water. They went up the circular stone staircase, and the guard unlocked the gate. The griffin was lying on the parapet, drooping over the edge to watch the traffic three stories below, and at times lifting its head to look at the pigeons cooing and bobbing, circling and fluttering. It was large and dark against the pale yellow haze of the setting sun, and its feathers were delicately ruffled.

"Doctor," said Gunar, "do not let me lose faith in you."

"I see it," the doctor assured him.

The attorney coughed in vicarious embarrassment.

Gunar stepped to the parapet, the doctor and attorney following. "Can we try our flight again?" he asked the griffin. The doctor turned pale, and Gunar, watching for just this response, continued, "Its back is broad enough and its neck the right size for my arms. I'll hamper it a bit, perhaps, but we'll manage. You think now that it's not here at all for me to climb upon, but an idea came to me while I was trying to mount it in the park: If I am afraid, then I am not certain of the griffin myself. In this way, by trusting myself to it, I prove its existence."

The doctor was plunged into remorse and self-doubt. He stood stockstill, his arms hanging numbly at his sides.

Suddenly the attorney was cognizant of Gunar Vries' kindliness, of depths to the man he had not considered. He placed his hand on Gunar's arm. "Gunar," he implored him, "we shall provide you with first-class accommodation by whatever means you care to travel. I shall see to it myself. I shall speak to the president and to the Chamber of Representatives. You will be authorized to go—indeed, dispatched."

But Gunar Vries had hold of the griffin's rear leg and drew himself onto the parapet. The guard, having taken the respite to smoke a cigarette, was leaning against the gate, watching the men, believing that anything was sanctioned. And Gunar Vries, knowing that in a moment the three men would toss off their stupefaction and converge upon him, threw himself upon the griffin.

They flew in a westerly direction, passing over the city. The night moved up from behind and overtook them. With the earth so far below them, Gunar was not sure whether they were still over Europe or had reached the Atlantic Ocean.

"Can you drop a bit closer to earth?" Gunar called forward, and his voice was not as he expected it to be, bounced or pummeled by the wind, but went out into calm air, the atmosphere into which an oracle speaks.

"What for?" the griffin asked.

"But can you see any lights?"

The griffin glanced sideways in derision, enabling Gunar to see its eye, which was a blue distilled from the night, like a pure blue flame, and in it were reflected, nebulously, the lights of a city he believed to be New York.

TAKING OUT UNCLE MONTAGUE

by DOROTHY MC CLEARY

IN THE TRESS HOUSE OF MOURNING ONLY TWO ROOMS STILL kept their familiar atmosphere—Uncle Montague's room, and Nettie's kitchen. The darkened parlor was given over to Miss Lida's casket. Miss Lida's bedroom was empty and probably ghost-infested. The guest room and dining room were occupied by out-of-town relatives, the Sawyers.

Mrs. Sawyer came into the kitchen every little while to issue an order to Nettie. "Now about lunch, Nettie—"

"Yes?" Nettie volunteered nothing. She stood immovable, looking out of the window above her sink at Miss Lida's rose-bushes.

"There's plenty of that steak left over, that Mr. Sawyer bought last night," said Mrs. Sawyer. "We'll have that warmed up on toast—"

"No." Nettie made free to send a broad smile out toward the back yard. "No steak left."

"Why, *Nettie!*"

"I took the whole shebang up to Mr. Montague for his breakfast."

"That whole big end?" cried Mrs. Sawyer.

"Sure thing!" said Nettie. "It's months he hasn't put steak between his teeth. He went wild last night over the piece I give him to his dinner. So this morning I kep' up the good work and let him finish it off."

"*Well!*" Mrs. Sawyer expressed her exasperation by picking up and setting down again heavily the big florist's box she had brought with her into the kitchen. "For just one person to have the major portion of that big, lovely steak, it does seem—Something to put these flowers in, Nettie," she added sharply. "And be sure to give me the card, afterward."

With a chuckle just barely concealed and showing plainly on her face, Nettie came over and lifted the cover of the flower box. "Um! That aroma!" she exclaimed, burying her face in the box. "Carnations! Miss Lida'd have a fit if she could see 'em."

"Very nice," said Mrs. Sawyer. "But *red*, that's a queer choice."

"Very welcome, I'll say," said Nettie. "We've got so much of that white stuff. Looks so dead, like, all the white in yonder."

"Where's the card?"

"Here." Nettie took it out of the envelope and read it. "Hooray!" she said happily. "From his lodge, it is. That's nice!"

"Whose lodge?"

"Why, his own!" said Nettie proudly. "Mr. Montague's! His Brothers of Woods and Rivers. Those men, they fish and they hunt, and they hold banquets—"

"How could Uncle Montague—"

"Oh no!" Nettie looked reproachfully at Mrs. Sawyer. "Not now he don't! Only in memory, you might say. When his mind's good he's great on memory. And every whichever the Brothers, they come and hold a meeting up in his room, to keep his hand in. He was Great High Shepherd for thirty-one years. Now he's Sublime King." Nettie got a quart jar out of the cupboard and arranged the carnations in it, saving one out. She stuck the florist's pieces of fern into the jar and bent them down all around to hide the plainness of the glass. "This'll have to go close to her head," she said, trotting into the parlor.

"Wait, Nettie—I don't know, now—" Mrs. Sawyer followed her.

Narrow bars of sunlight came into the parlor at either side of the lowered yellow shades, making the dust dance. One ray lighted full on Miss Lida's serene face. "Lookee there!" said Nettie in a hushed voice. "She's taken up to heaven on a gold ladder."

"Um," said Mrs. Sawyer.

Nettie brought over the claw-footed piano stool and set it beside the head of the casket for the carnations.

"No, Nettie—not that bare ugly jar there. That's where the minister has to stand."

"Here, then." Nettie moved it to the other side of the head. "See here?" she asked in a whisper of Miss Lida. "From the Brothers!" She stood gazing down, scrutinizing Miss Lida's face. "She's the last one I ever thought would go," she said. "Him, yes, someday. He's an old man. But never her. And not a good-by word to me about buying Mr. Montague's new nightshirts nor nothing. Am I to charge to Gilfillan as always? But who's to pay? and about his beef tea—"

"Nettie," said Mrs. Sawyer hastily, "you and I must have a little talk—"

"So kind she was!" Nettie hung over the still face. "We had such a happy life—always 'Please,' and 'Thank you,' and little jokes—I've laughed myself to death times untellable. And her too. Oh, glory—" A sudden pain of grief came over Nettie. She crumpled up against the casket, her face distorted with emotion. "She's gone all right," she whispered. "I see now for sure she's gone. Look at her mouth there—so unlike. That's the mouth of death, I tell you!"

"Come now, Nettie." Mrs. Sawyer laid an arm awkwardly across Nettie's shoulders. "At times like this we must all control ourselves."

"*He*'ll never believe it," said Nettie, "no more than me. 'Just one of her sulks,' Mr. Montague'll say. 'Let Daughter be—she'll come out of it—' "

"*Nettie*," said Mrs. Sawyer severely. "We can't have such wild talk!"

But now Nettie fell to weeping—great heavy sobs which shook her chest and disfigured her face. "I never felt it before this minute," she gasped out, looking piteously to Mrs. Sawyer. "All yesterday, and the night before, I never truly believed it. But now—"

Mrs. Sawyer went into the hall and called, "*Alfred!*"

Presently Mr. Sawyer appeared at the door, a newspaper in his hand.

"Alfred—look at Nettie!" said Mrs. Sawyer.

"What's up?" he asked.

"*Grief!*" said Mrs. Sawyer, shrugging her shoulders. "Nettie feels very badly."

Mr. Sawyer came gingerly into the parlor. "I say, old girl—" He touched one of Nettie's elbows. "It's a damned shame, and that's a fact, but—"

"Leave me be!" cried Nettie, pulling away from him. New tears started to flow. Nettie took a handkerchief from her apron pocket. "Why couldn't things go on like they were?" she asked. "Here we were, all so quiet and nice. This is the day I was to have washed her hair! This is a Thursday, ain't it?"

"Yes," said Mr. Sawyer. "Thursday the 14th."

"I was to have washed her hair this day regular as clockwork," said Nettie with deep sorrow. Every second Thursday. Now our reckoning's all spoilt."

One at either side of her, the Sawyers managed to convey Nettie out of the parlor and back into the kitchen. "Where's it all gone to?" she moaned, "our happy times?"

"Nettie," said Mrs. Sawyer, "sit down, please. We must have a little talk together, the three of us. Something very important!" She seated Nettie in the kitchen rocker.

"I don't think she's in any shape just now—" said Mr. Sawyer in a low voice.

"Sit down!" Mrs. Sawyer said to him exasperatedly. "If you're determined to catch the eight-twenty tonight—"

"I damn well have to!" he said. "But common humanity—"

"Nettie—" Mrs. Sawyer spoke in a kindly, confidential tone. "We all have a great big problem on our hands, you know."

Nettie, sitting limp with her eyes shut, made no response.

"Yes, we must put our heads together and do a little plotting—a little planning, I mean," said Mrs. Sawyer. "About Uncle Montague, I mean."

Nettie roused herself to lean forward earnestly in her chair. "Have no fear there," she said. "I'll do for him till the last. So long as I hold out I'll serve him with all my breath."

"Yes, but Nettie—" Mrs. Sawyer looked uncomfortably to her husband for aid. Mr. Sawyer began to scratch with his thumbnail on the kitchen table. "As you know quite well," continued Mrs. Sawyer, "Uncle Montague's in no condition—"

"Ah, he's no worse," said Nettie. "There's been no change for four or five years. He still knows to drag hisself into the bath. But if you think best I'll start and sleep in—just to be on the safe side. *This*—" She waved her hand in the direction of the parlor, "this won't worsen him. He won't take it in. He'll quiz me about Miss Lida for a few days, then he'll forget. Like a baby, he is—so sweet and jolly!"

Mr. Sawyer finally spoke up, in a low, embarrassed voice. "It's about getting him out of here," he said bluntly.

"Yes!" said Mrs. Sawyer, sighing in relief. "That's it—in a way, Nettie. That's just it."

"Getting who—him or her?" Nettie asked, bewildered.

"Uncle Montague, of course," said Mrs. Sawyer.

"But he's *alive!*" cried Nettie, shocked. "He's alive as you or me!"

"See what I mean, Lorah?" put in Mr. Sawyer. "This is no time—"

"*Please!*" Mrs. Sawyer waved him away. "Listen to me, Nettie," she said, speaking slowly and emphasizing every word, "we'll have to *close this house*—do you understand? There isn't any money now to keep it up—*nothing*. We'll have to get Uncle Montague out—"

"You mean take him out of his *room?*" asked Nettie in horror.

"Well, we can't leave him here in an empty house, can we?" said Mrs. Sawyer, at the end of her patience. "In a rented house that belongs to somebody else? There are such little matters as rent, food, heat—"

"Ah!" Nettie saw, at last. "You mean there's no *money* for him?"

"That's it," said Mr. Sawyer. "Cousin Lida had her little annuity, and while she lived we all did what we could to help her and Uncle Montague, but—"

"We can't maintain *him* here alone," said Mrs. Sawyer brusquely. "I don't suppose it's his fault, but during all this he's made himself so thoroughly objectionable, so—so—"

"Lorah!" her husband warned her.

"Why, you'd think it's God Himself sitting up there!" Mrs. Sawyer shot out.

"Oh, the poor babe in arms!" mourned Nettie. "Well, wherever he goes, I go."

"Nettie," said Mrs. Sawyer, "we've made all arrangements to place Uncle Montague in an institution."

"*Him?*" gasped Nettie.

"A mental sanitorium," Mr. Sawyer amended.

"Lord God!" Nettie fell back as though her rocking chair, her whole kitchen, were crumbling under her. "Oh, Miss Lida—come back!" she prayed in an undertone. "Help! Help!"

"But he won't go, if you please!" said Mrs. Sawyer. "Mr. Sawyer has talked to him and I've talked to him. Mrs. Waite from across the street has done her best, too. But he just laughs. That awful laugh—"

Nettie jumped up out of her chair and faced them angrily. "What did you say to him, you?" she cried. "Did you fret him? Did you scold the darling? I tell you the Lord will not hold you guiltless! I'll—" Furiously she looked toward the wall where her mop and broom hung. Oh, to broom them out of her kitchen, out of the house, like marauding rats—to mop out Miss Lida's death, too, and to have all as it was before!

"Well then, *you* talk to him, Nettie," implored Mr. Sawyer. "*You* explain to him."

"Yes, he'd do anything for you," said Mrs. Sawyer. "We thought if you just said to go, he'd go—and maybe you'd promise to go along with him. Then he'd be there, you see, and they could handle him once he got inside—"

"Play the Judas on him, is it?" asked Nettie in hot scorn.

"No, no. Just the one little white fib that the two of you, together—" said Mrs. Sawyer.

"It's only up on Caldee Street," Mr. Sawyer put in. "You can go to see him, you know, any time. He'll get the best of care there! Will you do it, Nettie?" He walked over to the window and looked out into the sunny yard. "Oh God," he murmured. "Why do we have to get into this mess?"

"The only other way, Nettie," said Mrs. Sawyer, "would be for the men from the institution to come here—and *take* him, by force. You know the rumpus he'd set up then."

There was a long silence in the kitchen while Nettie stood, her face flushed, her fingers pressing into the oilcloth on her kitchen table. At last she spoke. "There'll no men come here," she said quietly, "to lay hand on him."

"But—" Mrs. Sawyer started to protest.

"Let her be," said Mr. Sawyer quickly. "Let Nettie handle it. Will you handle it, Nettie?"

Nettie made no answer. Moving about with leisurely deliberation, she got a bowl out of the cupboard, poured milk into it and emptied in the yolks of two eggs. This mixture she beat long and noisily with the egg beater, then poured it, frothy, into a tall glass, added a pinch of salt and a spoonful of sugar. She took a bottle of rye from a cupboard shelf and, casting one glance of flintlike disdain at Mr. and Mrs. Sawyer, she poured about two tablespoonfuls of the liquor into the drink. Then she removed her gingham apron.

"Are you going to talk to him?" Mrs. Sawyer asked.

"Sh!" said her husband.

Nettie took the eggnog and the spare carnation and went silently out of the kitchen and up the stairs to the second floor. "What do you mean, 'Common humanity'?" she heard Mrs. Sawyer ask her husband angrily. Nettie's lips curled up as she knocked at the rear bedroom door. "Trash!" she muttered. "Scum!"

"You may enter," a benign voice called.

Nettie flung the door open and anxiously scanned Mr. Montague's face for signs of wounded pride. With relief she saw there were none; propped up high against the many pillows of his bed, his face bristled with well-being. "Ah ha!" he cried, seeing what Nettie had in her hand. "My nectar!"

"That's what!" Nettie handed him the glass, and he hungrily drank a third of it down at one gulp, getting it all over his mustache and beard.

"Look at you now. Look at you, my little pet!" said Nettie, wiping him dry.

"Is she still sulking?" he asked, eyeing Nettie closely.

"What?"

"Little Lida."

"Oh help us, no!" said Nettie.

"Hasn't been in my presence for five or six years," he complained.

"Days," said Nettie sadly, "five or six *days*."

"Is she afraid I'll banish her?" he asked with amusement. He swallowed down the rest of the eggnog, turning the glass upside down over his mouth to drain it.

"Here," said Nettie, "look what she sent you in." She handed him the long red carnation.

He pushed away the eggnog glass and snatched at the flower, smelling it avidly, crushing it against his cheeks and lips. "Declare a holiday!" he cried out with joy. "Bid the populace rejoice!"

"Mr. Montague, my dearie—" said Nettie, wiping his beard.

"The dianthus caryophyllous," he said joyfully, cupping his thin fingers around the carnation's head. "Cardinalis," he added.

"Mr. Montague," said Nettie, seating herself on the bed, "you and me are going to get dressed."

"Send this to the King of England with my compliments," he commanded, handing Nettie the crushed carnation.

"Yes, sir." Nettie took the flower and put it in a glass of water.

"Yes, *sire*," said Uncle Montague. He yawned and stretched heavily on his pillows. Nettie pulled down his dressing-gown sleeves and, holding his head a little forward, smoothed his pillows. "You may withdraw," he said. "I will compose a proclamation." He drew from under a pillow a thick, blunt pencil and a tablet covered with meaningless marks.

"You'll listen to Nettie, that's what you'll do," she said firmly. "Your scribbling can wait."

"Oh ho! *Rebellion?*" He drew himself up in regal ferocity;

but feeling Nettie's hands on his wrists, he began to giggle childishly. "What is it now, girl—do you want to wash me?" he asked.

"I'm going to dress you," she said urgently. "I'm going to put on your pretty suit, your socks, shoes—everything. You and Nettie are going bye-bye." She ran to his clothespress and from the extreme back of it brought out an old-fashioned gray cutaway smelling of mothballs. "Come now—you and Nettie, we're going for a little jaunt," she said, turning back the bed covers clear to his bare feet. "Swing your legs around now. Hump!"

"What infamy is this?" he demanded, shivering and stiffening himself against the bed.

"Will you come or won't you?" asked Nettie angrily, tugging at his legs.

"Here I remain," he said quietly.

"Oh, what a time to be stubborn!" Nettie looked at his long foolish length—such a handsome figure of a man, but the brain end so contrary! "Hark to Nettie, now—" She drew the covers over him again and seated herself on the bed near his head. "Listen, my petling—"

"Not so familiar!" he said, pushing her away with an upturned palm.

"Oh, you know your Nettie. Listen!" She spoke in a whisper. "You're to come with me to where I live—how would you like that? I've only got the one room, but you're to have it. I'll sleep I don't care where. But you'll have your bed there same as here. And the Brothers can come and welcome. We'll have meetings, meetings to burn—"

He began to laugh.

"No, no," begged Nettie, taking hold of his hands. "Don't fall into the laughter. It's now—*today*—do you understand? Before it's too late."

He looked into her face. His forehead began to wrinkle.

"That's it!" said Nettie, tears coming into her eyes. "*Think!* I say you're to come and live with your dear Nettie that loves you."

"No. I'm too tired," he said slowly. "I'm too old a man to contract a morganatic marriage."

"Oh, not marriage, no sir!" said Nettie weeping. "I'm but a plain woman. Shame on you with such talk!"

"I've lived too long," he said sadly. "The pleasures of the flesh have lost their glitter. Matters of state—matters of state—matters of state—"

"Mr. Montague!" cried Nettie, shaking his shoulders peremptorily. "Come, get dressed. The Brothers and you and Nettie are going for a little outing. We're goin' a-riding in a taxicab!"

"No," he said, taking up his tablet and pencil. "I will not leave my kingdom. I will not abdicate."

"If I get the Brothers here, will you come?"

"Those paltry men? Those buffoons and commoners?" he asked. "*Knights!*" he said scornfully. "Call themselves Knights of the Hunt! Did *I* knight them? Nay. I, Montague Rex, proclaim a holiday—" he announced, making wide, sweeping marks on the tablet.

"Darling pet," said Nettie desperately. She took one of his cheeks in either hand. "You're my all on earth—just like you were Miss Lida's. Now I'll tell you the solemn truth. If you don't come with Nettie they'll lock you up, that's what! They'll put you under lock and key! Oh, my precious, would Nettie tell you wrong? It's God's honest word—they'll lock you up!"

With his powerful head he shook her hands away from his face. "Present your petition in due order," he commanded.

"Look!" She got down on her knees beside his bed. "To please *Nettie*," she exhorted him, wringing her hands in the air. "To please *Nettie!*"

"Denied!" he said, breaking into loud laughter.

"Oh, sir—there you go!" Nettie rose to her feet and listened helplessly as the laughter grew and spread piercingly over the room.

Only one remedy for the laughter once it got a good start—a sleeping tablet. Nettie went into his bathroom and dropped the dosage, one tablet, into half a glass of water.

But instead of hurrying back, as usual, to stifle his uproar with the drink, she stood still, her feet weighted to the floor. As the high-pitched, maniacal laughter rose about her ears, she put her hand to her heart. "Oh, Lord God," she whispered fearfully. "Oh, Miss Lida—tell me what!" She looked hesitatingly, then with frantic searching, up at the ceiling of the bathroom. But no answer came.

Finally her hand, as if of itself, began to add another tablet to the one in the glass, then another, another, another. . . . Mechanically she stirred it up.

Going back to Uncle Montague, she put a hand on his wrist. "Here," she said. "Drink this, pet—it's poor Nettie's wish."

Eagerly, between bursts of laughter, he drained the glass upside down.

"I won't let them fret you," she said, combing his wild hair with shaking fingers.

THE GREATEST THING IN THE WORLD

by NORMAN K. MAILER

INSIDE, OUT OF THE RAIN, THE LUNCH WAGON WAS HOT AND sticky. Al Groot stopped in front of the doorway, wiped his hands and wrung his hat out, and scuffed his shoes against the dirt-brown mat. He stood there, a small, old, wrinkled boy of eighteen or nineteen, with round beady eyes that seemed incapable of looking at you unless you were in back of him. He stopped at the door and waited, not sure of his reception, examining the place carefully, as if he might have need of this knowledge soon after. It was a little fancier than the ordinary lunchroom, having dark, old wood booths at the left that fronted the sharp, glittering stools and counter of well-polished chromium. A clock on the wall showed that it was after ten, which might have explained why the place was almost empty. There was no one at the counter and the few truck drivers, sprawled out on two adjoining booths to catch a late dinner, were tired, and very quiet, engrossed only in their sandwiches and hamburgers. Only one man was left behind the counter, and he was carefully cleaning the grease from the frankfurter griddle, with the slow motions of a man who has a great deal of time on his hands and is desperately afraid of finishing his work, to face the prospect of empty tables and silent people. He looked at Al, uncertain for a moment how to take him, and then he turned back to the griddle and gave it a last studious wipe. He spoke, without looking up, but his tone was friendly.

"Hi," he said.

Al said hello, watching the man scrape some crumblings off.

"It's a hell of a night, ain't it?" the counterman asked.

"Lousy."

"It sure is. Guess we needed it," he said. "The crops are hit bad when it don't rain enough."

"Sure," said Al. "Look, what does coffee and doughnuts cost?"

"Ten."

"Two doughnuts?"

"That's it."

"Uh-huh," said Al. "Could you let me have one doughnut and half a cup of coffee for five cents? I ain't got but a nickel."

"I don't know," he said. "I could, but why should I?"

"I ain't had nothing to eat today," Al pleaded. "Come on."

The man looked up. Al sucked expertly on his cheeks, just pulling them in enough to make it look good.

"I guess you could stand it. Only, pay me now."

Al reached into his pocket, and tenderly extracted a nickel from two halves of a dollar bill. He finished over one-third of the doughnut in the first bite, and realizing how extravagant he had been, he took a small begrudging sip of the coffee.

"Nice place," he said.

"I like it," the man said.

"You own it?"

"You're damn right, buddy. I worked to get this place. It's all mine. You don't find me giving anything away on it. Every cup of coffee a guy drinks feeds me too."

"Top of the world," Al said.

"Nyahr," he answered bitterly. "Lot of good it does me. You see anybody in here? You see me clicking the cash register? The hell you do."

Al was thinking of how tough his luck was that the truck drivers should be uniformed, which was as good as a 'no rider' sign. He grinned sympathetically at the owner, trying to look as wet as he could.

"Boy," he said. "I sure am stuck."

"Been hitching, huh?"

"Yeah, walked the last three miles, ever since it started to rain."

"Must be kind of tough."

"Sure, I figure I won't be able to sleep if it don't stop raining. That was my last nickel. Say, look, you wouldn't have a job for me?" he said stupidly.

"What'll I do, watch you work?"

"Then let me sleep here tonight. It won't cost you nothing."

"I don't run a flophouse."

"Skip it, forget it," Al said. "Only let me stay here a while to dry off. When somebody comes in, maybe they'll give me a ride."

"Stay," he said. "I have such a fancy trade. New chromium, brass fixtures. Ahhhhr."

Al slipped off the stool, and sat down at a table in the rear, out of sight of the counterman. He slouched down against the side of the booth and picked up a menu, supported between the salt and pepper shakers, looking at it interestedly, but past all craving or desire. He thought that it had been almost a year since he had had a steak. He tried to remember what it tasted like, but his memory failed, and to distract him from the tantalizing picture he started examining the spelling on the sheet, guessing at a word first, then seeing how close he had been. Another company truck driver had come in, and Al shot a quick look back to see where the owner was. Finding him up front, almost out of sight, he quickly picked up the ketchup bottle and shook large gobs of it into his mouth as fast as he could get it out. It burned and stung inside his stomach, and he kept blowing, trying to cool his mouth. Noticing a few drops on the table, he took a paper napkin, and squeezed them over to the edge, where they hung, ready to fall. He ran his little finger along underneath, gathering them up, and catching the drops in his mouth as they dripped off.

He felt for the split dollar bill, and fingered it. This time, he thought, it was really his last. Once, three months ago, he had five dollars. He thought back and tried to remember how he had gotten it. It was very vague, and he wondered whether he had stolen it or not. The image of five separate bills, and all that he could do with them, hit him then with all its beauty and impossibility. He thought of cigarettes, and a meal, and a clean woman in a good place, and new soles to his shoes, but most of all he thought of the soft leathery feel of money, and the tight wad it made in his pants. "By God," he said thickly, "there's nothing like it. You can't beat it. If I just had five dollars again."

He withdrew his hand, taking the two pieces out, smoothing them lovely on the table. He considered breaking the bill for another doughnut, but he knew he couldn't. It was the last thing between him and. . . . He stopped, realizing that he had passed the last thing—there was no 'and.' Still, he did not think any more of spending this last bill. Tomorrow or tonight he would be in Chicago, and he could find something to eat for a day or two. He might even pick up half a buck by mooching. In the meantime he felt hungry. He stayed in the booth, staring at the end wall, and dreaming of his one-time hoard.

Three men came in to eat. Al saw them hesitate at the door, wondering whether to eat in a booth or at the counter.

"Take a booth," one said.

Al looked at them. This might be a ride, he thought. He waited until they had started eating, and then he went over to them, hitching at his faded gray-blue dungarees.

"Hi, sports," he said.

"Hello, sweet-face," one of them said.

"They call me Al Groot."

"His father's name was Groot," said one of them turning to the others.

"I ain't asking for any dough."

They eased up a little. "Boy, you sure ain't, sweet-face," one of them said. "Sit down, sit down," he said. "My name's Cataract, account of my eye, it's no good, and this here is Pickles, and this is Cousin."

They all looked alike.

"I guess you know what I want," Al said.

"Ride?"

"Yeah, where you going?"

"Chicago."

"Start warming the seat up for me," Al said.

They grinned, and continued eating. Al watched Cataract go to work on a hamburger. He held it between thick, grease-stained fingers that dug into it, much as they might have sunk into a woman. He swallowed a large piece, slobbering a little, and slapping his tongue noisily against the roof of his mouth as he ate. Al watched him, fascinated. Wild thoughts of seizing the hamburger, and fighting the man for it, deviled him. He moved his head, in time to Cataract's jaws, and he felt madly frustrated as Cataract dropped the last bit into his mouth. Cataract lit a cigarette, and exhaled noisily, with a little belch of content.

"Jesus Christ," Al whispered.

He turned his attention to the other two, and watched them eat each piece down to the very bitter end. He hated them, and felt sick.

"Let's go," shouted Pickles. "Come on, sweet-face."

The car was an old Auburn sedan, with a short, humped-up body. Al sat in back with Cataract; Cousin was driving. Cataract took out a pack of Luckies, and passed them around. Al took the pack, and fumbled with it, acting as if he were having trouble extracting a cigarette. When he handed it back, he had a bonus of two more cuddled next to his dollar bill.

"Where you from?" Pickles asked.

"Easton," Al said. "It's in Pennsy."

Cataract rolled his tongue around. "Good town," he said, extending his arm, fist closed, twisting it in little circles at the wrist.

"Yeh," Al said. "One of the best. I ain't been there in four, no three years. Been on the road since."

"Hitching?"

"Hell, no," Al exploded with contempt. "It's a suckers game hitching. I work the trains; you know, 'Ride the rails in comfort with Pullman'."

"Yeahr. How're the hobo camps?" Cousin asked.

It was Al's turn to extend his arm.

They all started laughing with wise, knowing, lewd laughs.

"What do you boys do?" Al asked.

They laughed again.

"We're partners in business," Cataract said.

Al looked at them, discarding one thing after another, trying to narrow down the possibilities. He decided they were sucker players of some sort.

"You guys know of any jobs in Chicago?" Al asked.

"How much you want?"

"About twenty a week. I'm in now. Got thirty-four bucks."

Pickles whistled. "What're you mooching meals for, then?"

"Who's mooching?" Al demanded. "Did I ask you guys for anything besides a ride?"

"Noooo."

"Awright, then don't go around being a wise guy."

Pickles looked out the window, grinning. "Sorry, bud."

"Well, awright then," Al said, acting sore.

"Well, awright then, dig, dig, dig, well awright," Cousin mimicked.

Cataract laughed, trying to be friendly. "They're funny boys, you know, just smart. They wish they had your thirty-four, that's all."

It worked, Al thought. He let himself grin. "It's okay," he said.

He looked out the window. They weren't in Chicago yet, but the lights shining from the houses on the side of the road were more frequent, making a steady yellow glare against the wet windows, and he knew that they must be almost at the outskirts by now. Just then, he saw a City Limits and Welcome sign flash past. Cousin turned off the highway, and went along for a way on a dirt road that in time turned onto an old oil-stained asphalt street. They passed a few factories, and Al thought of dropping off, but he wondered if it might not pay him to stay with the men a while.

Cataract yawned. "What about a game of pool now, boys?" he asked.

So that's what they are, Al thought.

"Say," he said, "I'd like to play too. I ain't very good, but I like the game." He had played exactly three times in his life.

Pickles assured him. "We're no good either, that is, I'm no good. You and me can play."

"Yeah," Al said, "it ought to be fun."

Cousin was driving up Milwaukee Avenue now. He turned left, slowing down very carefully as he did so, although there were no cars in sight.

"That Cousin drives like an old woman," Pickles commented. "I could drive faster going backwards."

Cousin jeered at him. "You couldn't drive my aunt's wheelbarrow. I'm the only guy left who hasn't lost his license," he said speaking to Al. It's because I take it easy when I drive a car."

Al said he didn't know much about cars, but he guessed maybe Cousin was right.

The car pulled up in front of a dark gray building on the corner of a long row of old brownstone homes. It was a dark street, and the only evidence that people lived on it were the overflowing garbage and ash cans spaced at irregular intervals in front of the houses. The poolroom itself was down in the cellar, underneath a beauty parlor and a secretarial school. On the steps going down, Al could see penciled scribblings on the walls; some hasty calculation of odds, a woman's telephone number with a comment underneath it, a few bits of profanity, and one very well-drawn nude woman.

The foot of the stairs opened right onto the tables, which were strung out in one long narrow line of five. The place was almost dark, only the first table being used, and no lights were on in the back. Pickles stepped over to the counter and started talking to the boss, calling him familiarly, and for some reason annoyingly, by the name Nick. Nick was a short, very broad and sweaty Italian. He and Pickles looked up at Al at the same time, and Pickles motioned to him.

"Nick, this is a pal of mine. I want you to treat him nice if he ever comes in again. Tell thick Nick your name, sweet-face."

"Call me sweet-face," Al said.

"H'lo," Nick said. "Pleased to meet you."

"Where we play?" Al asked. He noticed that Cataract and Cousin had not come down yet.

"Take number four."

"Sweet-face and me on number four," Pickles said. "Got it."

He walked down turning on a few lights. He stopped at the cue rack, and picked one at random. Al followed him, selected one carefully, sighting along it to see if there was any warp, and sprinkling some talc over it. "Should we play a rack for table?" he asked.

"Sure," said Pickles. "You mind if we play straight? I don't know any fancy stuff.

"Me neither."

They tossed a coin, and Al had to break. He shot poorly, hit the wrong ball and scratched. Pickles overshot and splattered balls all over the table. Al sunk two, shooting as well as he could, knowing that Pickles would notice any attempts at faking. They both played sloppily and it took fifteen minutes to clear the table. Al won, eight balls to seven.

"We're pretty close," Pickles said. "What about playing for a couple of bucks this next table?"

He watched Cataract and Cousin who had just come in and were starting to play.

Al could feel the sweat starting up in the small of his back and on his thighs. I can still get out of it, he thought. At least I'll have my buck. The thought of another five dollars, however, was too strong for him. He tried to think of what would happen to him if he didn't get away with it, but he kept remembering how it felt to have money in his hands. He heard himself speaking, feeling that it was not he but some one right in back, or on top of him.

"Make it a buck," he said.

Pickles broke, again shooting too hard. Al watched him flub balls all over the table, slightly overdoing it this time. They finished the rack, Al getting a run of three at the end, to win, ten to five. Pickles handed him a dollar, and placed another on the side of the table. Al covered it with the one he had won. I wonder when he starts winning, Al thought. If I can only quit then. They played for a dollar twice more. Al winning both times. A first drop of perspiration drew together, and raced down his back. He saw Cataract watching them play, juggling two balls in his hand. They played for three dollars, Al winning, after being behind, five to two.

He straightened up, making an almost visible effort to relax. "That makes six bucks," he said.

"Sure," said Pickles. "Let's make it five this time. I want to win my dough back."

This time Pickles won. Al handed him five dollars, separating the bills with difficulty, and handing them over painfully.

"Another one for five," Pickles said.

Al looked around him desperately, wondering if he could get out. "Five," he croaked. Cataract was still juggling the balls.

It was the longest game he ever played. After every shot he stopped to wipe his hands. In the middle, he realized that this game was going to be given to him. He couldn't relax, however, because he knew the showdown would merely be delayed for another game or so.

He won, as he knew he would, but immediately the pressure was on again. They played once more for five, and he won. After it was over, he didn't trust himself to stand, and he leaned against the cue rack, trying to draw satisfaction from the money in his pocket. He dreamed of getting out, and having it all to do as he pleased, until he saw Pickles and Cataract looking at each other. Cataract threw a ball up, and closed his fingers too soon, missing it. It came down with a loud shattering crack that made Nick look up from his counter. That's the signal, Al thought.

They were the only ones in the place now.

Pickles stroked his cue, grinning. "Your luck's been too good, sweet-face. I think this is going to be my game. I got twenty bucks left. I'm laying it down."

"No," said Al. "I don't want to."

"Listen, I been losing dough. You're playing."

They all looked at him menacingly.

"I want to quit," Al said.

"I wouldn't try it," Cousin said.

Al looked about him, trapped, thoughts of fighting them, mixing with mad ideas of flight.

Cataract stepped toward him, holding a cue in his hand.

"All right," Al said, "I'll play."

Pickles broke, making a very beautiful "safe," leaving Al helpless. He bent over his stick to shoot. The balls wavered in front of him, and he could see the tip of the cue shaking up and down. He wiped his face and looked around to loosen his muscles. When he tried again, it was useless. He laid his cue on the table and walked to the back.

"Where you going?" asked Pickles.

"To the can. Want to come along?" He forced a laugh from the very bottom of his throat.

He passed through a small littered room, where old soda boxes were stored. The bathroom was small and filthy; the ceiling higher than the distance from wall to wall. Once inside he bolted the door, and sank down on the floor, whimpering softly.

After a while he quieted and looked around. The only other possible exit was a window, high up on the wall facing the door. He looked at it, not realizing its significance, until a chance sound from outside made him realize where he was and what was happening to him. He got up, and looked at the wall, examining its surface for some possible boost. He saw there was none, crouched down, and jumped. His hands just grasped the edge, clung for a fraction of a second, and then scraped off. He knelt again, as close to the wall as he could possibly get, flexed himself, and leaped up. This time his palms grasped hold. He pressed his fingertips against the stone surface and chinned up enough to work his elbows over. He rested a moment, and then squeezed his stomach in and hung there on the ledge against the window, his legs dangling behind. He inched the window open noiselessly and, forgetting he was in the cellar, looked down into blackness. For a moment he was panic stricken, until he remembered he was in the cellar, and had to look up. He shifted his position, and raised his head. There was a grating at right angles to the window, fixed above a dump heap, much like the one beneath a subway grill. It was very dark outside, but he could make out that it opened into an alley. Overjoyed, he took his money out, almost falling off in the act, kissed it, put it back, and tried to open the grating. He placed his hands under it and pushed up as hard as he could in his cramped position. The grille didn't move. He stuck one foot through the open window, and straddled the ledge, one foot in, one foot out. Bracing himself, he pushed calmly against the grating, trying to dislodge it from the grime imbedded in it. Finding his efforts useless, he pushed harder and harder until his arms were almost pushed into his chest and his back and crotch felt as if they would crack. Breathing heavily, he stopped and stared up past the grating. Suddenly, with a cry of desperation, he flung himself up, beating against it with his hands and arms, until the blood ran down them. Half crazy, he gripped the bars and shook, with impassioned groans. His fingers slipped against a little obstruction on one of the end bars. His hand felt it, caressed it, hoping to find some lever point, and discovered it to be a rivet between the foundation and the grille. He sat there, huge sobs torn from him, his eyes gazing hungrily at the sky above. After a bit, he withdrew his leg, wormed his body in again, closed the window, and dropped heavily to the floor, lying in a heap, as he had fallen, his face to the wall. I'll just wait till till they come for me, he thought. He could hear someone coming toward the door. Pickles knocked. "Hey, kid," he yelled from the other side of the partition, "hurry up."

Al stood up, a mad flare of hope running through him as he thought of the money he still had. He held his hand to his throat, and struggled to control his voice. "Be right out," he said, managing to hold it through to the end. He heard Pickles walk away, and felt a little stronger. He started to wash himself, to get the blood off. His hands were still bleeding dully, the blood oozing out thickly and sluggishly, but he was able to stop the flow somewhat. He backed away, glanced out the window once more, and took his money out. He held it in his hands, and let the bills slip through his fingers. Gathering them up, he kissed them feverishly, rubbing the paper against his face and arms. He folded them tenderly, let down his pants and slipped the cash into a little secret pocket, just under the crotch. He flattened out the bump it made, and unlocked the door to go out. His heart was still pounding, but he felt calmer, and more determined.

They were waiting for him impatiently, smoking quickly and nervously.

Al took out one of Cataract's cigarettes and asked for a match. He lit it, sucking deeply and gratefully from it. They glared at him, their nerves almost as tight as his.

"Come on," said Pickles, "it's your turn to shoot."

Al picked up his cue, gripping it hard to make his hand bleed faster. He bent over, made a pretence of sighting, and then laid his cue down, exposing the place where his hand had stained it.

"What's the matter?" Cousin snapped.

"I can't hold a cue," Al said. "I cut my hand in there."

"What do you mean you can't play?" Pickles shouted. "My money's up. You got to play."

"You can't force me. I'm not going to play. It's my money, it's mine see, and you can't make me. You guys can't pull this on me; you're just trying to work a sucker game."

It was the wrong thing to say. Cataract caught him by the shirt, and shook him. "Grab ahold of that stick," he said.

Al wrenched loose. "Go to hell," he said. "I'm quitting."

He picked up his hat, and started walking down past the tables to go out. He had to pass three tables and the counter to get to the stairs. He walked slowly, hoping to bluff his way out. He knew he had no chance if he ran. He could feel the sweat starting up much faster this time. His shoulders were twitching, and he was very conscious of the effort of forming each step, expecting something to hit him at every second. His face was wet, and he fought down an agonizing desire to turn and look at them. Behind him, they were silent. He could see Nick at the entrance, watching him walk toward him, his face expressionless. Fascinated, he hung onto Nick's eyes, pleading silently with him. A slight smile grew on Nick's face. It broke into a high unnatural laugh, squeaking off abruptly. Terrified, Al threw a quick glance back, and promptly threw himself on his face. A cue whizzed by, shattering on the far wall with a terrific smash. Before he could get up, they were on him. Cataract turned him on his back, and knelt over him. He brought the heel of his hand down hard on Al's face, knocking his head on the floor. He saw them swirl around him, the pool tables mixed in somewhere, and he shook his head furiously, to keep from going out. Cataract hit him again.

Al struck out with his foot, and hit him in the shin.

"You dirty little bastard," Cataract said. "I'll teach you."

He slammed his knee down into Al's stomach. Al choked and writhed, the fight out of him for a moment. They turned him over, and stripped his pockets, looking for his money. They shook him. "Where is it, sweet-face?" Pickles asked.

Al choked for breath.

"I lost it," he said mockingly.

"It's in his pants somewhere," Cousin said. "These rats always got a secret pocket." They tried to open his pants. He fought crazily, kicking, biting, screaming, using his elbows and knees.

"Come on," Cataract commanded, "get it off him."

Al yelled as loud as he could. Nick came over. "Get him out," he said. "The cops'll be dropping in soon. I don't want trouble."

"What'll we do with him?"

"Take him out on the road where no one will hear you. After that, it's your imagination." He squealed with laughter again.

They picked him up, and forced him out. He went with them peacefully, too dazed to care. They shoved him in the car, and Cousin turned it around. Al was in front, Cataract in the back seat, holding his wrist so he couldn't break loose before they started.

Al sat there silently, his head clearing, remembering how slowly Cousin drove. He looked out, watching the ground shoot by, and thought of jumping out. Hopelessly, he looked at the speedometer. They were going around a turn, and Cousin had slowed down to less than twenty miles an hour. He had jumped off freight trains going faster than that, but there had been no door in the way, and no one had been holding him. Discouraged, he gave up the idea.

Cousin taunted him. "See that white sign, sweet-face? We turn left there, just around it, and after that it won't be long."

Anger and rebellion surged through him. They were taking away something that he had earned dangerously, and they were going to beat him up, because they had not been as smart as he. It was not fair. He wanted the money more than they did. In a fury, he decided to jump at the turn. The sign was about a hundred yards away; it would be his last chance. He figured it would take seven seconds to reach it.

He turned around to face Cataract, his left elbow resting loosely against the door handle. He had turned the way his wrist was twisted, holding it steady, so that Cataract would not realize the pressure was slackened. One, he counted to himself. "Look," he begged Cataract, "let me off. I ain't got the money, let me off." Maybe thirty yards gone by. Cataract was talking, "Oh, you're a funny boy, sweet-face. I like you, sweet-face." Another twenty. "Yeh, sure I'm funny, I'm a scream," he said. "Oh, I'm so funny." The sign, where is it? We should have reached it. Oh please God, show me the sign, you got to, it's my money, not theirs, oh please. "Goddam you, please," he shouted. "What?" Cataract yelled. Cousin slowed down. The sign slipped by. They started to turn. Al spat full in Cataract's face, and lashed out with his wrist against the thumb. His elbow kicked the door open, and he yanked his hand loose, whirled about, and leaped out, the door just missing him in its swing back.

His feet were pumping wildly as he hit the ground. He staggered in a broken run for a few steps, before his knees crumpled under him, and he went sprawling in the dust. His face went grinding into it, the dirt mashing up into his cheeks and hands. He lay there stunned for a very long second, and then he pushed hard with his hands against the ground, forcing himself up. The car had continued around the turn, and in the confusion had gone at least a hundred feet before it stopped. Al threw a stone at the men scrambling out, and plunged off into a field. It had stopped raining, but the sky was black, and he knew they would never catch him. He heard them in the distance, yelling to each other, and he kept running, his legs dead, his head lolling sideways, his breath coming in long ripping bursts. He stumbled over a weed and fell, his body spreading out on soft wet grass. Exhausted, he lay there, his ear close to the ground, but no longer hearing them, he sat up, plucking weakly at bits of grass, saying over and over again. "Oh, those suckers, those big, dumb, suckers. Oh, those dopes, those suckers. . . ."

At two-thirty, Al Groot, his stomach full, swung off a streetcar near Madison Street, and went into a flophouse. He gave the night man a new dollar bill, and tied the eighty-five cents change in a rag that he fastened to his wrist. He stood over his bed, and lit some matches, moving them slowly over the surface of his mattress. A few bedbugs started out of their burrows, and crept across the bed. He picked them up, and squashed them methodically. The last one he held in his hand, watching it squirm. He felt uneasy for a moment, and impulsively let it escape, whirling his hand in a circle to throw it away from the bed. He stretched himself out, and looked off in the distance for a while, thinking of women, and hamburgers, and billiard balls, and ketchup bottles, and shoes and, most of all, of the thrill of breaking a five-dollar bill. Lighting the last of Cataract's cigarettes, he thought of how different things had been, when he had first palmed them. He smoked openly, not caring if someone should see him, for it was his last. Al smoked happily, tremendously excited, letting each little ache and pain well into the bed. When the cigarette was finished he tried to fall asleep. He felt wide awake, though, and after some time he propped himself on an elbow, and thought of what he would to the next day. First he would buy a pack of cigarettes, and then he would have a breakfast, and then a clean woman; he would pay a buck if he had to, and then a dinner and another woman, He stopped suddenly, unable to continue, so great was his ecstasy. He lay over his pillow and addressed it.

"By God," Al Groot said, about to say something he had never uttered before, "by God, this is the happiest moment of my life."

FULVOUS YELLOW

by STANLEY KAUFFMANN

MR. AND MRS. SPRAGUE WERE A VERY NICE MIDDLE-AGED COUPLE. They lived in Albany, New York, and they had managed to remain mentally alive. They read a lot of books, some of them not chosen by book clubs, owned a few nice paintings, and had quite a good collection of phonograph records, including "Scheherazade."

They were proudest, however, of their son Everett. He was an unusual and talented boy. In six months down in New York City he had done well. He was already top assistant to one of the most important dress designers in the business.

"Fashion stylists," Mrs. Sprague had corrected her husband once. "Ev says they don't call them dress designers any more."

"Fashion stylists," Mr. Sprague agreed quickly.

They were on their way down to New York now to visit Ev. They hadn't seen him in almost four months. When he had first got his New York job, he had come home every week end. Then his visits had slacked off to every two weeks. Then four months had gone by without his visiting them. But Mr. and Mrs. Sprague were not foolish or demanding parents. They understood that their son was in a new life, making new friends, finding new interests, and as long as his letters once a week told them that he was well and happy, they were reasonably content.

Now Mr. Sprague had managed to get Friday off from the office and they were going down for a long week end. They hadn't told Ev in advance; they wanted it to be a surprise. They sent a wire just before they got on the train.

"Make sure you send it to the new address," said Mrs. Sprague. "Remember, he moved last month."

"I know that as well as you do," Mr. Sprague replied testily. Ev was as much his son as hers.

They had lunch in the dining car. The steward put them at a table for four and then seated a big bald man next to Mr. Sprague. They fell into talk and the big bald man told them that he was on his way to his son's wedding in Brooklyn Heights. The Spragues agreed that that was fine and envied the bald man. Then they told him about Ev's progress in six short months.

"What's your son's work?" asked the bald man, impressed.

"He's a dress de—he's in fashion styling," Mr. Sprague said. "Always had an eye for color, and things like that."

"Always," agreed his mother. "Ever since he was a very little boy."

"Oh," said the man, with the hint of a wrinkle between his brows. "That's fine. Fine."

Mr. Sprague noticed the wrinkle. "You know," he said with a laugh, "lots of people have the wrong idea about the fashion field. It takes ability and business sense just like any other business."

"Oh, sure, I know," nodded the bald man quickly. I saw an article about it in *Life*."

Ev wasn't at the station to meet them, but Mr. Sprague said that probably the wire hadn't given him time enough to get away. On an off chance, he called the apartment before he tried the office and was surprised to hear Ev answer.

Ev was glad to hear his father's voice. Yes, he'd received the wire but he hadn't been able to meet the train. He had some things he had to finish up for Ty. Ty was his roommate. Also his boss. Why didn't they take a cab and come right over before they went to their hotel?

It was a remodeled private house in the East Fifties, not far from the river. The card for Apt. 3 said "Emmet" with "Sprague" written in below it. Mr. Sprague gave the bell two pokes.

Ev stood at the top of the stairs in a striped basque shirt and a pair of slacks. "Hello, Mother," he said. "Gosh, it's good to see you. What a wonderful surprise. Hello, Father."

He used to call Mr. Sprague "Dad." Mr. Sprague thought he looked a little pale. Working too hard, probably.

The apartment was eye-filling. The furniture was low and modern, pearl gray and coral red. There were good reproductions of Picasso and Matisse and Utrillo in wide natural-wood frames. And there were small white-enameled wrought-iron gates between the living room and the tiny kitchen.

Ev gave his parents each a glass of sherry and apologized for not having been up to Albany for so long. "But gosh, I've been busy," he said. He indicated the drawing board at the side of the room; there was a large colored sketch of a woman in a coat tacked on it. "We're doing some rush work on a new line of casual clothes and Ty's given me some of the tougher things. But I don't mind. It's pretty exciting."

"Do you always work at home, Ev?" his mother asked.

"When I've got something really tough, yes. Because that office is a madhouse." He laughed. It was Mr. Sprague's boy's laugh, all right. "That's one advantage of living with your boss."

"It's certainly a nice place to work," said Mr. Sprague. He cleared his throat. "Ev—er, you mind if I ask? This is all pretty expensive, isn't it? And—"

"Oh, I pay my share," Ev replied. "Of the rent, anyway. Ty had the place for years before I moved in, of course, so I got the use of the furnishings for nothing. But when he saw that hole I was boarding in on Forty-fifth Street, he insisted on my coming in with him."

"He sounds like a very nice man," said his mother.

"Ty?" laughed Ev. "You'll love him. He ought to be along pretty soon. I phoned him when I got your wire and he said he'd come home early."

"By the way, Ev," said Mr. Sprague, "I've got regards for you. Or a bawling out, depending on how you look at it. Joanie Carson wants to be remembered, and she says she's not going to write to you again until you answer her last letter."

Ev laughed shortly. "Joanie Carson. That child."

"She still talks about you, Ev," said his mother.

"Does she?" said Ev.

Ty came in soon. He was a big man with a large, roundish face. He wore a beautiful gabardine suit and brown suède shoes. He had two boxes under his arm, and he gave one—a corsage box—to Mrs. Sprague.

"I'm so happy to meet Ev's parents," he said with a pleasant smile. "I hope you won't mind—I've brought you these, and I've taken the liberty of arranging things for this evening." He took a ticket envelope from his pocket. "There's a new musical—a smash—but a friend of mine did the costumes and he got tickets for me. 'Ice to the Eskimos.' Have you heard of it?"

"Oh, yes," said Mr. Sprague, who kept up on things. "I read the review of it. We'd love to see it. That's very nice of you, Mr. Emmet."

Mrs. Sprague opened her box. "Orchids!" she exclaimed. "How lovely! Oh, Mr. Emmet, you shouldn't have—really."

Ty bowed, almost from the waist. "Pleasure, I assure you. It's only once that I'll meet Ev's parents for the first time. Talented Ev." He put his hand briefly on Ev's shoulder. "Which reminds me—this other box." He opened it as he spoke. "I was passing Quentin's at lunch time today—" He explained to the Spragues. "Quentin's a friend of mine who keeps a shop. Men's accessories. Really unusual things." From the box he took a silk muffler, a beautiful tawny yellow. "There, Ev. What do you think of it?"

"It's stunning," said Ev. "But—"

Ty proceeded to wind it around Ev's neck and to knot it. "It'll go nicely with your chocolate-brown jacket."

Ev shook his head. "Ty, as Mother says, you shouldn't have—really."

"Nonsense." Ty hushed him grandly. "Anniversary present. You know," he said to the Spragues, "it's a wonderful coincidence, your coming down today. It's just a month today that Ev's been living here."

"Yes," said Mr. Sprague, "that's right, I guess it is. I remember Ev's letter telling us about it came right on my birthday."

"But just the same, Ty," said Ev, stroking the silken scarf

around his neck, "you're much too extravagant and generous."

Ty shrugged. "When I saw it in the window, I thought of you at once. It seemed your color somehow. A kind of—" he hesitated for a word, "—fulvous yellow."

"What kind?" asked Mr. Sprague.

"Fulvous," said Ty. "Tawny. Smoky yellow."

"Oh," said Mr. Sprague. He nodded thoughtfully. Then he sighed and got up. "Well, I suppose we ought to go on to our hotel."

They agreed to meet in the hotel lobby to go out to dinner, and Ev put them in a cab. On the way to the hotel, which was not far, Mrs. Sprague held the flower box carefully and Mr. Sprague sat with his hands in his lap, one on each leg, palms down.

After a while, Mrs. Sprague said, "It's a lovely apartment, don't you think?"

"Very pretty," he replied.

She looked at him. "Mr. Emmet's a nice man, don't you think?"

The taxi stopped for a light. Then the light changed and they went on.

"Very nice," said Mr. Sprague.

That night Ty took the Spragues to a French restaurant where the headwaiter knew him quite well and where the specialty was little soufflé potatoes. At dinner Ty told them what a fine future he thought Ev had in designing. He said he felt no hesitancy in telling them, even at this early date, that he was training Ev for the time when they might operate a studio together.

"I think there are really great things ahead for Ev," said Ty.

Ev flushed happily and turned to his mother. "Gosh, Mother, wasn't I lucky to meet him? Some people have to struggle for years before they get a real break."

"Not the ones like you, Ev," said Ty, patting his arm. "Not the ones with real talent."

"Well, Ev," said his mother gently, "we've been bragging all over Albany about your wonderful progress."

"Yes," said his father, "we have been."

In the cab on the way to the theater Ty explained that their seats wouldn't be together; he'd had to take what he could get. But he and Ev would be sitting almost directly behind the Spragues. Mr. Sprague wanted to take the second row, but Ty insisted that his guests have the better seats.

The show was loud and fast. The audience expected it to be funny, and where the show fell short of the mark, the audience's expectation filled up the gap and they laughed anyway. There was a scene in the first act in which a girl in a tight sweater threw herself on a bashful sailor's lap and made love to him. While the audience was howling, Mr. Sprague, vaguely disinterested, glanced around at the row behind. Ev was chuckling and Ty, his arm linked with Ev's, was smiling; the smile made his face seem larger.

Later, Ty wanted to take them to a supper club for drinks, but Mr. and Mrs. Sprague asked to be excused after their long day. Ty promised to pick them up in his car next morning at ten-thirty; they would drive out to his beach club on Long Island for lunch.

The Spragues were in the lobby next morning promptly at ten-thirty. They had not wanted much breakfast, but the coffee was very good and Mr. Sprague had had a barbershop shave, complete with hot towel, which had refreshed him.

Ty came smiling through the revolving doors and behind him came Ev in his chocolate-brown jacket with the new muffler knotted about his neck. Mr. Sprague thought that Ty was right, the muffler went very well with the jacket.

"Good morning," beamed Ty. "A wonderful day. I'll get you some suits out at the club so you can take a dip."

"Goodness," laughed Mrs. Sprague, "do you think they'd have any to fit me?"

"Why, they must have," said Mr. Sprague. "Lots of fellows' mothers must come to visit them, don't they, Ev?"

"Sure, I suppose so," Ev nodded.

"It's a long time since Ev and I went swimming together," said Mr. Sprague. "Can you still do that shallow dive I taught you, Ev?"

Ty's car was a roadster and Mr. and Mrs. Sprague sat together in the little back seat. Mr. Sprague was busy most of the time keeping his hat on his head, but Ty wore a beret when he drove and Ev's hair never seemed the worse for wind. Mr. Sprague sat right behind his son and could see Ev's hair.

They got suits quickly enough at the club and Mrs. Sprague dabbled in the shallow end of the pool while the men swam. Mr. Sprague was very good for his age but he soon climbed up on the edge of the pool, puffing, and dangled his legs in the water. Ty swam over soon after and hoisted himself up next to Mr. Sprague.

"Those are nice trunks," said Mr. Sprague. Ty had Hawaiian trunks, yellow with a blue flower design.

"These?" smiled Ty. "They're Ev's idea. He picked them out for me. Said he liked them but didn't quite dare to wear them himself." Ev's trunks were a solid light blue. "Ev," he called, "let's see you dive."

Ev, swimming in toward the board, laughed and said, "Right. The professor will be happy to oblige."

"Where did he learn to dive, Mr. Sprague?" asked Ty.

"Oh, I taught him some," said Mr. Sprague, "and he was on the team at school."

Ev climbed to the board and walked to the end. He raised his arms and arched himself.

"Watch this, now," said Ty, watching.

Ev leaped into the air, then spread his arms wide in the sun and came sailing down. Just before he hit the water, he brought his hands together over his head.

Ty applauded. "Ah, perfect," he said. "That was perfect."

"Pretty good," said Mr. Sprague. "Knees might have been a little straighter."

They had lunch on the terrace overlooking the pool. Ty was dissatisfied with the salad dressing and asked the waiter to bring him oil and seasoning so that he could mix a dressing himself. "It seems a shame to invite you all the way out here and then just give you run-of-the-mill fare," he said to the Spragues.

"Wait till you taste this, Mother," said Ev. "You've never tasted anything like this salad dressing."

Mr. Sprague thought it was very good indeed, but he wasn't especially hungry. When he had finished lunch, he lit a pipe and said, "I thought maybe tonight we'd all have dinner and go up to the Stadium concert to hear Lily Pons. The ticket man in the hotel said he might get me tickets."

"Oh, I always love Lily Pons," said Mrs. Sprague. "So do you, Ev."

Ev glanced at Ty, then said, "Yes, Mother, I do. But I'm afraid I can't go tonight. I should have told you yesterday. I'm terribly sorry, but gosh, I didn't know that you were coming this week end."

"Oh," said Mrs. Sprague.

"It's my fault, Mrs. Sprague," Ty said. "You see, we were invited to this dinner party about a week ago and I accepted for us. Business friends, and some people from out of town. It's really rather important, but I suppose I could make excuses for you, Ev, if you wanted to go with your parents."

"Well—" said Ev.

"No, no," said Mr. Sprague, "I wouldn't want to interfere. I know how these things are, I'm a businessman myself. It's our fault for not letting you know far enough ahead. No, you go out to your party, Ev. Your mother and I will make out."

When they started back, Ty invited Mrs. Sprague to sit in front with him. Ev sat in back next to his father and they talked for a while of things in New York, then they talked a little about things in Albany. Then they just sat and enjoyed the ride.

Ty dropped them at their hotel and Ev apologized for not being able to see them again that night. They said they understood perfectly. They all agreed to have dinner next day at three so that the Spragues could catch the five-o'clock train, and Mrs. Sprague thanked Ty for the pleasant day. Then Ev got into the front seat next to Ty and they drove off.

Mr. Sprague watched them go. Mrs. Sprague said, "Well, do you want to see the man about Lily Pons?"

"Oh," said Mr. Sprague, "sure."

They went to the agency counter, but the man said he had only one seat left for that night and it wasn't a very good one. "I guess it's just as well that Ev went to his party," said Mrs. Sprague.

"Yes," replied Mr. Sprague thoughtfully. He said, "Anyway, that Stadium's awfully far uptown."

They rested for a while in their room, then went to an Italian restaurant which Ev had recommended. They couldn't understand most of the things on the menu and finally ordered meat balls and spaghetti.

"What would you like to do tonight?" asked Mrs. Sprague.

"Oh, I don't know," he answered. "I don't much care. What would you like to do?"

"Would you like to go to the Music Hall?" she asked. "You always like to go to the Music Hall."

"Well, it's probably pretty crowded," he said. "What's playing there?"

"That life-of-a-composer picture," she said. "They say it's very good."

Mr. Sprague moved his spoon over close to his knife and lined it up exactly parallel. Then he pushed the knife ahead gently until the bottom was precisely level with the spoon. "Well," he said, "I don't know. I suppose we can see it up home."

"Sure," said Mrs. Sprague. "Sure we can."

They bought some papers and magazines after dinner and went back to their room. Later, when he undressed for bed, Mr. Sprague took his wallet out of his pocket, as was his custom, to put it in a drawer. He remembered a picture of Ev and himself that he carried in his wallet and found it. It had been snapped on an Adirondacks fishing trip about six years before. The boy was wearing high-top shoes and breeches and a plaid shirt open at the throat. He was grinning and squinting into the sun. In his hands he held the string of bass and pickerel he had caught that day.

When Mrs. Sprague came out of the bathroom, she scolded

her husband for reading in the dark; and he went in and brushed his teeth.

They waited in the lobby next day until half-past three before Mr. Sprague called the apartment. Ev answered sleepily. When he recognized his father's voice, he seemed to wake up. "Oh, gosh, Father," he said, "what time is it?"

Mr. Sprague told him.

"Good Lord," said Ev. "I had no idea. We were up terribly late. Gosh, I'm sorry, Father. I'm awfully sorry."

"Well," said Mr. Sprague, "those things happen."

"Are you still going to catch the five-o'clock?" Ev asked.

"I'm afraid we have to, Ev," answered Mr. Sprague.

"Then that spoils our dinner date," Ev said. "That's terrible."

"Oh, well," Mr. Sprague said, "we had a late breakfast. It doesn't matter."

"Well, at least we'll come over and take you to the train," Ev said. "We'll be right over."

Ty had dark circles under his eyes, but Ev looked all right. He had on a hound's-tooth jacket today, but he was still wearing the muffler.

Ty let go of Ev's arm to gesture apologetically. "A fine thing," he smiled ruefully, "a fine thing. And I wanted to make a good impression on you both. What ever are you going to think of me now?"

"Well," said Mr. Sprague, "as I told Ev, these things happen."

They drove to the station, and Ty and Ev put them aboard the train. Ty shook hands with both of them, said how happy he'd been to meet them, and hoped they'd forgive them for oversleeping. Then Ev kissed his mother's cheek and shook hands with his father.

"Ev," said Mr. Sprague calmly, "please. I know how busy you are. But try to come up next Friday, won't you? I'd like to have one of our old-fashioned week ends. Real old walk and talk. Try. Won't you, Ev?"

"All right, Father," nodded Ev, "I'll try. I really will. It was awfully nice to see you again."

Harlem, Hastings, Harmon. Change of engines. Mr. and Mrs. Sprague sat in the coach and didn't talk much. They train was really quite comfortably air-conditioned, but Mr. Sprague had buttoned his jacket to the top.

The waiter came through with the last call for dinner. Mrs. Sprague said, "We'd better have something, dear," and they went into the dining car. She ordered a sandwich and tea; he ordered a piece of pie and coffee.

The waiter brought their food. Mr. Sprague had been staring out the window, but he picked up his fork automatically and turned his attention to the pumpkin pie. He stared at it a minute, then he prodded the viscous, flabby filling with his fork. Then he dropped his fork sharply.

His wife looked up anxiously, and after a moment, he spoke.

"Fulvous yellow," he said.

THE LITTLE TROUT

by HALLIE SOUTHGATE BURNETT

THEY STARTED OUT AT SIX IN THE MORNING, THEIR FISHING tackle neatly packed on the back seat, their lunch in the brown wicker basket on the floor where it was coolest. The sky was warming to the sun in the east, but it was still undefined, and the Nevada sandland was gray and undisturbed by sunlight or movement as the night had left it.

"We've got it all to ourselves," the girl said. "It's so peaceful—so clean. It's hard to remember there's a war. You *can* just forget here—can't you, Max?"

The man nodded, being kind about the plea in her voice. She was asking him again to forget the things he knew, that they had not known together. Earlier in their relationship he had tried to answer her, reasonably, when she spoke like this. He had tried to warn her that there would be times he saw things in a way she would not understand, but now he only tried to be kind. There was no need for her also to be aware of the shadows behind him, that he was putting behind him here in Reno. The wife he had divorced, still in Germany and a Nazi, with their son: these things need not concern Jessie. Her own quiet academic past, let her grieve for that, a little, if need be. She would not. . . .

He smiled at her, and being a foreigner many things seemed to be in his smile. It had a special kind of communication, because he was handsome and accomplished as a lover (many women had been content to have him so and no more); because he had been through a tragedy in his world; but also, because of the girl, there was a belief, a feeling of faith in their future, together.

"You can forget," he assured her, and she returned his smile.

It took them half an hour to reach the bend in the river where they'd caught the six trout the day before; but when they got there it did not appeal to them. Yesterday they had cast long from its banks—they knew it too well, the large rocks broken off sharply, jagged-toothed beneath the water. They knew the minnows that robbed the red salmon eggs she used on her hook, so that for every pull but one in twenty would be a fish important enough for combat. The water had become over-explicit, like a person who talks much and seldom produces an arresting thought; so that even from the depths of the water they felt today there could be no trout large enough, beautiful enough to satisfy them.

"I think the fish have all been evacuated since yesterday," he said, softly, not looking at her. "This water is like a swimming pool. All it does not have is the little walk around it," and he made a walking gesture with his hands.

They looked though at the green around the banks and for an instant were tempted, the green touched the outer nerves of senses other than those used in fishing—sight, and the something felt, the fine magnetized wire strung through their bodies drawing them to the fish, the fish (so they could believe) to them. But a moment later they were walking back to the car without having set up their rods.

The thing that really affected them was that they had been here before. They did not want to return to anything in the past, even the most recent past. They were trying so hard to shut out each reminder of what had been, what still *was* for others in the world. They were cutting off the world—and the war—from their thoughts, and their emotions. They were doing this with discipline, allowing the pull of immediacy to take precedence over the inclination to dwell on things. Moreover, their love needed no buttressing of past associations, each moment between them was bright and new and sufficient. No need to say "Remember the day—". It was the quick that must be kept alive, and because they both wanted this they believed it to be possible. Because at the moment a thing is said, or done, nothing else can touch it, the words and actions stand alone; but remembered, there are the others standing by, the sounds outside oneself, the objects. They took pride in not using these props, like small boys walking the points of a picket fence, if they fell, well then. . . .

"No letters for a while," she said. "No telegrams, no news, no questions—."

She was happy, at this moment; she knew she was happy, and that was important. As she looked back on the smooth water they had left she saw the surface broken by the quick rise of a fish, so quick she could only be sure it was a fish by the beautiful expanding circle that spread out from the spot, and she smiled and touched his arm.

"The one we didn't catch," she said, and he leaned down and touched her lips, softly.

"Now," he asked, his face smoother than it was before, "where to, as you say—"

She spoke suddenly, delighted with her thought. "The state line, the stream beside the park."

"That is a very fast one. You do not have boots—"

"Then I'll get my feet wet. I *like* to get my feet wet," and she made him laugh, she could make him laugh now at things like an American, so his smile this time had gratitude in it as well.

They had to drive for another forty minutes before they came up against the mountains of the California side. And there at the base of them wound the shallow stream, white and lively, bursting in quick spray and foam over the rocks. Here and there were trees large enough to shade the water, and under each of these was a pool, a deepening of the water, as though the current had paused to rest.

They got out on opposite sides of the car, and without speaking took their rods from the metal cases and fitted the pieces together, secured the reels and threaded the long fine line through the ferrules. She was finished first, and with her creel and net crossing over her shoulders she started off, half skipping down the foot-path from the bridge.

A few minutes later she saw him on the opposite side of the stream, stepping out on the rocks in his high rubber boots that gave him such an unreal, romantic look. His legs rising straight and black from the water, and the loose jacket swelling like doublets above them. It was a distortion that always struck her, poignantly, although she could not have said why. It was such a little, man-made way of clothing himself against the current.

Patiently casting the red salmon eggs into the pool, avoiding the limbs of the tree above her, she watched his stronger arm swinging higher, more freely out over the water; and she thought for a moment, traitorous to their philsosphy, how he compared with her past. How no man had seemed so personal to her, engaged in an impersonal action, how other men, other persons lacked his ability to become one with the image of love that no one ever knows the source of.

It is an occupation that makes me think of his making love to me, she thought, I do not know why; but at the moment he looked up and she waved, impersonally.

Still, it is in this moment, she thought, that we have most completely shut out the others—and she smiled at him, knowing he could not see from that distance how her lip was trembling.

It was at her next cast that the hook was jerked violently to one side, and if her awareness had not been often practised she would have been caught off guard. The trout had provided its own lock by the violence of its attack, she did not need to thrust it further, just then. For an instant she waited, to make sure, and then cautiously, firmly, began pulling in the line she had held slack in her left hand. The trout was securely caught, and his slender, vivid body twisted and beat through the water helplessly. For an instant more he tried to swim; but as she continued the slow inexorable drawing, in a panic of fright he dipped, and then flung himself out of the water, his body curved like a scimitar with which he would cut himself free. Then, for a moment, it was as if he was resigned, and the line lay still and slack upon the water.

Carefully she had followed his movements, and now with a tense patience she drew the line closer and closer. Cautiously she lifted the landing net from about her neck as the trout flapped in the shallow water a few feet below her. With a nearly breathless motion, careful not to break the line on her rod—you could not see how big he was threshing about or throbbing deep on the bottom of the pool—she drew in the last few feet, quickly, and swept her net under him and lifted him on the bank beside her. And now the breath that she had been holding so long in her excitement came out in a rush and made a little whistling sound against the air.

Radiantly she lifted the net high for Max to see. His own rod was idle as he watched her, and he was grinning.

"How big?" he called, and she held the net out across the water toward him.

"Oh—" and she gasped. "It's big, Max, it's the biggest I *ever* caught. Oh, look, darling, look!"

The excitement was lifting her even above the present, she was remembering all of her life now in one breath because never before had anything seemed so good, so wonderful, not any moment— But as he stepped into the stream to cross it, coming toward her in his big wet boots and his thin brown face smiling, she knew better, suddenly she could remember moments that had been the same, breathless, all the blood of memory rushing back and then ahead to the moments to come. But by the time he was beside her she was able to speak quite calmly of her catch, disparaging her prize as a man might do.

"It's nothing—just a *little* old trout, darling," she protested, and they both could not keep from laughing again, it was so ridiculous her imitating the false modest people they had known, saying the thing that was polite and was not so.

And then she betrayed it by wanting to kiss him; she could not hold herself too long to an excitement so impersonal. That's the hell of being female, she thought; no emotion is enough in itself for long unless it is shared.

Lightly he brushed her lips with his, arrested in his action of taking the trout from the net, killing it, and then holding it limp and shining in his hand.

"And you brought him in so easily," he said, starting his sentence almost before his lips had left hers. "Just right. I could not have done it with so little effort—"

"You just *say* those things," she simpered, and then caught him wildly about the waist, dancing him around so that he held the fish high above their heads, protesting, both of them laughing; like fools, she thought, like irresponsible fools—

They stopped abruptly, but how good he felt now. No letters all day, only the two of them, and the silly beautiful fish they would catch.

"Oh, the fish!" she cried, as it went spinning out of Max's hand, landing perilously close to the bank. And the proximity of the water must have revived the trout, for quickly he wriggled closer, and they threw themselves down on him. They lay there together when Max got him in his hand, its last breath used and gone. They lay touching in excitement, her body awkwardly across his where she had fallen, her arms still outstretched.

The sun was shining at them obliquely now and on the road high above, on the ridge of the mountain, a car circled out of sight; but otherwise the wide flat land of the valley was theirs, used only by themselves. Rolling over and over, only half laughing now, they found a hollow for themselves on the other side of the tree, a little clearing with the bushes around it. And there the excitement that had been generated a few moments before, that she had forgotten to hold in check was released, safely, she felt, but spinning, spinning, to a beautiful, high green arc against the sky. . . .

They went back to their fishing after awhile. The sun pressed deeper and deeper into their bodies, and the same fluid of contentment ran through them both. Their limbs moved freely, at ease, and their contentment was shared, and unlimited. Jessie looked at Max and could see no sign of that strange, unpersonal guilt that was sometimes there, the pushing up from the soil of the past new green shoots of obligations. He was no longer remembering the things he had cut away from, the strange and terrible actions he had seen in the world apart from them, or that ghosts and reflected images had long shadows. None of these things had form in the present, because their love had bolted the doors against the world.

They caught eleven trout, four for her, and seven for him.

The first remained the largest, but they fished until it was quite dark, wishing, without expressing the thought, to surpass the one caught at the beginning. It was somehow not quite regular that this could not be surpassed, it was as if the day had begun at the wrong end. It even, vaguely, gave Jessie a feeling of uneasiness, as the day wore on, as they moved apart on the stream (but always in sight of one another) and their fishing was a little feverish for the brief half hour they had after the sun went down, before the dark came on. But when, by the light from the flashlight, they had cleaned all eleven, there was not much difference in the sizes of them, and two others could hardly be distinguished from the first one.

They felt very tender with one another now, as the moon soared, slight and golden, into the sky ahead of them.

They walked up the bank with their fish cleaned, and wrapped in wet leaves, the water from the stream still cold upon their hands. They placed the fish carefully on the wooden table before the open fireplace the park provided and wiped their hands on a towel from the car, then Max made a fire. The wood was dry and waiting, and it was only a matter of minutes before it blazed brightly through the iron grill on top. They waited until the blaze subsided, and then laid the frying pan with its strips of bacon upon it.

Now the world was very dark: a cloud had come upon the moon and the light from their fire had softened to a contracted glow, small in the vastness of the night. The dark rim of the hills was heavy and undistinguishable, and from the rim to their camp was blackness. They could not see, and they waited now for the moon; or for the fire to blaze again, drawing close to it, shivering a little. There had been so much light around them all day, and just suddenly they had become poignantly aware of the dark.

"Shall we turn on the headlights of the car?" but she shook her head, and although he could not see her, he did not get up.

With the darkness, also, the silence seemed to rise new and strangely felt; it became a positive thing, the silence had strength, like the presence of death, or of God. And now they held their breaths, going along with it in their philosophy of the natural, the immediate—

"We've got it all to ourselves," the girl said, suddenly, repeating, as though doggedly, her words of the morning. "It is what we want, isn't it, Max? You can forget—here, can't you?"

"Yes, Jessie," he said, but even as he spoke, the cats crept out from the darkness, and sat just on the outskirts of their small circle of light. Seeing the long shadowy forms around them, the girl and the man knew it was animal life; they knew it could not be harmful, they knew also that now, at this moment they must not express fear or doubt, they could not let their hands in one another's grasp grow tight, or self-consciously slack. They must accept these creatures as though they were of no consequence, as though the soft padding of their feet was a welcome thing—

It was when one of the cats brushed softly against Jessie's leg that she drew away, sharply, shuddering; so that when she did draw her hand from Max's, putting it behind her on the bench, she gripped the board until her whole arm was aching with tension. And after all, it should have been Max who was affected most, there was an element of reappearance about the creatures that should have been closer to him than to her. But he sat there most quietly than ever, and let the cats brush against him, even to leap softly through the air, half unseen, on to the table where the trout lay.

"They're only cats," he said, but his voice had gone white and she was glad of this, for it meant she was not alone in the strange fear suddenly upon her. "Just poor hungry cats," he said. "They're not even wild, Jessie."

But then the moon came out again, brightly, and they could see the poor starved creatures, even in the moonlight their ribs sharp and bare beneath their dark skins. There were four, or five or six of them, one larger and fuller than the others, and when Jessie saw this pregnant fulness she felt such shock that she could not answer him. Of course, it was inevitable that one at least should be in this condition, it must not move her more than the rest. Max stooped and picked this one up from the ground, and for a brief instant it allowed itself to be held.

Quickly turning away the girl bent over the pan where the bacon was frying crisply, and dropped in the fish, all she could get in the pan at one time. She turned her back on the man, and on the cats, and passionately, deeply absorbed, she watched the fish cooking, turning them with great deliberation when the time came for this, and with the utmost concentration taking them from the fire when they were done. The grease spattered out of the pan and into the fire, touching the grill and hissing, and she could sense the startled movement of the cats behind her at the sound. Then it dropped into the fire, and the flames grew suddenly large and tall, and extended the small lighted area fantastically into the darkness. But still she continued, methodically, removing the cooked fish, laying the raw cleaned ones into the pan, turning them until they were brown and crisp all over and then removing them from the fire. Until at last they were all done, the pan was put to one side, and she turned to butter the rolls, and get out the fruit. These things kept her busy and she made herself unaware of him behind her, so silent. She kept herself busy, and pretended she was not jealous, and when she looked around at last because she had to let him know she was finished with the meal, she still would not speak of the mother cat lying now on the table beside him, on its back, rubbing the side of her bony head against Max's rough sleeve.

He took the plate with the fish and the fruit from the girl, and she pretended not to watch him, but she was alert to his every movement, wondering just when he would give the cats his portion, all the cats all the portions, this food they had spent the day upon, this part of their love. And she was really surprised to see he held the plate away from the table, and ate quickly, with great appetite, saying, "It's good, Jessie, it is cooked to perfection."

It was with an unbearably growing feeling of amazement that she watched him now, occasionally warding off a cat that came hungrily near, pushing it gently away, but sharing nothing with it. His compassion extended so far, he did feel for them, yet still he could eat quietly until there was nothing left on his plate but the bones! And then, then only, did he allow the cats to come to him (and by now they were drawn close to his hands in a certain anger, smelling the food); then carefully, a look of great sadness on his face, he divided the bones among them, and where the portion was larger this he gave (and the heads) to the cat big with kittens.

Jessie watched until he had finished, watched the starved cats' lightning motions, snarling now, as they devoured the remains of what the man had eaten.

But as he looked up to share his feeling with her, she had to turn away suddenly, she needed a moment more, unshared. She looked down at the plate on her own lap, and saw the cats now watching her, warily, there was nothing left of what he had divided among them. She felt nothing, she assured herself, nothing—but suddenly, with all the strength of a reaction, of an emotion greater than any she had known, she flung the contents of her own plate on the ground among them. Threw it, prodigally, wastefully, passionately, and let the cats crawl over one another, quarreling, until in a few brief moments there was nothing left of that either, and the cats still moved about hungrily, although the mother cat was lying down now, close to Max's feet.

Not until then could the girl let herself cry, for the past that would always be waiting for them, for the shadows that could not be held back, the intrusions that could not be controlled. And Max looked at her tenderly, as if he had known from the beginning that which she saw only now, how for all their closeness a world yet lay between them.

THE TWO CRANES

by REARDEN CONNER

ALL DAY LONG THE YOUNG CRANE HAD FOLLOWED THE OLD crane. From one fishing ground to another it had flown in the wake of the older bird, haunting it like a shadow. Toward evening the old crane came to a neck of the river hemmed in by low-growing willows. This was its favorite fishing ground. Up to now it had not shared it with any other bird, nor had any of the lively younger ones dared to follow it so far upriver.

The old crane was wise and slow of movement. It flapped down to the edge of the bank and rested, almost motionless, waiting for the younger bird to follow it. The young crane resented its wisdom and its slow definite movements, slow not with age but with the experience that the years bring. The old crane stood very still, with its long sharp beak pressed down on its breast as though it were about to sleep. It did not attempt to fish. It did not seem to be observing the river at all. It looked a very old bird in that position. The young crane despised it.

The young crane was restless. It strutted up and down the river bank. It entered the water and waded past a clump of reeds. A water hen darted out from the reeds and gave its shrill cry. The sound startled the young crane, although it knew it did not mean danger. It turned down river and passed the old crane, now seemingly asleep on the bank. It was angry and wanted to attack this old bird that was so indifferent to the need of food.

The fishing had not been good that day and the young crane was hungry. In an hour it would be dusk. Already the sky was beginning to tinge with the first faint smoke of night. The young crane jerked at the water with its beak, but it was not fishing. It was standing in front of the old crane, jerking with its beak and throwing back its head as though it were swallowing fish rapidly. The old crane watched it without changing its position or opening its eyes too wide.

After a while the young crane grew wild with anger. It seemed to grow larger as though its wrath were puffing it up. It rose into the air and flapped its wings wildly, dropping down to the water now and again with noisy splashes. The old crane continued to watch it and felt irritated because it was frightening the fish by its foolish tactics.

Presently the young crane grew weary. It thought that it, too, would display wisdom. It rose high into the air and flew away across the field as though it were leaving the older bird to its slumbers. This was a ruse to make the old bird fish. But the old bird did not move. The young crane was drunk with rage now. It flew higher, then dived like a bolt at the old crane. The older bird heard its approach and seemed to sense its purpose. It dodged, without seeming to surrender its position on the bank, and flashed its beak sideways. The young crane shot past its head, out across the river, baffled and dazed with rage, a red spot appearing on its breast where the beak of the older bird had ripped into the flesh.

It dropped to the water and waded down river. In the shelter of a clump of reeds it began to plume its damaged breast, dipping its beak in the clear water and rubbing its blood-dyed feathers. The old crane did not seem to heed its movements. It stretched up its body, shook out its wings, and settled down on the bank once more, as though the young crane were not in existence.

The young crane's rage had died down now. It began to feel respect for the older bird. It, too, settled itself on the bank. It was waiting for the old crane to begin fishing. But it grew impatient soon and rose into the air again. It flew upriver, keeping a sharp eye on the water. A hundred yards above on the river bank a goat and kid stood, studying its progress. The kid was nervous at the sight of the big bird, looking so ungainly as it flapped along. It began to bleat unhappily, edging nearer to its mother.

Out in the field an old ass was resting, lying on its side, almost motionless like the old crane. The young crane was curious. It flew toward the ass, rising high into the air. From a height the gray-brown ass looked like a sprawling rock. The young crane swooped down and landed some yards away from the ass. It saw the ass's ears move as flies tickled them. That satisfied its curiosity. It began to plume its wounded breast once more.

Shortly afterward a man came into the field and began to shout in a strong voice. The old ass leaped to its feet and ran across the field, away from the man. The man beat the turf with a stick and shouted louder than ever. The young crane was terrified. It flew toward the river, seeking the comforting presence of the older bird.

The old crane was in no way perturbed. It was holding its head erect, watching the man and the ass. It did not look at the young crane, now standing below it in the river. It saw the ass come to a halt in mid-field and wait for the man to approach. Then it watched the man and the ass amble toward the gate in the far corner of the field.

It wore an expression of satisfaction in its wise eyes now, as though it had known that the man would fetch the ass from the field and had been waiting patiently for him to come and go. It shook out its wings, folded them carefully again, looked up and down the river, then stepped gently into the water. It began to move upriver, away from the young crane. It lifted its feet with great deliberation and set them down tenderly as though the water were overwarm from the day's hot sun. It paused for a moment, looking up at the sky as though measuring its time.

Then it began to fish. Its beak flashed down and lifted in one sweeping movement. It had swallowed a small sleeping fish in a twinkling. The young crane was startled afresh at this exhibition. It was jealous of the old crane's ability to find fish where fish did not seem to exist.

It followed the older bird closely, watching the ready beak with eyes that glistened with new rage. Suddenly the old crane paused over a deep pool under the river bank. It stood staring into the water, as though it had come upon the pool unexpectedly instead of merely reaching its goal. Then its beak flashed down and was upraised holding a wriggling eel. But with a speed even quicker the young crane had dived forward and upward and had seized hold of the eel's tail, lifting the prize clean away from the oler bird's beak.

Up, up, rose the young crane, swallowing hard, gorging its stolen meal. It swept out over the field. For a moment, the old crane stood as though it had been stunned by a falling branch. Then it, too, rose and dived after the younger bird. Now its turn had come to be gripped by rage. All day long it had borne the young bird's interference with dignified patience. It had permitted this intruder to share its private fishing ground. But now, at the close of the day, there was murder in its heart. Its rage was not the hot rage of youth, but a cold and callous feeling that would not be quelled until its purpose had been fulfilled.

Three years before it had killed a crane of its own age. It knew how to kill its kind. There would be a swift and steady flight until the younger bird tired, then a maneuvering for position, then a downward dive and the fatal blow.

The young crane sensed the fearful mood of the older bird. It rose higher, higher still, heading all the time toward a cluster of houses beyond the fields. Here it hoped, somehow, to shake off the older bird. Over the houses it began to circle. It saw the old crane still pursuing it relentlessly. It was tiring already. It was so young that its wings were still weak. Suddenly beyond the roof tops it saw the fringes of a wood. It dropped down, dived below the old crane, and skimmed over the roofs toward the wood. In a second it had left clear space and had shot like a weighted arrow into a bunch of telegraph wires. Its wings were smashed and entangled before it had recovered from the shock of contact. It tried to turn, to rise up, to drop down. But it was held tighter than any fish had ever been clutched in its own beak.

Above it the old crane soared, turned, and disappeared below the houses behind the telegraph wires, making steadily for the river. The film of smoke over the sky had deepened now and dusk had come at last. No one in that sleepy place seemed to heed the twanging of the wires.

In the morning small boys discovered the body of the young crane. They flung stones at it and laughed at the way its feet and neck hung down from the wires. Then they went away and forgot it, leaving it to the hundreds of flies that came out with the bright sun of the early day.

THE APOTHEOSIS OF FRANCIS JAMES O'DONOVAN

by LEO DILLON MURTAGH

WITH A RHYTHMICAL SWAY OF THE HIPS MRS. MULCAHY emerged from the basement of her rooming house at 339 West 13th Street. It was eight o'clock in the morning and the month was June. A pleasant morning and Mrs. Mulcahy was duly appreciative. A little wind from the Hudson catfooted up the street and swung playfully from window blinds. With it came an exciting smell of smoke from the funnels of the big and little ships moving on the waters. At the top of the steps she stood to give the street the once-over as she had been doing every morning for twenty years. Once at a standstill, the slight sway of her body was scarcely noticeable. It was really due to the fact that Mrs. Mulcahy did not like orange juice and for her it was natural to use alcohol instead. It was very good alcohol. She had made it herself and each morning was convinced anew that it was indeed an admirable substitute for orange juice. Mrs. Mulcahy often wondered why people drank that latter beverage at all.

Now with benign gray-green eyes she surveyed the street and thought everything was wonderful. If God was in His heaven then Mrs. Mulcahy was quite content to be where she was. She was now in the mood to really appreciate God and to approve of all His works. Under the anaesthetic of potato alcohol she even forgot about O'Donovan and the troubles of O'Donovan.

For all her sixty years she was as straight and lissom as a girl. Her thin sallow face drew more than one appreciative stare from passers-by. It was a face worth a stare. A high proud nose and a mouth twisted by an enigmatical grin. A Mona Lisa grown old and forced by circumstances to preside over the destinies of a third-class rooming house. Yet in spite of the twisted grin and the cynical glint in the gray-green eyes, there was something of tragedy in her face. Not a Mona Lisa grown old but rather a Lady Macbeth who had cast ambition aside and had lived to regard the murder of a king as a mere misdemeanor. Mrs. Mulcahy was in fact a tall and queenly figure.

From the house next door a fat Buddha-bellied woman waddled out on the steps. A snubnosed, loose-mouthed, laughing woman with porcine eyes.

"Morrow to you, Mrs. Mulcahy," she greeted. "A grand mornin' that's in it, thanks be to God."

"You said it, Bid. A grand mornin' surely. To be alive is joy and to be young must be very heaven."

The other laughed. "Arrah, Mrs. Mulcahy, but it's crazier you are gettin' every day. And I always say it's no wonder and that place you're runnin' little better than a bughouse. Seems to me you never had an honest-to-God rent-payin' roomer since you went into business."

Mrs. Mulcahy made no reply.

"That little half-pint Murphy, with his back teeth awash in beer and he owin' you seven months rent!"

"Craziness," said Mrs. Mulcahy, as if talking to herself, "is very often the last refuge left to decent folk." She turned and stared directly at the fat Bid Durfy. "I never knew a decent person yet that wasn't a little crazy."

The other ignored this ambiguous insult. "Badger O'Donovan upstairs is crazy enough. Do you mean to tell me he's a decent man? It's over in Bellevue he ought to be right now. Yes indeedy. It's a pair of Bellevue bracelets Francis James O'Donovan ought to be wearin' this minute. How is he gettin' on anyway?"

Before replying Mrs. Mulcahy turned and stared at a window on the second floor of her house. The blind was drawn and noting this she shook her head sadly. "Bid," she said, "since his wife died on him six weeks ago he's a changed man."

"If there's any change in the Badger then it can't be for the worse. That man was the terror of the neighborhood and, even if he was a cop once, a disgrace to the Irish people. Don't tell me he ever loved that poor little wife of his. The big savage." The fat woman leaned her weight upon the railing and panted with indignation.

"What would you know about love, Bid Durfy?" Mrs. Mulcahy demanded coldly. "No man ever yet loved a fat laughin' woman and don't ask me why. Anyway I'm worried about poor O'Donovan and wonderin' what's goin' to become of him at all."

Bid Durfy disappeared momentarily and returned with a broom. Red-faced and angry, she swept the steps vigorously. "Worryin' about him indeed," she panted. "Then it's a poor employ you have. Myself, I'd just as soon worry about the welfare of Barney's bull. Love. Says you. If O'Donovan really loved that wisp of a wife he had, then it's a strange way he showed it. I'd just as soon be fat and laughin' as have a love like that."

"Maybe you would and maybe you'd be wise," Mrs. Mulcahy answered sadly. "But for all that he's wastin' away for the past six weeks. Poor O'Donovan is as gaunt as a crucifix."

"If he is, then it's the curse of God come upon him, snarlin' as he was at the whole world and raisin' trouble everywhere he went. To my own knowledge he never said a civil word to a soul on this street since he came here."

"It's the bitter tongue you have, Bid."

"Is it so! You know as well as me he had the whole parish in a stew and a ferment. If it wasn't one thing then it was another. It was bad enough he not ever goin' to Mass but he had to start his Irish-American Catholic crusade for the overthrow of his Holiness the Pope of Rome. Wantin' a Pope with an Irish name he was. As if anyone ever heard of such a thing." At the very idea she began again to sweep the steps as if symbolically sweeping the O'Donovan and all his works into the garbage can.

Mrs. Mulcahy watched with cynical good humor. "What's the harm in that?" she asked easily. "O'Donovan would make a good Pope."

Bid Durfy was genuinely shocked. "Him on the throne of St. Peter! Foggin' his old pipe and spittin' up catarrh like moth balls and you could light a candle at every curse comin' from his mouth." The other seemed not to hear and Bid continued energetically. "No one but yourself would have him in the house and I'm thinkin' you keep him just to annoy your decent God-fearing neighbors."

"He was a fine figure of a man the day he first came here," said Mrs. Mulcahy reminiscently. "A big mustache sweepin' across his face like Halley's comet across the skies. Him, shaved to the hatband and the crease in his pants sharp enough to cut bread. And that Derby hat of his polished until it reflected light on all sides like those mirrors you'd see in a hock shop window. He not carin' a fiddler's curse for man, dog, or devil."

"Yea. And his poor little wife scared to death of him. Even the kids on the street would run when they saw him comin' with every foot under him like the lid of a manhole cover. Even insultin' Mrs. Hughes, as decent and cleanly a body as you'd wish to meet."

"What did he say to her?" Mrs. Mulcahy enquired politely.

"What did he say indeed! Me boyo lifted his big foot and kicked her garbage pail down into the basement. Claimed it smelled. Mrs. Hughes claimed it didn't. 'Madam,' says he, 'the smell around here would gag a buzzard and it's either you or it.' Now what do you think of the man who would say a thing like that? I tell you he's neither a Christian nor a gentleman. God forgive him."

Mrs. Mulcahy swayed easily to and fro and smiled enigmatically. Before she could reply a slight sound caught her ear. She turned and with surprise watched the blind upon the window of O'Donovan's room go slowly up.

Bid Durfy also watched but with real alarm. "That's the first time in six weeks that the light of day got into that room," she said. "I wonder what devilment he's up to now?"

The other held up a slender and somewhat dirty hand in an imperious demand for silence. Heavy footsteps slowly decended the stairs. The two women waited motionless and silent, until a huge and pathetic scarecrow of a man stood in the doorway. He seemed but a rack of bones over which the skin had been tossed carelessly. It hung in bags from the many bony promontories of his face. He was unshaven and the big mustaches hung as if they were dying at the roots. The once famous Derby hat was white with dust and the unpressed pants concertinaed about his shoes. There was indeed in his appearance something of the leanness and aridity of the crucifix. But for all that, the face of O'Donovan, with its beaked nose and jutting chin, was a fighting face, until one saw his eyes. They were blue eyes, bright and frustrate. The eyes of a child in pain. He was weeping and the tears cascaded through the dingy gray stubble of his cheeks.

"Glory be to God," Bid Durfy ejaculated. All her anger evaporated at the sight of the weeping man.

"What's the trouble on you, Mr. O'Donovan?" Mrs. Mulcahy asked and her voice was the voice of a woman speaking to a lost and lonely child.

With the sleeve of his dusty coat O'Donovan slowly and very methodically dried his eyes. His voice was as low and spiritless as a beggar's whine. "The heart is dead inside me, Ma'am."

Mrs. Mulcahy reached out and her hand rested lightly on his shoulder. "Don't you cry any more now," she soothed.

"No Ma'am. I won't. In spite of myself the tears would keep coming and now I feel as if I've wept them all. It's dry-eyed I'll be from now on."

" 'Tis better so," she agreed. "Do you still keep missin' her then?"

"Aye, I do. Waking in the dark I keep forgetting that she's gone until my hand reaches out to meet the cold wall. Daytimes I keep moving from one room to another thinking maybe I'd find her. When the front door opens I keep listening for her step on the stairs. Now I know I'll never see her on God's earth again." Like pebbles the words dropped into a silence from which, it seemed, no echo would ever come.

Mrs. Mulcahy looked on him with pity but could find no word to say.

It was Bid Durfy broke the silence. That good woman's eyes were wet but her voice and words were sharp.

"Arrah Mr. O'Donovan. Isn't it the shame on you to be

grievin' so. Is it have her back here you would in all this misery and she happy walkin' through the green fields of Heaven?"

The words had an extraordinary effect upon O'Donovan. He straightened up and there was a bright glint of anger in his eyes. "She is not in Heaven," he announced coldly.

Bid Durfy gasped like a waterless fish and even the imperturbable Mrs. Mulcahy was puzzled and silent for a moment. "But where is she?"

"She's in Purgatory, Ma'am. In Purgatory these long six weeks."

"But Mr. O'Donovan—"

"To be suffering in the flames. Her that never did an ugly thing or said a hard word. The thought of it is drivin' me crazy."

"But there's some mistake, Mr. O'Donovan. What would a harmless little soul like her be doing in Purgatory? It's in Heaven she is surely."

The big man, his anger gone, shook his head hopelessly. "I wouldn't have believed it if she had not come and told me herself."

The two women exchanged glances and the lips of Bid Durfy trembled to the vibration of an unspoken prayer. But Mrs. Mulcahy, after a moment's thought, looked up to meet the situation with a new hope. "So she came to you herself. When was that?" she asked.

"Last night it was. Even if it was the bad husband I was, it was to me she came with her trouble. She always said there was nothing I couldn't do if I once set my mind to it." Almost proudly his shoulders went back only to sag again. "But Purgatory. It's a long way from here."

"Did she appear to you. Did you see her plain?" Bid Durfy asked tremulously.

"Aye. I saw her plain." He turned to Mrs. Mulcahy and the plea in his voice stirred that woman to the heart. "She's depending on me and on no one else. Ma'am, what am I going to do?"

Mrs. Mulcahy reached out and drew him gently to her. Her own eyes, dry for many a long day, were now wet. "Franky," she said to him very solemnly, "it's all a mistake. We'll have her out of there before the sun of this day sets."

"Do you say so, Mrs. Mulcahy? Do you say so?" His eyes were alight with hope.

"I do that. It's a mistake. It happens often."

"But Mrs. Mulcahy. Purgatory—"

"It's the same there as everywhere else. Now, Franky. You used to be a cop and it's many a tale you must have heard of poor fellows brought in for the night and then forgotten for a week or even a month." She was playing a part now and playing it for all she was worth. Her steady eyes held his and her hand was tight upon his arm.

As if under a spell he nodded, but doubtfully. "I have heard such tales, Ma'am. I have heard such tales. But up there—"

"But up there it's just the same. People don't hear about it, that's all. It's only natural for mistakes to occur and thousands of prisoners arriving every hour of the day and night."

The eyes of O'Donovan had a faraway look as if he were considering the possibility. Then he nodded agreement. Meanwhile the scandalized Bid Durfy stood in speechless amazement at such heretical goings-on.

Almost sure of herself now, Mrs. Mulcahy went on happily. Her voice became a thin and sibilant whisper. "Not many people know this, Franky, but it's a little clique of Italian saints that's in charge of Purgatory."

"Dagoes?" he asked.

She nodded. "That's why the mistakes occur. You know yourself those Wops are a lazy easy-going bunch and becoming saints doesn't change them. They look after their own folk all right but what do they care what becomes of a little Irish soul?"

O'Donovan stood to attention stiffly. His big hands clenched. "And isn't there any Irish or American saints there?" he demanded.

"Devil a one. That is if you except St. Fintan who is there to look after the interests of the Irish people. But the poor man has a big job on his hands and can't be everywhere. You know yourself, Franky, that the Irish people, God help them, go to Purgatory in droves."

This statement he considered for a few moments and then nodded complete agreement. "That's true for you, Ma'am. St. Fintan must be a very busy man. There must be thousands of complaints every day. Doesn't he have any one at all to help him prepare his cases? There must be plenty of Irish saints who would be glad to donate their services."

"So there is. So there is." Mrs. Mulcahy agreed readily. "But the Italians have the inside track on all matters purgatorial."

Here the horrified and hitherto speechless Bid Durfy gasped up a low "God save us" and turned porcine eyes to heaven as if fearful of some cosmic catastrophe.

"And another thing, Mr. O'Donovan," the sibilant whisper drilled on. "Another thing. In the case of your poor wife it sticks in my mind that the mistake is due to sheer carelessness on the part of those Italians. It would be just like them."

From the face of O'Donovan the dewlaps and skinbags seemed to disappear. The blue eyes were bright with anger and the whine was gone from his voice. He was a cop again. An angry cop asking a question. He pronounced each word with such precision that the uttering of it seemed to give him a whole new countenance. "Do you mean to stand there, Mrs. Mulcahy, and tell me that due to gross carelessness and criminal negligence an innocent woman is suffering? My own poor wife."

His vehemence shook her poise and for a moment she was wordless. It was now or never she knew. Nervousness made her voice sound hard and staccato. "It has happened before, Mr. O'Donovan. It has happened before. To my own poor husband no less. Died on the front steps of a bawdy house over on East 12th Street. Circumstantial evidence. He drew a hundred and eighty days. The Wops forgot all about him for fifteen solid months and it was only by accident he ever got out, the poor man." Mrs. Mulcahy dabbed her eyes with a small and very dirty piece of cloth. She glanced at him furtively.

"Who," demanded the latter, "is in charge up there now?" His voice sounded like a piece of iron sliding down a tin chute.

Mrs. Mulcahy continued to dab her eyes furiously. In vain she combed her memory for the name of one suitable Italian saint. Rapidly she recalled the few sanctified names she knew. St. Patrick, St. Colum, St. Bride, Blessed Oliver Plunkett. All Irish. She was praying now herself. If she could not remember a good Italian saint then everything had gone for naught. The situation was becoming more desperate by the moment. Tautly she stood listening to the sound of O'Donovan's big impatient feet scrape the flags. Beyond, Mrs. Durfy was praying aloud to St. Anthony. She was asking him to intercede for the immortal soul of her uncanonical neighbor.

"Who, I ask you, is in charge there now?" His voice was the bellow of an angry bull.

Mrs. Mulcahy took the handkerchief from her eyes and met his gaze calmly. "St. Anthony," she said.

"Of Padua?"

"The same."

O'Donovan growled like a dog. "He's no good," he asserted flatly. "I lost my badge once and lit half a dozen candles for him but it never turned up."

"No, Franky. And I'm afraid it won't be any use talking to him about your poor wife. He's too busy lookin' after his own to bother about one poor little Irish soul."

The big man sagged and the old pain dimmed the brightness of his eyes. "Then what am I to do?" he pleaded hopelessly.

"What will you do? That's easy, Franky. Pull yourself together. Walk down there to the chapel and have a talk with the Man himself. Tell Him the whole story."

"Ah. It's little chance He'd listen to me. Me that was a sinner all my life."

"He'll listen to you, Frank O'Donovan. Make no doubt of that. He's a decent Man. He'll listen to saint or sinner. A word from you will be as good as a Latin mass sung by the College of Cardinals before an altar of marble and gold. There is only one sin and that's to be doubting His Goodness."

Again her steady eyes held his and again he nodded. "It's maybe right you are. It's maybe that what she meant me to do," he said almost with confidence. "She said herself last night that I could do it."

"Sure you can. It's that very thing she meant you to do."

"It's true," he answered placidly. "It's down to the church I'll go now, Mrs. Mulcahy, and I'll tell Him a few of the things that's happening behind His back."

"Do that, Franky boy. Do that. Before the hour is out Maura will be smilin' down at you from the terraces of Heaven."

He was smiling as he hobbled down the steps. His gaunt figure in the unbrushed and ill-fitting clothes seemed grotesque and almost obscenely out of place in the bright splendor of the June morning. At the foot of the steps he turned and still smiling said, "Maybe I'll see her tonight again. Maybe—maybe she might come again to tell me how everything went."

"She will. She will surely," Mrs. Mulcahy answered with conviction. "Be on your way now, boy, and God be good to you."

Her heart was glad as she watched him down the street but her limbs were trembling. When the black blot of his figure had disappeared she went down the steps into the basement. Once there she carefully measured out four ounces of home fermented. It was a milky and poisonous-looking brew which seemed to explode when it hit the stomach. But it suited Mrs. Mulcahy. Ten minutes later she was herself again and swaying like a sally branch in an April breeze. To her eyes the rain-rotted, sun-blighted buildings of West 13th Street were not things of stone and wood but the airy towers and temples of New Jerusalem.

Meanwhile the dilapidated O'Donovan was ponderously dragging himself up the steps of St. Bernard's Church. Inside, it was cool and quiet and very empty. From the stained glass windows patches of summer sunlight carpeted the floor. For a while he stood hesitant in the doorway and then began to shuffle up the long aisle toward where the gold and marble of the altar gleamed whitely in the shadows. Then again he stood and courage was drained from him. What if his prayer was not answered? At the thought his heart contracted agonizingly. He felt weak and the altar seemed but a mirage and very very far away. Gradually his eyes became accustomed to the lights and half-lights of the place. He saw the amorphous shapes of figures standing in niches about the walls. There was one just opposite to where he stood. It was St. Patrick. To him O'Donovan turned anxious eyes. There was no doubt about it. St. Patrick smiled through his plaster beard and murmured softly but very distinctly. "Stout fella, Frank. Go to it." O'Donovan smiled back and a great peace such as he had never known came to him. He continued resolutely up the aisle. There was a faint pleasant smell of summer flowers there and above his head the Sanctuary lamp burned bright and steady. . . . He stood very straight as he once used to stand when giving evidence in court. With both hands he held the dirty Derby hat across his breast. His tremulous tones echoed through the empty places of the shadowy church.

"This, Your Honor," he said, "is Francis James O'Donovan speaking. It was my landlady, Mrs. Mulcahy, told me to come straight to You. It's You she said would help me. 'Go to the Man Himself,' she said, 'and even if it's a sinner you are He'll help you. He'll listen to what you say and in a little while your wife will be walking happy with the Shining Ones on the green terraces of Heaven. Sure it would be a sin to doubt it,' she said. And Judge, Your Honor, I'm not doubting it. It's maybe it's a little queer with grief I am but I will give You the facts of the case to the best of my knowledge and ability. Amen."

He remained silent a short while and it seemed to him as if the very church and all the painted icons there were hushed and expectant. When he spoke again his voice was firm and low. "Your Honor. It's thirty years ago this week since I brought Maura Conners to the altar. It was a day just like today with a bright sun shining. Her hair was the color of wheat through the white veil she wore and I can remember the smell of the flowers she held in her hand. She was a frail little girl and shy but her eyes were holy-bright and I can feel again the feel of her hand in mine. I can't begin to tell You how beautiful she was but maybe You remember her Yourself because I'm thinking it's not often any human thing as beautiful walks the earth. Strange as it was she thought the world and all of me. Thirty years and every day of it she spent with me and every night of it she was by my side. The happiness we had I can't bear to be recalling now. If it wasn't happy I was all the time, it was my own fault. A bad sullen kind of a man I was always, and often enough I was a bad sullen husband. But I loved her. I loved her always. Your Honor, You'll forgive me saying this but she was more to me than any hope of Heaven, more to me than the safety of my own immortal soul. Even the sound of her foot upon the stairs and she coming back from the store was happy music to me and I'd forget my bitterness when she'd call me by the pet name she had for me. Six weeks ago she died. She had no fear of going but she didn't want to go knowing I'd be lost here without her. It's lost I am too."

He ceased and a sob racked the big frame. "Forgive me saying it but it was a hard and bitter thing You did taking her and leaving me to walk in pain and loneliness always. It's hard for a man like me to be journeying down to the grave alone. Maura used to say that You knew best but it's poor comfort I get from that. But I didn't come down here to be talking about my own pain. But about Maura. Standing here humble and contrite before You—all I ask is that You right the wrong that has been done. Do that for me, Your Honor, and I'll bless Your name from this hour to the dawning of my dying day."

With bowed head he stood waiting. He stood a long time. A patch of sunlight moved imperceptibly across the floor and gilded his dingy shoes. Then suddenly and as if in answer to a question he looked up and spoke with surety. "Oh yes, Your Honor. There is no doubt of it. She came last night to me and told me so. There's things going on behind Your back that You ought to know. As Mrs. Mulcahy said—it's a shame that a lazy bunch of Wop saints should be taking advantage of Your trust in them. St. Anthony is no fit person for such a responsible position or he wouldn't be keeping Maura in there. In Heaven she belongs and in Heaven she ought to be, happy with all the Bright Ones there. When You see her You'll say so Yourself and it's proud You'll be that You listened to the prayer of a poor lost and lonely man."

He genuflected stiffly and turned away. He was very weary and in a dark corner under the gallery he knelt to wait. From a pocket he pulled a string of rosary beads and began to pray. Before the first Ave Maria was said he was sound asleep.

O'Donovan's sleep was a short sleep but it was long enough for a miracle to happen. No sleep no matter how refreshing could have brought such a happy and peaceful light to his eyes. No rest no matter how complete could have brought such a joyous smile to the once sullen mouth, nor could have given such youthful lightness to the once heavy limbs. Like a giant refreshed he arose and walked easily up the aisle. At the altar he knelt and prayed a prayer of thanks. He also promised to carry out his new duties faithfully. He also smiled his thanks to St. Patrick and looked happily up at St. Bride.

Two candles were burning in front of the niche where St. Anthony stood in studious absorption of a plaster book. O'Donovan marched over briskly and blew out both candles. He placed his big hand upon St. Anthony's sandalled foot and spoke in a friendly way. "You'll hear no recriminations from me. I'm too happy for that. But you heard the news. You're no longer in control up there and I expect you to get out of there straight away. No delays, mind you. I won't have it." He admonished the saint with a warning finger and took a turnip watch from a vest pocket. "I'll give you one hour and not a minute longer to get out of there bag and baggage."

He turned and walked briskly out of the church and into the brazen midday sun that now baked West 13th Street. He rubbed the gray stubble on his cheeks and noted the unpressed pants and unpolished shoes. Forthwith he headed across the street to Dooley's cleaning and tailoring establishment. An hour later when he emerged from there his clothes had been sponged and pressed. A new tie of divers colors glowed under his chin. His Derby hat shone like a mirror. It was something more than just a black hat; it was in truth a shining nimbus on the head of Francis James O'Donovan. A haircut and a shave completed the transformation. A handsome and commanding figure, he was the object of admiring and incredulous stares as he hurried up the street.

The heliophiliac Mrs. Mulcahy was dozing peacefully on her steps. The voice of O'Donovan brought her to complete awareness. It also brought Bid Durfy out on her stoop.

"Mrs. Mulcahy, Ma'am," he announced. "I am a most remarkable man."

"Faith, I never doubted it," was the easy answer. With a wonder that was almost awe, she heard the youthful timbre of his voice and noted the smile that had transfigured his face.

"Yes, Ma'am. A most remarkable man. Upon me has been conferred a great and sacred honor. An honor such as has never been conferred on any human being in the history of mankind."

"Tell me all about it, Mr. O'Donovan. Sure it's easy to see that something grand has happened to you and you the very picture of happiness and exaltation."

He removed his hat and sat down beside her. Bid Durfy with both ears cocked leant over the railing.

"It was like this, Ma'am. I did what you said and dragged myself and my weight of sorrow down to the church. God forgive me, but it's little hope I had then. Once I was inside, I was afraid, until St. Patrick gave me the nod to carry on."

"Gallant lad, Pat. I wouldn't doubt him," said Mrs. Mulcahy.

"I spoke to the Man Himself. I told Him all about Maura and me and I told Him about the goings-on behind His back although I didn't mention any names."

"Well now. That was nice of you."

"When I had told Him all I went and knelt down to wait for an answer. My eyes were closed and I was saying a wee bit of a prayer. Then—then do you know what happened?" His blue eyes danced with joyous anticipation as he asked the question. Mrs. Mulcahy fixed her gaze on the spot where the bright radiance of the Empire State tower stained the summer sky.

"No, Franky, I don't. What happened?"

"Maura."

"Did you see her?"

"As plain as I see you and heard her as clear as I hear you."

"Ah. But isn't God good. How was she lookin'?"

"More beautiful than I ever saw her—even when she was

young. Heaven itself was in her eyes. She had flowers in her hand. The very same flowers she had upon our wedding day."

"She was in heaven surely."

"Surely. She told me that no sooner had I spoken to Him than she was walking with the Bright Ones. Her being in Purgatory was all due to a mistake."

"The lazy lemon-suckers," said Mrs. Mulcahy tartly. "It's a shame. The like of them in charge in such a place."

"Don't fuss yourself, Mrs. Mulcahy. Don't fuss yourself. This is the other great news I have for you. St. Anthony is no longer in command there as from eleven o'clock this morning." He was almost pompous as he made the announcement. A knot of the neighbors had gathered and stood unnoticed at the foot of the steps. Bid Durfy sent another frantic prayer winging skyward.

"Who's the big shot up there now?" Mrs. Mulcahy casually asked.

He did not answer for a moment. A dramatic and perfect moment. He stood up to his full height. "I am. Me. Francis James O'Donovan."

The group about the steps was frozen into immobility. Bid Durfy was out of prayers. Mrs. Mulcahy was silent lest a word of hers might mar this high and perfect hour of O'Donovan's.

"Yes," he said briskly. "Now I'm in charge and whatever I say goes." He pulled a notebook and pencil from his pocket and stood poised and businesslike. "Mrs. Mulcahy. Give me the names of all your friends and relatives you think are in Purgatory. I'll have every man and woman of them out within the hour."

"More power to you," said the good woman feelingly. For half an hour he was busy writing down names.

"Is that all now, Ma'am?"

"That's all right now. I'll think of the others tomorrow. They're a tough bunch of scallywags and it mayn't be easy to get them out."

"Never you mind that, Ma'am. I'll see to it that they'll be out."

"I wouldn't doubt you, Franky. It's an honor you are to my house and to the whole street. Sure I'll live to see the day when your statue in brass and marble will weigh countless tons. Maybe the neighbors here would like you to exercise your great and sacred powers on behalf of their friends."

"Certainly, Mrs. Mulcahy, Ma'am. Anything you say."

An hour later when he returned the notebook to his pocket its pages were black with names. Then the happiest man in all New York, Francis James O'Donovan, went down to St. Bernard's to release them en masse.

Mrs. Mulcahy watched until the dark nimbus of his hat had disappeared in the distance. Then feeling tired and strangely old she headed for the Fountain of Youth in the basement.

Bid Durfy accosted her. "It's a grievous sin you committed this day and it's my prayers you'll be having," she announced piously.

Mrs. Mulcahy regarded her with a humorous glint in her gray-green eyes. "Your prayers can't harm me, Bid Durfy. You are, if I may say so, an ignorant old hypothenuse."

Then, walking like a slightly moth-eaten queen, she descended into the basement for the third time that apocalyptic day.

THE LONG DEBUT OF LOIS TAGGETT

by J. D. SALINGER

LOIS TAGGETT WAS GRADUATED FROM MISS HASCOMB'S SCHOOL, standing twenty-sixth in a class of fifty-eight, and the following autumn her parents thought it was time for her to come out, charge out, into what they called Society. So they gave her a five-figure, la-de-da Hotel Pierre affair, and save for a few horrible colds and Fred-hasn't-been-well-lately's, most of the preferred trade attended. Lois wore a white dress, an orchid corsage, and a rather lovely, awkward smile. The elderly gentlemen guests said, "She's a Taggett, all right"; the elderly ladies said, "She's a *very* sweet child"; the young ladies said, "Hey. Look at Lois. Not bad. What'd she do to her hair?"; and the young gentlemen said, "Where's the liquor?"

That winter Lois did her best to swish around Manhattan with the most photogenic of the young men who drank scotch-and-sodas in the God-and-Walter Winchell section of the Stork Club. She didn't do badly. She had a good figure, dressed expensively and in good taste, and was considered Intelligent. That was the first season when Intelligent was the thing to be.

In the spring, Lois' Uncle Roger agreed to give her a job as receptionist in one of his offices. It was the first big year for debutantes to Do Something. Sally Walker was singing nightly at Alberti's Club; Phyll Mercer was designing clothes or something; Allie Tumbleston was getting that screen test. So Lois took the job as receptionist in Uncle Roger's downtown office. She worked for exactly eleven days, with three afternoons off, when she learned suddenly that Ellie Podds, Vera Gallishaw, and Cookie Benson were going to take a cruise to Rio. The news reached Lois on a Thursday evening. Everybody said it was a perfect *riot* down in Rio. Lois didn't go to work the following morning. She decided instead, while she sat on the floor painting her toenails red, that most of the men who came into Uncle Roger's downtown office were a bunch of *dopes.*

Lois sailed with the girls, returning to Manhattan early in the fall—still single, six pounds heavier, and off speaking terms with Ellie Podds. The remainder of the year Lois took courses at Columbia, three of them entitled Dutch and Flemish Painters, Technique of the Modern Novel, and Everyday Spanish.

Come springtime again and air-conditioning at the Stork Club, Lois fell in love. He was a tall press agent named Bill Tedderton, with a deep, dirty voice. He certainly wasn't anything to bring home to Mr. and Mrs. Taggett, but Lois figured he certainly was something to bring home. She fell hard, and Bill, who had been around plenty since he'd left Kansas City, trained himself to look deep enough into Lois' eyes to see the door to the family vault.

Lois became Mrs. Tedderton, and the Taggetts didn't do very much about it. It wasn't fashionable any longer to make a row if your daughter preferred the iceman to that nice Astorbilt boy. Everybody knew, of course, that press agents were icemen. Same thing.

Lois and Bill took an apartment in Sutton Place. It was a three-room, kitchenette job, and the closets were big enough to hold Lois' dresses and Bill's wide-shouldered suits.

When her friends asked her if she were happy, Lois replied, "Madly." But she wasn't quite sure if she were madly happy. Bill had the most gorgeous rack of ties; wore such luxurious broadcloth shirts; was so marvelous, so masterful, when he spoke to people over the telephone; had such a fascinating way of hanging up his trousers. And he was so sweet about—well, you know—everything. But. . . .

Then suddenly Lois knew for sure that she was Madly Happy, because one day soon after they were married, Bill fell in love with Lois. Getting up to go to work one morning, he looked over at the other bed and saw Lois as he'd never seen her before. Her face was jammed against the pillow, puffy, sleep-distorted, lip-dry. She never looked worse in her life—and at that instant Bill fell in love with her. He was used to women who didn't let him get a good look at their morning faces. He stared at Lois for a long moment, thought about the way she looked as he rode down in the elevator; then in the subway he remembered one of the crazy questions Lois had asked him the other night. Bill had to laugh right out loud in the subway.

When he got home that night, Lois was sitting in the morris chair. Her feet, in red mules, were tucked underneath her. She was just sitting there filing her nails and listening to Sancho's rhumba music over the radio. Seeing her, Bill was never so happy in his life. He wanted to jump in the air. He wanted to grit his teeth, then let out a mad, treble note of ecstasy. But he didn't dare. He would have had trouble accounting for it. He couldn't say to Lois, "Lois. I love you for the first time. I used to think you were just a nice little drip. I married you for your money, but now I don't care about it. You're my girl. My sweetheart. My wife. My baby. Oh, Jesus, I'm happy." Of course, he couldn't say that to her; so he just walked over where she sat, very casually. He bent down, kissed her, gently pulled her to her feet. Lois said, "Hey! What's goin' on?" And Bill made her rhumba with him around the room.

For fifteen days following Bill's discovery, Lois couldn't even stand at the glove counter at Saks' without whistling *Begin the Beguine* between her teeth. She began to like all her friends. She had a smile for conductors on Fifth Avenue busses; was sorry she didn't have any small change with her when she handed them dollar bills. She took walks in the zoo. She spoke to her mother over the telephone every day. Mother became a Grand Person. Father, Lois noticed, worked too hard. They should both take a vacation. Or at least come to dinner Friday night, and no *arguments*, now.

Sixteen days after Bill fell in love with Lois, something terrible happened. Late on that sixteenth night Bill was sitting in the morris chair, and Lois was sitting on his lap, her head back on his shoulder. From the radio pealed the sweet blare of Chick West's orchestra. Chick himself, with a mute in his horn, was taking the refrain of that swell oldie, *Smoke Gets in Your Eyes.*

"Oh, darling," Lois breathed.

"Baby," answered Bill softly.

They came out of a clinch. Lois replaced her head on Bill's big shoulder. Bill picked up his cigarette from the ash tray. But instead of dragging on it, he took it between his fingers, as though it were a pencil, and with it made tiny circles in the air just over the back of Lois' hand.

"Better not," said Lois, with mock warning. "Burny, burny."

But Bill, as though he hadn't heard, deliberately, yet almost idly, did what he had to do. Lois screamed horribly, wrenched herself to her feet, and ran crazily out of the room.

Bill pounded on the bathroom door. Lois had locked it.

"Lois. Lois, baby. Darling. Honest to God. I didn't know what I was doing. Lois. Darling. Open the door."

Inside the bathroom, Lois sat on the edge of the bathtub and stared at the laundry hamper. With her right hand she squeezed the other, the injured one, as though pressure might stop the pain or undo what had been done.

On the other side of the door, Bill kept talking to her with his dry mouth.

"Lois. Lois, Jesus. I tellya I didn't know what I was doing. Lois, for God's sake open the door. Please, for God's sake."

Finally Lois came out and into Bill's arms.

But the same thing happened a week later. Only not with a cigarette. Bill, on a Sunday morning, was teaching Lois how to swing a golf club. Lois wanted to learn to play the game, because everybody said Bill was a crackerjack. They were both in their pajamas and bare feet. It was a helluva lot of fun. Giggles, kisses, guffaws, and twice they both had to sit down, they were laughing so hard.

Then suddenly Bill brought down the head-end of his brassie on Lois' bare foot. Fortunately, his leverage was faulty, because he struck with all his might.

That did it, all right. Lois moved back into her old bedroom in her family's apartment. Her mother bought her new furniture and curtains, and when Lois was able to walk again, her father immediately gave her a check for a thousand dollars. "Buy yourself some dresses," he told her. "Go ahead." So Lois went down to Saks' and Bonwit Teller's and spent the thousand dollars. Then she had a lot of clothes to wear.

New York didn't get much snow that winter, and Central Park never looked right. But the weather was very cold. One morning, looking out her window facing Fifth, Lois saw somebody walking a wire-haired terrier. She thought to herself, "I want a dog." So that afternoon she went to a pet shop and bought a three-months-old scotty. She put a bright red collar and leash on it, and brought the whimpering animal home in a cab. "Isn't it *darling?*" she asked Fred, the doorman. Fred patted the dog and said it sure was a cute little fella. "Gus," Lois said happily, "meet Fred. Fred meet Gus." She dragged the dog into the elevator. "In ya go, Gussie," Lois said. "In ya go, ya little cutie. *Yes.* You're a little *cutie.* That's what you are. A little *cutie.*" Gus stood shivering in the middle of the elevator and wet the floor.

Lois gave him away a few days later. After Gus consistently refused to be housebroken, Lois began to agree with her parents that it was cruel to keep a dog in the city.

The night she gave away Gus, Lois told her parents it was *dumb* to wait till spring to go to Reno. It was better to get it *over* with. So early in January Lois flew West. She lived at a dude ranch just outside Reno and made the acquaintance of Betty Walker, from Chicago, and Sylvia Haggerty, from Rochester. Betty Walker, whose insight was as penetrating as any rubber knife, told Lois a thing or two about men. Sylvia Haggerty was a quiet dumpy little brunette, and never said much, but she could drink more scotch-and-sodas than any girl Lois had ever known. When their divorces all came through, Betty Walker gave a party at the Barclay in Reno. The boys from the ranch were invited, and Red, the good-looking one, made a big play for Lois, but in a nice way. "*Keep away from me!*" Lois suddenly screamed at Red. Everybody said Lois was a rotten sport. They didn't know she was afraid of tall, good-looking men.

She saw Bill again, of course. About two months after she'd returned from Reno, Bill sat down at her table in the Stork Club.

"Hello, Lois."

"Hello, Bill. I'd rather you didn't sit down."

"I've been up at this psychoanalyst's place. He says I'll be all right."

"I'm glad to hear that. Bill, I'm waiting for somebody. Please leave."

"Will you have lunch with me sometime?" Bill asked.

"Bill, they just came in. Please *leave*."

Bill got up. "Can I phone you?" he asked.

"No."

Bill left, and Middie Weaver and Liz Watson sat down. Lois ordered a scotch-and-soda, drank it, and four more like it. When she left the Stork Club she was feeling pretty drunk. She walked and she walked and she walked. Finally she sat down on a bench in front of the zebras' cage at the zoo. She sat there till she was sober and her knees had stopped shaking. Then she went home.

Home was a place with parents, news commentators on the radio, and starched maids who were always coming around to your left to deposit a small chilled glass of tomato juice in front of you.

After dinner, when Lois returned from the telephone, Mrs. Taggett looked up from her book, and asked, "Who was it? Carl Curfman, dear?"

"Yes," said Lois, sitting down. "What a dope."

"He's not a dope," contradicted Mrs. Taggett.

Carl Curfman was a thick-ankled, short young man who always wore white socks because colored socks irritated his feet. He was full of information. If you were going to drive to the game on Saturday, Carl would ask what route you were taking. If you said, "I don't know. I guess Route 26," Carl would suggest eagerly that you take Route 7 instead, and he'd take out a notebook and pencil and chart out the whole thing for you. You'd thank him profusely for his trouble, and he'd sort of nod quickly and remind you not for *anything* to turn off at Cleveland Turnpike despite the road signs. You always felt a little sorry for Carl when he put away his notebook and pencil.

Several months after Lois was back from Reno, Carl asked

her to marry him. He put it to her in the negative. They had just come from a charity ball at the Waldorf. The battery in Carl's sedan was dead, and he had started to get all worked up about it, but Lois said, "Take it easy, Carl. Let's smoke a cigarette first." They sat in the car smoking cigarettes, and it was then that Carl put it to Lois in the negative.

"You wouldn't wanna marry me, would you, Lois?"

Lois had been watching him smoke. He didn't inhale.

"Gee, Carl. You *are* sweet to ask me."

Lois had felt the question coming for a long time; but she had never quite planned an answer.

"I'd do my damnedest to make you happy, Lois. I mean I'd do my damnedest."

He shifted his position in the seat, and Lois could see his white socks.

"You're very sweet to ask me, Carl," Lois said. "But I just don't wanna think about marriage for a while yet."

"Sure," said Carl quickly.

"Hey," said Lois, "there's a garage on Fiftieth and Third. I'll walk down with you."

One day the following week Lois had lunch at the Stork with Middie Weaver. Middie Weaver served the conversation as nodder and cigarette-ash-tipper. Lois told Middie that at first she had thought Carl was a dope. Well, not exactly a *dope*, but, well, Middie knew what Lois meant. Middie nodded and tipped the ashes of her cigarette. But he *wasn't* a dope. He was just sensitive and shy, and terribly sweet. And terribly intelligent. Did Middie know that Carl really *ran* Curfman and Sons? Yes. He really did. And he was a marvelous dancer, too. And he really had nice hair. It actually was *curly* when he didn't slick it down. It really was gorgeous hair. And he wasn't really *fat*. He was solid. And he was terribly sweet.

Middie Weaver said, "Well, *I* always liked Carl. I think he's a grand person."

Lois thought about Middie Weaver on the way home in the cab. Middie was swell. Middie really was a swell person. So intelligent. So few people were intelligent, *really* intelligent. Middie was perfect. Lois hoped Bob Walker would marry Middie. She was too good for him. The rat.

Lois and Carl got married in the spring, and less than a month after they were married, Carl stopped wearing white socks. He also stopped wearing a winged collar with his dinner jacket. And he stopped giving people directions to get to Manasquan by avoiding the shore route. If people want to take the shore route, let them *take* it, Lois told Carl. She also told him not to lend any more money to Bud Masterson. And when Carl danced, would he please take longer steps. If Carl noticed, only short fat men *minced* around the floor. And if Carl put any more of that greasy stuff on his hair, Lois would go mad.

They weren't married three months when Lois started going to the movies at eleven o'clock in the morning. She'd sit up in the loges and chain-smoke cigarettes. It was better than sitting in the damned apartment. It was better than going to see her mother. These days her mother had a four-word vocabulary consisting of, "You're too thin, dear." Going to the movies was also better than seeing the girls. As it was, Lois couldn't go anywhere without bumping into one of them. They were all such ninnies.

So Lois started going to the movies at eleven o'clock in the morning. She'd sit through the show and then she'd go to the ladies room and comb her hair and put on fresh make-up. Then she'd look at herself in the mirror, and wonder, "Well. What the hell should I do now?"

Sometimes Lois went to another movie. Sometimes she went shopping, but rarely these days did she see anything she wanted to buy. Sometimes she met Cookie Benson. When Lois came to think of it, Cookie was the only one of her friends who was intelligent, *really* intelligent. Cookie was swell. Swell sense of humor. Lois and Cookie could sit in the Stork Club for hours, telling dirty jokes and criticizing their friends.

Cookie was perfect. Lois wondered why she had never liked Cookie before. A grand, intelligent person like Cookie.

Carl complained frequently to Lois about his feet. One evening when they were sitting at home, Carl took off his shoes and black socks, and examined his bare feet carefully. He discovered Lois staring at him.

"They itch," he said to Lois, laughing. "I just can't wear colored socks."

"It's your imagination," Lois told him.

"My father had the same thing," Carl said. "It's a form of eczema, the doctors say."

Lois tried to make her voice sound casual. "The way you go into such a stew about it, you'd think you had leprosy."

Carl laughed. "No," he said, still laughing, "I hardly think it's leprosy." He picked up his cigarette from the ash tray.

"Good Lord," said Lois, forcing a little laugh. "Why don't you inhale when you smoke? What possible pleasure can you get out of smoking if you don't inhale?"

Carl laughed again, and examined the end of his cigarette, as though the end of his cigarette might have something to do with his not inhaling.

"I don't know," he said, laughing. "I just never did inhale."

When Lois discovered she was going to have a baby, she stopped going to the movies so much. She began to meet her mother a great deal for lunch at Schrafft's, where they ate vegetable salads and talked about maternity clothes. Men in busses got up to give Lois their seats. Elevator operators spoke to her with quiet new respect in their nondescript voices. With curiosity, Lois began to peek under the hoods of baby carriages.

Carl always slept heavily, and never heard Lois cry in her sleep.

When the baby was born it was generally spoken of as *darling*. It was a fat little boy with tiny ears and blond hair, and it slobbered sweetly for all those who liked babies to slobber sweetly. Lois loved it. Carl loved it. The in-laws loved it. It was, in short, a most successful production. And as the weeks went by, Lois found she couldn't kiss Thomas Taggett Curfman half enough. She couldn't pat his little bottom enough. She couldn't talk to him enough.

"*Yes*. Somebody's gonna get a *bath*. Yes. Somebody I know is gonna get a nice clean *bath*. Bertha, is the water right?"

"*Yes. Some*body's gonna get a *bath*. Bertha, the water's too hot. I don't *care*, Bertha. It's too hot."

Once Carl finally got home in time to see Tommy get his bath. Lois took her hand out of the scientific bathtub, and pointed wetly at Carl.

"Tommy. Who's that? Who's that big man? Tommy, who's that?"

"He doesn't know me," said Carl, but hopefully.

"That's your *Daddy*. That's your *Daddy*, Tommy."

"He doesn't know me from Adam," said Carl.

"Tommy. Tommy, look where Mommy's pointing. Look at Daddy. Look at the big man. Look at Daddy."

That fall Lois' father gave her a mink coat, and if you had lived near Seventy-Fourth and Fifth, many a Thursday you might have seen Lois in her mink coat, wheeling a big black carriage across the Avenue into the park.

Then finally she made it. And when she did, everybody seemed to know about it. Butchers began to give Lois the best cuts of meat. Cab drivers began to tell her about their kids' whooping cough. Bertha, the maid, began to clean with a wet cloth instead of a duster. Poor Cookie Benson during her crying jags began to telephone Lois from the Stork Club. Women in general began to look more closely at Lois' face than at her clothes. Men in theater-boxes, looking down at the women in the audience, began to single out Lois, if for no other reason than they liked the way she put on her glasses.

It happened about six months after young Thomas Taggett Curfman tossed peculiarly in his sleep and a fuzzy woolen blanket snuffed out his little life.

The man Lois didn't love was sitting in his chair one evening, staring at a pattern on the rug. Lois had just come in from the bedroom where she had stood for nearly a half-hour, looking out the window. She sat down in the chair opposite Carl. Never in his life had he looked more stupid and gross. But there was something Lois had to say to him. And suddenly it was said.

"Put on your white socks. Go ahead," Lois said quietly. "Put them on, dear."

THE WONDERFUL WHITE PAPER

by RUTH DOMINO

A story of Spain before the Civil War

AT THE EDGE OF THE PROVINCE OF LA MANCHA, ON ONE OF the huge sandy plains somewhat withdrawn from the great highways leading to Madrid, stood a little village called Cueva. On the horizon before and behind it rose bald mountains of reddish stone which, toward evening when the sun went down, shone in lilac hues.

The village was exactly like every other poor village in the land. The houses were small and white with flat roofs; and in summer when the heat seemed inescapable, they had sackcloth curtains instead of doors. The biggest space in every house was the courtyard which, enclosed by the henhouses and goatsheds and living quarters, was like a room surrounded by four walls. This courtyard had the same trampled clay floor as that in the living quarters. The peasants, too, were exactly like those in the other villages. They wore black shirts which hung over their trousers. In summer they wore large broadbrimmed straw hats, and the whole year round canvas sandals with matted soles and a cloth around their neck.

The women had black dresses and black headcloths. It was as if they went constantly in mourning in their white houses because hundreds of years since the water had dried from their fields together with the trees in the woods. On the other side of the village was a small river whose bed was usually dried up in summer, exposing gray rocks like weather-beaten tombstones.

The priests had told the people that the dearth of water came from their sins. So they bore the heat, the drought, the flies and their poverty as the curse of God, and thought no more about it; they sinned and brought children into the world who, as long as they were tiny, crept about naked on the courtyard clay.

The peasants had dark brown faces, the older ones with many wrinkles and deeply wrought furrows. Their skin hung like supple leather, though not like tired flesh, about their joints. And in that, too, they were exactly like poor peasants the world over whose fat poured from their bodies, together with their sweat, as they bent over the earth. And finally—like peasants everywhere—they had a passion: they sang. They sang after their work when they sat by the side of the road; the women sang in the evenings in their tiny rooms, and the young girls on Sundays when they tied a colored ribbon in their hair. Their songs were called *flamencos*. They were wild monotonous melodies that suddenly soared and swelled out of their throats. The heads of the singers lifted high as if about to fly from their necks. Then the voices would subside again. The more suddenly and fiercely the song mounted, the more highly esteemed was the singer's art. On Sundays the people of the village would sit about such a leader and as he sang shrill and loud, they would clap hands and cry, "*Olè, olè, olè!*"

The words of the songs were very simple, generally only one short sentence, "The landlord is powerful, he does with us what he pleases." Or, "The earth is dry and quivers like a fish on dry land." And the young girls sang that they were so poor the sun and the moon belonged to them, but nothing on earth; there was no man who would look upon them.

Only one thing was more remote from these peasants' imagination than a moist earth with constantly flowing streams: that was a land without colors, in which the sky did not appear blue and the earth was neither red or violet. Faced with such a prospect they would certainly have replied that the people who lived there must be much, much poorer even than themselves.

Though the rich gentlemen still sat in their castles, the King had already been turned out of the country. Gradually teachers went into the districts to instruct the children; and to Cueva there came a young man, Fernando.

Before this when the monastery was still occupied, a few children had gone there to study, but they were the exception. Fernando brought with him maps that were very colorful. The children realized with astonishment that the land on the maps was only a plain without mountains. Moreover the mountains were shown in folds, brown like the earth; the rivers were as blue as the heavens and as sinuous as a goat's limb; the cities were thick black points like goat turds and the villages little black points like flyspecks.

The children learned that on the map their village lay directly to the right of the capital of Madrid, that the land near Valencia looked so green because it was a valley with abundant water and many green plants and that behind it, like unending and multitudinous confluent rivers, was the sea. And the teacher taught those who already knew a few letters that the various curves and lines in the letters of the alphabet imitated objects in nature; and that when, for example, they placed a large O on its back or stomach, it resembled the shape of a lemon, only without the little nose. And he taught those who knew no letters that, conversely, lines and curves could be joined together to form letters. He distributed colored crayons, water colors and paintbrushes to the children.

For their first lesson they all drew a lemon which the teacher had laid on his desk as a model.

Suddenly a titter swept over the class. The teacher, who was reading a book, looked up in surprise. Then the children held their painted lemons high and waved them like yellow drapes toward the desk. Fernando laughed too. There was not a child in the class who was bored.

After a few drawing and painting lessons the teacher divided his class. He asked his most diligent pupils to set down on paper objects out of their own imagination. He told them also that in the evening their older brothers and sisters, if they had time, could come to school. A few of the children tried to portray Bible stories in pictures, others attempted to make maps.

At home the mothers clad in black made the sign of the cross when they saw the paintings. To be sure, they had learned how to embroider in their youth but they had not drawn objects from nature. They had made patterns which had no meaning, or which depicted the cross of Christ and the loose swaddling-clothes of a Christ child on his Mother's lap. The fathers, for their part, gazed long at the maps. The children explained that the blue lines represented flowing water and that where there was much water everything was green, and that near Valencia there were three crops in the year.

To reproduce mountains, rivers and fruits on a small white piece of paper so that one could recognize and find meaning in colors and spaces as easily as in words, even if one could not read and write, that fascinated everyone. But then began what the priests and the authorities later called "the plague."

In the houses where there were boys, a colored map soon hung next to the oil painting of the Virgin Mother and the calendar of the Saints. Water-color paintings of biblical events were pasted over the sleeping-places of the girls. And where there were both boys and girls, colored drawings were grouped both to the right and the left of the Virgin.

Little Juanita wanted to show the rain of manna in the wilderness. But since she was unfamiliar with manna and tomatoes seemed to her good, tasty food, a gift of God worthy of the unfortunate Jews, she let tomatoes rain down from heaven. So her paper was filled with many beautiful, red tomato plants. Nine-year-old Angelita had a weakness for matches so she made an angel walk from star to star, at the coming of night, with a burning match in order to light the star spots which by day were colorless.

Not far from the village lay the landlord's house. The peasants had to bring payments to him for the arid little fields they rented from him. The tribute consisted of vegetables, eggs and a little wine. But the vineyards bore badly in the years of drought and exacted much toil. The landlord's house stood on the same broad expanse as the village; white rectangular, it faced the high red mountains. It had an outer courtyard and an inner courtyard around which the living quarters were grouped. At each of its corners there was a spire. The peasants knew only the outer courtyard where the bailiff stripped them of their food payments. But once little Pedro, peering from behind his father's black shirt, had glimpsed the inner court. There in the center stood a well with magnificently embossed iron troughs. A stream of water jetted forth and fairly flooded the surrounding flower beds. It struck him as the height of earthly splendor: water which was not laboriously drawn by bending over a thousand times, water which did not have to be stolen from the sparse rains, water which poured lavishly forth and yet was neither river nor rain!

When the teacher placed colored crayons at Pedro's desk, he chose a blue one. Then he drew a white, wavy rectangle with pointed spires at the corners. And in the middle he drew a blue stream gushing high and away over the walls and over the brown fields, right into the middle of the village. At home he laid the sheet of paper on the table. His mother wrung her hands; his father took the picture in his hands and murmured in his black beard, "Is this not the landlord's castle?" His wife asked, "What are you saying, husband?" But Pedro's father fell silent again, so the matter was left as if unspoken.

And therewith, the priests and authorities later said, sin came to the village because of the plague of the drawings.

In the evening before the sun had completely set, the father said to Pedro, "Give me a piece of paper and the drawing pencil!" And he sat himself in the yard, not by the edge of the road as was his custom, and drew his house and the blue stream of water which he let fall on his field behind the house.

That night it rained mightily, and the pails that had been set out were filled to the brim with water. The next morning the leaves were crisp and green.

"The Holy Virgin is pleased with the picture," said little Pedro's mother. Word spread throughout the village. "The Holy Virgin grants us water and painting to the children," the people said. Pedro's father did not listen to the women's prattle; and before the sun went down he again sat in his courtyard and painted a garden to his house, and colored his field green, red and blue. The blue came from the water of a little river which he depicted leading through canals and then flowed richly through all his fields. He painted the red of tomatoes and the green of the vine and the onion plant. The next day he sat down again and added a few more hills covered with vineyards, to which a little path led from his house.

The news of the painting by Pedro's father did not remain secret, and the neighbors with whom he used to sit before the house now came and watched over his shoulder. They liked the joyous colors of the garden and especially the water in it; and since their children also had crayons at home, one after the other began to sketch and paint his house with a big garden beside it and much water—in short, everything which did not in reality exist. And since they did not have much water, they copied from the stream which Pedro had sketched in his painting of the landlord's house. They made their little fields and gardens abundant in water and added vineyards which rose higher and higher, almost as high as the red mountains but in green. They extended their painted fields so much that they soon came close to the landlord's house. And now instead of singing *flamencos*, the peasants sat on Sundays before their houses and painted. Even those who could not write thus gave expression in paint to their desires on this earth. Fernando the teacher, who sometimes strolled in the evening through the village streets, would correct here and there an uneven line by one of the artists. He also showed them how to use water colors.

Then one evening a peasant said, "Yes, we're really painting our fields too big; the land no longer belongs to us."

Pedro's older brother sketched a white rectangle with spires and made it quite small next to the many-colored fields and blue canals. But no one yet said aloud to whom the great fields really belonged and what kind of a house that white rectangle with the ornamental spires was.

It seized them like a wild wind from the fields. Almost everyone painted; and if it was not a father, then it was his sons and small daughters who painted the white rectangle with spires as well as they could. Some painted the Egyptian plagues, and huge grasshoppers rained down over the little white rectangle with spires. The rectangle remained unchanged, as little Pedro had first drawn it. Some painted the Flood like a mighty blue pinion which started in one corner of the paper and moved down to the other where stood a small white rectangle with spires, tottering and wavelike. And there was a second picture, "After the Flood," in which green plots of ground with houses and fruit orchards rose up; one who could also write drew an inscription on the green plot of land, "Fields of the peasants of Cueva, the village is swimming far behind."

After two months the supply of drawing crayons and paper was exhausted, so the teacher went into the city to get new materials. The proprietor of the stationery store told Fernando that he did not have so many supplies in stock and asked him what he was doing with so much paper and so many crayons. Fernando replied that he was only the teacher of the village of Cueva and that his pupils and several of the peasants were now actively painting.

"And what do they paint all the time?"

"They paint water, always water, so much water that it almost drowns out the landlord's house," smiled Fernando.

But the merchant did not smile. He remarked that that was very serious, but Fernando did not agree with him.

In the evening at the tavern the tradesman told the mayor and the doctor of the town, and they all shook their heads. They had never bothered with the village of Cueva because none of the peasants there had ever brought them any money. But now times were uncertain in the country, they said, and even churches and monasteries had been burned. The monks had long since been driven from the district of Cueva and undoubtedly the peasants no longer went to church, and now this young and worldly teacher—the authorities should really begin to pay attention to the village now that insubordination was so rife among the people. On Sunday they even voiced their opinions to the priest.

And that Sunday the peasants of Cueva sat before their houses and Pedro's older brother sang a *flamenco* with a new text. He sang, "Oh wonderful white paper, you are getting fruits and fields! Oh wonderful little white paper, the water flows blue on you and the vineyards grow. Little white paper, you will be bigger than the house with the spires facing the red mountains!"

The peasants were silent a moment after the song had ended, then they cried loudly, "*Olè, olè, olè!*" They clapped their hands and sang, "Little white paper, oh wonderful white paper."

The following week a priest visited the schoolhouse and inspected the children's paintings on the walls. He wrung his hands and hastened back to the city.

The next Sunday there came four men of the *Guardia Civil*. It was about noon. They had revolvers and swords in their belts. They strode through the village streets until they came to the schoolhouse which was closed. They knocked. The young teacher looked out of the window. What did they want? Just let him open the door, he'd see soon enough! He opened the schoolroom. The many pictures of the children and grown ups hung roundabout on large thick nails.

"Who has painted these pictures?"

"The children," answered the teacher.

Didn't he know that the pictures were subversive? And they placed handcuffs on him. Two of them began to tear the pictures down from the walls. The children came running to the schoolhouse. They pressed themselves against the classroom door. Suddenly little Pedro sprang forward and cried, "Leave our pictures alone!" And he grasped the gendarme by the arm to stop him. When the man tried to shake him off, Pedro bit hard into his arm.

"*Now* will you!" the gendarme roared.

A gust of wind blew into the schoolroom and drove the pile of pictures into the street. The children watched with eyes wide open. Now the men of the village stood behind them; they too stood silent, their eyes staring.

Meanwhile the soldier had hurled the child from him with a powerful blow. The small body fairly flew across the room and lay on the threshold, stunned by the impact of his fall. His head hung down, his eyes were closed.

"That is my son," said Pedro's father taking a step toward the child.

"And so much the worse for you," shouted the soldier, "for he is the son of a dog!" Provoked by the silence of the children and the men, he kicked the senseless child from the threshold.

At that Pedro's father clenched his fist and held it ready for a blow. But the gendarme drew his saber and made as if to strike the peasant over the head. Perhaps he meant to use only the flat side. Pedro's father tried with his other hand to ward off the upstretched arm, but the blade turned and fell downward, slashing him right across the face. Blood spurted forth and gushed on his new sandals. He staggered toward his son. The gendarme, still more infuriated, pointed to the red drops in the sand. "There you have colors to paint with!" Then all four of the *Guardia Civil* turned to go, dragging the handcuffed teacher after them. A cry arose from the crowd of peasants. But the four men soon disappeared around a bend of the village street.

Perhaps it was this cry, a long echo, grown audible, of the drops of blood in the sand—all of them suddenly had the oppressive feeling that they had been robbed, and that still more would be stolen from them. So they went swiftly home, and those who had paintings took them from their walls and hid them in the darkest corners of their closets.

Early next morning a party of horsemen drew near the village. A few children, seeing the glint of harnesses in the sun, ran into the fields to tell their fathers. The peasants dropped their implements at once and ran back with their children. The vanguard of the riders had already entered the village. They rode on beautiful white horses that shimmered even more brightly than the little white houses. Then they shouted to the men and women that they must hand over those accursed pictures or else they would soon see what would befall them. And they set about searching the bedding and the few pieces of furniture, smashing them to bits. The men stood silently by but when a soldier found a picture, they would unfold their arms and leap furiously at him.

That lasted about an hour. When the soldiers left the village, they dragged behind them ten peasants in chains.

In the afternoon three dead men lay outstretched on the square before the schoolhouse. Among them was Pedro's father. The blackclad women stood at the foot of the biers staring into the faces of the dead. Then Pedro's mother and another woman stepped forth and loosened something from the stiff hands of the corpses. They were fragments of the torn pictures. They smoothed them with loving care and brought them home. Then they again hid the bits of paper in the darkest corners of their closets.

MR. NAB

by FERENC MOLNAR

MR. NAB WAS A MAN WITH A BIG NOSE, HIGHLY RESPECTED by the students in the boardinghouse. The boardinghouse was kept by a terribly old woman. This old woman had a daughter. The daughter had been married and was now a widow. She was only twenty-six years old and Nab and she were in love with each other. What Nab's real name was I don't remember. It was Russian—very long and unpronounceable and contained the "Nab" syllable. When I came to the boardinghouse this man Nab, as he was called, and the old woman's young widowed daughter had been very much in love with each other.

The liaison lasted for a long time. Nab had long passed his doctor's exam, but for the young woman's sake still stayed on at the boardinghouse. His father wrote and begged him to come back to Odessa. He said that he had got him a job, and also selected a wife for him. In short, he should come home, as all preparations for his life were arranged; however Nab did not go. They quarreled in their letters, and the old Russian wrote no more. And then suddenly Nab grew tired of the little woman. He no longer thrilled when the green silk petticoat rustled along the corridor, or the little feet tripped up the wooden stairs.

Nab was a satisfied man—he was no man of culture, but a primitive Russian peasant; Nab was ungrateful.

In the evening at half past seven, the gong sounded, which meant that supper was served. And one fine evening, the following happened—the gong sounded, everyone sat down to the table, but the little German boy's seat was vacant. The hot but tasteless soup arrived and still the little German boy did not take his seat.

Then the young woman with the green petticoat called to

the manservant. "Please sound the gong once more, it seems that Kurt did not hear it."

Outside the gong boomed again but still Kurt did not appear.

"Please," said the little woman with the dreamy eyes, "go up to the fourth floor to the German boy and tell him that we are already at supper."

Nab was the oldest at the table, all the others were school boys and the little woman turned to Nab.

"Why doesn't he come to supper?"

"I don't know."

"Is he ill? He complained to me that he did not feel well."

"He came to my room too. 'I cannot sleep,' he said. But I know what it is. The boy is only here a few weeks. Homesickness. . . . Homesickness. . . ."

Everyone at the table smiled. Homesickness in a boarding-house is the same as seasickness is to passengers on a boat. But when they are used to it, they are very apt to become amused at those who are still in its throes. Thus they laughed at the little spectacled German boy, who at the age of sixteen came away from home at Erfurt and who now tossed about every night, crying in his bed—for at such times the strangest things make one cry. One cries because of the windows, because of the blankets at home, the servant, the narrow gold bands on the plates. One cries over the wood box on which one used to sit in the kitchen while waiting for supper to be ready.

The manservant returned. "I can't get into his room . . . his door is locked."

"Perhaps he is not at home."

"Yes he is, for I heard him fumbling about in the room."

The handsome little woman cast a languid glance toward Nab. "I've so much trouble with him . . . please go upstairs and see what's the matter. If he cries, console him and bring him down. They cry and cry, then they get thin and their parents think that they don't get enough to eat here."

Nab put his table napkin down and left the room. He walked up the stairs and began to detest his life. Now he belongs to the household; they send him to the little German boys. Sometime ago this was love . . . just as every filthy, bad, dark, disreputable liaison was love once. And on account of that long-past love he must now wipe the little well-to-do German boys' noses, wet from homesickness.

"The devil may take this spoiled life of mine," thought Nab as he climbed the wooden staircase. "I'll box this boy's ears for him . . . I'll. . . ."

Upstairs, on the fourth floor, he looked for Kurt's room. He peeped through the keyhole, but he could not see anything since a handkerchief was hanging over it. "Oh, ho," thought Nab, "there is trouble here."

He knocked. "Please open the door."

No answer.

"Please open . . . it's Nab; Nab with the long nose."

Instead of a reply, something fell with a crash in the room, like the sound of a chair falling.

"Do you hear?" shouted Nab. "If you don't open it, I'll kick the door in. What are you doing there? I say, I have the right to break the door in since I am . . . what should I say . . . inspector here in the boardinghouse."

He grinned bitterly when he said that he was inspector here. He amused himself with this ironical title. He quietly added, "Hang it all."

The key turned in the lock and the door opened. Kurt was standing near the threshold, pale as death. His hands were trembling. Nab noticed that from the attic window a rope was hanging down, the upper end of which was fastened to the beam and the lower end finished in a loop.

Nab swallowed hard, closed the door, caught hold of the little German boy's hand and took him to the window. "What is your name?"

"Kurt."

"Well, Kurt, not much cleverness is needed to see that you wanted to hang yourself, judging from the rope, from your pallor and from the fact that you did not come down to supper. Kurt, you are tormented by homesickness."

The spectacled boy smiled sadly and said, "Yes."

Nab swallowed again. "Homesickness is a very fine thing, and everyone must love his country. I love mine too, although I am a Russian; everybody loves his country, even animals. I once knew a dog which came home to Odessa from Tobolsk, merely by following the scent. What's this if not love of country?"

"Yes," said Kurt with ever increasing breath which was bound to end in sobbing.

"I never heard that anybody hanged himself for the love of his country. Sometimes the executioner hangs him who loves his country, but that is quite different. In your case, the rope doesn't help, or do you expect to get home by hanging yourself?" Thus spoke Nab, gently and touchingly, blending humor with tender love, like an inebriated, impecunious philosopher gone to the dogs.

But now Kurt began to weep. "No," he sobbed, "you don't know why I wanted to die."

Nab stared at him. "Why . . . isn't that the reason?"

"No. You have a kind face. You have the most sympathetic face in this strange country. Mr. Nab, I'll tell you everything. . . . Mr. Nab, I wanted to die for love."

"There is some sense to that, but with whom are you in love?"

The boy's face shone through his tears. He took off his glasses and wiped them, smiled, cried, laughed, closed his eyes and turned his head aside like a bewildered little bird, then he spoke. "I am in love with the little woman—with the widow, the daughter of the boardinghouse-keeper, with the divine one—the one in the rustling petticoat—the scented one, because she is so nice."

"Yes," said Nab, "and . . . ?"

"And I want to die . . . as I can never be happy."

"And?"

"And she is twenty-six and I am only sixteen and she is round and beautiful—a full grown woman and I am only a young boy —a half-grown man, without a moustache, with soft hands . . .

and I know that I am not a man yet, and I know she wants a real man . . . a he-man."

"A he-man?" repeated Nab.

"You know, I should like to have broad shoulders . . . tanned, sunburnt muscles. A handsome, savage, athletic face, and I would be sullen, would look severe, wouldn't bother about her and she would secretly admire me, long for me, but I wouldn't speak to her . . . just pass her that she would yearn for me still more . . . but that can't be. I am thin, and spectacled, and my face is the color of milk, and I am sweet, Mr. Nab, so sweet and gentle and well brought up, just fit to be stroked, and the dear beautiful one will never even look at me, not even spit on me."

Kurt was now crying terribly. Somewhere in Erfurt his parents were sitting at supper and might have said with a gentle smile, "What is our Kurt doing now?" They did not know that Kurt is tossing about on a grass-green couch and is crying and that his first fierce torment shakes his stomach, bowels and heart, and they did not know that he had looked into the face of death and he had lived through that moment when man is so near death, as near as he will ever be to it only once more—one moment before his real death.

"Now that I have howled so much, I feel better," he said, and then shook hands with Nab, "but I shall die tonight. Bid farewell to me, Mr. Nab."

"Yes, yes," said Nab, "Just wait a little."

He rose, pulled the key out of the lock, unfastened the rope from the window and crammed it in his pocket. . . .

"Wait, I am coming back soon."

"You won't tell the woman?"

The young boy asked this in a way that if Nab had replied "No," the boy's heart would have broken.

"I told you to wait."

He went down to the dining room and called the woman aside.

"Kurt wanted to hang himself," he whispered to her.

"Why?"

"Because he is in love with you, he is crying upstairs and he wants to die."

The woman smiled.

"Splendid," she said.

"Yes," said Nab and looked at her. She was beautiful now, her eyes were shining with vanity, her mouth was moist and red.

"Yes," said Nab again and felt some kind of choking in his throat when he looked at the woman.

Four stories higher, cold death was waiting in the corridor, and here the woman was—beautiful, round and warm.

"Come up to him," Nab said aloud, that the other boys should hear it too. The woman threw her table napkin down and went out, Nab behind her, but could not overtake her as she hurried quickly. She ran up the stairs like one expecting great bliss.

They entered the room. The German boy was lying on the couch and jumped up when they came in. He blushed and then turned pale.

The woman smiled at him and spoke in a sweet, flattering tone, "Mr. Nab just told me that you are suffering from homesickness."

"Yes," said the boy, and cast a grateful glance toward Nab for his discretion.

"Don't fret," whispered the woman in a tone meant for a grown-up man and for those only in the most intimate moment, "make yourself at home. Here we all love you, isn't that so, Mr. Nab?"

"Yes," mumbled Nab and looked out of the window.

"Well, pull yourself together, will you?"

She stroked his scanty, fair hair, then drew his head onto her bosom. The young boy closed his eyes and thus clung to the full, womanly bosom. His gesture was childish, but his lips were burning, and he would have liked to cry, laugh—to kiss her lips, to catch hold of her head with both hands, to look into her knowing eyes with deathly desire, with a terrifying, great and complete love, which exists only in such young boys, whose head a bad woman presses against her expansive bosom with motherly care—a bad, strange, hot woman who makes the blood boil, while in Erfurt two old people are sitting at supper and ask with gentle smiles, "What is our Kurt doing now?" Nab turned toward them and said slightly angered, "Well, let us go down to supper."

The woman released the young boy's head. His hair was disheveled. He smiled, and said in a trembling voice, "I won't go down tonight, tell them that I am not well. . . . no, I can't go down . . . my eyes are red from crying. . . ."

Nab and the woman went down. Kurt threw himself down on the couch and closed his eyes. Tears were falling from under his closed eyelids. He decided that he would stay here in the boardinghouse for eight. . . . for ten years, then perhaps the woman would be his. Why should he die, when secretly he had already kissed her bosom? Downstairs, supper was proceeding; when it was finished all the boarders went to their rooms—only Nab and the woman remained at the table (supper had been set aside for them)—then they too rose.

Nab looked at the woman—at this moment he was not tired of her. They went into the drawing room; there was nobody there. They did not speak for a long time. The woman was staring in front of her with glowing cheeks and a secret, happy smile. Nab smoked a cigarette. Before supper he had decided to escape to a theater immediately after supper, but now he had no desire to go away.

He looked at the woman, then she said, "Won't the boy harm himself?"

"No," said Nab and threw his cigarette away.

He went to the woman and stroked away the hair from her forehead and looked into her eyes.

The woman quietly said, "Don't you think he might harm himself?"

"No," said Nab and kissed her mouth. The woman rose and pressed Nab's head to her face, purring softly.

"Such a boy . . . such . . . a . . . boy. . . ."

"No, no," said the Russian, "no, the rope is here in my pocket."

He showed her the rope and they both laughed. The woman's eyes were half closed. Then they went out of the drawing room, embracing each other. They stopped on the threshold as Nab had not finished a long kiss.

"They will see us," whispered the woman, "don't kiss me here . . ." She ran in advance. Nab threw the rope away and hurried after her. "The stupid little German," he mumbled on the way . . . "stupid little German."

SEEDLING

by HELEN MC CUNE

SHE WAS FOURTEEN, AND HAD LIED ABOUT HER AGE WHEN she started to work at Balfor's Cafeteria. Her breasts were ripe and her lips as tempting as the strawberry pie on the glass counter in front of her. She came in after school, her arms loaded with books, and a little after nine she left, the books held schoolgirl fashion under her arm.

At first the other girls were jealous of her unusual fascination for the men who came to the cafeteria. But as she continued to ignore their attentions and even tried to give them a slightly resentful look when they tried to be friendly, the girls felt more kindly toward her.

Then Damon came to work at Balfor's. His dark eyes laughed with those of every girl in the place. But toward Alees he was casual and remote. And her coolness and indifference to him were more pronounced than to any of the others.

One night after work they both reached the employee entrance at the same instant. "Carry your books?" he said. It was the first time he had spoken to her.

Alees looked at him an instant or two, her eyes cold. "All right," she said tonelessly. "If you want to."

He took the books and followed her out. For a few blocks they walked in silence. "I thought you took the streetcar at the corner." He watched the crimson color start up in her cheeks.

"I walk home sometimes," she said quickly. "Do you live this way?"

She looked down at his fine hands beneath the thick black sweater cuffs.

"I have an apartment in town." He said it casually, knowing the fact would impress her.

"A girl at work said you were in the Navy for two years."

"Yes. Yeoman. I had a little crack-up in a plane."

"That's too bad," she said.

He glanced at the childish tilt of her nose and the plumpness of her cheeks and wanted her suddenly, desperately. Her silence baffled and intrigued him and awed him in a way. He wanted to catch her hand in his but couldn't quite decide to do it.

"Do you live with your folks?"

"My mother."

She said "mother" with a certain intonation that made him wonder if it was a joke and she was really living with a fellow. He was about to catch her hand when she said, "I'll take my books. Thanks a lot."

"Oh, I'll walk you home. Nothing else to do."

Her hands reaching for the books dropped back to her sides.

He had expected her to live in an apartment or court, some small place. The house wasn't really large, but there were huge trees about it and a deep front yard. What might once have been grass was a stretch of weeds. A large unkempt hedge bordered the gravel drive to the house. He could see the front room brightly lit and all the blinds up.

"Thanks," she said. "I'll take them."

It seemed to him she was afraid of something. He saw a woman's figure cross the room.

"That your mother?"

She looked toward the windows. "Yes. Uh huh. Well, good night."

Her mother is probably strict with her, he decided as he started back. She was a nice kid, no doubt. He liked her. But he wasn't especially looking for nice kids. She had treated him pretty cool. No need to let anything go on.

At work the next day he paid no attention to her except to say hello when he first saw her. As the evening progressed he saw that she meant to pay as little attention to him. Several times he left the floor to comb back his dark hair. Toward closing time he found occasion to joke with some of the prettier girls, which sent them into bursts of controlled but appreciative laughter.

A few minutes after nine he waited outside. She gave him a faint, suppressed smile, the resentful look gone from her face for the moment. She didn't release her books.

She's all right, he thought. Lovely and childish when she didn't wear a stand-offish expression. He wondered about her age. Seventeen or eighteen, perhaps. She was pretty rounded and well built.

At the corner she stopped. "Thanks. Guess I'll take the street-car."

"I'll ride out with you. I haven't anything much to do."

She didn't say anything. He was undecided whether to get on with her. As the car pulled up she gave him another faint smile. Bashful, he thought. Sure she liked him. He had never met a girl who didn't like him.

They got a seat together in back. After a few minutes he took her hand and found it cool and unresisting. "Care to go to a show?" he asked.

The long yellow of her lashes fell down over her eyes and lifted again. "I have a lot of studying to do."

The silence continued until they got off. He reached for her hand again. "Don't you like me?"

She started to pull her hand away, then left it in his, her fingers clinging a little. "Of course I do."

When they got to her place he turned up the drive with her. The air was warm. It looked black and inviting beneath the overhanging trees.

"Well, good night," she said.

"Can't we sit out here and talk for a while?"

She glanced toward the house. It was dark. Her voice came hushed. "I guess so. For a little while."

Under one of the trees near the porch was a bench. She went over to it and let her books slide into a corner of it. She sighed softly and stretched her arms languidly above her head. He reached around her and she pulled away.

"Don't!"

He took out a cigarette and watched her as he lit it. She sat down, smoothing her skirt over her hips and tilting back her head. He couldn't figure it out. Her gestures and expressions didn't seem to fit in with the "don't" business.

A car came up the drive. He could hear a gurgle of feminine laughter and a woman jumped out. From the driver's seat a man emerged more leisurely. He had a heavy-set, solid figure. He dropped his cigarette to the gravel and ground it with the toe of his shoe. The woman had come around and stood beside him. He reached an arm possessively about her shoulders and they went onto the porch and into the house.

"They didn't see us here," Damon said.

She didn't answer. He noticed her hands clasped on her knees and her rounded arms stretched out stiffly.

"Your dad?" he asked.

"No. Just a friend of Mother's."

He picked up the largest of her books. "Ancient History," he said. "I had that in the ninth grade."

"I'm in the ninth grade."

"At seventeen!" He didn't mean to say it that way.

"I'm fourteen. They don't know it at work."

He whistled softly to give it time to sink in. The lights in the front room were bright. He could see the woman filling two glasses from a bottle. After a few minutes the lights went off.

"They're coming back out," he said.

The front door didn't open. A light shone on the driveway from one of the side rooms.

Alees began to gather up her books. "I'd better go in."

He took a shot in the dark. "With them there in the bedroom!"

She looked at him a moment blankly, her lips twisted. "I've got to study. She always has someone in the bedroom."

It was easier to talk to her after that. She allowed him to hold her hand and began to act the way a lot of girls had acted when they thought themselves in love with him.

But it was annoying walking home with her almost every night and just talking, nothing else. She seemed to want him to kiss her, her lips parted at moments and her movements definitely meant to be alluring. If he made any obvious move to do so, she became immediately cold to him and stood up as if to go in.

"Why don't you let me kiss you?" he said one night.

Her voice was cool. "Kissing's silly."

"It's silly, is it?"

He pulled her harshly to him and bit his lips into hers. She went limp like a rag doll in his arms. Then a car came up the drive. Her mother and a young fellow got out.

He judged the fellow to be around twenty-three or twenty-four, a few years older than himself. "Robbing the cradle!" he said, a little louder than he should have.

"Who is it?" the mother called. "Alees!"

"Yes," Alees said.

"Who is with you, Alees?" she asked pleasantly, stepping over. The man with her took a few steps forward, then stopped to light a cigarette.

"Mother, this is Damon, a boy who works at the cafeteria," Alees said in low tones.

"Hello, Damon." The pleasing fragility of her voice matched somehow the fragility of her body. By contrast Alees seemed suddenly a buxom little farm girl.

"Hello," Damon said. He took in rapidly the red-gold wispiness of her short hair and her eyes, dark, laughing, and naked.

"So you're the young man that Alees keeps out in the cold!"

"Not very cold these nights," he said and she laughed merrily, turning aside.

"Come in, you two, if you want to." The way she said it made it seem she was casually inviting him into a seventh heaven of loveliness and iniquity. He felt a rapid-fire rhythm in his heart.

"Let's go for a walk," Alees suggested.

The front door had closed and the lights came on bright. Alees glanced toward the house. He could see the knotted jealousy in her eyes and lips. Her hand came over warm and soft and enclosed his fingers. She was a child!

"I'd better go," he said. "Don't want you neglecting your studies." He placed a kiss on her cheek. "Good night, Alees."

The next few nights she responded to him with fervent little embraces. He could feel the youth beating and aching within her. She thought this was love, the door of the whole world opening before her. He remembered how he felt when he was younger, much younger.

"Do you want to go swimming tomorrow?"

"Sunday?" The words quavered on her lips.

"You mean you go to *church?*"

"I can skip it."

"No, don't skip it. I'll come over in the afternoon."

"No! Meet me at the church," she said excitedly.

"No. Why?" He made his voice sound annoyed. "I'll come over and get you."

The next day no one answered when he knocked. He could hear dishes rattling from the back of the house and he strolled around, brushing his fingers back through his dark hair.

"Oh, hello there," came the mother's voice from the kitchen window. "Come on in the back."

He wanted to take the three wooden steps at a bound, but came up them slowly and scuffed his feet a bit on the door mat. She didn't turn from the drainboard as he entered. Flour and measuring cups and a mixing bowl stood jumbled in front of her.

"Making a cake," she said. "Just putting it in the oven."

He liked the rounded contour of her limbs that accented her daintiness. He liked looking at her back. She turned around with the cake pans filled, smiled at him, and went toward the oven.

"Perfect little homebody," he told himself.

She slammed the oven door and took off her apron, looking up at him naïvely as she did so. It was a certain, composed naïveté he had run across before.

"Would you like a drink?"

"Thanks," he said and followed her into the living room. He stood near her as she poured it. She handed it to him and her breathing became more rapid as her eyes rested on his lips and went down to his hands.

"Alees isn't home?"

"No. She's at church. She never gets here until one-thirty or two. It's—" She glanced at the slender watch on her wrist. "It's eleven. Did she know you were coming?"

"Yes, but I guess I said afternoon. I'll come back."

Her eyes laughed at him. "Sit down and read the funnies, why don't you?"

"Maybe I will."

She went into the kitchen. He thought her movements a little angry. She didn't like his attitude and it amused him. He sprawled in one corner of the davenport. In a little while she came in again and seated herself on the other end of the davenport and picked up a section of the paper from the confusion in the center. His eyes slanted over. She was reading the drama section.

After a while they began to make disconnected remarks while continuing to read, almost as if each of them were alone and hardly expected an answer. Then at the same moment, they reached for a new section and their hands met and held. He looked into her eyes and smiled very slowly.

"You have nice hands, Damon."

He moved closer and slid a hand over her shoulder.

"I suppose Alees is crazy about you," she said.

"She's pretty young."

"Yes. But I was *married* before I was sixteen."

He added it up quickly but didn't say anything. He wanted to crush her fragility in his hands, but removed his hand from her shoulder, absently.

"It's a lazy day, isn't it?" she sighed.

He could feel the anger mounting in her and it gave life to the tempest in him.

"Yes. Sort of lazy."

"Another drink, Damon?"

She brought it over and took a small one herself. He sipped it slowly, looking into her eyes. He wanted to crush her in his hands. But he wasn't going to do it. Her eyes were cold in their depths, two dark frozen pools. He could see the cold fires dancing deep in them.

The drink swirled in his brain. He wasn't going to touch her. Let her get angry and sizzle her allure away. He wouldn't touch her. Then out of her stillness she moved a shoulder slightly and let her eyes go shut for an instant. His hands dropped quickly on her upper arms and she let her head drop back for his lips.

Alees left church before it was out. Her small green-sandaled feet hurried along the green parkway. She cut across a vacant lot behind the house and came in the back way. Before she had reached the porch she smelled the cake. It was a sweet smell. But there was something else. It was burning!

She hurried up the steps into the kitchen and crossed to the oven. She pulled down the oven door and looked at the three round, charred layers.

"Mother," she called and went into the living room. The bedroom door beyond had started to open, then shut quietly.

"Mother," she called through the door, "your cake is burnt to pieces. It's ruined."

THE WINDFALL

by ERSKINE CALDWELL

WHEN WALDO MURDOCK, WHOSE TRADE, WHEN HE FELT LIKE working at it was rendering creatures, came into the unexpected inheritance, there had been no commotion in Brighton to equal it since the time when, eleven years before, one of the Perkins brothers, with no more forewarning than a stroke of summer lightning, ran away in broad daylight with the resident minister's second wife.

As for the townspeople, none of them, not even Aunt Susie Shook, who told fortunes by reading tea leaves or coffee grounds if necessary, had ever had the remotest idea that anything in the nature of sudden wealth would fall into Waldo Murdock's scrawny lap, while at the same time, of course, people were quick to say that if he had not been sitting down, as usual, instead of being up and doing, there would have been no lap of his for it to fall into; and certainly Waldo himself, even though he daydreamed about almost everything else under the sun, had never entertained such a farfetched thought in his mind.

Waldo did not even know he had a brother in Australia and, even if he had known it, he would never have imagined that he would be remembered in a will. From Bangor to Burlington, all the Murdocks, especially the home-owning branch of the family, were known throughout the entire region north of Boston for their trait, which relatives-by-marriage and other outsiders called cussedness, of not acknowledging kinship with one another. And as it was, it was all Waldo could do to force himself, after having cast aside pride of long standing, publicly to admit blood relationship with another Murdock, even if he had lived in Australia, long enough to go to the bank in Waterville and cash the check the lawyer from Portland had handed him.

"Pay no mind to what the people say," he told the clerk in the bank. "There may be others in the State of Maine bearing the name of Murdock, but there's not a single drop of mingling blood that I would own to. I'd sooner claim kinship with my old black cow than I would with a so-called Murdock."

Dessie, Waldo's wife, was, at the beginning, the most level-headed of all. She maintained her mental balance, if only at the start, much better than Waldo and some of the townspeople. Dessie, although afterward she regretted not having gone along, even remained at home and tended the house chores while Waldo was away in Waterville cashing the check. There was only one thing she did out of the ordinary that forenoon, and that was to make Justine, the hired girl, air the parlor and shake out the scatter rugs, even if it were not Saturday.

During all that time the neighbors were ringing her up on the phone and asking what she was going to do with all that money, but that, too, in the beginning, failed to veer the even measure of her thoughts.

"When the check is cashed, if it's not worthless, and it'll be a wonder if it's not, there'll be ample time at hand for me to go out of my way to think about it," she told them. "Right now, and likely forever after, it's nothing but a scrawl and a promise on a slip of paper."

Dessie went back to work with her lips a little tighter each time she finished talking to one of the neighbors on the phone. She was not exactly worried, she told Justine, but she was feeling impatient. Waldo failed to come home at the noon hour for dinner, and it was not long after that before she, like everybody else in Brighton who was working himself into a frenzy over Waldo's sudden windfall, began thinking of the things that could be done with the money.

Late that afternoon Waldo drove up to the dooryard and left the automobile standing there instead of putting it away in the shed where it belonged.

Justine came running to tell her.

Dessie was so on edge by that time that she jumped several

inches off the chair seat when Justine, who was as excited as she by then, ran into the room where she was.

"Mr. Murdock's back!" Justine cried, twisting her fingers.

"He'd better be!" Dessie said. "If he hadn't got home when he did, he could have just kept on traveling, for all the concern I'd ever have."

"I guess Mr. Murdock has the real money," Justine said, looking over her shoulder. "He looked like he was feeling good about it when he got out of the auto."

Dessie leaped to her feet.

"Go on about your tasks, whatever they be, Justine," she said crossly. "It's none of your money, if there is any, anyway."

Justine went to the kitchen and watched Waldo come along the path to the side door.

Waldo came in, throwing his hat on the table. He looked at Dessie for a moment, cocking his head a little to one side. His coat pocket sagged heavily.

Neither Dessie nor Waldo spoke for a while.

Presently Dessie walked up to him and held out her hand.

"Guess I'll take charge for the time being, Waldo," she said stiffly. "Hand it over."

Waldo reached into his coat pocket, drawing out a mostly empty bottle and handing it to her. She stepped back, looking at it severely. Then, without a word, she grabbed the bottle by the neck and slung it with all her might across the room. It struck the wall, shattering into dozens of pieces.

"I might have known it, and I would have, if I had only had the sense God has given most people!" she said, raising her voice. "I've got only myself to blame!"

Waldo reached for a chair.

"Now, there's no cause for a human to take on so, Dessie," he said. "Everything turned out, from here to there and back again, like it was made to order."

He reached into his pants pocket and drew out a bulging roll of greenbacks. The bills were tied tightly around the center with a piece of heavy twine. Dessie forgot her anger the instant she saw the money. The scowling lines on her face disappeared completely while she watched Waldo bounce the roll up and down in his hand.

"All I've got to say," she began, "is that I never thought I'd live to breathe the air of the day when a deceasing Murdock would have the decency to do the honorable thing with his money, even if he couldn't find means of taking it along with him when he went, which would be a wonder if he didn't try to do, and he probably did, anyway."

Waldo leaned back and let her talk to her heart's content. He felt so good himself that he wanted her to have a good time, too. He let her speak what came to mind without uttering a single grumble.

"Have you any more blood relations that we've neglected to remind ourselves of, Waldo?" she asked, leaning toward him. "It seems to me that I recall your second cousin in Skowhegan saying once some years ago that a Murdock went to California at the end of the Spanish-American War and prospected for gold. It might be that he struck it rich out there, which a lot of people did, so I've read, if reading can be believed. If we'd been more particular about your blood relations in the past, we wouldn't have to sit here now and wrack our brains trying to call them to mind at a time like this."

"Guess I have no blood relations of the name of Murdock," Waldo said firmly.

Dessie drew a deep breath and looked longingly at the large roll of greenbacks bouncing up and down in her husband's hand.

Suddenly she leaned forward and grasped the roll desperately. Waldo snatched it from her.

"I think we ought to start making plans," she said.

"This is Murdock money, woman," he said quickly. "A Murdock made it, and a Murdock shall spend it."

Dessie sat up decisively.

"Well, anyway, we'll be sensible," she said calmly. "We won't throw it away on trifles like a lot of people would who I could mention, if I had a mind to."

"I've got it all settled, Dessie," Waldo told her, smiling as a kindly feeling came over him. "Guess we can afford to have a good time now at our age. Maybe we won't be lingering here much longer, which would be a shame if we hadn't taken full advantage of it by the time we went. Wouldn't be no sense in hoarding it only to have to pass it along to somebody else after we are gone."

Dessie nodded approvingly, her spirits rising again.

"I've always wanted a fur neckpiece, Waldo," she said, her face bright with hope.

Dessie did not sleep a single wink that night. For an hour after they had gone to bed, she lay silently tense, listening. Waldo did not stir. He lay on his back listening to Dessie's labored breathing.

Just before midnight Dessie got up as quietly as she possibly could and tiptoed to the foot of the bed where Waldo had laid his pants over the back of a chair. It was dark in the room with the shades drawn, and she took care in feeling her way to the chair. She was trembling nervously when she touched it, and the jerking of her breath had started a pain in her chest. Without losing any more time she slid her hand into the pants pocket.

"Get your hand out of my pants, Dessie," Waldo said, rising up in bed. "Leave that money be."

Dessie dropped the pants without having touched the money, and went back to bed without a word. Neither of them spoke as she lay down again and tried to make herself as comfortable as possible for the remainder of the night. After that both of them lay staring into the blackness of the room.

Just as dawn was beginning to show the first signs of breaking, Dessie slid carefully from the bed and crawled on her hands and knees toward the chair. As she was rising up to reach the pants, Waldo sat up erectly.

"Don't want to have to mention it again about you putting your hand in my pants pocket," he said. "Leave that money be, Dessie."

Dessie dropped the pants and went to the window. She stood there watching a red dawn break in the east. After a while she began dressing, and as she was leaving the chamber she heard Justine starting a fire in the kitchen stove.

While she and Justine were preparing breakfast, she began to realize how uneasy she really was about the money. She had spent a sleepless night worrying over the wealth, and she was afraid she would not get a chance to spend a single penny of it herself.

"Mrs. Murdock," Justine said, coming and standing beside her, "Carl and I could get mated right away if we had the money for a chamber suite."

"Let Carl Friend make his own money," Dessie said sharply, turning on the girl. "Me and my husband have worked hard all our lives for what we possess. It won't hurt Carl Friend to do the same for you, if he wants a family."

"I couldn't sleep much last night for staying awake wondering if you and Mr. Murdock wouldn't want to help me out," Justine said persistently. "Especially because I've worked here for you six years without asking favors, and I didn't think you'd miss a little of all that big inheritance from Australia."

"Mind your own affairs, Justine!" she said sharply. "Besides, Carl Friend can get the money from his own family if he wants to furnish a house for you. Those Friends have made plenty of profit in roof-tinning in the past."

"They won't help any, Mrs. Murdock," Justine said sadly. "And Carl and I don't want to have to wait and wait and wait."

"You don't have to hurry the marriage for any reason, do you?" Dessie asked suspiciously.

Justine looked at her for several moments, her thoughts racing through her mind.

"Not exactly," she admitted at last.

"Well, then," Dessie said, turning away, "in that case, you can afford to wait."

In turning abruptly she almost walked headlong into Waldo. He had come into the kitchen and was going toward the pantry. After Dessie had stepped out of the way, she watched him go into the pantry and pick up several cans off the shelf. He found an empty coffee can and left, going through the kitchen and out the door without a word being spoken. Dessie watched him leave, wondering what he was about to do. She went to the window and watched as he walked to the tool shed and came out a moment later carrying a spade. With the coffee can in one hand and the spade over his shoulder, he disappeared out of sight behind the barn.

It was not until almost ten minutes had passed that Dessie realized what Waldo was doing behind the barn.

Just as she was opening the door to run out there and observe him from the corner of the barn, Waldo walked into view. He came toward the house, carrying the spade but not the coffee can. Dessie's heart sank. He had buried the can, and the money with it, and she had failed to get out there in time to see where the wealth had been hidden. She walked back into the kitchen and placed breakfast on the table.

Waldo came in a few minutes later, washed his hands at the pump, and sat down at his place. He began eating as though nothing out of the ordinary had taken place out behind the barn. Neither she nor Waldo had anything to say to each other during the whole twenty minutes they were at the table. When he finished eating, he got up and put on his hat.

"Have some affairs to attend to in the village," he said shortly. "Will be away for the forenoon, the whole of it."

Dessie nodded. She had to grip her hands tightly in order to hide her impatience. She waited until Waldo had got into the car and driven over the hill out of sight, and then she grabbed Justine by the arm and pulled her through the door. Pushing Justine ahead, Dessie ran as fast as she could to the tool shed, where she quickly snatched up two spades, and then hurried toward the back of the barn.

She set Justine to digging right away, while she looked the ground over carefully, hoping to find evidence of a freshly covered hole. She searched for nearly half an hour without finding a single trace of the hole she was positive Waldo had dug, and after that she went to work, digging methodically.

After several hours Justine slumped to the ground, completely exhausted. Dessie was tired, too, and the blisters on her hands made digging so painful that she could hardly bear to hold the spade. But she forced herself to keep on, allowing Justine to rest a few minutes.

"Get up and dig, Justine," she called breathlessly, not being able to bear seeing her idle any longer.

Justine crawled to her feet and tried to push the blade of the spade into the stony earth. She wanted to beg Dessie to let her rest some more, but when she glanced up and saw Dessie's closely clamped lips, she knew it would be useless to ask.

Dessie stopped for a moment to ease her back. When her eyes were raised from the ground, she saw Fred Paxton leaning over the stonewall beside the road a hundred feet away.

"Going fishing, Dessie?" he called. "See you're digging fishing worms."

Dessie thrust her hand against the small of her aching back and straightened up a little more.

"Thought I might," she said slowly. "It's been a long time since I went."

"Now that you and Waldo have all that money to falute on," Fred said, "I guess you and him can afford to spend all your time doing nothing but fish, if you have a mind to."

"Maybe," she said, tightening her lips.

The mere mention of the money inflamed her thoughts until she could not see clearly. She bent over the spade, thrusting the blade into the rough, stony ground with all her might. She kept doggedly at it until she was certain Fred had walked out of sight over the hill.

Later she sent Justine to the kitchen for some bread and potatoes left over from breakfast, and when Justine returned, Dessie sat down in the shade of the barn and ate hurriedly.

"While I was in the house, Mr. Murdock phoned and said he wouldn't be back in the forenoon," Justine said. "He told me to tell you he would be away in the afternoon, too, the whole of it."

Dessie leaped to her feet.

"Why didn't you tell me right away when you came back a minute ago?" she said angrily.

Justine glanced at the stony ground.

"We're not going to dig out here the whole afternoon, too, are we, Mrs. Murdock?" she inquired pleadingly. "My hands are raw with blisters, and—"

"Never mind that," Dessie said firmly. "We are going to dig this afternoon, the whole of it!"

"But, Mrs. Murdock—"

"Shut up, Justine, and do as you are told!"

When Dessie fell on the bed at dusk that evening, she had never before in all her life felt so thoroughly miserable. Not only had she spent the entire day digging in the stony ground behind the barn, but, moreover, she had not been able to find the coffee can. Her back felt as if she would never be able to use it again.

Once upon the bed, she moved her body carefully, easing herself into a prone position. Justine had gone out earlier in the evening with Carl Friend, and Waldo still had not returned. Dessie felt so tired and lonely that she wanted to cry. Just as she felt tears coming into her eyes, the phone began to ring. She lay motionless, listening to it ring for several minutes, hoping all the while that it would stop so she could begin crying.

The phone did not stop, and it sounded as if it never would as long as she lived. She got to her feet, pressing her hands over her ears in order to keep out the sound, and stumbled painfully to the hall. There she sat down in the chair beside the stand and lifted the receiver.

"Hello," she said unsteadily.

"Is this Waldo Murdock's wife?" a voice boomed.

"Yes," she answered, wondering who it could be.

"Then you'd better bestir yourself and fetch Waldo home where he belongs before it's too late. This is Charles Mason. Waldo is over here at my place, in the east part of town, annoying my household, and if he was a Democrat, I'd shoot him myself, instead of turning the job over to his wife. I've never in my life seen a man behave like he's doing. I guess it's public knowledge by now, otherwise I wouldn't be repeating it that sudden wealth has gone to his head, but that's still no excuse for the way he's doing."

"What's Waldo doing?" Dessie asked, shouting impulsively into the phone.

"He's befuddling Miss Wilson, the schoolteacher who boards at my house, into going away with him. He says he's going to set sail for Australia or somewhere."

"But he can't do that!" Dessie protested.

"That's what any average, normal, level-minded human being would think, too, but I don't know what's going to stop Waldo if you don't come and get him right away, because he's already befuddled Miss Wilson into going to Boston with him tonight, and starting out again from there the first thing in the morning. He's got Miss Wilson believing everything he says, the lies along with the common truth. Looks like she would be on her guard, knowing she's associating with a newlyrich, but she's too far gone now to listen to reason. Waldo pulls out his wealth every few minutes and waves it in front of her, and the sight of that big roll of greenbacks acts on her just like chloroform would on an average being. I've done my best to—"

Dessie gripped the phone.

"Did you say Waldo has a big roll of money?" she shouted. "Greenbacks tied with a string around the middle?"

"He surely has, Mrs. Murdock. It's the biggest roll of money I've seen on a man since the Democrats took over."

Dessie, who had risen from the chair until she was almost erect, sat down, hard.

"Let him be!" she said coldly. "I don't want part or parcel of him. He had me digging in stony ground all day looking for that money in a coffee can, and it wasn't there at all. Let the schoolteacher take him. I've had my share, and more, of suffering, and now I'd be comforted to see somebody else have a goodly portion of it. Sudden wealth will show up a man's true nature every time, and I'm glad I found out the true size and shape of Waldo Murdock's nature before I wasted another single day of my life on him."

"You mean you're not going to try to stop Waldo from going away to the other end of the world with Miss Wilson?"

"No!" Dessie said emphatically. "Waldo Murdock has a free hand from now on!"

She hung up the receiver. A moment later she slumped brokenly in the chair. She called Justine several times before remembering that Justine had gone out with Carl Friend.

After that she hurried into her clothes and went back to the phone. She rang up Thornton Blanchard, her lawyer, and told him to come right away. He lived only a few miles distant, and he promised to be there within fifteen minutes.

While waiting for Thornton Blanchard, Dessie paced up and down the hallway, her face grim and determined. Her mind was made up, and she knew the sooner she acted the better she would feel.

After a few more minutes, he drove up to the house and stopped his car in the dooryard. Dessie went to the step, holding the door open for him. Thornton Blanchard hurried inside and went directly to the table in the center of the living room.

"Is there something wrong, Mrs. Murdock?" he asked anxiously.

"There is now, but it won't be much longer," she said, sitting down at the table, "not after I set things right I should have attended to twenty years ago."

Blanchard sat down and opened his briefcase, slipping out a pad of ruled yellow writing paper and a pencil. He watched Dessie's face, waiting for her to begin.

"Are you ready?" she asked.

"Yes, Mrs. Murdock," he told her, adjusting the pad on the table.

"I want a divorce," she said quickly, "and I want it in a hurry. How soon can I get it, or do I have to go find myself a better lawyer?"

Blanchard sat up.

"Joking aside, Mrs. Murdock, right after you and your husband inherited all that wealth, you want a divorce?" he asked unbelievingly.

"That's what I said."

"But, why?"

"Never mind my reasons," she answered. "When I go to the store and ask for a pound of sugar, I don't have to tell the clerk my reasons for wanting it, do I?"

"No, but—"

"Then go ahead and get me my divorce."

Blanchard fingered the writing pad nervously. After several moments he shook himself, and glanced across the table at Dessie.

"Have you any grounds, Mrs. Murdock?" he inquired cautiously.

"Of course, I've got grounds. I've got all the grounds needed, and a plentiful supply to spare."

"What are to be the grounds on which the suit is to be based, Mrs. Murdock?" he asked, bending over the pad and gripping the pencil tightly.

"Cussedness," she said, leaning back.

Blanchard looked up.

"That's what I said," she nodded. "Cussedness!"

"The judge that hears this suit might not—"

"I don't care what the judge thinks," she retorted. "It's my divorce, and I'll have grounds of my own choosing whether the judge likes them or not."

Blanchard tapped the pencil on the table several times, his mind deep in thought.

"As your attorney, Mrs. Murdock," he said finally, "would you mind telling me in confidence on just what grounds you do base your contention?"

"Waldo Murdock tricked me," she said angrily, relieved to have an opportunity to talk about her troubles. "He went and made as if to bury the inheritance in a coffee can behind the barn, but didn't, and then went off and stayed from home all day while I broke my back, and Justine's too, digging in stony ground for it."

Blanchard drew the palm of his right hand slowly over his face. He leaned back after that and gazed professionally at the ceiling. He was doing his best to keep from saying, on the spur of the moment, anything of a rash nature.

"And I want alimony, too," Dessie spoke up. "I want all of it."

Blanchard sat up.

"What do you mean by all of it?"

"All the inheritance, of course," she replied.

Blanchard was silent for some time. He looked down at the pad, studying the texture of the paper minutely. After a while he looked up at Dessie, fortifying himself with several deep breaths.

"It's going to be difficult, if not impossible," he said gravely. "Downright difficult, Mrs. Murdock."

"That's your job," Dessie told him. "I've worked hard for my living, too."

Blanchard expelled the breath from his lungs and took a fresh start.

"For one thing, Mrs. Murdock, we have no community property law in this state." He leaned back, rolling the pencil between the palms of his hands. "Naturally, that rules out automatically any possibility of a legal division of Waldo's wealth, whatever it may amount to. But let me put it another way. I'll review briefly the background of the whole matter. A wife is subject, more or less, to the will of the husband, all things being equal, of course. However, the marriage contract also subjects the husband to the will of the wife, placing the shoe on the other foot, so to speak. Now we arrive at the conclusion that the two members of the partnership are each and individually subject to the will of the other. But, and let me speak frankly, in our present society, it is the wife's own responsibility to devise, instate, and employ methods, means, and opportunities for enticement that will cause her spouse to desire of his own free will and accord to bestow, shall we say, a single largess, or, as the case often is, continuing largesses, upon her while united in wedlock. Now, as you no doubt realize, Mrs. Murdock, the average wife, to put it bluntly, by showering her favors upon her spouse obtains, in most instances, a bountiful portion of his goods, chattels, and wealth, in some cases benefits that, judged by worldly standards, are far out of proportion to the value—"

"No!" Dessie said emphatically.

Blanchard cleared his throat and bit his underlip.

"It might be best, in the long run, to let the presiding judge set the sum you might obtain from your present husband," he said wearily. "I'm afraid I won't be of much help in that connection. However, I can proceed with filing the divorce papers, and the matter of alimony can be taken up in due course."

"When can I see the judge about getting the money?" Dessie asked. "Tomorrow morning?"

"I'm afraid not," he said, shaking his head. "Your suit couldn't possibly come up for trial until the next term of court, come autumn."

"Come autumn!" Dessie cried.

Blanchard nodded.

"You mean wait all that time!" she cried excitedly. "Why! Waldo Murdock will have every penny of the wealth spent long before then. There wouldn't be anything left for me to sue for!"

"Well," Blanchard said, shaking his head, "I don't know what can be done, then. The terms of court are set by statute."

The side door burst open, and they both turned around to find Waldo standing in the doorway blinking his eyes in the bright light! After adjusting his vision, he walked into the room and went to the vacant chair between Dessie and Blanchard.

"How be you, Thornton?" Waldo said, reaching out and grasping Blanchard's hand. He shook it hard.

"Fair," Blanchard said uneasily. He glanced at Dessie. She was staring at Waldo. "Fair," he said again.

Waldo seated himself.

"Thought for a while today I needed to see you about a matter, but I changed my mind. There's no need, now."

"Well, I'm glad you handled the matter without needing any help," Blanchard said, stumbling over the words.

"Decided not to bother handling it," Waldo said, "so, I just dropped it."

"That's fine," Blanchard said, wondering.

Waldo made himself comfortable.

"Was trying to figure out a way to have a good time and keep the money, too. Figured it couldn't be done. So, I decided to get shed of it."

Dessie was about to leap from her chair when Waldo reached into his pants pocket and tossed the big roll of greenbacks across the table to her. The tightly bound roll of money tumbled into her lap.

For a moment Dessie looked as if she did not know what in the world had happened. Then slowly her eyes began to bulge and she looked down into her lap. She stared at the money dazedly.

"Waldo—" she said, her speech choked.

Tears began to flow down her cheeks, and Waldo squirmed uneasily in his chair. He dropped his head, glancing up at her from beneath his eyebrows every now and then.

"Waldo—" she began again. She could not continue.

Waldo wiped his mouth with the back of his hand.

"Figured a man with no more sense than I've got ought not be allowed to possess that much wealth," he said, still looking down. "So, I decided there was only one thing to do and that was to get shed of it." He glanced from Dessie to Blanchard. "It makes me feel better to be shed of it, the whole three hundred and fifty dollars of it."

Her chair falling over backward as she jumped to her feet, Dessie ran to Waldo. She dropped on her knees beside him and threw her arms around him.

"Waldo—that schoolteacher—"

"The mind was weaker than the eye," he said, glancing up at Blanchard. "The mind was weaker than the eye until she said she wanted me to give her the money to carry."

He looked down admiringly at Dessie.

"Waldo," she said haltingly, "I needed that exercise out behind the barn." She looked up into his face. "It did me a lot of good."

Blanchard pushed back his chair as quietly as possible, gathering up his pad and pencil as he backed away from the table. He had almost reached the door when he was startled to hear somebody singing in the kitchen. He stopped and listened, and by that time Dessie had heard it, too. She raised her head and listened intently. It was Justine singing at the top of her voice. She had never sung like that before, not even during the day.

Dessie got up and went to the kitchen door. She threw it open and stood back.

"Come in here, Justine," she called into the next room.

Justine walked slowly past her and went as far as the table. She stood trembling, fearing she was going to be scolded for singing in such a loud voice at that time of night.

Dessie followed her to the table.

"What did you tell me this morning about not having cause to hurry marriage with Carl Friend, Justine?" she asked her.

Justine gripped her fingers tightly.

"That's what I said this morning, Mrs. Murdock," she replied after hesitating to answer for several moments. She glanced quickly around the room at Waldo and Blanchard. "But—"

Dessie nodded.

"You can't fool me when I hear such singing as I heard a minute ago, Justine," she said. "I think it would be a good thing if you and Carl Friend went ahead right away and bought that chamber suite you were speaking to me about this morning."

She handed Justine the roll of bills and walked around the table to the chair where Waldo sat. Justine looked at the greenbacks in her hand, gripping them tightly before she could bring herself to believe they were real.

"Thank you, Mrs. Murdock!" she said, tears beginning to trickle down her cheeks. "How did you know?"

"Never mind, Justine," Dessie said quickly.

Justine began backing toward the kitchen doorway.

"That money never was intended for us in the first place,"

Waldo said. "We couldn't have managed it, even if we had had a smart lawyer to help."

Dessie dropped on her knees beside Waldo, throwing her arms around him again. They both turned and looked toward the door where Blanchard was standing. Without a word, he turned, opened the door quickly, and stepped out into the night.

THE VIGIL OF BROTHER FERNANDO

by JOAN VATSEK

BROTHER FERNANDO STOOD NEAR THE CHURCH DOOR, IN THE side chapel where Guido Reni's painting had hung for the last hundred and fifty years. Just now it was a little dusty, but the blue of St. George's tunic still held its original soft hue, hanging in Grecian brevity below the breastplate which seemed made of gray velvet scales rather than hard metal. The dragon under his feet writhed with unfaded, greenish contortions, bright gore spumed from its wounds, and the flying draperies, that somehow managed to be there in the background, wind-blown and billowing, glowed with color.

The head of St. George was really the head of Lucrezia, who had gone to visit Guido in prison. Even if one did not know that she had been his model, it was evident that the head was out of proportion, reflected Brother Fernando. It perched, in small blonde glory, on a massive warrior's neck, over a gigantic masculine torso with one muscled, sandaled leg held straight, like a piece of bronze, and the other gouging into the dragon's side.

Yes, one would have surely known the head was the head of a woman. It was delicate and dreamy, with blue eyes that gazed out, blandly unaware of the dragon's twisting, and her own enormous hand that poised negligently, holding a slim, wand-like spear, in preparation to plunging it once more into the dragon's many-tinted flesh.

It was obvious that when Guido had come to the head of St. George, he forgot all the extravagant paraphernalia of dragon and spear and blood, and painted Lucrezia as he saw her, looking at him.

Brother Fernando was not primarily concerned with this curious effect, he had observed it before. Neither was he praying before this attractive and ineffectual tableau, to be delivered from evil. As a matter of fact, he was trying to get some joy out of the color. For the singular thing had happened to him, that all colors seemed the same.

Now in the years that had hurried him so imperceptibly and quietly toward forty, color had been one of his greatest pleasures. The mellow splendor of stained glass windows were a continual joy to him. He had spent hours toiling through difficult old Latin books, for the illumination—the tiny, miraculously clear figures, the gay unstinted splattering of gold leaf and minute flowers—electrified his labors.

He was not given to moods. Occasionally some one of his pupils chafed at him for his lack of imagination, but this did not disturb him in the least. He had originally entered orders because a regulated, religious and scholarly life was the only one that appealed to him. This was the first time that anything had gone wrong, and Brother Fernando would far rather have lost his imperturable capacity for sleep, or his equable temper, or his appetite, than his appreciation of color.

It was not that his eyes were growing weak. His eyes were clear, and fine. His eyes saw sharply everything that passed in the classroom.

But instead of being glad when he got up in the morning and looked out of his tight little window, and saw the clipped, gem-like green of the hedges, and the crowding fertility of the grass, it seemed to him that grass and trees and sky, all shared the same dreadful abnegation of color.

He greeted his companions at the refectory, and noted with an unfamiliar sourness, that their faces all looked the same, and that the dark carved woodwork of the panels, which had seemed to him always unobtrusively magnificent, was drab, uninspiring and dull.

He walked along the aisle among the congregation, and thought how heavy and cloddish they were. The rainbow of hats the women wore, in which he had always taken a half humorous interest, with the unpredictable conceits that varied from season to season—for it was a fashionable church, one of the richest little churches in Rome, in fact—the whole crowd looked to him a vague, dark gray.

And now, even Guido's picture, to which Brother Fernando had come as a last resort, for all its soft gaudiness, had failed him. The oil was certainly a little mottled, he admitted to himself reluctantly. Odd that he had never thought so before.

The tall, bronze-studded church door was heaved open just then, and a little group of tourists was ushered in by one of the innumerable cocky guides who lead strangers like sheep about Rome.

"And this great masterpiece," declared the guide at once, in spluttering English, "is by Guido Reni. By Guido Reni, ladies and gentlemen, the same who painted 'Aurora.' "

Brother Fernando moved off in solitary scorn, his brown robes lightly brushing his bare legs as he moved, his sandals making a little echo on the stone.

The guide suddenly left his charges and began to pursue him. Brother Fernando covered distance swiftly, and the rather stout guide had a hard time to catch him before he entered the sacristy.

"Ecco!" exclaimed the guide. "How fast you hurry, Father! Would the sacristan take us below? I have promised these people that they should see the place of skulls. They will put something in the box," he added placatingly.

"The sacristan is at dinner," replied Brother Fernando shortly. "Let them come back later, if they wish."

"But—but this tour is all arranged!" exclaimed the guide. "We cannot come back to the same place twice! There is no time! We are going to the Coliseum now, and the baths, and the Vatican" —he checked them off on his pudgy fingers.

"What is that to me?" said Brother Fernando.

"But they will be angry! I promised them this, and they won't be satisfied if they don't have it! I beg of you, Father!"

Brother Fernando shrugged.

"Oh, very well. I will get the keys."

The guide, beaming, returned to his flock.

They were waiting when Brother Fernando returned. He could not help smiling a little, tourists had always struck him as so childish.

"Tell them to be careful of their heads," he said to the guide.

"Be careful!" cried the guide. "*Prenez garde!*"

They all obediently ducked, when they entered the winding passage which led to the vaults below.

"Now, I am telling you," said the guide, "you are about to see the most unique, the most extraordinary curiosity in Rome. I am telling you."

The place which was usually kept for the special tombs of prelates and for monuments was, instead, crowded with little chapels side by side, like booths. Brother Fernando led them to the first one and there was a gasp of astonishment from the group behind him. He turned and looked at their faces with ironical amusement. Horror, shock, disbelief, and the kind of unnatural smile that is struck from the face by strong and unexpected emotion, were all present, in varying degrees.

Then they all broke out in exclamations, and laughter burst from them. It was too grotesque to take seriously.

Skulls were placed, with meticulous exactitude, into the plaster of the wall. They formed a geometrical design, varied with a nice eye for effect, by crossbones and hip bones and collarbones, and, in fact, by every bone in the human anatomy. During the Middle Ages a monk, with a penchant for the unusual, had begun the game and it was kept up by generation after generation of the order, with a scrupulous perseverance and ever growing rivalry.

The first chapel was quite modest in its basic pattern; the next was more ambitious, attempting a little flourish with ribs; the third had a rather terrifying pyramid effect; the fourth had managed two great rosettes of skulls, and a circular design, and so on, sixteen in all.

"Tell them these are the heads of my predecessors," said Brother Fernando.

The guide translated with gusto, into three languages.

There was a little flurry, and Brother Fernando could feel that they were looking at him for the first time as a living man, instead of an impersonal brown robe.

"Yes," said Brother Fernando, "these are all the bodies of monks. They are piled here, in this offhand manner, to remind us that we must die also. Have your charges examined them to their satisfaction?"

The guide said, a little nonplussed, that they had.

And so, thanking Brother Fernando with nods and rather hesitant smiles, the visitors were herded up again, and whisked off by their competent manager, presumably to the Coliseum, the baths, and the Vatican.

Brother Fernando followed them slowly, locked the door, and went to take a short rest before going to his class of eager and argumentative theological students.

But he had no spirit for argument that day, his research, his knowledge, his insight, seemed things of the past. He listened to the words falling drearily from his own lips, and longed to escape from the eyes that fastened on him first with expectation, then with puzzled disappointment. In the end he apologized, before leaving them.

"Brother Fernando is not well," said one to the other, in explanation.

Brother Fernando, indeed, felt like a ghost. Intensity had left him, there was nothing to be explored, or learned, or discovered. Vaguely he wandered up to his room, looked around, and wandered disconsolately down again, into the courtyard. There he stood for a moment in the sunshine, looking at the small fountain that had seemed so peaceful to him a short time ago. Now the continuous trickle of water made him irritable.

Across the courtyard, on a stone bench under the portico, he could see Brother Luigi sitting, reading. It seemed peculiarly fitting that he should be there, in just that position, with his delicate and noble head like a fine fresco against the wall. His tonsure had grown over again, and his head was a mass of brown curls. His body, young and supple, showed its elasticity beneath the graceful folds of his robe. As Brother Fernando's glance rested on him, he looked up and waved his hand cheerfully. He yawned and got up.

"I don't believe him for a moment," he said, coming to join Brother Fernando.

"Who?"

"This man. He is all mixed up. He doesn't know enough history to put in a teaspoon."

"Well," said Brother Fernando.

They began to walk up and down, under the eaves, and around the courtyard, getting the most out of the little square of space.

Suddenly Brother Luigi began to talk about the Last Judgment.

It was evident that he had been reading heavily on the subject, for his phantasy caught fire as he spoke, and described the coming of the angels and the rising of the dead.

"Do you think it will be so?" he asked at last.

"I don't know," said Brother Fernando, and left him abruptly.

For many days after that, Brother Fernando looked for color, but could not find it. He became more and more morose. At last he decided to go to his superior, a man whom he did not care for, whom in fact he despised a little, for certainly his erudition was not equal to Brother Fernando's own, and he had a rough manner that was more becoming a butcher than a monk.

When Brother Fernando knocked and entered he did not alter his comfortable slump in an old easy chair.

"What is it, Brother?" he asked. Brother Fernando looked at his florid face over his large and well-fed paunch, and felt unable to begin.

He stood silent for a moment, his rather long and earnestly enquiring face unrelieved by any trace of his usual half ironical smile.

"Father," he said, "I am at the end of my usefulness."

"Indeed?" said Father Jerome. He did not move, only his eyes narrowed a little, shrewdly. "I would say that you were at the height of it: active, healthy—how old are you, forty,

forty-two?—at any rate, you have always seemed to me one of our best men."

"Thank you. At this moment, I am no good to anybody, least of all to myself."

"Well, well," said Father Jerome, and he got up and began to stump about the room. "It is a pity you had to disturb my siesta with this unpleasant news," he said with a grimace.

"I am sorry." Brother Fernando wished he could explain more fully. He could not state, bluntly, that he could not see color any more.

"Yes, now I shan't be able to sleep as well as usual. It is a great pity."

Brother Fernando smiled slightly, apologetically. His lips felt quite strange when he did so: he realized that he had not smiled for a long time.

"Now, if it were another man," said Father Jerome, talking to himself and gesticulating with his heavy, ham-like hands, "I would dismiss it as temperament, and humor him out of it. Or I would bully him a little," he added, reflectively. "But you, now, that's a different case." He sighed. "What is the matter?" he asked.

Brother Fernando shook his head. "That's what I should like to know," he said. "I've never been depressed before—I don't know what to do about it."

Father Jerome sat down again, puffing a little in annoyance. But he was not unkindly, in fact he had already rather lifted the weight from Brother Fernando.

"Sit down, sit down," he said, motioning. "Why can't you sit down by yourself? Are you a little boy?"

Brother Fernando sat down. This time he laughed a little. "Forgive my saying so, Father," he remarked, "but I have never appreciated you before."

"You did not need me before," retorted his superior. "Well, I shall tell you something at which you will laugh, but all the same, I suggest that you try it. Spend a night in the chapels below, as I did once. There is nothing like death to make you enjoy life. It is since then that I have taken on so much weight."

Brother Fernando stared, frankly astonished.

"I know, I know!" said Father Jerome, shaking one hand dismissively, "I know what you are thinking! An old fool if there ever was one! Well, well. But try it. Spend tonight down there, and let me know in the morning how you fare."

Brother Fernando shrugged. "I will fall asleep," he said, "and that is all." He got up. "But," he added, "I shall certainly do as you say. I am under your orders." And he made a rather questionable bow. It was a little too humble.

He was deeply annoyed with Father Jerome. What idiocy! he thought, as he took his leave.

But at nine o'clock he said good night gravely, took a blanket, a flashlight, and the keys, and locked himself in the underground chapels. He wrapped himself in the blanket, lay down on the cold stone floor, and fell promptly asleep, in spite of the dank chilliness.

At night he awoke with a start, and sat up. He was perfectly convinced that he was not alone. He groped for the flashlight, and turned it on, sweeping the bright arc into every one of the little chapels set with skeletons. There was nothing, nobody. He lay down and tried to go to sleep again, but his senses were keenly awake. He listened, and listening made him sweat a little, for it was so quiet.

He felt helpless, lying straight on his back, as though he were being kept down by a stone on his chest. So he sat up again, cross-legged, turned on his flashlight dimly, and waited. He wondered what he was waiting for. What were the dead waiting for? There was certainly something disconcertingly expectant in the way a skull faced your gaze, with sockets just as good as yours, except that they were empty.

He was sitting up opposite the third chapel, with the heads placed in a rising pile. The one at the summit was of singularly fine structure. It looked familiar, and Brother Fernando could not imagine why. It reminded him of someone.

He got up, and went into the small enclosure, going quite close to the central skull. It had a high brow, narrow cheekbones, and gave the impression, even in that stark state, of having contained a highly intelligent brain. But when he was near it, the familiarity vanished. He went further away again, experimentally. Again it seemed as if he had known the man, as if he had seen him often. But bones look much alike, and perhaps it was only the dominant position, enjoyed by the central skull, that made it stand out so.

His thoughts slipped into the past, when the monks were, say, halfway through this very chapel. Did some artistic fingers itch for just one more bone to complete a design. He smiled at the thought. Were any of the monks disturbed at the idea that, when their bones were blanched enough, they would be dug up again and apportioned a place in the wall?

His mind began to play with words, conversationally, in his solitude. Entertaining custom, he thought—undress burial. Three or four centuries ago, they enjoyed such things.

Perhaps it is Brother Luigi, he thought suddenly, for his eyes were drawn again to the central skull, and he remembered Brother Luigi's fine contour against the shadowed wall that afternoon. But concentrating on the skull, he saw that it was much longer, and guessed, at a hazard, that it had belonged to an older man.

He had an impulse to examine some of the other chapels, but hesitated. He had become used to this one. There's nothing to look at anyway! he thought crossly.

But after a little while, since he felt no hint of sleepiness, he got up and looked at some length, at each design, weighing their relative merits.

One could see the historic deterioration from the primal simple arrangement, no more than an array of heads, to a veritable orgy of Byzantine curlicues and complications. He preferred the third chapel, with his friend at the top of the pyramidal pattern. His friend was really a royal conclusion; the monk who unearthed him must have been very well pleased.

It struck Brother Fernando that even for as large an order as it had been, there were a few too many well-preserved remains. He laughed a little to himself, and his laughter was scattered softly in the silence. He was laughing at the creative eagerness of his colleagues that had made them rob graves.

"Weren't you afraid?" he asked out loud, in a mild bantering tone, "that a few murderers would slip into the company?"

"Imagine, my friends," he went on, finding it a relief to talk, "imagine if, as Brother Luigi believes, the dead will rise? What a scrambling for bones there will be! And what a surprise to find, perhaps, a woman or two in your midst?" He laughed again.

He thought of Lucrezia's head, on the body of St. George. It was a pity that it, too, had not a niche somewhere. He looked at his watch. "Witching hour," he remarked.

Of course he did not expect anything to happen, but once he had spoken, it was more than ever as though he were waiting for something. He became annoyed. He began to stalk up and down, angrily. Tomorrow he would be exhausted, not having slept all night. What a fool Father Jerome was. It was really a pity that Brother Fernando was not in his shoes—he would be so much more dignified, and give so much better advice. He wondered what Father Jerome had thought about when he spent the night in the chapels. He had probably had lugubrious thoughts about death. Brother Fernando sneered. "This has no power over me," he said coldly, and as he spoke more loudly than before, the words were thrown back at him, startlingly.

When, at that moment, a bit of bone, loosened from the plaster, crumbled away and fell, making a tiny noise, Brother Fernando was seized with a fit of shuddering. Even his teeth chattered. He sat down, and put the blanket around his shoulders.

For distraction, he decided to go over the theological lesson he was planning for the next day. He did not often do this, formally, but it was as good a way to spend the time as any.

"Now, class," he began, with jesting bravado, and choked. All the white skulls gleamed at him.

"There is heaven and earth," he whispered, and paused for a long time.

He could say nothing that the gathering before him did not question, though listening quietly enough.

He recalled his powerful sensation of not being alone when he woke up. This feeling had not been dispelled, but he had grown used to it. He realized now that it was not a single presence, but made up by the piles and piles of chalky remains, which appealed to him mutely, making his bones ache in sympathy.

He thought with wistful longing, of the sunny garden in the afternoon, and the blades of pushing, crowding grass.

"My poor friend," he said to the skull on top of the pyamid, "You won't know the sun's brave warmth again."

Suddenly, with a horror-stricken shriek, he leaped up. He knew who the skull reminded him of—it was himself.

His hands went to his head in a wild gesture, and he tried to press its warmth in, to catch it and hold it there forever. He fell on his knees.

Father Jerome always had his breakfast brought to him in his room. It began with pale purple smoked ham and fresh cantaloupe. He was just beginning on the sweet, flushed orange of the cantaloupe when Brother Fernando entered, looking haggard and woebegone.

Father Jerome put down his fork, regretfully but firmly.

"Well, my son," he said, "what did you find in the chapels?"

"Nothing," replied Brother Fernando.

Because Father Jerome's eyes looked at him so piercingly, and he felt so weak, he turned and went to the window, which was as small as his own and latticed. But it was open, and the balmy air of Rome blew in lazily, bringing the smell of grass from the garden plot below. A few doves had settled by the fountain, and were ruffling their white feathers in the morning sun, and darting their pink bills into the clear water.

He saw that Brother Luigi was out early, walking up and down the narrow pebbled path—under the eaved porticos, and that he had pulled a little blue gentian, from the border of carefully planted flowers, and was swinging it in one hand in an inconsequential manner and looking at the sky—which, as Brother Fernando noted with a start, was certainly blue. Every wisp of cloud had been melted against its deep dye, and it stretched in lazy and casual perfection before his unexpectedly delighted eyes.

He turned back to Father Jerome slowly, and looked at his red, round face worriedly gazing at him, and the smoked ham and juicy cantaloupe on his plate, untouched. It struck him as very funny.

"Eat, Father," he said. He sat down on the window ledge, and threw back his head in a long, refreshing laugh. The sun was very warm on his back. "It is certainly good to be alive," he remarked lightly.

Then he jumped up. "I must have a look at St. George's mantle," he said.

MY SIDE OF THE MATTER

by TRUMAN CAPOTE

I KNOW WHAT IS BEING SAID ABOUT ME AND YOU CAN TAKE my side or theirs, that's your own business. It's my word against Eunice's and Olivia-Ann's and it should be plain enough to anyone with two good eyes which one of us has their wits about them. I just want the citizens of the U.S.A. to know the facts, that's all.

The facts: On Sunday, August 12, this year of our Lord, Eunice tried to kill me with her papa's Civil-War sword and Olivia-Ann cut up all over the place with a fourteen-inch hog knife. This is not even to mention lots of other things.

It began six months ago when I married Marge. That was the first thing I did wrong. We were married in Mobile after an acquaintance of only four days. We were both sixteen and she was visiting my cousin Georgia. Now that I've had plenty of time to think it over I can't for the life of me figure how I fell for the likes of her. She has no looks, no body, and no brains whatsoever. But Marge is a natural blonde and maybe that's the answer. Well, we were married going on three months when Marge ups and gets pregnant; the second thing I did wrong. Then she starts hollering that she's got to go home to Mama—only she hasn't got no mama, just these two aunts, Eunice and Olivia-Ann. So she makes me quit my perfectly swell position clerking at the Cash'n' Carry and move here to Admiral's Mill which is nothing but a damn gap in the road any way you care to consider it.

The day Marge and I got off the train at the L&N depot it was raining cats and dogs and do you think anyone came to meet us? I'd shelled out forty-one cents for a telegram, too! Here my wife's pregnant and we have to tramp seven miles in a downpour. It was bad on Marge as I couldn't carry hardly any of our stuff on account of I have terrible trouble with my back. When I first caught sight of this house I must say I was impressed. It's big and yellow and has real columns out in front and japonica trees, both red and white, lining the yard.

Eunice and Olivia-Ann had seen us coming and were waiting in the hall. I swear I wish you could get a look at these two. Honest, you'd die! Eunice is this big old fat thing with a behind that must weigh a tenth of a ton. She troops around the house, rain or shine, in this real old-fashioned nighty, calls it a kimono, but it isn't anything in this world but a dirty flannel nighty. Furthermore she chews tobacco and tries to pretend so lady-like, spitting on the sly. She keeps gabbing about what a fine education she had, which is her way of attempting to make me feel bad although, personally, it never bothers me so much as one whit as I know for a fact she can't even read the funnies without she spells out every single, solitary word. You've got to hand her one thing, though—she can add and subtract money so fast that there's no doubt but what she could be up in Washington, D. C., working where they make the stuff. Not that she hasn't got plenty of money! Naturally she says she hasn't but I know she has because one day, accidentally, I happened to find close to a thousand dollars hidden in a flower pot on the side porch. I didn't touch one cent only Eunice says I stole a hundred-dollar bill which is a venomous lie from start to finish. Of course anything Eunice says is an order from headquarters as not a breathing soul in Admiral's Mill can stand up and say he doesn't owe her money and if she said Charlie Carson (a blind, ninety-year-old invalid who hasn't taken a step since 1896) threw her on her back and raped her everybody in this county would swear the same on a stack of Bibles.

Now Olivia-Ann is worse, and that's the truth! Only she's not so bad on the nerves as Eunice for she is a natural-born half-wit and ought really to be kept in somebody's attic. She's real pale and skinny and has a mustache. She squats around most of the time whittling on a stick with her fourteen-inch hog knife, otherwise she's up to some devilment, like what she did to Mrs. Harry Steller Smith. I swore not ever to tell anyone that, but when a vicious attempt has been made on a person's life, I say the hell with promises.

Mrs. Harry Steller Smith was Eunice's canary named after a woman from Pensacola who makes home-made cure-all that Eunice takes for the gout. One day I heard this terrible racket in the parlor and upon investigating, what did I find but Olivia-Ann shooing Mrs. Harry Steller Smith out an open window with a broom and the door to the bird cage wide. If I hadn't walked in at exactly that moment she might never have been caught. She got scared that I would tell Eunice and blurted out the whole thing, said it wasn't fair to keep one of God's creatures locked up that way, besides which she couldn't stand Mrs. Harry Steller Smith's singing. Well, I felt kind of sorry for her and she gave me two dollars, so I helped her cook up a story for Eunice. Of course I wouldn't have taken the money except I thought it would ease her conscience.

The very *first* words Eunice said when I stepped inside this house were, "So this is what you ran off behind our backs and married, Marge?"

Marge says, "Isn't he the best looking thing, Aunt Eunice?"

Eunice eyes me u-p and d-o-w-n and says, "Tell him to turn around."

While my back is turned, Eunice says, "You sure must've picked the runt of the litter. Why, this isn't any sort of man at all."

I've never been so taken back in my life! True, I'm slightly stocky, but then I haven't got my full growth yet.

"He is too," says Marge.

Olivia-Ann, who's been standing there with her mouth so wide the flies could buzz in and out, says, "You heard what Sister said. He's not any sort of a man whatsoever. The very idea of this little runt running around claiming to be a man! Why, he isn't even of the male sex!"

Marge says, "You seem to forget, Aunt Olivia-Ann, that this is my husband, the father of my unborn child."

Eunice made a nasty sound like only she can and said, "Well, all I can say is I most certainly wouldn't be bragging about it."

Isn't that a nice welcome? And after I gave up my perfectly swell position clerking at the Cash'n' Carry.

But it's not a drop in the bucket to what came later that same evening. After Bluebell cleared away the supper dishes, Marge asked, just as nice as she could, if we could borrow the car and drive over to the picture show at Phoenix City.

"You must be clear out of your head," says Eunice and honest you'd think we'd asked for the kimono off her back.

"You must be clear out of your head," says Olivia-Ann.

"It's six o'clock," says Eunice, "and if you think I'd let that runt drive my just as good as brand-new 1934 Chevrolet as far as the privy and back you must've gone clear out of your head."

Naturally such language makes Marge cry.

"Never you mind, honey," I said, "I've driven pu-lenty of Cadillacs in my time."

"Humf," says Eunice. "Yeah," says I.

Eunice says, "If he's ever so much as driven a plow I'll eat a dozen gophers fried in turpentine."

"I won't have you refer to my husband in any such manner," says Marge. "You're acting simply outlandish! Why, you'd think I'd picked up some absolutely strange man in some absolutely strange place."

"If the shoe fits, wear it!" says Eunice.

"Don't think you can pull the sheep over our eyes," says Olivia-Ann in that braying voice of hers so much like the mating call of a jackass you can't rightly tell the difference.

"We weren't born just around the corner, you know," says Eunice.

Marge says, "I'll give you to understand that I'm legally wed till death do us part to this man by a certified justice of the peace as of three and one-half months ago. Ask anybody. Furthermore, Aunt Eunice, he is free, white and sixteen. Furthermore, George Far Sylvester does not appreciate hearing his father referred to in any such manner."

George Far Sylvester is the name we've planned for the baby. Has a strong sound, don't you think? Only the way things stand I have positively no feelings in the matter now whatsoever.

"How can a girl have a baby with a girl?" says Olivia-Ann which was a calculated attack on my manhood. "I do declare there's something new every day."

"Oh, shush up," says Eunice. "Let us hear no more about the picture show in Phoenix City."

Marge sobs, "Oh-h-h, but it's Judy Garland."

"Never mind, honey," I said, "I most likely saw the show in Mobile ten years ago."

"That's a deliberate falsehood," shouts Olivia-Ann. "Oh, you are a scoundrel, you are. Judy hasn't been in the pictures ten years." Olivia-Ann's never seen not even one picture show in her entire fifty-two years (she won't tell anybody how old she is but I dropped a card to the capitol in Montgomery and they were very nice about answering) but she subscribes to eight movie books. According to Postmistress Delancey it's the only mail she ever gets outside of the Sears & Roebuck. She has this positively morbid crush on Gary Cooper and has one trunk and two suitcases full of his photos.

So we got up from the table and Eunice lumbers over to the window and looks out to the chinaberry tree and says, "Birds settling in their roost—time we went to bed. You have your old room, Marge, and I've fixed a cot for this gentleman on the back porch."

It took a solid minute for that to sink in.

I said, "And what, if I'm not too bold to ask, is the objection to my sleeping with my lawful wife?"

Then they both started yelling at me.

So Marge threw a conniption fit right then and there, "Stop it, stop it, stop it! I can't stand any more. Go on, baby-doll . . . go on and sleep wherever they say. Tomorrow we'll see. . . ."

Eunice says, "I swanee if the child hasn't got a grain of sense after all."

"Poor dear," says Olivia-Ann, wrapping her arm around Marge's waist and herding her off, "poor dear, so young, so innocent. Let's us just go and have a good cry on Olivia-Ann's shoulder."

May, June, July and the best part of August I've squatted and sweltered on that damn back porch without an ounce of screening. And Marge—she hasn't opened her mouth in protest, not once! This part of Alabama is swampy, with mosquitoes that could murder a buffalo given half a chance, not to mention dangerous flying roaches and a posse of local rats big enough to haul a wagon train from here to Timbuctoo. Oh, if it wasn't for that little unborn George I would've been making dust tracks on the road, way before now. I mean to say I haven't had five seconds alone with Marge since that first night. One or the other is always chaperoning and last week they like to have blown their tops when Marge locked herself in her room and they couldn't find me nowhere. The truth is I'd been down watching the niggers bale cotton but just for spite I let on to Eunice like Marge and I'd been up to no good. After that they added Bluebell to the shift.

And all this time I haven't even had cigarette change.

Eunice has hounded me day in and day out about getting a job. "Why don't the little heathen go out and get some honest work?" says she. As you've probably noticed, she never speaks to me directly, though more often than not I am the only one in her royal presence. "If he was any sort of man you could call a man he'd be trying to put a crust of bread in that girl's mouth instead of stuffing his own off my vittels." I think you should know that I've been living almost exclusively on cold yams and leftover grits for three months and thirteen days and I've been down to consult Dr. A. N. Carter twice. He's not exactly sure whether I have the scurvy or not.

And as for my not working, I'd like to know what a man of my abilities, a man who held a perfectly swell position with the Cash'n' Carry would find to do in a flea-bag like Admiral's Mill? There is all of one store here and Mr. Tubberville, the proprietor, is actually so lazy it's painful for him to have to sell anything. Then we have the Morning Star Baptist Church but they already have a preacher, an awful old character named Shell whom Eunice drug over one day to see about the salvation of my soul. I heard him with my own ears tell her I was too far gone.

But it's what Eunice has done to Marge that really takes the cake. She has turned that girl against me in the most villainous fashion that words could not describe. Why, she even reached the point where she was sassing me back, but I provided her with a couple of good slaps and put a stop to that. No wife of mine is ever going to be disrespectful to me, not on your life!

The enemy lines are stretched tight: Bluebell, Olivia-Ann, Eunice, Marge, and the whole rest of Admiral's Mill (pop. 342). Allies: none. Such was the situation as of Sunday, August 12, when the attempt was made upon my very life.

Yesterday was quiet and hot enough to melt rock. The trouble began at exactly two o'clock. I know because Eunice has one of those fool cuckoo contraptions and it scares the daylights out of me. I was minding my own personal business in the parlor composing a song on the upright piano which Eunice bought for Olivia-Ann and hired her a teacher to come all the way from Columbus, Georgia, once a week. Postmistress Delancey, who was my friend till she decided that it was maybe not so wise, says that the fancy teacher tore out of this house one afternoon like old Adolf Hitler was on his tail and leaped in his Ford coupé, never to be heard from again. Like I say, I'm trying to keep cool in the parlor not bothering a living soul when Olivia-Ann trots in with her hair all twisted up in curlers and shrieks, "Cease that infernal racket this very instant! Can't you give a body a minute's rest? And get off my piano right smart. It's not your piano, it's my piano and if you don't get off it right smart I'll have you in court like a shot the first Monday in September."

She's not anything in this world but jealous on account of I'm a natural-born musician and the songs I make up out of my own head are absolutely marvelous.

"And just look what you've done to my genuine ivory keys, Mr. Sylvester," says she, trotting over to the piano, "torn nearly every one of them off right at roots for purentee meanness, that's what you've done."

She knows good and well that the piano was ready for the junk heap the moment I entered this house.

I said, "Seeing as you're such a know-it-all, Miss Olivia-Ann, maybe it would interest you to know that I'm in the possession of a few interesting tales myself. A few things that maybe other people would be very grateful to know. Like what happened to Mrs. Harry Steller Smith, as for instance."

Remember Mrs. Harry Steller Smith?

She paused and looked at the empty bird cage. "You gave me your oath," says she and turned the most terrifying shade of purple.

"Maybe I did and again maybe I didn't," says I. "You did an evil thing when you betrayed Eunice that way but if some people will leave other people alone then maybe I can overlook it."

Well, sir, she walked out of there just as *nice* and *quiet* as you please. So I went and stretched out on the sofa which is the most horrible piece of furniture I've ever seen and is part of a matched set Eunice bought in Atlanta in 1912 and paid two thousand dollars for, cash—or so she claims. This set is black and olive plush and smells like wet chicken feathers on a damp day. There is a big table in one corner of the parlor which supports two pictures of Miss E and O-A's mama and papa. Papa is kind of handsome but just between you and me I'm convinced he has black blood in him from somewhere. He was a captain in the Civil War and that is one thing I'll never forget on account of his sword which is displayed over the mantel and figures prominently in the action yet to come. Mamma has that hangdog, half-wit look like Olivia-Ann though I must say Mama carries it better.

So I had just about dozed off when I heard Eunice bellowing, "Where is he? Where is he?" And the next thing I know she's framed in the doorway with her hands planted plump on those hippo hips and the whole pack scrunched up behind her; Bluebell, Olivia-Ann, and Marge.

Several seconds passed with Eunice tapping her big old bare foot just as fast and furious as she could and fanning her fat face with this cardboard picture of Niagara Falls.

"Where is it?" says she. "Where's my hundred dollars that he made away with while my trusting back was turned?"

"*This* is the straw that broke the camel's back," says I, but I was too hot and tired to get up.

"That's not the only back that's going to be broke," says she, her bug eyes about to pop clear out of their sockets. "That was my funeral money and I want it back. Wouldn't you know he'd steal from the dead?"

"Maybe he didn't take it," says Marge.

"You keep your mouth out of this, missy," says Olivia-Ann.

"He stole my money sure as shooting," says Eunice. "Why, look at his eyes . . . black with guilt!"

I yawned and said, "Like they say in the courts . . . if the party of the first part falsely accuses the party of the second part then the party of the first part can be locked away in jail even if the State Home is where they rightfully belong for the protection of all concerned."

"God will punish him," says Eunice.

"Oh, Sister," says Olivia-Ann, "let us not wait for God."

Whereupon Eunice advances on me with this most peculiar look, her dirty flannel nighty jerking along the floor. And Olivia-Ann leeches after her and Bluebell lets forth this moan that must have been heard clear to Eufala and back while Marge stands there wringing her hands and whimpering.

"Oh-h-h," sobs Marge, "please give her back that money, baby-doll."

I said, "Et tu Brute?" which is from William Shakespeare.

"Look at the likes of him," says Eunice, "lying around all day not doing so much as licking a postage stamp."

"Pitiful," clucks Olivia-Ann.

"You'd think he was having a baby instead of that poor child." Eunice speaking.

Bluebell tosses in her two cents, "Ain't it the truth?"

"Well, if it isn't the old pots calling the kettle black," says I.

"After loafing here for three months does this runt have the audacity to cast aspersions in my direction?" says Eunice.

I merely flicked a bit of ash from my sleeve and not the least bit fazed, said, "Dr. A. N. Carter has informed me that I am in a dangerous scurvy condition and can't stand the least excitement whatsoever—otherwise I'm liable to foam at the mouth and bite somebody."

Then Bluebell says, "Why don't he go back to that trash in Mobile, Miss Eunice? I'se sick an' tired of carryin' his ol' slop jar."

Naturally that coal-black character made me so mad I couldn't see straight.

So just as calm as a cucumber I arose and picked up this umbrella off the hat tree and rapped her across the head with it until it cracked smack in two.

"My real Japanese silk parasol!" shrieks Olivia-Ann.

Marge cries, "You've killed Bluebell, you've killed poor old Bluebell!"

Eunice shoves Olivia-Ann and says, "He's gone clear out of his head, Sister! Run! Run and get Mr. Tubberville!"

"I don't like Mr. Tubberville," says Olivia-Ann staunchly. "I'll go get my hog knife." And she makes a dash for the door but seeing as I care nothing for death I brought her down with a sort of tackle. It wrenched my back something terrible.

"He's going to kill her!" hollers Eunice loud enough to bring the house down. "He's going to murder us all! I warned you, Marge. Quick, child, get Papa's sword!"

So Marge gets Papa's sword and hands it to Eunice. Talk about wifely devotion! And if that's not bad enough Olivia-Ann gives me this terrific knee punch and I had to let go. The next thing you know we hear her out in the yard bellowing hymns.

Mine eyes have seen the glory of the coming of the Lord;
He is trampling out the vintage where the grapes of wrath are stored. . . .

Meanwhile Eunice is sashaying all over the place wildly thrashing Papa's sword and somehow I've managed to clamber atop the piano. Then Eunice climbs up on the piano stool and how that rickety contraption survived a monster like her I'll never be the one to tell.

"Come down from there, you yellow coward, before I run you through," says she and takes a whack and I've got a half-inch cut to prove it.

By this time Bluebell has recovered and skittered away to join Olivia-Ann holding services in the front yard. I guess they were expecting my body and God knows it would've been theirs if Marge hadn't passed out cold.

That's the only good thing I've got to say for Marge.

What happened after that I can't rightly remember except for Olivia-Ann reappearing with her fourteen-inch hog knife and a bunch of the neighbors. But suddenly Marge was the star attraction and I suppose they carried her to her room. Anyway, as soon as they left I barricaded the parlor door.

I've got all those black and olive plush chairs pushed against it and that big mahogany table that must weigh a couple of tons and the hat tree and lots of other stuff. I've locked the windows and pulled down the shades. Also I've found a five-pound box of Sweet Love candy and this very minute I'm munching a juicy, creamy, chocolate cherry. Sometimes they come to the door and knock and yell and plead. Oh yes, they've started singing a song of a very different color. But as for me—I give them a tune on the piano every now and then just to let them know I'm cheerful.

THE CALLING CARDS

by IVAN BUNIN

IT WAS THE BEGINNING OF AUTUMN, AND THE RIVER STEAMER *Goncharov* coursed along an empty Volga. The chill of early morning enveloped the vessel, and an icy wind swept the Asiatic expanse of water and beat head on against the steamer. The wind whipped the flag at the stern, tore at the hats, caps, and clothing of the people walking the decks, wrinkled their faces and snapped at their sleeves and skirts. A single gull followed the ship aimlessly and dully—now drifting just astern of the vessel, a sharp-pointed crescent swinging in the air, now soaring away slantwise into the distance, as if it did not know what to do with itself in the emptiness of the great river and gray autumn sky.

The steamer was almost empty, too. There was a small group of peasants on the lower deck and only three passengers on the upper. The three walked back and forth, meeting and passing: the two from the second class, both bound for the same destination, always inseparable, always pacing the deck together, constantly talking about something in a business-like manner, and alike inconspicuous; and the passenger from the first class. The latter was a man of about thirty, a newly renowned writer, distinguished by his serious air—not quite sad and not quite angry—and also by his outward appearance. He was tall and robust—he even stooped a bit, as some strong people do—well-dressed, and, in his way, handsome; a brunette of that Russian-eastern type one met among the old merchant families of Moscow. He came of such a family, although he no longer had anything in common with it.

He walked alone, with a firm step. In his checkered English cap, black cheviot coat, and expensive, well-made shoes, he paced the deck, breathing deeply of the bracing air. He reached the stern and stood watching the spreading, running surge of river behind the vessel.

Then, turning sharply, he walked toward the prow once more, lowering his head against the wind that clutched at his cap, and hearing the loud, regular pulsation of the sidewheel as each blade lifted to shed its glasslike cascade of rushing water.

A cheap black bonnet rose above the stairs that led from the third class, and he stopped short, smiling stiffly. Below the bonnet appeared the thin, sweet face of a young woman, his chance acquaintance of the previous evening. He hastened toward her. She was also smiling as she came forward awkwardly, bent over to fight the wind and holding her bonnet in place with a bony hand. She wore a light coat and her legs below it were thin.

"Did you sleep well?" he asked loudy and cheerily as he approached her.

"Marvelously!" she replied, a shade too gaily. "I always sleep like a top."

He retained her hand in his large palm and looked into her eyes. She met his glance with radiant intensity.

"You overslept, my angel," he said familiarly. "Good folk should be at the breakfast table by now."

"I lay in bed dreaming!" she answered, with an animation quite out of keeping with her appearance.

"What were you dreaming of?"

"Just—things!"

"Oh, oh—watch out! Dreams can be dangerous," he said. "Breakfasting is better. Let's have some vodka and fish soup," he added, thinking: probably she can't afford breakfast in the dining salon.

"Yes, vodka would be just right!" She stamped her feet. "It's devilish cold."

They set off for the first class dining salon, walking briskly. She led the way and he, following behind, observed her almost greedily.

He had thought of her during the night. The previous evening he had struck up a conversation with her as the vessel approached a high black bank in the twilight. A scattering of lights shone at the foot of the dark shore. Later he sat with her on the long bench which went all the way around the deck, beneath the white shutters of the first class cabins. But they did not sit there long, and at night, alone, he regretted they had not lingered. That night he realized, to his surprise, that he wanted her. Why? Because of the customary attraction of a brief encounter with a chance traveling companion?

Seated beside her in the dining salon, clinking glasses with her between mouthfuls of cold black caviar and hot white rolls, he knew now why she attracted him, and he waited impatiently for the affair to reach its culmination. The fact that all this—the vodka, her uninhibited bearing—was in strange contradiction to her normal self excited him the more.

"Well, another drink, and enough!" he said.

"It certainly will be enough!" she replied, in the same bantering tone he employed. "Excellent vodka!"

Of course, he had been touched by her confusion upon learning his name the previous evening. She had been astonished at thus unexpectedly meeting a well known writer. It was always pleasant to witness this confusion. It is usually enough to warm one toward any woman, if she is not absolutely ugly or stupid. Immediately a certain intimacy arises, one becomes daring in address, and somehow one feels a right to her. But it was not merely this that had stirred him: evidently he impressed her as a man, too—and he was touched by her very shabbiness and artlessness. He already had acquired a lack of constraint with admirers: he knew how to make a light and rapid shift from the first few moments of acquaintance to a free and easy, pseudo-bohemian manner, and from that to the studied simplicity of the questions: Who are you? Where are you from? Married or not? Thus had he questioned her the previous evening as they watched the varicolored lights of the forecastle reflected on the black water. The reflections stretched far out over the surface of the river. They could see the red glow of a bonfire on a river barge. "This scene is worth remembering," he thought. The smoke drifting up from the fire carried the smell of fish soup.

"May one ask your name?" he had said.

She told him her name and surname quickly.

"Are you on your way home?"

"I have been visiting my sister in Sviyazhk. Her husband died suddenly and—well, you understand—she was left in a terrible position. . . ."

At first she was embarrassed and looked away, gazing into the distance. Then she began to answer more boldly.

"Are you married?"

She smiled wrily. "Yes, I'm married—alas! This is not my first year as a wife."

"Why alas?"

"I was stupid enough to marry very young. One hardly has time to look about before life passes one by."

"It will be a long time before you need worry about life passing you by."

"Alas, not so long! And I haven't seen anything of life yet."

"It isn't too late to start."

Here she suddenly nodded her head, smiling. "I'm starting!"

"Who is your husband? An official?"

"Oh, he is a very good and kind man. But unfortunately not at all interesting. . . . The secretary of our rural district court."

"How sweet she is, and how unhappy," he thought. He opened his cigarette case.

"Do you want a cigarette?"

"Very much!"

She took a light bravely but clumsily, and then drew on the cigarette with quick, woman-like puffs. Pity for her quivered within him—pity for her confusion, and tenderness; and with all that, a sensuous desire to take advantage of her naïveté and inexperience. The inexperience, he felt, would surely be accompanied by extreme daring.

Now, seated in the dining salon, he glanced impatiently at her thin hands, her faded features that were all the more pathetic for being faded, and the dark hair, done up somewhat carelessly. After removing her bonnet she had slipped her gray coat off her shoulders and over the back of the chair, revealing a dark cotton dress. She kept tucking back stray strands of hair.

He was moved and stirred by the frankness with which she had spoken of her family life and her lost youth, and now her sudden boldness excited him; she was saying and doing the very things that least became her. The vodka brought color to her face. Even her pale lips grew red, and her eyes took on a starry, merry brightness.

"You know," she said suddenly, "we were speaking of dreams. Do you know what my fondest dream was in high school? To have calling cards. We were quite poor then. We had sold the last of the estate and moved to the city, and there was absolutely no one to call on anyway, but how I dreamed of having calling cards! It was so silly."

He pressed her hand, feeling all the bones through the gaunt flesh. Misunderstanding completely, she raised her hand to his lips like an experienced coquette and gave him a languorous glance.

"Let's go to my cabin."

"Let's. It's so stuffy here, with all this smoke."

Tossing her head, she reached for her bonnet.

In the corridor he embraced her. She glanced back at him over her shoulder, proudly and ecstatically. He almost bit her cheek out of the hatred that comes with passion and love. Over her shoulder she presented her lips voluptuously.

In the cabin, hastening to please him and to take full and audacious advantage of the unexpected happiness that had suddenly fallen to her lot in the person of this handsome, strong, and famous man, she tugged at the buttons of her dress and stepped out of it, letting it fall to the floor. She remained in her light petticoat and white underpants, her shoulders and arms bare; and in the half light that entered the cabin through the shutters she was shapely as a boy. The poignant naïveté of it all pierced him.

"Shall I take everything off?" she whispered, just like a young girl.

"Everything, everything," he said, growing sadder and sadder.

Obediently and swiftly she stepped out of her underwear

and stood naked, her flesh gray-purple with that peculiarity of the female body when it shivers nervously and the skin becomes taut and transparent and is covered with goose pimples. She stood there in only cheap stockings, worn garters, and cheap black shoes, and she gave him a triumphant, drunken glance as she reached back to remove her hairpins. Chilling, he watched her.

Her figure was better and younger than one might have thought. Her collar bone and ribs were clearly outlined, as might have been expected from her pinched face and bony shins. But her thighs were large. Her belly was flat, with a small, deep navel, and the curving triangle of dark, beautiful hair below the belly conformed to the thick mass of hair on her head. She removed the hairpins, and her hair fell down her gaunt spine, with its protruding vertebrae.

She bent over to pull up her slipping stockings; her little breasts, with their cold, shrivelled brown nipples, hung like small pears, charming in their meagerness. And he forced her to experience the extreme of shamelessness, so unbecoming to her and therefore so exciting to his senses, rousing all his pity, tenderness, and passion. . . . Nothing could be seen through the slats of the shutter, but she kept glancing toward the shutter in rapturous fright, hearing the unconcerned voices and steps of people passing on the deck outside the window; and this exaggerated still more his terrible exultation at her depravity. Oh, how close these people stood talking and moving—and none of them would imagine what was going on in this white cabin, only one step away!

Afterward he placed her on the bunk. She lay as if dead, her teeth clenched, her eyes closed, and a sad sense of peace settling on her now pale and quite youthful features.

Toward evening, when the steamer docked at the stop where she was to land, she stood alongside him, silent, with lowered lashes. He kissed her cold hand with that love that remains somewhere in the heart for all one's life, and she, without looking back, ran down the gangway into the rude, jostling crowd on the dock. *—Translated from the Russian by Leo Gruliont.*

MY GRANDMOTHER MILLARD AND GENERAL BEDFORD FORREST AND THE BATTLE OF HARRYKIN CREEK

by WILLIAM FAULKNER

I

IT WOULD BE RIGHT AFTER SUPPER, BEFORE WE HAD LEFT THE table. At first, beginning with the day the news came that the Yankees had taken Memphis, we did it three nights in succession. But after that, as we got better and better and faster and faster, once a week suited Granny. Then after Cousin Melisandre finally got out of Memphis and came to live with us, it would be just once a month, and when the regiment in Virginia voted Father out of the colonelcy and he came home and stayed three months while he made a crop and got over his mad and organized his cavalry troop for General Forrest's command, we quit doing it at all. That is, we did it one time with Father there too, watching, and that night Ringo and I heard him laughing in the library, the first time he had laughed since he came home, until in about a half a minute Granny came out already holding her skirts up and went sailing up the stairs. So we didn't do it any more until Father had organized his troop and was gone again.

Granny would fold her napkin beside her plate. She would speak to Ringo standing behind her chair without even turning her head. "Go call Joby and Lucius."

And Ringo would go back through the kitchen without stopping. He would just say, "All right. Look out," at Louvinia's back and go to the cabin and come back with not only Joby and Lucius and the lighted lantern but Philadelphia too, even though Philadelphia wasn't going to do anything but stand and watch and then follow to the orchard and back to the house until Granny said we were done for that time and she and Lucius could go back home to bed. And we would bring down from the attic the big trunk (we had done it so many times by now that we didn't even need the lantern any more to go to the attic and get the trunk (whose lock it was my job to oil every Monday morning with a feather dipped in chicken fat, and Louvinia would come in from the kitchen with the unwashed silver from supper in a dishpan under one arm and the kitchen clock under the other and set the clock and the dishpan on the table and take from her apron pocket a pair of Granny's rolled-up stockings and hand them to Granny and Granny would unroll the stockings and take from the toe of one of them a wadded rag and open the rag and take out the key to the trunk and unpin her watch from her bosom and fold it into the rag and put the rag back into the stocking and roll the stocking back into a ball and put the ball into the trunk. Then with Cousin Melisandre and Philadelphia watching, and Father too on that one time when he was there, Granny would stand facing the clock, her hands raised and about eight inches apart and her neck bowed so she could watch the clock face over her spectacles, until the big hand reached the nearest hour mark.

The rest of us watched her hands. She wouldn't speak again. She didn't need to. There would be just the single light loud pop of her palms when the hand came to the nearest hour mark; sometimes we would be already moving, even before her hands came together, all of us that is except Philadelphia. Granny wouldn't let her help at all, because of Lucius, even though Lucius had done nearly all the digging of the pit and did most of the carrying of the trunk each time. But Philadelphia had to be there. Granny didn't have to tell her but once. "I want the wives of all the free men here too," Granny said. "I want all of you free folks to watch what the rest of us that ain't free have to do to keep that way."

That began about eight months ago. One day even I realized that something had happened to Lucius. Then I knew that Ringo had already seen it and that he knew what it was, so that when at last Louvinia came and told Granny, it was not as if Lucius had dared his mother to tell her but as if he had actually forced somebody, he didn't care who, to tell her. He had said it more than once, in the cabin one night probably for the first time, then after that in other places and to other people, to Negroes from other plantations even. Memphis was already gone then, and New Orleans, and all we had left of the River was Vicksburg and although we didn't believe it then, we wouldn't have that long. Then one morning Louvinia came in where Granny was cutting down the worn-out uniform pants Father had worn home from Virginia so they would fit me, and told Granny how Lucius was saying that soon the Yankees would have all of Mississippi and Yoknapatawpha County too and all the niggers would be free and that when that happened, he was going to be long gone. Lucius was working in the garden that morning. Granny went out to the back gallery, still carrying the pants and the needle. She didn't even push her spectacles up. She said, "You, Lucius," just once, and Lucius came out of the garden with the hoe and Granny stood looking down at him over the spectacles as she looked over them at everything she did, from reading or sewing to watching the clock face until the instant came to start burying the silver.

"You can go now," she said. "You needn't wait on the Yankees."

"Go?" Lucius said. "I ain't free."

"You've been free for almost three minutes," Granny said. "Go on."

Lucius blinked his eyes while you could have counted about ten. "Go where?" he said.

"I can't tell you," Granny said. "I ain't free. I would imagine you will have all Yankeedom to move around in."

Lucius blinked his eyes. He didn't look at Granny now. "Was that all you wanted?" he said.

"Yes," Granny said. So he went back to the garden. And that was the last we heard about being free from him. That is, it quit showing in the way he acted, and if he talked any more of it, even Louvinia never thought it was worth bothering Granny with. It was Granny who would do the reminding of it, especially to Philadelphia, especially on the nights when we would stand like race horses at the barrier, watching Granny's hands until they clapped together.

Each one of us knew exactly what he was to do. I would go upstairs for Granny's gold hatpin and her silver-headed umbrella and her plumed Sunday hat because she had already sent her ear rings and brooch to Richmond a long time ago, and to Father's room for his silver-backed brushes, and to Cousin Melisandre's room after she came to live with us for her things because the one time Granny let Cousin Melisandre try to help too, Cousin Melisandre brought all her dresses down. Ringo would go to the parlor for the candlesticks and Granny's dulcimer and the medallion of Father's mother back in Carolina. And we would run back to the dining room where Louvinia and Lucius would have the sideboard almost cleared, and Granny still standing there and watching the clockface and the trunk both now with her hands ready to pop again and they would pop and Ringo and I would stop at the cellar door just long enough to snatch up the shovels and run on to the orchard and snatch the brush and grass and the criss-crossed sticks away and have the pit open and ready by the time we saw them coming: first Louvinia with the lantern, then Joby and Lucius with the trunk and Granny walking beside it, and Cousin Melisandre and Philadelphia (and on that one time Father, walking along and laughing) following behind. And on that first night, the kitchen clock wasn't in the trunk. Granny was carrying it, and while Louvinia held the lantern so that Granny could watch the hand, Granny made us put the trunk into the pit and shovel the dirt back and smooth it off and lay the brush and grass back over it again and then dig up the trunk and carry it back to the house. And one night, it seemed like we had been bringing the trunk down from the attic and putting the silver into it and carrying it out to the pit and uncovering the pit and then covering the pit again and turning around and carrying the trunk back to the house and taking the silver out and putting it back where we got it from all winter and all summer too;—that night, and I don't know who thought of it first, maybe it was all of us at once. But anyway the clock hand had passed four hour marks before Granny's hands even popped for Ringo and me to run and open the pit. And they came with the trunk and Ringo and I hadn't even put down the last armful of brush and sticks, to save having to stoop to pick it up again, and Lucius hadn't even put down his end of the trunk for the same reason and I reckon Louvinia was the only one that knew what was coming next because Ringo and I didn't know that the kitchen clock was still sitting on the dining-room table. Then Granny spoke. It was the first time we had ever heard her speak between when she would tell Ringo, "Go call Joby and Lucius," and then tell us both about thirty minutes later, "Wash your feet and go to bed." It was not loud and not long, just two words, "Bury it." And we lowered the trunk into the pit and Joby and Lucius threw the dirt back in and even then Ringo and I didn't move with the brush until Granny spoke again, not loud this time either, "Go on. Hide the pit." And we put the brush back and Granny said, "Dig it up." And we dug up the trunk and carried it back into the house and put the things back where we got them from and that was when I saw the kitchen clock still sitting on the dining-room table. And we all stood there watching Granny's hands until they popped together and that time we filled the trunk and carried it out to the orchard and lowered it into the pit quicker than we had ever done before.

2

And then when the time came to really bury the silver, it was too late. After it was all over and Cousin Melisandre and Cousin Philip were finally married and Father had got done laughing, Father said that always happened when a heterogeneous collection of people who were cohered simply by an uncomplex will for freedom, engaged with a tyrannous machine. He said they would always lose the first battles, and if they were outnumbered and outweighed enough, it would seem to an outsider that they were going to lose them all. But they would not. They could not be defeated; if they just willed that freedom strongly and completely enough to sacrifice all else for it—ease and comfort and fatness of spirit and all, until whatever it was they had left would be enough, no matter how little it was—that very freedom itself would finally conquer the machine as a negative force like drouth or flood could strangle it. And later still, after two more years and we knew we were going to lose the war, he was still saying that. He said, "I won't see it but you will. You will see it in the next war, and in all the wars Americans will have to fight from then on. There will be men from the South in the fore-front of all the battles, even leading some of them, helping those who conquered us defend that same freedom which they believed they had taken from us." And that happened: thirty years later, and General Wheeler, whom Father would have called apostate, commanding in Cuba, and whom old General Early did call apostate and matricide too in the office of the Richmond editor when he said, "I would like to have lived so that when my time comes, I will see Robert Lee again. But since I haven't, I'm certainly going to enjoy watching the devil burn that blue coat off Joe Wheeler."

We didn't have time. We didn't even know there were any Yankees in Jefferson, let alone within a mile of Sartoris. There never had been many. There was no railroad then and no river big enough for big boats and nothing in Jefferson they would have wanted even if they had come, since this was before Father had had time to worry them enough for General Grant to issue a general order with a reward for his capture. So we had got used to the war. We thought of it as being definitely fixed and established as a railroad or a river is, moving east along the railroad from Memphis and south along the River toward Vicksburg. We had heard tales of Yankee pillage and most of the people around Jefferson stayed ready to bury their silver fast too, though I don't reckon any of them practised doing it like we did. But nobody we knew was even kin to anyone who had been pillaged, and so I don't think that even Lucius really expected any Yankees until that morning.

It was about eleven o'clock. The table was already set for dinner and everybody was beginning to kind of ease up so we would be sure to hear when Louvinia went out to the back gallery and rang the bell, when Ab Snopes came in at a dead run, on a strange horse as usual. He was a member of Father's troop. Not a fighting member; he called himself father's horse-captain, whatever he meant by it, though we had a pretty good idea, and none of us at least knew what he was doing in Jefferson when the troop was supposed to be up in Tennessee with General Bragg, and probably nobody anywhere knew the actual truth about how he got the horse, galloping across the yard and right through one of Granny's flower beds because I reckon he figured that carrying a message he could risk it, and on around to the back because he knew that, message or no message, he better not come to Granny's front door hollering that way, sitting that strange blown horse with a U. S. army brand on it you could read three hundred yards, and yelling up at Granny that General Forrest was in Jefferson but there was a whole regiment of Yankee cavalry not a half a mile down the road.

So we never had time. Afterward Father admitted that Granny's error was not in strategy nor tactics either, even though she had copied from someone else. Because he said it had been a long time now since originality had been a component of military success. It just happened too fast. I went for Joby and Lucius and Philadelphia because Granny had already sent Ringo down to the road with a cup towel to wave when they came in sight. Then she sent me to the front window where I could watch Ringo. When Ab Snopes came back from hiding his new Yankee horse, he offered to go upstairs to get the things there. Granny had told us a long time ago never to let Ab Snopes go anywhere about the house unless somebody was with him. She said she would rather have Yankees in the house any day because at least Yankees would have more delicacy, even if it wasn't anything but good sense, than to steal a spoon or candlestick and then try to sell it to one of her own neighbors, as Ab Snopes would probably do. She didn't even answer him. She just said, "Stand over there by that door and be quiet." So Cousin Melisandre went upstairs after all and Granny and Philadelphia went to the parlor for the candlesticks and the medallion and the dulcimer, Philadelphia not only helping this time, free or not, but Granny wasn't even using the clock.

It just all happened at once. One second Ringo was sitting on the gatepost, looking up the road. The next second he was standing on it and waving the cup towel and then I was running and hollering, back to the dining room, and I remember the whites of Joby's and Lucius's and Philadelphia's eyes and I remember Cousin Melisandre's eyes where she leaned against the sideboard with the back of her hand against her mouth, and Granny and Louvinia and Ab Snopes glaring at one another across the trunk and I could hear Louvinia's voice even louder than mine, "Miz Cawmpson! Miz Cawmpson!"

"What?" Granny cried. "What? Mrs. Compson?" Then we all remembered. It was when the first Yankee scouting patrol entered Jefferson over a year ago. The war was new then and I suppose General Compson was the only Jefferson soldier they had heard of yet. Anyway, the officer asked someone in the Square where General Compson lived and old Doctor Holston sent his Negro boy by back alleys and across lots to warn Mrs. Compson in time, and the story was how the Yankee officer sent some of his men through the empty house and himself rode around to the back where old Aunt Roxanne was standing in front of the outhouse behind the closed door of which Mrs. Compson was sitting, fully dressed even to her hat and parasol, on the wicker hamper containing her plate and silver. "Miss in dar," Roxanne said. "Stop where you is." And the story told how the Yankee officer said, "Excuse me," and raised his hat and even backed the horse a few steps before he turned and called his men and rode away. "The privvy!" Granny cried.

"Hell fire, Miz Millard!" Ab Snopes said. And Granny never said anything. It wasn't like she didn't hear, because she was looking right at him. It was like she didn't care; that she might have even said it herself. And that shows how things were then: we just never had time for anything. "Hell fire," Ab Snopes said, "all north Mississippi has done heard about that! There ain't a white lady between here and Memphis that ain't setting in the back house on a grip full of silver right this minute."

"Then we're already late," Granny said. "Hurry."

"Wait!" Ab Snopes said. "Wait! Even them Yankees have done caught onto that by now!"

"Then let's hope these are different Yankees," Granny said. "Hurry."

"But Miz Millard!" Ab Snopes cried. "Wait! Wait!"

But then we could hear Ringo yelling down at the gate and I remember Joby and Lucius and Philadelphia and Louvinia and the balloon-like swaying of Cousin Melisandre's skirts as they ran across the back yard, the trunk somewhere among them; I remember how Joby and Lucius tumbled the trunk into the little tall narrow flimsy sentry-box and Louvinia thrust Cousin Melisandre in and slammed the door and we could hear Ringo yelling good now, almost to the house, and then I was back at the front window and I saw them just as they swept around the house in a kind of straggling clump—six men in blue, riding fast yet with something curious in the action of the horses, as if they were not only yoked together in spans but were hitched to a single wagon tongue, then Ringo on foot running and not yelling now, and last of all the seventh rider, bareheaded and standing in his stirrups and with a sabre over his head. Then I was on the back gallery again, standing beside Granny above that moil of horses and men in the yard, and she was wrong. It was as if these were not only the same ones who had been at Mrs. Compson's last year, but somebody had even told them exactly where our outhouse was. The horses were yoked in pairs, but it was not a wagon tongue, it was a pole, almost a log, twenty feet long, slung from saddle to saddle between the three span; and I remember the faces, unshaven and wan and not so much jeering as frantically gleeful, glaring up at us for an instant before the men leaped down and unslung the pole and jerked the horses aside and picked up the pole, three to a side, and began to run across the yard with it as the last rider came around the house, in gray (an officer: it was Cousin Philip, though of course we didn't know that then, and there was going to be a considerable more uproar and confusion before he finally became Cousin Philip and of course we didn't know that either), the sabre still lifted and not only standing in the stirrups but almost lying down along the horse's neck. The six Yankees never saw him. And we used to watch Father drilling his troop in the pasture, changing them from column to troop front at full gallop, and you could hear his voice even above the sound of the galloping hooves but it wasn't a bit louder than Granny's. "There's a lady in there!" she said. But the Yankees never heard her any more than they had seen Cousin Philip yet, the whole mass of them, the six men running with the pole and Cousin Philip on the horse, leaning out above them with the lifted sabre, rushing on across the yard until the end of the pole struck the outhouse door. It didn't just overturn, it exploded. One second it stood there, tall and narrow and flimsy; the next second it was gone and there was a boil of yelling men in blue coats darting and dodging around under Cousin Philip's horse and the flashing sabre until they could find a chance to turn and run. Then there was a scatter of planks and shingles and Cousin Melisandre sitting beside the trunk in the middle of it, in the spread of her hoops, her eyes shut and her mouth open, still screaming, and after a while a feeble popping of pistol shots from down along the creek that didn't sound any more like war than a boy with firecrackers.

"I tried to tell you to wait!" Ab Snopes said behind us, "I tried to tell you them Yankees had done caught on!"

After Joby and Lucius and Ringo and I finished burying the trunk in the pit and hiding the shovel-marks, I found Cousin Philip in the summerhouse. His sabre and belt were propped against the wall but I don't reckon even he knew what had become of his hat. He had his coat off too and was wiping it with his handkerchief and watching the house with one eye around the edge of the door. When I came in he straightened up and I thought at first he was looking at me. Then I don't know what he was looking at. "That beautiful girl," he said. "Fetch me a comb."

"They're waiting for you in the house," I said. "Granny wants to know what's the matter." Cousin Melisandre was all right now. It took Louvinia and Philadelphia both and finally Granny to get her into the house but Louvinia brought the elder-flower wine before Granny had time to send her after it and now Cousin Melisandre and Granny were waiting in the parlor.

"Your sister," Cousin Philip said. "And a hand mirror."

"No sir," I said. "She's just our cousin. From Memphis. Granny says—" Because he didn't know Granny. It was pretty good for her to wait any time for anybody. But he didn't even let me finish.

"That beautiful, tender girl," he said. "And send a nigger with a basin of water and a towel." I went back toward the house. This time when I looked back I couldn't see his eye around the dooredge. "And a clothes brush," he said.

Granny wasn't waiting very much. She was at the front door. "Now what?" she said. I told her. "Does the man think we are giving a ball here in the middle of the day? Tell him I said to come on in and wash on the back gallery like we do. Louvinia's putting dinner on, and we're already late." But Granny didn't know Cousin Philip either. I told her again. She looked at me. "What did he say?" she said.

"He didn't say anything," I said. "Just that beautiful girl."

"That's all he said to me too," Ringo said. I hadn't heard him come in. "'Sides the soap and water. Just that beautiful girl."

"Was he looking at you either when he said it?" I said.

"No," Ringo said. "I just thought for a minute he was."

Now Granny looked at Ringo and me both. "Hah," she said, and afterward when I was older I found out that Granny already knew Cousin Philip too, that she could look at one of them and know all the other Cousin Melisandres and Cousin Philips both without having to see them. "I sometimes think that bullets are just about the least fatal things that fly, especially in war. All right," she said, "Take him his soap and water. But hurry."

We did. This time he didn't say "that beautiful girl." He said it twice. He took off his coat and handed it to Ringo. "Brush it good," he said. "Your sister, I heard you say."

"No you didn't," I said.

"No matter," he said. "I want a nosegay. To carry in my hand."

"Those flowers are Granny's," I said.

"No matter," he said. He rolled up his sleeves and began to wash. "A small one. About a dozen blooms. Get something pink."

I went and got the flowers. I don't know whether Granny was still at the front door or not. Maybe she wasn't. At least she never said anything. So I picked the ones Ab Snopes's new Yankee horse had already trompled down and wiped the dirt off of them and straightened them out and went back to the summer house where Ringo was holding the hand glass while Cousin Philip combed his hair. Then he put on his coat and buckled on his sabre again and held his feet out one at a time for Ringo to wipe his boots off with the towel, and Ringo saw it. I wouldn't have spoken at all because we were already later for dinner than ever now, even if there hadn't never been a Yankee on the place. "You tore your britches on them Yankees," Ringo said.

So I went back to the house. Granny was standing in the hall. This time she just said, "Yes?" It was almost quiet.

"He tore his britches," I said. And she knew more about Cousin Philip than even Ringo could find out by looking at him. She had the needle already threaded in the bosom of her dress. And I went back to the summerhouse and then we came back to the house and up to the front door and I waited for him to go into the hall but he didn't, he just stood there holding the nosegay in one hand and his hat in the other, not very old, looking at that moment anyway not very much older than Ringo and me for all his braid and sash and sabre and boots and spurs, and even after just two years looking like all our soldiers and most of the other people too did: as if it had been so long now since he had had all he wanted to eat at one time that even his memory and palate had forgotten it and only his body remembered, standing there with his nosegay and that beautiful girl look in his face like he couldn't have seen anything even if he had been looking at it.

"No," he said. "Announce me. It should be your nigger. But no matter." He said his full name, all three of them, twice, as if he thought I might forget them before I could reach the parlor.

"Go on in," I said. "They're waiting for you. They had already been waiting for you even before you found your pants were torn."

"Announce me," he said. He said his name again. "Of Tennessee. Lieutenant, Savage's Battalion, Forrest's Command, Provisional Army, Department of the West."

So I did. We crossed the hall to the parlor, where Granny stood between Cousin Melisandre's chair and the table where the decanter of elder-flower wine and three fresh glasses and even a plate of the tea cakes Louvinia had learned to make from cornmeal and molasses were sitting, and he stopped again at that door too and I know he couldn't even see Cousin Melisandre for a minute, even though he never had looked at anything else but her. "Lieutenant Philip St-Just Backhouse," I said. I said it loud, because he had repeated it to me three times so I would be sure to get it right and I wanted to say it to suit him too since even if he had made us a good hour late for dinner, at least he had saved the silver. "Of Tennessee," I said. "Savage's Battalion, Forrest's Command, Provisional Army, Department of the West."

While you could count maybe five, there wasn't anything at all. Then Cousin Melisandre screamed. She sat bolt upright on the chair like she had sat beside the trunk in the litter of planks and shingles in the back yard this morning, with her eyes shut and her mouth open again, screaming.

3

So we were still another half an hour late for dinner. Though this time it never needed anybody but Cousin Philip to get Cousin Melisandre upstairs. All he needed to do was to try to speak to her again. Then Granny came back down and said, "Well, if we don't want to just quit and start calling it supper, we'd better walk in and eat it within the next hour and a half at least." So we walked in. Ab Snopes was already waiting in the dining room. I reckon he had been waiting longer than anybody, because after all Cousin Melisandre wasn't any kin to him. Ringo drew Granny's chair and we sat down. Some of it was cold. The rest of it had been on the stove so long now that when you ate it it didn't matter whether it was cold or not. But Cousin Philip didn't seem to mind. And maybe it didn't take his memory very long to remember again what it was like to have all he wanted to eat, but I don't think his palate ever tasted any of it. He would sit there eating like he hadn't seen any food of any kind in at least a week, and like he was expecting what was even already on his fork to vanish before he could get it into his mouth. Then he would stop with the fork halfway to his mouth and sit there looking at Cousin Melisandre's empty place, laughing. That is, I don't know what else to call it but laughing. Until at last I said, "Why don't you change your name?"

Then Granny quit eating too. She looked at me over her spectacles. Then she took both hands and lifted the spectacles up her nose until she could look at me through them. Then she even pushed the spectacles up into her front hair and looked at me. "That's the first sensible thing I've heard said on this place since eleven o'clock this morning," she said. "It's so sensible and simple that I reckon only a child could have thought of it." She looked at him. "Why don't you?"

He laughed some more. That is, his face did the same way and he made the same sound again. "My grandfather was at King's Mountain, with Marion all through Carolina. My uncle was defeated for Governor of Tennessee by a corrupt and traitorous cabal of tavern keepers and Republican Abolitionists and my father died at Chapultepec. After that, the name they bore is not mine to change. Even my life is not mine so long as my country lies bleeding and ravished beneath an invader's iron heel." Then he stopped laughing, or whatever it was. Then his face looked surprised. Then it quit looking surprised, the surprise fading out of it steady at first and gradually faster but not very much faster like the heat fades out of a piece of iron on a blacksmith's anvil until his face just looked amazed and quiet and almost peaceful. "Unless I lose it in battle," he said.

"You can't very well do that sitting here," Granny said.

"No," he said. But I don't think he even heard her except with his ears. He stood up. Even Ab Snopes was watching him now, his knife stopped halfway to his mouth with a wad of greens on the end of the blade. "Yes," Cousin Philip said. His face even had the beautiful-girl-look on it again. "Yes," he said. He thanked Granny for his dinner. That is, I reckon that's what he had told his mouth to say. It didn't make much sense to us, but I don't think he was paying any attention to it at all. He bowed. He wasn't looking at Granny nor at anything else. He said "Yes" again. Then he went out. Ringo and I followed to the front door and watched him mount his horse and sit there for a minute, bareheaded, looking up at the upstairs windows. It was Granny's room he was looking at, with mine and Ringo's room next to it. But Cousin Melisandre couldn't have seen him even if she had been in either one of them since she was in bed on the other side of the house with Philadelphia probably still wringing the cloths out in cold water to lay on her head. He sat the horse well. He rode it well too: light and easy and back in the saddle and toes in and perpendicular from angle to knee as Father had taught me. It was a good horse too.

"It's a damn good horse," I said.

"Git the soap," Ringo said.

But even then I looked quick back down the hall, even if I could hear Granny talking to Ab Snopes in the dining room. "She's still in there," I said.

"Hah," Ringo said. "I done tasted soap in my mouth for a cuss I thought was a heap further off than that."

Then Cousin Philip spurred the horse and was gone. Or so Ringo and I thought. Two hours ago none of us had ever even heard of him; Cousin Melisandre had seen him twice and sat with her eyes shut screaming both times. But after we were older, Ringo and I realized that Cousin Philip was probably the only one in the whole lot of us that really believed even for one moment that he had said good-by forever, that not only Granny and Louvinia knew better but Cousin Melisandre did too, no matter what his last name had the bad luck to be.

We went back to the dining room. Then I realized that Ab Snopes had been waiting for us to come back. Then we both knew he was going to ask Granny something because nobody wanted to be alone when they had to ask Granny something even when they didn't know they were going to have trouble with it. We had known Ab for over a year now. I should have known what it was like. Granny already did. He stood up. "Well, Miz Millard," he said. "I figger you'll be safe all right from now on, with Bed Forrest and his boys right there in Jefferson. But until things quiet down a mite more, I'll just leave the horses in your lot for a day or two."

"What horses?" Granny said. She and Ab didn't just look at one another. They watched one another.

"Them fresh-captured horses from this morning," Ab said.

"What horses?" Granny said. Then Ab said it.

"My horses." Ab watched her.

"Why?" Granny said. But Ab knew what she meant.

"I'm the only grown man here," he said. Then he said, "I seen them first. They were chasing me before. . . ." Then he said, talking fast now; his eyes had gone kind of glazed for a second but now they were bright again, looking in the stubbly dirt-covered fuzz on his face like two chips of broken plate in a worn-out door mat, "Spoils of war! I brought them here! I tolled them in here: a military and-bush! And as the only and ranking Confedrit military soldier present. . . ."

"You ain't a soldier," Granny said. "You stipulated that to Colonel Sartoris yourself while I was listening. You told him yourself you would be his independent horse-captain but nothing more."

"Ain't that just exactly what I am trying to be?" he said. "Didn't I bring all six of them horses in here in my own possession, the same as if I was leading them on a rope?"

"Hah," Granny said. "A spoil of war or any other kind of spoil don't belong to a man or a woman either until they can take it home and put it down and turn their back on it. You never had time to get home with even the one you were riding. You ran in the first open gate you came to, no matter whose gate it was."

"Except it was the wrong one," he said. His eyes quit looking like china. They didn't look like anything. But I reckon his face would still look like an old doormat even after he had turned all the way white. "So I reckon I got to even walk back to town," he said. "The woman that would. . . ." His voice stopped. He and Granny looked at one another.

"Don't you say it," Granny said.

"Nome," he said. He didn't say it. ". . . a man of seven horses ain't likely to lend him a mule."

"No," Granny said. "But you won't have to walk."

We all went out to the lot. I don't reckon that even Ab knew until then that Granny had already found where he thought he had hidden the first horse and had it brought up to the lot with the other six. But at least he already had his saddle and bridle with him. But it was too late. Six of the horses moved about loose in the lot. The seventh one was tied just inside the gate with a piece of plow-line. It wasn't the horse Ab had come on because that horse had a blaze. Ab had known Granny long enough too. He should have known. Maybe he did. But at least he tried. He opened the gate.

"Well," he said, "it ain't getting no earlier. I reckon I better. . . ."

"Wait," Granny said. Then we looked at the horse which was tied to the fence. At first glance it looked the best one of the seven. You had to see it just right to tell its near leg was sprung a little, maybe from being worked too hard too young under too much weight. "Take that one," Granny said.

"That ain't mine," Ab said. "That's yourn. I'll just. . . ."

"Take that one," Granny said. Ab looked at her. You could have counted at least ten.

"Hell fire, Miz Millard," he said.

"I've told you before about cursing on this place," Granny said.

"Yessum," Ab said. Then he said it again, "Hell fire." He went into the lot and rammed the bit into the tied horse's mouth and clapped the saddle on and snatched the piece of plow-line off and threw it over the fence and got up and Granny stood there until he had ridden out of the lot and Ringo closed the gate and that was the first time I noticed the chain and padlock from the smokehouse door and Ringo locked it and handed Granny the key and Ab sat for a minute, looking down at her. "Well, good day," he said. "I just hope for the sake of the Confedricy that Bed Forrest don't never tangle with you with all the horses he's got." Then he said it again, maybe worse this time because now he was already on a horse pointed toward the gate, "Or you'll damn shore leave him just one more passel of infantry before he can spit twice."

Then he was gone too. Except for hearing Cousin Melisandre now and then, and those six horses with U. S. branded on their hips standing in the lot, it might never have happened. At least Ringo and I thought that was all of it. Every now and then Philadelphia would come downstairs with the pitcher and draw some more cold water for Cousin Melisandre's cloths but we thought that after a while even that would just wear out and quit. Then Philadelphia came down again and came into where Granny was cutting down a pair of Yankee pants that Father had worn home last time so they would fit Ringo. She didn't say anything. She just stood in the door until Granny said, "All right. What now?"

"She want the banjo," Philadelphia said.

"What?" Granny said. "My dulcimer? She can't play it. Go back upstairs."

But Philadelphia didn't move. "Could I ax Mammy to come help me?"

"No," Granny said. "Louvinia's resting. She's had about as much of this as I want her to stand. Go back upstairs. Give her some more wine if you can't think of anything else." And she told Ringo and me to go somewhere else, anywhere else, but even in the yard you could still hear Cousin Melisandre talking to Philadelphia. And once we even heard Granny though it was still mostly Cousin Melisandre telling Granny that she had already forgiven her, that nothing whatever had happened and that all she wanted now was peace. And after a while Louvinia came up from the cabin without even being sent for and went upstairs and then it began to look like we were going to be late for supper too. But Philadelphia finally came down and cooked it and carried Cousin Melisandre's tray up and then we quit eating, we could hear Louvinia overhead, in Granny's room now, and she came down and set the untasted tray on the table and stood beside Granny's chair with the key to the trunk in her hand.

"All right," Granny said. "Go call Joby and Lucius." We got the lantern and the shovels. We went to the orchard and removed the brush and dug up the trunk and got the dulcimer and buried the trunk and put the brush back and brought the key in to Granny. And Ringo and I could hear her from our room and Granny was right. We heard her for a long time and Granny was surely right; she just never said but half of it. The moon came up after a while and we could look down from our window into the garden, at Cousin Melisandre sitting on the bench with the moonlight glinting on the pearl inlay of the dulcimer, and Philadelphia squatting on the sill of the gate with her apron over her head. Maybe she was asleep. It was already late. But I don't see how.

So we didn't hear Granny until she was already in the room, her shawl over her nightgown and carrying a candle. "In a minute I'm going to have about all of this I aim to stand too," she said. "Go wake Lucius and tell him to saddle the mule," she told Ringo. "Bring me the pen and ink and a sheet of paper." I fetched them. She didn't sit down. She stood at the bureau while I held the candle, writing even and steady and not very much, and signed her name and let the paper lie open to dry until Lucius came in. "Ab Snopes said that Mr. Forrest is in Jefferson," she told Lucius. "Find him. Tell him I will expect him here for breakfast in the morning and to bring that boy." She used to know General Forrest in Memphis before he got to be a general. He used to trade with Grandfather Millard's supply house and sometimes he would come out to sit with Grandfather on the front gallery and sometimes he would eat with them. "You can tell him I have six captured horses for him," she said. "And never mind patter-rollers or soldiers either. Haven't you got my signature on that paper?"

"I ain't worrying about them," Lucius said. "But suppose them Yankees. . . ."

"I see," Granny said. "Hah. I forgot. You've been waiting for Yankees, haven't you? But those this morning seemed to be too busy trying to stay free to have much time to talk about it, didn't they? Get along," she said. "Do you think any Yankee is going to dare ignore what a Southern soldier or even a patter-roller wouldn't? And you go to bed," she said.

We lay down, both of us on Ringo's pallet. We heard the mule when Lucius left. Then we heard the mule and at first we didn't know we had been asleep, the mule coming back now and the moon had started down the west and Cousin Melisandre and Philadelphia were gone from the garden, to where Philadelphia at least could sleep better than sitting on a square sill with an apron over her head, or at least where it was quieter. And we heard Lucius fumbling up the stairs but we never heard Granny at all because she was already at the top of the stairs, talking down at the noise Lucius was trying not to make. "Speak up," she said. "I ain't asleep but I ain't a lipreader either. Not in the dark."

"Genl Fawhrest say he respectful compliments," Lucius said, "and he can't come to breakfast this morning because he gonter to be whupping Genl Smith at Tallahatchie Crossing about that time. But providin he ain't too fur away in the wrong direction when him and Genl Smith git done, he be proud to accept your invitation next time he in the neighborhood. And he say 'whut boy.' "

While you could count about five, Granny didn't say anything. Then she said, "What?"

"He say 'whut boy,' " Lucius said.

Then you could have counted ten. All we could hear was

Lucius breathing. Then Granny said, "Did you wipe the mule down?"

"Yessum," Lucius said.

"Did you turn her back into the pasture?"

"Yessum," Lucius said.

"Then go to bed," Granny said. "And you too," she said.

General Forrest found out what boy. This time we didn't know we had been asleep either, and it was no one mule now. The sun was just rising. When we heard Granny and scrambled to the window, yesterday wasn't a patch on it. There were at least fifty of them now, in gray; the whole outdoors was full of men on horses, with Cousin Philip out in front of them, sitting his horse in almost exactly the same spot where he had been yesterday, looking up at Granny's window and not seeing it or anything else this time either. He had a hat now. He was holding it clamped over his heart and he hadn't shaved and yesterday he had looked younger than Ringo because Ringo always had looked about ten years older than me. But now, with the first sun-ray making a little soft fuzz in the gold-colored stubble on his face, he looked even younger than I did, and gaunt and worn in the face like he hadn't slept any last night and something else in his face too: like he not only hadn't slept last night but by godfrey he wasn't going to sleep tonight either as long as he had anything to do with it. "Good-by," he said. "Good-by," and whirled his horse, spurring, and raised the new hat over his head like he had carried the sabre yesterday and the whole mass of them went piling back across flower beds and lawns and all and back down the drive toward the gate while Granny still stood at her window in her nightgown, her voice louder than any man's anywhere, I don't care who he is or what he would be doing, "Backhouse! Backhouse! You, Backhouse!"

So we ate breakfast early. Granny sent Ringo in his nightshirt to wake Louvinia and Lucius both. So Lucius had the mule saddled before Louvinia even got the fire lit. This time Granny didn't write a note. "Go to Tallahatchie Crossing," she told Lucius. "Sit there and wait for him if necessary."

"Suppose they done already started the battle?" Lucius said.

"Suppose they have?" Granny said. "What business is that of yours or mine either? You find Bedford Forrest. Tell him this is important; it won't take long. But don't you show your face here again without him."

Lucius rode away. He was gone four days. He didn't even get back in time for the wedding, coming back up the drive about sundown on the fourth day with two soldiers in one of General Forrest's forage wagons with the mule tied to the tail gate.

He didn't know where he had been and he never did catch up with the battle. "I never even heard it," he told Joby and Louvinia and Philadelphia and Ringo and me. "If wars always moves that far and that fast, I don't see how they ever have time to fight."

But it was all over then. It was the second day, the day after Lucius left. It was just after dinner this time and by now we were used to soldiers. But these were different, just five of them, and we never had seen just that few of them before and we had come to think of soldiers as either jumping on and off horses in the yard or going back and forth through Granny's flower beds at full gallop. These were all officers and I reckon maybe I hadn't seen so many soldiers after all because I never saw this much braid before. They came up the drive at a trot, like people just taking a ride, and stopped without trompling even one flower bed and General Forrest got down and came up the walk toward where Granny waited on the front gallery—a big, dusty man with a big beard so black it looked almost blue and eyes like a sleepy owl, already taking off his hat. "Well, Miss Rosie," he said.

"Don't call me Rosie," Granny said. "Come in. Ask your gentlemen to alight and come in."

"They'll wait there," General Forrest said. "We are a little rushed. My plans have. . . ." Then we were in the library. He wouldn't sit down. He looked tired all right, but there was something else a good deal livelier than just tired. "Well, Miss Rosie," he said. "I. . . ."

"Don't call me Rosie," Granny said. "Can't you even say Rosa?"

"Yessum," he said. But he couldn't. At least, he never did. "I reckon we both have had about enough of this. That boy. . . ."

"Hah," Granny said. "Night before last you were saying what boy. Where is he? I sent you word to bring him with you."

"Under arrest," General Forrest said. It was a considerable more than just tired. "I spent four days getting Smith just where I wanted him. After that, this boy here could have fought the battle." He said "fit" for fought just as he said "druv" for drove and "drug" for dragged. But maybe when you fought battles like he did, even Granny didn't mind how you talked. "I won't bother you with details. He didn't know them either. All he had to do was exactly what I told him. I did everything but draw a diagram on his coat tail of exactly what he was to do, no more and no less, from the time he left me until he saw me again: which was to make contact and then fall back. I gave him just exactly the right number of men so that he couldn't do anything else but that. I told him exactly how fast to fall back and how much racket to make doing it and even how to make the racket. But what do you think he did?"

"I can tell you," Granny said. "He sat on his horse at five o'clock yesterday morning, with my whole yard full of men behind him, yelling good-by at my window."

"He divided his men and sent half of them into the bushes to make a noise and took the other half who were the nearest to complete fools and led a sabre charge on that outpost. He didn't fire a shot. He drove it clean back with sabres onto Smith's main body and scared Smith so that he threw out all his cavalry and pulled out behind it and now I don't know whether I'm about to catch him or he's about to catch me. My Provost finally caught the boy last night. He had come back and got the other thirty men of his company and was twenty miles ahead again, trying to find something to lead another charge against. 'Do you want to be killed?' I said. 'Not especially,' he said. 'That is, I don't especially care one way or the other.' 'Then neither do

I,' I said. 'But you risked a whole company of my men.' 'Ain't that what they enlisted for?' he said. 'They enlisted into a military establishment the purpose of which is to expend each man only at a profit. Or maybe you don't consider me a shrewd enough trader in human meat?' 'I can't say,' he said. 'Since day before yesterday I ain't thought very much about how you or anybody else runs this war.' 'And just what were you doing day before yesterday that changed your ideas and habits?' I said. 'Fighting some of it,' he said. 'Dispersing the enemy.' 'Where?' I said. 'At a lady's house a few miles from Jefferson,' he said. 'One of the niggers called her Granny like the white boy did. The others called her Miss Rosie.' " This time Granny didn't say anything. She just waited.

"Go on," she said.

" 'I'm still trying to win battles, even if since day before yesterday you ain't,' I said. 'I'll send you down to Johnston at Jackson,' I said. 'He'll put you inside Vicksburg, where you can lead private charges day and night too if you want.' 'Like hell you will,' he said. And I said—excuse me—'Like hell I won't.' " And Granny didn't say anything. It was like day before yesterday with Ab Snopes: not like she hadn't heard but as if right now it didn't matter, that this was no time either to bother with such.

"And did you?" she said.

"I can't. He knows it. You can't punish a man for routing an enemy four times his weight. What would I say back there in Tennessee, where we both live, let alone that uncle of his, the one they licked for Governor six years ago, on Bragg's personal staff now, with his face over Bragg's shoulder every time Bragg opens a dispatch or picks up a pen. And I'm still trying to win battles. But I can't. Because of a girl, one single lone young female girl that ain't got anything under the sun against him except that, since it was his misfortune to save her from a passel of raiding enemy in a situation that everybody but her is trying to forget, she can't seem to bear to hear his last name. Yet because of that, every battle I plan from now on will be at the mercy of a twenty-two-year-old shavetail—excuse me again—who might decide to lead a private charge any time he can holler at least two men in gray coats into moving in the same direction." He stopped. He looked at Granny. "Well?" he said.

"So now you've got to it," Granny said. "Well what, Mr. Forrest?"

"Why, just have done with this foolishness. I told you I've got that boy, in close arrest, with a guard with a bayonet. But there won't be any trouble there. I figured even yesterday morning that he had already lost his mind. But I reckon he's recovered enough of it since the Provost took him last night to comprehend that I still consider myself his commander even if he don't. So all that's necessary now is for you to put your foot down. Put it down hard. Now. You're her grandma. She lives in your home. And it looks like she is going to live in it a good while yet before she gets back to Memphis to that uncle or whoever it is that calls himself her guardian. So just put your foot down. Make her. Mr. Millard would have already done that if he had been here. And I know when. It would have been two days ago by now."

Granny waited until he got done. She stood with her arms crossed, holding each elbow in the other hand. "Is that all I'm to do?" she said.

"Yes," General Forrest said. "If she don't want to listen to you right at first, maybe as his commander. . . ."

Granny didn't even say "Hah." She didn't even send me. She didn't even stop in the hall and call. She went upstairs herself and we stood there and I thought maybe she was going to bring the dulcimer too and I thought how if I was General Forrest I would go back and get Cousin Philip and make him sit in the library until about supper-time while Cousin Melisandre played the dulcimer and sang. Then he could take Cousin Philip on back and then he could finish the war without worrying.

She didn't have the dulcimer. She just had Cousin Melisandre. They came in and Granny stood to one side again with her arms crossed, holding her elbows. "Here she is," she said. "Say it . . . this is Mr. Bedford Forrest," she told Cousin Melisandre. "Say it," she told General Forrest.

He didn't have time. When Cousin Melisandre first came, she tried to read aloud to Ringo and me. It wasn't much. That is, what she insisted on reading to us wasn't so bad, even if it was mostly about ladies looking out windows and playing on something (maybe they were dulcimers too) while somebody else was off somewhere fighting. It was the way she read it. When Granny said this is Mister Forrest, Cousin Melisandre's face looked exactly like her voice would sound when she read to us. She took two steps into the library, and curtsied, spreading her hoops back, and stood up. "General Forrest," she said. "I am acquainted with an associate of his. Will the General please give him the sincerest wishes for triumph in war and success in love, from one who will never see him again?" Then she curtsied again and spread her hoops backward and stood up and took two steps backward and turned and went out.

After a while Granny said, "Well, Mr. Forrest?"

General Forrest began to cough. He lifted his coattail with one hand and reached the other into his hip pocket like he was going to pull at least a musket out of it and got his handkerchief and coughed into it a while. It wasn't very clean. It looked about like the one Cousin Philip was trying to wipe his coat off with in the summerhouse day before yesterday. Then he put the handkerchief back. He didn't say "Hah" either. "Can I reach the Holly Branch road without having to go through Jefferson?" he said.

Then Granny moved. "Open the desk," she said. "Lay out a sheet of note paper." I did. And I remember how I stood at one side of the desk and General Forrest at the other, and watched Granny's hand move the pen steady and not very slow and not very long across the paper because it never did take her very long to say anything, no matter what it was, whether she was talking it or writing it. Though I didn't see it then, but only later, when it hung framed under glass above Cousin Melisandre's and Cousin Philip's mantel: the fine steady slant of Granny's hand and General Forrest's sprawling signatures below it that looked itself a good deal like a charge of massed cavalry:

Lieutenant P. S. Backhouse, Company D, Tennessee Cavalry, was this day raised to the honorary rank of Brevet Major General & killed while engaging the enemy. Vice whom Philip St-Just Backus is hereby appointed Lieutenant, Company D, Tennessee Cavalry.
N. B. Forrest Genl.

I didn't see it then. General Forrest picked it up. "Now I've got to have a battle," he said. "Another sheet, son." I laid that one out on the desk.

"A battle?" Granny said.

"To give Johnston," he said. "Confound it, Miss Rosie, can't you understand either that I'm just a fallible mortal man trying to run a military command according to certain fixed and inviolable rules, no matter how foolish the business looks to superior outside folks?"

"All right," Granny said. "You had one. I was looking at it."

"So I did," General Forrest said. "Hah," he said. "The battle of Sartoris."

"No," Granny said. "Not at my house."

"They did all the shooting down at the creek," I said.

"What creek?" he said.

So I told him. It ran through the pasture. Its name was Hurricane Creek but not even the white people called it hurricane except Granny. General Forrest didn't either when he sat down at the desk and wrote the report to General Johnston at Jackson:

A unit of my command on detached duty engaged a body of the enemy & drove him from the field & dispersed him this day 28th ult. April 1862 at Harrykin Creek. With loss of one man.
N. B. Forrest Genl.

I saw that. I watched him write it. Then he got up and folded the sheets into his pocket and was already going toward the table where his hat was.

"Wait," Granny said. "Lay out another sheet," she said. "Come back here."

General Forrest stopped and turned. "Another one?"

"Yes!" Granny said. "A furlough, pass—whatever you busy

military establishments call them! So John Sartoris can come home long enough. . . ." and she said it herself, she looked straight at me and even backed up and said some of it over as though to make sure there wouldn't be any mistake, ". . . can come back home and give away that damn bride!"

4

And that was all. The day came and Granny waked Ringo and me before sunup and we ate what breakfast we had from two plates on the back steps. And we dug up the trunk and brought it into the house and polished the silver and Ringo and I brought dogwood and redbud branches from the pasture and Granny cut the flowers, all of them, cutting them herself with Cousin Melisandre and Philadelphia just carrying the baskets; so many of them until the house was so full that Ringo and I would believe we smelled them even across the pasture each time we came up. Though of course we could, it was just the food—the last ham from the smokehouse and the chickens and the flour which Granny had been saving and the last of the sugar which she had been saving along with the bottle of champagne for the day when the North surrendered—which Louvinia had been cooking for two days now, to remind us each time we approached the house of what was going on and that the flowers were there. As if we could have forgotten about the food. And they dressed Cousin Melisandre and, Ringo in his new blue pants and I in my gray ones which were not so new, we stood in the late afternoon on the gallery—Granny and Cousin Melisandre and Louvinia and Philadelphia and Ringo and I—and watched them enter the gate. General Forrest was not one. Ringo and I had thought maybe he might be, if only to bring Cousin Philip. Then we thought that maybe, since Father was coming anyway, General Forrest would let Father bring him, with Cousin Philip maybe handcuffed to Father and the soldier with the bayonet following, or maybe still just handcuffed to the soldier until he and Cousin Melisandre were married and Father unlocked him.

But General Forrest wasn't one, and Cousin Philip wasn't

handcuffed to anybody and there was no bayonet and not even a soldier because these were all officers too. And we stood in the parlor while the home-made candles burnt in the last of sunset in the bright candlesticks which Philadelphia and Ringo and I had polished with the rest of the silver because Granny and Louvinia were both busy cooking and even Cousin Melisandre polished a little of it although Louvinia could pick out the ones she polished without hardly looking and hand them to Philadelphia to polish again:—Cousin Melisandre in the dress which hadn't needed to be altered for her at all because Mother wasn't much older than Cousin Melisandre even when she died, and which would still button on Granny too just like it did the day she married in it, and the chaplain and Father and Cousin Philip and the four others in their gray and braid and sabres and Cousin Melisandre's face was all right now and Cousin Philip's was too because it just had the beautiful girl look on it and none of us had ever seen him look any other way.

Then we ate, and Ringo and I anyway had been waiting on that for three days and then we did it and then it was over too, fading just a little each day until the palate no longer remembered and only our mouths would run a little water as we would name the dishes aloud to one another, until even the water would run less and less and less and it would take something we just hoped to eat someday if they ever got done fighting, to make it run at all.

And that was all. The last sound of wheel and hoof died away, Philadelphia came in from the parlor carrying the candlesticks and blowing out the candles as she came, and Louvinia set the kitchen clock on the table and gathered the last of soiled silver from supper into the dishpan and it might never have even been. "Well," Granny said. She didn't move, leaning her forearms on the table a little and we had never seen that before. She spoke to Ringo without turning her head, "Go call Joby and Lucius." And even when we brought the trunk in and set it against the wall and opened back the lid, she didn't move. She didn't even look at Louvinia either. "Put the clock in too," she said. "I don't think we'll bother to time ourselves tonight."

BLUE BIRD

by FREDA THOMPSON

DANNY DROPPED A NICKEL INTO THE SLOT TELEPHONE, AND held the receiver several inches away from his ear until the bell had rung. Then he dialed his number and listened for the long burring sound that meant the telephone was ringing on the other end. Once, twice, it burred; then, "Hello?"

"That you, Stell? Say, Stell, I got to go out on a job for the boss tonight."

"You mean you're not showing up on a Saturday night?" Stell's voice had a vulgar note in it.

"Now, listen, Stell, be reasonable. I got to work. Gas leak—"

"Oh, yeah?" Stell cut him short. "Well, you listen, Mr. Husky; I've heard that one before."

"But Stell," he protested, "you don't think I'd lie to you, do you?"

"Not much," she answered, "you and George Washington. Come up and see me some time," and she hung up the receiver.

Danny shrugged his shoulders irritably as he left the telephone booth, chewing his gum reflectively. Stell was a good kid, but too suspicious. He liked the trusting type, like Louise. There was a girl who was on the level, and figured you were, too. He guessed that's why he had married her.

But as he headed down into the subway, he began worrying again. Had Louise gotten wise to him or something? It was Johnny's crack about him thinking he could eat his cake and have it, too, that had gotten him to worrying. Johnny was the boss plumber's right-hand man—an odd duck, with a lot of screwy ideas. He had laughed derisively at Danny. There was always something back of it when Johnny grinned in just that way.

"What's the matter with you, fella?" Danny had asked him, "you're human, aren't you?"

"Sure," Johnny answered, "I'm human. But I've got this thing figured. Everything's got to balance, see? You can't beat the scales. I figure this way: I keep my life on the level, and I get a lot of pleasure out of nothing—"

"How do you mean, nothing?"

Johnny looked self-conscious. "Well, like when I'm sitting on the front porch of our summer shack; I hear the crickets, and the fog comes in, rolling over the fields—stuff like that."

Danny had grunted his bewilderment, and Johnny continued thoughtfully, "It's like this: I'm right there in anything I'm doing, and I'm satisfied doing it. See what I mean? If I helled around, I'd lose that—and I figure the price is too high for me, that's all."

It sounded screwy to Danny. You had to take life the way it was, and it was only human to run around. He was glad that he hadn't gone on foursomes with Johnny and his wife, the way they had wanted him and Louise to do. Johnny might let something slip out; he knew too much about Danny. Better to keep Louise away from anybody he knew.

When Johnny made the crack about his thinking he could eat his cake and have it, too, he wondered what the idea was. He hadn't done anything to Johnny, unless he was sore about his loafing on the job this morning; but he had a hang-over and he felt rotten.

But his crack had gotten Danny to thinking about Louise. The more he thought about her, the more he thought he had better find out what was wrong with her, and if she knew about his running around. That's why he had broken his date with Stell. He thought if he got Louise good and tight, she would tell him what she was hiding inside. He automatically touched the bottle of rye whiskey in his pocket to reassure himself that it was there. Louise couldn't take much to drink, just a little beer once in a while, and rye would make her tighter than a tick. She was a quiet one, but once or twice she had had too much to drink and had talked her head off.

The subway train pulled in at the station, and he found a seat easily; it was past the busy hour. The doors slammed together, and the train rushing on and on through the blackness of the underground tunnel lulled him, and started his memories going. He remembered the way Louise had looked the first time he saw her. It was a Monday morning, and he had gotten into the office late to pick up his calls. There she was, typing in her halting fashion, a slip of a thing with beautiful legs and big black eyes. He liked her hands, too; they were slender and soft, but they were strong, as though she weren't afraid to use them. He had approached her politely, and deferential-like; you had to go easy with the refined type. No wisecracks. She had blushed when she handed him his calls for the day, and he thanked her with his hat off. She was standoffish; not easy to get acquainted with the way most of the girls he knew were; but he had burned with a desire to possess her, like a collector after a rare gem.

And she had turned out to be a rare gem, too. Besides being a lady, she had turned out to be regular. It was an agreeable surprise to Danny, Louise's response to his love-making. It seemed to him in spite of all his experience, he had never known what sex was like before. With Louise it was like singing on a mountain top. Danny thought of it that way because he had sung in a choir when he was a kid, and the church had sent the choir to the mountains one wonderful summer for a month as a reward for their work.

There was another thing that was different about Louise, too; and that was the beautiful things she said afterwards. She wasn't one to talk much, but she had a way of saying things you couldn't forget. Like the time she said, "The word 'husband' is a wonderful word. I think and think about it and what it means. It's wonderful." And she said another time, "To think that every night, for the rest of our lives, we will share the lovely sleeping hours together. Every single night we'll close our eyes and go to sleep, right here together." Things like that. It made it all different.

But for a long time now she hadn't said anything at all afterwards. He even wondered if it had gotten to the place where he just filled the need in her life that everybody had—like eating so that hunger wouldn't torment you. He'd find out tonight what had brought the change about; whether she was sore that he was running around without letting on she knew about it.

The train stopped; passengers got off and others got on. The doors closed and the train was in motion again. Danny looked across at a tall blonde who had just taken a seat opposite him, his eyes traveling from the ankle bracelet up. She had the mask-like face of a mannequin, and heavy make-up. Her dress was one of the new pencil silhouettes, black satin, cut low in the neck, with short sleeves; a late summer model that came in just before the fall models, for girls who were tired of their summer things. Danny knew, because he was crazy about clothes. He was wearing a Palm Beach suit that he had bought at De Pinna's; a rich tan that contrasted nicely with his sandy hair and made his gray eyes look a sort of golden. He wished, however, that he had been wearing his new fall outfit; there was class to that, and it made him look like Somebody.

The girl returned his bold stare coolly; he could smell the heavy spicy perfume she was wearing: sophisticated. He liked the smell.

They looked at one another without so much as a flicker of an eyelash; then several people got up and stood in front of the girl, hanging to the straps, waiting for the train to pull in at the next station. The girl got up, too, and when the train had left the station, an elderly gentleman was in her place.

"She's an expensive doll, anyway, good riddance to her," Danny told himself, "she'd want to ritz around at the Fork Club, and those places, or you'd be a cheap skate—"

The long subway ride was getting on his nerves. Why did Louise have to live on Washington Heights? She said the air was better up there for the kid, and they got more space for their money. But it was hard on him, and after all, wasn't he the breadwinner? He should have first consideration. His eyes wandered up to the ads, but he knew them by heart already; then he tried reading the headlines on the back of the paper the old gentleman opposite him was holding out at full length. Danny wasn't much for reading; he was too restless to put his mind on it. He liked the tabloids all right; there were plenty of pictures to look at, and you got the stuff quickly.

At last he reached his station. He walked into the street with an air of relief; the August evenings were cool, although the subway still held the heat. He climbed up the hill to the apartment house where he lived, and told himself the entrance wasn't half bad; two imposing lions and good-looking plate-glass doors. He might not be able to afford a summer shack the way Johnny did for his family; but Johnny was a different type, he didn't have personal expenses.

He got into the self-service elevator, and pushed the button for the fifth floor. He could hear the voices of his wife and son even before he put his key into the lock. He couldn't hear what they were saying, but they seemed to be having fun. He came home so seldom at this hour, before Junior was in bed, that for a moment he felt like an intruder. He resented feeling this way, and it put him out of sorts.

Louise looked up with a smile of welcome as he came into the small living room. She was sitting on the rag rug she had chosen to carry out the Early American scheme of the room when they couldn't afford the hooked rugs she had wanted. The child was picking up wooden animals from the floor and putting them into a bright yellow ark trimmed with red.

Danny looked at his gold wrist watch with an air of disapproval. "Isn't he in bed yet?" he asked.

"He takes a nap in the afternoon," Louise explained, "he doesn't go to sleep if he's put to bed too early." Then anxiously, "Have you had dinner? I didn't wait for you, you said you had to work—"

"I've eaten," he said briefly. He didn't want any discussion about his night work. He dropped into one of the maple wing chairs and stretched his long legs out on the gray-and-yellow-striped ottoman before it.

"Now the camel—" Louise said to Junior.

Junior picked up the camel and put it into the ark, saying: "Now the camel will go to sleep."

"Now the giraffe," Louise said; and Danny thought how alike they looked, the mother and the child with their dark eyes and brown hair.

Junior picked up the giraffe and put him into the ark. He said, "Now the gir-affe will go to sleep."

Danny watched while half a dozen more animals were put through this ceremony, and he became impatient.

"You could scoop them up in about five minutes or less," he said to Louise, "this seems the hard way to clean up, if you ask me."

Louise looked hurt. "The idea is to teach Junior to pick up his things and put them away," she said. "At the same time, he's learning the names of the animals."

"He's only three," Danny said, "in a couple of years he will just scoop them up, and a lot of energy will be saved."

Louise did not answer him, but turned to Junior. "Daddy's going to put the animals to bed tonight," she said. "Come now, and you'll have your bath."

"But my animals want me to put them to bed," Junior protested, and his underlip began to quiver.

Danny swung his legs from the ottoman to the floor and got up. He put his arms about Junior and gave him a hug. "Daddy will do it tonight," he said. "Now run along to bed."

"I have to have my bath," Junior said, "and Mama will read Black Sambo."

"Not tonight," Danny said, "you have to go to bed tonight, and Mama will read about Black Sambo another night."

Junior began to cry, great tears running down his cheeks. Louise came over and took him from Danny's arms. "Mama will read Black Sambo," she said, drying his tears with her apron, "and we'll have a nice bath, too."

She winked at Danny behind Junior's back. "You w-a-s-t-e more time if you u-p-s-e-t the routine," she explained.

Danny watched her as she disappeared into the bathroom

carrying the child. Her figure had gotten a little plump, he reflected; and that reassured him somewhat. Women who kept themselves pencil slim were still interested in men; and if she thought he was running around, she might feel she had to keep herself attractive. She was satisfied with inexpensive little dresses, too, as long as she was neat; and she always bought serviceable shoes, which would point to the same thing.

Still, he thought, you never could tell. She was so wrapped up in the child, that might be the answer. You'd think once in a long time when he came home early, she would just put the child to bed without all this fol-de-rol. She could waste her time and fool around when he wasn't home and she had nothing else to do. He felt sorry for himself, and justified for seeking solace elsewhere. Hadn't he started running around for the first time right after Junior was born? He hadn't before that—well, not regularly; just once in a while. He was only human. And it was pleasant to go out with somebody who wasn't worrying about the check, and whether they could afford it or not.

He could still recall his annoyance with Louise the first time they had gone out after Junior was born. She had gotten an old woman whom the church had recommended to stay with the baby, and you would think that that would have made everything O.K. But no; she was uneasy. She thought the old woman wouldn't know whether the kid was crying from pain or just plain crying; or maybe she'd just let him cry and not bother. It seemed the doctor had told Louise to be careful he didn't get a rupture; his navel was too prominent or something. It had gotten on Danny's nerves; killed the evening for him entirely. He had taken a couple of quick drinks and said he was ready to go home. He had thought, sullenly, that there were plenty of girls he knew who would enjoy a good time, if she didn't.

He could hear the water running in the bath tub, and Junior's piping voice raised above the sound of the water, questioning his mother. She answered regularly, in monosyllables, but in a patient, kind voice.

Danny went over to the radio, and fumbled with the stations until he got some jazz music; South American stuff, he liked the rhythm of it. He sat down on the large day bed that served as a couch by day and a bed by night for him and Louise. He had always hated the thing, it spoiled the room—it was too large in proportion to the rest of the things, and the size of the room itself. When Junior was born, Louise had insisted upon their giving up the bedroom to him, and had bought the day bed. She said it was practical, and if it spoiled the room, it couldn't be helped. Danny never had had the same pride in showing off the apartment to callers after that; he had been proud of having the room just for a living room, and a bedroom separate.

He took three of the turquoise-blue homespun pillows that matched the couch cover, and propped them behind his back; he kept his feet carefully over the side of the day bed. He heard the sound of the water being let out of the tub, and he switched the dial and got some war news. It was all right if he listened to jazz, he thought, but no use putting any ideas in Louise's head. He never took her dancing any more, and pretended not to care for it himself now. You couldn't be too careful!

Louise came out of the bathroom, a glowing Junior in her arms, dressed in a white seersucker sleeping garment.

"Throw Daddy a good-night kiss," she said.

Junior threw a great noisy kiss to Danny from the palm of his hand, and Louise disappeared into the bedroom with him.

Danny got up and wandered restlessly around the living room. He picked up a magazine from the maple gate-leg table which was a reproduction in cheap wood of an antique, like the rest of the furniture. Danny opened the magazine idly, and saw the Public Library card inside the cover. Just like Louise to borrow magazines from the library, and save money—to wait until the magazines were a month old, rather than to buy them. She had her good points.

He turned the leaves of the magazine idly, then laid it down again. There was nothing interesting in it that he could see. Then his eye was caught by a large envelope, with "Department of Labor" as the return address. Danny picked it up quickly, his interest aroused. What on earth could Louise be doing with the Department of Labor? He opened the envelope, and found inside a phamplet on child training. He began reading the introduction to it, a look of black anger on his face. When he was halfway down the first page, Louise came back into the room.

Her face shone. "Isn't it interesting?" she asked; and her voice seemed to thank him for being interested in something pertaining to his home.

He turned toward her; and as he did he caught a glimpse of his face in the eagle-topped mirror above the mantelpiece, and he could see that it was deadpan, the way he wanted it. "How did you come to send for this?"

She looked at him in surprise, as though she thought it a strange question. "Why, Johnny—you know, the fellow who works with you—he told me about it."

"That's what I figured," Danny said, trying to keep his voice casual. He thought he would let Louise talk, and he would listen. You always learned more that way. Johnny had spoken to him a number of times about these pamphlets on child training, but Danny had had no interest. He thought it was some more of Johnny's screwy ideas and had never mentioned the subject to Louise. He didn't like the idea of Louise talking to Johnny; and he wondered why Louise hadn't mentioned it to him. An ugly suspicion was gnawing at his mind. Had Johnny wised her up to his running around? Was that the answer to her change in attitude when he made love to her? He told himself that easy does it; and his tone did not betray what was going on in his mind when he remarked, "Johnny's sure hipped on those kids of his."

Louise got down on her knees and began picking up the rest of the animals lying on the floor, and put each one into the ark carefully. "He certainly is," she answered; and Danny thought how open and honest her attitude seemed.

"I called up your office one day," she explained, "one day when Junior had the measles—remember? The doctor told me to bathe him in soda water to take away the itching, and I didn't have any baking soda in the house. Johnny answered the telephone."

"It's a good thing the boss didn't answer," Danny said, ostensibly looking at the pamphlet, but actually watching her expression in a furtive way.

She stopped with a zebra in mid-air. "Why?" she demanded indignantly, "he certainly knows me. I worked for him, didn't I?"

"Yeah. But he's changed a lot lately. He got sore when Johnny's wife called a couple of times—and you know he's tops with the boss."

"I've spoken to him different times, and he's been very nice," Louise protested.

Danny put the pamphlet down on the table and looked at her in a way he knew was appealing. It never failed: it was his little-boy-abused look. "Well, to tell the truth, the boss has been picking on me lately. Everything I do is wrong, for some reason. So all I need is to have you calling up to finish me off for good."

Louise got up from her kneeling position and went over to him. She put her arms around his shoulders and kissed him on the cheek. "Oh, I didn't know," she said. "I won't call again, Danny." Then anxiously: "Do you think you'll lose your job?"

"Not while the war's on," he answered. "Plumbers are hard to find. But there's no use making an unpleasant atmosphere around the joint." He gave her a little hug and released her.

She went back to picking up the last of the animals, closed the cover to the ark, and latched it with the little brass latch. Danny was thinking that she was reacting all right; as long as they apologized to you when they were in the right and you were in the wrong, you had them where you wanted them. Evidently she didn't know he was running around; Johnny hadn't let the cat out of the bag after all.

He watched her put the ark into the closet off the foyer; he saw her take off her white apron, smooth her brown-and-yellow gingham, hang the apron in the closet, and close the door. She seemed very calm and untroubled, but still the problem remained unsolved. What did she really think, under this calm and sweet manner?

"Sit down on the day bed," he suggested, "and take it easy for a bit. I'll fix the drinks."

She sat down stiffly on the edge of the day bed and said, as though continuing her thoughts aloud, "I can't get over the boss being mean to you—and after all the extra work you've been doing for him nights, and all."

Danny took two of the sofa pillows and put them behind her back. "Relax," he said with a grin, "lean back, and wipe that worried look off your face! We're going to have fun."

"It's nice to have you home," she said, leaning back against the pillows and forcing a little smile, "especially Saturday night. You feel lonesome, you know, when you hear all the others laughing and talking through the courtyard—"

Danny took her face between his hands and shook it gently. "No fussing, either! That's an order."

She smiled at him happily, he thought; and he went into the kitchen. He felt a sense of satisfaction at the spotless order; the white porcelain shone against a background of blue-and-white-checked gingham. He liked the touches of red in the cannister set and the step-on garbage can, too. He couldn't help thinking of Stell when he opened the Frigidaire; the ice trays came out so smoothly, they had just the right amount of ice in them. Stell's refrigerator was always in need of defrosting; it never failed to irritate him. He thought about last Saturday night, when it had been raining so hard that Stell decided to stay in; she met him in that slinky negligee of coral silk that set off her dark beauty to such advantage. A little silk certainly did a lot for a woman, he thought. Stell knew it, too. She always wore necklines that showed off her small, firm breasts. They fitted perfectly into the cupped palms of his hand; that's the way he liked them. After a woman had a child, Danny thought, she lost a lot of her attractions; her breasts sagged or got flabby. It was tough, but you had to take life the way it was—and the way it was wasn't his fault.

Louise never seemed to think about such things. She always wore flannel nightgowns in winter, and cotton crepe ones in summer. She was always thinking about what was serviceable; she didn't seem to have any vanity.

As he got out the lemons, cut and squeezed them, he thought

to himself that Louise was really the most wonderful girl in the world. He admired her more than anybody he knew. He loved her, too; he thought darkly that if any man ever made a pass at her, he would kill the brute with his bare hands!

He laughed at himself for his intensity; he thought he didn't have to worry: Louise wasn't the type to give anybody an opening. He took out the tall, frosted glasses and poured two jiggers of whiskey into each one; then a little lemon juice, and finally some soda. He emptied the ice cubes into a glass bucket and put the whole business on a large tray.

The drinks were double strength, which wouldn't bother him any; but Louise wasn't accustomed to drinking, the way he was, and it would really give her a kick.

The banjo clock in the living room struck nine, and Danny wondered with a sudden twinge of jealousy what Stell was doing. Was she slinking around in that coral negligee, sweet with the smell of gardenia perfume, tantalizing someone else? Probably, he decided; he had figured before she was two-timing him; here were suspicious telephone calls, and she had acted evasive about them. He wouldn't take it if he were really sure; a girl had to be all for him.

He picked up the tray and went into the living room. Louise was stretched out on the day bed, and he thought how tired and pale she looked, in spite of the tan she had gotten taking Junior to the park twice a day. He felt a sudden compassion for her, and hoped for her sake as well as his own that she didn't know about the other women. After all, what she didn't know wouldn't hurt her. Johnny was all wet about not beating the scales, and all that baloney.

Louise got up quickly when she saw him coming with the tray, and pulled the maple coffee table over to the day bed. Danny set the tray down upon it; then he pulled one of the wing chairs up close to the table for himself. Louise sat down on the edge of the day bed again, and put her elbow into one of the pillows, leaning her weight against it. Danny sat down and handed her a drink.

"It isn't beer!" she protested, "I'll get tight—"

"Didn't I say we were celebrating?" Danny demanded. "Come on, be a sport."

Louise took a sip out of the tall glass, and Danny urged, "Oh, take a *real* swallow!"

Louise laughed, saying, "Don't say I didn't warn you," and swallowed down half the drink.

Her cheeks flushed and her eyes got bright. Danny watched her narrowly, but her expression did not change. "I feel fine," she said, "I could dance on the clouds—"

"You and Johnny," he put the feeler out cautiously, "he goes for the clouds, and fogs, and what have you!"

"He's very nice," Louise defended him.

"Sure, he's okay," Danny agreed, "but he's a funny one, just the same. He's got a lot of screwy ideas. You'd think he would have told me that time you called up—about the baking soda."

"Oh, that," Louise replied, putting her glass down, "that was all right. Mrs. Lieberman, from across the hall, came in while we were talking on the telephone and she said she had some soda, not to bother you with it."

Danny reached for her half-empty glass, put some whiskey and another ice cube into it. "*Please*," Louise protested.

Danny laughed and poured himself a drink. "I thought you were glad I came home?" he asked pensively.

"Of course, I'm glad!" she replied earnestly. "You've no idea how empty the house seems at times. Like Saturday night—and when it begins to get dark—"

Danny interrupted her, "Here's to more celebrations!" and lifted his glass.

Louise lifted hers, too, drank a little, and put it down on the table. "I feel dizzy," she said.

"Bunkum," he protested. "You won't feel that way after a few minutes, Come on, here's to us."

They both drank to that. In the background the radio was playing, "All alone, I'm so all alone—," only a jazzed-up version, with a quicker tempo than it had originally.

Louise hummed the tune for a moment, then broke off, saying, "It's funny about loneliness. There are different kinds—"

"How do you mean, different kinds?" Danny asked, putting her glass into her hand and picking his up. He nodded for her to take a sip, and she did. He could tell by her eyes that she was feeling the drinks a lot.

She put down her glass and leaned against the pillows again. "Oh, I don't know. It's a funny thing."

He felt the time was ripe now to find out just what was what in their relationship, so he shot the question at her quickly: "Is that why—the loneliness, I mean—you don't say nice things to me after I make love to you any more?"

She nodded her head, puzzled. "Maybe that's it."

They both sat silent for a few minutes, and Danny waited for her to speak. "Maybe that is it—the loneliness," she said. "I used to think that when you came home, I wouldn't be lonely any more. You know, with you here. But then, after a while, I realized I was lonely even when you were home."

He watched her cagily. She was talking half to herself and half to him; he knew from the careful way she brought out each word that she had been figuring this out in her mind for a long time.

She leaned back against the pillow again, and Danny pretended to be busy measuring the drinks. He waited without a word for her to continue. After a while, she did.

"I found out after a while that even when you *were* home, I was lonely because it was as though you were away at the same time. It was tormenting. You hear about the soul leaving the body when people die. It was like that. Only your body was here; your soul seemed away."

Danny handed her the glass, but she set it down without taking any of it. He sipped slowly at his, waiting. There was no expression whatever on his face.

Louise's face looked drawn as she continued thoughtfully, "I figured to myself that when you made love to me, I wouldn't be lonely *then*; but it was the same. And instead of feeling I wanted to pray and laugh at the same time, the way I used to, I felt bitter disappointment that the loneliness hadn't gone."

She did not speak again for quite a long time, so Danny reached out her drink to her. "Come on," he said pleasantly, "you're going dead on *me*."

She smiled sadly, and took the proffered drink. She drank a little, held it, and drank a little more. "I guess I'm not very exciting company," she said. "I guess I'm not worth much attention."

The muscles in Danny's jaw tightened. He thought, "She *does* know! Well, here goes. Let's get it over with!"

Aloud he said, "You know you're the only girl for me, Louise."

To his surprise, she looked straight into his eyes and smiled gently. "You're a good boy, Danny. I know you work hard."

Danny was stumped. She didn't know he ran around. She didn't even suspect. Yet she had changed toward him. Why? He said, "Then what's the trouble, anyway, Louise?"

She leaned forward, clasping her hands tightly together. He avoided her eyes; he glued his attention on her hands. He noticed how shiny her gold wedding band had become, and how tiny the diamond was that he had given her for an engagement ring. How thrilled she had been with it! She couldn't have liked it more if it had cost a thousand.

"I had a dream one night," she began, "it's still vivid in my mind. I dreamed it was the middle of the night, and you got up to go to the bathroom. It was very dark, there was no moon. Suddenly, I was afraid of the dark, the way I used to be when I was a little girl. I got up out of bed and lay down on the floor outside the bathroom, because you had left the door to the bathroom ajar and some light streamed out. Also, I felt close to you there, and I wasn't afraid then."

Her face was pale again, and she pushed the damp curls back from her forehead. "You knew I was there outside the door, and you were annoyed. You closed the door. . . . A frenzy of fear gripped me, and I begged you to open the door. You didn't answer. I said, 'Oh, please, *please*, open the door just a little bit!"

But still you did not answer, and I knew you would not. I knew you were even irritated with me for asking. So I just lay there on the cold floor, yearning toward the door, and knowing it was useless. It was helpless agony. That's how it was."

Danny made an impatient gesture. "For God's sakes, is that all? It's nothing but a dream, for crying out loud!"

Louise stood up uncertainly. She looked terribly tired. "Yes," she said, "it was only a dream."

"Where are you going?" he asked.

"To see if the baby's all right," she answered. "He might kick the covers off, or something." She swayed slighty for a moment, but her steps were firm as she walked toward the bedroom door.

Danny poured himself a stiff drink and swallowed it down angrily. He had wasted a whole evening to find out nothing. He might have known she wasn't wise to his running around! And for no reason at all, as far as he could see, she had lost him the feeling of singing on the mountain top, the one thing she had given him that nobody else could.

Because he knew now it was gone forever, that feeling; and it was Louise's fault with all her screwy ideas. He felt sorry for himself and sore at Louise. She should have kept that feeling for him.

THE SONG THE SOLDIERS SANG

by ALICE FARNHAM

THE SOLDIERS WERE COMING. THEY CAME MARCHING DOWN THE narrow back street to avoid traffic, and the little girl's heart began to pound the way it always did. She stood quite still, her eyes big and brilliant in her little sallow face, her lips parted. She was trembling.

The little colored children who lived in the block were hilarious, as they always were when it was time for the soldiers. The boys, in their ragged pants, strutted barefoot up the middle of the street with rich gurgles of laughter.

They mimicked, "Hup-hup-hup! *One*, two, three, four!"

The smallest of them, in a half-unfastened sunsuit, jumped up and down the curb beside her in an ecstasy.

"Come the *sodgers*, come the *sodgers!*"

Now the little girl could hear them. Above the noises of the city streets she heard it. First only a beat—then, stronger and stronger, the deep boys' voices as the soldiers came singing home from classes to the hotel that was their barracks.

The little girl's hands were like ice. Would they be singing The Song?

Twice a day the soldiers passed, the wonderful singing soldiers. All the days were glowing and bright and alive now, even though she had no one to play with, no one at all in the big dingy house but herself and Cousin Ella. Things didn't matter so much, now that the soldiers had come—things like not living with your mother, and never having anyone to talk to. Sunday was a lonesome day, but you could make up fine conversations with imaginary soldiers while you looked out the gray lace curtains at the littered street. And you could sing snatches of their rollicking song that you'd never heard before, and try to imagine how it would sound if you could only hear all of it at once.

Word ran down the street ahead of them. The soldiers!

They didn't always sing. Sometimes they just whistled, and sometimes they had a yell that started *R.O.T.C.*, and sometimes they were tired and just marched with their eyes straight ahead. Then all you could hear was the tramp of their feet, a tired, heavy sound. It made you want to cry because you felt that the soldiers couldn't stop, that they must march on like that forever.

But today they were singing, and it was The Song.

The little colored boys marched with them, pompous and swaggering and very serious. The younger children ran beside them as they marched, shrieking with laughter. The little girl wanted to follow the soldiers too, but it was not dignified to make a game of it as the colored children did. She stood there very stiff and straight.

"*—twopence to* spend, *and twopence to* lend, *And twopence to send home to my wife!*" sang the soldiers as they swung past. They pronounced it toopence.

"*Poor wife!*" sang the soldiers who followed. But the ones in the middle weren't singing, and the boys in the rear ranks had started "Pistol-Packin' Mamma" in opposition to the song up front.

The little girl winked back angry tears. That was always the way. You never got to hear the whole thing at one time, so you could learn it.

When the soldiers had gone, she walked along the curb moodily, teetering off balance now and then because the heels of her open-toed shoes were much too high. Even the sight of her bright-red toenails didn't help.

She wanted someone to talk to about the soldiers. Cousin Ella was old. She didn't care about anything any more. There were other children in the block, but Cousin Ella wouldn't let her play with them. There was only Mrs. Holmstrom.

She was off down the street like an arrow, the soiled, backless white playshoes clattering over the uneven brick pavement.

At a frowning little house behind an old-fashioned iron railing, she unlatched the gate and clumped noisily up the steps. She rang the doorbell once and then moved anxiously to the window, shading her eyes to peer through.

"Mrs. Holmstrom! Mrs. Holmstrom!" she shouted. "Are you in, Mrs. Holmstrom?"

"It's you then, is it, Katey?" said Mrs. Holmstrom, opening the door.

The little girl had already gone to the scarred piano that stood in a corner of the little living room.

"Did you hear the soldiers today, Mrs. Holmstrom?" Her tone was excited.

"How should I not hear them?" Mrs. Holmstrom shook her head. "They'd wake the dead, them boys would."

The little girl turned from the piano. Her eyes were shining again, and much too large for her face. Her little skinny hand lingered lovingly over the yellow keys.

"But the song, you know, Mrs. Holmstrom—they were singing a different line today. Didn't you notice?"

"I can't say I did. But go ahead and pick out your little tunes on the piano, Katey. You'll get it yet," said Mrs. Holmstrom. "Just close the door behind you when you go out. I got to get back. The mister's waitin' on his supper."

The little girl scarcely heard her. In utter absorption, with the most frowning and concentrated care, she was picking out the disjointed fragments of a little tune. Sometimes she would seem to stop and listen for something, head sharply back and body tense; and then, with a quick gleam of satisfaction, she would bend absorbed over the keys again.

"I *got toopence, jolly, jolly toopence*," sang the little girl with gusto. "*Toopence to* lend, *and toopence to* spend, *and toopence to send home to my wife*. Poor wife!"

But her face clouded as she slid off the stool. There was more to it than that, lots more—parts about happy is the day, and the silvery mooo-oo-oon, when the boys' voices swooped up into a joyous shout.

But always it eluded her. Always they had gone by before

she could fix the words or the tune in her mind, or they'd change songs in the middle of the block, or start whistling and not sing at all. You just couldn't depend on them.

Back in the kitchen, Mrs. Holmstrom said deprecatingly to her husband, "The little motherless one from down the street."

"Don't give a man no peace."

But his grumbling was only perfunctory. He sat awhile over his paper, in his soiled and bedaubed painter's overalls, with his shoes off, and then he said suddenly, "*There's* a mother."

"*Hah!*" said Mrs. Holmstrom, and slammed the oven door.

When the little girl went home, Cousin Ella didn't notice her, as usual. There was a cold frankfurter in the refrigerator and she ate it, then a pork chop she found on the bottom shelf. The pork chop was greasy but all right.

Slowly she went upstairs. From a bureau drawer she took the enormous, peeling, red patent leather handbag that contained her treasures. A broken charm bracelet, a comb with several teeth missing, a chromo of the Madonna, a ten-cent compact, a card dispensed by the Your Weight and Fortune machine in the five-and-ten: "You possess great energy and determination, and are extremely popular with the opposite sex."

In the money-pocket was a dime. With a forlorn hope she probed the lining, though she knew it would be empty. A dime wouldn't be enough. She closed the pocketbook, her eyes darting to the door.

She stole to the head of the stairs and listened. There was only the rustle of the evening paper, Cousin Ella's occasional cough.

She took off her shoes and tiptoed into Cousin Ella's bedroom. The marbletopped bureau, the dark heavy furniture, all had an accusing look of Cousin Ella. The little girl paid no attention. With quick sure fingers she opened Cousin Ella's pocketbook and took out a quarter. That was all she'd need. She'd priced sheet music before.

"Where you going?" Cousin Ella looked up from the crossword puzzle on the back page.

"Friday night," the little girl said glibly. "Stores all open. I want to walk through the five-and-dime."

The fat old woman grunted, turned back to her puzzle. The little puzzle that was Katey slipped out the door, her heart racing. Now—now she would find it!

The girl at the music counter wouldn't even look. She sat up there at her piano, laughing and flirting with two sailors. She wouldn't even look at the tense little girl who stood there clutching the big red pocketbook.

Finally she heard, or could no longer not hear, a pleading voice. With a frown of annoyance, she turned away from the sailors.

"I never heard of a song about toopence," she said coldly.

The little girl's eyes were stricken. "Jolly, *jolly* toopence?" she quavered.

"Not any kind of toopence," said the salesgirl with finality. She returned to the sailors.

That's it, the child thought dully. It's never any use to steal. You think that maybe God won't notice, just this once; but He always does. Stolen money won't bring you any luck.

She felt a flicker of hope when she heard the man who sold little folders of popular songs hawking his wares at the door as she went out.

"Here they are, folks! Most popular hits of screen and radio, the songs you want to know! Only a dime, here they are, folks!"

The little girl got out her dime with fingers that suddenly trembled.

"Mister, have you got a song about toopence? Jolly, jolly toopence?"

"Sis, we got them *all*," said the hawker, with conviction. "Here, run along home with it and see for yourself. Here they are, folks, only a dime!"

The little girl stood by a lighted store window. Her quick eager eyes ran up and down the pages. There was no song about twopence.

Her feet dragged as she scuffed through the dark streets toward home. She would put the quarter back, when she got there. Stealing is something you pay for, after all.

She didn't want to go home yet. On an impulse she didn't turn at the corner but went on. Straight up Chestnut Street was the hotel where the soldiers stayed.

She walked fast till she came to it, and then she walked very, very slowly. Soldiers were in twos and threes about the door, but she affected not to notice them. A subtle change came over her gait; she swung her flat hips slightly and swayed a little from the shoulders. Mincing along with tiny steps, her gaze was fastened on something intensely interesting, incredibly fascinating, in the middle distance. Her eyes were bright with it, her lips parted in a little smile. Now she was no longer a little girl; she was beauty and sophistication and allure; she was Rita Hayworth and Lana Turner and Hedy Lamarr.

No one recognized her. No one ever did. The soldiers went on laughing and talking just as before. No one even knew she'd passed by.

The little girl gave one lingering, wistful, backward look. With a sigh she turned away again and began kicking her way along in the aimless, moody shuffle peculiar to disconsolate youth.

As she turned the drugstore corner she became erect and tense again. There on a stool at the empty fountain, close to the door, sat one of the soldiers! The tall one, with the freckles and the blue eyes, who always marched on her side of the street on the outside of the fifth row—oh, she'd know him anywhere, that one! He always roared The Song in a cheerful bass that just made you feel good all over, and sometimes he'd grin at you as he went by, so close you could reach out and touch him.

Her walk was self-conscious as she went in, blinking at the lights. She sidled onto the stool beside him with a deprecating cough.

"Hi!" said the soldier, grinning down amiably. "Keep late hours for your size, don't you?"

"I'm eleven," she said, with a touch of hauteur. "I always stay up late. Cousin Ella never minds."

"Well, Katey, what'll it be?" said the proprietor, with a look of disfavor.

She cleared her throat. "Just a—a glass of water, please, Mr. Greenberg."

"Bring the kid a soda," the soldier ordered. "What flavor, kid?"

For a dizzy moment she thought she might fall off the stool. It was like a dream—the beautiful dream that came a thousand times, in a thousand guises—but Mr. Greenberg couldn't be a dream. Nobody would dream Mr. Greenberg.

"Well, tell us about yourself," said the soldier carelessly. He poured out a little more of his milk shake. "So Cousin Ella don't mind you staying out late, huh? What about your old man and your old lady? Don't they care either?"

Katey turned very pale. She put down the straw for a minute, carefully.

"They don't—" she swallowed. "They don't—exactly—care either."

She pushed the soda away. Then she turned on the soldier a look of such burning misery that it penetrated even his offhand good humor.

"They don't—want me," she said rapidly. "They're divorced and I live with Cousin Ella because nobody wants me. My father went away. A long time ago, he went away."

"That's tough." The soldier's voice was gentle.

"My *mother* wants me." The little girl held her head up, as though by saying a thing many, many times one could make it so. "I know she wants me. Only she works in a beauty parlor, and has to room downtown. But she comes to see me sometimes," she added defiantly.

"Sure," said the soldier.

"Of course, she's very pretty, and when a person's mother is very pretty, it's natural she should have a lot of gentleman friends, and they take up most of her time. It's only natural."

"*Very* natural," the soldier agreed. He took out a pack of cigarettes from his pocket. There was only one in it, and he crumpled the empty pack and threw it on the floor. "So what do you do with yourself all day?"

She hesitated. "I take walks and pretend I'm people. Or I read movie magazines or look around in the five-and-ten. But mostly," she brightened, "mostly I go calling on Mrs. Holmstrom, because she has a piano."

"Does, eh?"

The little girl nodded several times, her eyes alight.

"I pick tunes out, you know—ones I hear in the movies or on the radio or places. I get so I can play them real good without any music. Mrs. Holmstrom says I'm a wonder," she added modestly.

"I'll bet you are."

The soldier looked at her with amusement. He saw a bony little figure in a cheap, pink rayon slack-suit, indifferently ironed; a sallow, wistful, little face and stringy dark hair; a huge red pocketbook, importantly held and displayed.

"I'm *musical*," she explained. "I like to sing better than anything." She opened the handbag and took out the folded sheet of printed song stanzas. "See, here are some of the ones I'm working on now. Right now I'm learning 'East of the Rockies.' "

The soldier whistled. "That's a humdinger. How about—"

All at once she remembered it. The Song!

"Oh, tell me what it is!" The words tumbled out in a breathless rush as she leaned tensely forward. "The song the soldiers sing—oh, you know the one! Every day, on their way back from school—*you* know!" Her face was flushed. "Toopence!"

"*That* one?" The soldier laughed. "Sure—I'll teach it to you." He looked around, and cleared his throat. "Well—er—not here. I'll walk you part way home. It won't take you long to get it."

As she slid down from the high white stool Katey's knees almost buckled under her. She was weak with happiness.

She broke into a giggle when they were out in the street. "The first time I heard it, you know what I thought they were saying, 'Two *pants!' Two pants to lend, two pants to send home to my wife.*"

"Now, the first part goes like this," said the soldier seriously. "*I've got sixpence*—starts out with sixpence, see, and works on down—I've got sixpence—"

"*To last me all my life!*" she finished, with an improvised little dance step as she sang.

The soldier took out a harmonica, polished it on his sleeve with loving care. "All right, you sing and I'll give you the tune."

"*I've got*—"

There were running footsteps behind them.

"Bill! Hey, Gallagher! Telephone, you GI Casanova!"

The sodier put his harmonica away hurriedly. "So long, Katey—see you again sometime. OK, I'm coming!"

She reached desperately for his sleeve. "Tomorrow night? Will you teach me the song tomorrow?"

"OK," he assented hastily. "See you later!"

He sprinted up the street toward the hotel. She stood there a moment under the street light, watching him, till he ran in at the lighted lobby. She started down the dark street toward home, the darkness still warm and bright and quivering with his presence; and then she stopped.

At the door of the drugstore she stood for a moment with bright eyes to reconnoiter. Mr. Greenberg was behind the prescription counter, in back; there was no one else in the store.

With a tremulous rush, she had swooped on something that lay on the floor beside the soda fountain, in triumph bore it away. The discarded cigarette wrapper.

The soldiers marched by again next day, and her heart swelled as she stood on the curb to watch. They sang, "Let Me Call You Sweetheart," and then they sang "Hinky-Dinky Parlez-Vous," and then all at once, while they were singing, swaggering past, she wanted to cry with the beauty of them.

They were beautiful, beautiful, all of them. Some of them wore glasses, and some were too short; the little one who was always falling out of step had such a pug nose you could scarcely call it a nose at all. But it didn't matter. They were beautiful. All of them were beautiful.

And then she saw him swinging along in the sunlight, his

books under one arm, trench cap balanced on one sunburned eyebrow, and her heart seemed to stop. Her eyes clung adoringly to his face. He saw her. As he went by, he turned his face toward her and winked.

She knew then that he was the most beautiful soldier of all.

Night was very long in coming. The unwanted sun still hung in the sky, the hands of every clock stood motionless. Only the clock in the shoemaker's window held out any hope: he kept it an hour fast.

When it said eight o'clock, she started slowly up the street. She didn't run. There was a funny trembling at the pit of her stomach, and her hands were cold.

It was still too early. She'd known that. That was why he wasn't anywhere around.

She walked past the hotel again. This time she didn't look in. She'd walk by without looking, until the tenth time. No—the fifth. Ten was too many.

The fourth time past she looked in the hotel again. Even now, he might be coming toward her—for a moment she couldn't breathe. No.

She had been walking up and down for almost an hour when at last she saw him. A blonde girl was on his arm, and both of them were laughing as they came.

The child stood there motionless.

The soldier's face wore a look of surprise, just tinged with embarrassment. "Hello, Katey—what are you doing up here?"

She swallowed. That other girl was looking down at her in amusement.

"Competition, Bill?"

The little girl ignored her. She took one step toward the soldier, her eyes in desperate beseeching on his face. "You told me to come." Her voice was tremulous, almost inaudible. "You said you'd meet me tonight and teach me the song. You said it last night."

The soldier glanced sidewise at his companion and cleared his throat. "Sure I did, Katey—I remember now. But I didn't realize we'd said tonight. Now be a good girl and run along home. Some other night, huh?"

With great dignity the little girl turned and walked away. Her feet dragged a little and there was a mist over things. Once she walked into a fat man who asked where she thought she was going, but she kept straight on.

Cousin Ella didn't look up when she went in. She went slowly, very slowly, up the stairs. It was as if she bore a tremendous load on her shoulders, bowing them down.

"I'm walking all bent over," she thought in surprise. "I'm walking like Cousin Ella." It scared her a little. Could you really turn old in a single night, in a single hour?

Not till she was safely in the dark bedroom and the door locked between her and all the world, did she break down. She sank beside the bed and buried her face.

How could she live? How do you go on living, when your heart is broken, when in all the busy world there is no one who loves you?

Long was the night, that had been so long in coming.

Katey sat at the piano in Mrs. Holmstrom's neat little parlor. With one hand she picked out a tune she had made up that morning, but her eyes looked through the piano and far away. It was a sad little tune that said over and over, "I'm lonely, I'm so lonely," but no one knew the words but Katey.

There was a beat of music in the distance.

"Here comes the soldiers, Katey," called Mrs. Holmstrom.

"Yes'm," the little girl said listlessly. She sat listening, her sallow face flushing as the beat came closer. For a moment she stood by the window irresolute, and then, as if drawn against her will, went slowly out.

The soldiers were almost there now. It was one of their tired days, and they had stopped singing. They didn't even whistle as they came past her, four abreast.

The sergeant swung smartly along the brick sidewalk.

"Hup! hup! *Three*, four! Hup!"

Katey didn't want to look. She kept her face turned away. Her chin was quivering.

"Psst! *Katey!*"

Oh beloved, well-remembered voice! She looked up, tremulous, flushed with delight.

Grinning, he tossed a little folded wad of paper at her feet as he went by. She snatched it up and darted away, her whole face alight. The words blurred a little as she read them.

Dear Katey:

I'm sorry about last night. Honest I never meant to disappoint you. Don't be mad, will you?

Here's the words of that song you wanted. You learn them like a good girl and meet me in front of the drugstore tonight. I'll teach you the tune. Honest.

Bill

P.S. Will be alone this time.

Through the endless hours of the day she idled. She mustn't get there too soon. But at sight of the shoemaker's clock she began to run, and so she arrived out of breath after all.

She slowed down before he saw her. With a haughty, a world-weary face she studied the roof lines of the houses opposite. She was a young lady out for an evening stroll, a stroll which just chanced to bring her in this direction of all others, and her mind was detached from the things of the street.

So much so, in fact, that she tripped over a loose brick and went sprawling.

The soldier caught her. "Here, look where you're goin', Star-Dust! Wanta break your neck?"

"Oh!" She looked at him, her eyes wide with a fine amazement. "Why, I really never even thought of *you* being here, Mr. Gallagher! I just happened to be out for a walk—" Her voice was high, her gestures elaborate with airy unconcern.

The corners of the soldier's mouth quirked as he looked at her. "Just happened along, eh?"

"I *often* walk here," she said loftily. "Almost every night.

Looking at the stars and things. I forgot all *about* you being here."

"I'm sure of it," said the soldier. "Now that you're here, how about a soda?"

She unbent. "Well—since I *am* here. Choc'lit."

Ambrosia through a straw, ice-cold and heavenly chocolate-flavored and fizzing a little in your nose!

As she sipped, she cast sidelong glances at the soldier's face. He looked like the pictures of the Greek gods in the fifth grade reader. Her throat ached with the beauty and wonder of him, so that she almost choked in her chocolate soda for love.

The soldier was oblivious of his godhood.

"You learn all those words yet, kid?" he asked, lighting a cigarette and looking down at her.

She glowed. "Yes, every single one! *I've got sixpence, jolly, jolly—*"

"OK, OK," he said hastily. "Outside. Not here."

They went across the street. A low wall ran around the Methodist church, and they sat there under the street-light.

"Now, let's hear you. No, wait till I get the Stradivarius oiled up." He took out the harmonica and wiped it with a handkerchief. "Let's go!"

Away they went. "*—to send home to my wife. Poor wife!*" sang the little girl joyously. Suddenly she couldn't sit still. She sprang up and danced the rollicking tune as she sang it.

The soldier's feet tapped on the pavement. The harmonica wheezed manfully into the chorus.

> *—by the light of the sil-vurr-rry moo-oo-oon,*
> Hap-*py is the day that we* line *up for our pay,*
> *As we go rolling home!*

"Oh, it's the finest song I ever heard!" the little girl panted. "Isn't it the best song you ever heard too?" And she danced a little more, in the fancy high-heeled shoes that were too big. "I'*ve got sixpence—*"

The soldier was smiling as he looked at her, but there was

pity in his eyes too, and a sadness. The little girl felt it, and her song trailed away uncertainly.

She sat down again and looked up at him anxiously. "I sang it all *right?*"

"You sang it swell." The soldier was looking at his harmonica. He wiped it off again with slow thoroughness.

"You know your song now, don't you, kid?"

She nodded mutely, her eyes never leaving his face. Foreboding fluttered in her heart.

"I want you to sing it when I'm gone, Katey." The soldier didn't look at her. The light from the street lamp was lavender as it shone on him, like moonlight in a dream. "They're sending us to camp tomorrow. Tomorrow night. We won't be around any more."

The little girl sat there without speaking for a moment. Her voice seemed to come from a great distance as she said, not very distinctly, "The camp—is your camp far off?"

"Georgia."

The little girl's shoulders sagged. He reached over and put the harmonica in her hand. It felt icy to his touch.

"Look, Katey, I want you to have it while I'm gone. And I want you to play it and sing and be happy, Katey, and not go feeling lonely because things aren't—just the way they oughta be. And remember, Katey," he tilted her chin up, "I'll be back!"

She seized his hand, covered it with kisses, pressed it to her cheek. "Oh, I'll never see you again! I'll never see you again!" she cried in a passion of grief. "You'll be gone and I'll never see you any more! I can't bear it, I can't! I can't!"

The soldier stroked her hair clumsily. "Katey, I'll see you! I'm coming back!"

She raised a dirty little tear-stained face. "Swear it! swear that you will!"

"OK, so I swear it," said the soldier uncomfortably, looking around to see that no one heard. "And I'll write to you. Every week, if you'll promise to be a good girl and not cry. And I want you to play that harmonica real good when I get back, you hear?"

Feverishly she searched in her bag. "A pencil—write down your address!"

He felt in his pockets. "Damn, I haven't got one either. Never mind, I'll write it out when I get home and toss it to you tomorrow when I go by."

When you go by. When you go by. The last time I'll ever see you. But the feel of the harmonica in her hand gave her comfort.

"You'll be there, won't you?" The soldier glanced at his watch. "To wave good-by."

Her fingers closed round the harmonica.

"I'll be there," she said steadily.

"That's fine." He sounded relieved as he rose. "Be a good girl and keep your chin up. I'll write. There!"

He had hurriedly kissed her forehead and was gone. Gone up the street to the hotel, where his date sat waiting in the lobby.

The little girl walked home in a dream, a confusion of pain and joy. Around the harmonica her fingers were tight.

He was going, tomorrow he was going. All the singing soldiers would go tomorrow, and the little back street would be gray desolation once more.

But he would write; he had promised. He would come back. He had sworn it. And when he came, it would not be a child Katey who greeted him. No, a woman—beautiful, queenly, poised! *Much* more beautiful than the blonde girl last night.

Starry-eyed, she strained the harmonica to her thin bosom and spoke in an exhalted hush. "Oh, I *will* wait for you, my darling! I'll be true! True to the end of time." And despite her heartbreak, she felt a little thrill of pleasure in the phrase.

She went in the door and up the dark staircase in a trance.

"I'll be true!" she murmured, pressing the harmonica to her cheek. "Oh, beloved—true to the end of time!"

She knelt by the window to gaze out at the stars hanging bright over the alley—the same stars that looked down upon him!—and an improvement occurred to her.

Reverently she whispered, "To the end of time—and beyond!"

When Cousin Ella woke her, she knew by the look of the sun on the carpet that the soldiers had already gone by.

"But I'll see him this afternoon," she thought, reaching hurriedly for her shoes. "This afternoon, when they come back. For the last time."

She shivered and took the harmonica out from under her pillow.

Cousin Ella was in the room, showing unusual activity.

"I declare, they might have told a body," she mumbled. Cousin Ella wore tight, black high-buttoned boots, and always walked as if her feet hurt. "Just call on the phone as cool as you please—'coming out for Katey at ten-thirty, please have her ready!' " she mimicked, in a high falsetto.

A giant hand seemed to close round Katey's heart. She sat on the edge of the bed, watching the old woman with frightened eyes. "Who—who called, Cousin Ella? You mean they're coming *today?*"

Cousin Ella handed out her clean underwear from the bureau and straightened up. "Your mother is who I mean, Miss. And that latest friend of hers—Mr. *Mordie*, he calls himself. They're taking you off somewheres for the day. Nonsense, I call it."

When she got home, he'd be gone. Slowly, like a sleepwalker, the little girl dressed in her best clothes. She would miss him, and he'd be gone. Forever, forever he'd be gone.

When her mother came, her new gentleman friend Mr. Mordie expansive and beaming behind her, the little girl pushed away her cereal untouched.

"Hello, sweetie-pie!" Her mother kissed her carelessly. "Gee, you're gettin' big, isn't she, Lew? Come on, hon', finish up and don't keep Mr. Mordie and I waiting. We're going to give you a real treat, aren't we, Mr. Mordie?"

Katey kept her eyes on her plate.

"You bet!" said Mr. Mordie fondly. "We're gonna show the kid a good time. A whole day out at Moonlight Park!"

Cousin Ella sniffed.

"Come on, come on!" said Katey's mother impatiently. "I'm surprised at you, Katey. When a person's going to use his car and give up his whole day to give you a good time, the least you can do is show a little appreciation and not keep them waiting."

She moistened a corner of her handkerchief with her tongue and rubbed a spot from the child's cheek.

"Now what do you say to Mr. Mordie?"

The little girl swallowed. "Thank—you, Mr. Mordie."

She sat between them in the front seat, her eyes glazed with misery. She felt a dull surprise that people could hurt so and live.

Now and then, at her mother's insistence, she would arouse to say mechanically, "That'll be fine, Mr. Mordie," or "Yes, Mr. Mordie, I like the amusements a lot."

"Kids are funny," her mother apologized. "Get so excited they can't hardly talk," She gave Katey an angry look under her mascara-ed lashes.

Once the little girl asked faintly, "Are we—going to stay long, Mr. Mordie? All day, I mean?"

"Of course we are!" Her mother sounded snappish. "We're going to stay here and have supper at the pavilion. For goodness sake, Katey, you might act less like it was a funeral when a person tries to give you a little enjoyment!"

Numb with despair, the child sat silent.

When they reached the park, Mr. Mordie helped them out with heavy joviality. "Now we'll all go for a ride on the roller coaster! How about it, Katey?"

It was on the roller coaster that she began to feel sick. That terrible moment when the car hung poised on the brink, the swoop through space—

"Boy, give me the old roller coaster every time! Couldn't keep me off it when I was a kid!"

"You said it!" Katey's mother laughed gaily. She pinched her daughter's arm. "Wasn't that great, hon'?"

White-lipped, the child managed, "It was swell, Mr. Mordie!"

For lunch they had hot dogs and bottled pop at a stand under the trees—because, as Katey's mother said, they'd have supper at the pavilion and didn't really need much. Dessert was ice-cream and popcorn. The little girl ate automatically, scarcely tasting what she swallowed.

Soon now, only two more hours, he would be marching past her house for the last time. The boys would be jolly and laughing, for their classes now were over. And they'd be singing The Song, and it would be for the last time, and all her life she'd remember that she wasn't there to hear it, that she wasn't there to wave good-by.

A huge lump hurt her throat. The people and trees began to blur.

Mr. Mordie looked at her curiously.

He said in a low voice, "Marie, that kid don't look just right to me. You suppose there's anything wrong with her?"

"Forget it!" Katey's pretty mother compressed her lips. "Stubborn spell, that's all! Just don't pay no attention."

On the Tumble-Bug, Katey clung desperately to the sides of the car. The ground was still in motion around her when they got off. She staggered and would have fallen but for Mr. Mordie.

He stared at her. "Hey, this kid's sick! Look at her!"

A pale-green Katey lurched to the nearest tree and proved his point. She leaned her head against the tree. Her thin child's body shook with sobs.

"I want to go home!" she wailed. "I want to go home, I want to go home!"

No one said much during the ride. Katey was handed over at the door in disgrace, to be put to bed by Cousin Ella.

When he was nearly down to the car, Mr. Mordie came back up the steps again. Apologetically he patted her hand. "Here, kiddo, here's a quarter. Buy yourself somethin' when you're feelin' better, see?"

Cousin Ella scolded all the way upstairs, but Katey didn't mind. She had seen the dining-room clock, and it said ten minutes after four. An hour, an hour, an hour!

"Might've known how it would turn out, but no one asks *me!*" Cousin Ella's voice was shrill and vindictive. "Now you'll just lie there, young lady, for the rest of the day. And no supper!" She banged the door behind her.

For a few moments the little girl lay there, weak tears of thankfulness streaming down her face, wetting her hair and her ears. Nothing mattered, nothing mattered! Not mother, not Cousin Ella, nothing. God had brought her safely home, in time to wave good-by. Only God could have done it.

When she had waited for what seemed years, she lifted herself cautiously from the bed. The house was silent. Cousin Ella's voice came faintly from the back yard. Noiselessly she stole down the stairs. In the street, she began to run.

As she made her purchase in the five-and-ten, she looked at the clock. Ten minutes till the soldiers came. "Don't wrap it up," she said quickly. "I want to carry it that way."

Out in the street, she looked down at it lovingly. It was a small, silk American flag, with yellow fringe. Holding it tight, in a hand suddenly wet with perspiration, she hurried through the streets. Soon, soon—

At the corner she stopped to lean dizzily against a telephone pole. The colored children were noisy in the street.

"Yay man, they *comin'!* Hup! Hup!"

Above the city noises came a rhythmic beat that swelled into song, and the sound of marching feet. The soldiers were singing, their voices deep and rich against the sounds of traffic, throbbing, growing, till the air seemed to ring with their song. They were singing The Song.

The little girl's heart beat very loud. She felt as though she would suffocate. She held herself very erect.

On they came. They were laughing as they marched, as they sang. It was their last day. And then she saw him.

The sun touched his head with a special light. He was sunshine itself. Warmth and radiance enwrapped her as he passed.

Unconsciously she reached out her hand. He pressed a fold of paper into it, squeezed her cold fingers with a little special smile—tender, half-rueful—as he looked back. And then he had passed, still in step with the others.

The boys who followed him roared the song in their deep young voices.

No-o cares have I to *grie-eve me,*
Pretty little girl to decei-eve me—

Happy as a king, belie-eve me,
As we go rolling home!

Still singing, the voices began to die away, to fade in the noise of city traffic. The little girl stood at attention, the twenty-five-cent flag draped across her flat chest.

The voices came faint and fainter. A big truck rumbled by, a news commentator's voice crackled from a radio somewhere in the block. In the distance a far-off beat of music hung in the air and was dispersed.

The soldiers were gone. The beautiful soldiers were gone.

THE INFAMOUS MANSION

by RICHARD COLEMAN

EDITH BEGAN TO WISH THAT SHE HAD WAITED FOR MARGARET to come with her to the auction and that she had not gone on alone. With a companion, she would have enjoyed the moonlight and shadows in these old streets. The moonlight was bright enough on the rooftops but between the tall houses darkness filled the narrow street in which no window shone with reassuring light. It was narrower than most streets in Charleston, and the Lord knows most of them were narrow enough. This one was no wider than an alley. She left the string of a sidewalk and went into the middle of the street. She felt that if she put her arms akimbo she would knock the houses down.

There was light and supper beyond those tight-shuttered windows because the smell of catfish frying came right through the walls, and occasionally there were the sounds of shut-in voices and distant kitchen laughter. George would think she was crazy if he knew she was walking this street alone at night. He would be so astonished that his facial muscles would be stirred into a bit of movement that would form a fleeting expression of some sort. She wondered how long it had been since she had ceased to think that he had "a good quiet face, so restful after all the grimaces and overplayed expressions people go in for today," and just when it was that she had begun to feel that George's expressionlessness did not indicate "a rich spirit at peace, a spirit with the calm and poise of a Taoist," and had decided that his spirit wasn't serene at all, it was just always upstairs lying down.

This was no way to be thinking about George when she was going to marry him next month. Here she was, on her way to an antique auction, hoping to find just the right things for their home, just the fine old things that would make a suitable background for George, a period piece himself. He *was* a tranquil soul, and she should stop thinking such things. Maybe with both husband and furniture of an antique composure, she too would achieve a little serenity.

The trouble was that for some time now, George and thoughts of George made her less at ease than she had ever been in her life.

And the most upsetting thing of all was that she was always thinking, "I don't *have* to marry him." Maybe a trip was all she needed. There was too much talk about a woman who's not getting any younger needing a husband and a home. Well now, that was undoubtedly the truth. Then it must be that she had lived by herself so much in the last few years that she was probably just worried about losing a freedom that was no freedom at all. At forty-four a still, hushed life in the high-ceilinged rooms of an old Charleston house with a placid, gentle husband would be wonderful, whereas a restless unsettled life with never a husband would grow more and more restless and settle only into loneliness.

As she went down the middle of the dark narrow street, she began to hope that when she turned the corner she would see some friendly lights. She saw a shutter open slowly but there was little light in the room beyond. She was sure someone was watching her and she yearned to turn the corner. When she did, she stopped to catch her breath, because three blocks down, light filled the street and the way right in front of her was bright with moonlight.

She walked slowly because it was still early and now she could enjoy the shadows of the palmettos against old garden walls, the silhouettes of chimney pots, and once the lacy shadow of a grillwork gallery made her pause, its edges softened out because it was a moon shadow, and not the bold black image it would have been upon the white wall if the glaring sun were where the moon was. She thought pleasantly that some of these shadows were over a hundred years old, and that they had been falling just so on every night like this one for generations. This was the sort of thing that had made her love Charleston during the two years that she had been here, and put her into a long-sustained mood that made her love George too.

She was glad now that she had not waited for Margaret. She was never good at this Charleston habit of evoking the past when Margaret was around.

She hurried along, thinking that now she would be able to choose well at the auction. She was in just the mood for antiques. There were always many fine old pieces at an auction like this one in an old house, but mistakes could be made if one didn't look things over carefully before the bidding started. Well, here was the house with four or five cars already in front of it and the door lights were shining beneath the fanlight which she recognized as one she had seen pictured in an art and architecture magazine once. She had even clipped the picture out and put it into a book about Charleston. She hadn't realized that the auction was to be held in this house, but then she had never been on this particular street before. No wonder she had never been able to find it while walking, it wasn't even below Broad Street. Well, in such a house the antiques should be real treasures.

Judging from the cars there were other people who had sense enough to come very early so they could look things over. She went up the worn marble steps and pulled open the big white door.

She turned to admire the extremely handsome fanlight from inside the spacious hall, but when she heard low voices from the room on her left she went toward them. There was a Chinese screen (much too battered for her consideration) set halfway across the door so that she could not see the people in the room, and she felt that she had better not go in just yet. After all, it was quite early and the auctioneer might have matters to attend to, before the overeager ones like herself would be welcome.

She wondered at the worn linoleum runner with the big green and red checkered squares that ran to the foot of a great curving staircase. Some of the things that people did to these fine old houses were unbelievable. The place smelled of collard greens. But when she saw the glow of the light falling through the fanlight on the staircase she forgot these things and walked to the foot of the stairs. It was an infinitely graceful staircase and she felt a profound nostalgia for a time and a manner of living that she knew only through her imagination. That staircase was made for great entrances. One would have to come sweepingly down those stairs, and could never come down just casually whether alone or to an audience.

Farther down the hall and on the opposite side to the room where the voices were, Edith looked into a big shadowy drawing room and saw a floor-to-ceiling mirror with an intricate carved frame that was over a foot wide. She saw the outline of a little Oriental table and many other interesting-looking pieces in the dim light. She'd go in there and look around, perhaps some of the things would be put up at auction later, and the room was sure to be beautiful in the half-darkness.

She went first to the mirror and pleasurably touched the figures in the elaborate design of the frame but quickly drew her hand away as she saw the figures plainly. There were countless satyrs and nymphs in many attitudes of zestful pleasure, some in Cyprian poses depicted in extraordinary detail. No wonder there was no light on in this room. They'd never sell the things in here without moving them away from that outrageous mirror.

It was then that she saw the painting. The nude was so mammoth that its luminous flesh seemed to be the source of what light was in the room. It was a dazzling copy of Prud'hon's "Psyche enlevée par l'Amour," with certain variations that made it a monumental and breath-taking example of pornographic art. Edith backed away from it to the door.

She found that by edging over to the left she could look up the hall and into the room where she had heard people talking. What the screen had hidden before were three men and three women who could not possibly have anything to do with an antique auction. Certainly the furniture could not.

There were two-battered Morris chairs, two tumorous horsehair sofas, four or five green and yellow cane-seated kitchen chairs, an old-fashioned drugstore table with looped and twisted wire legs, and in the corner a big cold, dark, silent juke box, evidently dead. There were no blazing and blaring eruptions from the thing, no internal scarlet and yellow streams of writhing lava, its devils were driven out, and several empty beer bottles were standing on its top.

One of the men was the fat man Edith sometimes saw selling oranges out of the back of a truck on upper King Street. He still had on his cap with the lumpy misshapen peak, and he was holding an unwieldy woman who was striving to sit on his lap which was already crowded with the fat man himself. The woman was kissing him tappingly on his stubbly cheek like a tireless woodpecker. When the impulse or her determination wore out at last, she took to the meaningless caressing sounds some people make to a baby when they are beside themselves with doting. The fat man was enormously pleased with the woman and with himself. He even let her take off his cap and muss his hair with an excessive fondness that left it in a rigid peak in front of a large bald spot.

One of the other couples was dancing. The man had a shrunken leg and had to dance on his crutches but he was managing very well indeed. Because of the extinct juke box the woman was humming and she held her hands on his thin shoulders and now and then would tell him with an awful archness how well he danced. This man was enormously pleased with the woman and with himself also. He became so pleased that he tried to jitterbug and his poor withered leg would dangle wildly and hit against a crutch as he danced faster and faster.

The other couple was watching this strange performance. Edith recognized the man, but this was the first time she had ever seen him without his wife. He was wearing the blue suit he generally wore when he and his wife sat listlessly through sermons, community concerts, and amateur theatricals. He looked different now because he was enjoying himself.

He would turn to the woman beside him and say something about the dancers and then would slap her on the thigh and laugh, and she would seem to like the things he said so much that she would kiss him impetuously on the ear. Every time he spoke for a moment or two she glowed with attentiveness, and kept looking worshipfully from his hair down to his eyes and then to his lips, then slowly back up the same route, and down again, in the way she had seen stars portray rapturous adoration in the movies. But when he wasn't looking at her, she stared at the dancers abjectly and with a malevolent boredom. The man in the blue suit beamed happily even when he wasn't looking at anything in particular. Like the other two men, he was enormously pleased with himself.

The relentless fondness of the woman on the fat man's knee, the relentless admiration of the woman dancing with the man with the withered leg, and the relentless attentiveness and adoration of the woman with the man in the blue suit made Edith realize that this place that she had wandered into by mistake had been in the same business for about seven generations. Of course she had known where she was ever since she saw that painting.

How many times she had heard of this house, but she had never really believed it. Even now she did not believe everything she had heard. It was the subject of the most unlikely stories of one of the fantastically romantic Charlestons that she felt existed only in people's imagination. She was always creating Charlestons of her own, it was an endemic disease. But everyone shared in the creation of this house, whispering more extravagant fancies from year to year as the legend grew.

This house was said to have stood side by side with another fine old house (the one where the auction would be held), in some lost street, nobody ever quite knew where as many fine old houses stood in many forsaken streets, and then, too, all the stories she had heard had been told by women, who were vague about everything but some of the persistent details, such as the painting, which were a part of each retelling. No one seemed to think that the house was actually standing today; its reality would have robbed the legends of most of their fascination. If it were standing, the women said, it had probably become a Negro tenement, or a miserable boardinghouse over a wretched beauty parlor, and it was best to think of it as gone. They liked to idealize the life of this mansion's great day just as they did the life of those of good fame. And every addition to the legend was sure to add fresh elegance, grandeur, and enchantment to the fabulous wickedness of the place.

The house had been one of the most famous brothels in the world. The beautiful girls had been chosen with the utmost care in both Europe and Asia, and the two most beautiful had been an Andalusian and a Hindu. Great dinners had been held in the stately dining room, many magnificent balls marked each winter, and *soirées intimes* each summer. The master chef had made a fortune and gone back to France to luxurious idleness. Many remarkable dishes had been created here and tasted only in this house. One of the girls had played that harp over there so exquisitely that she never had to leave this drawing room, as the others did upon polite entreaty. Little groups of excellent musicians had played charmingly behind screens at the end of both long halls.

This room was no doubt being kept as a museum. The rest of the place had gone down from *poularde toulousaine* to collard greens and butts meat, from lovely nocturnes to a juke box. Upstairs the fabled boudoirs were certain to be unbearably dreary with iron beds with the paint cracked off, and cockroached walls.

Edith remembered now that the painting was said to have been done by a notorious student of Fragonard, whose work hung only in the most famous *maisons de joie* of Europe, and was represented in America only in this mansion in Charleston. The artist had been commissioned to come from Paris to paint the most overpowering woman of his career.

There was one story that told of a scandal many years before when a well-known European critic had come to Charleston and asked to see this nude of which he had read in the notebooks of the notorious student of Fragonard. He had said that it was a masterpiece with a little difference, and that it was a much better thing than the real Prud'hon. A pity that the galleries would call it lewd. He was also delighted with the mirror's frame.

Later Oscar Wilde was said to have come to see these outrageous works of art, but he had not waited for dinner (the dinners were very indifferent by 1882) and had ignored everyone in the house. The legends always stopped with Wilde's visit, as though the mansion and everything in it had vanished after that.

No man had ever entered this house without a proper introduction, and many who came a great distance were not received, just as some have always been by the more justly renowned houses of Charleston. This house no doubt represented the strangest form of fallen tradition.

Well, the thing to do now was to get out of this place and safely into the house next door where the auction would soon begin. Edith started to think of all the things she had heard about brothels and felt afraid for the first time. Once she had overheard a woman on a bus say, "If they ever caught a regular woman in one of those houses, spying on them, those women would tear her to pieces like wild tigers." The woman with the man in the blue suit looked as though she would do that. When she was not paying servile attention to the man, her mouth sagged so that she had the brutal look of one of Roualt's terrifying prostitutes.

Edith was about to tiptoe into the hall when the front door opened and two very young men came in. She hid behind a chair and waited. The boys rang a little hand bell and she could hear someone coming out of a room in the back hall. The boys were so unsure of themselves that they whispered to each other as they went behind the large woman who didn't even bother to talk to them, but led them right up the great staircase, knowing that they weren't ready yet for the unselfconscious fun of the parlor.

Edith breathed easier. For a minute she thought they were coming into the room with her. But then this museum room was undoubtedly never used. She heard the bell ring in the front hall again and a man calling for a girl named Marilyn.

It must have been Marilyn who came from the back room, and went past Edith's door. In the other room the newcomer had already started to sing and all the others were joining in.

All except the woman with the man in blue. When she wasn't looking at him as though he were Sinatra, she was surely looking as though she would like to slit his throat.

"*Now*," Edith thought, "now I can get out of here," but the front door opened again and again the little bell rang in the hall. The large silent woman who had gone with the boys came down the staircase and as she clumped heavily on each step, Edith thought of the great entrances she had dreamed of when she stood before that staircase.

The woman had stopped. "Oh, it's you, is it?" she said. "Well, you can just go back to the old man's home or wherever you came from. I told you the other night not to come here again."

The old man was very close to Edith's door. "I just wanted to join in the singing in the parlor. They used to make an awful fuss over me here. All I want to do is sing and watch the fun."

The big woman came heavily toward him. "All right," he said. "All right, I don't want to be anywhere that I'm not wanted. I thought I'd always be wanted here. That's why I came back from the island."

"Do you think the girls want an old man like you sitting and watching them work?" the big woman said. "This ain't no play-party I'm running here. You don't expect them to play up to *you*, do you? They gotta draw the line *some*where. Now go on, go *onnnnn!*"

The old man went without another word and the woman was grumbling as she went into the back room.

In the safety of the museum room, Edith had been thinking that this was an infirmary, with brutish nurses, for men with famine-stricken egos. All brothels were undoubtedly just that, with their pandering, and toadying, and fawning. And for all the alluring legends, this place had been no more than that in its great day. A few, like those young men, came here because of an irresistible curiosity, and perhaps a lusty urgency, but most men came to a place like this out of a desperate need to be pleased with themselves. If the women they met every day gave them the meager attention and response necessary to keep a man from having scurvy of the ego and pellagra of the personality then they would not need the drastic treatment of the fawning ministrations of those dreadful women in there. Every wretch must be "Big Boy" to a harlot.

Except the very old.

That man with the withered leg was not to be pitied because of the leg but because of his shriveled spirit. No man in that room had ever tilled his heart. Having no warmth of his own he came here to the old rag fire that these women kept burning, and which would only stifle a man without warming him.

There was nothing *fleur du mal* about this place, it was just forlorn and desolate. She wanted to get out of here more than ever.

Suddenly she thought of George. She could never tell him about this experience and what she thought of it. She couldn't imagine talking to him about it. She felt another uneasy twinge about George. He was so restrained, or without the need of restraint, that he was always upset on hearing about people who did not restrain themselves. He hated ladies' men, and hearing about "affairs." He was terribly uncomfortable any time sex got into a conversation, and made everyone else uncomfortable. It would be inconceivable to talk to him about a brothel. Oh, well, he was bound to prove a gentle, complaisant, and faithful husband, and she should be grateful that he wouldn't want to hear about a degrading place like this.

She wished she wasn't going to meet him later at the auction. She didn't want to see George for a few days until she had time to feel farther away from this. The reek of the collards was like the stench of corruption. She felt that it would cling to her hair and clothes. She would leave word at the auction that she had to go home because of a sudden migraine. He would not even phone her after he got the message knowing that she would not want to leave her darkened bedroom for at least twenty-four hours. He had the rare gift of being able to leave one to oneself. There were times when she felt he was ineffectual because he was not importunate, but it was all part of his tranquillity and she would bless him for it many times, just as she was doing now. If he got to the auction in time to get some of the things she was sure to want, he and the antiques would wait for her.

Two people who had been talking in the back hall went into the room back there and she decided to make a run for it.

But the bell rang again. She felt sick. If this kept up she'd dart out in front of them. But no, she couldn't do that. If anyone saw her she felt she would never be able to shrug this business off.

She didn't let herself think that someone going to the auction might see her come out of this dreadful place. Surely some people must know that it didn't really vanish after Oscar Wilde's visit.

Her mistaking this house for the one next door would be too good a story to keep. Everyone in town would be laughing about it. They might even expect George to laugh.

The bell was rung in a special way, as some sort of a signal. A girl hurried by and almost before Edith had time to get behind the covered harp, the girl brought the signaler into the drawing room.

The man said, "I've got a little time on my hands, so I thought I'd slip in and see you." It was George.

She didn't hear what the two were saying for a few moments after that. Unaccountably her first thought was, "This room isn't a museum after all. It's being kept like this for the exclusive use of those who like to think they would have been received in the old days."

The door had been closed and a little table lamp turned on, and Edith was still hidden in the corner behind the big harp. She was back of the two on the sofa and she peered around the harp cautiously. The girl was not like those in the parlor, she was pretty in a way, and she had on a rather pretty dress, but her technique wasn't very much different. She was already sitting on George's lap and cooing and kissing him. He sat there as passively as if he were reading the paper, inertly accepting the girl's embraces, but Edith knew from his unfamiliar little laughs now and then that he was enormously pleased with himself.

He was always telling Edith that he hated a "demonstrative

man." What he meant was that he wasn't up to loving a woman himself. All her life she would have had to coo and fawn over him like this harlot, or he would have become so limp that life with him would be impossible. He would have kept coming here, as he must have been coming most of his life to one girl or another, to have his ego nourished to the degree that it could be nourished, by being satiated with ready-to-serve caresses.

She remembered how, upon occasion, when she had sat on the arm of his chair and asked him if he was tired, he had smiled with self-pity (the one emotion that she was sure now that he felt) and had waited for her to kiss him and put her arms around him. He seemed then to be settling down in his chair for her to make love to him. There was no sign that he would ever take over himself. She had gone to his chair like that because she felt that if she kissed him he would start making love to her. But he never did. And she knew now that it was after those times that she had first started thinking that George's spirit was always upstairs lying down, and that he had such an empty expressionless face.

She suddenly realized, too, that she had never given George's ego any nourishment and that she never would have, even though that must have been what he had hoped for; that she would learn to fawn over him. He had gone so long without attention that he had to sop up what he could pay for in a place like this. The kisses and endearments and loving attention that keep many men content would never satisfy George after a lifetime of being ignored. She had come along too late. Nothing less than the tireless, smothering, servile rites of these women would keep him pleased with himself.

While she was thinking how desperate George must have always been to need the treatment of this clinic, she had the sickening thought that she must have been more desperate than George because she had been ready to marry him. What need had always forced her to see him in a good light? Did she want desperately to be pleased with *herself*, and could not be without his help?

No, she had loved others in her life, and George never had.

As long as she never lost the ability to love she would never be desperate.

Like those men in the other room George came here because this was the haven of the unwanted. And the only people on earth who are unwanted are the unloving.

It was only since she had known him, and for some apprehensive reason, that came from worrying about growing no younger, had forced herself to believe that she was in love with him, that she had felt a profound frustration. She had never really been lonely until then. And she would never in her life be as lonely again as she had been with George.

The girl was saying that she would fix him his drink, and after making a great show of hating to leave him for a second, she kissed him fervently while he just sat there. Edith was glad that she had never seen him thoroughly pleased with himself before. His smugness was obscene.

The girl ran out of the room and down the hall, and Edith tried to get out of the room behind George's back, but suddenly he turned and saw her.

"It's too bad the auction *wasn't* being held here," she said. "There are some good things."

George's face was full of more expression than it had ever been in his life.

Edith walked out of the room and up the strip of checkered linoleum to the big door. Someone came out of the parlor behind her, but she went out hurriedly and down the marble steps into the warm fresh air.

TATTOO

by WALLACE GRAVES

BANTY'S FOREHEAD WAS ALIVE WITH PERSPIRATION. HE BIT HIS lips as the tattoo machine dug once again into his shoulder, tearing, grinding, clawing away at his living flesh. He looked down. The design was almost finished. In a few minutes the Chinaman sitting beside him, holding the devilish little black tattoo machine, would be through, and Banty's shoulder would be permanently marked.

Banty turned to Chief Charley, the squat, pot-bellied man standing beside him.

"Light me a cigarette, will you, Chief?" Banty said.

"Sure, kid, sure." Chief Charley lit a cigarette and stuck it between Banty's lips. Banty puffed hard on it. The smoke curled up in his eyes. The smarting of his eyes seemed to ease the pain of the tattoo machine working against his shoulder. He tried to take his mind off this dingy little tattoo shop. He thought about the ship. About Donald, for whom Banty was currently playing hero. He wondered what little Donald would think of him now, coming back to the ship with a dull, brown, staring bull tattooed on his shoulder. Banty sighed. The breath came from his throat jerkily. His lips quivered. He wished he had never come to the tattoo shop.

Banty hadn't intended coming to Honolulu on liberty with Chief Charley. They had met accidentally outside the Navy Yard gate, then ridden side by side to town.

Honolulu this afternoon was hot, sultry, spicy. Chief Charley had told Banty to come have a beer with him. They had turned into a tavern teeming with loud smells and sounds. They drank beer, several beers, served by a waitress with full, round curves. Banty looked. He heard Charley talk about his tattoos.

"I been in the Navy seventeen years," Charley said. "When I

first joined up an old sailor told me that if I once got a tattoo, I wouldn't be satisfied till I got another, and another, and another, and it sure has worked out that way." He held out his hairy, apelike, tattooed arms. They both admired them.

"It must hurt," Banty said.

Charley shook his head. "Naw," he said. "You can feel it, but it ain't bad." He laughed. "It ain't the pain, it's the idea of the thing. Why, I've seen guys pass out cold just from watching the needle. You oughta see them." A sound rumbled deep in his throat. "When we get through here I'll take you down to one of the shops."

Half an hour later they left the tavern and walked down Beratania Street. Banty had drunk four bottles of beer. The city was crowded. There seemed to be millions of sailors in white uniforms. They walked past a huge, loud, dark dance hall filled with colored soldiers. Past souvenir shops. Incense smells, musty cardboard smells, taverns, honky-tonk shooting galleries that popped innocuously in the afternoon heat. Past the corner where the old Chinese woman and her daughter cooked rice and rabbit over a charcoal fire.

Half a block down Banty saw a red painted sign. "Great China Art Shop," it said. "Ling Lee. World's Greatest Tattoo Artist." And in smaller letters, "Puts up Wonderful Faces." Banty laughed loosely at the sign.

"What are you giggling at?" Charley asked.

"Oh, nothing."

The shop was dark and dank, humid and warm; ten feet wide and a little longer. As they stepped inside a sailor emerged, rolling down his jumper sleeve. His face was covered with perspiration. The shop was empty except for Ling Lee, a wizened little Chinaman who sat silently at the rear beneath a huge overhead light. He wore a white shirt. Thin, sinewy arms jutted sticklike from his rolled shirt sleeves. He wore black-rimmed glasses. In front of him sat a white porcelain stand with five small bowls holding red, blue, black, brown, and green dye. He was cleaning his tattoo needles. The black tattoo machine lay beside him. A wire cord coiled from it to an attachment overhead. Behind him, on a wooden shelf, were cotton daubers, and a huge bottle of pink disinfectant.

Charley walked toward him, his hand outstretched. "Hiya, Ling, remember me?" No flash of recognition crossed Ling Lee's face. He extended a limp thin hand.

Banty looked around the shop. High on the walls were glassed frames filled with sample tattoos. Battleships and hearts and flowers; To Mother, To Sister, nudes. Bluebirds, bulls, eagles, flags; designs to adorn your arms and navel. The shop smelled tropical and humid, as though someone had recently perspired profusely; it left a strange metallic taste at the base of Banty's tongue.

Charley took off his shirt, revealing a gray, tattooed battleship on his chest. He sat down in a chair by Ling Lee. His hairy belly sagged over his lap. Ling saw the battleship and his face brightened. "Ah," he said. He sucked air. "I rememba' you by tattoo, not by face." They both laughed.

"Come here, kid," Charley said. "I'll show you how it's done." He turned to Ling. "This punk has never seen a man tattooed. We'll show him today, eh, Ling?" Charley laughed. He pointed to a red heart on his right forearm. "I want you to put the name 'Peggy' underneath this heart," he said.

Ling nodded. Banty watched him shave a neat patch of hair from beneath the heart, then wipe the bare space with disinfectant. He traced the name 'Peggy' across Charley's flesh with an indelible pen. Then he put a needle in his tattoo machine and turned the power on. It buzzed. The buzz sent a chill running through Banty.

"Light me a cigarette, will you, kid?" Banty lit a cigarette and put it between Charley's lips. Ling Lee held Charley's fleshy forearm taut with his left hand. He rested his right hand on Charley's arm, then lowered the whirring needle.

Charley's body jerked forward, almost imperceptibly, as the needle bit in on the first sweep of the letter P. A few beads of perspiration broke out on his forehead. They glistened in the light. Banty watched the needle as it traced the letter in blue dye across Charley's arm. He wondered how it felt.

"Peggy's my sister," Charley said. He looked up and winked. Banty blushed, for no reason. The heat oppressed him. He felt moisture on his forehead.

"Ever thought of getting a tattoo, kid?" Charley asked.

Banty stepped back. He shook his head. "Nope," he said. His eyes were fixed on the needle biting into Charley's arm. Ling Lee was tracing the letter E. It might hurt, Banty thought. Or, on the other hand, it might just be a tickling sensation.

"That's too bad," Charley said. "They're nice to have. Can't be a real Navy man without a tattoo." He laughed.

"Who wants to be a real Navy man?" Banty said. He still looked at the needle as he talked. He wondered how it would feel on his own flesh.

"You're in the Navy, aren't you?" Charley paused. The cigarette between his lips moved convulsively as he spoke. He was nervous. "They'll never believe you was in the Navy if you don't go home with a tattoo." Charley laughed. "In the Navy and no tattoo!" He chuckled deeply, spasmodically.

The needle began tracing the first G. Charley tightened his fist.

"Better get at least a little one," Charley said. "You and Don are about the only boys in our division that ain't got one."

"I don't know if I'd like it," Banty said.

"You mean you wouldn't like the *feel* of it?" Charley said. He looked hard at Banty.

"I didn't say that," Banty said. "I'm not scared. I just wonder if I want a tattoo." The high whining buzz of the machine rang swiftly in his ears. The heat heightened it. He put his hand on the back of Charley's chair for support. He felt the vibration through the chair on the palm of his hand. It was a sweet, sensual feeling. The needle was tracing the last G.

"Better get one," Charley said. His cigarette was almost burned out. He puffed thick, jerky billows of smoke. "It'd be awful if I went back to the ship and passed the word you was scared of a tattoo needle."

Charley guffawed. Cigarette smoke got in his throat. He

coughed, and as he coughed he spat the remains of his cigarette from his lips. Ling Lee glanced up.

"Light me another, will you, kid?" Charley said. Ling Lee began tracing the Y. Banty lit Charley another cigarette and put it between his lips. He puffed heavily.

"You wouldn't be just a little yellow, would you?" Charley said through the smoke.

"Hell, no, I'm not yellow," Banty said. The words came louder than he meant them. The buzz rang violently in his head. The shop seemed much too small. "Hell, no!" he shouted. Banty spread his legs wide apart. He reached down and twisted off his white jumper.

"Atta boy, kid," Charley said, standing up. He laughed deeply. Banty sat in the chair. He was impatient for the needle to begin.

"What'll it be?" Charley asked.

Banty looked at the wall. The first thing he saw clearly was the picture of the bull staring at him from one of the framed pictures. "Gimme that bull," he said. He pointed to his left shoulder. "Here."

Ling Lee wiped cool cotton across his shoulder. He traced the design. Banty turned his head away, waiting for the needle to bite into his flesh. It seemed too long before it happened.

The next morning the tattoo didn't ache as it had, but was still too sore to touch. Banty showed it to Donald and watched closely at Donald's thin face as he peered at the tattoo. He saw an expression of intense interest which might have been envy, or perhaps only morbid curiosity. Banty tried to act casual about it all, but he couldn't help noting how smooth, how white, how presumptuously unmarked Donald's thin arms and shoulders were.

"I can't get over you having a tattoo," Donald said. His eyes were alive with interest. Banty said nothing. As he looked at the smoothness of Donald's arms, Banty felt a pang of jealousy run through him. He tried to disregard it. Him jealous of Donald? He laughed, but the feeling grew.

At noon Banty and Donald changed to their white uniforms. Donald often suggested going on liberty with Banty, and today Banty condescendingly agreed. He tried to appear as if it made no difference to him whether they went to Honolulu together. He acted with great unconcern.

On the bus to Honolulu Banty felt feverishly warm. He told Donald he wanted to stop at the tattoo shop. "Ling Lee said he'd put some oil on this tattoo if it itched—and it itches," he said. He tried to sound casual.

Donald laughed. He still couldn't get over Banty having a tattoo.

"It's not a bad deal," Banty said. "Didn't hurt as much as I thought it would." He watched Donald closely.

"The way you talked this morning, it didn't hurt at all."

"Oh, it stings a little, but not enough to worry about," Banty said. He felt the bull itch and burn under his jumper. He wanted to rip his clothes off and dive into a cool pool of water. "It's not bad," he said. He felt a gush of desire rise in him. He looked at Donald. "I'm not sorry I got it." He was surprised how easily the lie came for him.

"It's one way to get in solid with Chief Charley," Donald said.

"It sure is."

Banty and Donald got off the bus in the heart of the humid honky-tonk district. Banty led the way to Ling Lee's tattoo shop. As he stepped inside, the oppressive sorrow of the place reminded him of the fear he had felt yesterday. It had been fear, all right. It was like Charley had said. Not so much the pain, but oh, the little needle biting and clawing away at your flesh; the poisonous dye going under your skin. Something you couldn't wash off. Banty's spine tingled with the horror of it. He looked at Donald lolling beside him, looking bug-eyed at the pictures of nudes and battleships and lovers' designs that hung around the room, with prices quoted underneath.

Ling Lee was sitting under his light, working with his needles. He was lining them up in neat rows waiting for the next customer. He looked up.

"I was in here yesterday," Banty said. "You said come back if it itches." He took off his jumper and laid it on the chair next to the Chinaman.

"Oh, yes," Ling Lee said. He reached for a bottle filled with livid green oil. He soaked a piece of cotton soggy. Banty sat down. Ling Lee rubbed the cotton across his shoulder, back and forth. It soothed the burning tattoo.

Banty turned to Donald. "Look at the different colored dyes," he said. "And the needles." Donald looked at them. He was strangely quiet. His quietness irritated Banty.

"Why don't you get a tattoo?" he said. "Charley says you're the only guy left in our division without one." He was amazed at the belligerent tone of his voice.

"I don't think I'd like one," Donald said.

"You're not afraid it'll hurt, are you?" Banty looked at Donald and laughed nervously. He felt tensely alert.

"I didn't say that," Donald said. He wiped a pale thin hand across his forehead. "It's hot in here. Let's go."

"What's your hurry?" Banty said. "I'm in no hurry." He stood up. His head felt bloody full. He walked deliberately over to Donald. "Come on, Junior, better get a tattoo." The words flowed from his mouth uncontrolled. "You wouldn't want the rest of the boys to know that you were scared, would you?" Donald seemed distant to him, as though Banty were talking from a high peak, or a valley.

Donald eyed him soberly. "You wouldn't do *that*," he said. His lips remained parted. They were moist.

"The hell I wouldn't," Banty said. He felt desirous. His face was warm. "It'd be awful if I told the Chief you were yellow!" With the words out of him he felt calm. His face softened. He turned away, casually. "Well, if you don't want one I guess there's nothing I can do about it."

"Who said I didn't want one?" he heard Donald say.

"Why *you* did."

"I did not." There was a touch of bravado in Donald's voice. Banty thrilled as he saw his lips quiver. A moment of charged silence; then Donald's thin arms moved hesitantly toward his jumper.

Banty forced a grin. "Atta boy," he said. His voice was weak. Donald's face was tense. Banty clapped his hand across Donald's shoulder. The act seemed unnatural and cold. "Ling Lee'll fix you up." He felt nauseatingly weak. He helped Donald off with his jumper. Donald's flesh looked deathly white in the darkness of the shop. He sank down in the chair.

"Which one do you want?" Banty asked. Ling Lee was ready with the disinfectant. Donald looked up. His eyes were frightened.

"Oh, I guess I'll, get a—bluebird," he said. His voice cracked. Banty saw a faint line of perspiration above his lip. The insides of his hands were damp.

Ling Lee rubbed Donald's arm with strong-smelling disinfectant, then traced a bluebird across the trembling flesh. As he grasped the tattoo machine Banty's eyes were intent on the needle. The high, whining buzz began, and the tremendous desire within Banty changed to fear—the same fear he had felt yesterday. But with it there was no bitter satisfaction of pain; only a sense of shame and sorrow.

THE CHRISTMAS STAR

by MINA LEWITON

THE SOFT, ENORMOUS SNOWFLAKES ATTACHED THEMSELVES briefly to the windows of Class IX and melted into wavering wetness. Inside the classroom, the children's excitement and wonder at the snow had died down. It had worn off in an hour, early in the morning, and it was now midafternoon. The children did not look up at the snow any longer but were working with clay, shaping it laboriously into thick stars. When the children had finished two stars each, Miss Cobb gave them two candles apiece, green or yellow or red, which they stuck into the soft center of the stars. Miss Cobb spread a newspaper over the long radiator that was also the window sill and each child brought his stars and set them out to dry.

"Now," said Miss Cobb, "you may choose a color to match or contrast with the candles. When the stars are dry you can paint them." She began to distribute the paintboxes.

The children no sooner had set out the stars than they began to run back, first to the radiator to see if they were dry, then to the basin to get water to mix the paint. The whole room was in hubbub and movement and Miss Cobb's head was aching. She held up both hands and told the children that the stars would not be dry until the big hand on the clock on her desk was on the ten and the little hand on the three. But they could have stories until then, and who would like to tell them?

Peter Bellman tiptoed up to look at the clock and Miss Cobb said she would tell them as soon as it was the right time, and to go back to his chair.

"Stories about animals?" asked Dicky.

"About anything at all," said tired Miss Cobb.

"But could they be about animals?" asked Dicky.

"Yes," said Miss Cobb.

"I have a kitten," said Mark, "it has six paws."

"Six paws?" asked Miss Cobb, shaking her aching head doubtfully.

"Six toes, I mean," Mark said, and the children laughed noisily, but they would have been just as ready to believe it had six paws.

"What's its name?" asked Stephen.

"Tiger. It has six toes on each paw and its name is Tiger," Mark said, repeating himself in a boring monotone.

"That's a nice story," said Miss Cobb. "Has anyone else a story to tell?"

Walter said, "I can tell a story."

"All right, Walter, tell us a story."

"It's about a dog," Walter said, "and no one could make him go if he didn't want to. My father couldn't take him for a walk. And my mother couldn't. He'd sit down until they both took him out. Both together."

"And did they both together have to take him for a walk *every day?*" Miss Cobb inquired.

"Oh, sometimes he didn't mind," Walter said. "But mostly he wanted them both together."

"Your mother could carry him," said Freddy. "That's what my mother does when Tootsie doesn't want to go out."

"Oh," Walter said, "he was too big. Much too big."

"And so they both took him for a walk," Miss Cobb rounded out the story.

"His name was Captain Flagg," said Walter.

"He must have been a fine dog," Miss Cobb said, but because she knew what had happened in Walter's home she did not ask where Captain Flagg was now.

A little girl named Dove said, "Miss Cobb, may I see if my stars are ready?"

"I will tell you when they are," said Miss Cobb and glanced at her clock, then went to the radiator to see.

"Are they, Miss Cobb?" called the children, one after the other.

The clay had hardened and was dry and warm to the touch and she began to hand the stars back to the children.

They began mixing their paint in their small tin dishes and the room became quiet while they absorbed themselves in their painting.

Miss Cobb's head began to feel better and she looked out at the white snowflakes that seemed suspended in mist and thought she would start the children dressing a bit earlier to allow for rubbers, and how nice it was going to feel to walk home with the soft snowflakes falling. For Miss Cobb was a person who liked dreary weather and wet weather. It made her feel cozier when she was indoors, and when she was out it made her look forward to being soon in a comfortable, warm room cheerfully lit.

She straightened her desk and tore the leaf for Friday off her calendar, then Saturday and Sunday also, feeling while she did so that already those days were gone, torn, spent. Then she saw there would be only Monday and Tuesday before it was Christmas day, and a whole week of calendar leaves to tear off. A vaguely regretful feeling came over her at this flagrant speeding of time.

Then she saw that Dove had finished her candlesticks and had begun to paint her fingernails with the red water-color paint. Miss Cobb said, "Dove and Marianne, please help me to collect the pans and pour the water down the drain. Then George and William begin to collect the paintboxes. Don't touch the stars until the paint has dried," warned Miss Cobb. "Let them get nice and dry. They'll be perfect little Christmas stars if you let them dry, and you can use them for candlesticks."

The children were very proud of their stars. Those who could write their names turned the stars upside down and printed as much of their names as could be put in the small space, and Miss Cobb wrote their names for the others.

The children had been saving paper bags for the stars and now each had one. When Miss Cobb gave his to Walter, he said, "I'll put one away for my mother but I'll leave this one out for my father."

"It's snowing," said Miss Cobb, "and the paint may run. I've an extra bag if you like."

But Walter shook his head. "My father's coming for me. I'll give it to him in his hand."

When they were downstairs standing in line, Miss Cobb went to Walter and whispered, "I'll keep the bag for you if this is Daddy's week end. Shall I?"

He gave it up at once and then she opened the outside door. Miss Cobb stood by and saw that each child was called for. A whole group went home in a bus. Only a handful were left with her.

Walter stood watching the children pile into the bus, and he began jumping up and down on the slippery, muddy step. Then suddenly he pulled his raincoat tightly about him and holding the star with its candle in one hand sat down. He opened his mouth and let his tongue loll out to one side.

"Walter, get up at once from the cold wet step. Your father will be here in a minute. You don't want him to see your nice raincoat all muddy."

"I'm Captain Flagg," Walter said. "When my daddy comes I won't go away with him. I'll sit here and wait till my mother comes too."

Miss Cobb felt herself becoming very warm.

"But you're not a dog, Walter. You're a boy. Boys don't act the way poor dumb animals do. Besides, it's impossible because it's an agreement. You understand, don't you? This is Daddy's week end and all next week is Mother's week, isn't it? You have to play it like a game—with rules. That's how it *must be*, Walter." She was gently tugging at his hand. "It's the best way," Miss Cobb went on, sounding unconvincing to herself, "and you'll have a lovely week end, *if* you don't start off wrong. And here he comes."

"I'm Captain Flagg," he whispered, but he had stopped playing it and stood up when he saw his father smiling at him out of the car window.

The car stopped in front of them and she saw that they had both come, the child's father and his new wife.

"Daddy," Walter called, "look," and held up his star with its bright red candle.

The little girl named Dove stood on the steps waiting too, and as she saw her mother round the corner, skimmed down the steps and snatching Walter's candlestick out of his hand, let it fall. It made a flat, small noise and broke into three pieces and the candle rolled away, while Dove ran into her mother's arms.

The child did not cry at once but stared down in disbelief at the broken star. Then slowly his face became tortured and miserable and hopeless.

"Now everything's broken," thought Miss Cobb. "Everything."

Walter's father and his new wife got out of the car. His father stood beside him trying to console him, talking to him but not wanting to lift him up, not wanting to treat him like a baby. At last the child began to cry. Miss Cobb heard his long, deep sobs and could not bear it.

"Walter dear, don't cry," she said, coming quickly to him. "Take this one and we'll make another one on Monday." She thrust the paper bag toward him and there was a pause in his crying. Then he said, "No, that's the one to keep," and looked at her searchingly to see if she had forgotten. The blood rushed to Miss Cobb's face.

Then the girl with the reddish hair who was his father's new wife picked up the three pieces of candlestick and the candle.

"I've got very fine glue," she said, "that can mend this. It comes in a bottle and anyone can do it with a little care. I think you can. Then when it dries it will be as strong as ever." She bent toward Walter. "We'll have a Christmas party a little ahead of Christmas day. And we'll put the candlestick on the table and light the candle. Let's do it right away." The girl had put together the star while she talked to him, and put back the candle. She held it in the palm of her hand to show him.

Miss Cobb put her arm gently round his shoulders, "Good-by, Walter, I'll see you on Monday."

"Dove shouldn't have pushed me," he said.

"No," Miss Cobb said. "She shouldn't have."

"But keep the other for me," he said, touching the paper bag.

"I will," she said eagerly, seeing that everything was not broken after all.

Walter's father got into the car, the girl helping Walter in, and they drove off. Miss Cobb went down the street in the soft winter twilight, breathing quickly, the cool snow falling and melting on her warm face.

I BROKE MY BACK ON A ROSEBUD

by WILLIAM MARCH

THIS IS A STORY WHICH CORPORAL CURTAIN TELLS TO THOSE who will listen, and this is the way he told it to me:

I'm talking about the last war, remember—not about this new, fancy one. . . . Say, how old do you take me to be? All right. Go on. Go on and say sixty. It won't hurt my feelings any. But you'll be wrong if you think that, because I was forty-eight years old on my last birthday.

Okay. Okay. So I'm forty-eight on my last birthday, and that makes me twenty-four in 1919, now don't it? And you want to know something else? My birthday falls on the eleventh of November—Armistice Day—remember that far back? I was luckier than most, I used to say to myself, because I went through the fighting and didn't get a scratch. Didn't get gassed, either. Didn't even get flu or trench-feet. Didn't get anything, see?

Then, after it was all over, comes this parade in New York City, up Fifth Avenue, and as we marched along, I kept thinking that my army days were about over—that it wouldn't be long before I was on the outside. And so we paraded up the avenue at attention, according to regulations. People stood on both sides of the pavement, waving flags and cheering, but I didn't pay them any mind. I was too busy checking off each landmark as we went by. "That's Fourteenth Street ahead," I'd think; or, "There's Madison Square to the left, as big as life and right on schedule." So finally we got into the public library neighborhood, and I knew we'd be passing the reviewing stand before long.

There was some sort of commotion taking place near the south side of the library steps. I looked in that direction, without really turning my head, and there, standing on a pedestal above the crowd, between the front feet of one of the stone lions, was a good-looking woman. A pink basket was hung around her neck on a wide, pink ribbon; and what's more, the pink basket was full of pink rosebuds. Not the stems and leaves, too, mind you—just the pink heads. . . . And every once in a while she'd show all her pretty teeth, blow a kiss to the troops and sing out, "Welcome home to each and every one!" Then with a little twitch which started at her ankles and ended in a shake of her yellow curls, she'd reach in her pink basket and toss a pink rosebud to the boys.

Now listen carefully to me, because here comes the pay-off. . . . When my platoon was almost flush with the stone lion and the dame standing there above the heads of everybody else, I cut my glance up and around a little—and there she was, looking straight into my eyes. So she reached in her silk basket, picked out a fat rosebud, all for me, and tossed it in my direction. "Welcome back!" she called out, while people on the sidewalk looked at her and clapped their hands. "Welcome back to the United States of America!"

I felt the rosebud hit me on the chest, and I saw it bounce off; and the next thing I knew, there was something soft and sliding under my foot, like a big, pink eyeball. I tried to get my balance back, but I couldn't; and then I was lying flat on my back, right in the middle of the street, with the men of my company detouring around me. I didn't feel pain anywhere—the only thing was, I couldn't get up when I tried. So first they carried me into a store. After that an ambulance took me to the hospital, but it wasn't until a couple of days later that I knew, for certain, my back was broken. . . . You know the rest, I imagine. Somebody must have told you already that I've been lying on a board since 1919. Figure it out for yourself. That's almost a quarter of a century. Well, that's the way it is, and there's nothing I can do to change it. . . .

Pull down the shade a little, will you fellow? The God damned sun's in my eyes.

All right! All right, let's get on with the story. . . . Anybody would think I'd be downhearted, knowing I had a fractured spine, but I wasn't. Well, not right away. I kept saying to myself, "Look at the discoveries doctors are making these days. Somebody is sure to find out what to do for me." And so I lived on hope for ten years or more, and every time something new came up, why, I'd let 'em do it to me first, saying to myself that this time everything was going to be all right; but it never was. The Government took good care of me, and sometimes when visitors came, the doctors would point to me and say, "This is Corporal Curtain. He sets us all an example in fortitude."

Hope dies hard in a man, but it does die finally. . . . Am I telling you something new? Am I telling you something you haven't heard before? I don't know how hope died in me, but one morning I woke up wise to myself. I knew, then, what the doctors had known all along, and that was, I'd never be any better, no matter what they did for me. That's when I started to see the woman's face again. I'd close my eyes and try to shut it out, but I couldn't. I cursed her and damned her from morning to night, like a crazy man. "Why wasn't she home, where she belonged, cooking her husband some dinner?" I'd say. "Why did she have to show herself off like she did?"

I'd known from the beginning, you see, that she didn't come out that morning to look at the soldiers. She came out to have the soldiers look at her. . . . And she didn't throw me a rosebud because I was a returning hero in her eyes. Oh, no! Not that one! She did it so people could see how nice she *looked* throwing a rosebud! That was the worst thought of all, and when it came to me, I'd close my eyes and lay my head deep in the pillow. . . .

Lift my neck up some and give me a drink of water, will you? My throat's dry. . . .

Now, here's a thing I never figured out to my satisfaction: You'd think hate would last longer than hope, but it didn't work out like that. Not with me, anyway. And so after a year or two I wasn't able to see her face any more. I didn't blame her for anything, either. I leaned over backwards to be fair and reasonable. She couldn't know that I was going to slip and fall, now could she? How could anybody anticipate such a thing? It was probably something which had never happened to a man before in the whole history of the world, so why hold her responsible? Then I had another thought, and it was this: Maybe the woman was an instrument in the hands of God. Maybe I was being punished for something I did once, but couldn't remember. So I said to myself, "If that's the way it is, that's the way it's going to be, and I've got to accept it." So you see? First I hoped, and then I hated—but at last I was resigned.

Then a year or so later I saw things in another light, and now I laugh to myself when I think back. Can you figure out what changed me? I've already given you a hint or two. You can't? Okay. I'll tell you before long, but let me lead up to it gradual. Let me tell you first about the man who wrote a piece about me in the newspapers.

It was Richard Emery Simms, the famous columnist, and the story was printed all over the country, in I don't know how many papers. A lot of people read about my case, and it wasn't long afterwards before some of the boys I knew in the old outfit, who had forgot me years ago, started writing me letters, or even coming to see me here at the hospital.

Now, hardly a day passes without somebody dropping in—strangers or otherwise. The boys from my old outfit talk about themselves for the most part. I guess they figure that since I never had a real life of my own, I'd be glad to hear about theirs. They tell me who they married, and how many kids they got. They tell me everything that's happened to them since we saw each other last—what they had hoped to get out of their lives, and what they had really got.

So one morning a fellow named Jamie Ethridge (he used to be a sergeant in the old second platoon) came to pay me a visit. He talked about his troubles even more than the others. All he had ever asked was a little peace and security, he said. Once he thought that he had it, too, and then something had gone wrong somehow. He had hoped so much, he said. He had tried so hard, and then something had happened, although he didn't know how or why. I quit listening to him about that time, and my mind went back to my own troubles. . . .

At first, what happened to me seemed like an accident without sense, then it seemed like something planned for me alone. All at once I knew both ideas were wrong, and I've been a changed man from that minute on. This may sound dopey to you. But now I think of that woman as something made out of paper and wires. Something curled and painted pink for the people. Something that lives right there in the library, with the romances and poems. . . . And every once in awhile the authorities get her out, dust her off, and send her out for the world to see—like a beauty contest winner with Miss Universal Dream across her belly.

When that thought came into my head I started to laugh in earnest, while Sergeant Ethridge looked at me and wondered what had happened. . . . You see, I used to think that no other man was in my particular fix. That was my mistake, and I know better now. Oh, no, fellow! I'm not the only man who broke his back on a rosebud. Not by a long shot. Sometimes it seems to me that everybody in my generation done the same thing one way or another. "I'm not the only one," I say to people now. "There's many another. Oh, many and many a one."

Light a cigarette and put it between my lips, will you, bud?

SAWDUST

by ARTHUR FOFF

I WALKED INTO JOE'S AND THERE WAS MY OLD MAN AT THE bar as usual. He was oiled pretty good and kept arguing with a skinny, yellow-faced guy I figured I'd seen someplace before.

"Pop," I said, "Maggie just had five pups, four males and a bitch, why don't you come home and look them over?"

"Tom," Pop said, "you remember Mr. Finley here. He had Danny Day." I remembered Finley now and I remembered Danny Day. Danny Day had been a good dog. It had been about seven years ago when I'd seen Danny's last fight. If you've maybe ever seen a sick dog try and fight you know why it stuck in my mind though I was only ten. Finley had lost a lot of good dogs besides Danny.

"Mr. Finley says he has a better dog than Danny ever was, a dog that can whip anything I got. What do you think about that, Tom?"

"He maybe has, and he maybe hasn't. We're not fighting dogs any more, what do we care?"

My Pop turned back to the bar with his foot on the brass rail and took a swallow of beer. He wiped his lips with his coat sleeve. "Sure, I know we aren't going in the pit no more O.K., but Mr. Finley here says his Snatcher can lick anything I got. And I say he can't. And I'm willing to bet my drawers even a pup like Moby Dick can lick the hell out of him." I felt sick when he said that. I wanted to get out of the bar and away from all the guys who hung around it. I wanted to get back into the afternoon sunshine.

"You still talk a lot, like always," Finley spat into the spitoon, "but I ain't interested in your talking. Three hundred bucks: put up or shut up."

Pop turned back to the bar and pretended to drink his beer,

but I could see the roll of flesh on the back of his neck turn red. I said, "How old is Moby? How old is he?" I said.

"Two."

"Eighteen months."

"There isn't much difference," Pop said. He knew there was.

"Not much difference?" I stepped right up alongside him and shook his arm. He wouldn't look at me, so I thought he was sore until I saw his reflection in the mahogany mirror. It was a big mirror and his face seemed little in it, little and frightened and mad all at the same time. Then Joe, the bartender, moved in front of him and I couldn't see his face any more. Finley had been watching him too, but now he turned and looked at me.

"Gentlemen," he said, staring hard, "you can't, you can't get good apples," he sneered at Pop, "off a bad tree." The crowd laughed, even some of the racing men at the far end of the bar.

Pop faced Finley. He stood on his toes and shouted into Finley's face, "Damn you! Damn you, we'll fight you and your crossbred cur!"

"The three hundred?" Finley acted like he wasn't interested. "Joe, bring another bottle."

"Don't worry about me, don't worry about me," Pop yelled in his ear, trying to pull him away from the bottle Joe had just set down in front of him.

Finley nodded. "Have a drink," he said.

A lot of guys had gathered around us and they were all talking at once, betting and swearing and asking when and where it was to be. Pop said would next month at the old pit outside Mill Valley be all right and Finley said any time, any place. Pop was bragging about what Moby would do to the Snatcher when I pushed through the circle of cigars, derbies, and fancy watch fobs to start home. Dick was my dog. He'd never been in a fight in his life.

The month passed like nothing. My old man didn't even bother to try and train Moby Dick. He stayed at Joe's all day, sometimes playing stud in back and sometimes standing at the bar with his beer. He talked about the fight whatever he was doing and there were big racing guys who hung onto everything he said, he told me, who'd never noticed him before. I tried to teach the dog a little myself, but he was my dog and I couldn't drive him and sweat him the way he needed. When Pop came home nights, which was usually late, he brought Moby into the parlor to pet him and talk to him. If he had a snoot full he'd feed him sausages on the sofa until he fell asleep. In the mornings he'd still be snoring on the sofa with his mouth open and Moby beside him.

When the first Thursday of the month rolled around, the time of the fight, I was shaky in my pants. The pit, which was in an old barn, had been fixed up by a half-brained nigger named George who'd been a good jockey until he got rheumatism. He'd made plenty of money for others but he didn't have any himself. He sold newspapers in front of Joe's now, bumming a drink when he could and doing errands for the guys who remembered him.

Pop and I took the ferry to Sausalito, driving the rest of the way to the old lumber barn outside Mill Valley. All the way over I rubbed Moby's head while Pop drove. "Moby," I'd say to him, "you'll win in no time, you're a cinch. You won't get a scratch and you'll win in no time." He'd wrinkle his nose up so his teeth showed in a smile because he liked to be talked to and have his head rubbed. He didn't know what I meant and I don't think I did myself. Whenever the car stopped suddenly he slobbered lightly but kept his cookies. That was lucky, I thought, it showed he wasn't too nervous.

We parked the car under some redwoods outside the barn and left Moby locked in it. After we'd opened up a few guys drifted in, then more, and finally there was a big noisy crowd. I knew some of them and recalled others from when I'd been a kid. A couple of cops came in, but they were off duty. Pop shook hands with them and they said wasn't it just like the old days, and he said by God if it wasn't. Finley came in at eight-thirty on the dot just as Pop was walking around inside the pit inspecting it and cleaning his fingernails with his big jackknife, the way he does when he's worried.

Finley carried the Snatcher wrapped in a white towel through the crowd, set him in the pit, and took the towel off. It was the first time the Snatcher had been out to the coast and the crowd stopped talking to stare at him. He was an oversize brindle with a scar clean across the back of his head, and there were other marks from fighting on his chest and legs and muzzle. His chest was heavy as a beer keg; when he closed his mouth you could see the jaw muscles stand out like thick fists. Finley walked him around the pit twice to give the boys a chance to look him over and bet some more. Pop brought in Moby Dick and did the same. For a while you couldn't hear yourself think for the noise. New bets were placed. The odds went up in favor of the Snatcher to ten to one, but my old man kept putting down even money. Then at last it was quiet. Pop and Finley took the customary drink from the same bottle. The pup looked fine, you understand, but for all that he was a pup. He came from a good fighting line, only a fighting line don't mean a hell of a lot to a dog that hasn't ever been in a fight.

The dogs were placed opposite each other. The pit was closed. Pop leaned over the rail, talking low to Dick. The barn was almost black but for the yellow light dim in smoke over the pit. The sweet hard smell of whiskey seemed everywhere. The crowd pressed to the rail. On the other side of the ring I could barely make out Finley's face, yellow as the light and blurred as the smoke. Moby stood with his head cocked at us. The Snatcher moved toward him and he stepped stiff and high away.

"Pop," I said, "look!"

Pop took a shot out of his bottle. "Don't worry, Tom," he said to me. "Moby'll lick him."

Just then the Snatcher flattened his small sharp trimmed ears and braced his hind legs in the sawdust. Moby was moving away when the Snatcher lunged. The hold missed but there was a nasty rip down Moby's shoulder. Right away he knew what it was about. His brown, pink-circled eyes became close and black and his lips curled back over his teeth in a snarl. He rumbled in his chest and braced his body until the muscles in his back quivered and bulged. The Snatcher moved in again and Dick met him with a hold for the throat that just missed. He struck again, fast and hard, for the same place. He missed. His teeth slid and tore along the base of the Snatcher's skull, reopening the scar and pouring blood down the Snatcher's neck. The Snatcher got his head away in a smooth rolling move that brought him right back. He slashed Moby's left ear into shreds, but missed the real hold he was trying for once more. The two of them backed away for a minute and for the first time I could see how the once white body of Dick was stained gold and red with sawdust and blood. Pop took another drink and swore under his breath.

The two snarls came at once. Moby moved too late. The Snatcher was on top of him. His teeth shone white for the second his mouth was open and then he fastened them in the lump of shoulder muscle, forced his legs deeper into the sawdust so that he could sink the teeth to the bone. Once those teeth got there the bone would be mashed like a paper box.

"Roll, Moby, you damned fool, roll!" Pop finished the whiskey in his bottle with a final gulp.

Instead of rolling away Moby tore away, and the shoulder flesh tore wide open with him. He blurred in white, the flank of skin hanging like a flag, stained with blood and flecked with gold. I heard his jaws snap together once and miss, clean across the ring. I waited to hear the next empty smash. It didn't come.

I opened my eyes and saw he had the Snatcher solid by the throat. It must have been luck because he was a dog that didn't know enough to roll yet. The Snatcher tried uselessly to underslice at his gut. Moby held him away, threshing him back and forth, working in his hold. His thews jutted like rocks and the tendons in his legs got larger as they filled with blood from the strain. Slowly he began the slope of his shoulders to one side to bring the Snatcher down on his back into the sawdust. For a minute the two dogs stood there, stuck in space, not moving and yet fighting with everything they had. Then the hump of muscle ridged across the Snatcher's shoulder line relaxed and Moby drove him to the ground. He worked the hold deeper and surer until the Snatcher could not even raise his head.

My old man raised the whiskey bottle and cracked it over the rail. "By God, I told you. I told you he'd lick him. I told you, didn't I?"

The Snatcher gave one last fine brave jerk to get away, then he settled back easy to the sawdust as if he'd decided to go to sleep. Finley, at the rail opposite us, screwed his lips and spat cleanly into the ring onto the side of his dog's head where his eye was closed. He climbed the rail, walked across the pit without looking at the dogs, and stood in front of us. He said, "That was the luckiest hold I've seen in twenty years. A better dog wouldn't have even tried it."

"Lucky? Lucky?" Pop said, his voice getting louder. "A better dog? There ain't no better dog nor no better line! See that Pit, see him out there? He wouldn't ever let loose his hold on the Snatcher's throat without you pry open his jaws. That's my kind of dog. He don't let loose!"

"Yeah?" said Finley, tilting back his hat.

One guy who had his arm around Pop's shoulder answered yeah, that dog couldn't take his teeth out of the Snatcher's throat if he wanted to. It was inside him to hold on. You could turn a fire hose on him and he wouldn't let go!

Everyone yelled and laughed. Sure, that was right. Moby Dick wouldn't give up his hold even if you turned a fire hose on him. Then, above all their voices, came my old man's. "A fire hose? By Jesus, you could cut his legs off and he wouldn't let go that throat hold!"

Finley took out his wallet and the barn became still. He looked at Pop, and Pop looked at him, and he said, "How much would you like to bet? Double or nothing?"

My old man stared at Finley, at me, at the faces of all the guys standing around him. Nobody said anything. A guy passed Pop a bottle and Pop took a big shot. The dim yellow light patched shadows on his face as he tilted his head back to drink and I could see the sweat oozing from the creases under his chin. He handed the bottle back and wiped his mouth with his sleeve. When he turned his head toward the pit everybody watched him. Moby was still holding fast. Then some wiseacre in the back yelled that he was yellow.

Pop wheeled around, clumsy, trying to keep his voice down. "Double it is," he shouted. "Who wants another C?"

"I'll take that, pal." The voice was from the back again. Right away everyone went nuts.

"Another ten?"

"Hell, where's my dough?"

"Keep that damned cigar out of my face."

"Twenty-five'll get you fifty the dog gets loose. Here we go, boys. Who wants to take my easy money?"

"Hand me that bottle, you bastard."

"He won't go through with it, I tell you."

"I told you to keep that cigar out of my face."

"Don't listen to them, Pop," I shouted. "Don't listen."

My old man looked at me once over his shoulder before the crowd surged forward, driving him toward the ring. He grabbed the rail. "Just a minute, just a minute!" he yelled. "Who's going to do it?"

"It's your dog's legs," Finley said.

"It's impossible, impossible. He can't go through with it."

"That's right," shouted the wiseacre in the back, "he's yellow!"

Pop's face went hard. His chest rose and fell beneath his old brown sweater. Without a word he turned, climbed over the rail, walked across the pit to where Moby was holding onto the Snatcher.

"Don't, Pop," I screamed, "for the love of God, please don't!"

Some guy grabbed me and told me to shut up. He shoved me back and took my place at the rail. It seemed like everybody was shoving me. Pretty soon I was way in the back with nothing in front of me but heads. I clawed to the front again. It was too late. My old man was kneeling over the dogs so that his belly touched his knee. The light above him spilled yellow on his bald spot and gleamed in the sweat streaming off his cheeks.

The man next to me heaved when it was all over and he ran from the barn with his hand over his mouth. The whole place was wild with screaming. Two guys who'd bet Moby would hold on gave Pop another drink and helped him out of the pit. After he got out it didn't seem as if he'd needed any help because he was talking and bragging the loudest of them all. "What'd I tell you? Licked the living—what do you think of the apple tree now, Finley? Here, here, who's got a drink? Yellow, boys, did you ever see the day I was yellow? Feel, feel? Feel a hundred percent, boys. Six hundred percent. Drinks on me at Joe's. No, no, didn't hurt him; only thinking about his hold—that's the way I breed them."

I just stood there and watched him go out with a big wad of greenbacks stuck in one fist and a bottle in the other. He went out and they went with him. Pretty soon I looked around and the barn was empty. Even the nigger George had left. There was nothing there but me and the two dogs and the yellow light.

I went into the pit and sat in the sawdust by Moby and the Snatcher: two good dogs, one of them mine, and both of them dead. I saw something shine on the ground. It was the jackknife, the blade still open. I shook off the blood, closed it, put it into my pocket.

I buried the two dogs under the redwoods in back of the barn. There were two trees close together. I buried Moby under the one, and the Snatcher under the other. The earth was soft and dark. I wanted to get into it too. I patted the last dirt into place with my hands because it seemed the thing to do.

It took me four hours to get to San Francisco. My old man had taken the car and I had to walk from the barn into Sausalito where I caught the last night ferry. When I walked into Joe's it was nearly morning and the stars were beginning to fade out of the sky. All the lights were on in Joe's and most of the guys were still there, laughing and patting Pop on the back, smoking cigars and drinking his whiskey. I walked through the crowd. Pretty soon I came to him. I stood in back of him while the crowd gradually moved away until it was him and me there alone. "Pop," I said, "I want to talk to you." I maybe guess he'd seen me come towards him in the mahogany mirror because without turning he said,

"Sure, sure, Tom." He yelled to his friends, "Hell, don't go away, boys. I'm standing them again soon's I put the kid in his place." He was very jolly. The guys began to move back to the bar.

I walked out the back door. Pop followed me. He shut the door and stood next to the big slop can with his back against the brick wall of the alley. I took the jackknife from my pocket. The alley was dirty and cold, with a mean wind blowing old papers down it that made scraping sounds. Above us the sky was purple and gray lighted by the first streaks of the sun coming through the night clouds a golden red. I got the blade of the jackknife open.

"Well," I said, "this isn't going to be as fine and courageous as cutting off your legs, but I maybe guess it'll have to do."

I put the point of the knife against his belly. There was a hole in the sweater where I put the knife. The threads had worn out and broke.

Pop didn't move. I looked up from the knife to his face, seeing the wetness on his cheeks.

"Best kid you ever seen, by Jesus," he said. He was smiling and the goldred light of the sun was flush on his forehead. I closed the blade and handed him the jackknife. "It's yours," I said. I turned around and walked down the alley with the wind and the papers.

VERY SPECIAL SHOES

by MORLEY CALLAGHAN

All that winter and into the spring while the rest of the Johnson family waited anxiously for the doctor to decide what was really the matter with Mrs. Johnson, eleven-year-old Mary, who had only been told that her mother was troubled with pains in the legs from varicose veins, stayed home from school to help with the housework and dreamed of a pair of red leather shoes. The shoes had been in a shoestore window over on the avenue. Mary had seen them one day in the winter when she had been walking along slowly with her mother, doing the shopping.

All winter she had dreamed of the shoes. Now she could hardly believe that the day she had been waiting for had come at last. Every Saturday she got twenty-five cents for doing the housework all by herself and today it finally added up to the six dollars which was the price of the shoes. Moving around quietly so she would not wake her Mother, Mary finished up the last of the dusting in the living room. She hurried to the window and looked out: on such a day she had been afraid it might rain but the street was bright in the afternoon sunlight. Then she went quickly into the bedroom where her mother slept, with one light cover thrown half over her. "Mother, wake up," she whispered excitedly.

Mrs. Johnson, a handsome woman of fifty with a plump figure and a high color in her cheeks, was lying on her left side with her right arm hanging loosely over the side of the bed: her mouth was open a little, but she was breathing so softly Mary could hardly hear her. Every day now she seemed to need more sleep, a fact which worried Mary's older sisters, Barbara and Helen, and was the subject of their long whispering conversations in their bedroom at night. It seemed to trouble Mr. Johnson too, for he had started taking long walks by himself and he came home with his breath smelling of whiskey. But to Mary her mother looked as lovely and as healthy as ever. "Mother," she called again. She reached over and gave her shoulder a little shake, and then watched her mother's face eagerly when she opened her eyes to see if she had remembered about the shoes.

When her mother, still half asleep, only murmured, "Bring me my purse, Mary, and we'll have our little treat," Mary was not disappointed. She gleefully kept her secret. She took the dime her mother gave her and went up to the store to get the two ice-cream cones, just as she did on other days, only it seemed that she could already see herself coming down the street in the red leather shoes: she seemed to pass herself on the street, wearing the outfit she had planned to wear with the shoes, a red hat and a blue dress. By the time she got back to the house she had eaten most of her own cone. It was always like that. But then she sat down at the end of the kitchen table to enjoy herself watching her mother eat her share of the ice cream. It was like watching a big eager girl. Mrs. Johnson sat down, spread her legs, and sighed with pleasure and licked the ice cream softly and smiled with satisfaction and her mouth looked beautiful. And then when she was finished and was wiping her fingers with her apron Mary blurted out, "Are we going to get my shoes now, Mother?"

"Shoes. What shoes?" Mrs. Johnson asked.

"The red leather shoes I've been saving for," Mary said, looking puzzled. "The ones in the window that we talked about."

"Oh. Oh, I see," Mrs. Johnson said slowly as if she hadn't thought of those particular shoes since that day months ago. "Why, Mary, have you been thinking of those shoes all this time?" And then as Mary only kept looking up at her she went on fretfully, "Why, I told you at the time, child, that your father was in debt and we couldn't afford such shoes."

"I've got the six dollars saved, haven't I? Today."

"Well, your father. . . ."

"It's my six dollars, isn't it?"

"Mary, darling, listen. Those shoes are far too old for a little girl like you."

"I'm twelve next month. You know I am."

"Shoes like that are no good for running around, Mary. A pair of good serviceable shoes is what you need, Mary."

"I can wear them on Sunday, can't I?"

"Look, Mary," her mother tried to reason with her, "I know I said I'd get you a pair of shoes. But a good pair of shoes. Proper shoes. Your father is going to have a lot more expense soon. Why, he'd drop dead if he found I'd paid six dollars for a pair of red leather shoes for you.

"You promised I could save the money," Mary whispered. And then when she saw that worried, unyielding expression on her mother's face she knew she was not going to get the shoes; she turned away and ran into the bedroom and threw herself on the bed and pulled the pillow over her face and started to cry. Never in her life had she wanted anything as much as she wanted the red shoes. When she heard the sound of her mother moving pots and pans in the kitchen she felt that she had been cheated deliberately.

It began to get dark and she was still crying, and then she heard her mother's slow step coming toward the bedroom. "Mary, listen to me," she said, her voice almost rough as she reached down and shook Mary. "Get up and wipe your face, do you hear?" She had her own hat and coat on. "We're going to get those shoes right now," she said.

"You said I couldn't get them," Mary said.

"Don't argue with me," her mother said. She sounded blunt and grim and somehow faraway from Mary. "I want you to get them. I say you're going to. Come on."

Mary got up and wiped her face, and on the way up to the store her mother's grim, silent determination made her feel lonely and guilty. They bought a pair of red leather shoes. As Mary walked up and down in them on the store carpet her mother watched her, unsmiling and resolute. Coming back home Mary longed for her mother to speak to her, but Mrs. Johnson, holding Mary's hand tight, walked along, looking straight ahead.

"Now if only your father doesn't make a fuss," Mrs. Johnson said when they were standing together in the hall, listening.

From the living room came the sound of a rustled newspaper. Mr. Johnson, who worked in a publishing house, was home. In the last few months Mary had grown afraid of her father: she did not understand why he had become so moody and short-tempered. As her mother, standing there, hesitated nervously, Mary began to get scared. "Go on into the bedroom," Mrs. Johnson whispered to her. She followed Mary and had her sit down on the bed and she knelt down and put the red shoes on Mary's feet. It was a strangely solemn, secret little ceremony. Mrs. Johnson's breathing was heavy and labored as she straightened up. "Now don't you come in until I call you," she warned Mary.

But Mary tiptoed into the kitchen and her heart was pounding as she tried to listen. For a while she heard only the sound of her mother's quiet voice, and then suddenly her father cried angrily, "Are you serious? Money for luxuries at a time like this!" His voice became explosive. "Are we going crazy? You'll take them back, do you hear?" But her mother's voice flowed on, the one quiet voice, slow and even. Then there was a long, strange silence. "Mary, come here," her father suddenly called.

"Come on and show your father your shoes, Mary," her mother urged her.

The new shoes squeaked as Mary went into the living room and they felt like heavy weights that might prevent her from fleeing from her father's wrath. Her father was sitting at the little table by the light and Mary watched his face desperately to see if the big vein at the side of his head had started to swell. As he turned slowly to her and fumbled with his glasses a wild hope shone in Mary's scared brown eyes.

Her father did not seem to be looking at the shoes. With a kind of pain in his eyes he was looking steadily at her as if he had never really been aware of her before. "They're fine shoes, aren't they?" he asked.

"Can I keep them? Can I really?" Mary asked breathlessly.

"Why, sure you can," he said quietly.

Shouting with joy Mary skipped out of the room and along the hall, for she had heard her sisters come in. "Look, Barbara, look, Helen," she cried. Her two older sisters, who were stenographers, and a bit prim, were slightly scandalized. "Why, they're far too old for you," Barbara said. "Get out, get out," Mary laughed. "Mother knows better than you do." Then she went out to the kitchen to help her mother with the dinner and watch her face steadily with a kind of rapt wonder, as if she was trying to understand the strange power her mother possessed that could make an angry man like her father suddenly gentle and quiet.

Mary intended to wear the shoes to church that Sunday, but it rained, so she put them back in the box and decided to wait a week. But in the middle of the week her father told her that her mother was going to the hospital for an operation.

"Is it for the pains in her legs?" Mary asked.

"Well, you see, Mary, if everything comes off all right," her father answered, "she may not have any pains at all."

It was to be an operation for cancer, and the doctor said the operation was successful. But Mrs. Johnson died under the anaesthetic. The two older sisters and Mr. Johnson kept repeating dumbly to the doctor, "But she looked all right. She looked fine." Then they all went home. They seemed to huddle first in one room then in another. They took turns trying to comfort Mary, but no one could console her.

In the preparations for the funeral they were all busy for a while because the older sisters were arranging for everyone to have the proper clothes for mourning. The new blue dress that Helen, the fairhaired one, had bought only a few weeks ago, was sent to the cleaners to be dyed black, and of course Mary had to have a black dress and black stockings too. On the night when they were arranging these things Mary suddenly blurted out, "I'm going to wear my red shoes."

"Have some sense, Mary. That would be terrible," Helen said.

"You can't wear red shoes," Barbara said crossly.

"Yes, I can," Mary said stubbornly. "Mother wanted me to wear them. I know she did. I know why she bought them." She was confronting them all with her fists clenched desperately.

"For heaven's sake, tell her she can't do a thing like that," Helen said irritably to Mr. Johnson. Yet he only shook his head, looking at Mary with that same gentle, puzzled expression he had had on his face the night his wife had talked to him about the shoes. "I kind of think Mary's right," he began, rubbing his hand slowly over his face.

"Red shoes. Good Lord, it would be terrible," said Helen, now outraged.

"You'd think we'd all want to be proper," Barbara agreed.

"Proper. It would be simply terrible, I tell you. It would look as if we had no respect."

"Well, I guess that's right. All the relatives will be here," Mr. Johnson agreed reluctantly. Then he turned hopefully to Mary, "Look, Mary," he began. "If you get the shoes dyed you can wear them to the funeral and then you'll be able to wear them to school every day too. How about it?"

But it had frightened Mary to think that anyone might say she hadn't shown the proper respect for her mother. She got the red shoes and handed them to her father that he might take them up to the shoemaker. As her father took the box from her, he fumbled with a few apologetic words. "It's just what people might say. Do you see, Mary?" he said.

When the shoes, now dyed black, were returned to Mary the next day she put them on slowly, and then she put her feet together and looked at the shoes a long time. They were no longer the beautiful red shoes, and yet as she stared at them, solemn-faced, she suddenly felt a strange kind of secret joy, a feeling of certainty that her mother had got her the shoes so that she might understand at this time that she still had her special blessing and protection.

At the funeral the shoes hurt Mary's feet for they were new and hadn't been worn. Yet she was fiercely glad that she had them on. After that she wore them every day. Of course now that they were black they were not noticed by other children. But she was very careful with them. Every night she polished them up and looked at them and was touched again by that secret joy. She wanted them to last a long time.

PATCHES ON MY PANTS

by JOHN MODESTO

IT WAS THE BIG NIGHT OF THE WEEK-LONG FESTIVAL, AND I went home with a black eye and a bloody nose.

"What happened?" my wife cried out, sitting up in bed the instant I turned on the light.

"There was a fight," I said.

With a sigh she lay down again, and it was as though she had a sack of flour on her belly.

"What was it about?"

"I don't know, " I said.

"Then why did you fight?"

"Because somebody hit me."

She placed a forearm over her eyes to shield them from the light, and again she sighed.

"That's a good excuse," she said.

I lost my temper.

"Now look here, Toniella, I'm not in the mood for argument. Understand? So turn over and go to sleep."

"Well," her voice was soft as a kitten's, "I only wanted to know."

"So you want to know! Well, there's nothing to tell. I was listening to the band. That's all. Except that I noticed a rumpus down the street and went to see what was going on. Somebody in the crowd hit me and I got mad and let go at some fellow, and someone else let go at me. That's all."

After doctoring myself as well as I could, I put out the light and crawled into bed.

"Don't try to crowd me onto the floor," she protested. "Remember, I'm not so small as I used to be."

"I'm sorry," I said. "We'll simply have to get a bigger bed."

"After this one is born there'll be no more," she mewed.

This was to be her first, and she was afraid. That was why she talked as if she already had had a dozen.

I tossed about.

"You can't fall asleep," she said.

"You're right," I assured her. "I can't."

I reached out toward the bedstand for a cigarette.

"Livy?"

"Now what?"

"Livy, you forgot to bring me something."

"So that's what you're mewing about, eh?"

"Well, I was good enough to wait up for you. But a lot you care!"

"Please forgive me, Toniella," I pleaded. "I didn't want to go walking around like this. You understand, don't you?"

"It would have taken only a second for you to stop to buy me something."

I jumped out of bed as if she had pitchforked me. "All right, then," I said. "It's not too late. The booths are still open. I'll go right out and buy you something. Anything—just so you'll stop your mewing."

She began to cry.

"You don't realize," she sobbed.

Believe me, I hadn't run away from the fight until the cops were upon us, which proves I'm not a coward; but now, as she cried so piteously, I felt myself to be more than a coward—a criminal.

I snuffed out my cigarette; and in my awkwardly humble way I tried to make amends. I sat down on the edge of the bed and caressed her as though she were a maimed pet.

"Toniella," I murmured, "please forgive me."

"You don't realize," she sobbed.

"But of course I do. I know how it is, darling. If I've spoken a little too harshly it's because of what happened to me out there. But just think! It might have been worse. I might have been dragged off to jail with the others."

"Oh, dear me! Were the police after you, too?"

"Well, I'm sorry it slipped out—but otherwise I couldn't

make you understand why I didn't stop to buy you something." I kissed her. Then I began dressing in the dark.

"Where are you going?" she asked.

"Toniella," I said, fagged out with patience, "I thought you just now said you wanted . . ."

"My feet are getting cold," she chattered.

I arranged the coverlet about her.

"Livy?"

"Yes, darling?"

"Livy, I was thinking of figs while waiting for you. Oh, not baked figs imported from Italy with almonds in the center, not dried figs strung on a straw, not sulphured figs in Cellophane, not canned figs, either . . . but fresh figs—right off a tree."

"*O mama mia,*" I groaned. "Toniella, have mercy on me—we aren't in California."

"I know. I knew it all along. And that's why I tried not to think of them. But the more I tried not to think, the more I . . ."

"But this is Manhattan," I broke in, desperately trying to spare both her and myself. "Where am I going to find a fig tree around here? It might not be so bad if we knew someone to ask. But whom do we know?"

Yes, whom did we know? Whom could anyone get to know in less than a lifetime in New York?

I turned on the light and finished dressing.

"I shouldn't have told you," she said half whimpering.

"Don't let it worry you," I said. "It's still September and there must be some *paesano* in this burg who has a fig tree with a fig or two on it."

"But you will be careful, Livy?"

"Don't worry, darling," I said, kissing her.

On the streets again, I made my way toward the festival. A man who was somewhat tipsy bumped into me.

"It's all right, *paesano,*" I said as he excused himself.

"I'm sorry," he insisted. "I'm not the type to go around molesting people."

"Me neither," I said.

"Ah, I see somebody has already taught you a lesson tonight."

I laughed.

"It was a wild party," I said, "and everything was in fun."

"That's the spirit, *walyo*. Life isn't meant for crybabies."

"Is the *festa* over yet?"

"No, not yet. They haven't carried the saint in yet. There's still time to confess your sins, if you know what I mean. They say he still performs miracles. I stuck a dollar bill on his vestments and made a prayer. I have a child who was born blind."

"I'm sorry to hear that, *paesano*. But have you tried the doctors? Sometimes they perform miracles where the saints can't."

"What are you talking about? I've tried even sorcerers who get their commands straight from the devil, may he melt on my threshold. It's useless, my good friend. And yet my eldest daughter read in the paper the other day . . ."

"I know. Where in West Virginia a girl who was born blind has been made to see."

"Tell me something," he said, clutching my arm. "You look like you ought to know. Tell me—can this affair really be true? Is it possible? Or is it just another story they made up to fill the papers with?"

"It must be true. The best doctors in America have attested to it. Have courage, *paesano*. Perhaps someday your own child . . ."

"Yes, have courage! That's why I get drunk at times—so as not to lose my courage. Ah, I wish I could have afforded to stick a five-dollar bill on that saint. But I'm the only one working and how much do I make! And there are five others besides me and my wife. Yes, and bless my everlasting good fortune, there's still another on the way, too."

"Well," I said timidly, "my wife is about to have her first."

I thought he might at least congratulate me or even say something to buck me up. But instead—

"My first one lost an arm hopping freights."

"I'm sorry to hear that," I said. "You sure must have had your share of bad luck."

"What are you talking about? I was born with the cross hung around my neck. Yes, *walyo*, do me a favor and don't talk of hard luck. My litany is not all sung yet by a long shot. It began when I came over from the other side. The ship almost sank. I wish it had."

"Listen, *paesano*," I said, changing tracks without a puff or whistle, "I've already told you about my wife. She's pretty big now, going from day to day, any minute now. And you know how it is with women. Just tonight she had a desire for figs—yes, a hankering for figs fresh off a tree. I was thinking there must be somebody in this great big city with a fig tree, but the tough part of it is that we're strangers here from Pennsylvania. I don't know a soul. I'm like one lost. I don't know where to turn. And my wife, poor thing, she's back there in her room thinking of figs, fresh off a tree."

"Figs?" echoed the man. "You're lucky. They're still in season. Now's just the time to pick them off, if you can find them. But just think what a fix I was in a few nights ago when my wife couldn't rest in bed from thinking of strawberries. Why can't they desire such things except at midnight? Just the same, I was lucky she didn't want them fresh off a bush. . . . Do you know something, *walyo?* There are blockheads who will laugh at you for running around in circles over a thing like that. If they could only realize what it is to be a father—or about to become one!"

"Yes," I said, "if they could only realize."

"Figs did you say? Well, Patsy the shoemaker has a fig tree. But he lives in Brooklyn, and that isn't just around the corner."

"That's all right, *paesano*," I said, feeling a lift. "Just give me the address and I'll try my luck."

"Wait! Maybe you won't have to make the trip. I'm not sure now and I can't promise a thing. But come along with me. We'll see."

He took me to a house where a man was arguing with his wife. My friend introduced me to him and acquainted him with my case.

"*Oh caro Pompeo mio*," said the man of the house, "you've brought your friend too late. Yes, it's true—I still have that fig tree, but it's as bare as if the north wind had hit it. Those children of mine, good and dear as they are, didn't give the figs half a chance to ripen."

"That's right—blame it on the children," his wife said with a look that could have split atoms.

"Here, boys," said the master of the house, as if he had suddenly hit upon a more pleasant subject. "Here, let's have a glass of wine."

We had a tumbler each.

"Well, Dominic," said Pompey, "thanks very much and excuse us for the inconvenience. The only one I know besides you who has a fig tree is a shoemaker in Brooklyn. That's why we came to see you first."

"Hold on," said Dominic. "I have a Saint John who lives down in the Village who has a fig tree. Here, drink! Let's have another glass and we'll jump in my boy's machine and go down to see my godparent."

"But it's pretty late," I protested, with a furtive glance at his glowering wife. "I don't wish to drag you out of your home at this hour."

"That's all right, it's a matter of nothing," said Dominic, who appeared overexuberant at the prospect of escape. "Tomorrow's Sunday. We can sleep all day. Can you drive?"

"Yes," I replied, "but I don't have a license."

"Damn the licenses!" stormed Dominic. "This is a free country. Besides, think of your wife."

At the house down in the Village a group of men were playing cards.

"Good evening, *Compare* Secondo," said Dominic. "Excuse the late visit. Here, I want you to meet two friends of mine."

"That's fine," said Secondo, shaking hands with us; then to a boy looking on at the game, "Hey, Pippy, go and fill this pitcher."

We drank one another's health all around.

"Excuse me, friend," said Dominic to me. "I didn't want to be rude and ask you in front of my wife. But what happened to you, anyhow? Don't tell me your wife gave you such a fine grooming before sending you out on your errand."

I laughed.

"I fell down some steps," I said.

"Well, boys," said Secondo, like a judge calling for the verdict, "how does this wine strike you? I started the barrel this very day."

"Well, *Compare*," said Dominic, smacking his lips with the gusto of a connoisseur, "you have a nice glass of wine here."

"Come on," said Secondo, "let's have another glass all around."

Well, I have always been told that if you don't know how to be polite the best thing is to stay at home. And so I drank along.

"I'm very sorry," said Secondo when he heard the purpose of our visit. "I don't have that fig tree any more. I cut it down this past week. That was better, I decided, than going to jail. You see how it is—the yard fence is pretty low and the people next door, what with all their other virtues, have long reaches. You tell me—what was I to do? I'm a mild man. Better chop that fig tree down, I said to myself, than go to the electric chair for murdering somebody. And so there you are, boys. That's the kind of fellow I am. . . . Hey, Pippy, go and bring us another pitcher."

"Well," said Pompey to me, "it looks as though we'll have to jump in the car and go to Brooklyn after all."

Secondo protested fiercely at our apparent haste to leave.

"Wait till the boy comes up with the wine," he insisted, "and have at least another glass."

Right at that point we were startled by a cry of anguish from below.

"Help, pop! Quick! Help!"

"By the Madonna!" exclaimed Secondo in a horrified whisper as he dashed from the room. When he returned some minutes later he was the most woebegone man in creation, and spattered with wine, besides.

"How could it have happened?" he was groaning.

"I couldn't help it," Pippy was whimpering, cringing before him. "The tap popped out just as I . . ."

"How could it have happened?" groaned Secondo. "A half

barrel of wine spilled . . . more precious than the tears of Christ! What sin have I committed to merit this agony?"

"It's good luck," said one of the card players by way of consolation. "Spilled wine means good luck."

"Oh," groaned Secondo, "how could it have happened?"

"Courage, *Compare*, courage," said Dominic. "The good earth gives and takes. It's a matter of nothing."

All the way to Brooklyn I denounced myself as the primary agent of Secondo's misfortune.

"Think nothing of it," said Dominic. "It will do my *compare* good. He'll go to church in the morning and confess his sins."

We found Patsy the shoemaker sitting on his front step, smoking a long-stemmed pipe.

"Well, well," he said in greeting as Pompey strode forward. "What a grand surprise! I was wondering who it could be when I saw the car stop. You might call it a coincidence, *caro* Pompeo, but I was just thinking of the good times we used to have going around playing at weddings, baptisms, and christenings. Oh, how you could make that guitar hum!"

"Ah, the guitar!" reminisced Pompey sadly after a hearty handshake and the mutual inanities. "It's among the relics of the past now. With the troubles I've got, it would be blasphemy to pluck a chord. Please, old friend, as a favor, spare me further agony."

"Well, come on in, boys," said Patsy, leading the way. "I was just sitting out there smoking and thinking. What a beautiful night! I was thinking. And I thought of the old country. That was enough to make me sad."

He led us through the semidarkness of his shop like a guide in a mined field.

"Look out, boys," he warned. "Be careful and don't bump your shins or stumble. This place is in a terrible mess. I used to take great pride in this shop once. But now my pride is gone . . . everything is gone for me nowadays."

We entered a dimly lit back room.

"These are my quarters, boys," he said, as if that statement precluded an apology for the disorderliness of the place. "I eat, sleep, and get drunk in here. I live the life of a hermit. There was a point to it some years back. Now I continue merely out of force of habit. There's no point to anything any more. I was just saying to myself . . . oh, excuse me for rattling on like this. Well, sit down, boys. Let's not have any ceremony. All I've got is a gallon of wine here, and to tell you the truth I don't even know how it is. A customer of mine brought it to me today. He can't pay his bills to me in money, so he goes out, buys grapes, makes wine and pays me in wine. This is what America has come to!"

He poured our wine, and then brought out bread, cheese, olives, anchovies, and a few sticks of dried sausage.

"Forgive me, Patsy," said Pompey. "I believe I'm losing manners every day. I forgot to introduce my two friends."

Dominic and I shook hands with him.

"Go on, boys," he said, as if even that semblance of formality were a waste of time. "Eat and drink."

"With all due respect," said Pompey, "speaking of eating, how is that fig tree of yours doing?"

"Oh, that fig tree," said Patsy, like one recovering a long-lost memory. "I've still got it. Yes, it's still out there. But I'm beginning to lose pride in that, too. It reminds me too much of the old country. Yes, it's thriving well, but the way I feel nowadays about everything, I guess I'll give it the ax this fall."

"For the love of God, no!" cried Pompey, horrified as by a vision of sacrilege. "No matter where you go in New York you hear of Patsy the shoemaker's fig tree. Now even the people of Pennsylvania will hear of it, for this young friend I've introduced to you is from there and that's why we're here. *Walyo*, you tell him."

Patsy stared at me as if I were changing identities before his very eyes.

"Only, for charity's sake," he said, "don't tell it to me as it was told to you."

I laughed. "I slipped getting out of the car," I said.

"His wife is making him his first baby," said Dominic.

"That brings us back to the subject of figs," said Pompey.

"Yes, my good sir," I said, "she's getting her first, and tonight she had an enormous craving for figs—fresh off a tree, as she put it. We've gone to several places, but without luck. That's why we're here now, though I don't know how we can be pardoned for the intrusion at this hour."

"Oh, my good son, you're the boss of my house any time. My door is always open to friends and everything I've got is theirs. Ah, now I know why I had no appetite for those figs. It was just like Saint Peter telling me to lay off. Well, let's get a light and see what we can gather."

In a drawer bulging over with odds and ends he found an old flashlight. Its beam was a feeble one and he gave us repeated warnings as we followed him into the tiny patch of ground he called his garden.

"Watch out where you put your foot," he said. "This garden's in a terrible mess. I'm going to clean it up some Sunday. Look out! Don't fall over this bench. Be careful of that washtub. . . . Well, boys, here it is!"

He might have been exhibiting to the world the rarest of jewels for all his voice had to do with it.

"Look!" he said, tenderly raising leaf after leaf to uncover the luscious fruit. "Turn that light a little more this way, Pompeo. Look, my friend, these figs are crying to melt in somebody's mouth. Where's that plate I gave you to hold, son?"

"Only a few," I insisted respectfully as I proffered the plate. "Only two or three to satisfy her craving."

"The mellowest of honey can't match the goodness of these figs," he went on, so that the tree well might have withered from his inordinate praise.

At last, satisfied that he had plucked the choicest of the fruit, he stepped down from his perch.

"Be careful with that plate there, son. If you were to stumble now it would be a sin no priest would dare hear you confess."

I turned to follow Pompey and Dominic back to the house, with our host steering me from behind with all manner of cautions as to where to step in the littered yard. Then, of a sudden, he fairly frightened me with a yell, calling out for the Madonna to save him. I swung round.

"Oh, my good son!" he groaned as he lay sprawled out on the ground. "I've had my feast day."

"How did it happen?" asked Pompey, helping him up.

"I always knew I'd break my neck in this garden," groaned Patsy. "Only this time it's my right leg."

"But of course you're joking," said Dominic.

"It's my ankle, then," groaned Patsy. "But that puts the benediction on this fig tree for sure. The ax will do for it."

"It's all my fault," I said, overwhelmed with a sense of guilt. "If I hadn't come in search of figs . . ."

"When your fate is black there's nothing that can be done about it," he complained as Pompey and Dominic helped him inside. "The fault is all mine for tolerating the conditions I live in. I was just thinking the other day . . . easy, boys . . . here, let me slide into this chair."

Pompey helped him off with his shoe and sock.

"Just a sprain," said Dominic. "It's a matter of nothing. A basin of hot water and some Epsom salts is all that's necessary."

"Look in that cabinet there, my son," said Patsy. "There ought to be some there. But whoever would have thought I'd have such a use for it!"

I grew distressingly sad in realizing how brave as a stoic he tried to be, for I sensed his hurts went rather deep and did not originate with his personal welfare.

"An estimable man," said Pompey when, at last, we got back into the car. "As good as bread."

"Here, let me hold the figs while you drive," said Dominic.

Whereupon I consigned to him the paper bag containing the eight precious figs.

"Now," I said, "how do we get back to where we started from?"

"Leave it to me," said Pompey. "I know Brooklyn like the palm of my hand. . . . Turn right here, *walyo*."

"I lived here awhile myself some years ago," said Dominic,

like a citizen of the world. "If I'm not mistaken, you turn left at the next corner."

"That's correct," said Pompey.

But a few blocks further on, instead of corroborating each other, they began to disagree; and then, finally, the one resorted to disparaging the other's knowledge of the town's layout. Until—

"Turn right here, *walyo*," said Pompey.

"Speaking with respect, *caro* Pompeo," said Dominic, "I think you're drunk. I'm positive you turn left here."

"I know this town like the seven of diamonds," said Pompey. "Turn right, *walyo*."

"We'll never get home this way," said Dominic. "Turn left."

"Right!"

"Left!"

"Right!"

It happened so suddenly that I hardly knew how it happened at all. We came to an abrupt stop with a crash.

"Are you all right, *walyo?*" I heard someone say from above.

I felt myself being shaken as if I were a bag of wool to be emptied.

"How did it happen?" asked Dominic, jerking me to my feet.

"Where'd this pole come from?" demanded Pompey.

"It's a matter of nothing," said Dominic. "Just a smashed grill."

"Where's this water coming from?" demanded Pompey.

"Run!" said Dominic, giving me a shove to start me on my way. "Run! You have no license!"

"But . . ." I mumbled.

"Run!" shouted Pompey. "Think of your wife!"

"But . . ."

"Run!" shouted Dominic. "Before the police are upon us!"

"But . . ."

"The subway! Quick!"

"Run! We'll stay and make excuses. Run!"

I found myself running, but with a difficulty I could not account for offhand. Going down the steps of the subway entrance, I located the trouble in my right knee. I paused to examine it; and through the rent in my trousers leg I saw that it was bruised rather badly. And, on top of that, I remembered the figs I had left behind.

"Oh!" I groaned, like one who is going down for the last time.

It was well past midnight when I got home. And, hobbling as quietly as I could through the hallway to our room, I unaccountably went cold with fear. I saw the streak of light under the door, but I knew there was scarcely anything ominous in that. Yet, I could not shake from me the fear of I knew not what. Somehow I felt that something horrendous had occurred during my absence—that Toniella had gotten sick, that she had been taken to the hospital, that she had prematurely given birth to my child, that . . .

I turned the knob softly and entered like an intruder. I stood a longish while staring at her asleep in bed. It seemed, after the premonition I had had, that my life was about to begin anew.

There was a flutter of her eyelids. "Livy?" she mewed.

"Yes, Toniella?"

And with the assurance of my safe return, she fell off to sleep again.

I slid into a chair. And I sat there gazing at her heavenly face so that it would do for me for all eternity. I kept watch over her as if she were a stricken lamb. Stricken? And with what? Why, stricken with her holy bondage to me—a ne'er-do-well who, her irate parents had ceaselessly reminded her, had nothing to recommend him but the patches on his pants.

I grew melancholy because I felt so inadequate, because I knew I could hardly ever compensate her for all that she had sacrificed for me, because my every effort to make myself worthy of her was so futile. I could bequeath her nothing except the ashes, so to speak, of my good intentions.

And, fresh in mind, simmered the remembrance of my bungling quest for figs and the grief it had caused others. Little could she dream, as she so innocently lay sleeping there, that because of my ardor to serve her merest whim a man's half barrel of wine had been spilled, another good soul might well have broken a leg instead of spraining an ankle, still another had his son's automobile smashed . . . and . . . and . . . I looked down at my bruised and swollen knee and contemplated the long rent in my trousers leg.

"Another patch," I muttered.

BEAUTIFUL SUMMER IN NEWPORT

by FELICIA GIZYCKA

"YOU WILL NOW WRITE YOUR FATHER," SAID FRÄULEIN.

Rue sat with the pen in her hand. She stared at the thin gray paper with the letterhead "Beach Cottage, Newport, Rhode Island."

"I wrote Poppy," said Audrey. "I wrote him a long letter the way Fräulein said. I got it all finished."

Rue looked over at her sister, virtuous and golden-headed, sitting in a chair. Her own face felt thick and ugly, and all of her was swelled up into a stony immobility. The hand, with the pen in it, lay there. Near her chair stood Fräulein, like a snake staring at a bird, her tiny black eyes fixed with an excited malevolence. She had a fat red-cheeked face, and a mouth that was sunken like a very old woman's but that was nevertheless red and wet.

"Do you want I should give you castor oil?" said Fräulein, amiably, with a smile.

And now, as always at some point in their struggles, Rue moved forward in obedience. Blood flowed into her hand. It tingled as though it had been asleep. She was able to move it.

Dear Father, she wrote. *I am having a lovely time.*

Fräulein came and stood behind her. "The beach is beautiful," she said. "The children are very nice. Newport is a very nice place."

Rue started writing again. Fräulein's whaleboned stomach was pressed against the back of the chair. She watched Rue writing the words. "Is that all you're going to say?" she demanded.

She took Rue's chin in her hand and tilted her face up. Rue had to look up into the small black eyes, the hanging cheeks like two balloon-pink breasts, and the ripe, terrible mouth.

"Darling," said Fräulein in a sweet whine, "aren't you going to say something nice about your Lina?"

Rue held her face very still. She shut her eyes. Inside of her something was crying, Don't listen! Don't look! It was like something frantic, caught, fluttering, tearing itself to get away. The outside of her felt like stone. She thought, I won't be able to move my hands any more. She wriggled her hand with the pen in it.

"My neck hurts," she said. "Let me go."

The governess let go. She said, "My Little Liebchen! I know two little girls who are going to get i-scrim tonight. If they're good."

She was still pressed against the chair.

"Now you write 'Poppy, I have a nice Fräulein.' Go on: 'I have a very nice Fräulein. Nicer than Nanny. I like her better than Nanny.' "

"I don't like you better than Nanny," Rue said. She thought that she might have to cry.

"You'd better say so," Audrey said. "I did."

"Do you want i-scrim or castor oil?" asked Fräulein.

We have a very nice governess, wrote Rue. *I like her very much.*

"Good. Now go on: I like her better than Nanny, and hope she comes back to Chicago with us."

Rue wrote it and signed her name quickly.

"Address it," said Fräulein.

Rue jumped out of her chair. "I have to pick some flowers for Aunt Agnes," she said.

They were already dressed for the beach. They wore white English eyelet embroidery, below-knee length, tall white socks, black patent leather shoes, and black sashes around the hips. Fräulein opened the closet door where hung the rows of starched and perfect clothes, with hats to match perched above, and rows of shoes all wonderfully clean as though no child had ever worn them. The first week when Nanny had come on from Chicago with them she'd let them wear their less-good clothes to the beach. She had let them take their shoes and stockings off, and run in the sand. But they had been lonely in their pleasure. Nanny had been told she had to sit with the nurses, down the beach. They had had to play with the little children, and everybody had stared at their bare feet. "Nobody lets their children go barefoot so early," another nurse had told Nanny. And in a week Aunt Agnes had found Fräulein, and told Nanny she could go. She had sprung all this on them very suddenly. In one day Nanny had kissed them and they had said "Why are you crying?" and a few hours later Fräulein had arrived.

Rue let Fräulein put the white Panama on the back of her head. Then she ran downstairs, fast. She ran into the drawing room and picked up the phone.

She sat trembling in the stuffy pretentious little room. The brocades, the lamps with fringes.

She was afraid the long-distance operator would know she was just a child. She made her voice controlled and rather affected.

"This telegram goes to Mr. Anthony Peterson, Hayfarms, Lake Forest, Illinois. *Poppy. Come and get me. Please, please, please.* Sign it Rue."

"What's the name?" Rue spelled out her aunt's name.

"What's your number?" the operator asked.

Just then Rue heard Fräulein coming down the stairs.

"This is Newport 271," she said frantically.

"Shall I charge it to that number?" inquired the operator.

"What are you doing?" cried Fräulein.

"Yes," said Rue, hanging up.

Fräulein grabbed the receiver, said hello, and listened.

"I was going to get some flowers and some people called up. They wanted to speak to somebody—" Rue said.

"Was it the wrong number?" Fräulein asked sharply.

"Yes," Rue said.

"Well, here's your coat. Everything you do looks sneaking. You are nothing but a sneak."

Audrey and Aunt Agnes were out in the hall. Aunt Agnes was just rushing out. She was a thin, pretty little woman, forever flying past them like a molting bird. Now in the hall her heels made a fast tapping sound as she ran to call the maid for something. Her heavy hat was a mushroom besieged with flowers, and this was pulled awry by her veil, so that some wan hair had escaped from her pompadour. Her looped *mousseline de soie* rustled elegantly around her ankles, and her thin stupid-looking feet.

"Why aren't they out on the beach?" she asked Fräulein shrilly.

"They were writing to their father, Mrs. Peterson," Fräulein said, and now her speech and accent were foreign and ladylike. "I have here the letters. They write slowly. They need more discipline. Curtsy to your *Tante!*"

They both curtsied, sticking out their small bottoms so that their skirts flew out like ballet dancers'. Rue then saw her aunt smiling, pleased and amused.

"I must say your manners are better since Nanny *departed,*" she said. "You already show you are being taught by a *gentlewoman.*"

"Is Mrs. van Deusen coming to your dinner party tonight?" Audrey asked.

"Why, of course," Aunt Agnes said. She gave Audrey a brief look as though she were looking at a woman her own age.

"She didn't come to the other parties you gave," Audrey said.

"I don't think that's very nice," Aunt Agnes said mincingly. "Now you run along. Don't let them stay in the sun too long," she said to Fräulein. "And don't let them go into the water yet. It's too cold."

"When are we ever going in the water?" Audrey asked. "We were supposed to come here to go swimming."

"Run out at once. I am going to get my parasol."

Outside they strolled around aimlessly, waiting. It was too hot for the clothes they wore.

Audrey made a line in the gravel with her toe. "Mrs. van Deusen won't come," she said. "She'll call up again and say she's sick. That'll be twice."

"Is she sick?"

"No, you little ninny. She doesn't *want* to come. I heard the Phellps' governess tell another governess that Aunt Agnes was here to crash society."

"But she told Poppy she wanted to bring us here for our good," Rue said, surprised.

She looked toward the house, the closed front door, the steps down which Fräulein would come. This new thing that Audrey had just said seemed to seal something. Some doom, as though now the telegram would surely not get there. Would surely be lost. She had a vision of the yellow envelope forever fluttering in outer darkness like a distress signal from a sinking ship, unanswered. And now she actually let out a little cry.

"What's the matter with you?" Audrey asked in her new mincing voice. "Are you shocked, dear?" And Rue saw a crafty look in her face, spiteful and mature.

"You're only ten years old," Audrey said. "You don't know what a widow is."

"Aunt Agnes is a widow."

"No, I mean *what* a widow is, silly. A widow is a woman trying to get married again. Aunt Agnes is here to get in society and marry a rich man."

"But Poppy is rich," Rue said.

"He's only a meat packer and he's only her brother-in-law."

"I don't care what he is, I want to go home. I want to go home to Poppy."

"You can't go home."

Fräulein was now coming down the steps. Her white leghorn hat with the red roses flopped hideously. She wore a white blouse and a long white skirt. Her black-button boots pointed out daintily as she walked. She was absorbed with her parasol which wouldn't open.

"Audrey," Rue whispered desperately, "don't you want to go back to the farm and Poppy and Nanny? We can't play here. Nanny let us go any place we wanted and she never liked punishing us. I bet Poppy wants us back."

"You're no longer a baby," Audrey whispered back. "You need a governess. Besides, if we stay here long enough, we'll get in society. Then I can grow up and marry any boy I like."

"Stop whispering," Fräulein said sharply. "Start walking toward the gate."

"You were running around the farm like an Indian," Audrey said out loud. "How would you like somebody to take you for a red Indian with your thin face and dark hair, and no curls like me?" She walked sedately along with her new mincing steps. She wasn't a bit the way she'd been on the farm.

"They all hate us here," Rue said, looking behind her at Fräulein. "The children hate us. I want to go home."

Her mouth trembled. She thought of the telegram. Please, God, let Poppy get the telegram.

"They'll get used to us," Audrey said. "Don't you see? Aunt Agnes will get a break. Someway. That's what they say. They say she's pretty and clever and that she'll get an opportunity."

Fräulein came up suddenly behind Rue and hit her on the legs with the closed parasol.

"You are walking crooked!" she cried. "Straight! March!"

Rue could feel her right there behind them. Her legs burned like fire. She tried to walk like Audrey. Somewhere inside her mind was the wild thing, fluttering and scratching. She thought, Don't. Don't. Hold still and wait.

The beach at Newport is beautiful and desirable because it is enclosed. It is a slip of sand pearly and pure as a saint's heart. It was created to keep people out. A club. All those people like the grandfathers, grandmothers, and great-grandparents of the club members. The dirty swarm, the money-makers who came over in steerage, who started as bootblacks, as jailbirds, as farm boys, as madames, and murderers. These, who made millions, and left it all to their descendants so that the descendants might become picky and choosy, social and different.

For instance, on this beautiful summer in 1915, no stage people were allowed on the beach.

Rue and Audrey each took Fräulein by the hand and started walking through the gates and down the steps to the sand. In the middle sat the governesses with the older children. Now in these morning hours, until noon, the governesses were great ladies. They were everything. They played the game of being ladies with one another, queening it to the hilt. But then at noon the parents began arriving. Then the governesses rose hurriedly, gathering their embroidery and their knitting, with shocked silent faces like people who have been aroused from a rich and guilt-laden dream. They would almost run from the beach, pausing only long enough to send the children to the parents to say Hello and Good-by for the day.

"Now you play nicely, and don't get those shoes wet. Do you hear?" Fräulein said. She moved off toward the governesses, fixing upon her face a ladylike smile.

All the little girls were in a group playing. With their starched lovely clothes they looked like ballet dancers. They were digging, making something in the sand. Audrey began walking toward them slowly. She was like a fisherman with a rod who has not caught a single fish all season and who for this very reason feels the keenest excitement, the most romantic and hopeless yearning. Audrey, moving down the beach, had a greedy, bright look. Today, perhaps today she would catch the prize: a bright smile from Nona van Deusen, a nice TL from one of the Phellps girls.

Rue said to herself, if I stand still here, if I shut my eyes and squint, I won't see it. I won't see Audrey looking like that. But today, because escape was now possible, it all seemed more than she could stand. Maybe Poppy will be here tomorrow, she told herself. Maybe tomorrow night I'll be on the train, going home. Her patience was squeezed to the limit, so that she thought she would stop breathing. This hateful place, dry sand. (No, you can't go in the water!) Those little girls, clean, good, sweet-smelling and beautiful, and every one of them mean. Mean as sin. And Fräulein, any minute Fräulein like a cruel jailer who will not let his prisoner fall asleep, descending on her, yanking her arm. "Get up! Get up! What did I tell you? Look at your dress!" And a pinch, cruel and tweaking, making her eyes and mouth fill with water.

Poppy will take me home, she told herself. And then she said, Supposing he doesn't? She stood still, rooted to despair.

"You go and play with the children," Fräulein cried. "Don't stand there like an imbecile!"

She ran quickly toward the children.

Nona van Deusen raised her beautiful, stupid face. "We need more children to dig this canal," she said. Her voice was clear and British, like her governess's. It cut the air like a military command. She was Mrs. van Deusen's great-granddaughter, and everybody on the beach did what she said. Sometimes, when she didn't get her way, she grew stiff and lay on the ground jerking.

Audrey squatted down next to her. "Where do you want me to start?" she asked.

Nona leaned over sideways, her mouth pinched up in a fury. She pushed Audrey so that she fell over on the sand. "Go away," she said. "I don't want you next to me. Go to the end of the line. You're a slave, digging the canal. We're the architects."

Then she saw Rue standing there. "You're a slave, too," she said. "Go and dig. Do as you're told."

Rue walked over and squatted down next to Audrey. The long canal was seeping in water from the sea.

"Whoever doesn't dig gets their eye poked out with a hot stick," said Angie Phellps.

"Whoever doesn't dig doesn't get asked to our house to play," said Maggie Phellps.

"We're not going to ask *everybody* to our house anyway," Angie said. Rue could feel their sly eyes sliding over to watch her and Audrey. She bent her head over the narrow ribbon of water and dug, saying nothing.

"We don't want *hoi polloi* in our house," Angie said with her clear, beautiful enunciation.

Suddenly Rue jumped up. "Shut up or I'll kill you!" she shouted.

"Is that *so?*" they all said.

Now they looked pleased beyond words, smiling. They stopped digging and looked up at her slyly with their beautiful eyes. Suddenly there was sand hitting Rue's face. It burned her eyes so that she screamed.

"Haha," someone yelled at her. "We've come to help you, little girly-girls."

It was the boys and Dina Marlboro who always played with them. They were jumping on the canal, kicking it and throwing in sand. All the girls were running, covering their faces. The sand in Rue's eyes hurt so that she stood there, weeping.

"Cry baby," said Dina Marlboro. "Little cry baby!"

Rue could just see the thin tough child, looking exactly like a boy. She had no governess and she dressed in sweaters and skirts, and was always filthy. Three or four boys were jumping up and down on the canal, yelling. Something in Rue burst open. She jumped, grabbing Dina's hair and yanking it. Dina pushed her back and laughed.

"Ooh, you're hurting me!" she said. "I wouldn't do dat, little girl."

Her fist landed in Rue's mouth and Rue sank back in the sand sobbing.

Dina and the boys started walking off as though nothing had happened. The governesses were coming in a body. Rue couldn't stop crying. The pain in her eyes and mouth was terrible. When Fräulein jerked her to her feet she spit out bloody sand and made a few sick swallowing noises.

"How nicely you play!" cried Fräulein. "How sweet and dainty!" She shook Rue but Rue didn't feel it. She sank down on her knees in the sand, with her hand still in Fräulein's.

"Get up this minute," said Fräulein.

The great rabbit face of Nona's governess looked suddenly down at Rue. She saw the long dry teeth and the gray circular lips.

"Mrs. van Deusen wants to see you," said Miss Miffin. "Don't ask me why," she added, looking around with an injured air.

"She wants to see Rue?" asked Fräulein. She let Rue's hand go, and Rue sat on the sand. The beach spun around, like a bright carrousel. She saw the clean straight legs of the little girls.

"Go and see her," commanded Fräulein with a new sort of urgency in her voice.

She pulled Rue up and took her by the hand.

"She says alone. Without you," said Miss Miffin, grieved. Fräulein scrubbed Rue's face with her handkerchief.

Never did Mrs. van Deusen come to the beach so early. It was perhaps a new whim, to ease boredom. Like someone on a sickbed, who tries everlastingly to find a new position that will ease the monotony of pain, which is worse than the pain itself. Everybody in Newport knew that she was bored. Rue, walking along the beach, knew this, and felt scared and angry. She thought, This old woman is why we're here. This is Newport, *the reason.*

Here she was, under the blue parasol, sitting in the beach chair. Her maid and butler were just leaving. The iced champagne was already in its bucket, and the shriveled hand concealed by a long white glove was already holding the first bubbling glass. Rue could see the bronze slippers with the bronze steel buckles, and the brown chiffon skirt looped over the ankles. Under the blue shadow of the parasol the old shrunken face looked fearful and hideous in purple shadow. The small brown eyes were too full of light. Rue stopped dead.

Mrs. van Deusen stared at her with a little smile, like someone looking into a tank of fascinating fish.

"Come here, dear," she said.

Rue came closer, and suddenly sat down. She thought that she was going to be sick.

"Here," said Mrs. van Deusen. "Take a big swallow."

Rue took the glass and swallowed the sharp sour stuff.

Mrs. van Deusen laughed. She had a coarse broken voice like an old actress, and the laugh was startling and unpleasant. Rue looked down at the sand.

"See?" she said. "You're better. It's the shock. I wish I could get a shock. Almost any shock."

Rue was afraid to look at her.

"What's your name?"

"Rue Peterson."

"Oh, a Peterson child. You aren't sweet, like your aunt." And again the coarse, shattering laughter. "Why did you pull Dina's hair?"

Rue looked up and saw her waiting for the answer, waiting to laugh again.

"She hit me," Rue said.

But now there was silence. Rue kept looking down at the sand.

"Why don't you come and play with Nona tomorrow?" Mrs. van Deusen said. "Just girls. No boys. No Dina. No governesses."

"I'll have to ask my aunt."

"Do by all means." There was another pause, Rue looked nervously up and down the beach.

"Good-by," Rue said. She started walking off slowly, afraid to run. She thought that any minute Mrs. van Deusen might start to laugh again. And at last she had to stop and look around. Mrs. van Deusen was staring at her, smiling. Rue had to smile back. Her lips jerked into a smile, like a muscle spasm. She thought, She's going to make me laugh! The thought scared her so that she ran. Now she thought she could hear the hideous laughter starting up again.

"Well, so you're in society," said Fräulein. "You're in society, Mrs. Astor."

Her heavy red-faced pleasure was like a too hot sun, unbearable. All that afternoon, Fräulein hung over her. When she and Audrey were having their naps in the thin gray rooms in the back of the house Fräulein came tiptoeing in twice, smiling secretly, like a madwoman who now intends to be pleasant, who intends for the moment to conceal the dripping knife.

Rue kept her eyes shut, almost afraid to breathe.

"You are not sleeping," cried Fräulein with coy pleasure. "My little Liebchen is not sleeping at all!"

She sat heavily on the bed. "Tell me what the old hag said to you," said Fräulein. And she leaned toward Rue, obscenely.

"She didn't say anything."

"Oh, but yes! We all watched you. All the children, all the

governesses watched you. Mrs. Astor, talking to Mrs. van Deusen. Two great ladies. Ha, ha."

"Go away. I want to sleep."

"You tell *me* to go away?" Fräulein cried. At once she grabbed Rue and dragged her off the bed.

"*Now* you're going to catch it," she said. "*Now.*"

Rue lay on the floor with her hands protecting her head. Now, now! She was already feeling the blows—the pinches.

But now there was nothing. Fräulein didn't touch her. The door was creaking open. Aunt Agnes's voice cried out in shrill refinement, "What are you doing on the floor? One would think you didn't *have* a bed."

Rue got back on the bed and sat staring, saying nothing.

At once Fräulein poured forth a torrent, a soft complaint.

"Mrs. Peterson," she said, gently, "she is *such* a naughty girl. I can do nothing, sometimes. This morning she had some champagne. Mrs. van Deusen gave her some champagne, and she drank almost a glass."

"Mrs. van Deusen?" said Aunt Agnes. In her face and voice was a shock, a sort of multiple alarm.

Fräulein stood there as though her corsets were extra tight.

Audrey came running into the room. "And now you!" said Fräulein. "Get back in your bed."

"Mrs. van Deusen gave Rue some champagne?" cried Aunt Agnes. "Why—why, what does this mean?"

"I bet she doesn't come to the party anyway," Audrey said. She stood there in her white cotton underwear strung with pink ribbons. "She invited *us*, though," Audrey said, with relish. Rue could see that both she and Fräulein were watching Aunt Agnes in a peculiar way.

"She invited *you?* To what, may I ask?"

"To Wavelands," said Audrey. "We are on the first rung of the ladder."

"Audrey! Don't talk like that! What do you mean? What does all this mean?"

"Rue amuses her. So she asked us to Wavelands."

"She is a very old lady," said Fräulein, with mock sweetness. "And she *does* drink that champagne in the hot sun."

"That's because she's bored," Rue said.

"I bet she doesn't come tonight," Audrey said. "Bet you she's already telephoned to say she won't come."

"Be quiet," Aunt Agnes said thinly.

"But it's true, isn't it?" Audrey persisted. "It's really truly true. I bet you already know."

"Will you and Fräulein leave the room, please? I want to talk to Rue."

The two of them left, closing the door. Outside Rue could hear angry whispering as they pushed each other trying to listen. Rue turned and saw her aunt looking at her. She was astonished, for it was a totally new look, loaded with charm and friendliness. Rue stared back at her, not smiling. Aunt Agnes came over and patted her on the cheek. It was a tentative gesture, experimental.

"Rue," she said, "let's be friends. Shall we?"

Rue had no idea what she meant. She lowered her eyes in embarrassment. Aunt Agnes sat down on the bed beside her.

"Dear Rue," she said. "You don't want to leave Newport just as you're getting acquainted. Do you? You and Audrey want to *make* something of yourselves, don't you? You have no mother. It's up to me to see that you grow up and occupy your rightful position in society."

Rue stared at her.

"Your father wants me to do everything I can for you," Aunt Agnes continued. And her voice was her sweetest, most social voice.

"Don't you think you're a rather ungrateful little girl? I have this large expensive house. Your father has to foot the bills—"

"Poppy!" cried Rue. "Did you speak to Poppy?"

"Well, now that's very clever of you, dear. You see. I'm not cross with you. Now at all cross."

"What did you say? Did he call up, or telegraph? Is he coming?" Now, in her moment of hope, she had forgotten to be careful. She stared at her aunt's pale narrow face, which was so close to hers.

"Well, dear, I'm glad you admit it," said Aunt Agnes gently. "I must say, I'm glad. No matter how bad a thing is, it's better to be truthful, isn't it?"

"Am I going home?"

"My dear child," said Aunt Agnes. "*My dear child!* He telephoned me at great expense. He thought you were sick. He was worried."

Now, at once, Rue knew it was hopeless. She stared hard at the wall, keeping her face away from Aunt Agnes.

"Isn't he coming?" she asked, knowing the answer.

"What would people say, I'd like to know, if your father appeared suddenly and whisked you off? As though I starved or beat you!"

"Fräulein beats me," Rue said. She had not meant to say it. This shaming thing, this frightfulness. But the words flew out of her. She turned her face away again. Aunt Agnes seized her chin, turning her face around. Now the displeasure in her face was uppermost, and the smile was nearly gone.

"Look at me and say that again, dear," she said.

Rue's mouth jerked upward into a smile. She began to giggle hysterically, shamefully. Hot tears filled her eyes.

"I *thought* so," said Aunt Agnes, and her voice was conclusive. She rose, drawing her chest up and away from her corsets, so that she looked like a thin pigeon, virtuous and triumphant. "Say, 'Aunt Agnes, I'm a little liar.' "

"Aunt Agnes, I'm a little liar."

The words escaped Rue, like the air from a punctured balloon. She lay on the bed, face down.

"Fräulein was with Lord and Lady Borstal's children when they were here last year. Do you think that Lord and Lady Borstal would hire a *bad* governess?"

There was a pause.

"I realize you don't like Fräulein." And here Aunt Agnes reseated herself on the bed. "I realize a great deal more than you suppose. I know that you don't want Fräulein to go back to Chicago with you."

Her voice had dropped almost to a whisper. Rue's heart beat with shame. She felt that something terrible, something shaming was about to occur.

"I will make a bargain with you," Aunt Agnes whispered. "If you do something for me, I'll do something for you."

Rue kept her face buried.

"You don't want to have Fräulein go back to Chicago with you, do you?"

Aunt Agnes's voice was still too low for Fräulein and Audrey, listening at the door, to hear. But the sweetness had come back into it. She tapped Rue lightly on the shoulders, as though bestowing a caress.

"Well, then you would do something, wouldn't you? If I promised to send her away?"

"What do you want me to do?"

"Well now, sit up! Look at me!" Aunt Agnes said sweetly. "And don't talk loudly. This is a secret. A big secret between you and me!"

"What is it?"

"Why don't you say you're giving a party, and why don't you ask her to come? As though it were your idea?"

"Ask who to come?"

"Now, dear, don't be stupid. That isn't like you!"

"Mrs. van Deusen? But I'm not giving a party."

"Well, that's just it, dear. It's time you had a nice party. I'd like to *give* you a party. You and Audrey. And if you could just get Mrs. van Deusen to drop in. To your party. She likes you. Don't you see?"

"You mean if I could get her to come, you'd send Fräulein away?"

"Yes, dear. I do."

"Could I go home?"

"No. But I'd send Fräulein away."

"Now?"

Aunt Agnes laughed, and it was sweet and careful, like notes preserved in sugar.

"Now, dear, be practical. I will send her away if you get Mrs. van Deusen here."

"What shall I say to her?"

"Just be your own natural self. That's best. Just say you're giving a party and ask her to come. Say next Wednesday. And then, if she accepts, you can ask all the little girls. You're so natural. It will be sweet."

Once more Aunt Agnes released the sugared laughter.

They were in the car, going to Wavelands, and Rue sat in the middle, Fräulein's great hot corseted hips crowded against her side. She and Audrey were dressed in pink organdie dresses, with ruffles all down the front, pink organdie picture hats to match, pink socks, and black patent leather shoes. The clothes were of a museum-like quality, impossible to move in, without ruffling or soiling them in some way.

"The old hag has a mood," said Fräulein. "She wants no governesses. I come back for you at six sharp. And if I see so much as one little spot on either dress—" her voice trailed off, leaving the threat wide open.

"Yes, Lina darling," Audrey said.

"If you are good girls today," said Fräulein, "I'll take you next week to Newport News. To the interned submarine Prince Wilhelm. Your Lina knows an officer on board. He said to me, 'Britannia Rules the Waves. But *Deutschland unter Alles*.' With the submarine. Do you see, or are you too dumb like all Americans?"

"England is going to win the war," Audrey said.

"Do you want I should slap you for a change?" Fräulein inquired.

"No, Lina dear. Slap Rue. She's sulking."

"She is snooty. She is Mrs. Astor," said Fräulein. They both looked at Rue and laughed.

Rue thought, I have to ask her to the party. I have to make her come. I'll wait till she's alone. I'll tell her in a whisper. And then she thought, I can't. I just can't. But if I don't, we'll have Fräulein forever. She felt that she was moving through some curious sort of nightmare, some fairy story where it was necessary to do a dangerous, awful, and impossible deed. Her heart squeezed together with fear and despair. She felt the numbness come over her, and she thought that she wouldn't be able to get out of the car.

Now they were going through the colossal wrought-iron portals. A lodge keeper stood watching them drive by. The gray-blue immaculate gravel crunched as they drove, and everywhere was green lawn, like a great sterile rolling plain. Avenues of clipped hedges and rows of box trees clipped in the shapes of birds went winding here and there. You could see dozens of flower beds, with the earth showing black between the design. There were greenhouses, and stables. In the distance the great lawn ended suddenly at the sea wall above the private beach, like a long, long story that has gone away past the point, or the bounds of reason, and which ends abruptly, pointlessly. Then there was the house itself, a startled palace of raw red brick.

Ahead of them were two pony carts with grooms, governesses, and miserable, overdressed children.

"Those are the Phellpses and the Morrison brat," Fräulein said.

"We should have a carriage," Audrey said. "Poppy's mother, my grandmother, had carriages in Chicago when we first got rich. I don't see why we can't," she whined. "Nona has two ponies and she can't even ride them. She foams at the mouth when she gets on a pony."

"Don't say things like that," said Fräulein sharply.

Now they pulled up at the front steps. The chauffeur opened the car door.

"Fräulein," Rue said desperately. "Fräulein. I can't move!"

"Shut up," Fräulein said. "Get out."

Imperceptibly her hand crept over to Rue. The thumb and forefinger, like steel pincers, twisted Rue's arm. Rue let out a scream and like someone cruelly roused from sleep crept out of the car. Her arm hurt. But she was stunned, and far away from tears. She saw the governesses and the other children filing up the great shallow steps. They were silent and self-conscious.

Rue walked up the steps. Her heart was moving unpleasantly in her breast. She thought, Perhaps she won't be here. Perhaps I won't see her. But almost immediately Rue did see her, standing in the front hall. She was like a majestic cascade of water, all green silk, a flowing dress looped over the ankles. Her stockings and shoes were green, and a tiny lorgnette of green emeralds hung by a diamond chain over her thin slack old breast. Beside her stood Nona in a white sailor suit. Not dressed up at all.

The hall was not like a home. It was like a cathedral. It soared into the air in great sheets of stone. Rue saw stained glass windows, a great double stairway, and a fountain which was a high waterfall, filled with bronze figures, ferns, and fish. She closed her eyes and said, This isn't real. This is a dream. Poppy, Poppy come and get me.

"Mrs. van Deusen," Rue said.

Everybody would stop now. They would stare. They would turn smiling in her direction.

But no one saw her, or heard her. The whisper had been tiny, almost nothing.

The old lady was leaning on her cane, and talking, and she was saying, "I have ordered the car. All of the governesses may go to town, to the motion picture. You may spend the afternoon"—and she smiled like an old reptile—"you may spend the afternoon with love and passion."

Rue saw their faces, like stone, and the staring children like a group of waxwork princesses.

"The children may take off their shoes and run in the grass."

"But Madame," Miss Miffin said. "But Madame, they aren't used to going barefoot. They'll catch cold."

"Let them catch cold," Mrs. van Deusen said, turning away. "What are you all for? You can take care of them."

Rue stared, watching her go. Now, she said to herself. Now! The governesses were talking together in low indignant tones, and the children were talking and giggling. Rue walked after her, slowly, hoping no one would see. Around a corner, she ran, and found Mrs. van Deusen entering a door.

"Mrs. van Deusen," she said, and her voice quivered desperately. "I have to ask you—"

"What do you have to ask me, dear? Come in. There's a bathroom in here."

Now they were in a small private sitting room. Now they were here, alone together. And in this green place hung everywhere with satin, stiffened with lace, starched everywhere with something rich and folded, some texture too beautiful for ordinary use, there was a silence, such as you hear in prison, when you have come to the end of things. And indeed Rue thought this was the end. Reality slipped from her. She was in a ghastly museum, and this figure, too, was waxwork, this mythical old woman waiting, with a grainy, staring quality, waiting like fate. The end.

Without knowing it, the words came out of her. She did not address Mrs. van Deusen, but Destiny and her own fate.

"If you don't come Wednesday," she said, saying it like a prayer, "if you don't come, Aunt Agnes will keep Fräulein forever. If I can make you come to tea she'll send her away."

And then at once everything broke, like some great glass object. The air seemed to shake, splintering on the sound of laughing. Rue ran to the door and Mrs. van Deusen, laughing as if it hurt her, as if any moment she would have to cough and die, called to her, "Come here, dear."

Rue stood, holding onto the door handle.

"You want me to come on Wednesday?" she asked. "To your house? Is that it?"

And she looked at Rue, with the expression of laughter still on her face, and perhaps a smile. Yes, perhaps smiling, perhaps even kindness.

Rue was afraid to answer. Before she said yes, Mrs. van Deusen was already moving toward the telephone.

"What is your aunt's number?" she asked, and then without

waiting for that answer she rang a bell. A footman came instantly, and she said, "Have Cassie get Mrs. Peterson's telephone number."

"Cassie is my secretary," she said to Rue.

Rue now had the door open, and was half squeezed through it. There, on the threshold, stood Audrey. She stood there stolidly, blinking, unashamed of having been listening.

At once she began whispering at Rue, a sort of fierce, hissing whisper like a spray of venom.

"You fool," she said. "You little chump. You didn't believe Aunt Agnes, did you? You don't believe she'll send Fräulein away, do you? And now you probably just made Mrs. van Deusen mad."

Audrey's solid unsympathetic body dressed in the fairy pink clothes was pressed against her own, as if to push her back through the door. And suddenly panic filled her. She felt her knees go out in front of her. The door, released, swung back into the room.

"Go out, children," Mrs. van Deusen called. "And close the door."

The voice sounded kind. And this, somehow, was an added cause for terror. Nothing was real any more. This was a dream, and yet, with the thick choking quality of truth, reality, unescapable.

She pushed at her sister in panic. "Let me go," she said. "Get out of the way."

But now Fräulein came up to them. "Well, here you are," she said furiously. "Now what?" She looked toward the closed door, and, as if guessing something, as if divining something, she croaked, "What have you been doing?" and stared straight at Rue.

"She's a little chump," Audrey said. Her voice was thick with pleasure. "She thought that Aunt Agnes would send you away, if she could get Mrs. van Deusen to come to tea. Aunt Agnes *told* her that," and her big blue eyes, filled with malice, slid around to Rue. She stared at Rue, from under thin pink lids.

Rue saw Fräulein's face turned to Audrey. She saw Fräulein forming the phrases, "What do you mean? Explain this."

And as they stood there, in that instant before action, Rue turned and fled. Her mind said, Run. Run, run! She rushed along the hall, toward the open front door, where the old butler stood, as if at attention. She could hear the children's voices, and in an instant she was running toward them as if to join them. There they stood on the green grass like a bunch of pale birds suddenly uncaged, not knowing how to fly. In a big car in front of the door sat the governesses waiting for Fräulein. They were whispering together, a bunch of old maids, a bunch of child haters. And now she fled past them all, not knowing whether they spoke to her or looked at her, not caring.

She ran away from them, and toward the cliffs. The great green lawn stretched all around her like some sort of mock freedom, and she ran in circles like a crazy pony. She thought, Run—hide. She ran toward the back of the great brick walls. She started running across a kitchen garden, stepping on flowers and vegetables. Then, suddenly, she stopped, staring around her. This was the servants' entrance, here was a gravel drive, ending in a circle of cinders, a long low red wing which was the garage and the back door itself, shabby wooden steps, and a row of garbage pails, the dreariness of the back of a palace. Near by she saw an open window and some bushes, and the window seemed to open on some sort of narrow hall. And then she heard purposeful steps coming around the house. She ran, and dived into the bushes. One of the pink ruffles gave a long tearing sound as she squatted down. She squatted, with the branches jabbing at her. She stayed as still as a wild rabbit hiding from a beast of prey. Through the branches she could see Fräulein in her hour of full revenge, coming to find her. She watched the flopping hat, the trembling red roses, and the face so afire with the delight of anger that it seemed to have some radiant light of its own. The little button boots were turned out comically, flung outward with each step like a cruel figure in a Punch and Judy show.

"I see you," Fräulein called, staring around her. "I see you." And the voice was loaded with a sort of fatal-sweet coyness, unbearable, irresistible. Something exploded in Rue's head. And now the frantic thing in her arose, and cried to her again, Run! Run!

She jumped up and headed past the vegetable bed, out toward the open lawns again, a rolling desert of green, going straight to the cliffs above the private beach. Her little pink dress flew on ahead of Fräulein, but Fräulein was also running: now she had all at stake. All her passions were gathered into running. Sex, love, hate, and murder, which were all the same thing in Fräulein, all this now was bunched into her running, and her screaming, which was a long steady scream, like a siren. Fräulein's flopping rose hat was now a shapelessness held to the back of her bun by a few pins, pulling her hair cruelly so that tears gathered in her eyes. Her skirts were gathered in her hands and her little boots twinkled comically across the grass. Rue got to the cliff and doubled back, dodging Fräulein. And now her eyes were on the last hope, the open window. She ran toward it, going for all she was worth. Get to the window, she said. Window, win-dow, and she ran like someone hypnotized, staring at the black open square, the last escape. It was even nearer the ground than she had hoped, but Fräulein, with a burst of speed, caught her just as she was astride the sill. As Fräulein's nails began to claw her leg, she gripped the sill, unable to move.

"I'm going to beat you to death," Fräulein sang. It was an ecstasy, like a religious climax. "I'm going to beat you to death," she sang. "I'm going to beat you to death."

On Rue's legs were long white furrows with beads of dark red blood. Now Fräulein grabbed Rue, trying almost gently to lift her off the sill. And as suddenly, she let go. She backed away, far, far away from the window. Her eyes slid in the direction of a sound, and she started fixing her hat, straightening her skirt, as demurely as a great beast of prey which has mauled its victim and is now licking itself, cleaning its whiskers, large and soft.

"Get off the sill. Get in the house," she said to Rue.

Rue sat there, gripping the sill, unable to move. She stared, watching Audrey come around the house, her face twisted into petulant distress. Audrey stopped, panting and whimpering.

"You're fighting again," she said. "You've spoiled everything anyway. Mrs. van Deusen called Aunt Agnes and said that Fräulein was cruel to you, and told her all sorts of things. I could hear Aunt Agnes right out in the hall. They had an awful fight, and now she's calling Poppy, and you're going to be sent home."

Fräulein straightened up. "Who?" she asked. "Who is calling Mr. Peterson?"

"Mrs. van Deusen. She has a call in, and she sent me to get Rue, to talk to him."

There was a silence, as Audrey stood there, sniffling. Then Fräulein, in another tone, as though she had been suddenly projected into the middle of some quite other play and scene, said, in soft tones,

"Darling, you are joking. You are teasing your Lina."

"You mean she's really calling Poppy?" Rue asked.

She stared at her sister, the spoiled face, twisted with crying. It seemed suddenly to be a focus for the truth, for hope, for everything. She sat immovable on the sill, concentrating on Audrey's open mouth, her closed weeping eyes, and the wail of despair, coming from this sudden inexplicable turn of events.

"You are joking," Fräulein insisted softly. "My little Liebchen is joking." She put a tentative hand on Audrey, and Audrey shrugged it away.

"She wants Rue to talk to him and tell him *everything*, and when he finds out how you treat her he'll come and get her himself, that's what she says," Audrey blubbered. Her eyes, wet, and piglike, suddenly opened upon Rue. "You're mean and selfish and I hate you," she said to Rue.

Over her head, Rue's eyes met Fräulein's. As Fräulein moved toward her, Rue did not budge. She stared at Fräulein coming toward her.

"Liebchen," Fräulein said, "you will not say naughty things about your Lina?"

The hideous face, spread in cajolery, was there beneath her. Now, from this smile, more than from Audrey's weeping, Rue understood that this was indeed all true. So swiftly, in one hour, she had undone them, all three of them, all three of her enemies. In this short time, she had accomplished their defeat and her own victory. Unexpectedly, without meaning to, she had turned this trick.

"Do you want me to kick you?" she asked Fräulein, and Fräulein backed away from the sill.

"Liebchen," she said. "My little girl. My little love. Fräulein is going to be good to you. You'll see."

Rue watched Audrey's open bawling mouth, and Fräulein standing there smiling and raising her eyebrows coyly like some wanton old flirt. She thought of the telephone conversation between Mrs. van Deusen and her aunt. Her aunt's voice over the telephone, the tones of spreading delight, upon hearing Mrs. van Deusen's voice at first, and then the shock, the silly squealing protests.

A footman opened the door of the back hall behind her.

"Oh, here you are, Miss," he said. "Mrs. van Deusen wants you to come and speak to your father."

THE FLAMINGOS

by FREDERIC PROKOSCH

THERE IS NO MORE BEGUILING PLACE IN THE WORLD. ITS beauty and its strangeness lie in this: that one breathes a sigh of surprise the moment one arrives, a haunting uneasiness is coupled with a rush of exhilaration, and a weird conviction arises that one has been here many years ago, generations ago, in some other incarnation perhaps; the place seems so intimate and yet so mythological, so golden.

The place is called Arrabida. It lies on the coast of Portugal some distance south of Lisbon, and gazes out on the Atlantic. But not the Atlantic we all have seen and heard; not that green, metallic, tossing expanse. It is as though a great shell of glass had descended from the sky and captured the cliffs, the beaches, and the sea; everything is lustrous and strangely immobile.

Still, when one looks at it prosaically, there is nothing at all exceptional about the place. There is a long sandy beach, and above that a wall of rock rising toward the rough, blue-tinted heather-covered hills that follow the coast of Alentejo. Only at Arrabida do these hills fold inward sufficiently to allow a tiny strip of green land to intervene between beach and cliff. On this strip has been built a small, rather commonplace hotel with accommodations for twenty or thirty guests. There are a few villagers' huts and fishermen's cabins. Above, poised on the edge of a crimson promontory, stands a medieval fortress of the kind one sees scattered the length of Portugal.

In the protective shadow of the old fortress lay a tiny villa, built by an Englishman thirty-odd years ago and in the ornate yet somehow barren style of that period. This Englishman, a novelist of mediocre talents and eccentric tastes, had died in 1935, and since then the villa had stood empty. It was already beginning to slip into a kind of salty decay when, some months after the fall of France, two American sisters happened to visit

Arrabida, saw the little villa, and decided to settle there "for the duration."

They could, perhaps, not have said quite what drew them to the place. The beauty, of course; the air of safety and seclusion; the air of unreality too, in a way, for they were women whom life had begun to terrify.

Their names were Anne and Eleanor. Anne was the older, and might not have been far from forty; yet she was still the more beautiful of the two. She was a black-haired, somber type, with an air of experience about her, and a strong low voice which suggested a habit of having her own way. She had married a young Alsatian aristocrat, a Baron Duchêne, about ten years ago; and four months previously he had been taken prisoner by the Germans at Sedan.

Eleanor was unmarried, and had remained Miss Chapman. She had lived in her sister's house in Paris for the past two years. She was still in her twenties, and looked as different from her sister as was conceivable. Anne was dark and shapely, Eleanor was ash-blond and slim; Anne looked sensual, shrewd, and stubborn, Eleanor looked pallid, helpless, and submissive. Anne had the air of a woman who knew all that men had to offer, but Eleanor had a virginal, prematurely chilled look. She did not lack a certain timorous beauty, but what everyone had said for the last several years was, "Poor Eleanor; she's already resigned herself to being an old maid."

They came of a wealthy family in New Haven, and were born and brought up in a fine old house on Whitney Avenue, with red bricks and white columns that shone agreeably through the overhanging elms. The Chapmans had always been associated with Yale University in a dusty, dutiful sort of way; and every male Chapman had attended that institution. But Anne and Eleanor had no brothers, and their father, with a well-calculated air of resignation, had sent them off to Bryn Mawr as the next best thing. There Anne had been a precocious but erratic student; Eleanor had become a bluestocking. Anne was attracted to music; Eleanor had studied geology. Anne had at an early age revealed a certain inclination toward bright dresses, high-heeled shoes, and piquant coiffures; Eleanor preferred mouse-colored suits and low sports shoes, and wore her hair in a simple, unpresumptuous knot.

For several weeks their life in the villa at Arrabida continued uneventfully. A Belgian lady in the neighborhood, a Madame Bouvier, sometimes dropped in at tea time and told them the latest Lisbon gossip. They themselves drove to Lisbon in a special taxi twice a week and there they visited the hairdresser, the milliner, the confectioner, and the little French bookseller, and ended up with cocktails at the Aviz, where occasionally they ran into acquaintances from Paris or London. Sometimes a friend would ask them, "Why don't you go back to America, my dears? You'd better, you know. Europe simply isn't safe any longer; the war will go on for years and years, mark my words." But they both replied with optimism; they loved Europe, they hoped for the best, and they somehow preferred, for the time being, Portinho de Arrabida to New Haven.

One evening a youth in bare feet and a dark blue shirt came to their door with the morning mail and a basket of fruit, eggs, butter, and milk. He explained to the cook, Maria, that his father Gabriello was ill, and that therefore he himself had come to bring the food and the letters. He smiled brightly at the two sisters, who were sitting in the garden under a eucalyptus tree, reading; then he vanished.

"What a handsome boy," said Anne. "I haven't seen him before."

"Nor have I," said Eleanor, without interest.

"As a rule, I must say I don't find the Portuguese handsome," continued Anne. "But this boy . . . he had such nice teeth; such a nice smile."

"Yes, he did," agreed Eleanor.

"Did you notice how dark he was? I suppose he goes out in a fishing boat all day."

"I suppose he does," commented Eleanor.

"They look so unspoiled; that's what I like about them.

So spontaneous," said Anne, and then she added suspiciously, "They're probably treacherous and dishonest, one and all. It's a decadent country, I can't help feeling."

"They look so openhearted," suggested Eleanor. "They look kind and helpful."

"You can't go by looks in these southern countries."

"I suppose not," said Eleanor sadly.

"The only way to handle these southern men," hinted Anne, "is to dominate them; otherwise they'll dominate you."

"I'm sure of it," murmured Eleanor.

This pattern of conversation between the sisters was not infrequent. Anne took a growing pleasure, condescending and faintly cruel, in parading her own amorous slant on life before Eleanor; she enjoyed shocking Eleanor; and she sought to tantalize her—from a mingled sense of her own guilt, from envy, from boredom, and from other motives too obscure to define. Such aimless relationships tend to become increasingly complex, marked as time goes on by a whole network of conspiring passions.

"Have you never," inquired Anne softly, "been interested in men, my dear Eleanor?"

Eleanor paused. "What a strange question, Anne!"

"Not at all strange; the most natural in the world."

"I'm accustomed to an unromantic life," said Eleanor. "You know that, dear."

"Nonsense, nonsense," said Anne, in a silky tone. "Come. Be frank, Eleanor. Don't you ever feel a certain—how shall I put it—sense of abandon?"

"I believe in self-discipline," said Eleanor primly.

"Well, someday," said Anne, "someday . . ."

"Yes?"

But Anne left the sentence unfinished.

It might have been a month later. It was early summer, and the heat carried a honeyed, insinuating flavor.

Anne was up in her room in bed, reading a book by Agatha Christie. Eleanor decided to walk down the path toward the sea, to breathe a bit of ocean air before retiring. She carried a little red book under her arm—the sonnets of Camoëns, which she was trying to read in the original Portuguese. She was beginning to love this country, but in an ill-defined, uncritical way which was not characteristic of her.

In fact, a curious change had been coming over Eleanor. She had grown more indolent. She would sit for half an hour at a time, watching the fishermen returning at dusk and hauling their boats ashore. Or at night she would sit on the bench among the cedars and watch, from a safe distance, the shaggy men in front of the softly lit *adega*, raising their tall blue wine glasses, laughing and singing.

And she had developed a sudden passionate interest in poetry. It had started with a volume of Rimbaud which she picked up in the little bookshop on the Rua Augusta one day. Then she sampled Baudelaire, and even tried her hand at translating *Femmes Damnées* into English. Now she was reading Camoëns.

She came to the edge of a large rock shaded by mimosa and sat down. She had formed a habit of visiting this same spot every night—it calmed her nerves, it helped her fall asleep. Only three months ago she had suffered cruelly from insomnia; but it troubled her no longer, or only rarely; and her health was improving in a remarkable way.

She sat down on the soft, aromatic ground. The Atlantic Ocean lay black and still. One by one the village lights were darkening.

Her thoughts began to rove. She thought of Paris and of London; of New Haven and Bryn Mawr. She thought of the garden parties her mother gave when she was a little girl with braids. She thought of May Day on the grassy slopes of the campus, when she used to dance around the flower-decked Maypole. She thought of her first visit to the Louvre. She thought of her first visit to the tennis matches at Wimbledon. She thought of many things, and she grew aware of a deep stirring within her, half sweet and half painful; and her memories grew flavored with a touch of resentment, almost of anger.

Then she noticed, with remarkably little surprise, that a stranger was walking softly down the path. She recognized him instantly. It was Vasco, the son of the village grocer, Gabriello. She knew him by the dark blue shirt, the bleached, tight-fitting trousers, the shaggy mane of hair and the lazy, barefooted tread.

He saw her, and looked startled. "Pardon me . . . I did not expect to find the *senhora* . . ."

"It is pleasant," stated Eleanor with composure, "to take a stroll at night; to cool off."

"Yes," nodded Vasco. "The weather has grown warm, very warm. Does the *senhora* . . ." He hesitated. The Portuguese, it might be noted, recoil from the use of the first and second person singular; they prefer the third.

"Yes?"

"Does the *senhora* like our country?"

She nodded. "It is charming." She spoke in a rather halting Portuguese; she used the word *linda*, which is more frequently applied to women than to countries.

Vasco smiled and nodded. "Yes, but old; too old. Old and poor. Too old, too poor."

"Sometimes," sighed Eleanor, "it is a relief to be in a place that is old and poor and simple."

"Simple?" Vasco smiled. "We are old, *senhora*, and we are poor. But we are far from simple. . . . No, we are not simple!" Then he added, "Look at the sea, *senhora*. It is very bright tonight!"

He stood on the edge of the rock and gazed over the sea. And Eleanor, for the first time in her life, felt a response to the keen, stirring beauty of a young man. As he looked over the sea with his bright black eyes, his brown arms folded, his long black curls stirred by the wind, a sense of antiquity came over her. She felt her mind and body caressed by the smells of the earth and the sea, and by the flavor of history which they engendered. She thought of the greatest of all explorers, this lad's namesake, who must have stared across this same water when he was young, and with the same simple yearning: with only a somewhat greater sense of mystery, perhaps, and more burning sense of combat.

Vasco turned and looked at her. "Would the *senhora* allow Vasco to sit down?"

"She would be pleased to do so. . . . Vasco likes the sea?"

"Vasco has seen the sea every day of his life; he feels that he is a part of the sea." He sat down on the soft warm ground beside her.

Then he pointed into the sky. "Look. Does the *senhora* see those stars over there?"

"Which ones?"

"The seven little stars just over the tip of the fortress. There."

"Yes. She sees them."

Vasco smiled. "We have a legend in Portugal about those stars. We call them the flamingos. We say that they have been flying for ten thousand years. On their way to an unexplored country, where they will find eternal peace and happiness. They keep flying and flying. They have not reached it. But someday . . ." The boy paused, and grew thoughtful. Then he sighed a little and said, "Does the *senhora* love the sea?"

Eleanor nodded. "But from a distance; only from a distance."

"Ah," whispered Vasco ardently. "Then the *senhora* has not lived! It is the sea which brings a man to life. . . . Vasco has watched the sea for seventeen years, and has watched children born and old men die in the arms of the sea. It is the sea which makes a man's soul grow wider!" He stretched his arms apart, as though to measure the spaces of man's being.

"Is Vasco . . ." began Eleanor, and hesitated.

"Yes, *senhora?*"

"Is Vasco only seventeen?"

"Seventeen, *senhora.* But a wise and strong seventeen. Seventeen is no longer young, *senhora.* In Portugal a boy can become a man at sixteen, or fifteen, or even fourteen. . . ."

There was another question Eleanor was about to ask. But suddenly she found a breathless excitement pass through her, and she could not speak. Vasco had turned toward her and was smiling; the great warm smile was flowing toward her from his eyes, his lips, his warm body; from the warm night air, from the whispering stretches of the sea.

"Ah, *senhora!* May Vasco . . . Vasco would like . . . Vasco would be so happy if the *senhora* would allow . . ." She saw his brown arms open and his dark head move toward her; then she closed her eyes, and felt the firm, passionate touch of his mouth on her neck, and his arms surrounding her body.

The following evening, after dinner, Anne lit a cigarette and said calmly, "What did you do last night, dear?"

Eleanor thought, for a moment, that she had not heard correctly; for the words were the very words her own twisted spirit had been uttering all day long. A stab of terror passed through her. "I did nothing," she said blindly.

"Nothing?" repeated Anne, in a mild, insidious tone. "You're quite sure?"

"Nothing at all," muttered Eleanor.

"Don't lie to me, darling. . . . I can read you like a book. Something happened to you last night. I'm sure of it. What was it?"

"It was nothing," said Eleanor, in a groping, desperate, unreal tone of voice. "Nothing happened to me. Nothing."

Anne sighed. Her thin sharp voice rose again, playing like a needle upon her victim. "You have been secretive all your life, Eleanor. You have never been frank with me. You have always kept certain sides of your nature hidden. Why? Don't you trust me?"

Eleanor remained silent.

They were sitting in a small loggia which adjoined the living room. There was no light in the loggia itself but the yellow light from the room behind them passed through the curtains and fell on the blue-tiled columns and the cream-tiled floor. Eleanor could not see her sister's face, which was hidden in shadow; but she could see her long hands lying motionless on the arms of the chair, and the writhing cigarette smoke which rose slowly from one of them. There was a pause, and Eleanor heard nothing but the long, wild hiss of the Atlantic.

"Don't you trust me, Eleanor?" repeated Anne, in a caressing tone.

"I have always trusted you, Anne," said Eleanor weakly.

"Then tell me about last night, dear. Tell me, what happened?"

Eleanor paused. Then she cried softly, "Why should you wish to torment me, Anne? You have always done so. Why?"

"I do not wish to torment you, dear," said Anne gently. "I wish to help you. I wish to know what happened. Tell me. What did you do last night, after you left me and wandered down the path alone?"

Eleanor drew a deep breath, and then said in a voice suddenly calm and firm, "I shall not tell you, Anne."

Anne laughed lightly, in a brittle, porcelain tone. "No? Well, you needn't bother, my dear. I know everything. Everything." She paused, and her laughter grew silvery and triumphant. "I know every detail, my lamb. The dear boy told me all about it this morning. Yes, didn't you know? I've been having my little fling with him for the last three weeks. He's dark and impudent, just the type I like. You remember the morning we first saw him? Well, I looked him up in the village that very afternoon. I found him in old Gabriello's shop; it was all surprisingly easy. And surprisingly pleasant too, to be blunt about it. That night I met him in the garden. He's a nice boy, don't you agree? I'm rather experienced, you know, and frankly, I consider him exceptional. . . . Well, we arranged a little joke together. Of course, it took a bit of persuasion on my part; but he wasn't really reluctant. He was to meet you down there by the mimosas—oh, by the merest chance, of course. I coached him beautifully, I must say so myself. A bit of talk about poetry, the sea, the stars. . . . Well, I was happy to hear how superbly it all worked. There was real wit in the way he described it to me this morning; I shall never forget it! Don't let it upset you, darling. But from now on you must promise to be frank with me. I really shall insist, one of these days, that you tell me all about yourself. Perhaps you'll learn to take a more mellow view of life, someday. . . . After all, you too are human. Was it pleasant, my dear? Or were you a bit, shall we say, too overcome by it all? Do tell me. Tell me, dear. . . ."

THE CHAMPION

by JESSE STUART

"Now, Lester, you know that I can outeat you," Sam Whiteapple said as he followed me down the path from our house to the barn. "I ain't seen anybody yet that I can't outeat."

Sam stood in the path and looked me over. He slapped his big stummick with his big pitchfork hands. He had walked six miles to get me to try to outeat him.

"Right here's where I put the grub," he said. "This old nail keg will hold it."

Sam laughed a big horse laugh and showed two rows of yaller teeth. His beady, black eyes squinted when he looked into my eyes. Sam looked tough as a shelled-bark hickory too. His face was covered with black beard—so black that it made his yaller teeth look like two white rows of corn between his beardy lips. Sam was a hardworkin' man, too, fer his overall knees were threadbare and the seat of his overalls was good as new. His overall suspenders had faded on his blue workshirt. His gray-checked cap bill stood over his face like a front porch.

"I've heard you was a great eater," Sam said. "I've just come over to put you under the table. I want to show you who is the champion eater in these parts."

"It's in crop time, Sam," I said. "Any other time but now."

"Why not now?" Sam ast.

"It knocks me out," I said. "I don't want to be knocked out. I've got too much work to do."

"You know which side of your bread is buttered," Sam laughed. He bent over until he nearly touched the ground; he slapped his ragged overall knees, and laughed. "Old Beanpole Lester Pratt can't take it. You got a mouth big enough to shovel in grub, but you can't take it. The eatin' championship goes to

Raccoon Creek. There's where I winned it from Gnat Hornbuckle when I et a hog's head."

"That aint no eatin'," I said. "I could eat that much and still be hungry."

"What about five stewed hens and all the trimmings?" Sam said. "I winned the chicken eatin' contest over on Uling Branch. I was full to the neck. Didn't think I could get the last bite down my gullet but I did."

"You didn't eat that many hens."

"Ast Porky Sturgill," Sam said. "He et the least—just a couple of hens. He had to pay for all the hens six men et. I'll tell you it's fun to get a real square meal and let the other feller pat fer it. I've never paid fer a meal yet. I've winned every eatin' contest. I've got the nail keg to put it in and you've just got a hollow beanpole there."

Sam hit me on the stummick and laughed as I started to open the barnlot gate.

"Wonder if Sam could outeat a cow," I thought. "No, he couldn't eat corn nubbins, fodder or hay. Wonder if he could outeat a mule. No, a mule et more roughness than anything else. Sam couldn't eat hay or fodder." Then it flashed through my mind if Sam could outeat a hog. But Sam couldn't eat the things a hog et. Sam wouldn't get down and drink slop from a trough and gnaw corn from the cob on the ground. What could he eat with?

Just then my black game rooster run across the barnlot. He could always put away more corn than any chicken I'd ever seen. He'd eat so much corn I often wondered where he put it. He was tall with a long neck and a big craw. His face was red as a sliced beet. He didn't have any comb for it was cut off so other roosters couldn't peck it when I took him to fight.

"Sam, you're braggin' about your big nail-keg stummick," I said. "You can't eat as much shelled corn as that rooster."

"You wouldn't try to be funny would you?" Sam ast.

"No, I mean it."

"Huh, never et with a rooster but I'd just like to show you,"

Sam said. "If I could eat the same grub, I'd eat with a mule, horse, cow or hog. It wouldn't make no difference to me. I've fed livestock around the barn and I know how much they eat. I know how much I can eat. I'll tell you I've got a big capacity. When I drink water in the cornfield it takes a gallon bucket full of cold water to make me a swig. You talk about that little chicken! You make me laugh."

The rooster stopped in the barnlot. He held his head up to one side and cackled. He looked at us with the glassy-lookin' eye that was turned toward us. His red face beamed. It wasn't as large as the side of a big watch. I looked at the rooster and then I looked at Sam. He stood head and shoulders above me. I didn't know he was so tall. He looked short for his shoulders were so broad and his stummick bulged out so in front. His sleeveless arms looked like fence posts folded across the bibs of his overalls. Sam was bigger than a lot of fattenin' hogs I'd seen. Maybe he could outeat my tall slim game rooster; I didn't know. But if he did, he would have to put a lot of corn in his craw!

"Can old Sam outeat you, boy?" I ast my rooster.

My black game rooster cackled. He cocked his head to one side and looked at Sam. He cackled louder.

"He says that you can't outeat him, Sam," I told Sam. "Said he was ready to take you on!"

"That rooster can't understand what you say," Sam laughed. He looked at me as if he believed though that the rooster could understand what I said.

"Can he outeat you, boy?" I ast my rooster.

He cackled louder than ever. He cackled like he was skeered.

"W'y that silly chicken," Sam chuckled. "You shell the corn and I'll show you whose the champion of this barnlot in just a few minutes. I won't haf to swaller enough corn to spile my dinner to beat him."

We walked from the gate down to the corncrib. The chickens followed me to the crib for I allus shelled 'em corn in front of the crib. The rooster walked toward us cacklin' like he was tryin' to say somethin'.

"What's your rooster sayin' now?" Sam ast.

"He's cussin' you," I said. "He says that you can't eat corn with a chicken."

"Tell him in chicken talk that I got a good gullet," Sam said. "Tell him I got a place to put shelled corn that's bigger than his craw."

I opened the crib door and got an ear of corn. I shooed the rest of the chickens back from the crib. My rooster stood there. He wouldn't shoo. He wasn't a chicken that you could shoo easily. If you shooed him too much he was liable to fly at your face and try to spur you. He never had as much as he could eat for I left 'im in fightin' trim. Now I would give him all that he could eat. He stood with his neck feathers ruffled up like he was goin' to fight. His feathers were black and shiney as a crow's wing. His spurs were straight as sourwood sprouts and sharp as locust thorns. He acted like he owned the barnlot and that he would as soon spur Sam as to outeat him.

"Now, Sam, I'll give him a grain of corn everytime I give you one," I said.

"Any old way suits me," Sam said. "This eatin' contest aint going to last long nohow. I'm just doin' this fer fun to say that I outet Lester Pratt's black-game rooster since old Beanpole Lester was afraid to eat with me."

Sam ketched the grain of corn in his big mouth when I pitched it to him. It was fun fer Sam. He laughed and swallered the corn. Then I pitched my rooster a grain. He picked it up in his hooked bill and swallered it. He quirked and wanted more.

"He laughed at you, Sam," I said.

"Throw us the corn," Sam said. "We'll see who laughs last."

Sam stood there a big giant in our barnlot. I'd throw a grain of corn first to Sam and then one to my rooster. The hens stood back. They were wantin' the corn that I was throwin' to Sam and to my rooster but Sam thought they were lookin' on and hopin' that their hero would win.

That ear of corn didn't last as long as frost on a hot plate. I kept shellin' corn and pitchin' to Sam and my rooster until my arm got tired. Every time a hen quirked or made a funny noise in her throat Sam thought she was makin' fun of him. He would screw up his big beardy face and look sour at something little as a hen. Sam stood by the corncrib. He never moved out of his tracks. He would stand there and crane his big bull neck and swallow.

"Ain't your throat gettin' awful dry?" I ast.

"Nope, it aint," Sam said. "A little grain of corn just draps down my gullet. You'd better ast your rooster and see if his throat is gettin' dry."

Just then I pitched my rooster a grain of corn and he sneezed.

"My rooster says his throat is okay," I said.

Sam looked a little funny when the rooster sneezed. I could tell he didn't have the confidence that he did have when we started the contest. Sam was lookin' a little worried. Maybe it was because of all the noises the chickens made.

"Am I 'lowed to chew my corn?" Sam ast.

"Nope, you're not," I said. "The rooster aint got no teeth and you're supposed to swaller your corn like he does. What's a little grain of corn nohow?"

"Nothin' to look at it," Sam groaned, "but a lot of swallered corn gets heavy. I can feel a heavy lump right down at the end of my gullet."

"I guess my rooster feels it too," I said. "Watch him stretch his neck when he swallers a grain."

I looked down at my feet and there was a pile of corncobs big enough to start a fire in the fireplace. There was a pile of cobs big enough to cook a big dinner in our cookstove. I'll tell you it was horse and cat between Sam and my rooster. At first I thought Sam would swallow more corn than my game rooster. Now I doubted that he would. I wondered where my rooster was puttin' so much corn. His craw had begun to swell. When he reached down to get a grain he nearly toppled over from the weight of his craw. But he reached down and picked up a grain, stood up as straight as Sam, and swallowed it.

"I'd like to have a sip of water," Sam said. "I'd like to dampen my gullet. It's gettin' a little dry."

"My rooster aint ast fer water yet," I said. "You've got to

abide by the same rule he does. See, he's never made a sound. He just stands up straight and swallers his corn."

"It's gettin' hard to get down," Sam said as he craned his neck and twisted his head from first one side to the other.

I could see now that Sam was worried. His eyes showed it. He didn't have any confidence at all. My rooster looked cheerful. He acted that way when he picked up a grain of corn in his fightin' beak. His eyes looked bright. He was confident and in fine spirits.

"Where's that chicken puttin' all that corn?" Sam ast.

"I don't know," I said. "You will haf to ast the chicken."

But Sam Whiteapple didn't ast the chicken. Old Sam kept strugglin' with a grain of corn. He was tryin' to get it down. His eyes begin to look watery. And Sam didn't have his natural color. There was a place on Sam's cheek where the beard didn't reach and that was allus rosy-red. Now it was turning pale. Sam moved out of his tracks when he tried to get another grain down. He run a little circle like a dog followin' his tail when he lays down. I kept my eye on Sam to see that he didn't spit the grain of corn out. Finally Sam got it down. My rooster swallowed his but he acted like he was gettin' plum full up to his ears. His craw was swellin' all the time. But 'peared like he knowed what was up. And he was goin' to beat Sam.

I pitched Sam another grain of corn. He ketched it in his big mouth. I never saw a big man wrestle with a little grain of corn like Sam did. He worked and worked and finally he got it down by screwin' up his face, gruntin' and groanin' and runnin' a little circle. Tears come to his eyes and flowed down his beardy cheeks.

" 'Pears like I got a bushel of shelled corn in my gullet," Sam said. "It's lodgin' now in my windpipe. I'm gettin' short of breath."

I had just pitched my rooster another grain of corn and he had had time to grab it when Sam fell like a tree. If my rooster hadn't been a quick one, he wouldn't 've got out of Sam's way. Sam sprawled like a sawed-down oak on the barnlot. His arms fell limp as two rags. It skeered me nearly to death. I shook

Sam. He wouldn't talk. He didn't move or anything. His mouth was open and I saw three grains of corn on his tongue. I felt to see if his ticker was still goin'. I thanked my God that it was. My rooster walked away with his flock of hens. He was craw-heavy for he almost toppled over on his face. But he flew up on a fence post and crowed. He'd et more corn than Sam. I wanted to break the news to boys on Raccoon Creek that my rooster had outet their champion eater. But I had to get on a mule and get a doctor.

"A man's a fool that will do a thing like this," Doc Hornbuckle said. "A big fine-lookin' man like Sam Whiteapple ought to have more sense than to eat corn with the chickens. Swallowin' corn grains that have never been chewed. Get him home!"

I harnessed the mules and hitched them to the spring wagon. Doc helped me load Sam on the wagon. Doc strained his back liftin' on Sam. Finally we got him on the spring wagon, and I hauled him to Raccoon Creek. I left him with his people. His Pa was awful mad at me about it. But I didn't have nothin' to do with my rooster eatin' more corn than Sam. I told his Pa that too. He said his crop was in the weeds and he needed Sam's help.

It was a funny thing the way people talked when Sam was so bad off the next two weeks. We'd go there and sit up all night. We'd talk about the corn Sam swallered. Some thought that Sam would have to swallow pieces of broken dishes, egg shells and white gravels from the creek just like a chicken did to work on the corn in Sam's craw. I told them Sam didn't have a craw and that Doc Hornbuckle would bring him out of it if anybody could, if they'd just listen to Doc's orders.

The last night I was over to the settin-up, Doc Hornbuckle said, "Don't you ever try to outeat another chicken, Sam. You have ruint your stummick. You'll haf to go easy fer a year. You can't do much work. You'll just have to piddle about the place. I'm goin' to haf to put you on a cornflake diet. You'll haf to eat cornflakes and warm sweet milk mornin', noon and night."

Sam's eyes got awful big when Doc Hornbuckle said "cornflakes."

CONVERSATION BY THE SEA

by J. WILLIAM ARCHIBALD

A SOLITARY CLOUD MOVED OVER THE HILLS AT DAWN. THEY were beautiful hills; very green hills. At dawn, this dawn, they were green in their depths and golden in their crests, and the highest trees shone from the smallest leaf to the roughest bark. The cloud passed away from these hills and moved its shadow over the little town.

This town was scarcely more than a village; its houses were built in ugly or pleasant shapes; but seen together none of the houses, not even the largest that stood with its back to the sea and its face to its proud and carefully kept lawns, was ugly. The town was magnificent at dawn or at evening when the woods and paints of the walls of its houses dissolved into the color from the sky. And under the shade of the passing cloud the town, on this particular morning, was soft and almost still asleep, soft and now almost awake. Some people were still in their beds. Some were even then about their houses. Dreaming faces, rumpled faces, faces with the print of night disappearing into the cold water of the wash basin.

In a tiny house an old woman sat up in her bed and looked about her. There was nothing in her room that she did not know. The great cupboard in which she kept ancient dresses and worn shoes was standing in its place against the wall farthest from the window. The only chair with its low legs and tall slender back was, as always, four inches from the bed. The long mirror showed her face and arms as she pushed with her hands to lift herself. There was nothing in her room that she did not know. The moan that had awakened her must have been dreamed. She lay back to sleep that one hour more. She lay down to sleep and never again awoke. . . .

In the room below, her daughter lay across a bed that was a

hundred years old, as old as the house. She was a nice-looking woman with a slightly tanned face. During the past week she had been painting the outer walls of the house. She had climbed a ladder and had painted almost all of the outer walls. She had used a paint that was white. Even now minute specks of paint were under her nails. Where the thick blood had dripped onto her hands the specks of paint seemed whiter. Where the blood had left her neck the skin was pale. She was quite dead. She lay across the bed that was as old as the house. She was naked and quite dead.

Her two children in the small room beyond the kitchen had just awakened. They looked across at each other and smiled. It was a beautiful morning. The sun shone in through the large window and long bands of light crossed and recrossed themselves on the rafters above. The waves below the window threw bands of green light on the white outer walls. Little boats were tied to slanting poles in the knee-high water, minute fishes swam in between the piles. Larger fish seemed to hang in the deeper water that filled the strange hole that had been dug by the tides.

"Aren't you glad it's Saturday?"

"It's lovely! Saturday is the loveliest day!"

"I know what I'm going to do today! I know what I'm going to do today!"

"Don't make so much noise! You'll wake Granny up . . . then she'll be mad at you."

"Oh, she's up. I heard her a second ago."

"You couldn't have. You were asleep."

"I was not! I did too hear her."

"Well, I heard what you heard and it wasn't Granny at all."

"Who was it, then?"

"Was old Bandy Fraser. . . ."

"You can't frighten me. . . . It's bright now."

"You were frightened last night when I told you about him."

"I wasn't at all. Anyway it's bright now and I know what I'm going to do. I know what I'm going to do!"

"Oh, you're a little silly!"

"I'm not! You're a nasty person. I shan't speak to you ever again!"

They were nice little girls even as they quarreled. The older was twelve years old. She was Katherine, just at the age where she had stopped wondering about things and had started to find out for herself. The younger, Elizabeth, still was puzzled by everything that she saw or heard. She was not young enough to accept happenings, nor was she old enough to misunderstand them and so ignore them; she was in between and a lot of trouble to her sister who loved her nevertheless. In a little while she was crying.

"Now, Elizabeth . . . you're not a little silly . . . you know you're not. Why, didn't you swim ever so far out yesterday? And didn't you swim faster than I did? Well, almost faster —?"

"You—you let me almost beat you. . . ." And she wept some more.

"Now what's the matter? Didn't you sleep well? Don't you feel good? If Mama isn't up yet we can still get something to eat and then we can go to Peter's Point. Wouldn't you like that?"

"An' what about Bandy Fraser? Wouldn't he find out where we had gone and come after us?"

"No. . . . I was only fooling you about him. There isn't any Bandy Fraser. Why, do you think Mama would let him come into this house? Even if he was a person really?"

"Wouldn't she?"

"Of course not!"

Their Mama wouldn't, of course; even if there were such a person or anyone like him. Mama was wonderful about things like that. And about other things, too. Why, she could think of the most wonderful surprises! Hadn't she made that family of dolls for Elizabeth without even a birthday as an excuse? And made them out of the most wonderful things like shells, and pale dried seaweed for hair; there was no other family of dolls like that one. They were a very individual family of dolls. They were more like a family of mermaids. Actually they were more at home in the water than on the land. Elizabeth was cheered by all this and soon she was laughing and talking in a loud whisper. "Oh, it's going to be such fun! Such lovely, lovely fun!"

"But you mustn't shout so! We must be very quiet or it won't be any use leaving a note for Mama."

"Are we going to leave a note for Mama? Like we did the last time?"

"It would be fun, wouldn't it? But we must be very quiet."

"What're you going to write this time?"

"Well . . . I could write about how we are going away out in a boat . . . or any numerous things. . . ."

"Like what?"

"We might go and see Lu Timinson. . . ."

"Oh, not again! She was so rude to us the last time! She's not a lady at all.

"Elizabeth! I wish you would remember that the poor woman has all those children and can't really be actually polite when we just bounce in on her."

"Mama wouldn't like her. She picks her nose."

"She doesn't actually do that. I just told you that because I was annoyed with her at the time."

"Well, she isn't truly a person so I can think what I like about her. So there."

"If you're going to be difficult I won't waste my time with you. There are so many things I have to attend to, really. Saturday is my one free day. You shan't do a thing with me if you don't behave."

"Oh, now you're talking like Mama when she's angry. I shall play by myself. I shall do what I want and I shan't go to see Mrs. Timinson. I shan't."

"Then I'll tell Bandy Fraser to follow you wherever you go."

"You wouldn't . . . oh, you wouldn't, would you Kathy? Besides you did say he wasn't true, didn't you?"

"He is and he isn't. You're such a baby at times, Elizabeth!"

"I'm not! Not really . . . only I do want to play with you . . . only I don't want to visit Mrs. Timinson today. Don't let's see her today. Let's do something new. You think of something new, Kathy. Something really new!"

"Well, we must have something to eat and I wish you wouldn't fidget so, Elizabeth!"

Elizabeth wasn't fidgeting at all. But Katherine was being very happy and capable. The two little girls went softly into the kitchen and took several slices of bread that was a trifle stale. They buttered them and spread a thick portion of strawberry jam on each.

"Don't take so much, Elizabeth! Mama and Granny will be furious."

"Granny doesn't like strawberry jam at all. Why, only yesterday . . ."

"Shss! What's the use of having a surprise picnic if everyone knows about it! I wish you'd be quiet."

"Well, after all, Kathy, won't they know about it? Aren't you going to leave Mama a note?"

"I won't if you don't behave. That's quite enough jam. If you get ill you won't have a nice time at all."

Katherine wrote on a piece of wrapping paper that she and Elizabeth were going away for a month at least. She signed it: *Your always loving Daughter, Katherine*. Then as an afterthought she added Elizabeth's name. Then because it made it plural she added a large S onto the Daughter. Then she wrote it all over again. This time because she was a little sorry for the way in which she had spoken to Elizabeth, she put that name first, and, as a happy thought struck her, she encircled the word Mama with a little garland of penciled flowers.

Outside the sky was even clearer than one would have thought. The cloud that had crossed the hills at dawn now was far over the horizon. It almost shone. It was a pure white. It hung like a tiny bunch of cotton over the blue horizon, and the deep sea looked all the deeper for the highness and whiteness of this cloud.

The two little girls walked away from the house and along the road that was at this hour as bare as it had been just before dawn. The road wound up and up. But so gradually did it climb that there was hardly an effort needed to follow it. It was pleasant road because of this and also because of the view it afforded.

"You know," said Elizabeth, "Granny is ever so much stronger."

"Now, Elizabeth, what on earth are you talking about?"

"Granny. I just looked back and saw her dive from her window."

"You're so silly! Really I don't know why I should bother with you. Granny never dives. Don't you know that old people hate the water?"

"I never shall. Oh, I do love the water especially when it's the sea. Do you know, Kathy, that Timothy and Rebecca live by a river and have never even seen the sea! I shall ask them to spend a week or two with me ever so soon."

"You're making up people again. I'm too old to do that. I know there's no one else but people who you see. Like Granny and Mama. You really must try and break yourself of that habit, Elizabeth."

"You're talking like Mama again. I shan't play with you if you do that. I shall go away by myself."

"If you did Bandy might catch you. . . ."

"You made Bandy up. Oh, I'm not afraid of him. There's nothing to be afraid of even when it's dark. Mama said so. And it's light now, so there!"

"Well, I'm sure Mama wouldn't like you telling lies about Granny diving from her window."

"It wasn't any lie! I did too see her dive. It wasn't a very good dive in the first place. She's been in bed so long, you know. Poor thing."

"You're not to speak of Granny like that. It isn't polite."

"Why ever not? I am awfully sorry about her pains and everything. Besides, if you look hard you can see her swimming across the bay."

There was certainly someone swimming away from the house—someone churning the water and sending fine spray into the sunlight. Katherine became very impatient with her younger sister. "Why, anyone can swim in the sea! You mustn't go making up things about your relatives. It's bad manners. Would you like everybody to say how Granny jumps out of her window in the morning? Adults don't behave like that. It isn't dignified."

"Adults *do* do things like that. Adults can do very awful things."

"You're being a very silly little girl. I shan't let you walk with me if you go on like that."

"Well, I still think adults are able to do things younger people don't do. F'instance . . ."

"Now Elizabeth! You shan't have any bread and jam if you go on like that."

"I think you're a nasty person. A most nasty person. I do think so. You don't like conversations or anything. What's the fun of going on a picnic if you won't have a conversation?"

"You're too young to have conversations."

"I'm not! Why, only yesterday Granny said to me, 'My, my dear, you *are* like one of my own age,' she said."

"Oh, Elizabeth, how can you tell an awful lie like that!"

"It's not a lie! You couldn't hear her because you were out shopping with Mama. We had a very nice chat. And then I fixed her bed for her and made her most comfortable."

"You know very well that Granny hates people fussing over her. Now you mustn't go on telling me untruths like that or I shall leave you and do everything by myself."

"I don't care. I shall sit here and look at the view." And Elizabeth sat down under a shady tree and put her chin in her hands while Katherine, who was extremely upset, went walking on.

Elizabeth sat in this position for several minutes. She looked at the sea which was now such a lovely shade of blue. She looked at the tiny white cloud that had passed beyond the wind and that stayed in one place for ever so long. She looked at the road that wound far beneath her . . . and at the houses that seemed too small for anyone except a rabbit or a field mouse. Everything was so far away. It was all there, of course, but it had such a Sundayish look about it. Where was everybody? Of course they were all there. But where?

Well, Mrs. Parsons was probably marketing. So she would be in the market, and not on the road. And Mr. James would be in his field spraying his fruit trees, only the field was around the bend in the road and quite out of view.

"And what are you doing, little girl?"

"I am not a little girl!" Elizabeth answered sharply, for she was still upset.

"Ah! my mistake. A thousand pardons, Madam." And the elderly gentleman bowed so low that the water from his jacket ran in a thin trickle onto the road.

"Well, I'm not really very old, you know. But I do get tired of everyone calling me little. It's most undignigying, you know."

"Naturally. I feel exactly the same way about things like that."

"Oh, but you're not little at all."

"I am other things, though. Yes, it can be quite disturbing." Elizabeth settled herself comfortably and continued the conversation which was certainly the nicest she had ever had. Katherine would be mad, she thought. But then, Katherine never did understand about conversations.

"I see you have been in swimming?" She put it as a question for, after all, he might have fallen into the sea or anything else.

"I have. You are a most observing person, Madam."

"Oh. . . ."

The elderly gentleman sat down on the grass beside her and wiped his hands carefully on a silk handkerchief. "And what, if I may repeat myself, are you doing?"

Elizabeth thought a while. "I'm just sitting and looking at the view."

"Yes, that is a pleasant way to spend a morning. A very pleasant way, indeed."

"I didn't actually mean to do that. My sister and I—that's Katherine, and she's walking up the road over there—well, we were going to play. But we got angry at each other, I'm afraid, and I decided to be by myself. You see, it's most difficult with a sister who is older than you are."

"Yes, indeed."

"We live in that house down there. And Katherine likes to pretend she's so much older than me."

"Does she look after you, my dear?"

"Goodness, no! Mama looks after both of us. And Granny as well. Granny is very old."

"Very old, my dear?"

"Oh, terribly old! She hardly ever gets out of bed. Even when Mama is painting the house she just stays in bed and says things to her through the window."

"Through the window, my dear?"

"Oh, yes. Mama has been painting the outside of the house. So Granny just lies in bed and talks to her through the window. Though I did see her dive out into the sea this morning. But Katherine wouldn't believe me. That's really what made us angry with each other, you know."

"How perfectly charming!"

Elizabeth thought about this for a while. There was nothing charming about being angry with Katherine. It was only annoying.

"And which is your house, my dear?"

"The white one down there. At least, it's almost white."

The little white house and all the other houses seemed to shake themselves to attention and all along the sunny road a faint quiver of dust rose and scattered.

"Did you see that?"

"What, my dear?"

"Why, the window in Granny's room . . . it opened and shut. It might have been the wind, of course, but I think Mama must be up. Oh, Katherine and I mustn't be seen!"

"Why ever not, my dear?"

"Why, we left a letter for Mama. And we told her in it how we were going away. We always do that on Saturdays. And it wouldn't be any fun if she saw us before we came back. Would it?"

"Very true. We should be hurrying along, then."

The elderly gentleman helped Elizabeth to her feet and brushed some dust from the hem of his trousers. Then, hand in hand, they hurried on up the road. The road passed between trees bent down by the sea wind and rooted in rocks.

"Isn't it lovely here?"

"Very lovely, my dear. You are the loveliest thing amongst all these beautiful trees."

"Oh, thank you. Katherine couldn't have gotten very far, could she?"

"Why should we worry, my dear? Although I am sure she is a charming person, I don't think I would like your sister at all. Must we find her?"

"We should. She's really a nice person when you get to know her. I've known her an awfully long time, of course. Although she does try to tell me what to do. All the time. It's most undignifying, you know."

Above the sea that shone far below, the trees cast fat shadows upon the rocks. The air was salt and soft and moved past the branches and shook the green leaves. Through the twisted trunks of trees narrow patches of sky and sea glinted and gleamed; far, far away the little shining cloud was moving back to land. On a gentle breeze it changed its shape; at times it was a fish, as was proper over the sea. But now and then it was a floating face, or a turning swan. At other times it became a cloud and as such moved, larger and always of the purest white, in toward the shore. The elderly gentleman smiled.

"There's Katherine! Oh, there she is! Oh, doesn't she look funny from here!" Elizabeth was excited and she pulled her hand away and shook her finger severely at the elderly gentleman. "Now you mustn't spoil it. You really must do as I tell you. I shall go and meet my sister. But you . . ." she whispered softly, "you must hide behind a tree. It'll be such a surprise!"

The elderly gentleman obediently hid behind a tree.

"Katherine! O Katherine!" Elizabeth called as she ran, her feet stumbling over the pebbles, her clean cotton sash flying out behind her.

Katherine turned. Her mouth opened. Oh, doesn't she look silly! Oh, won't she be mad!

"I wish you wouldn't scream like that, Elizabeth!"

Elizabeth stopped and came walking toward her slowly. "I met a nice man," she said.

"Don't be silly. Now, you can walk with me if you behave."

"But I did meet a nice man. We had a long conversation."

"Really Elizabeth. You are annoying. Can't you think about anything else? First it's a conversation with Granny which wasn't true at all. Now it's a conversation with nobody at all. I wish you'd stop."

"But I did! I did! He had been in swimming. With all his clothes on. And he called me 'Madam' and everything."

"Don't be a little silly."

"And he doesn't think he'll like you. So there!"

"You're a little fool! You'd better behave or I'll leave you again."

"You didn't leave me. I sat down. And I looked at several things. And then this man said, 'What are you doing?' And then we had such a nice conversation. He's hiding behind a tree. And we were going to surprise you and now you're being nasty and I hate you!" And Elizabeth started to cry.

"Stop sniveling. There's no one behind any tree."

"He is! He is!" Elizabeth looked at the tree and called, "You can come out now."

Overhead the branches brushed against each other, a twig snapped under the running feet of a rabbit, a gust of wind shook a leaf onto Katherine's neck. She jumped and almost screamed. "You see! There's no one there at all!"

Elizabeth stamped her foot. "There is too! He's just shy, that's all. You probably frightened him." Then she called again, "You can come out now." The shadows under the trees were very still.

"Please, Elizabeth, please stop. You're being very silly. You're telling such horrible fibs. Now come on and we'll go up to the end of the road and play any sort of game you like."

"No. That would be rude. Why, I told him to hide behind that tree. I shall go and see if he's shy or something."

Katherine was not quite sure. There might be someone behind the tree. If there was someone there he shouldn't be. Adults don't hide behind trees. She didn't like it at all.

"Elizabeth! Come back here! Please come back!"

"But I'm not going away—I'm just going to peek and see."

The wind shook down another leaf. Two more leaves sailed down from the highest tree. Elizabeth, her cotton dress pale in amongst the shadows, gave a little cry.

"Why! He isn't here!" She ran around another tree.

"I told you there's no one there at all, Elizabeth! Please, please, stop it!" Katherine started to cry. She seldom cried, but now she wept as though she'd never stop. "It was such a nice day and now you're spoiling it all!" But that was not the reason. She was frightened and felt cold and she was tired all at once. Elizabeth was behaving so funnily.

Elizabeth came slowly toward her. "I know he was there. . . ."

"Never mind, Bethy. Shall we go on up the road? Shall we play up on that big rock on the hill? Let's play at camping out, shall we? And you can carry the bread and jam now. Shall we?"

"No. I want to go home. . . ."

"All right."

They walked, a little apart from each other, slowly as if feeling for the stones underfoot with their feet.

The highest trees shone from the smallest leaf to the roughest bark. The little white cloud was really quite large as it edged into the bay. Mrs. Parsons should be going home from marketing now. But there was no one on the road. People don't do things at the same time all the time. And why is one road such a lonely thing?

And why does my shadow run beside me always a little faster than I am walking? And why does it make a rustling sound as no other shadow ever did?

Elizabeth turned and looked at her. Her face was white and she looked as though she was going to laugh. "Katherine? Katherine? Katherine, he's down in front of our house."

"Elizabeth . . . please stop it. . . . I. . . ."

Elizabeth stood still and pushed a stone with the toe of her shoe.

"Elizabeth, that's only a ragged man. You said he was an elderly gentleman. You said you had a nice conversation with him. Why, that man is only a tramp. You can see that he's dirty —even from here."

They walked past the small square field where Mr. James should be spraying his fruit trees. The old horse stood alone amongst the tall weedy grass flicking his tail at some bothersome flies.

Then they were near enough to the little white house to see, between the garden palings, the fat cabbages Elizabeth had planted in her tiny square of soil.

Then they could see the old ragged man with his funny face. He stood leaning against the gatepost, his jacket all damp and wrinkled. He was pulling down one corner of his mouth and then the other. Every now and then he squeezed a little water from the sleeves of his jacket.

"Ah! There you are, Madam. And this is your sister, I presume?" He bowed until his head almost scraped his knees.

Katherine pulled Elizabeth toward her. "Don't say anything. . . . Don't speak to him."

Elizabeth looked out to the sea and the tiny hanging fish. What a bad old man! To run away as though she had told a fib about him. She held her head very high. She certainly would not speak to him. Why, he was only a tramp!

Katherine stopped at the gate. She was going to be very severe. Imagine, her sister, her little sister, had spoken with this horrible old man! "I don't think Mama has any money to give away. Please go away."

The elderly gentleman straightened himself. "Your mama? Why, I was only waiting to see you and your charming sister. I am not a beggar, Madam." He bowed again, "I have already seen your mama . . . and your grandmother. Charming. Charming." He giggled. "We had a most charming conversation just before dawn."

"You couldn't have. Mama wasn't even up. . . ." Then Katherine was frightened. She was tired. Elizabeth was holding her hand so tightly that it hurt.

"Go away, you nasty old man!" Elizabeth was crying. She, too, started to cry. She pulled Elizabeth with her and ran up the garden path. Between the broken bits of stone that lined the beds she ran. And Elizabeth was stammering all the time. "He's coming after us. . . ."

But what did it matter? The door was reached and Katherine shut it and locked it and hugged Elizabeth. Then she felt a lovely relief at being back home with Granny and Mama.

THE DREAM OF ANGELO ZARA

by GUIDO D'AGOSTINO

UNFORTUNATELY FOR ANGELO ZARA THE DREAM HAPPENED on Saturday night, and on Sunday there was no work and nothing to do but talk about it. Unfortunately he had to tell it to Matteo (Big Mouth) Grossi who lived downstairs in the same building. But most unfortunate of all was the fact that he wasn't built for a dream of such terrific and far-reaching proportions.

In the morning when Angelo Zara awoke in his furnished room on the top floor of the tenement building on Bleeker Street he was seized with a violent trembling sensation. He realized that he had actually been in the Villa Torlonia and what had happened had happened right before his very eyes and every word and gesture that had taken place was just as clear in his mind as the tips of his toes sticking out from under the bed sheet. He wanted to get up right away and rush downstairs to see his friend Matteo Grossi, the bricklayer; but then he remembered it was Sunday, and on Sunday Matteo had a passion for sleeping late. Once when Matteo's kid accidentally shot off his cap pistol before going to church, Matteo had leaped up out of the bed in a frenzy and held the child screaming out of the window. Angelo Zara did not approve of this kind of violence, but after all a friend was a friend and who was the man without some failing in one way or another? Just the same he didn't rush downstairs. He sat in his little room under the tenement roof, dressing slowly and going over every angle of the miraculous dream. Now and then his fingers would pause on a button and his features would light with an ecstatic glow mingled with bewilderment. He couldn't believe that such a dream had actually happened to him.

At fifteen minutes after nine, dressed in a clean shirt and wearing his good pants and his black Sunday shoes, he knocked on the door of Matteo Grossi's flat. There came the shuffling slippered footsteps of Mathilda Grossi and the door opened. "*Bon giorno, compare* Angelo," Mathilda greeted, stepping to one side for him to enter.

"Matteo!" Angelo said in a hushed voice, "He is up, no?"

"Ma, sure," Mathilda smiled.

Angelo followed her through the foyer and into the flat. In the bathroom he found Matteo shaving. One side of his face was lathered and the other side was already finished, but there still remained the cleft of his chin, and this was the most difficult part of all. Angelo Zara sat down on the edge of the bathtub and waited. He held his hands nervously in his lap, lost in the excitement of thoughts which packed his brain. As Matteo Grossi gave a last finishing stroke with the razor and reached for a towel, he blurted, "Last night, Matteo! Mussolini! He die. In the Villa Torlonia he kick the bucket!"

The towel fell from Matteo Grossi's hands. His square rugged face gaped in amazement. "Where you hear this?"

"No place," Angelo Zara answered. "Was there me. Plain. Joost like I stand in front you now. In that big room with the automatico bed that go down in the cellar when they have the airs raid."

Matteo Grossi picked up the towel again. "Bah, was joost a dream."

"Sure," Angelo said, growing excited. "Sure was joost a dream. But such a dream like never before I have in my life. Ma, plain! Plain like Jesu Cristo, you face. Mussolini he there on the bed. He gonna die and I watch. On his face is a big soomprise. Like he never believe he gonna die like this. Great big Mussolini gonna die joost like anybody else. He no can onderstand—"

"Was the pizza you eat last night," Matteo said. "The pizza and sleep is a bad combinash. Is like worms in the stomach." Nonetheless a change had come into his voice. He put on his shirt and walked out of the bathroom and through the living room and into the kitchen and sat down at the table. Angelo followed and sat across the table from him, while Mathilda set out an extra cup and poured coffee. Matteo tasted the coffee.

He picked up a loaf of bread, broke off a chunk and handed the loaf to Angelo. "Was joost you and Mussolini there?" he asked.

"Joost Il Duce and myself," Angelo Zara replied. He made a movement with his hand to indicate the vast silence of the scene. "On the fireplace from the marble de Carrara was the clock. Solid gold! And the hands silver. And could hear, ticka-tocka, ticka-tocka, ticka-tocka. When Mussolini he see me there he look in soomprise and he say, 'who you?' "

Matilda moved over from the stove, staring at him as if he'd lost his mind. She was about to say something but her husband waved her out of the kitchen. "*Sangue de la Madonna*, how many time I tell you when man talk politic no mix yourself up?" He turned to the table again. "And watch you say, Angelo, when Mussolini ask, who you?"

"What was I gonna tell him?" Angelo said. "I come to America from twenty years now and I press in the pants factory. What I was, gonna lie? Was the man gonna live maybe five minuts and I was gonna make up the storia about be rich or something like that! I tell the truth." He hunched his shoulders, undecided, wondering if maybe he'd said the wrong thing.

Matteo Grossi scratched his head disapprovingly. "Could say you was foreman in the factory. Was no too big lie, because last years the boss he proomise you that. Is no good tell politish like Mussolini the truth. He only believe half watch you say." He let out a deep breath. "If was only me there—" He stared at Angelo as if the rare opportunities of life always came to the wrong people. "Then what happen?"

"Then what happen happen the most curioose thing like you will never believe," Angelo Zara went on. "From the window on the garden come the moon very bright and I can seen him in the bed better from before even. But is no the Mussolini like you see in the paper and in the moonpitch. Is an old man with the face green like cheese and with the black line under the eyes. He get up lilla bit in the bed and he say, 'Is true, Angelo, you have good life in America? Is true all the things what they say? Is true everybody have the chance there like everybody else?' "

"Yeah, yeah—"

"And then more curioose than before even," Angelo said. "Mussolini he fall back on the bed with big—" exhaling a deep breath to indicate a sigh. "He close his eyes and then he open them again. Is choke and is the pain inside I can see. But joost the same he talk. 'Angelo,' he say. 'Si, I give you a job with my governmento, three thousand lire for month, you stay here with me?" He crossed his hands over his chest. "*Su mia madre!* I swear. He say that to me."

"And watch you say?" Matteo Grossi exclaimed, hanging onto every word, pushing his coffee cup aside.

"I say, no."

"Goddam fool!" Matteo Grossi shouted. "Is salario like a general. More. Badoglio he never make so much money."

"But I no wanna go back to Italy," Angelo Zara said. "I like here. I satisfy. What the hell I know I gonna find over there. Maybe two days Mussolini like me no more and I get the castorolio. Oh no. I no wants that propozish. Is no for me. Maybe for you is all right."

"Go to hell Il Duce," Matteo Grossi said. "Without contract I no trust him from here across the table. But three thousand lire! You say no too fast. If was me I make him come up to five thousand before I say no. Make you look more big. And after that?"

"Was nothing," Angelo answered. "Then he die. And was terrible to look. Stink in the room like never I smell before. And on the face was the expresh like somebody who have no more friend and no care what happen no more—"

"And finish," Matteo Grossi said.

"Finish," Angelo Zara added with a sigh. "But such a dream, and so plain like this coffee now."

For a few minutes Matteo Grossi was silent. Then his eyes spread like two peeled potatoes and he jumped up from the table. "Is a dream for Ignazio Ferro. Come on, we see what Ignazio Ferro say." Without letting Angelo finish his coffee he grabbed him by the arm and hurried him out of the flat in search of Ignazio Ferro, the shoemaker.

Walking along Bleeker Street in the quiet Sunday morning

sunlight, Matteo Grossi became more and more enamored of the dream. "Imagine, Mussolini with the automatico bed!" he laughed. "And the clock go ticka-tocka, ticka-tocka, and he die joost like any poor salamambitch you and me. Ho ho! And he wants make you general for five thousand lire for month." He wagged his head. "Where that salamangonia, Ignazio? Wait we tell that to him. He study dreams. I betch this mean something like never we can imagine—"

"Was no five thousand lire," Angelo Zara corrected. "Was only three thousand. And was joost a job, no general, like you say."

"The same differenza," Matteo Grossi exclaimed with a vague gesture. He stopped suddenly. "Salamambitch! Like that Mussolini he spend the money from the poor people what pay the tax! For what? Watch you know how to do in the governmento?" Then he grinned and continued walking. "Ticka-tocka, ticka-tocka! Was me I say, Goddam right, America foist-class place. Where in Italia I can have house with the hot and cold water and the toilet inside, and the Forda like what I got here? All right, I not got the gas no more, but joost the same I got the Forda."

Ahead, on the corner, they spied Ignazio Ferro. His squat rotund figure was propped against a lamp post and he was chewing a toothpick and twirling the ends of his huge iron-gray mustache. Angelo started to hurry toward him, but Matteo Grossi held him back. "Wait. Angelo! Leave me talk. If you tell him you spoil everything. Is no dream for you this kind dream."

"But was my dream!" Angelo Zara exclaimed. His small shriveled face assumed a hurt expression. "Was happen to me, not you. Why you mix up in my dream? Why you no leave me alone?"

"All right, is your dream. But for the part where Mussolini he give you the job, that belongs to me. That you let me tell, yes?"

"All right," Angelo agreed. "Joost that lilla part."

However, when they came up to Ignazio Ferro, Matteo Grossi planted his huge bricklayer's body in front of the shoemaker and before Angelo could open his mouth to draw a breath, he said, "Watch you think, Ignazio? Last night Mussolini he die."

"Please, Matteo," Angelo begged. "Was you have this dream or was me?"

"Never mind," Matteo Grossi said. "Is a dream like this no belong one man. Is pooblic property. We in America here. Everything for everybody."

Thrusting Angelo Zara aside he told the shoemaker the dream from beginning to end, pointing it up here and there, giving it the little artistic touches. Angelo Zara listened, tears beginning to glitter. His voice was a squeak, his entreaties futile against the booming thunderous speech of Matteo (Big Mouth) Grossi. "And salamangonia," Matteo finished off, "in front my eyes he was dead. And was a stink in the room like one million rotten sardines. And his face! Was no more the face of a man! Was the face of the devil who have lose his best wife."

As Matteo Grossi's words died away, even Angelo stood with his mouth open, as if he'd been hearing the dream for the first time. The shoemaker continued to pick his teeth in silence. Both Angelo Zara and Matteo Grossi waited breathless for his verdict. But in the matter of dreams, Ignazio Ferro didn't slap together verdicts like he slapped heels on a pair of shoes. He had to turn the dream over in his mind, give it proper consideration. Waiting for him to speak, Angelo thought it only right to set him straight on the ownership of the dream. "Was like Matteo say, but was my dream, Ignazio. And was—"

Ignazio Ferro didn't answer. He simply removed the toothpick from his mouth and gave him a look. That was all. The rest of the sentence died on Angelo's lips.

"Is a dream with big significanza," Ignazio Ferro said finally. "Very big. Is a dream I have to speculate." He glanced up at Matteo Grossi, at the same time pensively twirling the end of his mustache. "You sure was no Count Ciano in the room there?"

Angelo Zara shook his head vigorously. Matteo said, "Sure we sure. Ciano is no a cockroach he can hide in the floor."

"Very big significanza," the shoemaker repeated, his voice low and mysterious. He half closed his eyes and spread out his hand before him. "Is mean the finish for Mussolini. Is mean the finish for Il Fascismo, like I have been say for ten years. Is miracolo, this dream!"

Angelo Zara listened out of a haze. The shoemaker's words became like music, like the sound of a muted heavenly voice in his ears. He, Angelo Zara, had dreamed a miracle—a dream that would make him the envy of the whole neighborhood.

"See!" Matteo Grossi exclaimed, slapping him on the shoulder. "See what I tell you! Is no for you this kind dream. Is too big." He turned abruptly from Angelo and locked arms with the shoemaker. "We wake up Amalfio. We get Alfredo and Beppo. Salamangonia miracolo this dream we must tell the whole world. We get the priest too."

The shoemaker stiffened. "No the priest! For the kids and for confess the women the priest all right. But for the dream is need specialize study. No priest."

"Then, no priest," Matteo Grossi said.

They started along the street, walking arm in arm. Angelo Zara followed along. They kept talking about the dream and when he tried to interfere neither of them would listen. He could feel his dream slipping further and further away from him. It was hopeless to mutter, "Was my dream! Was me talk with Mussolini! Was me the last there before he die!"

Matteo Grossi and the shoemaker turned into Thompson Street and Angelo Zara fell a little behind. But he could hear Ignazio Ferro saying, "Five thousand lire! *Mannagia L'America!* Is no the king so much! But if was me that was there—"

Near the corner they turned from the sidewalk and went down a few steps to the door of Amalfio Testoni's pizzeria. It was early and Amalfio wasn't dressed yet. He opened the door in his nightshirt, rubbing his eyes, grumbling in annoyance. But he allowed them to enter. As they went inside they were joined by Alfredo, the butcher, who lived in the building next door.

"Wine!" Ignazio Ferro shouted to Amalfio. "Fillemup the glasses with wine. Is a miracolo happen today."

"You crazy," Amalfio said. "Is Sunday today. No wine before one o'clock say the law."

"Go to hell the law," Matteo Grossi said. "You fillemup the glasses and we tell you something like never before you have hear in you life."

"No joke?"

"Joke!" Ignazio Ferro said. "With the miracolo he wants play joke now."

Amalfio hesitated. He ambled over to the door and glanced furtively outside before bolting it. Then he hurried to draw a pitcher of wine from one of the barrels setting on wooden horses at the far end of the pizzeria.

Angelo sat down with the others. The most important place at the head of the long plank table was taken by Ignazio Ferro. On his right sat Matteo Grossi and on his left Alfredo, the butcher. When Amalfio returned with the wine and glasses, Angelo saw his opportunity and blurted, "Last night, Amalfio. I have dream . . ."

"Angelo!" Ignazio Ferro shouted, his eyes popping from their sockets, his mustache bristling. "Is you the specialist for the dreams, or is me?"

"Whatsamatter with you, Angelo," Matteo Grossi said.

"I don't care," Angelo Zara cried. The words choked him, but he had to get them out. "Was my dream. Why for everybody gotta take my dream?"

"Foolish, stupid," Ignazio Ferro said. "Anybody can have the dream. Even the jackass with the sick head. But to onderstand the dreams! Ah, that is something else. For that I have read two book. You have read these book too?"

"No. But joost the same—"

"Then keep quiet."

Amalfio poured the wine, his sleepy eyes now alive with wonderment as he gazed from the shoemaker to Alfredo the butcher, who sat with his mouth open. Ignazio Ferro pounded the table for silence and began. "Last night in the Villa Torlonia, Mussolini he kick the bucket—"

Angelo Zara rose quietly from the table and moved to the

door. Nobody paid any attention. As he slipped the bolt and went outside he could hear startled amazement and the two new voices echo in a breath, "Where you hear this?"

He climbed up the basement steps and onto the sidewalk again. It was no use. He had been cheated. Fate had played a trick on him. It had given him a dream and he wasn't big enough to carry it. He walked along slowly, filled with a growing consciousness of his utter insignificance. Glancing up he saw Beppo, the baker in Amalfio's pizzeria, hurrying toward him. He wanted to cross over to the other side of the street, but it was too late. Beppo accosted him. "Whatsamatter? Why Amalfio open the pizzeria? What happen?"

Angelo Zara shrugged his shoulders and moved on. He had it on the tip of his tongue, but it was no use. The dream was gone. It didn't belong to him any more. He continued to walk along lost in a surge of depressing thoughts.

Sometime later, reaching the park at Washington Square, he sat down on one of the benches. All around him birds were chirping and there were kids playing at the fountain and on the sidewalk a pigeon hopped along with its chest all puffed out. He began to feel better. When the comfortable happy face of Flannegan the cop greeted him, he smiled. "Meesta Flannegan," he said. "Last night Mussolini he is dead."

"Ye've been dreaming," Flannegan grinned.

"Me?" Angelo Zara said in astonishment. "Is too big only for me. Was five other men have this dream too!"

THE UNBOWED HEAD

by FRED E. ROSS

I WOKE UP HEARING OLD RAYMOND CROWING. HE WAS NOT really old, but not a stag by any means. He was three years old if he was a day, I judged, though I had no way of telling his real age, since I picked him up without inquiring as to his blood lines or age. I was just an interested bystander at a cockfight when the sheriff and a couple of deputies raided the place. In the resulting confusion I picked up old Raymond and fled the scene. That was over a year ago and nobody could dispute ownership now. He was a fine bird and today I would find out just how great a fighter he was.

He was as fit a warrior as ever crowed a challenge. I think he must have known that he was going to fight this day, for he crowed all night. Or maybe it was me that was the nervous one, for I woke up about a dozen times and every time I heard old Raymond crow. He had as rasping and insulting a crow as I ever heard a fowl utter. Most roosters, when they crow, sound like they mean they are the cock of their roost, but old Raymond sounded like he meant he was the cock of all roosts. And he was an evil bird. He lowered his head and raised his hackles at me every time I went near him. He was mean to his hens, too. They never knew whether to expect affection or brutal treatment.

I looked out the window and saw a streak of light in the east and decided to get up. I eased out of bed as quietly as I could, so as not to disturb Molly, my wife. She had gone to bed in a bad humor and I figured that she was more than apt to get up that way. Molly is a good woman, too good for the likes of me. She has wasted a lot of time and breath trying to show me the light regarding Christian living. We don't see eye to eye about some things. Cockfighting, mainly. I give over to Molly in nearly everything but that. I let her tell me when to sow, when to reap, when to go to bed, when to get up. But about cockfighting I let her talk into my deaf ear.

I pulled on my overalls and went into the kitchen barefooted. I built a fire in the cookstove and put the coffeepot on. I heard Molly turn over in the bed, slamming herself over so hard that the bed slats bounced and made a hell of a racket. I knew she was still mad and letting me know that she was awake and too mad to get up and cook my breakfast. I put on my shoes and went out on the back porch to wash my face. Old Raymond heard me and crowed at me. I went back in the kitchen and put on a few slices of ham to cook.

While the ham was cooking I thought about old Raymond. I had made him a member of my family and I had been good to him. I had fed him well, gave him game pullets to subdue to his will, and dropped Molly's fine dominecker roosters in his run every once in a while, to give him a taste of blood. Molly always thought her domineckers flew over the wire to get at old Raymond. Old Raymond never failed to eat his food, chase and catch his pullets, and to cut the other cocks to ribbons with his natural spurs. He always crowed after doing any of these things. He was a smart rooster, but a brag.

I had been training him for the past three weeks and I had scars on my arms and legs to show for my pains. He had an evil disposition to start with, and when I penned him up away from his hens he really got mean. I had two real pretty game pullets that I dropped in his lot for a few minutes every day. I penned them out by themselves and saved their eggs. I hid the eggs in a bucket I had hung up in old Raymond's lot. Molly didn't know about that. She was afraid to go in old Raymond's lot. I had fifteen of these eggs hidden and I aimed to sell them for a fancy price if old Raymond showed up well today. I had shaved him, trimming his comb and wattles so close that he was having trouble in picking up his food, due to loss of balance.

He was an Arkansas Traveler, of the best blood, judging by his desire for battle. He was a shake, weighing six pounds and fifteen ounces. So far as I knew he had never been pitted, but I was confident that if he ever was dropped in a pit he would let daylight into the vitals of his opponent.

I saw that the ham was done; so I took it off the stove. I wasn't hungry, though; so I just drank three cups of strong coffee. Then I went out to the lot to see how old Raymond was looking this morning. As I went out I heard Molly flop over in the bed and kick the footboard hard. She was working herself up into a lather. Old Raymond was strutting around his lot, fussing to himself in a treble key, and flapping his wings a little. He had a touch of red on him and a light touch of gray, but the white was his color. He showed up plainly there in the early morning fog. The broad feathers on each side of the fan of his tail were the prettiest shade of red I ever saw. Red like freshly let rooster blood. He had a broad back and a high, thick breast. What a sight this shake was as he challenged me there in the gray light! But it was old Raymond's eye that held me. I was a right good reader in my youth, and I read "The Ancient Mariner," and old Raymond put me in mind of that poem, for he certainly could hold me with his glittering eye. He was a cocky rooster, all right, and I had a soft spot in my heart for him. I think he was fond of me in his own way.

I gave him a little food, clean hulled oats and a little cracked flint corn. He ate it halfheartedly, threatening me all the time so that he was almost too busy to eat. I put in a pan of water and he tried to flog me, but I put my foot out and pushed him back. I went back to the house and wrapped up a couple of ham sandwiches and got my overall jacket. I was taking it in case it rained during the day. I put the sandwiches in one of the jacket pockets. I went to the chest of drawers in the bedroom and got my .38 special and slipped it into my front overall pocket. Molly raised up in bed and said, "Taking a pistol with you, eh? It's bad enough for you to go to a cockfight without you taking a deadly weapon along with you. You got no respect for the church, the law or me. I spend my life trying to do what's right and you undermine me at every turn. Why, oh why, did I ever go to that brush arbor revival the night that I did and meet you?"

"Now, Molly," I said, "just because you first met me at a brush arbor meeting is no sign that I am a regular brush arbor man. It was raining that night and I was curious to see what went on in them brush arbor meetings. I never done bad by you, Honey, in our years of wedded life."

"Not if you don't call rooster fighting, betting, and drinking corn liquor bad, you ain't, Jackson. That old Raymond of yours has killed my dominecker roosters, mixed with my dominecker hens, killed the only gander I had, and flogged me three or four times. Why you aim to take him off to a lawbreaking fight is beyond me. But go! Think nothing of your poor wife who has spent half the night praying over you."

While Molly was preaching to me I got a few papers out of a drawer and slipped them in my shirt pocket. I went over to the bed and tried to kiss her good-by. She turned her face to the pillow.

I went back out to the chicken yard and got the gaffs I had hidden there. I put those steel gaffs in my shirt pocket, after wrapping them carefully in a clean handkerchief. I had ordered those gaffs from Philadelphia and had paid twenty dollars for them. I had met the rural mail carrier every day for two weeks to be sure Molly didn't see them. She wouldn't have understood. They were listed in the catalogue as the "Little Rock Special." It was not a drop-blade gaff, as old Raymond was not a shuffler, but was a single stroker. By that I mean he would not sit on his tail and spar, but would bide his time and fly in the air and deal a deathblow with a single lightning stroke from his sturdy legs. I had filed those gaffs until they were as sharp as a needle, and I had a stone in my pocket to touch up the points in case I dulled them during the trip. The length of those gaffs was an even two inches, not too much for a high-flying shake such as old Raymond. I had trimmed his natural spurs a week or so ago with a hack saw and by this time they were healed and ready to have the gaffs slipped on. His natural spurs were as tough and sharp as any I ever saw, and he could have given a good account of himself without any steel on his heels. I got a pint of whiskey

I had hidden in the lot and slipped it in my hip pocket. I had a lot of small treasures hidden in old Raymond's lot. Molly was mighty shy of that place.

Then I caught old Raymond. This was not so easy to do, for he wanted to fight me and I had my arm spurred good and deep, even with his stubby spurs before I had him by his legs. I dropped him in a twenty-five-pound sugar sack and stuck his head out of a hole I had cut in the bottom of it. I tied the sack with a piece of binder twine and took old Raymond up under my arm. As I was leaving the yard Molly raised a window and yelled, "If you get arrested today you can batch it from here on out. There's a welcome waiting for me at my pa's house any time I got sense enough to leave you and your game chickens."

I pretended I didn't hear her, for I was fond of Molly. She was right pretty, and the only faults I could find with her were that she talked too long and too shrill. I set out for Duke's woods, where the fights were to be held. It was about five miles, so I had me a good start.

It was a nice May morning, warm with a threat of some heat in the afternoon. The dew was cool on the green stuff and the sky was as clear as crystal. I walked down the back side of my pasture and hit the woods road going part of the way to Duke's woods. Old Raymond had settled himself in the sugar sack and was riding like a good horseman, snaking out his evil head with every step I took. He must of had his eye on the foot near his side, for his head followed its every move. The arm he had spurred began to pain me; so I shifted him to the other arm. I reckon the move upset him, for he pecked me on the back of my hand and brought the blood again.

"That's the second time today, Raymond, that you have spilled blood. I hope you have the spunk and guts to draw blood from an enemy rooster when I drop you in the pit," I told him. He gave me another rake with his bill and squawked.

When I got to the railroad tracks I left the road and hit it down the tracks for about a mile, then I went down Dugan's branch for another mile and then I turned east and followed the ridge of pines that were growing on the edge of Duke's woods. I was just getting in the woods good when a tall man stepped out from behind a cedar bush and got in my way. He was toting a deer rifle and was chewing tobacco. His eyes looked mighty mean to a country yokel like me.

"Where you going with that bird?" he asked me.

"Oh, I'm going down here to set him on a dozen eggs he done slipped off and laid. What you doing deer hunting in May?" I asked him.

He stepped out closer to me, squarely in front of me, and spit a little stream of ambeer at my shoes, spraying them good.

"Live around here, Bud?" he asked me.

"I sure as hell do," I allowed to him. "Where was you raised?"

"Why?" he asked.

"Well, I just thought I'd ask where you wanted your limbs sent for burial after I get through cutting you up. You done asked me a personal question, blocked my path, give me a short answer, and spit at me. That rifle ain't pointed straight at me, but this .38 I got in my hand here under this chicken is aimed at your nable. If I ain't being too bold, would you mind dropping that firearm at your feet and then move to one side so I can get at it?"

He gaped at me and seen that a .38 special barrel was showing its blueing at him and he dropped his rifle like it was hot to the touch. I shifted old Raymond to the other arm and then laid him on the ground. I cocked my pistol and walked round this fellow once.

"What you doing that for, Mister?" he asked me. His voice was getting a shade trembly now and his Adam's apple was bobbing up and down in his throat like a cork just before a fish takes it under.

"Just to see which side of you gives the best target and to see which way you'll be apt to fall. I been a expert logger for many years and I like to throw my logs where I want them to fall. Same way with cutting down a man. If I shoot you in the back of the head you will probably fall face first. If I shoot you in the forehead you might fall most anyways, probably sideways. How would you like to be found laying?"

"Listen, boss man, I just been hired for this job, I got nothing for you but respect. I been hired to stop everything, man, or beast, or fowl, that comes across this side of the woods today. Seems like this pit was raided by the law a year or so ago and the boys don't want that to happen again. Please don't do nothing rash that you might regret in later life. I got a wife and seven kids at home crying for bread right this minute. Think how the little ones will weep and wail when their pore old pappy is brought home in a pine casket."

I was in a pretty good humor this morning, so I just took his gun and unloaded it, picked old Raymond up, and went on my way. I dropped the rifle in a honeysuckle thicket a hundred yards or so further on, as I didn't want him taking a potshot at me after I got out of pistol range. I slipped into a little hollow and was soon away and out of his sight.

After a half mile, more or less, I reached the clearing in the tall pines. There were a couple of dozen men already there and they turned as I broke through the underbrush. The ground in the clearing was level and covered deeply with pine needles that had fallen from the protecting trees. It was as if walking on a carpet. The tall trees broke the direct glare of the sun and it was a half-sun, half-shade in there.

"Hayo, Jackson, what you carrying in that there bag?" one of the men called to me. I didn't answer until I got among them and set my burden down.

"Oh, just a old banty rooster what has been getting gay with my wife's domineckers, and I decided to drop him with a really mean bird to break him."

They all crowded round me to look old Raymond over. He gave each of them a wicked glare from them red eyes of his.

"Strong looking breast," one of the men said.

"He got that from chasing pullets and crowing," I said. "He ain't never hurt another game rooster nor has he ever had gaffs on. Of course I got some steel here for him but I doubt if he will fight when I put them on him, since he ain't never been armed before in his life. Probably get hung in his own self the first pitting. I want to fight him in the first fight so's I can be on my way back home before the sun gets too high. I got to do some plowing this morning after I get old Raymond whipped."

The other cocks there were crowing and that made old Raymond perk up. He looked all round and begun talking to himself a little, kind of mean like. He knew he was tied fast, so he made no move to try to get out of the sack, but his hackles rose until I thought he would cast them.

The crowd was pouring in now, and I took a seat on a log at the edge of the clearing and watched. The men coming in now had carrying crates for their cocks. They had niggers to carry the crates and sometimes a man had as many as a dozen birds. I didn't see any as looked old Raymond's equal, though. Old Raymond didn't either, for he let out a sassy challenge every once in a while. Whenever he did, some of the newcomers would look him over and ask how many fights he had won and how old he was and who laid him. I looked as dumb as I could and kept my mouth shut. Finally the man in charge of the meet came over and told me to register my bird. I picked up old Raymond and went over to a table where he had a notebook and a set of scales. The kind that says in fine print, "Not legal in trade."

"What's your name, young man?" he asked me.

"Jackson Mahaffey, of Union County, Democrat, Presbyterian by choice, nothing by practice, white, wedded, and sober."

He gave me a funny look and said, "I ain't taking no census, Brother, so kindly confine your remarks to the limits of decency and respect."

I was reaching for my sidearm, but he asked me another question so quick that I failed to draw on him.

"How many birds you want to enter? Give me their names and blood lines, please."

"I got one bird, old Raymond by name, all his blood is bad, and I want to fight him in the first fight and then I challenge any winner, providing I get the right odds. About three to one on the other cock, I would say."

He gave me a sour look and said, "Seriously now, give me the names, if any, of this bird's ancestors."

"Well, his ma was as pretty a Traveler as ever set a nest. His pa was a killer that won twelve straight pit fights in Kentucky and died a noble death by the sheriff's ax, raising his hackles at it as it fell. I calls this bird old Raymond in memory of my fierce bulldog, name of Raymond, who met sudden death at the spurs of this here bird of prey. I demand here and now that you have every man what drops a bird against me be searched for weapons, as I have had trouble in the past by men wanting to spill my blood on account of the destructive manner in which old Raymond handled their cocks. It has got so that I have been gaffing him on one foot only, since I feel that to steel up both his legs would be holding the life of some poor rooster too lightly. However, today I fetched both gaffs on account I aim to fight old Raymond until he meets his master or else masters this here meet."

The man peered all about and then pulled a bottle out of his pocket and took a long pull on it. I listened to the bottle clucking and took out my bottle and had a short one.

The fellow behind the desk coughed, spat, wiped his mouth and said, "I ain't in the habit of doing this, but now I really need it. I'm going to enter this bird against my better reasoning, just to see you handle him in the pit."

He filled out some sort of a paper and pushed it over the desk to me. He shoved his pen in my hand and said, "Make your mark on that last line, Brother."

I made an X, but I could of signed my name with a flourish if he had asked me to. I shoved the paper back to him.

"The entrance fee is five dollars a bird, to help with the expenses, such as keeping this place up and buying off the law." He held his hand out to me, palm up. "And I'll thank you for my fountain pen, too."

I gave him his pen and said, "I didn't come here to spend no money. I come here to fight a cock. Put my name down and let's get a battle going, I ain't one to be wasting time."

"Supposing I was to enter this bird for you, you got any money to bet with? Surely you didn't come out here with just a rooster and a pint of liquor."

"I got less than five dollars cash on me, but I got the deed to a hundred acres of rich soil, fair stand of timber on it. Reckon I can raise a loan on it here today?"

He took another draw on his bottle and strangled a bit. When he got his breath back he said, "I first got the idea that I ain't plumb right in the head when I got married. Every day that I live with that woman I see more clearly that I am a little foolish. But the thing I'm fixing to do now marks me as a damn fool out and out. I am a notary public and it happens that I have my seal of office with me. Let's see that deed."

He looked it over and then yelled out towards the pit, "Les, you and Pee Wee come here a minute." Two straggly-looking fellows came over and the big man said, "Jackson, here, is mortgaging his place to me. You two sign here as witnesses." He tossed out a piece of blank paper and they signed it. "I'll fill it out later. Thank you, boys." They left, and he handed me the paper. "Make your mark, Jackson." I marked it. I figured that in a court of law my signature would outweigh a mark that could have been forged.

"I'll stand for any bets you make up to a couple of thousand dollars, Jackson. God help me!" He bowed his head in his hands for a minute and then raised up and said, "I got the very bird here for you, Jackson. I'll match your bird with Dewitt Bruton's Morning Thunder, a bad bird. Go on out and get your cock heeled, you're in the pit first. I hope you got a fire going at home to stew this bird."

I went back to the log and took Raymond out of his sack. I worked his legs a little to get the blood flowing quicker in them, tossed him in the air a couple of times to get him to spread his wings, and rubbed his hard head. I was winding the heeling strips around his gray legs when some fellow got up and yelled in a clear bass, "The first fight this morning, a battle between Mahaffey's Raymond and Bruton's Morning Thunder, two pit-wise veterans. Place your bets, gentlemen, while the birds are gaffed and brought up."

I slipped the bright shiny steel gaffs on old Raymond and saw that they were tight on his horny legs. The steel shone in the light and I ran my thumb across the points to see if they had lost any of their needle sharpness since the night before, when I had set up way past my bedtime to whet them. I took a mouthful of water and sprayed it over old Raymond's head as hard as I could blow it. I got a firm grip on him and walked down to the pit.

The pit was about three feet deep, dug in the soft red clay under the covering of pine needles, and twenty feet across. It was a circle of bright red in a clearing of drab brown. There was a picket fence round it about two feet high and there were seats rising in rows round the pit, reaching up about thirty feet, I would say. Good yellow pine in that grandstand, too. Somebody had sunk a sight of work or money in that pit.

I hopped down in the pit to handle my bird and saw a snuff dipper in the other corner, with a bunch of cotton lint sticking to his clothes; so I knew I was pitted against a mill hand and his bird. His cock looked like an ordinary bird, so I felt no fear, and the minute old Raymond laid eyes on him he squawked and tried to pull away from my hand and be at this bird. I held him firmly and roughed up his head a little to make him madder.

"You want to make a little bet, farmer?" the lint dodger called to me. He pulled a few bills out of his pocket and waved them in the air. "Here's thirty dollars as says you pick up a dead bird."

"Calling that bet and all bets around the pit," I yelled. I was beginning to feel good. The whiskey and the excitement were working on me.

My friend of the desk spoke up, "I'm taking care of Jackson's bets today, so place them with me. Tend to your cock, Mahaffey."

The referee examined the gaffs and brought us to the center of the pit and had us bill our cocks, which was a uncalled-for thing, since old Raymond was so worked up that he would of tackled a wildcat then and there. The birds pecked at each other a second or two and then me and the lint dodger stepped back to the far sides of the pit, on opposite sides, and the referee hollered, "Pit your cocks." We dropped the birds and old Raymond was across the pit in a flash, the other cock being a shade slower on his feet.

They met well up in the air, four or five feet if a inch. The other cock, a round head, was a shuffler, while old Raymond was a single stroker. The roundhead's gaffs were working like pistons, but he failed to strike my bird a fair blow. They landed, turned, and met again, this time not so high in the air. Old Raymond got in a quick blow to the head and the roundhead landed a bit addled. Raymond was at him quick as lightning, striking at his breast.

The steels caught sunlight and the next second they was dripping red. The town cock staggered, turned to run, and old Raymond was astride his back, gaffing his neck. It was soon over, with old Raymond standing on his enemy and crowing over his dead body. I took Raymond up and went out and sat on my log again. I offered him water, but he refused it, being too busy challenging every rooster on the lot. I unheeled him and sprayed some water on his head and rubbed his legs so he wouldn't get stiff. He was still talking to himself, so I decided to fight him again in an hour or so. The lust of battle was strong in us both.

My betting partner came out holding a wad of money out to me. "I bet a hundred and eighty dollars on the fight and here she is." He counted it out in my hand and I said, "Ain't you taking no commission?"

"They call me 'Honest Mott' in these here parts, Brother. I am interested solely in your bets as best benefits you. You fight that bird and leave the betting to me. I figure you ought to pick up maybe three hundred on this next fight." He walked away, calling back over his shoulder, "Let me know when Raymond gets his wind back."

I knew old Raymond hadn't lost no wind, but I didn't tell him so. I was just beginning to smell something dirty in the wind.

I lit a cigarette and gave the whole situation a thinking over. If we won I didn't know how much had been bet, and he probably took most of it. But if we should happen to lose he had my deed to pay off with and may have placed a sizeable bet with himself, in case there was something left over. I decided to know more about the betting the next pitting.

I tended old Raymond for about an hour, and then I went back to the pit and told the referee that I challenged any winner there. I didn't want to pit old Raymond against a fresh bird, but I figured that we had had more rest than any other team there, since we had been the first to fight that morning.

He called out the challenge for me, and in a minute or two a man with a Norwood Warhorse came up and said he had a thousand dollars he would bet that his bird could, and would, destroy old Raymond.

"Sir," I told him, "you got you a bet and a dead cock."

I turned to "Honest Mott" and said, "That is the only bet I am calling. Any other bet is out of your own pocket."

He turned purple in the face and began to splutter, "What's the matter? I done well by you in the other fight. You had better leave well enough alone. Ain't you got no faith in me?"

"Not as much as I could have," I admitted. "I ain't got much faith in anything here in this vale of tears but me and old Raymond. No telling how much you won on that first fight, so you might as well stop counting on me paying off for you in case we was to lose. Not that I fear this Warhorse any more than I would a white Leghorn, but you back your bets with your own money from here on out."

As I stepped down in the pit I whispered to old Raymond, "Raymond, if you lose this fight, yet come out of it alive, you still done lost your all. Remember that, boy, if the going gets rough." The referee looked the heeling over and we let the birds bill and retired to drop them. I turned, heard the referee shouting, and dropped old Raymond.

That was as short a fight as I ever saw. The cocks met in midair near the center of the pit. There was a short flurry of feathers, the quick click of fast-moving steel, and the birds were on the ground, old Raymond on top. Blood showed at the beak of the Warhorse and he acted like he was hit in the vitals. Raymond came in to make the kill and the Warhorse showed that he was full of grit and guts. He was too near dead to stand up, but he reached up and got a beakful of old Raymond's hackles and pulled himself up enough to make a dying shuffle. He raked Raymond good and must of hurt him, for Raymond pulled loose and made two of the most vicious thrusts shown that day at the pit. The Warhorse didn't live long enough after that to develop a loud rattle. Old Raymond hopped up on his dead breast and crowed. I collected my thousand bucks and retired to the shade with old Raymond. It was getting hot now, and I felt it best to rest and cool Raymond for a spell. I nursed him along and tried to get him to take some food, but he refused everything except a little onion water I fixed for him.

"Honest Mott" came up and old Raymond crowed another challenge to the lot. When it was answered he raised his hackles and begun talking to himself again.

"That bird is still raring to go," Honest Mott said.

"Give us a cock that can make it interesting and we'll show you a fight you won't forget to your dying day," I told him. "We been wasting time here this morning looking for a fighting cock, and all the time I got plowing waiting on me at home. Old Raymond here has a lot full of young pullets waiting on him, too. Maybe I could interest you in a setting of eggs from them pullets? You done witnessed the fighting qualities of the stock."

"I sure would like to have a stag from him, or better still, I'll buy Raymond. I'll give you two hundred dollars for him." He pulled out his pocketbook and began to peel off twenties like I peel off ones after I sell a bale of cotton.

"Hold your folding money, Mott," I told him. "Old Raymond ain't for sale at any price. I'm fighting this here bird until he either meets his master or else proves to me that he is as good as he has been crowing that he is. You ever been kept awake all night by a bird what is spoiling for a fight? I been tempted many a night to get up and bash his brains out and stew him up for the table. My wife has urged me to do just that. My wife has let this here bird come between us until she has threatened to leave me. This day he has got to fight if he aims to crow tonight. He knows it, too. That's why I been betting so heavy on him. Old Raymond has a stomping good time at home and he will battle to live to get back there and strut before his pullets. When you want them eggs?"

He wrote something on a piece of paper and handed it to me. "Mail them to this address whenever you get a setting. I'm giving you fifteen dollars, a dollar an egg, and if I get just one stag that looks like his pappy I'll get my money's worth. Raymond reminds me of a bird I lost about a year ago. Some thief stole him at a fight here when the law slipped up on us. I would give a pretty to get my hands on the thief that stole him, for he was as promising a bird as I ever called my own. He was a Traveler, like Raymond, only a bit prettier, and he looked like he was a blooded bird. You could tell at a glance that he was from championship stock, while Raymond, and don't take offense, looks like his mamma slipped a nest in the bushes. Blood lines will always tell."

I nodded and said, "Old Raymond ain't exactly of royal blood as I knows of, but he will do till a royal bird comes along. I had a chance to pick him up cheap and I took him. I been like a daddy to this wretch ever since and he spurs me for my pains. Fighting cocks are rough, tough birds, and like my wife says, I reckon a cockfighting man ain't a true Christian. I aim to repent after today and lead a better life, that is, providing I win a sizable amount of money. I better take old Raymond out here in some deeper shade. I'll send them eggs the first day I get a full setting."

I took old Raymond out to a deep shady spot and tied a stout cord to one of his legs and tied the loose end to my wrist. He tried to fly off and start a fight, but the cord pulled him up short. He sat down as far away from me as he could get and sulked. I threw some flint corn out to him but he never even looked at it. I opened my bottle of corn and had a couple of stiff drinks, and then I ate a fried-ham sandwich. I begun to feel better and I counted my winnings of the day. I had won eleven hundred and eighty dollars. I figured that my place wasn't worth more than eleven hundred dollars at the most, on account of it being off the main highway and the buildings being in bad shape. Old Raymond had won, to my knowledge, more than my farm was worth. "Honest Mott" probably had five or six hundred bucks in his pocket that by rights belonged to me. I decided to bet the whole eleven eighty on Raymond in our next fight. I figured that a bird with his strength could go three bouts in a day if properly rested.

We rested, old Raymond and me, until the shadows was lengthening, and then I picked him up and went down to the pit. I saw the finish of a good knife fight as I walked up. Some fool had made a slight remark about some man's bird and there was blood spilt on account of it. I walked up to the pit, reared back and hollered, "I got to be going on home, but I got time for one more fight. If any man here has a bird what can whip old Raymond here, I got eleven hundred and eighty dollars for him. Let's get this fight started, as its getting over towards the shank of the evening."

The men begun to crowd around the pit and they were arguing about which bird to pit against old Raymond. Finally they decided on a roundhead named Oscar. The man what was handling Oscar got his bird, we heeled them, I got my money covered, and then we got in the pit. Oscar was about the same size as old Raymond, but some younger. He had killed one cock today, the only fight he had had.

The referee examined the heeling, we billed the birds, retired to our places, and the well-known cry, "Pit your cocks," sounded in my ears. I let old Raymond to the ground and in a flash he was racing towards the roundhead. There was a thunder of sound from the crowd as a streak of white, old Raymond, and a streak of red, Oscar, met and a storm of feathers flew. Everything was still then except the whir of feathers and the click of steel. They hit the ground, paused, dashed out, sparred, rolled against the wall of the pit, and the referee called a handle. Old Raymond was in the red in the thigh. The red's handler pulled the gaff out and we pitted again. The red scored quickly with a hung gaff in old Raymond's neck. I pulled the steel out and saw that it wasn't such a bad blow, just caught the skin enough to hold. We pitted again and old Raymond flew high in the air and hung in the red to the socket. At the handle, red showed on the bill of the roundhead. We pitted again and this time the birds met so hard that they raised a cloud of dust and it was hard to see what was going on in the pit.

But soon from this cloud of dust there was heard a cracked blast of racket, a sound dear to my ears, old Raymond's victory crow, the dirge for the roundhead. When we could see, it was old Raymond standing on the roundhead, pecking his dead foe, and then he reared back and crowed again. He reached down and pecked the dead bird on the head and it sounded sort of like my ax does when I lay it into the side of a hard wood tree on a frosty morning. I went in and picked old Raymond up and put him in his sugar sack. I put his head out the hole and tied the other end of the sack. He didn't raise much Cain this time. Then I collected my bet and after shaking hands with the man what used to cherish Oscar, we set out for home. At the edge of the crowd I saw Mott. He was standing out by himself. "How much did you win that time?" I asked him.

He cleared his throat loudly and said, "I been picked clean, my boy, picked clean. I didn't see how in the world that rooster could win a third fight; so I bet every nickel I had on Oscar. I still don't see how you did it."

"I'll take my deed back now, if you please. And that note you fixed up against it."

"Oh yes. The deed." He fumbled around in his pocket and brought it out and handed it to me. "I wouldn't have thought of holding you to that deal, Jackson. I would have shared any loss with you gladly."

I didn't feel like answering that one; so I started off. He called to me after I had gone a few steps and said, "Oh, Jackson, could you spare a twenty until next week?"

I let him have the money and started home again. Old Raymond was a lot quieter this trip than he was coming over. I carried him on home and dropped him in his pen, after looking him over for serious wounds and finding none. I carried him some food and water and he ate and drank with me standing there watching him.

"Seems like winning a couple of battles has made a changed bird of you, Raymond," I said. He cocked his bloody head and gave me a long look from his wicked eyes and then went back to eating.

It was getting dark and time for me to feed the stock, but I went in the house first. Molly was pulling the straps tight on her suitcase.

"I done had supper, Jackson. The last supper I'll ever eat at this house or with you. I'm going back to my pa's house." She wiped her eyes with her handkerchief and said, "You been off all day gambling on rooster fights and us dirt pore. I can smell liquor on your breath, too. You made your choice today, Jackson, good-by."

She picked up her suitcase, but before she started out I said, "Now wait a minute, Molly. I done give up cockfighting this very day. Old Raymond put up such good battles that I retired him from the pit. No more bloody battles for him. He can sit back and take it easy."

Molly set her suitcase down and looked at me. "Jackson Mahaffey, you done told me so many lies in just a few short years that I don't believe you. Prove it to me."

I pulled the money out of my pocket, most of it, that is, and said, "I ain't had time to count this, Honey, but you got a good head for figures; so how about counting it in a hurry?"

I threw the pile of greenbacks on the table and Molly's eyes like to of popped out. She counted it fast once and stopped and gave me a long look. She counted it again, but slower this time. "Jackson, you got exactly two thousand dollars here. I'm taking care of it from here on out. I don't trust you to handle money on account of the way you like to gamble. Put that suitcase in the back room and set your bottle of whiskey out here on the table. If you got to drink you might as well drink it in your own house like a man."

I did as she told me and took a nice-sized drink. "I better be going out to the barn and feeding up, I reckon," I said.

As I was going out to the door Molly stopped me. "Jackson, remember, no more cockfights. You can let old Raymond spend the rest of his days here, but you can't fight him no more. You can't raise no more games, neither. You got to sell them game hens tomorrow."

"Honey, you got my promise," I told her.

I was dog tired so I went to bed early that night and soon dropped off to sleep. I woke up during the night and looked at my watch and saw that it was a little past midnight. I was fixing to go back to sleep when it dawned on me that I hadn't heard old Raymond crow. So I lay there waiting to hear him insult the world before I went back to sleep. I waited and waited, but he didn't crow. After an hour of this I was really worried; so I got up and lit a lantern and went out to see what ailed him, if anything. I was afraid that he might have got out and left the place, or been stolen. I went out to his pen, and there he was, stretched out on the ground, dead. His hackles was raised, like he didn't want to go. I sure felt bad. Me and old Raymond had been through a lot together. I sure would miss him. I took the bucket of game hen eggs I had hid in the pen and went in Molly's chicken yard. She had a dominecker that hadn't been setting but a day or two. I took the eggs from under her and slipped the game eggs in their place. Then I went back to the house, not feeling quite so bad.

PAUL'S TALE

by MARY NORTON

" 'Ho! HO!' SAID THE KING, SLAPPING HIS FAT THIGHS. 'Methinks this youth shows promise.' But, at that moment, the court magician stepped forward . . . What *is* the matter, Paul? Don't you like this story?"

"Yes, I like it."

"Then lie quiet, dear, and listen."

"It was just a sort of stalk of a feather pushing itself through the eiderdown."

"Well, you needn't help it, dear. It's destructive. Where were we?" Aunt Isobel's short-sighted eyes searched down the page of the book. She looked comfortable and pink and plump, rocking there in the firelight. ". . . stepped forward . . . you see the court magician knew that the witch had taken the magic music box, and that Colin—Paul, you aren't listening!"

"Yes, I am. I can hear."

"Of course you can't hear—right under the bed clothes! What are you doing, dear?"

"I'm seeing what a hot water bottle feels like."

"Don't you know what a hot water bottle feels like?"

"I know what it feels like to me. I don't know what it feels like to itself."

"Well, shall I go on or not?"

"Yes, go on," said Paul. He emerged from the bed clothes, his hair ruffled.

Aunt Isobel looked at him curiously. He was her godson; he had a bad feverish cold; and his mother had gone to London. "Does it tire you, dear, to be read to?" she said at last.

"No. But I like told stories better than read stories."

Aunt Isobel got up and put some more coal on the fire. Then she looked at the clock. She sighed. "Well, dear," she said brightly, as she sat down once more on the rocking chair, "What sort of story would you like?" She unfolded her knitting.

"I'd like a real story."

"How do you mean, dear?" Aunt Isobel began to cast on. The cord of her pince-nez, anchored to her bosom, rose and fell in gentle undulations.

Paul flung round on his back, staring at the ceiling. "*You* know," he said, "quite real—so you know it must have happened."

"Shall I tell you about Grace Darling?"

"No. Tell me about a little man."

"What sort of a little man?"

"A little man just as high—" Paul's eyes searched the room—"as that candlestick on the mantelshelf, but without the candle."

"But that's a very small candlestick. It's only about six inches."

"Well, about that big."

Aunt Isobel began knitting a few stitches. She was disappointed about the fairy story. She had been reading with so much expression, making a deep voice for the king, and a wicked, oily voice for the court magician, and a fine, cheerful, boyish voice for Colin, the swineherd. A little man—what could she say about a little man? "Ah," she exclaimed suddenly, and laid down her knitting, smiling at Paul. Little men . . . of course . . .

"Well," said Aunt Isobel, drawing in her breath. "Once upon a time, there was a little, tiny man, and he was no bigger than that candlestick—there on the mantelshelf."

Paul settled down, his cheek on his crook'd arm, his eyes on Aunt Isobel's face. The firelight flickered softly on the walls and ceiling.

"He was the sweetest little man you ever saw, and he wore a little red jerkin and a dear little cap made out of a foxglove. His boots . . ."

"He didn't have any," said Paul.

Aunt Isobel looked startled. "Yes," she exclaimed. "He had boots—little, pointed—"

"He didn't have any clothes," contradicted Paul. "He was quite bare."

Aunt Isobel looked perturbed. "But he would have been cold," she pointed out.

"He had thick skin," explained Paul. "Like a twig."

"Like a twig?"

"Yes. You know that sort of wrinkly, nubbly skin on a twig."

Aunt Isobel knitted in silence for a second or two. She didn't like the little naked man nearly as much as the little dressed man; she was trying to get used to him. After a while she went on.

"He lived in a bluebell wood, among the roots of a dear old tree. He had a dear little house, tunneled out of the soft, loamy earth, with a bright blue front door."

"Why didn't he live in it?" asked Paul.

"He did live in it, dear," exclaimed Aunt Isobel patiently.

"I thought he lived in the potting shed."

"In the potting shed?"

"Well, perhaps he had two houses. Some people do. I wish I'd seen the one with the blue front door."

"Did you see the one in the potting shed?" asked Aunt Isobel, after a second's bewildered silence.

"Not inside. Right inside. I'm too big. I just sort of saw into it with a flashlight."

"And what was it like?" asked Aunt Isobel, in spite of herself.

"Well, it was clean—in a potting-shed sort of way. He'd made the furniture himself. The floor was just earth but he'd trodden it down so that it was hard. It took him years."

"Well, dear, you seem to know more about him than I do."

Paul snuggled his head more comfortably against his elbow. He half-closed his eyes. "Go on," he said dreamily.

Aunt Isobel glanced at him hesitatingly. How beautiful he looked, she thought, lying there in the firelight with one curled hand lying lightly on the counterpane. "Well," she went on, "this little man had a little pipe made of a straw." She paused, rather pleased with this idea. "A little hollow straw, through which he played jiggity little tunes. And to which he danced." She hesitated. "Among the bluebells," she added. Really, this was quite a pretty story. She knitted hard for a few seconds, breathing heavily, before the next bit would come. "Now," she continued brightly, in a changed, higher, and more conversational voice, "up in the tree, there lived a fairy."

"In the tree?" asked Paul incredulously.

"Yes," said Aunt Isobel, "in the tree."

Paul raised his head. "Do you know that for certain?"

"Well, Paul," began Aunt Isobel. Then she added playfully, "Well, I suppose I do."

"Go on," said Paul.

"Well, this fairy—"

Paul raised his head again. "Couldn't you go on about the little man?"

"But, dear, we've done the little man—how he lived in the tree roots, and played a pipe, and all that."

"You didn't say about his hands and feet."

"His hands and feet?"

"How sort of big his hands and feet looked, and how he could scuttle along. Like a rat," Paul added.

"Like a rat!" exclaimed Aunt Isobel.

"And his voice. You didn't say anything about his voice."

"What sort of a voice," Aunt Isobel looked almost scared, "did he have?"

"A croaky sort of voice. Like a frog. And he says 'Will 'ee' and 'Do 'ee.' "

"Willy and Dooey . . ." repeated Aunt Isobel, as if fascinated.

"Instead of 'Will you' and 'Do you.' You know."

"Has he—got a Sussex accent?"

"Sort of. He isn't used to talking. He's the last one. He's been all alone, for years and years."

"Did he—" Aunt Isobel swallowed. "Did he tell you that?"

"Yes. He had an aunt and she died about fifteen years ago. But even when she was alive, he never spoke to her."

"Why?" asked Aunt Isobel.

"He didn't like her," said Paul.

There was silence. Paul stared dreamily into the fire. Aunt Isobel sat as if turned to stone, her hands idle in her lap. After a while, she cleared her throat. "When did you first see this little man, Paul?"

"Oh, ages and ages ago. When did you?"

"I—Where did you find him?"

"Under the chicken house."

"Did you—did you speak to him?"

Paul made a little snort. "No. I just popped a tin over him."

"You caught him!"

"Yes. There was an old rusty chicken-food tin near. I just popped it over him." Paul laughed. "He scrabbled away inside. Then I popped an old kitchen plate that was there on top of the tin."

Aunt Isobel sat staring at Paul. "What—did you do with him then?"

"I put him in a cake tin, and made holes in the lid. I gave him a bit of bread and milk."

"Didn't he—say anything?"

"Well, he was sort of croaking."

"And then?"

"Well, I sort of forgot I had him."

"You forgot!"

"I went fishing, you see. Then it was bedtime. And next day I didn't remember him. Then when I went to look for him, he was lying curled up at the bottom of the tin. He'd gone all soft. He just hung over my finger. All soft."

Aunt Isobel's eyes protruded dully. "What did you do then?"

"I gave him some cherry corjil in a fountain-pen filler."

"That revived him?"

"Yes, that's when he began to talk. And told me all about his aunt and everything. I harnessed him up, then, with a bit of string."

"Oh, Paul," exclaimed Aunt Isobel, "how cruel!"

"Well, he'd have got away. It didn't hurt him. Then I tamed him."

"How did you tame him?"

"Oh, how you tame anything. With food mostly. Chips of gelatine and raw sago he liked best. Cheese, he liked. I'd take him out and let him go down rabbit holes and things, on the string. Then he would come back and tell me what was going on. I put him down all kinds of holes in trees and things."

"Whatever for?"

"Just to know what was going on. I have all kinds of uses for him."

"Why," stammered Aunt Isobel, half rising from her chair, "you haven't still got him, have you?"

Paul sat up on his elbow. "Yes. I've got him. I'm going to keep him till I go to school. I'll need him at school like anything."

"But it isn't— You wouldn't be allowed—" Aunt Isobel became suddenly extremely grave. "Where is he now?"

"In the cake tin."

"Where is the cake tin?"

"Over there. In the toy cupboard."

Aunt Isobel looked fearfully across the shadowed room. She stood up. "I am going to put the light on, and I shall take that cake tin out into the garden."

"It's raining," Paul reminded her.

"I can't help that," said Aunt Isobel. "It is wrong and wicked to keep a little thing like that shut up in a cake tin. I shall take it out on to the back porch and open the lid."

"He can hear you," said Paul.

"I don't care if he can hear me." Aunt Isobel walked toward the door. "I'm thinking of his good, as much as of anyone else's. She switched on the light. "Now, which was the cupboard?"

"That one, near the fireplace."

The door was ajar. Timidly Aunt Isobel pulled it open with one finger. There stood the cake tin amid a medley of torn cardboard, playing cards, pieces of jigsaw puzzle, and an open paint box.

"What a mess, Paul!"

Nervously Aunt Isobel stared at the cake tin and, falsely innocent, the British Royal Family stared back at her, painted brightly on a background of Allied flags. The holes in the lid were narrow and wedge-shaped; made, no doubt, by the big blade of the best cutting-out scissors.

Aunt Isobel drew in her breath sharply. "If you weren't ill, I'd make you do this. I'd make you carry the tin out and watch you open the lid—" She hesitated as if unnerved by the stillness of the rain-darkened room and the sinister quiet within the cake tin.

Then bravely she put out her hand. Paul watched her, absorbed, as she stretched forward the other hand and, very gingerly, picked up the cake tin. His eyes were dark and deep. He saw the lid was not quite on. He saw the corner, in contact with that ample bosom, rise. He saw the sharp edge catch the cord of Aunt Isobel's pince-nez and, fearing for her rimless glasses, he sat up in bed.

Aunt Isobel felt the tension, the pressure of the pince-nez on the bridge of her nose. A pull, it was, a little steady pull as if a small dark claw, as wrinkled as a twig, had caught the hanging cord. . . .

"Look out!" cried Paul.

Loudly she shrieked and dropped the box. It bounced away and then lay still, gaping emptily upon its side. In the horrid hush, they heard the measured planking of the lid as it trundled off beneath the bed.

Paul broke the silence with a croupy cough. "Did you see him?" he asked, hoarse but interested.

"No," stammered Aunt Isobel, almost with a sob. "I didn't. I didn't see him."

"But you nearly did."

Aunt Isobel sat down limply in the upholstered chair. Her hand wavered vaguely round her brow and her cheeks looked white and pendulous, as if deflated. "Yes," she muttered, shivering slightly, "Heaven help me—I nearly did."

Paul gazed at her a moment longer. "That's what I mean," he said.

"What?" asked Aunt Isobel weakly, but as if she did not really care.

"About stories. Being real."

ON THE WAY HOME

by LANGSTON HUGHES

CARL WAS NOT WHAT YOU WOULD CALL A DRINKING MAN. NOT that he had any moral scruples about drinking, for he prided himself on being broad-minded. But he had always been told that his father (whom he couldn't remember) was a drunkard. So in the back of his head, he didn't really feel it was right to get drunk. Except for perhaps a glass of wine on holidays, or a mug of beer if he was out with a party and didn't want to be conspicuous, he never drank. He was almost a teetotaler.

Carl had promised his mother not to drink *at all*. He was an only child, fond of his mother, but she had raised him with almost too much kindness. To adjust himself to people who were less kind had been hard. But since there were no good jobs in Sommerville, he went away to Chicago to work. Every month he went back home for a Sunday, taking the four-o'clock bus Saturday afternoon, which put him off in front of the door of his boyhood home in time for supper—a supper with country butter, fresh milk, and homemade bread.

After supper he would go uptown with his mother in the cool of evening, if it was summer, to do her Saturday-night shopping. Or if it was winter, they might go over to a neighbor's house and pop corn or drink cider. Or friends might come to their house and sit around the parlor talking and playing old records on an old Victrola—Sousa's marches, Nora Bayes, Bert Williams, Caruso—records that most other people had long ago thrown away or forgotten. It was fun, old-fashioned, and very different from the rum parties most of his office friends gave in Chicago.

Carl had promised his mother and himself not to drink. But this particular afternoon, he stood in front of a long counter in a liquor store on Clark Street and heard himself say, strangely enough, "A bottle of wine."

"What kind of wine?" the clerk asked brusquely.

"That kind," Carl answered, pointing to a row of tall yellow bottles on the middle shelf. It just happened that his finger stopped at the yellow bottles. He did not know the names or brands of wines.

"That's sweet wine," the clerk told him.

"That's all right," Carl said, for he wanted to get the wine quickly and go.

The clerk wrapped the bottle, made change, and turned to another customer. Carl took the bottle and went out. He walked slowly, yet he could hardly wait to get to his room. He had never been so anxious to drink before. He might have stopped at a bar, since he passed many, but he was not used to drinking at bars. So he went to his room.

It was quiet in the big, dark, old rooming house. There was no one in the hall as he went up the wide creaking staircase. All the roomers were at work. It was Tuesday. He would have been at work, too, had he not received at the office that noon a wire that his mother was suddenly very ill, and he had better come home. He knew there was no bus until four o'clock. It was one now. He would get ready to go soon. But he needed a drink. Did not men sometimes drink to steady their nerves? In novels, they took a swig of brandy—but brandy made Carl sick. Wine would be better—milder.

In his room he tore open the package and uncorked the bottle, even before he hung his hat in the closet. He took his toothbrush out of a glass on his dresser and poured the glass a third full of amber-yellow wine. He tried to keep himself from wondering if his mother was going to die.

"Please, no!" he prayed. He drank the wine.

He sat down on the bed to get his breath back. That climb up the steps had never taken his breath before, but now his heart was beating fast and sweat came out on his brow; so he took off his coat, tie, shirt, and got ready to wash his face.

But no, he would pack his bag first. Then, he suddenly thought, he had no present for his mother—but he caught himself in the middle of the thought. This was not Saturday, not one of his monthly Saturdays when he went home. This was Tuesday and there was this telegram in his pocket that had suddenly broken the whole rhythm of his life: YOUR MOTHER GRAVELY ILL COME HOME AT ONCE.

John and Nellie Rossiter had been neighbors since childhood. They would not frighten him needlessly. His mother must be very ill indeed; so he need not think of taking her a present. He went to the closet door to pull out the suitcase, but his hands did not move. The wine, amber-yellow in its tall bottle, stood on the dresser beside him. Warm, sweet, forbidden.

There was no one in the room. Nobody in the whole house, perhaps, except the landlady. Nobody really in all Chicago to talk to in his trouble. With a mother to take care of on a small salary, room rent, a class at business college, books to buy, there's not much time left to make friends, or take girls out. In a big city it's hard for a young man to know people.

Carl poured the glass full of wine again—drank it. Then he opened the top drawer, took out his toilet articles, and put them on the bed. From the second drawer he took a couple of shirts. Maybe three would be better, or four. This was not a week end. Perhaps he had better take some extra clothing—in case his mother was ill long, and he had to stay a week or more. Perhaps he'd better take his dark suit in case she—

It hit him in the stomach like a fist. A pang of fear spread over his whole body. He sat down trembling on the bed.

"Buck up, old man." The sound of his own voice comforted him. He smiled weakly at his brown face in the mirror. "Be a man."

He filled the glass full this time and drank it without stopping. He had never drunk so much wine before, and this was warm, sweet, and palatable. He stood, threw his shoulders back, and felt suddenly tall as though his head were touching the ceiling. Then, for no reason at all, he looked at himself in the mirror and began to sing. He made up a song out of nowhere that repeated itself over and over:

In the spring the roses
In the spring begin to sing
Roses in the spring.
Begin to sing. . . .

He took off his clothes, put on his bathrobe, carefully drained the bottle, then went down the hall to the bathroom, still singing. He ran a tub full of water, climbed in, and sat down. The water in the tub was warm like the wine. He felt good, remembering a dark grassy slope in a corner of his mother's yard where he played with a little peach-colored girl when he was very young at home. His mother came out, separated them, and sent the little girl away because she wasn't of a decent family. But now his mother would never dismiss another little girl be—

Carl sat up quickly in the tub, splashed water over his back and over his head. Drunk? What's the matter? What's the matter with you? Thinking of your mother that way and maybe she's dy— Say! Listen, don't you know you have to catch a four-o'clock bus? And here he was getting drunk on the way home. He trembled. His heart beat very fast, so fast that he lay down in the tub to catch his breath, covered with the warm water—all but his head.

To lie quiet that way was fine. Still and quiet. Tuesday. Everybody working at the office. And here he was, Carl Anderson, lying quiet in a deep warm tub of water. Maybe someday after the war with a little money saved up, and no expenses at home, and a car to take girls out in the spring when the roses sing in the spring. . . .

He had a good voice and the song that he had made up about the roses sounded good with that sweet wine on his breath; so he stood up in the tub, grabbed a towel, and began to sing quite loudly and lustily. Suddenly there was a knock at the door.

"What's going on in there?" It was the landlady's voice in the hall outside. She must have heard him singing downstairs.

"Nothing, Mrs. Dyer! Nothing! I just feel like singing."

"Mr. Anderson? Is that you? What're you doing in the house this time of day?"

"I'm on the way home to see my mother. She's . . ."

"You sound happier than a lark about it. I couldn't imagine—"

He heard the landlady's feet shuffling off down the stairs.

"She's . . ." His head began to go round and round. "My mother's . . ." His eyes suddenly burned. To step out of the tub, he held tightly to the sides. Drunk, that's what he was! Drunk!

He lurched down the hall, fell across the bed in his room, and buried his head in the pillows. He stretched his arms above his head and held onto the rods of the bedstead. He felt ashamed.

With his head in the pillows all was dark. His mother dying? No! No! But he was drunk. In the dark he seemed to feel his mother's hand on his head when he was a little boy, and her voice saying, "Be sweet, Carl. Be a good boy. Keep clean. Mother loves you. She'll look out for you. Be sweet and remember what you're taught at home."

Then the roses in the song he had made up, and the wine he had drunk, began to go around and around in his head, and he felt as if he had betrayed his mother and home singing about roses and spring and dreaming of cars and pretty brown girls with that yellow telegram right there in his coat pocket on the back of the chair beside the bed that suddenly seemed to go around, too.

But when he closed his eyes, it stopped. He held his breath. He buried his head deeper in the pillows. He lay very still. It was dark and warm. And quiet, and darker than ever. A long time passed, a very long time, dark, and quiet, and peaceful, and still.

"Mr. Anderson! Hey, Mr. Anderson!"

In the darkness far off, somebody called, then nearer—but still very far away—then knocking on a distant door.

"Mr. Anderson!" The voice was quite near now, sharper. The door opened, light streamed in. A hand shook his shoulder. He opened his eyes. Mrs. Dyer stood there large and dark, looking down at him in indignant amazement. "Mr. Anderson, are you drunk?"

"No, Mrs. Dyer," he said in a daze, blinking at the landlady standing above him. The electric light bulb she had switched on hurt his eyes.

"Mr. Anderson, they's a long-distance call for you on the phone downstairs in the hall. Get up. Button up that bathrobe. Hurry on down there and get it, will you? I've been yelling for five minutes."

"What time is it?" Carl sat bolt upright. The landlady stopped in the door.

"It's way after dinner time," she said. "Must be six-thirty, seven o'clock."

"Seven o'clock?" Carl gasped. "I've missed my bus!"

"What bus?"

"The four-o'clock bus."

"I guess you have," said the landlady. "Alcohol and time-tables don't mix, young man. That must be your mother on the phone now." Disgusted, she went downstairs, leaving his door open.

The phone! Carl jumped. He felt sick and unsteady on his legs. He pulled his bathrobe together, stumbled down the stairs. The telephone! A kind of weakness rushed through his veins. The telephone! He had promised his mother not to drink. She said his father—he couldn't remember his father. He died long ago. And now, his mother was . . . anyhow, he should have been home by now, by seven o'clock, at her bedside, holding her hand. He could have been home an hour ago. Now, maybe she . . .

He picked up the receiver. His voice was hoarse, frightened. "Hello. . . . Yes, this is Carl. . . . Yes, Mrs. Rossiter. . . ."

"Carl, honey, we kept looking for you on that six-o'clock bus. My husband went out on the road a piece to meet you in his car. We thought it might be quicker. Carl, honey. . ."

"Yes, Mrs. Rossiter?"

"Your mother . . ."

"Yes, Mrs. Rossiter."

"Your mother just passed away. I thought maybe you ought to know in case you hadn't already started. I thought maybe . . ."

For a moment he couldn't hear what she said. Then he knew that she was asking him a question—that she was repeating it.

"I could have Jerry drive to Chicago and get you tonight. Would you like to have me do that, since there's no bus now until morning?"

"I wish you would, Mrs. Rossiter. But then, no—listen! Never mind! There's two or three things I ought to do before I come home. I ought to go to the bank. I must. But I'll catch that first bus in the morning. First thing in the morning, Mrs. Rossiter, I'll be home."

"We're your neighbors and your friends. You know *this* is your home, too, so come right here."

"Yes, Mrs. Rossiter, I know. I will. I'll be home."

He ran back upstairs, jumped into his clothes. He had to get out. Had to get out! His body burned. His throat was dry. He picked up the wine bottle and read the label. Good wine! Warm and easy on the throat! Hurry before the landlady comes. Hurry! She wouldn't understand this haste. I wonder—*did she die alone?* Quickly he put on his coat and plunged down the steps. Outside it was dark. The street lights seemed dimmer than usual. *Did she die alone?* At the corner there was a bar, palely lighted. He had never stopped there before, but this time he went in. He could drink all he wanted now. *Alone, at home, alone! Did she die alone?*

The bar was dismal, like a barn. A nickel machine played a raucous hit song. A brown-skinned woman stood near the machine singing to herself, her hair dark and curly under her little white cap.

Carl went up to the bar.

"What'll it be?" the bartender passed his towel over the counter in front of him.

"A drink," Carl said.

"Whiskey?"

"Yes."

"Can you make it two?" asked the curly-haired woman.

"Sure," Carl said. "Make it two."

"What's the matter? You're shivering!" she exclaimed.

"Cold," Carl said.

"You've been drinking?" the woman said, close beside him. "But it don't smell like whiskey."

"Wasn't," Carl said. "Was wine."

"Oh, so you mix your drinks, heh? O.K. But if that wine along with this whiskey knocks you out, I'll have to take you home to my house, little boy."

"Home?" he asked.

"Yes," the woman said, "home—with me. You and I alone—home."

She put her arm around his shoulders.

"Home?" Carl said.

"Home, sure, baby! Home to my house."

"Home?" Carl was about to repeat when suddenly a volley of sobs shook his body, choking the word "home." He leaned forward on the bar with his head in his arms and wept. The bartender and the woman looked at him in amazement.

Then the woman said gently, "You're drunk, kid! Come on, buck up. I'll take you home. It don't have to be my house, either, if you really want to go home."

THE COCOON

by JOHN B. L. GOODWIN

WHEREAS DOWNSTAIRS HIS FATHER HAD A ROOM THE WALLS of which were studded with the trophies of his aggressive quests: heads of ibex, chamois, eland, keitloa, peccary, and ounce, upstairs Denny had pinned upon his playroom walls the fragile bodies of Swallowtails, Nymphs, Fritillaries, Meadow Browns and Anglewings.

Although his father had maneuvered expeditions, experienced privation, waded through jungles, climbed upon crags for his specimens, Denny had blithely gathered his within the fields and gardens close to home. It was likely that his father's day as a collector was over; Denny's had just begun.

Denny was eleven and his father forty-six and the house in which they lived was a hundred or more years old though no one could be exact about it. Mr. Peatybog, the postmaster in the shriveled village, said as how he could recall when the circular window on the second-story landing hadn't been there and Mrs. Bliss said she knew that at one time what was now the kitchen had been a taproom because her father had told her about it. The heart of the house, as Denny's father put it, was very old but people had altered it and added on and covered up. Denny's father had added the room where his heads were hung, but Denny's playroom must have been the original attic because where the rafters of its high, abrupt ceiling were visible the nails in them were square-headed and here and there the timbers were still held together with wooden pegs.

But the playroom, where Denny also slept, appeared to the casual glance anything but old. The floor was carpeted in blue, the curtains were yellow and the bedspread blue and white. The wallpaper, which his mother had chosen for him before she left, was yellow willow trees on a pale blue ground and to an alien eye the butterflies pinned on the walls seemed part of the design. It had been a long time since Denny's father had been up in the room and although he knew that his son's collection of Lepidoptera, as he called them, was pinned upon the walls he did not know and therefore could not reprimand his son for the damage they had done the pretty wallpaper. Under each specimen a putty-colored blot was spreading over the blue paper. It was the oil exuding from the drying bodies of the dead insects.

In one corner of the room was a chintz-covered chest in which lay the remains of Denny's earlier loves; battered trains and sections of track, an old transformer, batteries covered with cavern-like crystals of zinc salts, trucks, and windmills no longer recognizable as much more than haphazard, wooden arrangements of fitted blocks and sticks, books crumpled and torn with Denny's name or current dream scrawled aggressively in crayon across the print and pictures, a gyroscope, a rubber ball, its cracked paint making a mosaic of antique red and gold around its sphere, and somewhere at the bottom weighed down with tin and lead and wood more than any corpse with earth and grass, lay a bear, a monkey, and a boy doll with a scar across one cheek where Denny had kicked it with a skate. In another corner the symbols of his present were proudly displayed. The butterfly net leaned against the wall, and close to the floor on a wooden box turned upside down stood Denny's cyanide bottle, tweezers, and pins, the last shining as dangerously bright as minute surgical instruments in their packet of black paper.

After almost a year of collecting butterflies, Denny had found that a certain equivocal quality could be added to his pursuit if he were to collect not only the butterflies but also the earlier stages of their mutations. By cramming milk bottles, shoe boxes, and whatever other receptacle the house might offer with caterpillars and pupae he was, in the cases of those that survived, able to participate in a sort of alchemy. Intently he would squat on his haunches and gaze into the receptacles, studying the laborious transformations, the caterpillar shedding skin, the exudation that it used to hitch its shroudlike chrysalid to twigs or undersides of leaves, and then the final unpredictable attainment of the imago. It was like opening a surprise package, for as yet Denny had not learned to tell what color, size, or shape worm would turn into a Dog's Head Sulphur, Mourning Cloak, or Tiger Swallowtail.

As late summer approached, Denny insisted that the servant girl refrain from opening the windows wide in order to air out his room. The sudden change in temperature, he said, would disturb the caterpillars and pupae. Even though the girl reported to his father that Denny's room smelled unhealthily from all the bugs and things, the man did no more than mention it to Denny in an offhand manner. Denny grunted to show that he had heard and did no more about it, and as his father was writing a book on his jungles and crags and beasts, he had really very little concern about what went on upstairs.

So it was that an arid smell of decaying vegetable matter resolving itself into insect flesh pervaded Denny's bright attic room and the oily blotches on the walls beneath his specimens spread ever so slightly, discoloring the paper more and more.

In a book, "Butterflies You Ought to Know Better," which an aunt had sent him for Christmas, Denny read that a suitable "castle" for a caterpillar could be made by placing a lamp chimney, closed at the top, upon a flowerpot filled with earth. He prepared this enclosure, purchasing the lamp chimney from the village store with his own money. It was such an elegant contrivance and yet so magical that he decided to save it for an especially unusual specimen. It was not until a late afternoon in October that Denny found one worthy of the "castle."

He was exploring a copse between two fields. Because of the stoniness of its ground it had never been cultivated and lay like a sword between the fertility of the fields on either side. Denny had never trespassed on it before and dared to now only because of his growing self-confidence in his power over nature. A month ago he would have shied away from the area entirely, even taking the precaution to circumvent the two fields enclosing it. But he felt a little now the way he thought God must feel when, abject within its glass and cardboard world, the life he watched took form, changed, and ceased. Protected from unpleasant touch or any unpredictable action, Denny watched the metamorphosis from worm to chrysalid to miraculously vibrant petal. It lay within his power to sever abruptly the magical chain of their evolution at any point he chose. In a little way he *was* a little like God. It was this conceit that now gave him the courage to climb over the stones of the old wall and enter the half acre of dense woodland.

The autumn sun, already low, ogled the brittle landscape like some improbable jack-o'-lantern hanging in the west. What birds were still in that country spoke in the rasping tone of the herd; the more melifluous and prosperous had already gone south. Although the leaves on the trees displayed the incautious yellows of senility and ochres of decay, the underbrush such as cat briar and wild grape were mostly green. Armed with his forceps and his omnipotence, Denny explored each living leaf and twig.

Brambles tore his stockings and scratched his knees but, except for vulgar tent caterpillars in the wild cherry trees, Denny's efforts went unrewarded. It was dusk when, searching among the speculatively shaped leaves of a sassafras, Denny found a specimen beyond his most arrogant expectations. At first sight, due in part to the twilight, it looked more like some shriveled dragon than a caterpillar. Between it and the twig a filament stretched and this, added to the fact that when Denny touched it gingerly he could feel its puffy flesh contract the way caterpillars do, convinced him that it was no freak of nature or if it was it was a caterpillar freak and therefore nothing to fear. Tearing it cautiously with his tweezers from the twig, he put the monster in the Diamond Match box he always carried with him and, running breathlessly, blind to briar and brambles, Denny headed home.

It was suppertime when he got there and his father was already at the table, his left hand turning the pages of a book while with his right hand he ladled soup into his mouth. Denny had clattered up the stairs before his father was aware of his presence.

"You're late, son," he said in the moment between two printed sentences and two spoonfuls of soup.

"I know, Father," Denny replied without stopping, "but I got something."

Another sentence and another spoonful.

"How many times have I told you to be explicit? *Something* can be anything from a captive balloon to a case of mumps."

From the second landing Denny called down, "It's just *something*. I don't know exactly what it is."

His father mumbled, and by the time he had finished a paragraph and scooped up the last nugget of meat out of his soup and had addressed his son with the words, "Whatever it is it will wait until you have your supper," Denny was peering at it through the glass of the lamp chimney.

Even in the bright electric glare it was reptilian. It was large for a caterpillar, between four and five inches long Denny guessed, and was a muddy purple color, its underside a yellowish black. At either extremity it bore a series of three horny protuberances of a vermilion shade; they were curved sharply inward and stiff little hairs grew from them. From its mouth there protruded a set of small grasping claws like those of a crustacean. Its skin was wrinkled like that of a tortoise and the abdominal segments were sharply defined. The feet lacked the usual suction-like apparatuses caterpillars have but were scaly and shaped like tiny claws.

It was indeed worthy of its "castle." It was not to be found in any of the illustrated books Denny had. He would guard it and keep it a secret and finally, when he presented its metamorphosis into a winged thing to the world, his father's renown as the captor of extraordinary beasts would pale beside his own. The only thing he could guess at, and that because of its size, was that it was the larva of a moth rather than that of a butterfly.

He was still peering at it when the servant girl brought up a tray. "Here," she said, "if you're such a busy little gentleman that you can't spare time for supper like an ordinary boy. If I had my way you'd go hungry." She set the tray down on a table. "Pugh!" she added. "The smell in this room is something awful.

What have you got there now?" And she was about to peer over Denny's shoulder.

"Get out!" he shrieked, turning on her. "Get out!"

"I'm not so sure I will if you speak like that."

He arose and in his fury pushed her hulk out the door, slamming it and locking it after her.

She started to say something on the other side, but what it was Denny never knew or cared, for his own voice screaming, "And stay out!" sent the young girl scurrying down the stairs to his father.

It was typical of the man that he merely commiserated with the girl, agreed with her on the urgency of some sort of discipline for his son, and then, settling back to his pipe and his manuscript, dismissed the matter from his mind.

The following day Denny told the girl that henceforth she was not to enter his room, neither to make the bed nor to clean.

"We shall see about that," she said, "though it would be a pleasure such as I never hoped for this side of heaven were I never to enter that horrid smelling room again."

Again his father was approached and this time he reluctantly called his son to him.

"Ethel tells me something about you not wanting her to go into your room," he said, peering over his glasses.

"I'd rather she didn't, Father," Denny replied, humble as pie. "You see, she doesn't understand about caterpillars and cocoons and things and she messes everything up."

"But who will see to the making of your bed and dusting and such?"

"I will," asserted Denny. "There's no reason why if I don't want anyone to go into my room I shouldn't have to make up for it somehow, like making my own bed and clearing up."

"Spoken like a soldier, son," the father said. "I know the way you feel and if you're willing to pay the price in responsibility I see no reason why you shouldn't have your wish. But," and he pointed a paper knife of walrus tusk at the boy, "if it isn't kept neat and tidy we'll have to rescind the privilege; remember that."

His father, grateful that the interview had not been as tedious as he had anticipated, told his son he could go. From then on Denny always kept the key to his room in his pocket.

Because caterpillars cease to eat prior to their chrysalis stage and Denny's caterpillar refused to eat whatever assortment of leaves he tried to tempt it with, Denny knew that it had definitely been preparing its cocoon when he had plucked it from the the sassafras branch. It was very restless, almost convulsive now, and within the lamp chimney it humped itself aimlessly from twig to twig, its scaly little claws searching for something to settle upon. After a day of such meanderings the caterpillar settled upon a particular crotch of the twig and commenced to spin its cocoon. By the end of twenty-four hours the silken alembic was complete.

Though there was now nothing for Denny to observe, he still squatted for hours on end staring at the cocoon that hung like some parasitic growth from the sassafras twig. His concentration upon the shape was so great as he sat hunched over it, that his eyes seemed to tear the silken shroud apart and to be intimately exploring the secret that was taking place within.

Now Denny spent less and less of the days out in the open searching for the more common types of chrysalid with which he was acquainted. Such were for him as garnets would be to a connoisseur of emeralds. His lean, tanned face became puffy and the palms of his hands were pale and moist.

The winter months dragged on and Denny was as listlessly impatient as what was inside the cocoon. His room was cold and airless, for a constant low temperature must be kept if the cocoon was to lie dormant until spring. His bed was seldom made and the floor was thick with dust and mud. Once a week the girl left the broom and dustpan along with the clean sheets outside his door, but Denny took only the sheets into his room where they would collect into a stack on the floor for weeks at a time. His father took no notice of his condition other than to write in a postscript to what was otherwise a legal and splenetic letter to his wife that their son looked peaked and upon receiving an apprehensive reply he casually asked Denny if he was feeling all right. The boy's affirmative though noncommital answer seemed to satisfy him and, dropping a card to his wife to the effect that their son professed to be in sound health, he considered himself released from any further responsibility.

When April was about gone Denny moved his treasure close to the window where the sun would induce the dormant thing within it into life. In a few days Denny was sure that it was struggling for release, for the cocoon seemed to dance up and down idiotically upon its thread. All that night he kept vigil, his red and swollen eyes focused on the cocoon as upon some hypnotic object. His father ate breakfast alone and by nine o'clock showed enough concern to send the servant girl up to see if everything was all right. She hurried back to report that his son was at least still alive enough to be rude to her. The father mumbled something in reply about the boy's mother having shirked her responsibilities. The girl said that if it pleased him, she would like to give notice. She was very willing to enumerate the reasons why, but the man dismissed her casually with the request that she stay until she found someone to take her place.

At ten Denny was positive that the cocoon was about to break; by ten-thirty there was no longer any doubt in his mind. Somewhat before eleven the eclosion took place. There was a convulsive movement inside and the cocoon opened at the top with the faint rustle of silk. The feathery antennae and the two forelegs issued forth, the legs clutching the cocoon in order to hoist the body through the narrow aperture. The furry and distended abdomen, upon which were hinged the crumpled wings, was drawn out with effort. Immediately the creature commenced awkwardly to climb the twig from which the cocoon was suspended. Denny watched the procedure in a trance. Having gained the tip of the branch and unable to proceed farther, the insect rested, its wings hanging moist and heavy from its bloated body. The abdomen with each pulsation shrank visibly and gradually, very gradually, the antennae unfurled and the wings expanded with the juices pumped into them from the body.

Within an hour the metamorphosis of many months was complete. The beast, its wings still slightly damp though fully spread, fluttered gently before the eyes of the boy. Though escaped from its cocoon, it lay imprisoned still behind the glass.

Denny's pallor was suddenly flushed. He grasped the lamp chimney as if he would hold the insect to him. This was his miracle, his alone. He watched with a possessive awe as the creature flexed its wings, although it was still too weak to attempt flight. Surely this specimen before him was unique. The wings were easily ten inches across and their color was so subtly gradated that it was impossible to say where black turned to purple and purple to green and green back into black. The only definite delineations were a crablike simulacrum centered on each hind wing and upon each fore wing, the imitation of an open mouth with teeth bared. Both the crabs and the mouths were chalked in white and vermilion.

By noon Denny was hungry, yet so overcome with nervous exhaustion that he almost decided to forego the midday meal. Aware, however, that an absence from two meals running would surely precipitate an intrusion by his father with the servant girl as proxy, he reluctantly left his room and went downstairs to face his father over luncheon.

Despite his complaisance, the father was immediately aware of the transformation in his son.

"Spring seems to have put new life into the lad," he said, turning over the page of a book. "You're like your mother in that respect and in that respect only, thank God. She never did do well in cold weather."

It was the first time he had mentioned the mother to the son since he had been forced to explain her departure obliquely some five years before. The boy was shocked. But as the opportunity had arisen, he hastily decided to follow up the mention of his mother. It was unseemly that he should disclose any sentiment, so he hesitated and calculated before putting his question. "Why doesn't she write or send me presents?" he asked.

His father's pause made him almost unbearably aware of the man's chagrin in having opened the subject. He didn't look up at the boy as he answered, "Because legally she is not allowed to."

The remainder of the meal was passed in silent and mutual embarrassment.

Denny returned to his room as soon as he could respectfully quit the table, and while unlocking the door for an awful moment the possibility that the moth might have escaped, might never really have been there, scorched Denny's mind. But it was there, almost as he had left it, only now it had changed its position; the spread of its wings being nearly horizontal and in this position Denny realized that the lamp chimney was too narrow to allow it free movement.

There was no receptacle in the room any larger and in Denny's mind there paraded the various jars, the vases, and other vessels in the house that had from time to time in the past served as enclosures for his specimens. None of them was large enough. Without sufficient room, the moth as soon as it attempted flight would in no time at all damage its wings. In a kind of frenzy Denny racked his brains for the memory of some container that would satisfy his need. Like a ferret his thoughts suddenly pounced on what had eluded them. In his father's room a huge crystal tobacco jar with a lid of repoussé silver stood on an ebony taboret beneath the smirking head of a tiger.

There was no time to lose; for within five hours after emerging from the cocoon a moth will try its wings in flight. Breathlessly Denny bounded down the stairs and for a moment only hesitated before he knocked upon his father's door.

"Yes?" his father asked querulously, and Denny turned the knob and walked in.

"Father—" he began, but he had not as yet caught his breath.

"Speak up, boy, and stop shaking. Why, even confronted by a rogue elephant I never shook so."

"I want to b-b-borrow something," the boy managed to stammer.

"Be more explicit! Be more explicit! What do you want? A ticket to Fall River? A hundred-dollar bill? A dose of ipecac? The last would seem the most logical, to judge from your looks."

Hating his father as he had never hated him before, the boy spoke up. "I want to borrow your tobacco jar."

"Which one?" the father parried. "The elephant foot the President gave me? The Benares brass? The Dutch pottery one? The music box?"

The boy could bear this bantering no longer. "I want that one." And he pointed directly where it stood half full of tobacco.

"What for?" his father asked.

The boy's bravura was suddenly extinguished.

"Speak up. If you make an extraordinary request you must be ready to back it up with a motive."

"I want it for a specimen."

"What's wrong with all the containers you have already appropriated from kitchen, pantry, and parlor?"

Denny would not say they were not big enough. It might arouse sufficient interest within his father so that he would insist on seeing for himself what this monster was. Denny had a vision of his father grabbing the moth and hastening to impale it upon the study wall, adding it to his other conquests.

"They won't do," Denny said.

"Why won't they do?"

"They just won't."

"Be explicit!" his father thundered at him.

"I want to put some stuff in it that won't fit in the others."

"You will stand where you are without moving until you can tell me what you mean by 'stuff.' " His father laid down his glasses and settled back in his chair to underscore the fact that he was prepared to wait all day if need be.

"Chrysalids and dirt and sticks and food for them," the boy mumbled.

The man stared at Denny as if he were an animal he had at bay.

"You intend to put *that* filth into *that* jar?"

Denny made no answer. His father continued.

"Are you by any chance aware that that jar was a gift from the Maharana of Udaipur? Have you any faintest conception of its intrinsic value aside from the sentimental one? And can you see from where you stand that, beside any other objections I might have, the jar is being employed for what it was intended for? And if for one moment you think I am going to remove my best tobacco from my best jar so that you can use it for a worm bowl you are, my lad, very much mistaken."

The man waited for the effect of his speech and then added, "Go and ask Ethel for a crock."

It was useless for Denny to attempt to explain that he wouldn't be able to see through a crock. Without a word he turned and walked out of the room, leaving the door open behind him.

His father called him back, but he paid no mind. As he reached the second landing Denny heard the door slam downstairs.

A half hour had been wasted and, as he had been sure it would, the moth, having gained control over itself, was in the first struggles of flight.

There was only one thing to do. Denny went to the corner where he kept his equipment. Returning, he lifted the lid from the lamp chimney and reaching inside with his forceps he clenched the moth with a certain brutality, though he took pains to avoid injury to its wings. Lifting it out, the beauty of so few hours, Denny once again felt his omnipotence. Without hesitation he plunged the moth into the cyanide jar and screwed down the lid.

The wings beat frantically with the effort that should have carried the moth on its first flight through the spring air. Breathless, Denny watched for fear the wings would be injured. The dusty abdomen throbbed faster and faster, the antennae twitched from side to side; with a spasm the abdomen formed a curve to meet the thorax. The eyes, still bearing the unenlightened glaze of birth, turned suddenly into the unknowing glaze of death. But in the moment that they turned Denny thought he saw his distorted image gleaming on their black, china surfaces as if in that instant the moth had stored his image in its memory.

Denny unscrewed the cap, plucked out the moth and, piercing its body with a pin from the black paper packet, he pinned the moth to the wall at the foot of his bed. He gave it a place of honor, centering it upon a yellow willow tree. From his bed he would see it first thing in the morning and last thing at night.

A few days and nights passed, and Denny, though still on edge, felt somewhat as a hero must returning from a labor. The untimely death of the moth had perhaps been fortuitous, because now in its death the creature was irrevocably his.

The meadows were already filled with cabbage butterflies, and Denny would go out with his net and catch them, but they were too common to preserve and so, having captured them, he would reach his hand into the net and squash them, wiping the mess in his palm off on the grass.

It was less than a week after the death of the moth when Denny was awakened in the night by a persistent beating on his windowpane. He jumped from bed, switched on the light, and peered outside. With the light on he could see nothing, and whatever it had been was gone. Realizing that though the light made anything outside invisible to him it would also act as a lure to whatever had tried to come in, he went back to bed leaving the light on and the window open. He tried to stay awake but soon fell back into sleep.

In the morning he looked about the room, but there was no sign of anything having entered. It must have been a June bug or possibly a lunar moth though it had sounded too heavy for one, thought Denny. He went over to look at the moth on the wall, a morning ritual with him. Although he could not be sure, the dust of one wing seemed to be smudged and the oily stain from the body had soaked into the wallpaper considerably since the day before. He put his face close to the insect to inspect it more fully. Instinctively he drew back; the odor was unbearable.

The following night Denny left his window wide open and shortly before midnight he was awakened by a beating of wings upon his face. Terrified and not fully conscious, he hit out with his open hands. He touched something and it wasn't pleasant. It was yielding and at the same time viscid. And something scratched against the palm of his hand like a tiny spur or horn.

Leaping from bed, Denny switched on the light. There was nothing in the room. It must have been a bat and the distasteful thought made him shudder. Whatever it had been, it left a stench behind not unlike the stench of the spot on the wall. Denny slammed the window shut and went back to bed and tried to sleep.

In the morning his red-rimmed eyes inspecting the moth plainly saw that not only were the wings smudged but that the simulacra of crabs and mouths upon the wings seemed to have grown more definite. The oily spot had spread still farther and the smell was stronger.

That night Denny slept with his window closed, but in his dreams he was beset by horned and squashy things that pounded his flesh with their fragile wings, and awakening in fright he heard the same sound as he had heard the previous night; something beating against the windowpane. All night it beat against the closed window and Denny lay rigid and sleepless in his bed and the smell within the room grew into something almost tangible.

At dawn Denny arose and forced himself to look at the moth. He held his nose as he did so and with horror he saw the stain on the paper and the crabs and the mouths which now not only seemed more definite but also considerably enlarged.

For the first time in months Denny left his room and did not return to it until it was his bedtime. Even that hour he contrived to postpone a little by asking his father to read to him. It was the lesser of two evils.

The stench in the room was such that although Denny dared not leave the window open he was forced to leave the door from the landing into his room ajar. What was left of the light in the hall below, after it had wormed its way up and around the stairs, crawled exhaustedly into the room. For some perverse reason it shone most brightly upon the wall where the moth was transfixed. From his bed Denny could not take his eyes off it. Though they made no progress, the two crabs on the hind wings appeared to be attempting to climb up into the two mouths on the fore wings. The mouths seemed to be very open and ready for them.

That night no sooner had the beating of wings upon the window awakened Denny than it abruptly ceased. The light downstairs was out and the room was now in darkness. Curling himself up into a ball and pulling the sheet over his head, Denny at length went off to sleep.

Sometime shortly afterward something came through the door and half crawled and half fluttered to the bed. Denny awoke with a scream, but it was too muffled for either his father or Ethel to hear because what caused him to scream had wormed its way beneath the sheet and was resting like a sticky pulp upon Denny's mouth.

Floundering like a drowning person, the boy threw back the covers and managed to dislodge whatever had been upon his mouth. When he dared to, he reached out and turned on the light. There was nothing in the room, but upon his sheets there were smudges of glistening dust almost black, almost purple, almost green, but not quite any of them.

Denny went down to breakfast without looking at the moth.

"No wonder you look ghastly," his father said to him, "if the smell in this house is half of what it must be in your room, it's a wonder you're not suffocated. What are you running up there? A Potters' Field for Lepidoptera? I'll give you until noon to get them out."

All day Denny left the window of his room wide open. It was the first of May and the sun was bright. As a sop to his father he brought down a box of duplicate specimens. He showed them to his father before disposing of them.

"Pugh!" said his father. "Dump them far away from the house."

That night Denny went to bed with both the door and window locked tight in spite of the smell. The moon was bright and shone all night unimpaired upon the wall. Denny could not keep his eyes off the moth.

By now both crabs and mouths were nearly as large as the

wings themselves and the crabs were moving, Denny could swear. They appeared in relief, perhaps through some trick of chiaroscuro induced by the moonlight upon the dusty white and red markings. The claws seemed upon the verge of attacking the mouths, or were the so terribly white teeth of the mouths waiting to clamp down upon the crabs? Denny shuddered and closed his eyes.

Sleep came eventually, only to be broken in upon by the beating of wings against the windowpane. And no sooner had that ceased and Denny become less rigid than the thing was at the door beating urgently as though it must be let in. The only relief from the tap-tapping was an occasional, more solid thud against the panel of the door. It was, Denny guessed, caused by the soft and fleshy body of the thing.

If he survived the night Denny vowed he would destroy the thing upon the wall or, better than losing it entirely, he would give it to his father and he in turn would present it to some museum in Denny's name. Denny for a moment was able to forget the persistent rapping which had now returned to the window, for in his mind he saw a glass case with the moth in it and a little card below upon which was printed *Unique Specimen Lepidoptera. Gift of Mr. Denny Longwood, Aged 12.*

All through the night, first at the window, then at the door, the beating of wings continued, relieved only by the occasional plop of the soft, heavy body.

Though having dozed for only an hour or two, with the bright light of day Denny felt his decision of the night before indefensible. The moth smelled; that was undeniable. The matter of the crab and mouthlike markings seeming to expand and become more intense in their color could probably he explained by somebody who knew about such things. As for the beating against the window and the door, it was probably as he had at first surmised, a bat or, if need be, two bats. The moth on the wall was dead, was his. He had hatched it and he knew the limitations of a moth dead or alive. He looked at it. The stain had spread so that now its diameter was as great as the spread of the wings. It was no longer exactly a stain, either. It looked as if a spoonful of dirty cereal had adhered to the wall; it was just about the color of mush. It will stop in time like the others; just as soon as the abdomen dries up, thought Denny.

At breakfast his father remarked that the smell as yet hadn't left the house, that it was in fact stronger if anything. Denny admitted it might take a day or two more before it was completely gone.

Before the meal was over his father told Denny that he was looking so badly that he had better see Dr. Phipps.

"How much do you weigh?" he asked.

Denny didn't know.

"You look," his father said, "all dried up like one of those pupae you had upstairs."

The moon shone bright again that night. In spite of his logic of the morning Denny felt sure that the movement of the white and vermilion crabs up to the white teeth and vermilion lips was more than just hallucination. And the beating of wings started at the window again. Then at the door. Then back to the window. And, in a way, worse than that was the plop now and then of the body against the barrier. Though he tried to rise and look out when it was at the window, his limbs would not obey him. Hopelessly his eyes turned to the wall again. The crablike spots clicked their tiny claws together each time the wings struck against the windowpane. And each time the plump, squashy body went plop the teeth snapped together between the thin-lipped mouths.

All at once the stench within the room became nauseating. There was nothing for Denny to do but make for the door while whatever it was still pounded at the window. As much as he feared and hated him, his father's cynical disbelief was to be preferred to this terror.

Denny refrained from switching on the light for fear that it would reveal his movements to the thing outside. Halfway across the room and shivering, he involuntarily turned his head and for a moment his feverish eyes saw what was outside before it disappeared.

Denny rushed for the door and unlocked it, but as he twisted the knob something beat against the other side of the door, pushing it open before Denny could shut the door against it.

When luncheon was over Ethel was sent upstairs to see what had happened. She was so hysterical when she came down that Denny's father went up to see for himself.

Denny lay in his pajamas on the floor just inside the door. The skin of his lonely and somewhat arrogant face was marred by the marks of something pincerlike and from his nose, eyes, ears, and mouth a network of viscid filaments stretched across his face and to the floor as though something had tried to bind his head up in them. His father had some trouble in lifting him up because the threads adhered so stubbornly to the nap of the blue carpet.

The body was feather light in the father's arms. The thought that the boy had certainly been underweight passed inanely through his father's mind.

As he carried his son out his eyes fell upon a spot on the wall at the foot of the bed. The pattern of a willow tree was completely obliterated by a creeping growth that looked like fungus. Still carrying his son, the man crossed over to it. A pin protruded from its center and it was from this spot, Mr. Longwood could tell, that the terrible smell came.

SCHMUEL SAVES THE SCHULE

by ALMA DENNY

ONE EVENING IN LATE NOVEMBER, SCHMUEL FEIGENBLATT sat down to supper with his family and alternately smiled and swallowed as though tasting some delicious thoughts. He lifted his fork and scratched lightly along the top of a mound of chopped liver. This unwonted finickiness toward a favorite dish prompted his daughter Annie to ask, "What's the matter, Papa? You aren't hungry?"

The old man chuckled. "Who can eat? I'm too excited."

"Excited? About what are you excited, Papa?" Annie prodded. "From business you can't be excited no more. You are retired. From the family? What's exciting? You got no worries from us. Moma's veins are better. Bernie's making out good in the grocery. Tillie's married. I'm going steady. Marty's learning pharmacy. So from us you can't be excited. . . . So tell us already, why all of a sudden are you excited and you can't eat your *geshmaka* liver?"

"I just met Schneiderman—" Schmuel began.

"So that's what it is, Papa," interrupted Bernie who was halfway through the soup course. "The schule again. Only this time for a change, you're not worrying about it. What happened now?"

Schmuel laid down his knife and fork and placed his hands on each side of his plate. "My dear family," he began again, looking over their heads and out of the kitchen window, "a big honor has come today to your father. Schneiderman told me now what it was decided last night by the officers' meeting."

"So tell us, Papa. Don't make us first *plotz*, please," scowled Marty.

"All right, but wait a minute. It's a whole long story and you got to hear what comes first." Settling back in his chair, the head of the house raised a glass of water with wine, took a few leisurely sips, replaced the glass painstakingly, and addressed his loved ones on the latest turn in his relationship with the Synagogue. He spoke from behind a smile which wouldn't straighten out and wait for its cue in the recital.

"You remember when I gave the store to Bernie and I retired. I promised the schule I would have time now to help them. Every year for forty-one years it's the same thing with them. In the red. They owe for electric, for coal, for painting. Every cent they collect they hurry and pay first the Rav he shouldn't have to take charity. But they never collect enough. I tell them they could charge more for the seats on the holidays. They could charge more for the honors. But they don't listen. One good businessman they need there, that's all. But Schneiderman, he's got no time with his drugstore, and Applebaum, his eyes are no good.

"So, you remember I said, Schneiderman, I never could help out the schule before, but now . . ."

Schmuel's wife, turning pancakes at the stove, hurried him along. "So we know all this, Papa," she complained. "Where then did you go all year, night after night after night, if not to the schule? So tell us now. What is the big honor?"

"Listen," Schmuel threatened, "*or* you let me tell the whole story like I want *or* I'll be quiet altogether. One way or the other."

He frowned and waited to see whether his ultimatum had been accepted. Slowly the smile reappeared and he resumed amid a silence broken only by the sound of pancakes sizzling in chicken fat.

"Schneiderman, I said, I'll show you how the schule can make money and get up on its own feet. But also, I told him, once I get everything fixed up, running good in the black, I want you should keep it like that yourself or else get somebody else for the job. Not me after that. Me and my wife, I told him," and here Schmuel glanced at her, "we want yet a few years to take it easy. Florida, Ferndale, Spring Valley, Edgemere . . .

"All right. So first thing I called together the officers for a meeting and showed them something. Every year they sell seats for New Year services, two dollars a seat, three dollars, maybe sometimes they get five. What kind of business is that? I told them leave it to me, I'll get ten dollars a seat this year. Some in the back, maybe only eight. Charity is charity, I said. Really poor people we can give a few seats for nothing. But our regular people, they can pay ten dollars easy. They had a good year, the most of them. Let them give to the schule. Why must you be broke all the time? I asked them."

"Papa, please, we *know* all this about the tickets," exclaimed Annie in exasperation. She had been noiselessly clearing away the dishes from the chopped liver and the soup, while the others at the table nibbled on crumbs of pumpernickel or munched slivers of sour tomato. Suppressing their impatience with this part of their father's report which they knew thoroughly, they had been concentrating upon their mother's expert juggling of matzoth balls into the hot chicken broth and then into each serving. Schmuel, feasting upon his well-chewed words, had no idea that no one was listening, for his gaze was upon the heavens visible beyond his wife's stooped shoulder. Annie's reproach was like a bone in his throat.

"That's all," he said with a sigh. "That's all I have to say. A man comes home, he wants to speak a few words to his family . . ."

"Please, Papa," soothed his wife, "say it like you want. What's the matter with you, Annie? You got maybe a train to catch? Let Papa talk however he wants it. Go ahead, Papa. It's all right like you saying it." And she patted the air in a gesture of placation.

Schmuel sighed again, and picked up his story, glaring at Annie during the first few words. "So I told them, just leave it to me. And just like I said it, they made plenty of money. They got a good ten dollars a seat from nearly everybody. And Kupperman, that thief, I wouldn't let him get away under twenty-five. You know how I ate my heart out over each ticket, I should get the best price.

"Also I gave them more ideas, good business ideas. For the

Honors I wouldn't let them take less than ten dollars, too. So what happens? Schindler wants to open up the Ark for the evening service on the Day of Atonement. He bids a little five dollars. They wait to see who will bid higher. Right away that same Schindler says twenty-five!

"Another thing. I made them clean it up, that room in the back of the schule. Now they get fifteen, twenty dollars every time for parties, weddings, a couple *bar mitzvahs*. And on the wall, I show them should be a memorial tablet and, believe me, from this alone, the money comes in so fast . . . one, two dollars a name should be painted there with gold paint for a remembrance. From us here only, look, they got a good twenty dollars, ain't it? From my father's name, my mother, my brothers, Momma's people, our little Hannah, they should all rest in peace. . . ."

At this point Schmuel's wife stopped stirring the mashed carrots and prunes, and heaved a long, trembling sigh. The rest, resigned to the unpredictable wordage of the account, cut into their potato *latkes* listlessly.

"Anyhow, Schneiderman tells me last night the officers, they had a meeting." Here Schmuel paused and the smile finally broke loose completely. "Applebaum, the treasurer, he shows them this year is the first time the schule is not in the red. Now the Congregation Sons of Novorodomsk don't owe nobody a penny and also they got in the bank four hundred and thirty dollars. This, Applebaum tells them, is the whole thing the work of one man all by himself. This is thanks, he says, to Schmuel Feigenblatt."

With this injection of the personal note, interest perked up. Eyes were diverted from the matzoth *kugel* long enough to indicate that attention was still on the recital.

Schmuel cleared his throat and his tone now resembled a purr. "Schneiderman says they all clapped their hands. Then he remembered what I said, how I wanted someone else to take over this job. Which it is so, absolutely so. Right away, they all start to worry. So Koplewitz, the secretary, he gets the smart idea, maybe they'll plead with me a little, maybe I'll keep on.

But also, he says, they should give me something for a thank-you. In his society he tells them, the members just presented last week a plaque, a beautiful piece bronze, to the chairman from the Cemetery Plots Committee. Which it says on it the whole story what the man did. . . ."

"Papa, what do you want with a plaque here, anyhow?" blurted Annie. The news, at last out, was something of a letdown to Papa's waiting public.

"Wait a minute, wait a minute, people." The beaming old man shrugged his shoulders. "What should I do? Is it nice they want to give me a beautiful plaque and I should say no? Maybe I'm still going to work there, maybe I'm not. That's got nothing to do with it. Ain't it nice your father is going to get a bronze plaque, a big one, to hang up here on the wall? My grandchildren, please God, will read it all about me, the whole story. What's so terrible? What do *you* think, Marty?"

Schmuel picked up his fork to return to the chopped liver. The rest of the family was on boiled chicken and salad. Marty squinted. He was the thoughtful member of the household.

"A plaque, Papa? What good is it? From all that hard work you'll have nothing. A piece of junk to hang on the wall! Who'll see it even, unless we pull them by the nose and say, Here, read it? And Momma's got enough work already. Now also she'll have to dust off your plaque every day, otherwise nobody will be able to read it."

"Never mind Momma's work," chimed Schmuel's wife, herself. "That kind of work I would like to get from all of you, don't worry." Schmuel nodded at her gratefully.

"Look, Marty," pleaded his father. "What do you want? I should go to Schneiderman and say No, a plaque is a piece of junk? It don't make enough noise? I want better a brass band? No. They want to give me a plaque, let it be a plaque." Schmuel went back to his meal, his *joie de vivre* somewhat soggy.

"Papa," said Marty, suddenly, "maybe you can hint to Schneiderman that it's a waste of money. Tell him to tell the officers you'll be satisfied with no plaque just as much as with one. Let them forget about the plaque. Of course, if they want to give you a gold pen or a ring, that's different. That's something sensible."

The rest of the family looked up from their tea and nodded in agreement with Marty. Schmuel's wife stopped slicing the mandelbrot and said, "The thing is the honor, that they *want* to give you something. A plaque, a ring . . . what's the difference? It's the big honor I like, that they realize what you did for the schule."

"Maybe you are right, children." Schmuel raised his hands from the table. "I'll see Schneiderman tonight when I go down. I'll tell him tell the officers . . . never mind the plaque."

The following Saturday Schmuel returned from schule, washed his hands, and offered a blessing over the privilege of doing same. Before sitting down to his meal he broke off a piece of bread and said grace. His wife was balancing two plates of hot noodle soup from stove to table, while the rest of the family was engrossed in balls of gefillte fish with bright red horseradish on the side.

Schmuel pushed his chair back slightly, took a deep breath, and spoke casually. "I saw Schneiderman again in schule this morning."

His sons slowed a bit, but continued eating. Annie and her mother were waiting for their soup to cool.

"Again the officers had a meeting," Schmuel went on tonelessly, "and they wouldn't take my No for an answer, Schneiderman said. If I work there or if I not work—whichever way, still they want to give me something. If not a plaque, Schneiderman said, maybe a wrist watch, but what—"

"That's it, Papa!" exclaimed Bernie. "You take a wrist watch. That's something I can use."

"Quiet, Bernie," his mother commanded. "Who's asking you?"

Schmuel was grinning. "Wait, you didn't hear nothing yet," he coaxed. "On the back of the watch they want it should be engraved exactly the same fine words just like it was going to be on the plaque!"

Annie was at the sink, rinsing out the fish dishes to get them out of the way before the drippings passed along a fish taste to the other utensils waiting to be washed.

"A nice idea, Papa. Personally, I like that. This way you got something you can carry around with you. You can use it. Not like a plaque that just hangs on the wall."

Marty asked, "When are you getting it, Papa? Who's going to buy it? How long must you wait now?"

"Listen, I only know what Schneiderman told me. But I still got something to say to them. I don't want them to throw out their money. This afternoon I'll meet Schneiderman at the Shass when we talk about Torah with the Rav. I'll say to him, Schneiderman, all right to give me a nice wrist watch. But one thing I insist: Let me go buy it. I got connections, wholesale, on Canal Street. Don't I know Wasserman yet from when he didn't have a dime? He'll give me a good buy. I can save the schule a nice piece of change."

"But, Papa," his wife asked softly, "the engraving? Those nice words? How would it be for you, Schmuel Feigenblatt, to tell Wasserman, Write it Schmuel Feigenblatt saved the schule from bankruptcy, he's a wonder, that Schmuel?"

They all smiled, reluctantly. "Don't worry, Momma," Bernie said. "Papa just picks out the watch and pays for it. Then he leaves it by Wasserman until Schneiderman comes with a paper. On the paper is written the words from the officers. Papa's got nothing to do with that part. That doesn't cost no extra money. That's none of your business, right, Papa?"

"So sure right," answered Schmuel. He clapped one hand on the table and said sharply, "All right. That's how it's got to be. I'll tell Schneiderman, that way or no watch at all."

He surveyed the large center bowl of *cholent*, a steamy slow-cooked roast with lima beans and sweet potatoes nestling in the syrupy gravy. "I'll see first how much they want to spend. Then I'll show them I'll save them a nice couple dollars," he mused.

"But pick out a nice one, Papa," urged his wife. "For a few dollars less, don't bring home a no-good piece of rag."

"A good one I'll get, don't worry." Schmuel tasted his meat.

"And still I'll show them I can get them six cents for every nickel."

"This is a wonderful idea, Schmuel," added his wife as she placed a large wedge of spicy noodle pudding in front of him. "Like this you got a nice honor and you also got a watch!"

Schmuel laughed openly. "Wait, people, wait. We'll talk first when the watch is already here on my arm—right here." And he pointed to his right wrist.

"The other hand, Papa," corrected Marty. "Everybody wears a watch on the left hand. See?" He raised his sweater sleeve to reveal his own timepiece. "After all, you eat with your right hand, you write with it, you shake hands, you talk with it. . . . It's better for the watch, on the left hand."

"This should be my only worry, Marty. Right hand, left hand." Schmuel bent his head first one way, then the other. "This is nothing."

Joining his family at supper a few nights later, Schmuel tackled a bowl of hot boiled potato and cold sour cream with the singleness of purpose of a dive bomber. He seemed too preoccupied with his food to attempt conversation. The others had already unburdened themselves of the top layer of the day's communiqués and had settled into a well-fed drowse. The silence, broken only by the ring of silver against china, was all the more conspicuous because Schmuel's arrival was usually the signal of a new wave of communication emanating from the head of the family himself. With the ace reporter so strangely reticent, no one else chose to initiate a topic for table talk. Each, as by habit, awaited Schmuel's cue on what to argue about. Then the flow of chatter would resume easily.

But there seemed to be nothing on Schmuel's horizon this evening except white potatoes, and finally Annie ventured, "What's the trouble, Papa? Something is wrong? You don't even say Hello tonight! You're quiet like you got a sore throat or something."

Her father raised his eyes, laid down his fork, wiped his mouth. He shrugged innocently. "What's the matter, she asks me.

Now she asks me," he reproached whimsically. "And what took you so long? Why do you all the time wait *I* should talk, talk, talk? You think I like it, to talk all the time about mineself? Today I made up my mind I'll just go home for once and shut up mine mouth. I told mineself, Schmuel Feigenblatt, you don't say a word. Be quiet. See if maybe they'll ask you something . . ."

"A haircut you got, Papa!" shouted Bernie. "See, I knew it was something different with you."

"Listen, smarty, the haircut I got yesterday and nobody said nothing. You people are blind or . . ." Schmuel was flushed.

"He got the watch already, I bet you," cried his wife. "Look at him!"

"So what else?" Schmuel sat back and crossed his arms, displaying a silver watch bound to his right wrist with a gray suede leather strap. "All right. Look! Seventeen jewelry, rubies, Wasserman said. You don't have to wind it up. I can even take a bath with this watch. It is waterproof. Believe me, I saw with mine own eyes Wasserman gets a good seventy-five dollars for this watch. A guarantee for a whole year."

Around the table, Schmuel's family stopped eating their chopped herring. "So take it off, Papa. Let's see it," urged Annie. "I knew it was something fishy when you didn't say nothing. All of a sudden so quiet. C'mon, let's look at it a minute."

"Listen, Wasserman himself put this on me. He wanted to put it on the other hand but I can see it better on this side. But Wasserman said it's not good to take it off. It's a new kind of watch. You got to leave it on." Schmuel opened the buckle slowly and passed the watch to Annie. "Only a minute, you hear?"

Turning the watch over, Annie squealed excitedly, "Look, look. See what it says about Papa. The engraving!"

Schmuel's wife scurried for her glasses as Annie read, *To Schmuel Feigenblatt for Supreme Service to Congregation Sons of Novorodomsk, New York, 1947.* Gee, that's nice, Papa. Ain't that nice, Momma?"

"Oh, it's wonderful, Schmuel. Congratulations." His wife

placed a portion of applesauce on the table, rubbed her hands against her apron, and grasped the watch. Fingering it delicately, she added, "Such a beautiful watch you got now. Like a college boy you look with it. But tell me, Schmuel, how much costed it, this present?"

"How much?" echoed Schmuel. "Go look. See. The ticket is there. I left it like it was, on the buckle there."

His wife adjusted her spectacles and examined the small tag dangling from the strap.

"Hand it over here, Momma," ordered Marty. "I'll tell you right away. . . . Here. It says forty-three dollars. How much with the tax also, Papa?"

Schmuel nodded. "I tell you I got a really good buy. With the tax and all it comes to forty-three dollars. Stainless steel, a special grind glass. Wasserman says it is like a rock, so strong. Believe me, I saved the schule plenty money. And the beauty part is, I can bring them yet change! Fifty dollars Schneiderman gave me, I should shop around first. Even more I could get, he said, in case it's a couple dollars more. So they got absolutely no kick coming. Seven dollars I'll bring them back to the meeting tomorrow night."

"You said it, Papa," chimed in Bernie. "They sure got no kick coming. Say, you gonna let me wear it some time, Papa?"

His mother turned to him quickly, "What's the matter with you anyhow, Bernie? You let your papa wear it for a long life in good health!" Then, more calmly, "You got time yet. You'll meet a nice girl, please God, you'll get engaged. So your girl will give you a nice watch, an engagement present. . . . Wear it, Papa, wear it in good health. It's very nice."

Noting that Schmuel rebuckled the strap without removing the price tag, Annie said, "Wait a minute, Papa, take off the ticket. You don't need it any more."

"Sure, Papa." Marty agreed. "You can't return it now, even if you wanted to. Not after the engraving. You know that."

Schmuel smoothed his coat sleeve over his wrist. "Who wants to return? This I would never want to do. Also, I would never take off this ticket. How do you like that?"

His children were exasperated. "Papa, who ever heard of such a thing?" scolded Annie.

"Nobody wears a piece of jewelry with the price still on. What's the matter with you, Papa?" Marty laughed, derisively. "You want to look like you just picked it up off a counter somewhere?"

"Listen, that's enough!" Schmuel warned. "I'm wearing it like I want and I'm wearing it like this. How would it be somebody in the schule should think I'm making a penny on the deal? I know my customers there. Like this, anybody wants to know how much cost the watch, let him see for himself. Never mind take my word. Here it's printed down black and white, forty-three dollars by Wasserman's store."

"What you gonna do, Papa, when it wears out? The ticket, I mean," teased Bernie.

"Don't worry, smarty," replied Schmuel. "I know what I'm doing. After, when every member from the whole Congregation Sons of Novorodomsk sees that this present costed forty-three dollars by Wasserman, maybe then I'll take off the label. I know these people. Next month maybe someone says Schmuel, he paid only twenty-five dollars for that piece of junk, the thief! You think I want that?"

"Do like you say, Papa," soothed his wife.

Schmuel relaxed. "All right. With the ticket the watch came. With the ticket the watch remains. They go together. That's how it's got to be." His horrified children were silent as he raised his glass of water. The little white square fluttered like a piece of clean linen in a lively breeze.

DIRTY MINNIE

by FRED URQUHART

Dirty Minnie said she had been going to wash her feet when Winnie the Wailer went. "I wasnie wantin' to wash them, mind ye," she said to the other women in the shelter, "but they were that sair that I thocht I'd gi'e them a bit steep in hot water. I was just tryin' to pluck up strength to take the kettle offen he fire when the sireen blew, so I said, Ach to hell, I'll wash them the morn!"

"Ay, if ye're still alive to tell the tale," the woman in the corner said dolorously.

"Ach you!" Dirty Minnie laughed. "Ye're aye lookin' for snaw afore it comes on! Here, tak' a wee sup o' stout. That'll cheer ye up a bit."

She peered over her enormous bust and fished in her message-bag, taking out two bottles of stout and a crumpled five of Woodbines. "This is a' I had time to bring wi' me," she said. "I just planked them in ma bag, put ma shawl ower ma head and dived doon the stair."

"Like a paper ship in full sail!" laughed Mrs. Ryan. "I met her in the entry, breezin' along. At first I thocht it was a bomb, then I saw it was Minnie. She seemed a' bust and a' belly!"

"Ye're jealous!" Minnie grinned and uncorked one of the bottles. "Ye're that wee and skinny, folk would never tak' ye for onythin' else but yer auld man's pipe-cleaner!"

"Mind and no' spill that stout on ma clean boards," the woman in the corner said sharply. "I scrubbed them a' wi' lysol this mornin', and I'm no' wantin' them a' mucked up."

"Tae hell wi' you and yer auld boards!" said Minnie cheerfully. "Ye'd think this shelter was a palace the way ye're aye scrubbin' and cleanin' at it. Shakin' oot the rugs every day and airin' the mattresses. It's a wonder ye dinnie bother to put fresh floo'ers in the jamjar!"

"Ay, it's easy seen that ye have nothin' better to dae, Mrs. Milligan," said Mrs. Ryan, reaching out for the cup of stout that Minnie handed to her. "If ye had twa or three bairns ye wouldnie bother aboot cleanin' oot the shelter."

"Ay, or a lodger or twa!" Minnie held up her cracked cup and said, "Here's tae us a' and tae hell wi' Hitler!" before gulping down her stout.

Mrs. Milligan sniffed and said, "Well, yer lodgers dinnie seem to get that much o' yer attention, Minnie. Any time I see ye ye're either oot gallivantin' or hangin' oot the window."

"Och, ma lodgers dinnie mind," Minnie said. "They just tak' me the way I am!"

"Sailors don't care!" Mrs. Ryan said, taking the cigarette Minnie held out.

"Was that an airyplane I heard?" Mrs. Milligan cried, cocking her shrewish face to the side.

"No, it was just ma belly rumblin'!" Minnie laughed and struck a match. "Ye're aye hearin' airyplanes! Ye're like Joe, yin o' ma sailors; he's aye hearin' submarines!"

"Well, he'll no' hear many submarines at the docks doon at Hollisfield," Mrs. Milligan said sarcastically. "Dry land sailors! They've got a grand cushy job."

"They're no' dry-land sailors at a'," Minnie said. "They've got a right dangerous job playin' aboot wi' a' thae mines. It's a' their chance if they can get into a comfortable bed every second nicht."

"Ay, if it is a comfortable bed!" said Mrs. Milligan.

Minnie blew a mouthful of cigarette smoke toward the sandbags at the opening of the shelter, and putting her hands on her fat thighs she leaned forward. "Listen here, is it a fight ye're lookin' for? Because if it is I'll paste the lights oot o' ye!"

"I never said onythin' oot o' place, did I?" Mrs. Milligan began to look scared. It was all very well baiting Dirty Minnie, but when she got that threatening look on her face it was time to call a halt.

"Well, just you leave ma beds alone," Minnie said, relaxing again into her usual comfortable easy-oziness. "Ma sailors have nothin' against them. They're damned glad to come up to ma hoose every second nicht and get a decent sleep after the bunks they ha'e on that wee cramped boat.

"And I'm damned glad to ha'e them!" She laughed. "I dinnie ken what I'd dae wi'oot them. They keep me supplied wi' a' the tea and meat and fags and stuff that I want. I never need to ken that there's a war on."

"Ye're lucky," Mrs. Milligan said, glad to see that the danger signal was past. "I wish I could get some lodgers like them. I've had dozens in ma time, but never one that stayed longer than a week or twa. I'm sure I did ma best for them, cleanin' and seein' that their beds were comfortable and that they got their meals on time. But they never stopped for mair than a week or twa. They aye had some excuse. Ardingtown was ower far awa' frae the centre o' Glasco or somethin'. They didnie like the neebors or they had ower far to go to their work. Yon last yin I had, Mr. Veitch. My God, I'll never forget what he said. The impiddent brute. I was glad to get rid o' him. He said. 'The people here come from the slums and they're makin' Ardingtown back into a slum as quick as they can.' "

Dirty Minnie laughed and drank off her stout, but the rest of the women began to speak indignantly about the uppishness of the unlamented Mr. Veitch. They were still airing their views when the All Clear sounded. Minnie picked up her bag and stuffed the empty bottles into it. "Well, I'd better get awa' up and get ma lads' tea ready for them," she said, pushing her way out of the shelter. "Or they'll be here afore I can cough."

"Dae ye never think what would happen to ye if yer lodgers' boat got blown up by a mine?" Mrs. Ryan said as they went into the entry.

"Och ay, I often think aboot it," Minnie said. "But och to pot, what's the guid o' thinkin' aboot things like that. It just turns yer hair gray, and mine's gray enough already!"

She stood and spoke to Mrs. Ryan for a while, then she stopped outside her door to have a few words with Mrs. McIntosh. She had just got in and was putting on the kettle when the three sailors came in. "Ay there, Minnie the Moocher!" Joe cried, slapping her bottom as he passed her on his way to the sink. "She was a great big hoochy-coocher!"

"G'out ye nasty brute!" Minnie grinned.

George flung his sailor's hat onto a chair, put a parcel on the table and began to rake inside his blouse. "That's your steak, Minnie. And here's your fags. I had a terrible job gettin' them from the Old Man. He raised blue hell. He was playin' Nap and he didn't want to be bothered goin' to the safe for them."

"The lazy auld devil," Minnie said. "Hoo does he think folk are goin' to live if they dinnie get their fags?" She unwrapped the parcel and sniffed the meat. "This is real fine steak. Better than the stuff ye buy in the butcher's. I dinnie ken what I'd dae if it wasnie for you laddies."

"We don't know what we'd do without you, Minnie!" George laughed. "You give us a home from home!"

"Home was never like this!" Toots said, settling himself in a chair by the fire and stretching out his legs over the cinder-covered hearth. "What have you been doin' today, Minnie?"

"Just muckin' aboot," Minnie said, slapping the steak into the frying pan.

"You're tellin' us!" George said, looking around and winking at the others. "You lazy old devil, you! You've never even swept up the shavings that Joe made on Tuesday night when he mended the table."

"Och to pot!" Minnie said. "Sweep them up yersel' if ye're no' pleased." She gave the frying pan a shake before turning over the steak. "Here, Toots, if you're wantin' ony tea ye'd better set the table."

Immediately the three young men began to get in each other's way, laying cups and saucers and plates of different shapes and patterns on the soiled crumby tablecloth. They jostled each other good-naturedly on their way to and from the cupboard. Joe still wore his sailor's hat cocked over his forehead. George kept sticking his chewing gum onto his front teeth and sucking it off noisily.

"Oh, Minnie was a slave driver!" Toots sang, banging two plates together like cymbals. "But Minnie had a heart as big as a whale. . . ."

They put their arms around each others shoulders and tried to harmonize:

"As big as a whale!"

"AS BIG AS A WHALE!"

"Oh, Minnie was as dirty as a tanker, but she had a heart bigger than a banker!"

"G'out ye daft devils!" Minnie brought the frying pan over to the table. "Haud yer tongues and haud oot yer plates!"

"Gosh, but the Old Man was in a right rage the night," George said, chewing his first mouthful. "Him and the Chief and yon P.O. with the pawly arm were playin' Nap when I went in to get the cigarettes, and the Old Man didn't want to bother his backside gettin' them for me. You'll get them tomorrow, he says. Tomorrow, I says, but what good'll they be to me tomorrow? I want them today. Well, you can't get them today, he says. But we're supposed to get them today, I says. You know the rule. Twenty cigarettes, duty free, to each man every day. See? But the old mucker didn't want to bother his ass. What do you want them for anyway? he says. You don't smoke. I know I don't smoke, I says. But the rest of the boys do. I always give my share of cigarettes to them. Ask any of them and they'll tell you. Jesus, but he was in a flamin' row at havin' to leave his Nap and go to the safe for them. 'I'll watch you for this, George,' he says. The old bastard. I'll watch him. If he knew the things I could pin on him. Gettin' meat from the store and sellin' it. And sellin' cigarettes and tobacco on the pier. Our cigarettes and tobacco! The graft that goes on down at that base! The Old Man's only one that's makin' a pile. All those bloody P.O.'s are pilin' in money hands down. It's a great war for some of them. It would make you sick."

"Come on and finish yer steak afore it gets cauld," Minnie said kindly. "Dinnie bother aboot what happens doon at the docks."

"Well, I can't help it," George said. "It fair makes my blood boil. All that graft."

"Aw, why worry?" Joe said. "Maybe you won't have to worry about it much longer."

The sailors were silent. They chewed their meat, swilling it down with strong tea. None of them looked at Minnie. They scowled at the grease-spots on the tablecloth.

"Er—Minnie. . . ."

"Ay, Joe, what's wrong wi' ye noo?" Minnie leaned back and picked her teeth with a hairpin, sucking away the scraps of meat that the pin loosened.

"We're maybe goin' away," Joe said. "Got the news today. Word of the boat bein' shifted to another base. Maybe Aberdeen or Hull."

Minnie went on picking her teeth. Nobody looked at anybody else. "We don't want to go, Minnie," Toots said gloomily. "We're fine and comfortable here."

"Anybody want mair tea?" Minnie said, reaching for the pot.

"Ah well," Minnie said after a while. "If ye have to go we cannie help it. It's the way of the world. But ye're no' shifted yet. There's time enough to worry aboot snaw when it comes on."

She put the hairpin back in her greasy gray bun and rose from the table. "What aboot goin' to the picters? There's a guid yin in the Embassy. Gene Autry and Smiley Burnett. It should be guid."

"Okay," Joe said. "Maybe we're not goin' away at all, mind. Only there's word about it. We just thought we'd better tell you in time."

"Well, ye're no' awa' yet," Minnie said. "But it's high time we were gettin' awa' to the picters if we're goin' to get in. Come on, hurry and get yer skates on! We'll leave the dishes till the morn."

THE LIFE OF THE HUNTED

by WILLIAM FIFIELD

TOWARD EVENING A MAN, NOT QUITE YOUNG, HAIR BEGINNING to gray at the temples, stepped out from behind a Norway spruce that lifted its dark plume skyward from amid the autumn scarlet of the sugar maples, sighted briefly down the cold blue of his gun barrel at a patch of russet framed by bright sassafras leaves, and pulled the trigger. At the report the girl started and looked up from her wood chopping. She turned around and gazed a moment up the hill slope, tawny and vivid with turning colors through which ran the darker markings of the spruce and pine.

The buck, at the shot, sprang with folded forelegs through the growth of sassafras and, his eyes flecking with little lights of fear, crashed down the bank. He crossed a clearing where a solitary aspen trembled, and the hunter, who had quietly held him in the sights all the way, pressed the trigger again.

The girl, a quarter of a mile below, lifted her head. She drove the hatchet into the block and stopped to listen.

The buck, driven frantic by the shattering noise and the accompanying man-smell that came from up the hill, plunged on down toward the area he was careful never to approach till nightfall, when sometimes he would slip in to nibble at the greens that grew out behind the little cabin. Now he breasted his way through the blackberry thicket and out onto open ground. "Oh!" cried the girl from less than a dozen yards away. The buck shied, wide-eyed, and without an instant's pause bounded off laterally into the woods again.

A little later the hunter emerged. He pushed aside the last of the blackberry brambles, thrust through the spiny hawthorn limbs, gun held up before his face, and came out into the clearing. He was surprised to see the slatternly cabin with the bare slab lean-to built off one side and the few fruit trees dangling their small bitter apples. He looked quickly to right and left in search of his quarry, and in doing so saw the girl.

"Hello . . ." he said. "Which way did he go?"

Mutely, the girl pointed.

"That way? Thanks, I'll—" He started off.

"He's gone now," the girl said.

He stopped and then grinned ruefully. "Yes, I suppose you're right." He came back a few steps and stood with the gun held at the end of one arm. With his free hand he reached up and pushed back the billed hunting cap, wiping the perspiration from his forehead. "Well, it's my own fault. I had two perfect shots."

"He'll go up the gully and across to Wrightwood Glenn," the girl said softly. The hunter looked at her more closely. In spite of the cold wind that belied the brightness of the late afternoon sun, she wore nothing but a short-sleeved gingham dress. It was checked in white and blue, and as he looked he saw that there was a rip down near the hem. Her yellow hair blew in the wind and the color bloomed in her fresh round face. He thought she was about sixteen.

"Are you sure he'll go that way?" he asked, smiling at the seriousness of the sweet young face.

"I think he will," she said. "I've watched them."

"What did you say the place was called?" the hunter asked.

"Wrightwood Glenn."

"Can you tell me how to get there?"

She nodded. "You go up the back road . . . that's the one that turns off to the right in about half a mile. And you follow that till you come to a big oak with a Listerine sign on it. Just past that there's a path that goes into the woods. It takes you into a little gully and on the other side of that you—" She went on a few minutes longer.

The hunter listened until she was finished, then grinned and shook his head. "You've lost me completely," he said. "I'm afraid I'm still back by that oak tree with the Listerine sign. I'm not even too sure how I got there." He looked up, the crow's-feet deepening as his eyes crinkled friendlily. "I know it's a lot to ask," he said, "but could you come along and show me? We'd be able to go most of the way in the car."

"Oh, no, I—" She drew back a step.

"I did want a deer," the hunter said. "I'm going back this evening and it's my last chance. I don't know if you'll understand this," he said thoughtfully, "but there's a young woman who'll say 'I told you so' if I come in empty-handed. She'll say it as only she can. . . . And I'd rather not have that happen." He was silent then, and for the moment seemed quite tired.

The young girl gazed at him with wide-open blue eyes. His face was creased with long lines and there was a close-cropped mustache on his upper lip. Just now he bent forward to light his pipe, and he looked up at her over the glow almost wistfully.

She hesitated a little longer, then said softly, "I don't know what you mean, but I'll go with you if you want me to."

As they walked down the hill to where the car was parked, she kept a little way away. She looked neither to right nor left. When they got into the car she wedged herself into the corner by the door. She gazed straight ahead.

"Warm enough?" the hunter asked when they'd started and the breeze came up.

She nodded but did not look at him. A soft flush colored her cheeks. The gingham skirt had slipped up over her bare knees and quickly she replaced it.

"Do many hunters get up into this area?" the hunter asked at length.

She shook her head.

They rode a little longer.

"You haven't told me your name," he said, taking the pipe from his mouth and turning to her.

"Laurie," she answered, not looking around. She did not ask him his.

He smiled slightly at this—his girls never asked. Though for a different reason. It was because they didn't need to. They always knew what it was . . . and just how many dollars it represented. And so they brushed back their sleek blond hair, or sleek dark hair, and said, "Oh, but of course I recognized Mr.—"

And they tilted their heads and smiled in a way that said, "Heavens, who wouldn't?" and slipped a slim hand through his arm and let their long lacquered nails pluck lightly at the stuff of his jacket as they chattered predatorily up into his face. . . . The current one was Jane. Jane—who, having read Dun & Bradstreet, had come clear up the Sound in August to hunt him down. The pity was he fell for it each time now—when they told him how marvelous he was. Perhaps now that forty was behind him he'd be more and more ready to believe that sort of thing. . . . He shook his head.

They turned into the back road and mounted into the hills. As they climbed higher it grew colder. In the places where the sun hadn't reached, frost still clung to the cobwebs that stretched from twig to twig or between blades of grass. At the marsh there was skin ice around the brown stems of the cattails. Then the road plunged between two barriers of hazel hedge and the cold rose chillingly in the tunnel of shadow.

"No, that way—" Laurie said suddenly, pointing to the left. There was a fork in the road and he'd taken the wrong turn. "This goes to the McCullough farm. The other one goes up the hill."

He stopped the sleek, expensive car and backed it, then swung its nose into the other fork. "I'm glad I didn't try to follow your directions," he grinned. "You know you neglected to tell me about this fork. . . ." He turned and looked at her, his crinkled gray eyes chiding her good-humoredly. Her shyness of him melted a little and she smiled.

"Is that the oak?" he asked a moment later. The twisted tree lifted leafless branches, and there was a sign nailed to the trunk. Laurie nodded. As they came nearer, the hunter could make out a few words of the faded Listerine ad on the split, weathered surface.

"You'd better stop now," Laurie said. "The path is right up there."

Laurie went ahead when they started in along the path. She walked swiftly, and the hunter following behind had to lengthen his stride to keep up with her. They went through a dip padded with pine needles and then up the hard shell-clay bank on the other side. Laurie, barelegged, her feet in soiled saddle shoes, trod lightly. She paused only when there were branches across the path. Then she held them back until the hunter arrived, so as not to switch him with them.

They came to a little meadow where the gentians bloomed. There was a three-strand barbed-wire fence. The hunter set his gun against the post and held out his arms to indicate he'd lift her over, but she backed away. Wide eyes on him, she shook her head. She was afraid. And before he could say anything, she bobbed swiftly under the bottom strand like some startled little animal and, in the gentians, stood waiting for him to come.

The sweat was breaking out on his brow by the time they reached the crest of the rise beyond the meadow. Laurie stopped ahead on the path and looked back over her shoulder to see if he was following. At his woebegone expression a smile touched her lips. "It isn't far now," she said. "Well, I can't say I'm sorry to hear that," he answered with his rueful grin.

A moment later she signaled him and they took a narrow trail that branched off from the path. She stopped and pointed. Black pellets of deer droppings dotted the ground.

They went a little farther, and then she waited for him and touched his arm. "Do you see that?" she whispered. The hunter looked, and there at the edge of a grove of cottonwoods that flickered golden leaves in the descending sunlight was a young hickory. The trunk was barkless from an inch or so above the ground to where the first limb branched out. The wood was gouged and deeply torn. The scars were old and partially healed. They had browned over from the weather. "That's where one of them scraped the velvet off his horns last spring," Laurie told him softly. "We're almost there."

And as though the barked hickory were a marker on some private itinerary of her own, she left the game trail and entered the untracked woods. She slipped along so soundlessly that the hunter laboring behind was chagrined at his awkwardness. He'd thought himself skillful in the woods, but now the dry branches seemed simply to appear under his feet, where they'd snap with a sharp sound. Where the girl walked there were none. She moved swiftly, now and then turning her hips or her shoulders, through the thick-growing tangle—and every minute she had to stop and wait till he came up.

Suddenly she pulled him down beside her in a pocket of shadow. Out across swaying heads of goldenrod they looked into a little clearing, bluish as the twilight fell. They crouched side by side, and in her intentness she forgot to remove her hand from his arm.

A buck moved out into the clearing, emerging as though out of vapor in the blue light. The hunter thumbed the safety of his gun, and at the faint metallic click Laurie pressed his arm and shook her head. "Wait," she whispered. He glanced at her, but she was gazing out into the clearing, a faint smile on her lips. Her young breast, under the gingham, stirred with her light breathing.

"There's the other one," she said softly to herself, as though she'd been expecting it. A second buck had appeared.

The two animals moved deliberately, heads lifted high over white-ruffed breasts. The hunter counted their points, making his selection. His hand slipped along the cold stock of his gun. He'd left it off the safety. Well, he'd have his deer now . . . and at least Jane wouldn't be able to impale him with her cool green eyes and say, "But darling, I *told* you. You really must try to remember, angel, that you're not a boy any longer."—in that mocking way of hers that somehow was the way she humbled and held him. Yes, he'd have his deer . . . and Jane would be silenced. But the girl's hand was lying lightly on his arm and he did not lift the gun.

Suddenly he realized that soft pairs of eyes looked out from the shifting, collecting shadows at the far side of the clearing. A brown shape moved, and for an instant was dappled with light as the branches blew above.

"The does have come to watch," the girl beside him whispered. "Now the bucks will show off." She smiled up at him quickly, shyly—and her expression was that of a child who wants to please. The hand that had held the gun stock lifted and closed over her fingers as they rested on his arm. She started, but the quiet gray eyes reassured her and she smiled.

The bucks approached one another on delicate legs, small feet lifting mincingly in the high grass. They constantly made ducking movements with their heads, now eyeing, now sniffing one another. Their long ears turned alertly, nervously apprehending every sound. The does watched, gathered in a pool of shadow in which the individual bodies were indistinct.

Then the larger of the bucks lowered his head and, nostrils dilating, cut a furrow in the ground with one sharp hoof. The other head dropped too, and instantly, without preliminary fencing, there was a gathering of haunches and a grinding crash. Antlers locked, the bucks strove up and down the clearing, the one advancing as the other retreated, then the reverse. The two forms battled unreally in the blue descent of twilight. But for the snorting and constant grinding, there was very little sound. Then they crashed into a block of bramble, and the smash was startling.

The smaller buck broke free. With quick movements that might have been mistaken for dancing, he bounded now to the right now to the left as though propelled on springs . . . then he sprang forward and with the dry crash the antlers joined again. The two beasts, head locked in a bowed, taut *V* beneath their thrusting shoulders, crossed and recrossed the spectral amphitheater. The does stood silent. The sentinel trees were encased in shadow as the darkness rose from the ground.

Suddenly all movement stopped. The bucks were as still as the hovering does or the rooted trees. With a quick, flirting motion they disengaged their antlers. Both heads went up, nostrils dilating, ears pointing across the clearing toward the spot where Laurie and the hunter knelt. For an instant the tableau held—the trees, the dying lights, the grouped mild does, the bucks poised on the point of flight. Then, with a sudden crashing that brought the hunter's gun halfway to the shoulder, the scene disintegrated. Nothing remained but the circle of trees and the trampled arena, which was now nearly dark.

Laurie and the hunter rose and walked into the clearing. Their hands were joined. Silently they stood and looked around them. Then she turned a troubled face up to his.

"The wind changed," she said. Then "I'm sorry."

"Sorry? Why are you sorry?"

The blue eyes darkened. "Will the lady say 'I told you so' now?"

The hunter's gray eyes crinkled as he looked down at her. "I don't know," he said. He stood musing a moment, looking as though with amusement at something far off. "Perhaps it doesn't matter very much after all," he said—and smiled down at her again.

THE GIRLS OF TONGATABU

by JOHN LANGDON

"THE GIRLS DRAG YOU INTO THE BUSHES HERE," SWEDE, THE four-to-eight oiler, said. "And they don't wear any clothes either, back in the hills."

"Yeah? Who told you?" Samish, the scullion, pushed his way into the group at the rail. His pasty-white face like a toy bull-dog's was thrust forward and his small, glassy-green eyes glared fiercely. Some of the guys turned away.

Swede balanced over the rail staring at the group of white, two-story houses with red tile roofs, standing stiffly among the tall coconut palms.

"Who told me!" he said. "Listen to 'im, willya! Why any-body who's been goin' to sea at all knows them things, chum. They don't have to be told. The Queen of the island's a Univer-sity of California graduate and she weighs three hundred and fifty pounds!"

"Here comes the first bumboat," the third cook, George, said. He pointed with an arm tattooed down to the knuckles in the direction of the two destroyer escorts near the shore.

"Bumboats?" the engine-room cadet said. "What's that?"

George looked at him. His small black eyes under heavy brows twinkled and a wad of snuff under his upper lip pulled it back against his yellow teeth when he smiled.

"Don't know what bumboats are, kid?" He shook his head. "They're natives. They come out to bum and trade with you. This one's lucky. He's been making those two cans, drummin' a little business on the Q.T. He'll be the only one for an hour. Guess we're the first freighter here in a long time."

The native in the outrigger was speeding toward them, send-ing the craft swiftly and lightly over the water with powerful strokes of his double-bladed paddle. A small boy kneeled in front.

Samish grunted and left the group. DuShane, the deck-hand delegate, looked around, a wide grin on his imp-like face.

"There he goes," he said. "The bastard. Knows all about it now. Gonna tell everyone from the skipper on down, just what's what."

"That ignorant hillbilly gives me a gut ache," Swede said. "Why the hell don't he stick to potato farming? It's those kinda guys that louse up these ships."

"Oh, you got him all wrong," George said seriously, his black brows drawing together. "He's had Maritime School training. Three months of it. Why, he's even got a ticket with 'Steward's Mate—Fourth Class' written on it. And a uniform too, by God. Good man." He shook his head. "Washes a plate cleaner'n a Junior Third Mate's uniform—" He broke off, staring down at the clear, blue-green water. "Bet there's some good fishing here."

"Lotta tuna," DuShane said, pointing to the long shadow that slid through the water as Samish came back, dragging along two of the armed guard crew and a messman. "They're pretty good fishing."

"Who wants to fish?" Samish said, pushing his way to the rail. "Who wants to fish with all them girls ashore?"

George's eyebrows arched. "Ashore? How do you know you're goin' ashore?"

"Who's gonna stop us?"

"Why, the Limies, kid," George said, scowling darkly. "They own the goddamn island. Might just decide they don't want us on it. You can't never tell how they'll act." He winked at Swede who grinned at DuShane over Samish's back.

The outrigger slid in against the hull and came to a stop, the native balancing the motion with his paddle. He looked up grinning, yellow stubs of teeth startling behind lips stained a purplish-red.

"Tapa? Nice tapa?" He unfolded a tapa cloth in crude native design. Samish leaned out.

"How much?"

The native held up four fingers. "Fou' dolla'."

"Four dollars!" Samish shouted. "For that piece 'a cloth! You're crazy!"

"It ain't cloth, kid. It's bark," George said. "Inside bark that's been pounded under water."

"I don't care what it is! Four dollars! I wouldn't give more'n one for it—"

"Take it easy—he'll hear you."

"I don't give a damn!"

"I do. I want it. And I'm gonna get it too—for nothing."

"For nothing!" Samish stuck his pug face toward George, his eyes narrowing belligerently. "How you figure? The coon ain't that dumb."

Several guys looked around quickly, uneasily. But none of the colored crew members were present.

"Just stick around and watch, kid." George winked at Swede and DuShane and leaned over the rail. "Hey, Joe!"

The native looked up, grinning and blinking. "Hello, Joe," he said. Swede and DuShane laughed. George grinned.

"Okay. You got me with that comeback, Joe." He studied the native a moment. "Joe," he said. "How about one shirt for two tapas?"

The man leaned forward and spoke to the boy. After a brief discussion, he turned to George.

"No. One shirt—one tapa."

"One shirt—*two* tapa."

The native shook his head. The boy said something and he twisted around. Along the far hook of the island, brown dots were visible on the blue-green water, three or four rusty-red sails among them.

"Now we got 'im," George said. "Competition." He watched the boy and the man whispering. "Well, Joe? One shirt—two tapa?"

The native looked up. "White shirt?" he asked hopefully.

"Blue shirt. Like this—" George pulled out the front of his own shirt. The native shook his head.

"One shirt—one tapa." There was a note of finality in his voice.

"Now comes the dirty work," DuShane said. Swede nodded. Samish breathed heavily, mouth open. His little green eyes kept looking from one to the other. George started.

"Joe," he said softly. "One towel—one *white* towel—one tapa?"

Swede said, "The Steward better lock up the linen right now."

The native held up two fingers. "Two towel—one tapa."

"Two small towel?"

"Two big towel."

"No. One big towel—" George spread his arms, "—one tapa."

The native hesitated, glancing anxiously toward the boats. "Let's see?"

"Okay." George left. He returned with two face and two bath towels. They were lowered to the native who examined them carefully. They finally settled for two tapas, the first and a smaller one, a grass bag beaded with shells, and four coconuts.

"Didn't cost a dime, either," George said, handing them around.

When they learned they weren't going ashore, the crew knocked off work for the day. By the time the boats arrived, they were strung along the sides in little groups. The ship's sheets, towels, and pillowcases and the crew's soap, cigarettes, cigars, socks, and undershirts went over the side. By late afternoon it looked like a carnival with tapas, hula-skirts, grass bags, beaded baskets, and other trinkets hanging over the rails and decorating the deck cargo. One sailboat with a fat young woman who giggled and smiled continually, did a rushing business. Samish went from group to group, telling about the girls, the Queen, and how theirs was the first ship here in six months, until nobody would pay any attention to him.

From back aft someone started shouting, "*Hula-hula!*" at the young fat woman. It was Andy, an armed guard. Every few seconds his raucous, "*Hula-hula!*" echoed.

The first few times it was funny. But he kept it up too long. From different parts of the ship came cries, "Lay off, moron!"

"Change records!" "Quiet, you farmer!" A couple of guys started back aft.

The other armed guards, sensing trouble, tried to quiet Andy who could be heard complaining, "But I wanna see her hula! I ain't never see a hula. . . ." Samish had gone back that way. An armed guard spotted him.

"Hey, Samish! Where them girls you was talking about?"

Samish waved a hand. "Up there, I guess. Waitin' for us."

"Well, they ain't doin' us no good up there," Andy said.

"Why don't you ask him?" another guard said, pointing to the boat below. Andy's dull eyes brightened. He licked his lips.

"Hey, Joe!" he called. "Got any girls? Young ones?"

The native in charge of the boat with the fat woman in it grinned and nodded.

"Well, why didn't you bring 'em?"

The native looked puzzled. He watched the row of faces. The engine-room cadet said, "Hey, fellas! Let's quit trading till they bring the girls!"

The idea caught on. "That's the ticket, kid!" "No girls, no trade!" The rest of the crew took it up. They stamped and yelled, "Girls! Girls!" "No girls—no trade!" until the natives, puzzled, drew their boats together. After a hurried conference, the native in charge of the boat with the fat woman stood up.

"What want?"

"Girls, Joe!" The chorus descended on him.

"Girls all there." He pointed to the far hook of the island.

"We know that, Joe! No girls—no trade! Catch, Joe?"

"Okay. Okay." Joe's head bobbed. "Me catch. We bring."

"Attaboy, Joe!" "Young ones, Joe!" "Yeah! No old bags!"

"Me know!" There was a flash of gold teeth. Another hurried discussion, two sailboats were emptied and dispatched and Joe looked up, grinning hopefully. "Trade now?"

"No soap, Joe!" "Girls first, Joe!" Joe's face fell. He tried another tack.

"Come ashore?" he inquired. "Plenty girl—"

"No can do, Joe!" "Next trip, Joe!"

It grew dark. The two boats returned. Flashlights were brought out and played on the empty boats.

"What's'matter, Joe? Where are the girls?"

Joe shook his head, blinking at the light. "Queen say no."

"Queen?" Andy said. "What queen?"

"The Queen of the island, you fathead."

"What the hell kind of a queen is she?" Andy wanted to know.

"A damn smart one," Samish said. "She's gone to a college in California and she weighs three hundred and fifty pounds."

"I don't care what she weighs!" Andy said. "Why no girls?"

Joe spread his hands. "Queen say no. She say, 'Come ashore. Plenty girl. Plenty drink. But no go to ship—' she say."

"*Goddamit!*"

"I hope the Japs take the damn island!"

The crew began turning in; the boats drifted away.

In the morning they were back. Joe and the fat woman had brought a girl who couudn't have been a day over fifteen. She wore a sarong from her sharp-pointed little breasts to her knees. The crew started calling her "Suzy."

Suzy was a born show girl. Smiling, throwing kisses, she made suggestive invitations with her body and did lewd dances to the armed guards' portable phonograph. Her English was pert and bawdy, and she was showered with presents—soap, candy, cigarettes. Samish gave her two bright-colored neckties. Suzy gave him an especially ecstatic wriggle, threw out her arms and invited him ashore. His creased face glowed.

In the afternoon, Suzy went for a swim. Immediately several guys stripped to their shorts and dove in. Suzy let them grab her before kicking and squirming free. Those who couldn't dive or swim well watched enviously.

At sundown the ship pulled out. A small crowd stood on the fantail until they could no longer see the brown dot of the boat.

That evening Samish lay in his bunk. His lined, pushed-in face now and then broke into a smile. He reached for a pencil and paper.

Dear Oscar—he wrote. *So you told me I was crazy to go to sea but wait till I tell you what happens to us on a little island—*

He looked up frowning. "How'n hell you spell that place?"

The other messman looked on the map. He was a long time finding the island.

—called Tongatabu. Samish grunted he he printed the letters. *The girls there just about pull you into the bushes and they are young and pretty too and not old hags like you see in pitchers and they all but drag us into the bushes and give us food and likker and make over us like we was kings or something wanting to do our washing and everything and we sure had a hard time getting away from them. The queen of the island went to a college in Calif. and talks good english but is she big and how—three hundred and fifty pounds and she lets the girls all go around nakkid and do what they like even if it is a Limey island. But it is late now and I am tired from two days of nothing but you know what and so I will write more later. Your brother Nathaniel.*

He folded the letter, addressed an envelope and put them away in his Bible. He lay back staring dreamily at the bunk above, smiling.

THE OLD DOG

by DONALD VINING

FROM TIME TO TIME, WHEN THE ROAD WAS STRAIGHT AWAY, Brad Turner glanced at the old red dog beside him on the front seat of the car. Benny had thrust his nose out the window into the breeze and his silky ears blew back along his head and neck. It was just like all the other times, the other years. But no, it wasn't. Benny was as thrilled as ever at the wild flame color of the autumn hills, at the hunting jacket his master wore, at the presence of the gun in the back seat, but somehow he seemed too weary to express all the joy he felt. The wind in his face made Benny's eyes water more than usual; that stiff and paralyzed rear left leg made it harder than ever for him to balance himself around curves, and while there were occasional joyous barks as of old, they were interspersed with an almost steady flow of those half-whine, half-growl noises that Benny made of late, as though he were holding protracted conversations with invisible tormentors. It was these senile mumblings which had disturbed Brad's wife and had forced Brad to exile Benny from the house nights and make a reluctant kennel dog of him after all those years. No, there was nothing for it but to admit that Benny was an old dog. After all, he was going on fifteen.

Fifteen years. That was a long time for a man and a dog to be together. This was the first hunting season in Brad's memory to which he had not looked forward.

For the past year Lucille had been at him. "Brad, I don't see why, when you claim you love the dog so much, you don't put him out of his misery at once. He's almost blind, he's partly paralyzed, he imagines he sees and hears things, and makes a lot of noise over nothing—"

"I know, I know," Brad would protest, "but he gets a lot of

fun out of life yet. You don't dispose of people when they get broken down and fanciful."

"People and dogs are different. We're more humane toward animals," Lucille would answer in disgust.

The argument went on and on. Brad came to dread every indication Benny gave of his failing faculties for it always brought up the subject of getting rid of him. The old dog, in the midst of perfect silence, would dart up from his rug and rush barking to the door to chase some imaginary intruder from the deserted front porch. Or he'd suddenly yelp and cower as though someone were beating him. It was a painful sight for Brad in any case, remembering as he did the days when Benny won annual ribbons in the Blairton dog show, but it was all the more painful because of the unpleasant discussions it brought up.

"A veterinarian could do it so quickly and easily, and it wouldn't cost much," Lucille would say for the fiftieth time.

"Hang the cost, if I thought it were the thing to do. But I won't have it that way," Brad said, stubbornly.

Benny had always been such an active, vital dog, especially in the hunting field, that death by needle seemed completely inappropriate. Then one day Brad had remembered an incident of one of his early hunting trips. He, Jerry, Doug, and some others had had their dogs in the field and one badly trained dog failed to hold for the scent, leaping just as Jerry shot. He had fallen among the browning field grasses without a cry. Jerry had been upset, of course, but somehow it had always struck Brad as the right kind of death for a dog, death in action. When that memory came back to Brad, he had a good answer ready for Lucille the next time the question came up.

"Next fall," he said, "I'll do it myself. In the fields, where Benny's happiest."

Now autumn was here and today was the day. Brad turned the car off the highway into the dirt road that led up and over the hills to where rabbits, pheasants, and quail were unfailingly to be found. In the senuous pleasure of breathing in the woody air, Brad's mind strayed for a while from its preoccupation with Benny. Benny, too, gave up his half-articulate noises and devoted himself to delight at homecoming.

Brad found a stretch of fields and woods which he knew of old and which he seemed to have to himself so far. Only as he opened the door of the car for Benny to get out did the business of the day flash back into his mind. Benny forgetfully jumped with abandon, but yelped as he landed painfully. He quickly recovered and ran about sniffing the ground and the withering weeds. Brad got his gun from the back seat and loaded it sadly.

There would be no real hunting today. Benny could not really do his job any more. The devils in his old mind and body were riding him too hard for him to be able to concentrate. No, no hunting today. Today was for Benny. They would roam the fields together as they had done for so many years, and then when the moment came—Brad would have no stomach for hunting after that. He locked the car and with the pathetically eager dog he waded knee-deep into the fields.

In his first joy Benny bobbed here and there, his plumy tail sometimes the only indication of his whereabouts, while at other times his head and floppy ears bobbed up on a leap over a run of brambled creeper or a fallen tree or fence post. Brad tried to let the autumn scene and smell flow over and drown his mind so that he should not think of Benny. But the trees lost their color, the air its snap, as he thought of what he must do. He watched Benny's rheumatic cavorting and thought back to the days when he was the supplest, quickest, most sensitive and best coordinated dog in the field. He remembered Benny's actual look of disdain at the body of the dog which had leapt in the way of Jerry's shot. And this poor wretch was also Benny. Brad remembered how in his childhood he had shed many secret tears over the sudden and early death of various pets; he knew now that that was much easier to bear than standing by and seeing the processes of age and decay.

Benny came running back to him, looking up with those nearly useless eyes. He wagged his tail and whined impatiently in a way that sounded to his master very much as though he himself were angry that his old body was not as it used to be. Brad felt the stock of his gun. It was good that he kept his marksmanship up to scratch between seasons by shooting clay pigeons. He'd not want to bungle the job. But no, he knew that he could make it clean and quick.

Across the fields rang the yelp of dogs. Brad stopped in the act of climbing a zigzag fence under which Benny was squeezing. Yes, there on the far side of the field plaid coats and gleaming barrels told of the approach of other hunters. The spots of their hounds showed now and then as they galloped through the fields. The dogs' vigor made a heartbreaking contrast with Benny's already weary gait. If anything they were a little too energetic and uncontrolled. Not fully trained, perhaps.

"Hello there," came the call from the approaching hunters. "Any luck?"

"Just out," Brad replied.

"Same with us."

The young dogs barked loudly at meeting Benny. They all sniffed each other and Benny stuck his neck out as though he were straining to see the newcomers with his dim eyes. The younger dogs seemed to toss their muzzles in the air patronizingly as they completed their inspection of Benny.

"Sort of an old dog you've got there, isn't it?" one of the hunters asked Brad.

"Yes, I'm afraid his hunting days are done. But I wanted him to die in the fields," Brad said, rather sharply lest the tightness in his throat betray his feelings.

"Oh," the others said, in chorus, and they looked at Benny in silence. He wagged his tail.

"Well—" the men said, somehow embarrassed, and gesturing their farewells, they moved on, their dogs doing a whirling dervish all over the fields, circling about and about. Benny started to amble lamely after them. Suddenly he stiffened and stopped. His tail stood motionless, only the plumes of soft fur moving in the breeze, and one front paw was held off the ground.

So ghosts were bedeviling Benny again. The younger dogs had romped right by the spot where Benny was now pointing and had picked up no scent. But now Benny thought. . . . This was the moment. Benny had almost some of his old beauty as he stood there, tense and ready. His old body was in ecstasy with the fantasy that he was pointing game for Brad. Swallowing hard, Brad took off the safety catch and put the gun to his shoulder.

Under his breath he murmured, "Good-by, Benny. I love you, old boy."

The shot sounded to Brad like the cracking of the world. Benny fell without a whimper. Up from the grass before him flew a covey of quail.

THE GREEN PALMS

by ROBERT PAYNE

THE AIR STEAMED UP FROM THE MUDBANKS AND THE JUNGLE, and far across the bay the red coastal oiler was waiting beside the palms. The palms hung there at the end of the jetty, listless, no leaves turning in the faint wind from the Sulu Sea, no breakers falling on the shore, the sea as smooth as blue silk, the harsh line of the horizon turning to black; and above that black harsh line, the sky was the same color as the sea. All morning, and every morning, there was the same changeless air of desolation on the shore. Sometimes a puff of smoke would come from the oiler, sometimes a Malay in a striped sarong would make his way along the road beside the glistening pipe line, tapping it with a steel hammer, and the sound, communicated along the whole length of the line, stirred the parakeets in the forests and the dazzling hothouse birds that screamed in the green silence of the place. A long winding road had been cut through the forest to the oil wells, where the varnished and continually re-painted derricks rose above the tallest trees; there were bungalows, frail patches of vegetables, stunted mangroves, coolie lines near the shore; and then there was the strip of red land forming a jetty, the palms and the coastal oiler.

The oppressive stillness of the morning, the faint powdery plumes from the oiler, and the tapping of the steel hammer seemed to be in some kind of harmony; impossible to imagine one without the other. But if you closed your eyes, overcome by the heat or by the shining of the immense sea, the thing that was impressed upon your retina was the clump of green palms. On Balik Tamang, the palms were a landmark. Sailors looked from the crows-nest for that long half-mile jetty and the ridiculous tall palm trees that shot up straight from the red sandy soil, the leaves glistening, brighter than the green of the forest.

Actually, the palm trees were dying, and the brightness of the green leaves came from the salt on them. These palm trees bore no fruit; they had been left standing when the mangroves and the forest near the shore had been cut down. No one knew why.

Dunhill lay on the long raffia chair of his porch, nursing his blood-poisoned hand, now heavily bandaged; the hot throbbing poison moved along his arm, festering the glands under the armpit, a sullen, endless throbbing like the rhythm of the whole island. The tapping infuriated him. He heard his servants clip-clopping at the back of the house, and once his wife called to him, but he paid no attention to her. He felt surly, ill, ill at ease; he wished he could leave with the coastal oiler; the sea dazzled him, so that another kind of throbbing began to inflame his eyes; a four-weeks-old *Strait Times* lay in a crumpled ball at his feet. He was thirty-seven, his face licked red by the sun, yet underneath the redness he felt worn out, drained by the malarial exhalations of the place, with no fight left in him. Every morning he had gone by buggy to the oil well in the interior, every afternoon he had returned, sick with loathing of the smell of the yellow-green oil, the sight of the drills and the derricks, the thud of the steam engines in the clearing. His wife had come from Singapore the previous year, and somehow her presence had only made him feel a more savage hatred of the place, the endless moist days broken only by the October monsoon, on this island off the coast of Borneo. He heard ice tinkling in a glass, then a shadow loomed over him. He knew by the scent of her body that it was Estelle.

"The doctor's coming over soon, darling," she said. "He just phoned."

She looked down at the enormous bandaged hand; she could almost feel the swollen pain that was mounting to his shoulder.

"I didn't hear the phone," he said quietly, looking up at her. "He told me this morning he would come."

Watching her, seeing her bright red hair falling in clusters over her shoulders, the young body moving with incomparable ease within the white dress, he felt some of the pain leave him; he screwed up his mouth, and waited for her kiss. But it didn't come—she, too, was looking out to sea toward the green palms. He hated her for lying about the telephone.

"We'll get a better job soon," he said, drinking the whiskey she brought.

"When, darling?"

"Oh, soon—two or three months. I've written to Sandy. I'll go to the Singapore Harbor Board. They'll take me. The important thing, sweetheart, is to hang on."

He spoke in a soft English drawl, every word prolonged, the sentences ending in a dying fall so that she nearly always had to guess the last words. The heat came up from the stone floor. She wondered how long she should remain with him—hating the proximity of the bandaged arm, the man ten years older than herself, the sullen composure of his burning blue eyes. He looked as though he might die, and she did not care, really; it would be better, there would be a pension from the superannuation fund, she could return to California, it was absurd to have to come out here—why, why, why in this heat should she remain?

Yet she knew perfectly well why she remained. Habit, and security. There were servants; the Chinese cook, the Malay boys, the Filipinos and Malays working in the forest; the strange sense of desolate security on this island, where food was plentiful, because every fortnight crates would arrive from the Philippines. It was an American oil company—everything streamlined, clean, the insect powder always within reach, the refrigerator always filled to the brim. She had nothing to do, and she liked that; she always wanted to be in a position where she could spend her mornings in bed. She said, "I'm so worried. Does it hurt, darling?" and he turned his face away, because at that moment the hot pain sprang again along his inflamed arm.

Then the telephone rang. It was the doctor, Estelle told Dunhill. He had spent the morning at the oil well, and would be right out. Dunhill felt grateful to him, although he did not like the doctor. He was a youngster, hardly out of medical college, a little younger than Estelle, with a low forehead and greasy hair. He had a pleasant smile and imitated a comfortable bedside manner. In the clubhouse he was always the first to suggest a drink, the last to leave; there was a dash about him; he liked classical music; he fitted into no pattern. Once Dunhill had been to his bungalow. The whole place was filled with baseball pennants, yet every fortnight a great crate of new records arrived for him. "Must have a fortune," Dunhill thought, and then he noticed that his wife had left him and returned inside the bungalow.

He continued to stare across the shore until the doctor came, worrying vaguely over Estelle, conscious that he had not done his best by her, his mouth hard and embittered whenever he conjured her up in his mind. "I ought to give her a break—take her to Singapore—dances—not always dancing with the same partners." And he was glad at that moment when his attention was distracted by something running across the beaten mud outside his bungalow.

At first he could not distinguish it clearly. In this hot light it resembled a ball of tawny yellow fur. Then he saw that it was a chicken, and suddenly one of the natives leaped from the shadow of the bungalow and ran after it, waving a knife. It was the tall, beautifully formed native servant Dunhill had hired shortly after landing at Balik Tamang, hardly more than a boy, with dark eyes, black oiled hair wound in a bun, long silky eyelashes and bright red lips stained with bete juice. The boy wore a short sarong, and seemed always to move with a slow, sulking, gliding motion, like a girl, proud of his beauty and his strength. Now he was swifter than the chicken, running like a ballet dancer with long graceful strides, the golden-brown body shining against the dull blue sea. Seeing the upraised knife, the flexing muscles, the eagerness and determination on the handsome beardless face, Dunhill found himself caught up in a wonderful sense of admiration for the boy's youth; but the admiration changed imperceptibly to an inexplicable fear for the ungainly idiotic bird that stopped, ran in zigzags, cawed loudly, opening its little metallic beak for gulps of hot air, then turned and almost lost its balance, the feathers scraping the sand. He had never felt such pity for a bird before. Perhaps it was the steely splendor of the upraised knife, the utter determination of the youth, the heavy momentum of the boy's black shadow on the ground. Dunhill wanted to shout out, "Stop it! Let the bird alone! If you want to kill it, kill it behind the house!" He said nothing. He was horrified by a sense of impending grief. The Malay boy was already straddling the chicken which was exhausted now, fluttering gamely between his legs. It made one last hesitant dash for freedom, and then the boy threw himself on it, his body falling at full length. It was only then that Dunhill realized that the boy had been performing a kind of dance.

Dunhill left his chair and with his free hand gripped the wooden rail of the bungalow with all his strength, incapable of tearing his eyes away from the spectacle of the boy lying at full length on the earth, holding the chicken in one hand and the knife in the other, playing with the chicken, even speaking to it, and then drawing his head away and bringing up the knife. The knife swam into the sun. The chicken gave a final scream, and then the neck was cut, near the breast, slowly and dramatically, so that everything seemed to occur like a slow-motion film. Almost crazed by the spectacle, Dunhill wanted to shout, "Take it behind the house! I don't want to see it, do you hear! Take it away!"

He was too late. The blood was springing from the neck, and like a crab the head was moving in the sand. The boy held the chicken by the legs and turned it upside down to let the blood drain away. Dunhill could feel even at a distance of twenty yards the pitiful reflex actions of the chicken which even now, headless, was attempting to escape the boy's hands. When sufficient blood had been spilled, the boy pinched the wound together with his thumb and forefinger and carried the chicken to the back of the house. Along the whole coast there was only the Malay tapper, the palms, the coastal oiler, and the head of a chicken in the sand.

There were moments afterward when Dunhill thought that nothing had happened, the scene was a nightmare brought on by the throbbing in his arm, a mirage, or even a deliberate invention of his own perturbed mind. The heat trembled, thickened. Sometimes on the black rim of the horizon, he reminded himself, he had seen flowering islands. A faint stagnant wind blew over the sand, coming from the towering and mysterious green forest through which men had tunneled their threadlike road, with its metal pipe line already rotting—it was necessary to paint it three times a year, the strangest kind of green growths appeared on it, and there were rumors that a new concrete pipe line would be built. Snakelike, it wound from the shore to the heart of that green darkness within. He steadied himself, drank the iced whiskey which his wife had brought him, and closed his eyes.

When he opened them, the boy was beating the *gamelan* gong for dinner, and the doctor, wearing white starched shorts, a polo shirt, white stockings and white shoes, was gazing down at him.

"Oh, it's you, Alderton. The damned thing aches. I suppose you want to see it." The reverberations of the sweet-toned gong were still hanging in the air. "You'd better stay for dinner, Doc."

Alderton did not answer. He was busy swinging a thermometer in the air; the sun shining on the thermometer reminded Dunhill of the boy's knife.

"You'll have to rest up," Alderton was saying, in his sharp North American accents.

"How long?"

"Oh, a couple of weeks, maybe. We don't know half enough about blood changes in the tropics. A thing like that would be cured in a day on the Tropic of Capricorn."

He was slowly unwrapping the bandage. The thermometer lay under Dunhill's tongue. Dunhill felt the skin of his hand swelling and straining against the loosening bandage; somewhere in the center of his palm there was the faint prick he had received from a hanging liana on the road to the oil well. The skin was stretched, ballooning up, throbbing—he knew all this without looking at it. The doctor's dark oily hair was almost touching Dunhill's face. The furnace heat of the bay seemed to be growing every moment stronger, but perhaps this was only one more effect of the pain. There was lint on the hand, pale pink. When it had been removed, the doctor whistled under his breath.

"What's the matter, Doc?" Dunhill said. It was the voice of an appealing, terrified child.

"Oh, nothing. Not very healthy. How does it feel?"

"Damnable."

"You bathed it?"

"Yes, my wife bathed it."

The doctor held the inflamed, inflated hand as though he were carefully weighing it.

"Any sore spots?"

"What the hell's a sore spot?"

"Glands."

The word was like a shock: it was the first time that Dunhill had admitted to himself the swelling under the armpit.

"That's what I thought. The body's doing it's job—getting the poison out of the hand and into the arm." He added, "Anywhere else?"

"No."

"Any other symptoms?"

"No. Except that I've got a damned headache, and I'm sick and tired of looking at the coaster."

"Oh, she'll leave tonight."

The conversation became desultory. The doctor was wondering whether to lance the hand, inject sulfanilamide—it was the time before sulfanilamide powder—or to use a new preparation, resembling molasses, which had arrived by the coastal steamer. Dunhill had heavy rings around his eyes. He looked played out, breathed heavily, and did not always seem to understand what Alderton was saying. Watching Dunhill carefully, the doctor spoke about the club, the new Gramophone records of "*Don Giovanni*" which had just arrived, gossip from the oil well, the prospects of a Japanese invasion, speaking hurriedly and effortlessly. The wind blew lightly over the rustling pages of *The Tatler* on the couch, but it was a hot, unconsoling wind, drugged with the scent of summer flowers, spices, decaying vegetable matter.

"What are you going to do, Doc?" Dunhill said at last, feeling for his pipe with his left hand—the curse of the thing was that it was his right hand that was wounded. "A fortnight's a hell of a long time. It's getting on Estelle's nerves." He could hear Estelle moving about in the bedroom. God knows what women did all day in their bedrooms.

"I tell you what I would like you to do. Go to Singapore on the coaster tonight. It'll get you there in a week. Take Estelle. Give her a good time."

Dunhill awoke from the drugged pain, conscious that Estelle was standing on the veranda in a print frock, the faint wind pressing her clothes to her skin. She wore nothing underneath, and in this light the print cloth was almost transparent. She half stood, half leaned there, smiling at the doctor, fresh and gleaming, her face freckled with little yellow sunspots, and the tremendous red flame of her hair blotting out the whole bay. There were women who had that effect—their faces coming across rooms obliterated everything, absorbed and reformed everything; Dunhill saw only her face, the golden-red hair, the brown-gold, quick, steady eyes. And seeing her there, while the blood rushed and hammered into his face, he knew she had been unfaithful to him. There was nothing he could do. It had happened recently, at most a day or two before, perhaps only a few hours before. He did not care any more, but he knew he would care later, there would be times near heartbreak, the future contained moments when a terrible dark emptiness would fill his heart. He had no hatred for her, only a sharp distaste.

He said, "Hear what the doctor says, Estelle? Would you like to go to Singapore?"

"If you want to, darling."

The doctor was saying, "It's partly psychological. These things cure better with a change of air. I'll sign a chit for a three-weeks absence on medical grounds."

"What's the alternative, Alderton?"

"I don't know. Frankly, I don't know. We've had some of these things with the natives—they've got tremendous resistance, but you can never tell. There are four alternatives—a rest, or a lancing, or some of that newfangled sulfanilamide in injection, or the new stuff. Or all of them. You can take your choice, Dunhill."

"I'd prefer a lancing," Dunhill said.

The doctor was feeling the raised place under the armpits; the smell of sweat suddenly filled the air.

Alderton shook his head. "No, you'd better have some of that newfangled stuff. I've read reports about it. The French have been doing wonders with it. You're sure you're not going on the coaster tonight?"

"No."

"You might regret it."

"Oh hell, I've regretted so many things in my life."

The doctor filled the hypodermic syringe in the sunlight—once more there was the knife shining across the sun and said, "Well, thank God, the temperature's steady. Don't have any alcohol. Remember that. Keep warm at night, and don't get excited. The usual things." Then he bared the left unwounded arm, searched for the vein in the elbow hollow and dug the needle in. At that moment the hooter sounded. Somewhere in the green forests the workers were mopping their foreheads and beginning to return to their bungalows. It was two o'clock in the afternoon, and for the rest of the day they would be free under the burning sun to do as they pleased. The clubhouse would fill up. Some of the younger women would be cycling to meet their husbands, while others, uncomplaining, with lined red faces, would be sitting at their dinner tables, waiting. Estelle was holding in her hand an iced lemonade. He drank it, watched the doctor daubing iodine on the faint prick in his left arm. Now there was no movement in the huge bay, no plumes of smoke came from the coastal oiler, the stiff leaves of the palm hung listless in the midsummer air, and already he had forgotten the place in the sand where the chicken's head lay.

He felt relieved of all responsibilities now, the pain gone, the throbbing nearly over, his wife smiling, the doctor snapping the metal prongs of his bag. Dunhill said, "You know, I've got a curious feeling it will be better in a day or two. Estelle will look after me. It's a damned silly idea to go to Singapore just when the company is doing so well." He held out his left hand, but before the doctor took it, he said, "Look here, Dunhill, you've got to take very good care of yourself. I've told you before that we don't know what these things are. Ever seen a case of *kurap?* It's a disease of the skin which makes it scaly. Oh, I'm not trying to frighten you, but you've had that for a week now, it doesn't seem to change, and then, too, there's something in the water here which makes resistance weaker. Are you sure you wouldn't go to Singapore?"

"No. I'll be well again in two days."

He knew somehow that in the end he would get over it, as the natives got over it. It happened often, other Europeans had suffered from it, it aged them for a while, but they always recovered. Not a single oilman had died since Balid Tamang was opened three years ago. Not one, and he was determined not to die; then he looked up at Estelle, who was whispering to the doctor at the other end of the veranda, and though he knew they were talking about his hand, a wild uncontrollable anger seized him, the throbbing increased, and with the greatest effort he turned his face away from them.

Sometimes Estelle played the Gramophone—they were cheap dance records, and he could hear her long heels clicking the floor in tune with the music, sometimes absent-mindedly she turned on the radio; through the heady atmospherics you could sometimes hear news from Singapore, Delhi, even from San Francisco. Dinner was brief, unceremonious, neither speaking much. The long afternoon wore away, the light faded from the sea, and then there was only the darkness. As the coastal oiler pushed away from the jetty, its deck lights lit the green palm tree. Once or twice during the dark evening they heard the animals growling in the forest.

Sometimes Dunhill would turn accusing glances at his wife, remembering the sudden motiveless fear of the morning; but at such moments he would be overcome with tenderness, admiring the graceful American girl whose hair was like flame. Her cheeks were highly colored, almost russet, and there was something about her unusual complexion which always delighted him; there was a hidden fire there, the girl's body bursting with sensual life. He said, "The headache's going. Alderton's a damned monkey. We'll go to Singapore as soon as I hear from Sandy, but it's no use losing the superannuation money." He turned over the pages of a mail-order catalogue. He said, "It's time you had a new dress." He wanted to say, "I've never seen you look so fresh, so beautiful," but something held him back, the knife glittered on the table, a faint wind was scouring the sand and through the window there was only the immensely high lamp at the end of the jetty throwing a stark incandescent light on the palms. He turned away from the window. A messenger had brought some reports from the oil well. He found them on the sideboard, where Estelle had placed them, and began to turn over the pages listlessly. He said to himself, "It's strange. I saw it only for a moment." He wondered whether he should talk to her about it. There had been, for a brief moment, an expression, not of horror or contempt, but of guilt, of someone enjoying guilt, on her face. He was certain she had been unfaithful, more certain of this than of anything in his whole life. But where? With whom? Alderton? But she had said so often how she disliked him, with a pitying voice, not troubling to conceal her distaste for him. The air was growing clammy, bats were wheeling outside, as always there was the strange exhalation from the forest, as though every evening and night the forest expelled its evil odors; malignantly evacuating the diseased combinations of oxygen and leaf mold which had gathered during the day. He heard voices from the coolie lines. Sometimes he heard a gibbon screaming in the dark mangrove swamps. His headache was gone, but he noticed that one of the effects of blood poisoning seemed to be that everything glinted more brightly than ever—the knives, his wife's face, the gold hair in the light. He said quietly, "One of those damned natives went after a chicken this morning. I do think they ought to do their executions in the kitchen. He left the head just outside the veranda."

Estelle was knitting for one of the oilmen's wives. "Darling, how's the hand?"

"I wish you would listen to me. It was Ambo, the tall one. I don't want him to do this kind of thing. You know. I've always been squeamish—there's something about beheading a chicken which is much worse than beheading a man. They're so damned pitifully weak against a knife, and I just don't like it."

He thought he saw the color mounting to her face, she looked more beautiful than ever, the young heavy body sitting there in an attitude of complete contentment and assurance. She looked up at him and then dropped her gaze. "You mean the Malay?" she asked.

"No, he's a Dusun, really, but have it your own way. Tell him not to make the front of the veranda his execution porch."

She nodded, the faintest inclination of the head, and then the knitting was resumed. His hand was numb, no longer aching, and he could hear the Chinese making the bed. It would be difficult. He could hardly caress her with a great wad of bandages on his hand, but he wanted her now more than he had wanted her for many weeks; wanted her with a kind of pure vengeful insistence, with that sudden motiveless desire which sprang so readily in the tropics. The bookcase glittered, the white enameled fan went ceaselessly round, whirring gently, the knitting needles clicked. He said, "Come on, redhead, let's go to bed," and then she laid the knitting aside and walked to the bedroom.

Far away he heard the breakers roaring on the other side of the island, twenty miles away. A moon came up, shining through the white silk mosquito netting, and in this light the torrential gold hair looked like a smoldering fire and his wife's body lay very quiet beside him. It was too hot for covers. He began to caress her slowly, at first with the unwounded hand, and then, more clumsily, with the other; but she was already asleep, and he had no heart to awake her. For perhaps an hour he stared through the mosquito netting into the surrounding darkness, wondering at the strange expression he had seen on her face, then at last he, too, slept.

There happens occasionally on Balik Tamang a sudden inexplicable storm which lasts hardly more than a day. At such time the sea whips up, turns steel gray, mists rise from the sea, rain beats against the forest, and everything more than ten paces away from you is hidden. You hear the forest animals above the sound of the rain, the creaking of branches and the drumming of the natives, who beat gongs to send the storm away, praying in their damp *sulaps*. At such times very often the electric generator fails, and instead of the unchanging electric lights you are forced to use hissing oil lamps. For days afterward hot gusts of steam rise from the land, and the peasants go over the drowned vegetable patches, searching for whatever can be saved from the long onslaught of the storm. The island changes beyond recognition. The path to the oil derricks is littered with broken branches, drowned animals, and sometimes even the road has been washed away and the workmen must be sent out again with their sickles and their great pounding hammers to make a new road. Then, too, the oil pipe is suddenly covered with a thickness of green forest growths which have to be cleaned away.

During the night the storm arose, at daybreak it was raging over the whole island, the telegraph wires from the oil derricks had been pulled down, a heavy mist covered the bungalows, and the jetty entirely disappeared from view. When Dunhill awoke the next morning, he was cold, the window was banging open, and through the window there was nothing visible at all except a smoking white square. He covered his wife with a feather-weight eiderdown, and then went to the bathroom. His hand felt better, though the pain under the shoulder blade was sharper. He had forgotten his suspicions of the previous day. In the cold humid bathroom—cold only because the temperature had dropped two or three degrees—he bathed, shaved, and dressed hurriedly, determined to go over to the company's offices for his reports of the day. Afterward he would go to the clubhouse. He would tell Alderton that the injection had worked wonderfully well. He would read a few papers, and perhaps take a drink at the bar and yarn with young Dogherty about the prospects of new drillings on the other side of the island, and how the new refinery machinery was going on. The rain was still pelting the corrugated iron roof, but the asbestos beneath dulled the sound. He passed through the bedroom barefoot, afraid of waking her, admiring even then in the drowsy downpour of rain and mist through the window the hot red mass of her hair.

He must have awakened her, for as soon as he reached the door he heard her moving and looked back. She had thrown off the eiderdown, and now the woman drowsily awakening looked younger than ever, and more than ever desirable. He said stupidly, "Did I wake you?" She turned, blinking in the unaccustomed white light of the storm.

"It's nothing—I had a bad dream."

He came back and sat on the edge of the bed, letting his fingers run through her red hair. She was still drowsy.

"Are you all right?" she asked.

"Yes, you know I'm all right," he answered, and once again he thought he detected that curious look of guilt in her eyes.

"You shouldn't go to the office. The doctor said you ought to rest."

He wondered why she said "the doctor," when usually they spoke of him as Alderton. He continued to play with her hair, and then, overcome by a strange and unusually tender affection for her, he began to stroke her with his bandaged hand over the high cheekbones, and along the face and neck and breasts. At last he said, "You mustn't worry. It doesn't hurt. And then we'll leave soon—you must hate it so much."

"I wish you wouldn't touch me," she said turning her face away.

He flared up. "Why the hell shouldn't I? I'm sorry. I didn't mean to talk like that. What's happened? There's nothing I can do nowadays that you approve of. You don't like sleeping with me lately—Why?"

He was determined upon an answer.

"It's too hot," she said, almost in a whisper, her face turned away from him, her sharp breath rippling the pillow.

Often at night on this island he wondered what he would do if she left him. He knew now. Everything would be the same, but the air would have changed; instead of breathing lightly, he would breathe heavily, against the air. He said, "I didn't mean a damn thing. You know it. Oh, darling, what the hell have I done?" She did not answer. "It's my fault," he went on. "I should have rested. This rotten blood poisoning poisons everything. Forgive me, darling. Can I get you something?" He was like a child. He looked distractedly round the room in search of something she might need, an emblem of surrender, the bone a dog brings to the master after being whipped—there was nothing she needed, for she was perfectly self-contained. In utter despair he began to babble, "Oh my God, you're so lovely, you're so soft, you're so smooth in bed."

She sat up suddenly, flinging her hair back. "Are you talking about a water bottle?" she said quietly.

He said, "What in God's name have I done? I'll do anything. You've never been like this before." But she had turned her face away, burying it in the pillow, as she sobbed quietly, the red hair shaking and her whole body quivering in the white sunlight.

He went away after that, knowing that there was nothing that could be done, not helpless any more, because he had begun to believe that when the storm was over, she would be herself again. He did not know why he believed this, but it kept him going through the day. He went to the office, remembering that she had been more restless than ever recently, drinking more, or perhaps it was the Chinese servant who was drinking—the level of whiskey was going down alarmingly.

Dogherty said, "Why the hell don't you rest up? It's getting us all down. If I had a blood-stained hand, I wouldn't come to the office."

"I suppose it's a sense of duty," he explained. "I can't bear things to go wrong."

Dogherty was a tremendous, weak-chinned, prematurely white-haired Irishman. Dunhill looked at the charts in the office, red lines showing expanding production of oil, blue lines showing the decrease of wages under the new mechanical drills. The office was a bare room made of nipa palms.

"Take it easy, Dunhill. Oh, for God's sake! You don't seem

to realize—" The fan was circling uneasily above his head. "Things are going from bad to worse."

"How?"

"Oh, the natives are talking about a mutiny. We've got the police going through the coolie lines. There's some damned agitator here. We don't know who he is yet, but we will; we'll have him flung out." Dunhill lit a cigarette, surprised that his hand was shaking. Gusts of white mist were pouring past the window, but the storm was abating. It would end as suddenly as it came.

"When did this happen?" he said.

"We noticed it three weeks ago for the first time. Not laziness—taking their time, complaining, whining. You shouldn't employ Malays or Dusuns. I've told them before—the best labor force is Chinese. *They* don't complain."

"I've never seen the Dusuns complain."

"It's not the way they complain so much, as the damned uncertainty—you don't know which way they're going to spring."

"Come, come. They're lazy, man. They don't spring," Dunhill heard himself saying. "What the devil should they spring about? They live in the sun, take coconuts from the palms, we've built them comfortable quarters, they've got their wives—"

Dogherty was infuriating with his calm air of assumption of superior knowledge. "In the first place," he said, "the Dusuns are not Malays—you seem to think anyone who wears a sarong is a Malay. They're Borneo head-hunters, I don't like the situation. Oh, we can't prove anything. We haven't found any Marxist literature. Only they sit around in their councils, as they call them, and they talk about the white men, not the usual stuff, and we know something goes on in the forest at night. They slip away. There's a notice saying no one should go into the forest after nightfall. They keep on going. You can't stop them. And some dynamite has disappeared." Dogherty said "dynamite" in a loud voice of inexplicable tension.

Dunhill wandered down to the sea, seeing the word "dynamite" in white-hot letters over the horizon. "Senseless," he muttered. "The man's too young for the job." The last white shreds of mist were dissolving over the opaque blueness of the sky; and standing there, in the shade of the green palms, his blood-poisoned hand still aching a little, he gazed back at the island with an expression of delighted amusement. It was good that Dogherty should see visions!"

"Oh my God!" he thought. "They need something to wake them up. They go to sleep here. They're such bloody bastards."

He did not know why he was being overwhelmed with a mounting sensation of horror of the white men there. They seemed to have no place on the island. They wore shorts and colored shirts, they even played golf, they were continually creeping into each other's beds, and somehow all this desperate motiveless life on the island gave proportion to the scene, fitted perfectly with the steaming forest in the distance and the coral sands. There was a corrugated iron shed under the palms with a smoke funnel—God knows why they put a smoke funnel there—that, too, was part of the providential arrangement of things, and you could not see the hut from the house, because the jetty sloped at this point. The women are worse, he told himself, looking toward the factory buildings, the terrible snakelike iron pipe, and high above him the palm trees stiff as telegraph poles, the bright yellow stems of the palms and the feathery green tufts waving in the soft sea wind. It was hot and moist, the terrible moisture that comes after a brief storm; and then looking up, he saw thin gray spider webs hanging from the palms.

The spiders were so small he thought they were harmless, till he saw the little green eyes and the curiously rough inflated skins. They were about the size of a penny, and they kept swinging slowly backward and forward in the wind. When everything else was silent and unmoving, he thought he heard the faint crepitation of the gray threads. Then he rubbed his eyes. It was odd. There were no spiders. Had they gone? No, very suddenly they had climbed up the long black silken ladders and five or six of them were hanging above his head; and he thought he saw the intensely small green eyes in the sun.

The heaviness which had oppressed him all morning remained.

The doctor was still at the oil well. He wondered why he had come here, what chance had brought him to those detestable green palms under the heavy sun. Of course, there were spiders everywhere on the island, perhaps it was a spider along the road in the forest that had pricked his hand. He was sure of it now, looking up at the gray dangling net of viscous silk, the spiders suddenly sent into a frenzy of movement because he had lifted his head, green eyes winking like lamps. "It's my fault. I shouldn't have come here," he thought, and he was about to return when he noticed twenty feet below, in the place where the water was transparent and shaded, some natives bathing.

He had to confess it to himself, they looked magnificent, the slow, lithe copper-colored limbs against the faint redness of coral. They were taller and better built than the Malays in Singapore, with crinkled hair and heavy mouths, almost Negroid. He could see their sarongs on the shore, a dark patch of browns and striped yellows; and as their young bodies caught the copper glint of the sun, as they swam slowly in the shade, a profound envy rose within him. He had never dared to bathe here. There were too many sharks, too many poisonous corals, too many uncharted pockets in the sea floor, giving rise to dangerous currents. Danger everywhere. The sun flashed white among them when they went beyond the shade, but how slowly, how effortlessly they moved in the shadow of the jetty. They were boys of about fourteen, the sons of the factory workers, and they spoke to one another across the waters, and a soft sound perfectly in keeping with the slumberous stretch of water, the colored rocks, the unwaving palms and the sand pipers which kept prancing along the jetty, the only quick-witted things in the whole island.

After a while the boys came out of the water and bathed in the sun, tawny bronze and gold, like young lion cubs sweltering through the sandy midsummer heat. For a long time he watched them from the shade of the green palms.

Estelle rose from the bed, trembling with rage. The mist was rising, and already the hot blue day was shining through. She took off the flowered dressing gown and lay full length on the bed, softly fanning herself, and there came to her, together with the sound of breakers and the still softer sound of the Malay servants whispering together, the distant throaty roar and sudden spout of oil leaping through the derricks, and almost at the same moment she imagined the yellow transparent oil towering into froth in the sky, then falling heavily and damply on the clearing in the forest. Then she rang the bell, and Ambo came silently through the curtains.

She had never asked him his age, but she knew he was still young. The bronze skin was warm, though there were menacing shadows under the eyes. He wore a sarong of dark brown and purple, carefully plaited and folded, and he was barefoot, coming silently across the wooden floor. Seeing her lying on the bed, he made a movement as though to go, but she beckoned him, throwing back the whole shock of her flame-red hair on the pillow.

"Massah no come?" Ambo said, falling beside the bed, and resting his hands on the edge of the bed—the fingers almost purple, soft yet bony.

She was oddly exhilarated, her breath coming in nervous jumps, smiling, arching her neck and gazing at her lover without tenderness but with a kind of insolent desire, almost a savagery.

Ambo said again, "Tuan Besar—he gone? What for? No place here. We go forest."

The urgency was being communicated to him, and she could see how much he desired her, his eyes becoming larger and more velvet.

"Tuan Besar says you mustn't kill chicken," she said softly, and so tenderly that the words were no more than a caress.

Ambo nodded. "I kill chicken before him. He no like. Massa good man, he no like dead chickens," and then his voice dropped again and he said, "We go forest."

"No, here."

It was like a summons, but it was a summons he had never obeyed before, and he was not accustomed to the thought of taking her there. There were a host of objections rising in his mind, but she was so beautiful, the flesh so firm and taut and alert, and the hair so red, that for a moment he surrendered, leaning forward and breathing over her, his face hardly an inch from her body. And while he did this, she held his head and put her hand through his dark crinkled hair, laughing softly in the pleasure of expectancy, already leaping a little toward him. "Come soon, come soon," she whispered, dragging him down, but there was a stiffness of repulsion in him, seeing the mosquito net and her husband's things all about the room.

"You come forest?" he said. "You come quick. He come back."

Once, three months ago, Ambo was with her when she heard her husband coming up the steps of the veranda. She had received a sudden stab of fright like a heavy blow in the chest which made her recoil from any more meetings with Ambo for a little while. Afterward they always went to the forest. She riding on the small pony and he following her at a distance, walking with long loping strides, or perhaps he would disappear altogether and they would meet in the little clearing he cut out of the hanging lianas with his *parang*. They had left cushions and blankets in a hollowed-out tree, protected from the rain by stones. Once or twice a week she met him there. They would remove the stones, lay the cushions carefully on the grass and for a long time they remained there; if her husband asked where she had been, there were always the flowers and orchids they collected from the forest to prove that she had been performing her wifely occupations. She loved flowers, and to her Ambo was like one of those hanging orchids which glow in terrifyingly compact clusters on the trees, spreading in every direction, entwining the branches, dark red and purple and soft to touch.

He was called Ambo because he was a native of Amboina.

"Yes, we go?" he said urgently, his hot breath more quickening to her than the touch of hands.

There were moments when it was best to humor him; so she dressed quickly and allowed him to go. She hated the lonely journey to the forest, the roads of red ants, the succulent greenness and sappiness of the undergrowth. Parakeets would scream at her from the trees, breaking the long silences; or she would hear in the distance, coming through warm pockets of air, the voices of the laborers at the derricks five or ten miles away. Always she feared she would come upon some Malays spying on her, yet fear gave her courage, she liked riding in the shaded green lanes beneath the huge *merantis,* and the thought of Ambo waiting for her drove her into a kind of frenzy. "He makes love like a dog," she thought, and then she was in despair that he might not come.

He came long after she had tethered the pony and laid the cushions on the grass, his chest streaked with sweat and his sarong wet with the dew of the long grasses. Handsome and young, the bony face lifted jauntily in the air, the shoulders delicately rounded, he came with the loping stride which she always admired. He squatted there beside her, mindless and alone, not seeing her, seeing only the hunger she had aroused in him, while the sunlight stippled him black and gold; and outside the small square of cushions and blankets there was only the forest and the pony. She unbuttoned the white blouse and waited for him to undress her, knowing that this, too, would be the same, all his gestures would be the same, he would undress her a little and then breathe lightly upon her, and there were some herbs in his mouth which gave his breath a smell as of long earth-buried flowers, or of those poisonous orchids which resemble crabs. But this morning there was a greater haste in his movements; he did not carefully unfold his sarong, but leaped upon her with his sarong still on him, pulling it above his waist, addressing her in terrible urgency, moaning and saying words in Malay she could not understand, till at last she said, "Speak more softly—someone might hear you."

"Who care?" he answered.

"Oh, you must be careful, Ambo—for my sake. Please don't be rough. You know how I hate you when you are rough."

She could feel the cold steel blade of the *parang* against her bare legs, for it was still buckled into his sarong. He was leaping like some wild thing, breathless with impatience. She tried to push him away, to quiet him, to hold him so close to her that his urgency would disappear. Ambo pressed himself down with all his strength, and suddenly she yelled at him, trying to push him away, "Don't you see, you've cut me! You clumsy fool! Why do you have the *parang* there?" and she tried to take it away from him, pulling it up through the belt of his sarong. The sunlight spilled over the blankets, and she was rolling away from him. Her legs were streaked with blood. She said, "What's happened to you?" She was cowering on the edge of the blankets, and suddenly he had leaped into a crouching position, breathing heavily, unrecognizable, a yellow soft thing in the sunlight with a hard shining face, all his teeth showing. He was looking at her leg, where the blood spilled. He was murmuring to himsef, and then she knew no more, for he had leapt at her again like a released tiger and he was so close to her that everything else was swallowed up in her passion for him. Now he was more tender than ever. He caressed her quietly, no longer wearing the sarong, the *parang* thrown away, and for a long time they lay there quietly.

The pony came toward them, and once a parakeet screamed so loud that they both jumped a little in fright and laughed nervously. The heat drained their surviving energy. In the sunlight her hair took on the quality of incandescence, and her skin glowed with sweat which rolled over her and turned into mist. She knew almost nothing about him. It was the springing stride, and the purple hands and the way he breathed all over her which made him so attractive to her, so that there were times when she wondered whether she could ever face life without him.

She remembered stepping through the kitchen and seeing the dark red guavas on a tray, overripe, but yet exciting to taste, and she wished she had brought some food with her. Nearly always she would remember food only when she had reached the place in the forest. Her temper had gone: the best part of love came afterward when you were drowsy in the sun, not thinking, perfectly at peace. She said, "I wish there was some food—we must bring something to drink next time," and he only nodded.

Then she remembered the wound. It was a long wound, and the blood made her leg hideous. She had not noticed it before, but now she began to be afraid—it had spotted her blouse, someone might see her before she could change it. There was no stream where she could wash off the blood.

She said, "They mustn't see this. What shall I say? I cut myself in the bathroom?"

It was the only answer. She hoped her husband would not see the deep cut; she would keep away from him. She looked at her watch. They had been there only five minutes together, but it seemed an age. Ambo was breathing all over her again, as he always did, and wherever his breath fell there was a dull center of pleasure; she half hated it now; it was like a terribly chaste and at the same time evil kiss; it was better when he lay against her.

He said, "I'll take you again, but in my own place."

"Where?"

"In the forest. We'll go away."

She thought for a while, fighting against the idea of him.

"I must go back to him, Ambo," she said sorrowfully. "I must go back."

He was smiling at her. She looked at the cut which was still bleeding. The *parang* was curved and had cut a crescent shape into her leg.

"You go back? I wait?" he said.

"Yes, I go back," she said, and she thought of the days that would follow, Dunhill's bandaged hand, swimming out in the moonlight in the blue sea, the trip to Singapore and always the rendezvous in the forest and the blankets and cushions hidden in the hollowed-out tree. "Yes, you wait," she said, looking up at the sun and leaning her face in the crook of his arm.

The sun fell through the trees, staining her, but she did not care. The other wives went about their accustomed duties, gossiped, helped their husbands, went to bridge parties, and longed for the boat bringing mail from Singapore or Kuching. It was not her world. She would grow old, but while she was young she would sleep with a striped tiger and have him at her mercy—she would do as she pleased. "Am I beautiful?" she said, and he answered, "Yes, beautiful—like the eye of the dawn, like the sea," and this pleased her, and once again she would allow him to breathe on her, all over, until every part of her body had quickened under the hot, scented breath. "I'm beautiful," she said, "I'm the eye of the dawn, as beautiful as the sea."

Dunhill did not know why he was gazing out to sea; there was nothing there, only the endless blue hard stretch leading to the thin dark line on the horizon. His arm ached still, and occasionally he would make infantile gestures, as though he could shake off the pain. When the bell rang over the factory shed, he went in search of the doctor.

In his surgery Alderton wore a white starched coat and the red stethoscope hung around his neck. He was washing his hands when Dunhill came in.

"Well, let's have a look at it," Alderton said. "How's the temperature?"

"Rotten."

Alderton looked up sharply. "Was that you standing in the sun?"

Dunhill nodded.

"You shouldn't, you know. You ought to have more sense. The best thing is to stay indoors. The sun inflames everything. You ought to be more careful." He went on, "It's partly psychological. I've got to have the patient's help, otherwise the whole treatment is worthless. You do understand that, don't you?"

Dunhill knew then that he wanted to die; he couldn't face Estelle again. She had treated him once too often as though he wasn't there. The doctor was undoing the bandage. The gland under the shoulder gave a sudden spurt, and he went pale, not so much because of the ache as because he was afraid to look at the swollen hand, the skin drawn so tight that the hand was characterless, like a monkey's hand.

But the hand was better—Dunhill himself could see no change in it, but Alderton swore that it was healthier altogether, the medicine had done its work, in a few days it would be over.

"Rest it, whatever you do, don't work or worry, and I'll give you another injection. Wonderful stuff. And there's another thing—keep it in ice, it will stop the pain." He said a little later, "I'm making some statistics. I think I can get the company to cut down our working hours and increase the holidays. The kind of life we are living drains hell out of us."

Dunhill nodded. He had no particular respect for the young doctor, who knew too much about the private lives of everyone on the island.

When the injection had been made, Alderton lit his pipe and said, "You know what is the best medicine for anyone in the tropics? A loving wife. It's taken me a hell of a time to learn that, but I shall never forget now. I'm going to get married next trip."

"Anyone in mind?"

"Oh hell, no. I had a childhood sweetheart, but she got married—but you don't have to pick and choose. Find someone who is handsome, like Estelle, really handsome, and then you can teach them the tricks. No children for three or four years, say five years, and then they're tamed."

"Yes, it's something like that," Dunhill said, and he went out into the sunlight, dazed, the arm thumping again from the injection and the prick of the needle still hurting.

He did not expect to find Estelle: she was always either rowing or gathering flowers or taking long walks or riding. He was accustomed to her absence, and indeed preferred it. He rang the bell. The Chinese number-one boy answered, and he ordered a bowlful of cubes of ice, an iced lemonade, and some aspirins. He waited impatiently, gazing out of the window, now at the green palms, now at the sandy shore and the birds hovering on blue waves. The sea had never looked more solid or more motionless.

When the number-one boy returned he stripped off his coat and plunged his hand in the ice; dropped an aspirin in the lemonade and lit his pipe. He turned on the electric Gramophone and listened to the chorus of lovers at the opening of "*Don Giovanni*." When dinner was laid, he asked if there was news from his wife, but when the boy shook his head, he was not distressed; she might be having lunch with the Naylors, or perhaps she had decided to spend the whole day riding or rowing. It had happened before. With his arm in the bowl of ice, he lost all sense of pain.

In the evening, when she had not arrived, he phoned the Naylors and asked whether she was there. It infuriated him when he heard Naylor's high-pitched voice saying, "No sirree, not a sign of her—I bet she's wandering again." He drank some whiskey in defiance of Alderton's orders, and after a short meal, during which he hardly touched his food, he went to bed, bringing another bowl of ice with him for his hand. On the way to the bedroom he saw Ambo squatting in the kitchen below, and he reminded himself that he would ask Estelle again when she came in to speak to him. He had seen the chicken's head again on his return from the doctor. Ambo should have picked it up and thrown it away.

He was content not to share his bed. When he first came to the island, Estelle had asked for twin beds, but he had told her that they were fatal for people in the tropics. "You see, Estelle," he said, "everyone has tiffs in this climate. You can't help yourself, but if you have a double bed, you can break through the anger, you don't just lie fuming at each other." He heard footsteps, thought it was Estelle, but it was only one of the Chinese boys turning out all the lights.

He slept heavily, drugged by the aspirin and the injection. When he awoke the next morning, he was calmer than ever and the pain was gone; he knew the swelling had gone down. He rang for the number-one boy and asked whether Estelle had returned.

"Me no know."

"Then what the hell's the matter with you? Go and look for her. Ask the number-two boy."

The Chinese giggled. It infuriated him. He lit a cigarette and went to the icebox, and poured himself a bowl of condensed milk, waiting till one of the other boys came in.

"They no see," the boy said. "They say no sign her she come, no sign her she go."

"Don't talk that bloody language. Who saw her last? I left her here. She was all right then. You go ask boys where she went." It suddenly staggered him to think that she might have got lost in the forest or drowned at sea. He hoped for her sake that she was drowned at sea rather than lost in the forest, for he hated the thought of her eaten by red ants. At that moment, standing on the veranda, he saw the boy Ambo running after a squawking red chicken, hardly large enough to make a meal. He shouted at the boy, "Stop it, do you hear? Leave the bloody thing alone, or do the killing in the kitchen. Come here. Who are you?"

The boy paused in his pursuit, with the *parang* in his hand, so graceful and lithe a thing in the yellow and purple sarong that Dunhill felt a momentary regret for bawling so loud. As the boy came nearer, the Englishman saw the slow white smile spreading in the heavy languorous face.

"Tuan Besar speak?"

"Yes, I want to tell you I don't want the front of the house cluttered up with chicken heads. Leave the bloody bird alone if you haven't strength enough to kill it in the kitchen. You always let them escape and run after them. It's a kind of game. Don't do it again."

The hot sun stretched over the sea, and there was no wind; the palms were tranquil in the sun. The boy moved away, nodding and bowing, the *parang* flashing in his hand, and Dunhill said aloud, "It's sheer laziness, or perhaps he wants to make an exhibition of himself—the bastards are all the same."

There was no sign of Estelle. He was angry and impatient now. He drank a short whiskey and followed it ten minutes later with a stiffer one. He thought of telephoning O'Brien, the manager, and then dismissed the thought from his mind. The radio was one continual crackle of atmospherics, as it was every morning of the year: it was only in the evening that you heard Delhi or Singapore with comparative clarity. He had pronounced views, and was furious with the Japanese: he wished Estelle were in the room, so that he could tell her what he thought of the Japanese.

After breakfast he read for the third time a month-old copy of the *Straits Times*, then he summoned the number-one boy again and told him that he must make inquiries about where Estelle had been last seen. There was a grapevine: the servants knew far more than the officials, and he had long ago come to the conclusion that the only way to deal with the servants was with alternate beatings and bribes. He gave the boy five dollars, and sent him away.

In the evening the boy returned to say that no one knew where she was, but she had gone into the forest.

"It's some damned trick of hers," he told himself. "Flaming hair, and as cold as ice. I don't know what's come over her lately."

He went to bed early, but he could not sleep. The pain had gone entirely from his arm, but in its going it had left an emptiness which nothing in the ill-furnished bungalow could fill. At night he dreamed of her. He was ashamed of his dreams, but they brought her so vividly before him that he switched on the light, thinking she was there. "She's a bloody fool. The way to deal with a woman is the way I deal with the servants—beatings and bribes. I never gave her enough beatings, I never gave her enough bribes."

He felt sick and lonely, in a black storm of despair. He heard one of the servants wandering about downstairs, and he thought he heard an animal howling. The little white transparent lizards were squeaking high up in the wall, and a moth, which had fluttered aimlessly around the electric lamp, suddenly fell to the floor, hopped, making a sound like starched cotton rubbing together, and then lay still. "Probably dead. The bloody ants will eat it. It's a hell of a place." Like someone mesmerized he watched the ants creeping in long columns from the wall, glittering metallic red, going straight as a plumb line; they burrowed around the dead moth, formed a circle, crawled over it, bit away portions of the face, bit off the wings one by one, and then forming three inexhaustible columns, carried off the three pieces of the still quivering moth. They did not carry it back to the hole where they had come from, but continued their journey across the floor. When they had gone, nothing was left except a faint stain of powder from the wings.

He had another drink, and knew he would not be able to sleep again that night—the death of a moth had kept him awake before. At dawn he rang for the Chinese boy.

"She may be hurt," he yelled at the boy. "Can you get that into your thoughtless, dumb, idiot head? She may be hurt. She must be found. Where did she go?"

"They say she go follest—"

"Yes."

"That's all. She no come back."

A sharp, ghastly fear struck him. He said, "You've got to come with me. Have you got any senses, man. We've got to find her."

His face was dead white with sleeplessness. He dressed hurriedly and strode across the intervening half mile of land toward the forest, looking in the grass for a sign of her, but there was no sign. He had strapped on his revolver, and because there was a land mist, he shivered a little in his shorts and shirt. Then he found a trail of hoofmarks. "She must have taken Jerry," he said. "What a fool I was not to see whether any of the ponies were missing." There were three ponies which were kept in the stable at the far end of the long kitchen. "Keep your eyes skinned," he shouted, unnecessarily loud. "Look out for her. I'll give you money if you find her, and I'll beat the living lights out of you if you don't." The boy did not understand what he was saying.

When they were in the forest, in one of the many lanes carved through the undergrowth, he wished he had brought a knife. Hidden lianas suddenly swung into his face. There were caves of greenness, walls of vines, a maze of footpaths. The sun began to rise, burning through white mists, turning them to dew and sun haze, and the heat rose from the grasses and exuded from the trees; parakeets swung like flashes of red hot blood across his eyes, and he heard, nearer at hand than he desired, the awakening sounds of beasts. He wished above all that he could hear the neighing of the pony, or his wife's voice. All thoughts of hatred had gone from him. He thought of her now only as she was in the early days of their marriage, when he lived thunderstruck by her red-gold hair. She was so beautiful that he knew he did not deserve her. It was like a pain, thinking of her. Now he felt he would promise her everything, even a lover, if only she would return. Loneliness faced him; a quick old age. You lose your bearings in the tropics, and you are no good for work at home after a few years in this stifling heat, which drains the saps and vigors from your body. He hated the forest. He hated the Chinese boy, waiting for bribes. If he found her, they would take the next boat to Singapore, take a holiday in Penang or the Cameroon Highlands, and never return to these sweatshop islands off the north coast of Borneo. He smiled grimly. He would be a good lover, and he would give her small beatings and big bribes.

Then in a clearing he saw a tree which had been struck by lightning, blue and chalky yellow, the height of a man, and there were blankets strewn at its feet. Estelle was lying naked in the sunlight, surrounded by hosts of silent fat magpies and by line upon line of red ants, but what was more awful was that there was only a swollen red stump where her head had been and the ants were pouring all over her. He looked up. On a tree branch, on a level with his eyes, she was looking at him, hanging by her red hair. The ants were all over the branch and the severed neck but her face was still recognizable. He shut his eyes, but the red hair, glinting in the sun, in great heaps, was so bright that even when he closed his eyes, he saw it—a slab of yellow and gold. He turned to the Chinese boy, who suddenly threw himself down on his knees and licked his shoes, in the gesture of a low-class Chinese avoiding arrest by the most complete subservience and self-surrender.

Without looking at the red-gold hair, he examined the body, squashed out whole lanes of ants, kicked the heavy blood-swollen birds which could no longer lift their wings and which fell with a dull sound, without sufficient energy after their feast to squawk; and then, sweating heavily, he rolled the headless body in the blankets and ordered the Chinese to carry it. The boy refused. Dunhill put his revolver against the boy's side, and said, "You'll do as you're told." The boy obeyed. Dunhill picked up his wife's clothes, the blouse and the riding breeches, socks and boots and some blood-stained handkerchiefs, and he did not know what he was doing; he knew only that he could not look at that head hanging on the branches. "Christ, Christ, Christ," he said. "Christ, Christ, Christ—you bloody fool," he kept on saying, while tears ran down his face in heavy streams. "I didn't want this—but you, you wanted it—gold hair in the trees." He was choking with horror and remorse. "You carry the head," he said to the boy, and held out the riding breeches; but the boy stepped back and refused to carry anything more. There were birds everywhere, even great hawks, and they were all screaming and flying about the head, and others were attempting to perch on the boy's shoulders. "They'll get to the face soon," Dunhill said. "We'll have to save it." He couldn't think why the birds had not pecked the face, which was still beautiful, though thinner; then, holding up the riding breeches to catch the head, he carefully uncurled the hair tied to the branch. "Oh Christ, oh my darling," he kept on saying. "What shall I do with it?" and then his voice changed and he asked accusingly, "What were you doing? Who was it? My darling, my sweet one, I forgive you—please believe me—I forgive you—you have suffered already—but never again."

Very slowly they walked through the trembling forest, hardly knowing where they were going or what they were doing. Dunhill held the riding breeches close to his chest with one hand; with the other he held the blood-stained blouse.

They walked blindly back to the house, laid the head and the body in the drawing room without saying a word to anyone. The other servants were not in sight. They had probably seen him coming and retreated into their own quarters. "Poor darling," Dunhill kept on saying, delirious with grief. For a moment he thought that if he could tie the head and the body together, and cover them with flowers, she would be made whole again. The boy was slipping away from the room.

"Come here—you can't go yet," he shouted after the boy. "It's not over. You've got to help me, you understand. I'll beat the heart out of you if I have any more nonsense. What's the matter with you?"

He went up to the boy and pulled him back in the room. "We can't have it here," he said dazedly. "We've got to get it away."

"Where to?"

"It doesn't matter, as long as we get it away. You carry again. You carry, or I'll beat your guts in—I'll make it worth your while, you've got to help me."

He knew where he was going now. He was going to the doctor's prerogative, not his, to care for the dead. They went out again. On the way he passed the chicken head and stopped, nearly dropping the riding breeches, for the head had shriveled in the sun, a little yellow thing with dead cracked eyes and an open beak, the blood dried up, no more than a dead twig or a stone. He said, "I told him not to do it. I wish she was here—she could tell him. I'll have to speak to him again when I get back."

When he reached the doctor's bungalow, he turned for a moment to look at the green palms. It was strange how they glinted there, the color of some savage metal, unmoving in the faint wind. No breakers fell on the shore, the sea was like steel or like glass and the heavy midsummer sun was still sucking all life from the earth; and there, halfway between sky and sea, like an unchanging green face, lay the green leaves of the palm. The red coastal steamer from Singapore was returning.

THE RUSSIAN GESTURE

by JOHN HEWLETT

SERGE IVANOVITCH LOVET-ZALINSKY (THAT'S NOT HIS REAL NAME) walked heavily eastward on Thirty-seventh Street. He was down on his luck.

A confident breeze which promised lower temperatures doodled nervous brown patterns on the pavement, off Park Avenue, with the last falling autumn leaves from the sidewalk maples.

Serge shivered. He would have to take his topcoat out of the Sixth Avenue pawnshop as soon as possible. He needed it now. And his suit! The one he wore was a tropical worsted summer garment. Lucky it was blue. Not too many persons, he was sure, had noticed. A wonderful and serviceable color, blue, he thought.

The Russian, however, could not fool himself. Already he had the sniffles. He had been chilly for a week. Serge was hungry, too. This, somehow, made it seem colder than it actually was. No, he could not blame it all on the suit.

As he walked ahead he thought of Peter. Good old Petrov! Petrov, his ever-faithful countryman, would fix things up. He and Trina. He had kept it from them for a long time, his best friends. He was on his way there, to their home, to see them now. How he loved them! How wonderful they were! The very thought of their goodness was a compelling thing. The emotional, unreconstructed Czarist let his heart fill and he brushed away a tear. This did him no end of good. Within him now was a stove which warmed his body. He forgot the chill in the air, ignored the presaging, jiving leaves, was oblivious to the prophecy of the breeze.

The Russian was only a few doors away from the Murray Hill house of his friends, the house of Petrov and Trina. It was near Lexington Avenue. There it was! The light from the living-room windows glowed a whole friendly hand of beckoning fingers. A new spring and snap entered his stride. Suddenly he felt good and confident, all over. He bounded up the steps, three at a time, and rang the bell.

"Petrov!"

It was his friend Peter, himself, who answered the door. He seemed the most surprised man in the world.

"Serge!" he cried. "God bless you! Where have you been?"

Good old Petrov! It was the sort of welcome he knew would be his.

Cozy air from the living room wafted odors of security to Serge's nostrils. He smelled borsch, vodka, roasts, and tallow from a candle melting before an ikon. Peter had guests, too. He heard the clanking of glasses, familiar toasts in his beloved native tongue, gay laughter.

"It's a party," said Peter. He embraced his friend warmly. "Come in. Join us. It's Trina's birthday."

But wait!

Peter held Serge by his shoulders at arms' length. He regarded him curiously. He looked him up and down.

"Serge! You are not yourself. You are shabby, and, my God, man, pale and thin! What is the reason for this?"

"Broke, Petrov. And for a long time."

Peter's face was constricted with grief and pity. "And you did not let me know! Shame on you, Serge. You, my friend. Come in here, you idiot, you lovable idiot. This is your house. Our house is your house. What we, Trina and I have, is yours."

Good old Petrov. Serge hugged him convulsively. No man could have a better friend than good old Petrov, his countryman.

Peter pulled Serge into the vestibule, slammed the door. He screamed impulsively, at the top of his voice, shaking the walls. He made himself heard above the party's din. "Hi, hi, hi! Everyone," he shouted. "Here is Serge, our countryman. Welcome him wildly!"

Trina, who cried easily, was so startled she dropped a glass of vodka on the floor. She ran over to Serge. She kissed him excitedly. "Serge, darling, where have you been?"

Peter answered for him, loudly. "Down on his luck," he shouted. "Serge has fallen on bad days, and only now has let us know."

This announcement hushed the party instantaneously. For a second no one said a word. You could hear only the gasps of incredulity as every pair of eyes now looked pityingly, appraisingly upon the formerly immaculate and dashing Serge. But this lasted, for but a second. It was followed by a general rush to Serge's side. Vodka glasses were left deserted upon a heavy mahogany table near steaming aluminum pots of borsch as all stampeded to express their sympathy.

Trina embraced Serge again. This time he felt her tears dropping on his neck, wetting his frayed collar.

Katia pushed up to Serge through the now babbling group about him. She kissed him, pinched his cheeks, patted his face affectionately. "Beautiful Serge, poor Serge," she said.

Then forward came Sonia and Pabla, and Mushia and Stacha and Helenka. They kissed Serge, on his face, on his mouth, on his neck and ears. His face soon was measled with lipstick, and new tears, not his own, drenched his shirt front.

Almost equally affectionate were the big Russian men, who embraced him characteristically, pressed his hands warmly, uttered words of praise and encouragement.

Serge stood flat-footed, overcome. "God!" he said. "What a welcome. Only a Russian could welcome a friend like this."

The sentimental thought touched him curiously. In a moment he, too, was weeping.

It was Trina who quickly put an end to this embarrassing tack. "Enough, everybody," she commanded. "Serge is hungry. Bring him food and vodka."

"Yes," everyone shouted together, "Serge is hungry. We are bringing him food and vodka."

Now the stampede was in the direction of the table. Forks full of borsch meat were stabbed from the aluminum pots, held aloft, carried triumphantly, pushed into Serge's mouth.

The man chewed wildly to keep up with the procession.

"Ah!" he burbled between desperate swallows. "Only the

Russians drink soup with a fork. The wonderful Russians!"

"Vodka," someone shouted. "Vodka for Serge."

"And get me a bowl," commanded Katia, "a big bowl."

"Drink vodka from a bowl?" asked Sonia in surprise.

"No," gleefully announced Katia, "Serge will need other meals. The bowl is for my diamond earrings. The bowl is for Serge."

A cheer went up and rang through the house and startled many a person on the street.

"A bowl of jewels for Serge!"

Hooray, this was genius!

Katia unscrewed earrings, dropped them into a china soup tureen. Pabla stripped a diamond bracelet from her wrist. Tania contributed her large diamond engagement ring, a lavaliere. Mushia tore a scarab necklace with golden links from her neck. The bottom of the bowl was full of jewels. Helenka added to the pile her emerald brooch. Sonia divested her shoulder of a golden pin shaped like a dandelion and ransacked her pocketbook until she found a broken string of pearls. All of these she tossed into the treasure bowl which now was brimming.

Each contribution brought new cheers. The men were hoarse. The rafters rang. Eardrums were splitting.

Suddenly everyone was tired.

"Let's all sit down," suggested Peter. Strangely now, almost miraculously, the hilarity disappeared. The hour of emotion had seemingly drained everyone of the last vestige of effervescence.

Nicholas, Wladislaw, Alexander, Sasha, Alexis, and Ivan slumped on a davenport before the big log fire. Others found seats around. Serge sat between Peter and Trina. Curiously, somehow, no one started a conversation of any sort. All seemed self-conscious and embarrassed.

A Negro butler brought new trays of glasses filled with vodka with a dash of grenadine. Everyone gulped his drink, reached for more. The pace was terrific.

Serge drank as much as anyone. He made a little speech.

"Ah! My friends," he said, "thank you. Only the Russians could make such a gesture."

Several of the guests did not hear him at all. They had fallen asleep. Serge was drowsy too. Everyone soon was snoring.

Serge dreamed of a castle in the air with diamond-studded walls. The others slept restlessly and nodded or tossed a great deal.

Katia was the first one to awaken. She felt for her earrings. She was startled. They were gone! Then she remembered. She shook her husband Nicholas.

"Let's go home," she commanded. She walked over to the "treasure bowl" and for a moment regarded the haul.

"The morning," she said, "is wiser than the night." Katia fished for her baubles. "He won't miss these," she said. She and Nicholas left quietly.

Then awakened Sonia and Mushia and Pabla and Helenka. All were fishing for their jewels when Trina awoke.

They all giggled guiltily when Trina came over to join them.

"Oh, well," said Trina, "Serge would be too proud to take the jewels, after all." She dipped into the dwindling trove for her contribution, a platinum pendant, an heirloom from the court. She went to her bedroom to retire for the day.

When Serge awoke finally, he stretched and groaned. He had a gigantic hangover. It took him several minutes to remember where he was. He stood up slowly and looked about the large room. Peter was sleeping, stretched out on a chaise longue like an awkward life-sized window dummy broken in two. Serge waded through a welter of broken glasses over to the china soup tureen on the big, splattered mahogany table.

It was empty.

Serge shrugged his shoulders.

"Anyway," he said aloud, "what a gesture! A real Russian gesture!"

He left the house noiselessly without awakening his host.

A SWORD FOR SERENA

by JEROME SELMAN

"GIT THE TNT, BENJY," RAFE SAID, HIS GREAT CHEST HEAVING beneath his faded twill shirt. "Git me a coupla-few blocks pronto! I seed him and I chased him and I got him holed up—the biggest, fattest Jap officer I ever did see. Fat as a hull new bag of corn flour."

Young Benjy ran off in a low crouch to the deserted Jap cistern where the demolition supplies had been left for them by the advancing patrol, and in a minute returned through the dense wood to Rafe. Rafe, he saw, sat on the footpath, hardly visible in the jungle light that filtered through the overhead translucent foliage, his carbine aimed at the side of the high ridge, frozen like a statue until Benjy neared him. He asked in a whisper, "What you gonna do now, Rafe?"

"Do!" Rafe said, tuning slightly toward Benjy, sun and shadow lengthening his lean, yellowed face. "Why, I'm gonna set you on my left flank with this here carbean, and I'm gonna scrounge on my belly till I kin toss a block into his cave. I want his sword. You kin have his automatic, and his watches, and any filthy pictures he has. I need that sword. I promised Serena another Jap sword. She's got one from Bougainville over her mantel. But you need two swords to have crossed swords. See him move in the cave! Cover me whilst I crawl. Keep his bullet head down, and when I git close I'll blow him to kingdom come. O.K.! Now! Fire away!"

Rafe crept low through the undergrowth, thick with wild cabbage, and was at the edge of the rock formation when the Jap fired his automatic pistol. Benjy let go a magazine while Rafe backed up like a giant lizard, and rested, panting, near him, his face buried in the wet leaf-and-timber mold. After a while Benjy said, "Let me try one time."

"You're no bigger nor a hopper, and you're spittin' molasses all over yourself," Rafe said. "This is a man's war, and I dunno why they send kids here in the fust place. I'd give you the TNT and you'd blow us all to kingdom come."

"No, I wouldn't. I wouldn't, Rafe. Just gimme the TNT in my hands, and you'll see."

Rafe kept glancing around, looking at the high cliff, sharp with shadows, the flat land to their rear, the coral reefs below them and surrounding the island. He did not seem to be aware of Benjy, and he was mumbling, "Serena needs two . . . that sharp cliff . . . the path by the orchids . . . my BAR . . ."

"Now what you gonna do, Rafe?" Benjy asked.

"Hold up that piece! Want my sword to git away?"

Young Benjy jumped up and down with excitement. "Look, Rafe, look here! He must have moved, cause you can see him in there now. He's just laying there on his belly, just looking and looking at us. If I only had my old M-1!"

"Well, my aching back, my GI feet! You jest wait there, fat Mr. Jap, whilst I run back and git my BAR and drill you through the head. You know what to do if he comes out, Benjy. Kill him dead, and don't you forgit it, neither. Japs ain't like people. I'm gonna run all the way for my BAR like a fire through the fields. So you jest hold him in there good!"

Benjy heard Rafe's dogtrot, fainter and fainter. Soon he found himself alone with the carbine guarding the entrance to a cave in a slope where the Jap was hiding. He peered into the blackness. It was a small tunnel for a big Jap, probably the lair of some large animal. The place was strange to begin with, with wild orchids and breadfruit, palm fronds, natives. His carbine grew heavy poised on his shoulder, and he rested it by his side. Once he heard a string of unmusical *yerts* from a bird, beady and metallic, like fife notes over the field. Otherwise, besides the buzz of insects and a parrot mimicking something, all was quiet. So very quiet Benjy thought he heard the beating of the Jap's heart against the earth, *thump, thump, thump.* The Jap looked big and very powerful when Rafe chased him off the path into the rocky cave. Benjy wished with all his heart that

Rafe would get back already, he wished that Rafe would get back with that BAR. What was keeping him, anyway?

The Jap had inched to the opening, his eyes growing larger and redder and fiercer. The quiet became audible. He knew he must do something, he must. "Eiyahhh!" The man sound of his voice made him brave. He raised the carbine, menaced the Jap, fired into the opening, loosening some dirt from the roof of the dugout. When the dust settled, he saw the Jap crouched in the entrance, darting his head from side to side, then leaping out with his arms held stiffly in front. He saw the Jap explode in a paroxysm of motion, and with a mechanical movement he brought his carbine to follow the blur. Tiny, short slugs cut deep in the flesh of the Jap, leaving a raw, red gash in the side of his neck. The Jap hit the bank sideways and rolled down. On level ground, below Benjy, he righted himself and staggered blindly, tripping on the vines, blood oozing bright scarlet on his soiled uniform. Fear forgotten, Benjy ran after the Jap, who could bleed like any old animal, like his first running rabbit. He aimed high but hit the shoulder. The Jap bled from both sides now. Benjy fired again. The Jap collapsed and with a spasm of coughs lay supine and pawed instinctively, feebly. Why don't he die? Benjy thought, his knees feeling like water. He prodded the Jap on his side with his boot. The eyeball he could see seemed to pop from its socket, and a lusterless film covered it. There was sweat on the Jap's forehead, and he tried to remember what Rafe had told him about Japs who played dead. When they sweat they stink, Rafe said, and when they stink they're alive. He reached for the Jap's sword that caught spires from the tropic sun. It was attached to the Jap by a braided cord, and he stooped quickly. That moment the Jap hit him in the face with his elbow, and tried to turn over on his side to pin Benjy's arm beneath his body, but the sword was too far out of the sheath for his trick to work. Benjy was stunned by the blow. What had happened? He looked around. He found himself about ten feet from the Jap, with the sword in his hands. The Jap was struggling to upright himself from the miry earth, slipping, panting loudly. It was kill or be killed. Me or you. Gone were his seventeen weeks of basic, his Geneva Convention, his Marquis of Queensberry rules. He lifted the heavy sword and lunged forward. It did not seem to make any difference that he had never used a sword before. He was alone in a nightmare with this fat Jap, down and down and down, he and the Jap might have been on some other planet, or from some former era, kill or be killed; gone was the thin crust of civilization; it might have happened a million years ago (and maybe it was) and he was Alley-oop or one of King Arthur's knights or a special agent of the F.B.I., and the Japs weren't people, Rafe said, and he swung and swung until hot tears welled up in his eyes. Suddenly he felt more tired than he had ever felt in all his life, he felt like a scarecrow that had its skeleton removed. The sword fell.

When he opened his eyes he saw the clouds like white horses galloping for the horizon, the trees fronting the wood, coconut palms, their greenish fronds, and the high grass running to the border of the wood, fringed by round-headed clumps, variegated brown and orange. A large bird sounded its hollow trumpet into the wind and flapped over the sunlit treetops toward the knobby hills to Mount Topotchau. He leaned against a tree and wiped his hands on his shirt. His hands felt sticky. It was actually the end of summer, yet in the tropics one day was like another, the smell of the rotted and decayed woods filled his nostrils with putrefaction so he could hardly breathe. Suppose, he thought, suppose the Jap had escaped. He would tell Rafe that the Jap had jumped high, over his head perhaps, before he could fire, like buck fever with his piece jammed. Rafe would chew him out good. Then they would go back to demolish the cistern. Rafe would fix the charges and they would get back low and Rafe would use his battery, and the cistern would mushroom upward and the leaves and the earth and the geyser would settle, and they would go back to the Observation Post and contact the patrol, mopping up the Japs hiding in the mountains.

Rafe's shout snapped him back to reality.

"What the hell's going on there? Did you git him?"

Soon Rafe was bending over the Jap, swatting away the robber flies. "I knew he was a big un," he exulted. "He's even biggern I estimated he was. By the looks of his uniform he gived you a fight. You musta hit him a nice coupla times. You'll be a man yet, Benjy." He wiped the sword on the Jap's chest, yanked off the rope with the sheath, and placed both between his body and the webbed belt he wore. In the sheath there was a wallet of bills with two photographs, one a wedding picture, the other of two moon-faced children. Rafe tore out the pictures and gave Benjy the empty wallet and the Jap's automatic pistol. "Here," he said. "I wonder if he's got any gold teeth. A fat Jap likes sweets." He pried open the jaws and broke out with a crunching sound the gold-filled teeth with some gum meat still attached. "What's the matter?" Rafe yelled after Benjy as he started to run. "Benjy! Benjy!"

Benjy ran past the palms notched by lightning, past the fist-shaped rock. He ran to the mud creek in the hollow, and sat down, exhausted, in the cool, green shadow of the shrub that grew on the sloping bank. The creek spilled along like a melody vaguely remembered. Oh, no. Would he ever forget that malignant look of hate that flashed like fire from the Jap's eyes? It was hate, but not the hate of animals, not a basic animal emotion, like the sadness of cows back home, or the frustration of cats. All at once he was crying again, his head between his knees, and everything, the sky, the trees growing old, the insects, the jabbering parrots, the strange animals, and the swampy soil he sat on seemed, somehow, kneaded into oneness with himself.

THE RETURN

by EDWIN A. GROSS

THE TRAIN WAS PULLING INTO THE STATION. TED ("MULEY") Clark looked at his wrist watch, the tough little talisman that had been with him overseas at Palau and in the Philippines. It was 10:39 P.M.

He lifted his light canvas bag and awkwardly hopped down the steps. He was one of the few who had dismounted. He was home!

A chilling flush pervaded his cheeks. Peculiar, he had forgotten the buff-colored brick of the station, its layout, its runways. Too late to give him any help, the conductor waved.

Ted suddenly felt cumbersome—curiously large—in this familiar territory. Too experienced. He spotted the bright neon sign over the new hotel. Well, he guessed as a civilian he would be green enough—the color of that sign—about plenty. He smiled, grimaced, and went out the gate.

He didn't know exactly why he hadn't let the folks or Ann know that he was catching an earlier train. A desire to be perverse, perhaps, to upset civilian life a little. Or to punish himself. For nothing. He had these moods now.

The thriving, compact East Texas town seemed to have tidied up and rearranged its buildings for his inspection. Otherwise, why were they so little changed? There was the bank, the grain elevator, the mail-order store. You'd think in two and a half years—oh, well, no bombs had dropped here.

It was on this corner that the band had been playing when he'd left for the induction center more than three years ago. From here his mother had waved good-by to him on his only furlough in the States. His father had waved from the store.

The noise of the crickets suddenly flayed his ears. Somehow, even the moon at last seemed familiar again.

Since he wasn't expected home yet, he'd go for a walk. He still liked to walk. He turned southeast, deliberately making himself climb Snake Hill. The short, crooked street didn't seem so steep as he'd remembered it, but for him, at least, it was a hard pull.

Odd. He was a native to this town, and yet its ground had never lived with him with the same intensity as the terrain where he'd done his training and his fighting. In the Pacific, a hill had been a hill, a ravine a ravine, rain was rain, more than they'd ever been at home. Shadows had grown important because they offered not only shade but places to hide in, foliage provided conealment, defilade gave protection. In the Army he had been more of a creature of this earth. From now on he must remember that he was an animal deposited on the earth—in another sense, a man endowed with it—and try to understand his environment. If anybody from another planet were to query him about this one now, he'd be able to give a much-better-than-prewar account of himself.

From now on he'd understand more that was in the newspapers, too, and follow events of all kinds more closely. This wasn't just baloney. World affairs were real as a bullet to him now—even if he lacked training in "politics," he guessed you'd have to call it; international relations; and what not. He'd read more, converse more—especially here at home—if he stayed here. And he might. His determination had grown stronger and stronger lately. This was his town.

He knew where he was headed now. He was going toward the ball park.

Yes, from now on he'd be a fan of the newspapers and magazines. He understood better now what it was to be hungry, miserable, sunk in obscenity, skyhappy over trivialities, vomiting with no attention near, loathing your work but compelled to cling to it, critically shot, drunk just like that, drunk because you nearly had to be, too tired to be sympathetic, relaxed mid comradery. He was positive he knew better now how to hate—he wasn't thinking of "the enemy," either, but of fellows he'd met in the Army. He guessed maybe he had never hated the things he didn't like enough before the war.

The main cluster of gas stations was behind him now. He was passing Hank Jorgenson's Foul Ball Café. He could hear voices and a juke box, but he felt no impulse to look inside. He would drop around in a few days, though. He wondered if old Walker with the crossed eye still worked here. His mother had written him that the girls who used to serve you in shorts at the curb were long since gone.

O.K., then, he understood more now about the earth, about what was in the papers. What else had the Santa Claus of all soldiers, working overtime—three hundred and sixty-five days a year—brought him? Continued life, of course. And there had been many other presents. He'd been having flashes of intuitive realization lately—especially lying in the hospital when his mind wasn't turning on Ann—but he was damned inept at assembling them. Or did he just have an inferiority complex because he wasn't "intellectual"? Wasn't he the guy who was going to read more, converse more? Very well—he'd see how much he could list.

Of course, he'd brought back with him memories that were exciting like history—that really were some pretty important history—and more appreciation of the customs of home that he'd remembered as he'd strayed. Of course, he understood more now about the *reasons* for things—the reason rope, for instance, is twisted just so—he'd never given much thought to such matters when he was a civilian; the reason coaches and gym teachers harp on the need for strength, agility, and physical conditioning; the reason older folks are often religious. He knew better now why Pa and Grandma had listened to the radio so intently before the war. War meant to him about what it did to them, now, he guessed. He'd seen famous American cities on both coasts, the magic California-Arizona desert, two large oceans, a lot of small Pacific islands. He had learned not to take factors even so basic as land, air, and water for granted. He probably understood more now about what artists were trying to do.

And, of course, his GI Santa Claus had let him see his first snow on a maneuver. That first snow was a symbol of his growing up, of his becoming a soldier in the ranks of Man. Yes, that was it. Hereafter he would think of snow as his symbol. And maybe rope.

He had crossed the highway and was passing through the Negro section now. He wasn't afraid at this time of night the way he had been as a civilian youth. It was the uniform; he felt it was a mighty bond. He supposed it always would be, even just hanging in the closet. The colored people needed to be given a better chance. He thought of some of the discussions on the Negro problem he'd heard in the Army—and shook his head. Suddenly he remembered Hi-Hat, the pumpkin-headed truck driver from Alabama, and chuckled.

Yes, they were *his* memories, those men he'd met in the Army. He thought of Bill whom he'd always called whacky because he insisted he was a Californian even though he'd been born in Texas; of Ruzicka who enjoyed all the spit and polish; of Foreman, the loud mouth, the first EM in the platoon to get shot and who won the DSC—loud mouths weren't always braggarts; of Nevins, who brought his wife with him to every training camp and yet was notoriously unfaithful to her as soon as he arrived overseas.

The ball park loomed ahead in the darkness. There were more weeds around it than you'd expect at this time of year, even though the season was over. The Owls must have played a curtailed schedule. Oh, yes—Ann had written him so. He had forgotten.

He leaned against a ticket window to continue his thoughts. To rest. He remembered one particular blazing Pacific sunset. He thought of Nieman, the German-Jewish refugee who'd made a daring escape from prewar Austria over the Alps—dead now; of Stammers, the artistic First Sergeant; of Byrne, who bragged so glowingly of his criminal record; of Grigo, the ex-carnival man who "woiked on a Ferris wheel one year but never rode on heem." Yes, you learned about people in the Army!

Remembering Byrne made him recall how he used to eat his

heart out over ratings during training—imagine that! When the blood started to gush, ratings hadn't meant much. He thought of Elly Watson, his Sunday-school classmate, who'd been attached to his battalion briefly on Luzon and had become officious, hard, lean, and a captain. Would Elly ever be able to live happily around this county again? He doubted it, unless he became a big shot. Aw, but maybe he was just being jealous because he hadn't become an officer. In a way he'd been something of a flop from the start, he guessed. And now—with this new handicap—

How he hoped nothing had happened to all those guys who were still O.K. when he left them! But that was impossible. He would have to get his hands on a casualty list somehow, a country-wide one. He would pore over it state by state, letter by letter. But there was so much duplication in names, you could never be sure two names represented a soldier you knew.

Someday, maybe soon after the end of the Jap war, he would take an automobile trip and look up most of the men in his platoon. He recalled how one night, feeling thrilled by the various parts of the United States his squad was from, he had conceived that plan. That had been in basic training. Or was it on Hawaii? His Army memories were beginning to dim on him already. But how many of his ex-buddies would care about seeing him in civilian life? What would they have to talk about, except a rehash? Then, too, perhaps he'd have a wife with him. He couldn't imagine many of the men sitting at ease with him in a restaurant, with Ann, let's say, at his side, or entertaining them in their homes. Not that he was snobbish—oh, well, he'd just remembered, a cross-country trip was probably exed for a long time, anyway. He couldn't gallivant around like a kid any more—not with only one leg. He was, as Pa said in trying to dissuade him from stealing melons from the Carathers' patch many years ago, "a big boy now."

Gosh, he hoped no more of the men in Company B got hurt!

Why was it the individual was what his memories almost always boiled down to? Maybe this was natural. He had a favorite idea that it was up to all of us after this war to emphasize the importance of the individual, and to dignify him. To raise the standards of his self-respect, down deep in his private insides. Life was too complicated to place hope for mankind anywhere but right there. Another pet notion of his was that beauty and grace were mostly women's responsibilities. This thought had first occurred to him in combat when he'd seen native skirts hung out to dry. He'd recaptured the idea recently; he couldn't remember where. It was why he'd stopped feeling sore at Ann for not becoming a nurse, or something. All the same, he still had a tremendous respect for women in uniform.

The doors of the ball park were locked. No guards here to challenge him. He went around to the first-base side where the stands gave way to a high fence, and wiggled in through a narrow opening where a plank was conveniently missing. One childhood knack he hadn't lost.

The grass was surprisingly high in the outfield. It must have been longer ago than he thought that Ann had written him the league had closed down. It was in mid-June that she'd described a fire in the stands. She must have referred to the park at least five other times in her letters. Oh, well, he thought, grinning and climbing up into the stands, she should remember it, all right. The first place they'd ever necked was right out there behind third base, the year the spring circus had played the park. That had been when they were juniors, just before the circus went back to Blalock's lot. The ball park looked eerily, hauntingly the same, gloomy and wide in the vacant dark. It stimulated him still, much as it used to when he'd sneaked out here alone in the evening in years past.

Gee rod! He'd think it corny as "Give My Love to Nelly, Jack" if anyone told him so much feeling could be wrapped up in a ball park. But there was no denying that much of his background was tied up here.

He sat down behind the visiting team dugout, a little way up in the stands.

It was here as a kid he'd caught sight of his first hero, old Hank Jorgenson, the third baseman, who owned the café he'd just passed. And of Tony Moore with the buck teeth, who'd stayed up for three years with the Boston Braves. It was here he'd played end in his senior year in the game for the state football championship. The contest was held here to accommodate a large crowd. Of course, he'd played only half the game, sharing the position with Rod Reilly. He grinned a bit shamefacedly. He'd never told the guys in Company B about *sharing* the position. Well, anyway, he'd played on a varsity. That was more than some of those other GI liars had. It was here he'd led cheers at several county track meets. And here, when he was only ten, Pa had spoken from the back of a truck in the infield at an all-candidate political rally the time he was licked badly for county clerk.

Here, one April night when he was eleven, he met a tramp who'd boasted about sleeping in dugouts in lots of ball parks, and about original ways he had of mooching, and how proud he was to be on the bum. He'd written about that man in compositions in seventh and eighth grade and in English classes all the way throughout high school.

He really should be getting up and going home soon. How screwy it would seem to his folks to hear that he'd walked out here like this! He was glad he had come, though. He was beginning to feel more like himself. He guessed he had always been a loner till he got in the Army. And now he had one lone leg. "Ted's peculiar," he remembered his Aunt Jenny used to say. There was one person who'd died while he was away, whom he'd never have a chance to know better. Aunt Jenny.

Some of the guys fighting in the Pacific and in CBI would understand his coming out here, though.

He'd tell his folks he had gotten a lift. Maybe he'd tell Ann he had been out here. Only Ann.

He really should be going home now.

He still sat motionless.

It was in a lane near here that he'd had relations with his first girl, a hussy, little Ida from Longview. Even that seemed like before he was born now, though it was only four years.

Here, too, was where he must have decided, sitting by himself under the stars, to become a chemical engineer and to set the world on fire—only in an American way, of course, not like Hitler. But his grades had been disappointing in Mr. Edmund's class. With the draft menacing, he hadn't been able to make himself study hard enough to win a scholarship. Anyway, there had been Ann. After all, she was a preoccupation. Oh, well, any gold brick could make up excuses. Now he could go to school at government expense—the GI Bill said so. Or work in Pa's store. He'd decide—soon.

It was here that the town had held memorial services for Monk Robertson, the butcher's sailor son who had been killed at Pearl Harbor. That seemed ages ago. It was shortly before he went in. Good God! He wanted to shout. He was here again, and he had only lost one leg, and it was only three and a quarter years.

He felt queasy at the thought that men from Texas had been killed on the very first day of this war, even before he had been drafted. But then, men from our side had been killed even before America's war began, if you counted the Chinese, and he counted them, all right. He had been convinced of that much by orientation.

Gosh, he hoped no more guys in Company B had got hurt! He wished he could have stayed over there with them.

But he was glad he was out of all that—that horror, that noise, that quiet, that confusion, all those screaming orders. When no one, not even God, could know exactly what to do. But he wished he was still over there. And could come back later. Whole.

Well—he rose and turned to go away. He was crying. This was no self-sympathy, though. He felt pretty strong, considering.

As he limped down the steps, he thought again of Ann. Why shouldn't he marry Ann? Why not? His conscience was clear. He was a heap of man—let that be resolved, once and for all—even with one leg.

He passed through the field, wiggled through the fence, and began to move a little faster. He had always enjoyed walking fast at night—the night air, somehow, made you think you were really putting on the steam. Boy, remember those forced marches in basic! He smiled and continued walking at a rapid pace till he had crossed the highway. He felt much better now.

On the way home he chose the road back through one of the wealthier residential districts. He was glad when he reached it. The streets were broader, whiter, the trees and lamps were nicer.

This was *his* town. His children would walk these streets yet. Or at the very least, they would know their father had grown up here. And their grandfather. And that their mother had worked at her first job here—that is, their mother, if he could help it. For his thoughts of a moment or so ago had been the clincher. He would ask Ann to marry him. Right away. He had been hesitant about this in the hospital, but now he knew. He loved her—he was positive she'd say bother the leg—and he had decided.

He was passing the large red house of Mr. Cady, the oil man. It had always felt good, in the Army, to be from East Texas and to know of oil. Men from other regions had shown much curiosity about it. And he had gotten a great deal of lift out of describing the drilling of a well, or Kilgore, for instance, with its derricks taking over the main plots of town. The fact that oil excited them excited him. He wanted to work with it, he realized now. He had decided irrevocably during his years of training and fighting. Pa's kind, the merchant, was important, but trade wasn't for him. Oil was. It was his crop.

And before the month was out, if she still wanted to, he would marry Ann. He would go to school for a short time, then set to work.

Life would never be easy, but he had his liberty. This was what he had been fighting for. He had been fighting so armies—including his own—and governments—including his own—would let him alone, provided he was a good citizen and discharged his debts to society. Now, once again, he could have his own moods and plans, even if he couldn't run fast at night the way he'd used to when thrilled with ideas of his own possibilities. He could never feel so free in Germany, or even Russia. Maybe other people could, but not he. In the last analysis, he had been fighting so he could continue to be he. Unlike some of the others, he had known all along it was his fight.

He was almost on Main Street now. This was a thrill like—like walking down Pennsylvania Avenue in Washington, D. C.

He turned down Main Street, south of the Courthouse Square. As a kid he'd sold lemonade on its lawn, under the big elm. Across the street in front of the radio store was where Forrest Hubbard, the seventy-year-old ex-circus performer, used to show up from his farm every Saturday with his wizened wife to dance their jig and prove to the whole town that they were still alive and kicking. The Square, dimly lit and densely treed, looked lovely, for once as good-looking as it was on the picture postcards sold in Dyke's drugstore.

He crossed Main Street in front of the old bank. "Fury in the Pacific," an Army documentary, was playing at the Strand. He had seen that picture only recently and had realized acutely the war wasn't over yet, even if he was honorably discharged. Wherever an American serviceman fought, it was still his war. Say—it was when seeing that picture that he'd recaptured the thought about beauty and grace being women's responsibility. When he'd seen a fifteen-year-old girl, the kind that didn't wear make-up, there to see the other features, squirming in horror at it.

He was surprised, peering through the plate-glass window, not to recognize the night clerk at the desk in the Fannin Hotel.

He did recognize Vincent Carrillo, night watchman at the power plant, though. He felt self-conscious before Vince, limping a lot. Vince didn't seem to recognize him, though. Just nodded. Probably the old man hadn't thought of him in a long time.

A woman carrying a child crossed the street ahead of him. A little child I've never seen, he thought.

He turned right and walked past the Negro dentist's and the library. He cut catty-cornered across Sawyer's lawn. See! Gee! What do you know about that? He hadn't lost the habit of taking the short cut! The one that made Mr. Sawyer so mad! Suddenly he wanted to chuck his plastic leg over his shoulder and run. His heart was in his mouth, and no Army doctor could tell him it wasn't, either. He felt strong. He felt exultant. This was *his* block. These were his trees, the dogs and cats of his neighbors, his across-the-street sky line.

He turned down the walk in front of the house—how often—often—he'd seen it when he couldn't—and rapped the knocker.

His father, mother, and Ann were all waiting for him. He could see them through the door. They were all up and dressed. In another hour they would be leaving to meet the late train.

He felt fine. Purged. Manly.

The door opened, and he went in.

THE DELEGATE FROM EVERYWHERE

by JAMES ATLEE PHILLIPS

IT WAS A WARM SUMMER EVENING, AND THE MEN IN THE BEDS were stirring restlessly. They lay in strange attitudes down the length of the ward, wrapped in splints and immobilized in casts. Some of them had their limbs strung up in awkward positions. Others, ambulatory, went sliding along hesitantly with probing canes and lurching crutch steps. A group of card players sat in a pool of brightness at the far end of the ward. They held their cards with one hand or the other, according to their incapacities, and one player with both arms broken was calling out his choices to a squatting orderly. Those who were up wore maroon corduroy robes with "U. S. Army, M.D." on the pockets. A hum of conversation was over the whole place, broken by sporadic cursings from the knot of card players. The orthopedic ward of Carnavon General Hospital was one of several lighted arms jutting off the main building. The huge hospital sprawled out over the Texas plains, and its wards were precise rows of diminishing yellow rectangles under the pale stars. Inside the buildings was the maimed fruit of war, the lucky ones, caught in an eddy of the violence and washed back into the long rows of beds.

One of the card players glanced at his watch, and shouted down the hall, "Hey, Eddie, give us the business. It's time for Frederick to save the world."

An orderly came out of the ward office and switched on the radio amplifier. Listening heads turned on the beds, and the card players put down their hands and clumsily moved their chairs. Nearly every one of the wounded soldiers was smiling faintly, almost tenderly. The patients with canes and crutches sat down and waited. The unguent voice came smoothly and intimately out of the amplifier.

"*Ladies*," said the modulated voice of the announcer, "*now that peace is here can you afford not to have soft, smooth hands? Now that your man is back from the fighting fronts, isn't it more than ever necessary to retain the charm of lovely hands? Because it fits in so well with gracious living, enhances the real You, we ask that you try three liberal applications of Carruther's Eden Lotion, available in the generous dollar size. You'll see the difference mirrored in His Eyes. And now, Eden Lotion proudly presents that distinguished world traveler and news analyst . . . Mr. George Frederick Starling!*"

Mr. Starling was a tradition with the armed forces. All during the war, he had been a beacon of cheer to the troops. Night after night, beginning with Pearl Harbor, he had saved the world in fifteen minutes. Like a stout, sweating Cassandra, he had viewed with alarm and then reassured himself. His elephantine delivery had been short-waved all over the world, and the armies being decimated on beachheads and in jungles had taken a certain wry, masochistic pleasure in listening to his reports. Surrounded by their own dead, many times in complete defeat, the soldiery had sought some measure of comfort in hearing Frederick announce their complete triumph. What they had not been able to do with their own arms and valor had not been unbearable. Because they knew that at 10:15 Frederick would pull them out, bullfrogging his triumphant reversal of actuality into millions of American homes.

"*. . . And so we come to the final meeting*," said Starling's heavy and ponderous voice. "*We come to the meeting of all the nations, bent on making peace, at New York City next Wednesday. There, on August 6, 1946, the emissaries of the Allied Nations will hold a solemn caucus, one which will determine the fate of the world for generations to come. . . .*"

The heads of the wounded soldiers were inclined gravely as the voice poured down over them. They listened to the voice say that the danger of power politics could send the very next generation back to war, that Russia's insistence upon a Manchurian mandate and the collapse of de Gaulle's government might imperil the success of the peace conference. Mr. Starling slowed to a quivering vibrato as he wondered what effect the passing of Chinese control to the Yenan Government would have. What of British insistence on Hong Kong? Mr. Starling didn't know these things; he just sighed and wondered.

The broken back in Bed 83 blinked his eyes at the ceiling. "He's hot tonight," the boy with the cropped blond hair said. "Must really take it out of him."

The amputee sitting on the end of the bed scratched his chin and grimaced. "Don't worry about it," he answered. "He'll pull out of it. Got six minutes left."

Starling did pull out of it, but it was close. In the last minute and a half, he regrouped and threw the book at them. He shouted that everything would be all right, had to be all right. He was rumbling about it so strenuously that the men in the quiet hospital ward could imagine that he had to be led away from the microphone, still shouting out hope. When he was gone and the fluent announcer was back, deftly shilling for Eden Lotion and its undeniable place in the world of today, the men held their usual forum. They agreed that it had been a little too close for comfort, and then they drifted apart. They got in bed, those that were not already there, and the orderly switched off the string of overhead lights. Only a faint radiance from the latrine and the nurse's cubicle remained.

The breathing of the men was audible and measured. Once in a while its tempo would be changed as pain stabbed below the casts, or an unwary movement made someone gasp. The broken back, who was cased from chin to knees in hard plaster mold, moved his head slightly.

"I wonder what they will do?" he asked.

"What who will do?" It was the amputee in the next bed, the one with the broken clavicles.

"The characters at that conference next week."

"Oh." The amputee flexed carefully inside his shoulder brace. "Same old song. Make a hell of a lot of high-sounding statements and carve up what's left."

"You think so?"

"Certainly. Look at Poland. Greece."

The broken back bit his lips thoughtfully. "Jesus," he said softly, "that would be rough."

The amputee sat up. Carefully, he lighted two cigarettes, holding his forearms out from the brace. Then he slid his good foot onto the floor, and pivoted across to the next bed. He put one of the cigarettes in the broken back's mouth.

"Thanks," said the broken back.

"Rough," said the amputee, balancing between the two beds. "Of course it's rough." They sucked on the cigarettes and exhaled with a faint sibilance. A man three beds down raised up.

"Don't worry, fellows," he called. "Argentina will have a delegation there. Everything will be all right."

He said it in a flat, bitter voice, and lay down again. The whole ward fell silent. A nurse went tapping down the long hall outside, her footsteps urgent. Someone way down the line growled a curse, impersonal and full of pure vitriol. The moon was rising; it was a sheen flooding in over the white beds.

"Good enough for me," said the broken back suddenly. "If Argentina can have a delegate, I guess we can too."

His voice fell over the ward plainly, and there was a stir among the wounded men. Those who could not move their bodies thrust their heads around helplessly, like turtles. They came up, those who could, and off their beds. In the silver radiance the canes came tapping and the rubber-tipped crutches came faintly squealing down the long hallway. They moved in around the bed of the man encased in the cast. "Dammit!" said a fierce whisper, "somebody roll me down." It was the double femur fracture at the far end, and one of the cane cases went back to push his wheeled bed down the aisle.

"It's no good; it's nuts," said the amputee, staring downward.

"No, it's not." The broken back said it plainly. "We'll elect a delegate, and we'll finance him."

"They won't let him in," said the amputee. The crippled soldiers were still moving in around the bed.

"Yes, he'll get in."

"From where, from where?" asked the amputee. "This ain't no movie. You can't just buy a ticket and walk in. . . ."

"No tickets," said the broken back. "Our man will be the delegate from everywhere."

"Nuts." The amputee hopped back on the edge of his bed.

"Don't be such a dumb bastard," said the broken back sharply. He sounded impatient, as though he could see the whole thing clearly. "Sound off out there, with the name of the place where you got your lumps. All of you!"

It was a command, and the names came with a rush. They were the names out of dead headlines, the strange foreign names. They had been the proving grounds for a million graveyards. The wounded men blurted them out, whispered them, said them bitterly and softly. It was a roll call for the whole world, spurting from between tense lips into the moonlit hall, and the broken men who said them stiffened with memory.

"Our delegate will get in," whispered the man with the broken back.

They chose a Marine corporal, one who was just beginning to handle himself well on artificial legs. The amputee from the infantry cried out bitterly against the selection. He said that the Marines had enough press agents already, and you'd think the lunkheads died differently from other people, to read the newspapers. This temporary schism was healed by the broken back, who announced that the Marine was a former assistant professor in history and was qualified to speak for them. For three nights, groups of ambulatory patients made all the wards, spreading the word and collecting money. In the eye ward, they knelt beside the blinded and patiently explained. Everywhere interest in the project grew and the money showered down. By Saturday the man with the broken back had over $4,000 under his cast. The nursing staff watched and wondered, and the doctors noticed the flushed cheeks without comment. Whatever was happening, they thought, was beneficial. It showed on the charts.

On Saturday night there was a near-wholesale exodus from the orthopedic ward. A soft chorus of farewells went up from the immobilized patients as the committee escorted the delegate out the back door. Three ambulances were waiting, and their wheels spun across the graveled road. Contrary to all regulation, the gate guards did not accost the ambulances. They merely stood like ramrods, at salute, as the cars went out of the hospital grounds and down toward the town.

Senator Ballard awoke as the train slowed down and came to a halt. He had been in a light sleep, and he lay in his drawing room listening to the disjointed noises out in the station. He turned over and looked at the lighted platform, that was like a stage set out in the darkness of the night. He was an old man, and he looked more shriveled in his pajamas than he did in the wing collar and string tie. The grayish, curling hair was all awry on his wrinkled neck. The senator could feel his heart pounding, in his wrists and shoulders. Better take some of that damned medicine, he thought, and slowly heaved up and reached for his bag. As he swung the enclosed lavatory open, he thought idly that the senior senator from New Mexico was going to have that extra heart twitch some night and become defunct. Since he had few illusions, the old machine politician smiled grimly at what a shattering loss that would be to the nation, and gulped his pills.

He was back on the bed when he saw the crowd coming onto the station platform. They were almost outside his drawing room. Nearly fifty boys in maroon corduroy robes, and one tall one in a Marine uniform. The senator had been through many military hospitals, and he watched the group curiously. As he watched, the Marine walked slowly down the platform and out of sight. The maroon robes followed him. A few minutes later, the train jolted slightly and began to roll. The wounded soldiers on the platform flowed by him. They were waving.

Senator Ballard lay down again, but sleep would not come back. He rolled slightly with the motion of the train, and wondered about his problems. He had a great many of them, and they seemed almost insoluble. An hour went by, and he got up and put on his robe and slippers. The green Pullman curtains wavered as he went down between them and turned into the men's toilet. The Marine was sitting there. The senator nodded at the dark-eyed boy, and brushed back his long hair with one hand.

"Evenin'," he said.

"Good evening, sir."

The boy's musette bag was on the seat beside him. The senator noticed this as he sat down and lighted a cigar. For a while, the old man puffed at his cheroot with silent dignity. The Marine wore no service ribbons, and he sat stiffly.

"No berth?" asked the senator casually, from around the cigar.

"No sir. All full."

Pallor around the eyes, thought the senator. Still, no service ribbons. "Just released?"

"In a way," said the tall boy, hesitantly. "Have to report back."

"Shame," said Ballard in his rich voice. "Could be worse, though, I guess."

"Sure it could," answered the Marine, and grinned suddenly. "You're Senator Ballard, aren't you, sir?"

"Yes." The senator flicked the ash from his cigar with his little finger. He nodded amiably when the soldier asked if he was on his way to the New York Peace Conference.

"So am I," said the Marine, and the senator threw a startled glance at him, at the corporal's chevrons on his sleeve.

"Are you indeed?" he asked. The thought came that the Marine might be unbalanced, a shock case. "Were you wounded?"

"Lost my legs at Iwo Jima," said the boy, and Senator Ballard bit his cigar in two. He spat the stub out and began pushing the bell for the porter. When the porter came, the senator began barking instructions. The porter knew big-tip talk when he heard it. In two minutes the Marine was installed, with his baggage, in Senator Ballard's drawing room. As the porter closed the door, the stooped old man and the young soldier were talking earnestly.

The place was a hive of confusion, buzzing with strange tongues and hurrying people. The vortex of the clamor was around the reception desk, where a well-scrubbed young man in a frock coat presided. The young man looked up and smiled pleasantly as Senator Ballard approached. The smile lessened somewhat as his eye fell on the Marine corporal.

"Good evening, Senator," he said, shaking hands in the best rising-young-diplomat manner. "Your guest, sir?"

"No," said the senator. "A delegate."

"I beg your pardon?"

"Permissible," said Senator Ballard. "Done countless times with impunity. My friend is the delegate from Iwo Jima."

The career man was caught bending over his ornate list, colorful with its seals and names of many nations. His mouth was partly open, and its sag detracted from his natural charm. "We don't have," he began helplessly, "any—"

"That was before," said Senator Ballard. "Now you do. The delegate from Iwo Jima will be seated with me, in the American section."

The impeccable young man moved his head like a fish trying to throw a plug. "The seating arrangements—"

"Are rearranged," said the senator crisply. He and the Marine moved past the flag-draped table into the huge amphitheater. As they went down the aisle, the senator nodded greetings with a casual air. Back of them, the young diplomat wrote in, on his American list, a hurried notation. "Delegate, Marine, name not given, from Iwo Jima."

The huge auditorium was filling rapidly. The speaker's platform was backed by the flags of all the United Nations, and braid glittered on hundreds of different uniforms. A battery of microphones squatted on the speaker's table, and technicians were working around them. The place pulsed with noise. In the first row of the wide balcony, the working press hammered out tentative leads, and sporadic cheers broke out as important personages were escorted down the main aisle. Senator Ballard sat on the second row, and pointed out the famous faces to the Marine. They were all there, with their claques. The corporal gazed at them, and twisted in his seat. He was nervous.

"They're all old," he said slowly. "All old men."

Senator Ballard's leonine head turned toward him. "I know," he said, his rheumy eyes contracting and the sparse hair curling away from his neck like a duck's tail. "That's always been the danger. But somewhere, someday, in a meeting like this, we've got to face it. Maybe this is the time."

"I hope so, sir."

"I do too. All your people ready?"

"Yes, sir."

"Good, good." They sat there together, and the corporal was trembling slightly, now that the time was so near.

It took two hours to get the roll called. When that was done, Senator Ballard slipped down the aisle and stepped on the rostrum. He was fixed in a glare of popping flash bulbs as he bent down to speak to Lord Harley, the chairman. His Lordship smiled and then sobered; he shook his graying head impatiently. Senator Ballard spoke on, in his ear, with great heat. Harley shook his head again, and leaned over to speak to the Russian representative on his right. The stolid Russian looked at him for a second, then half smiled and shrugged his heavy shoulders. The newsreel cameras were grinding. Senator Ballard stepped back down, and Lord Harley faced the microphone.

"The chair," he said in a clipped and worried voice, "recognizes the delegate from Iwo Jima."

The great hall quickened with motion. Men leaned forward to stare, and the heads in the press row bobbed as their owners thumbed hurriedly through the sheets of accredited representatives. The Marine was on his feet, moving stiffly forward, Senator Ballard's arm took him, and then he was facing the assembly in his plain olive-drab uniform. The doorways became jammed, and the flash bulbs flared again. The packed assembly seemed to lean forward together. The delegations were whispering among themselves, the French arabesquing their hands to indicate deep mystery. Gradually, the tumult died down.

"We shall take very little of your time," said the corporal in the plain uniform, "because you are met here on a most urgent business." His voice was shaky, and not strong. A man came running wildly down the center aisle, and signaled the radio engineers to cut him off the air. They did.

"Every eye, in every nation, is fixed on this place tonight," said the Marine. His tone was clear now; it carried out over the small sea of uplifted faces. "Your problems are difficult, and through them all run the conflicting questions of world good and national self-interest. Those who fought the war are appreciative of these latter problems, but they are not so important as ours. We are the young, not limited by national banners, and you will write this just peace for us. We come as delegates from everywhere to insist on that. Here are the reasons why you will write this peace fairly. . . ."

In the stillness, the young speaker stepped back. There was a moment of wholesale flurry. Someone yelped "monstrous disturbance" and ten or fifteen men in uniform and diplomatic dress swarmed onto the platform. Lord Harley began calling crisply for order, but there was no order. In the shuffle below him, the Marine was knocked off balance and fell down. He lay with his legs sticking straight out. Senator Ballard began pulling him up, and the foreign delegations bent eagerly toward their interpreters.

The greatest commotion was at the top of the crowded aisles. Through the men clotted at the doors came a strange cavalcade. Down the six lanes to the well of the chamber came wheel chairs followed by limping men with canes and crutches. Back of them came men being led, men with eyes staring out sightlessly over the glittering assembly. Hitching and crawling, the maimed parade filed down and stood below the speaker's table, facing the representatives of the nations. Women carrying babies were among them. The queer parade halted, and the noise slowly subsided again. As it dwindled, the members of the press row stared at each other with amazement, and their fingers went ticking rapidly over the keys.

The Marine was back on his feet. He waited. The radio technicians held a hurried parley, and by vote switched the battery of mikes back onto the open air.

"We are the delegation from many places," said the corporal finally. His voice cracked out over the hall like a whip lashed in anger. "You are all important men, in a certain ratio, and yet your considerations are not to rank with ours. We come from places, not from nations. Many of us could not come; millions of us were detained."

The hall was very quiet.

"We are the singing rats of Tobruk, the leveled wastes of Stalingrad, the rubble of Coventry. Will you hear us? We are the voices of violence, the fountains of beachhead death that spurted at Tarawa. We have many names and many colors, many ways of kneeling down to God. But all our blood was red, and it hurt to lose it. Here is the remnant of one Ploesti plane. . . ."

The corporal leaned forward and touched the head of a child, held below him in a woman's arms. His reaching fingers disarrayed the child's silken hair, and it turned, chortling gleefully. It was a delightful and frivolous sound.

"I bring you greetings, gentlemen," said the intense voice, "from Kweilin and Warsaw and the moist jungle graveyards of Burma. The boys send their regards from St. Lo and Okinawa. I bear a message from Salerno and Cassino. It is a message forged in a fiery crucible. Only this. That all nations have a right to self-determination, and to live in comity if they so desire. Small nations retain their honor, and must be allowed to preserve it. We ask no guarantee of economic bliss for any nation or any man. Systems that are not valid have no right to survive, but let there be no more trading in human unhappiness. Back of all your little national flags, we stand as one army, without medals or insignia of rank. Make this peace free of small thought or we shall rewrite it with the violence you taught us. The trumpets are crumpled, gentlemen, and the drumheads are smashed. Our eyes are open, and watching. . . ."

In the great stillness, the corporal stepped back. His face was shining with sweat. He came off the platform and went slowly up the middle aisle. Back of him were the halt and lame, the sightless, the women with their children, and the wheel chairs.

In silence, the delegates watched them go, and the only sound was the whispering of the interpreters. The seated men began to stand up, and when the last of the wounded had passed out the door at the head of the aisle, the whole assembly was erect. There was no music playing, nothing to jump the pulse or inflame the spirit. All the representatives of the victorious nations simply stood up in homage as the crippled delegation went out.

Three days later, the Marine delegate walked into the orthopedic ward at Carnavon Hospital. He had come back without any notice, and had taken a taxi from the little red brick station. As the cab turned through the gates, the guard halted it, peered briefly inside, and stood back to salute. When the Marine walked into the lighted ward, all the patients came crowding around. They shook his hand and asked him about the conference. He grinned, threw his bag on the bed, and sat down. The stumps of his legs were chafed and aching, and he bit his lips as he raised them carefully.

"Do any good?" asked Bed 83, the broken back.

"Yeh, how 'bout them big shots?" put in the amputee.

The corporal scooted back against the head of the bed and sighed with relief. "Hell, I don't know," he answered. His thin face was serious and meditative. "I got in, said my piece, and left. You can't tell."

He lay there nodding to the constant stream of patients that were coming in from the other wards. They crowded around him, faces eager and alight. What did Churchill look like? How had he met Senator Ballard? Why had this joker knocked him down? The Marine said that was an accident, and they all said it was a swell speech, that they had heard part of it on the radio. He was talking about the speech, and how he got knocked down, when someone shouted that it was time for Frederick. They all quieted as the announcer glibly promoted Eden Lotion and introduced Mr. George Frederick Starling. ". . . *to make a free world, every nation must compromise*," said the booming voice. "*Whether England can or Russia will meet the requirements for a lasting peace is something not yet . . .*"

The unctuous voice flowed over them. Packed in the confines of the ward, they listened carefully. They were calculating the bombast, appraising the talk. Like men caged in an antiseptic prison, the wounded soldiers stood motionless and lay twisting gently in the warm summer night. They hoped the news would be good. They were waiting.

HOW BEAUTIFUL THE SUN ON THE MOUNTAINS

by RUDOLPH UMLAND

THIS IS A STORY THAT THE CITIZENS OF THE LITTLE TOWN OF Glovers, Colorado, will tell you if you are a stranger and appear at all interested. What's more, to prove that it's not spun out of the whole cloth, they'll show you the little yellow house on the edge of town where Abigail Stevens used to live, the garden patch in which she used to grow tomatoes, and even, perhaps, the roadside along which she used to herd her two cows. They'll show you these things and tell you the story, and then, if you still express any doubt, they'll take you to Clancey's store and show you George Clancey. If seeing George Clancey doesn't entirely convince you, the villagers will give you up and close their doors to you. For they'll figure—and perhaps rightly enough—that anybody who fails to perceive in George Clancey the marks of a man who has lived through just such an experience as they've been talking about must indeed be simple. George Clancey certainly wasn't born with that surprised, hurt look on his face, as if maybe at one time he had touched a hot iron and never forgotten about it.

George Clancey is an old man now. This story happened years ago. It started when Abigail Stevens developed a bust. Abigail had lived in Glovers all her life and a sudden change in her physical appearance when she was about forty years old was something that was bound to cause astonishment in her neighbors. Heavens! the town folk had seen Abigail day after day going about her business; they had seen her digging in her garden, tending her chickens and ducks, herding her two cows along the roadside, and coming to trade at the stores. She had always been a small wiry woman with a peaked face, a chest flat as that of an adolescent boy, and feet so long that you could easily run a wheelbarrow over her toes without so much as brushing her skirt with the handles. Nature had erred in not having provided her with all the feminine essentials and as a result she had never appealed much to men. Then in a single week she had blossomed forth with a bust that was a wonder to behold. Such a thing had been nothing short of miraculous in a woman of her age.

It had set the whole town talking. The men were awed by it. "Why, dammit," they exclaimed, "Abigail's gone and got herself the purtiest bosoms of any woman hereabouts!" The women were immediately suspicious. "Abigail's done something to herself," they said. "It ain't natural, not a thing of that sort." They shook their heads and discussed it among themselves in mortified whispers.

Abigail became a changed woman after she acquired the bust. Gone was her shyness, her awkwardness. She became a fluttery, coquettish, and giggly woman. She flaunted her bust—thrust it forth as if it were the prow of a ship. She was such a little mite of a person that it was questionable whether to speak of her as a woman with a bust or a bust with a woman. Sometimes it seemed when Abigail came tripping along the streets that she was being partly lifted, partly dragged along, by her bosoms. Men's eyes followed her in speculative wonder. They no longer found her lacking in appeal. There wasn't one of them who didn't feel an uplift in spirit after exchanging sallies with Abigail Stevens.

But it wasn't long before the secret of Abigail's bust became known. Abigail confided in her sister, who in turn confided in a member of the church aid society, and then everybody in Glovers knew. Abigail had been getting lonely, pathetic thing, the sister said, living all by herself and felt it wasn't right that she should have to suffer because of an oversight on the Creator's part. For years she had tried to develop a bust such as other women had, but massage, oils and female medicines had failed to do the trick. Finally she had read in a mail-order catalogue about Dr. Zwingle's Patented Pneumatic Breasts and had ordered a pair. The contrivances, held together by an elastic band, were made of rubber and could be inflated to whatever size was desired by means of a small hand pump. The first day that Abigail wore Dr. Zwingle's boon to blighted womankind, she inflated them only a little. The next day, she inflated them more. Since the bust in this still nebulous stage did not seem to attract attention, she threw caution to the winds. All her life, Abigail had been envious of the banker's wife who sported the largest bust in town. A week after Abigail had received the contrivances in the mail, she had a bust which surpassed that of the banker's wife. And such an achievement, of course, could not pass unnoticed.

The men in Glovers felt a bit disappointed when they heard that Abigail's charms were artificial. It was something they did not want to believe. A few were even skeptical, knowing what talk the gossipy tongues of women could get started. "I'll be gol-blasted!" sputtered Max Elton, the curio dealer. "I can't believe that little Abigail would set out to fool a fellow that way." But Bill Mannering, the druggist, was of a different opinion. "A woman will do anything to snare her a man," he said. Despite their knowledge of Abigail's secret, however, the men continued to display an interest in her even while they muttered, "The little fraud!" under their breath. And Abigail continued to flaunt her bust and exchange sallies with them.

A couple months later, when George Clancey came to Glovers to clerk in his uncle's store, talk about Abigail's bust had died down. None of it reached George's ears. George was a tall, gangling fellow of about forty-five; he was not handsome but he was a quiet, industrious, and most obliging fellow. He was not particularly an educated sort either; for instance, if you asked him the location of the State of Massachusetts, he could probably tell you it was in the United States somewhere but that would be about as specifically as he would be able to locate it for you. It is doubtful if he ever completed grammar school but a man's worth isn't measured in such terms in a Western town like Glovers. George was a good store clerk; he knew where the dry goods and groceries were in his uncle's store and he could always find the articles you wanted.

There was something else about George Clancey. He liked the mountains. Some of the highest peaks of the Rockies could be seen from Glovers. On Sundays George drove his flivver to the mountains and spent the day climbing the trails through the timber and among the rocks and enjoying the beauty of Nature. He was an agile climber but wasn't one who climbed merely for the sake of reaching the summit. In fact, it was seldom that he climbed above timberline. Usually, when he found a high point that afforded him an interesting view, he lay down, ate the sandwiches his aunt had prepared for him, smoked his pipe, and relaxed. Sometimes he would lie for hours in the same place and look down at the ravines and rocks below or watch the sun on the neighboring peaks. George was a lonely man. The sun on the mountaintops was the most beautiful thing he had ever known. It gave him a feeling of quiet satisfaction to gaze at this beauty. Perhaps it was because he found himself wanting to share this experience with someone that he came to fall in love with Abigail Stevens. Or perhaps it was because of Abigail's bust. Anyhow it happened and so swiftly did the affair progress that it had reached the hand-holding stage before the citizens of Glovers were aware of it.

George had become acquainted with Abigail when she came to trade at the store. Then one day he had delivered some groceries to a customer living in the country and was returning home in his flivver when he saw Abigail walking along the road. He had stopped and asked, "Do you want a ride, ma'am?" Abigail had accepted the invitation and climbed in beside him. George had always been a bit shy with womenfolk but somehow he found he wasn't that way with Abigail. As the flivver jounced along the road, he told Abigail all about the beaver meadows he had found on his trip to the mountains the Sunday before. He told her many things about the beavers themselves, their habits, how they lived, and how they built their dams. All the while he was talking, however, George's eyes kept straying to Abigail's bust. The odd thought had struck him that it was about time he was marrying. When he stopped the car before Abigail's house to let her out, he hadn't really wanted her to leave. There were so many other things he found himself wanting to talk to her about. When she got out of the car, he had gathered sufficient courage to say, "If you don't mind, ma'am, I'd like to see you again."

"Well, Mr. Clancey," Abigail giggled, "I've always been wanting a man to fix the rainspout on my house. It leaks dreadfully."

George fixed the rainspout for Abigail the following evening and also found there were other things, such as the rose trellis and the garden fence, that needed fixing for Abigail. Each fixing took a separate visit and with each visit George and Abigail became better acquainted. Pretty soon they were calling each other by their first names and thrilling at the accidental touch of hand or sleeve. George also found opportunity to tell Abigail about the beauty of the sun on the mountaintops.

"Abigail, you don't know how pretty the sun is on the mountaintops," George said. "You'll have to come with me on a Sunday and see."

But Abigail was hesitant about accepting this invitation. Abigail had been seeing the mountains all her life from a distance but she had never been real close to one. The thought of climbing a mountain frightened her.

One evening when George went to see Abigail he took along a quart of wine. George and Abigail sat on the porch of Abigail's little yellow house and watched the shadows of night descend over the distant peaks. George poured two tin cups full of wine from the bottle and passed one to Abigail. Abigail took a snort of the wine and felt its warmth steal through her.

George talked about the mountains. He told Abiel about the crazy woman who used to live in a cabin at the foot of Herman Mountain. Folks called her Kiote Mary because when her own baby died she took a litter of coyotes to nurse. She disappeared later and nobody ever knew what happened to her. He told Abigail about Kayser's Peak, eternally snow-clad, whose summit had been scaled once by professional climbers who used ropes and other equipment. He told her again how beautiful the sun was on the mountaintops.

"Abigail," he said, "I want to take you to the mountains and show you how beautiful the sun is on the mountaintops. Will you come?"

When George asked this question, Abigail had drunk her third tin cup of wine. She was willing to do anything. She wiped her mouth with the back of her hand. She was ready to go lion hunting with a buggy whip.

"I'll go mountain hunting with you, George," she said. "I'll climb Kayser's Peak with you. I want to see how beautiful the sun is on the mountaintops, George."

The rest of the week George and Abigail were happy as two lovebirds. The town folk were awakening to the affair about this time and some of the men tried to draw George out on the subject. Tom Jeffers, the barber, was cutting George's hair and remarked casually, "You know, George, the men in this town think you're a mighty lucky fellow. You're the first man Abigail Stevens ever gave the nod to. It's as though Abigail had waited all these years for you to come along."

"That so?" said George Clancey. "I wish you wouldn't use the clippers so far front, Tom."

Tom Jeffers did not continue the subject.

Another one who attempted to draw George out was Bill Mannering, the druggist. George stopped at the drug store to buy a tube of tooth paste. While wrapping the purchase, Bill Mannering said, "Abigail Stevens was in here this morning and bought a pair of sun glasses. She said she was going mountain climbing. This is the first time in all the years I've known Abigail ever to see her show any enthusiasm about getting near a mountain. She always used to be afraid of the mountains. Know anything about it, George?"

"A lady can always get over being afraid of mountains, I reckon," said George, picking up his purchase and leaving.

The Sunday that George took Abigail to the mountains was a beautiful late summer day. The summit of Kayser's Peak was veiled with a cloud. George felt in a talkative mood as the flivver climbed the road leading to the mountains. He pointed out features of the landscape and told Abigail interesting things about them. After a time George noticed that Abigail held her hands over her bust and looked a bit uneasy.

George laughed. "Oh, it's the altitude that's affecting you, Abigail," he explained. "It's nothing. You'll get used to it."

"Well, I declare," said Abigail. "I feel light as a wren, almost as if I could fly."

When they reached the end of the road at the foot of Kayser's Peak, George and Abigail got out of the flivver and George slung the straps of their lunch kit over his shoulders. Then, hand in hand, they started their climb through the fragrant evergreens which extended up the sides of the mountain. But soon Abigail was running ahead, looking at the lichen on the rocks, pointing here, pointing there, and asking question after question.

"George, what is this?"

"George, what is that?"

Or she was exclaiming, "Oh, George, look up there! Isn't that pretty!"

George plodded behind, laughing at Abigail's child-like eagerness, marveling at the way she flitted from rock to rock. Frequently he called, "Come back and walk with me, Abigail! You'll wear yourself out." But the higher they climbed, the more nimble did Abigail seem to become. George labored to keep her in sight. Several times he stopped to mop his brow and rest.

"Abigail, oh, Abigail!" he called. "Come back and rest a minute."

Abigail would turn and come tripping down the mountain to join him, but she was always fresh and impatient to be off again. On these occasions, George never failed to observe Abigail's bust which seemed even more voluminous than before. It was perhaps due to the exertion, he figured. After they had rested, he took her hand and they would start climbing again. But soon, on some pretext or other, Abigail would pull her hand away and go laughing and giggling up the mountain ahead of him, taking ever greater skips and leaps.

"Abigail, oh, Abigail, be careful!" George begged.

At noon they ate their lunch under some trees on the edge of a rocky precipice and watched the shadows of clouds go racing over the rugged terrain and the treetops below. They watched the sunlight too on the neighboring peaks. "Oh, it's beautiful, George!" exclaimed Abigail. "It's so beautiful!" George had brought along a bottle of wine and when they had emptied the bottle they both felt deliriously happy.

"Let's start climbing again!" cried Abigail, springing suddenly from the rock on which she had been seated and starting up the trail. George was on his feet in an instant and had her in his arms. The feel of her taut bosoms against him caused him to grow amorous. He lowered his face to hers and started kissing her.

"George Clancey!" Abigail gasped terrified, beating him with her hands. "Stop it, stop it, oh, stop it, George!"

But George Clancey was reluctant to stop. He was in a most exhilarated and reckless mood.

"It's all right, Abigail," he tried to assure her. "There isn't any hurt in kissing."

He lowered his face and started kissing her again; but she squirmed, kicked him on the shins, and was out of his grasp and away. She ran up the mountain trail, her hands over her bosoms which bobbed before her like two great pumpkins. She scampered up and over the rocks as George Clancey had never seen mortal scamper before. The lightest touch of her feet on the rocky trail propelled her through the air almost as if she were part bird.

"Abigail, please!" George called as he pursued her. "Abigail, please!"

But Abigail paid no heed to his entreaties. Perhaps she had read the desire in George Clancey's eyes when he held her and was a little frightened. Up and over the rocks she ran, laughing and giggling, sometimes turning to taunt him for his slowness.

George continued to follow behind, mopping the sweat from his forehead and cajoling. He felt uneasy. The higher they went up the mountain, the more uneasy he became. Every time he looked up at Abigail, he was amazed to notice a further increase in the size of her bosoms. When Abigail reached timberline and turned for an instant to throw a taunt back at him, he was horrified at the great size to which they had grown. They were larger than bushel baskets! George rubbed his eyes, thinking he was not seeing right.

"Abigail, we had better start down," he called.

But Abigail giggled and ran on. Above timberline, Kayser's Peak continued in a jumbled pile of rocks, some of them rising sheer for fifty feet, terminating finally in a gigantic elephant's back. Snow lay over the summit and extended down the crevices between the rocks. Altogether it was a grand and formidable sight. Abigail started to climb the sheerest of the rocks.

George stared incredulously.

It was unbelievable! She went up the side of the rock as nimbly as if she were being pulled by ropes. When she had nearly reached the top, George saw her clutch suddenly at the rock. She had reached a height exposed to the winds which continually lash the high peaks above timberline. Her enormous bosoms bellied skyward as she clung desperately to the rock.

"Abigail, hold on!" shouted George, excitedly stumbling up over the rocks.

But the winds pulled at her, wrestled with her, and soon won the bout. Abigail's hands slipped from the rock and she was carried away into the air.

"George! George!" came her plaintive cry.

"Abigail, OH, ABIGAIL," shrieked George dumbfounded.

George stood, powerless to aid her, and watched her lifted higher and higher into the air. Her bosoms grew ever larger until, when she was in the far distance, they seemed to envelop her entire body. George watched her until he could see her no longer.

Then he turned and started running down the mountain.

When he told his amazing story to the men of Glovers, they organized a searching party and scoured the mountains. But to this day no further word has been heard regarding Abigail Stevens. Bill Mannering's theory about the occurrence is still generally accepted as the most likely explanation.

"A simple matter of physics," Bill Mannering declared.

"Those patented pneumatic breasts Abigail wore were just like a couple of balloons. If you inflate a toy balloon and carry it up a mountain, you'll find it expanding more and more the higher you climb. It might even burst before you reach the top of the mountain. Why? Because the greater the altitude, the lighter the air. Abigail was such a little mite of a person that when her pneumatic breasts got large they buoyed her up so it was no effort at all for her to climb. And when she got above timberline she probably was so buoyant that she didn't have enough weight to hold her to earth when the winds struck her."

George Clancey never climbed mountains again after the experience. He couldn't bear the thought of poor Abigail floating around in the high altitudes above timberline. And he always somewhat held it against the men because they hadn't told him about Abigail's bust being artificial.

George Clancey grew into a morose old man.

EXCHANGE OF MEN

by JOSEPH CROSS

WHEN THE TRAIN PULLED SLOWLY OUT OF GRAND CENTRAL, Francis Baron took the miniature chessboard from his pocket and began to contemplate it. He did not set out the pieces, but simply studied the sixty-four black and white squares on which, you might say, he played not only chess but his whole life as well. Already as he watched the vacant board, invisible pieces moved and combined in his mind's eye, developing of themselves the studied complexities of his games. It was as he had once said, "When one passes a certain stage, one no longer moves the pieces, but simply watches them move." Francis Baron had passed that stage by the time he was twenty years old. What he was doing now, and expected to be doing until the train reached Boston, might be compared to the five-finger exercises which a great virtuoso performs faithfully every day. A discipline, a regimen, and more: he knew that from these simple diversions might come the inspiration that would save a game, the subtle but definite variation that had never appeared in books. It had happened so before, and the books had modified themselves agreeably: "The following brilliant line of play was employed for the first time in any tournament by the American master, Francis Baron. . . ."

Now, at the age of forty, on his way to the International Tournament, his appearance certainly suggested nothing so artistic and out of the way as a chess master. He was a small man, neatly and not distinctively dressed, and his only peculiarity was a rather oversize round head from which large eyes peered through silver-rimmed glasses. This anonymity of appearance, coupled with his magnificent play, had caused someone to nickname him "the mighty pawn," a title which, with that other more grandiose one of "master" he had retained since his early tournaments.

Conductors and people passing through the car glanced curiously at the little man who nursed in his lap the unoccupied chessboard as though it were a treasure or a secret sorrow; and a personable young man, who sat with a pretty girl across the aisle, leaned over and asked, "Would you care to have a game?"

Baron looked up in some annoyance. "Thank you, no," he said primly, and while he spoke he exchanged queens with his invisible opponent, and came out with the advantage of a pawn. That was one thing about being a master: you could not play with anybody you happened to meet. Even a master dropped games surprisingly often, and such a loss to an unknown opponent in a railroad car would be embarrassing, not to mention the detriment to one's reputation. Also, though Baron was a young man compared to most of the masters he would meet in tournament play, he already had a strong respect, which soon would become fear, for the rising generation. He himself must have looked like a naïve innocent when, at twenty-three, he defeated Orimund in the first of many games. Now he could not blame Orimund for behaving so ungraciously afterward.

Fearing he might have been rude, he said now, "I'm terribly busy, you see," and realized that it must have sounded ridiculous.

"Are you going to watch the tournament in Boston?" the young man asked.

Baron hesitated. "Yes," he said finally. "Yes, I expect to be there." Firmly his mind told him, rook takes rook, pawn takes rook, check . . . the ending would be simplicity itself.

"I guess it's really between Orimund, Savard, and Baron," said the young man. "No one else has much chance against those three."

The mate, Baron thought, would be accomplished with a very small force, because the white king was blocked in three directions by his own pawns.

"I admire Orimund very much," the young man continued. "He's the last of the old grand masters. He has the most intense attack I've ever seen. I rather hope he becomes champion again.

It would be a victory not only for himself but for his style of play as well."

"You don't much care for the modern way?" asked Baron.

"Too much subtlety, too much caution," said the young man. "Modern chess isn't playing, it's waiting."

"It wins."

"Look," the young man offered. "How about a game? I'll spot you whatever you like—a rook, even."

Baron smiled slowly. "I don't think that will be necessary."

"Well, I feel I should tell you; I'm Richard James, that is—I don't suppose you've heard of me. I won the intercollegiate championship last year."

So this was Richard James. Baron remembered a piece in the papers, not about the intercollegiate tournament, but about another, a small affair in Chicago, in which a young man named Richard James had lost rather badly to Max Tarnes but carried off the brilliancy prize all the same for a rather exciting combination against Jacob Goldman. He could see the familiar old pattern as it began to repeat itself. In a year, or two years, or three, he would be facing the brilliant young master, Richard James, across the tournament board, and everything would be at stake. But nothing need be given away at this moment. He began to set up the pieces.

"I'd still prefer to play even," he said.

"Now are you satisfied?" asked the pretty girl. "You've trapped the innocent bystander into a game. That's what's such fun about being married to Dick," she explained to Baron, "you meet such a lot of interesting people. But by a strange coincidence, they all play chess."

The young man laughed. "I want you to meet my wife, Sally, Mr.—?"

Baron looked at the board. "Springer, John Springer," he said, using the German name for knight. His use of a pseudonym, he told himself, was not in the least disreputable. After all, he had a standing which must be jealously guarded at every moment. Suppose there should be a slip, an accident, the distraction of being aboard a rattling train, the disturbingly informal conditions generally—he did not intend that such an accident should affect the reputation or the tournament play of Francis Baron during the next week.

But in trying, temporarily, at least, to conceal his identity, he must not, he knew, employ his own style of play, which to an expert would at once reveal both his name and his quality. He must accept, then, the disadvantage of meeting Richard James on the latter's own ground, which would probably be the ground of a violent attack, initiated as rapidly as possible. Ordinarily Baron would withdraw before such an attack and use his whole development for defense, for subtle probing and slow exploiting of weaknesses, occupying more and more space in the long wait for his opponent's critical mistake, which must come in time. Then, rapidly, the complexion of the match would change. From the reticence of his beginnings and his control of strategic area, Baron would open out the penetrating, incisive, and fatal counterattack. That was the way, the modern style, which had made Baron a master. But now he must fight by older and riskier methods.

Young James drew the white and opened with the Max Lange attack, quick and straight down the center of the board. It was evident that he was trying for immediate victory, and accepting a disadvantageous position if the attempt failed.

Baron countered along conventional lines, vigorously fighting for the center, for the points from which well-masked and defended powers could extend their grasp on positions within the enemy's lines. Both men were slightly nervous. There was a quality of chess, thought Baron, which made it absurd to say, "It's only a game." On the contrary, as you could judge from the way people played it, it was a warlike and representative struggle for mastery. It was a conspectus of life itself, with the illusion of power over life, which is why, though unthinking people laugh to hear of it, the chess master often dies worn out, overstrained from an incredible depth and complexity of concentration prolonged over a period of years.

As they entered the end game with an exchange of queens,

James was a pawn behind, but occupied better immediate attacking position.

"You play extremely well, sir," he said deferentially to Baron, who nodded and smiled. The position, he saw, was critical. If Richard James possessed perfect book knowledge, he had what amounted to a winning game. On the other hand, he was nervous, just about trembling with eagerness for success. If that nervousness could be exploited properly, or improperly, for that matter, but exploited somehow—Francis Baron regretted exceedingly having been drawn into the match. This young man would be present at the tournament, he would recognize his opponent of the railroad car, there would surely be some publicity. He could imagine Savard's wry, crooked grin; and not alone Savard. Baron was not so well liked among the masters; they resented his youth and perhaps his manner as well. There would be a good deal of laughter over this.

Abruptly he said, "I'm afraid I didn't tell you my real name." He smiled in apology, held out his hand. "I'm Francis Baron."

On the surface it was all right. It was even a compliment to the younger man. The master, by revealing his identity, seemed to be acknowledging a worthy opponent. And Richard James tried desperately to take the acknowledgement in that spirit. But there was now too much at stake. He was no longer playing a chess game. He was playing, with a chance to win, against Francis Baron himself. He blushed and stammered, "I hope you didn't think me rude—about Orimund, I mean. I had no idea—"

"Of course not." Francis Baron smiled. "Orimund plays his way, I play mine. It's your move, Mr. James."

Two moves later Richard James moved the pawn that cost him the game. His famous antagonist was gracious in triumph, quiet and assured as he complimented the younger man on playing a very strong game.

"We shall be seeing you in tournament play very soon, I fear," he said cordially when they parted in Back Bay Station.

"You're very kind to say so; we look forward to watching your games."

Both men knew what had happened. For Baron the victory was rather empty, achieved by a trick in a class with blowing smoke in your opponent's face throughout a game (this being the favorite strategem of one Russian master), or whistling, or tapping your fingers on the table. And worst of all, he did not know if he could have won that particular game without such a device.

As for Richard James, he said to his wife, "I don't know why he had to pick that moment to tell me who he was. I was doing all right until then, but Lord! to be up against Francis Baron! I just collapsed right there."

"And that," said Sally, "is just about what he wanted. Your Francis Baron may be a great master, but it strikes me he's just a little bit of a heel at the same time."

"Now, darling, he could have beaten me anyhow."

"Don't 'now darling' me. I don't know much about chess, and he may have been able to beat you hollow; but from what I saw of his face at the time, he didn't think so."

The players in the tournament, thought Baron, had all the solemnity and high seriousness of a conclave of cardinals met to elect a new Pope, and all the jealousy, to be sure, of a boy's ball team electing a captain. It was the first international tournament since before the war, and the meeting was marked by the absence of a few faces formerly well known: Estignan, who was dead; Zinuccio, who had turned Fascist and was in prison; Einrich, who was not allowed to leave his country. But the others he knew well enough: the English master, Cranley, looking in his rich tweeds like an aged schoolboy; Savard, the Frenchman, a dumpy little man who resembled a chef and played the most eccentric games of any master; Jasoff, from Russia, looking more than usually peaked and unhappy; and several other masters from all over the world. Second-rate, thought Baron. And yet, not really second-rate: so little distance, in chess, separated the master from the expert, the merely brilliant player. It was more than probable, he reflected with distaste, that he would lose games to more than one of them. But fortunately, in a chess tournament one was not eliminated for losing a game. Elimination occurred at definite stages, on the basis of point score: one for a win, one-half for a draw. After a complete round, the contestants with the lowest scores went out and the remainder began again.

And there was Orimund, at last. The aged master whose white hair stood out like a wiry halo over his head, who always wore a high white collar and shiny black suit. Orimund, nearing seventy, with his trembling hands, his gentle voice and perfect manners, and that mind whose keenness had probably suffered somewhat during the last years. They said he had spent time in a concentration camp, and looking at him now, Baron found it easy to believe this. He had not remembered the old man as so gentle, so meek. They met in the lobby of the hotel, and Orimund seemed to have forgotten his resentment of Baron. They called each other, conventionally, Master, and were for a moment almost friendly.

"Ech, life passes, Master Baron," the old man said. "You, too, are no longer exactly of the youngsters."

Was that the way of it? Did one creep gently out of life, shedding the old antagonisms, ridding oneself gradually of the vicious desire for success?

"I am glad to have the honor once again, Master," he replied.

"Perhaps for the last time," Orimund said. "You know, years ago, when I was asked 'How can you waste your life playing chess?' I was able to reply 'How can you waste your life writing books, or making money, or painting pictures, or whatever?' And it was a good, an acceptable answer. Now, I confess, I begin to wonder, what have I done? I was given my life, and what have I made of it?"

"You leave an immortal name," replied Baron gravely.

"An immortal name—better to have died ten years ago, much better. Perhaps you will understand that someday, Master." This last, Baron recognized, was said with the familiar cold, deadly anger that he remembered as an element in the former Orimund. But Baron understood what the old man meant: better to have died champion of the world, rather than face the failing of one's powers, the uprising of the young just when one is no longer able to oppose them with success. Better than the last cold years in which, if a master makes a mistake, he believes himself to be losing his mind.

That was the last time they spoke together except over the board. Almost angrily, Baron put down the pity he felt for the old genius. If that's the way it is, that's all, he told himself. When my time comes, I don't expect to weep on the conqueror's shoulder. That's what life is, and if we were the same age I would still be confident of winning. For that matter, if the position were reversed would he show any mercy to me? I doubt it.

The tournament was not easy. Few can go through the nervous strain of game after game against excellent players without feeling a sense of desperation, and Francis Baron was no exception. The competition grew progressively more severe, and in the last matches of the opening round one came up against players who, knowing already that they would be eliminated, played with violence and extravagance in the hope of taking home by way of consolation at least one victory over a possible world's champion. Baron was beaten in this way by Jasoff and Cranley, while Orimund dropped games to Savard and to Baron himself.

Baron, however, was superbly confident. In the first round he had beaten Savard, and his victory over Orimund was achieved, if not easily, at least with certainty and power from the opening move of a solid, invulnerable game. The old man played with a brilliance matching his former great tournament play, but finding his attack met at all points he overextended his defenses slightly and was unable to withstand the vicious counterattack when it finally came.

Richard and Sally were present at all his matches, and though Baron did not in any way acknowledge their interest, he felt intensely and uncomfortably that they had in some sense seen through what had occurred on the train, that it would give them pleasure if he lost, that they were in fact simply waiting for him to make a mistake. He smiled ironically to himself. There would be no mistakes, there must be none—perfection. And forthwith he proceeded roundly to trounce Dr. Anderson, his last opponent in the first round.

Orimund, Savard, Francis Baron, and an Irishman named Brian alone escaped elimination. In the second round Brian realized suddenly that he was very close to being world's champion, and simply collapsed, losing to everyone. Savard lost to Baron and Orimund, and these last drew their games and entered the final with a score of two and a half each for the round.

On the night before the last match, Baron was sitting in the hotel lobby, reading, when he was approached by the secretary of the local chess club.

"We have about ten people collected," this functionary said, "and we wondered if you'd care to give some sort of exhibition. We should be honored, greatly honored, Master, and I can say definitely that there will be no publicity. Of course, I realize that you may not feel inclined to make the effort on the eve of the final, but I was instructed to ask you all the same." He hesitated, looked apologetic, and seemed, as though realizing the enormity of his request, to be ready to retire without an answer; but Baron stopped him.

"Under the conditions you specify," he said, "I shouldn't object to the exercise. In fact, I'm grateful for the compliment of your interest. But understand, I'll hold you to strict silence on the subject. In the first place, it would be a reflection on my opponent if it got out that I was so careless of him as to play for fun on the night before our game. I can play tonight only if it is understood that the results don't matter, that it is simply a relaxation from the tournament."

"I quite understand," the secretary said. "This is the arrangement. The members will be told that a master, whose name will not be given, will play blindfolded against all ten of them simultaneously. The master will be in a room apart, and will not meet the other players either before or after the match. In that way the secret of your identity can be kept between the president and myself until after tomorrow night. And besides, the other players will be asked to keep silent about the whole event."

These terms proving to Baron's satisfaction, he was driven to the quarters of the Copley Chess Club, where he was placed in a small antechamber and left alone. Presently the secretary came in.

"It has been arranged," he said, "that you are to have white in the even-numbered games and black in the odd. Fair enough?"

"Fair enough," replied Francis Baron.

"Then the first move in all the odd-numbered games is pawn to king four," said the secretary.

"My reply is the same, and my opening move in the even-numbered games is pawn to queen four."

That was the way of it, he thought. In this blindfolded game one allowed the opponents to open up a little, and then when the weak sisters among them disclosed themselves, they must be whipped rapidly, allowing one to concentrate on the difficult games.

The amateurs did show themselves very soon. Games one, two, four, eight, and nine took less than fifteen moves for the establishment of overwhelming superiority on Baron's side. Few of the boards presented any great difficulty. There was the usual zealot who felt that the queen-side pawns could do everything necessary, one who thought that to *fianchetto* both bishops was to solve all his troubles, another who brought out his queen and proceeded to do damage to the extent of a rook and a pawn before falling into a cleverly prepared trap. Few of the games were in any way rewarding, except as an exercise in concentration for the master.

At last game number seven sorted itself out from the rest; there was something there. A Max Lange attack, with a curious variation in the placement of the queen's knight. Going over the position in his mind, Baron began to recognize the style. His opponent, he was almost certain, could be no one but Richard James. A few minutes later an astonishingly rapid attack confirmed his belief. Baron felt himself being pressed with some severity and marshaled his forces to defend. It would be a close game.

The other games expired in something over the fortieth move.

He had won them all, but then, the competition had been very nearly nothing. The seventh game, however, was close and even threatening. James was playing for a brilliant win and as things stood it was well within the possible for him to achieve it. And this time there was no way of breaking the boy's nerve; instead, Baron knew, his own nerve might go. It was so easy to make a mistake; he was holding precariously in his mind the crossing, tangling threads of thirty-two pieces moving altogether more then eighty times over sixty-four squares. The possibilities were infinite. If one forgot a move, or misplaced a move in memory, it was over: defeat. One defeat, of course, in ten blindfold games, is nothing; but to lose to young James! And he was certain that James knew his opponent; he felt an intellectual rapport that enabled him to picture the handsome young face as it bent over the board, and realized that James knew perfectly that he was playing—and winning—against Francis Baron.

And then it came. The secretary entered, said, "Game number seven. Pawn to bishop six."

"Is he certain of that?" Baron asked, incredulous.

"That is his move, sir."

"My reply—queen takes rook."

Francis Baron breathed easily. Richard James had made a mistake, a subtle mistake, to be sure, and not immediately apparent, but the master could now foresee the imminent collapse of his opponent's game. After the sacrifice of the queen, knight and two rooks would accomplish the rest. He called after the secretary, "I announce checkmate in six moves."

It went as he planned, now. On the fifth move he forced the white rook to occupy the square adjacent to the white king, thus blocking all escape squares and enabling the knight to mate at bishop seven. He returned to his hotel.

But he was troubled in his mind. A mistake like that, it was unnatural, considering how masterful James's play had been up until then. It was tantamount to deliberate surrender, it was . . . it was deliberate surrender! He saw it now. James had recognized his adversary, had realized that Baron, strained by the tournament, could be upset beyond measure by a defeat of any sort at this moment, and he had deliberately opened up his board so as to be defeated. It was a gesture of the most subtle and keen sportsmanship; it was, in a way, a moral revelation. After all, he reflected, when you consider that he probably dislikes me intensely, and realized that he had it in his power to hurt my game and refrained—that shows the greatest delicacy.

Francis Baron found it difficult to get to sleep. His own face kept appearing to him, saying, "I am Francis Baron, I am Francis Baron," over and over with the utmost pomposity imaginable. What was it for? he asked himself. For a game of chess. Chess is not, after all, life itself. Chess, if you regard it properly, is a game. A great game, true; but is it worth the demands it makes? Fancy a man like Orimund, now, decrepit, feeling bitterly the decline of his powers, yet playing with the most religious courtesy and chivalry.

He could imagine Orimund after the final match, returning alone to Europe. There would still be many admirers, would still be the satisfaction of a good game, not a great game, mind; but deeply, essentially, he would be an old man, nearing death, alone.

Orimund won the final game. Francis Baron would never forget how the reporters gathered around after the game, nor how the old man wept far more over his success than he would have wept over his defeat. And how Orimund called him "Master" and said good-by in the most touching and friendly way, his hand on the younger man's shoulder. "After me," he had said, "in a year, less perhaps, who knows?"

Between dejection and satisfaction, Francis Baron, runner-up for the world's chess championship, packed his bag and prepared to return to New York. The analysis of that final game, he knew, would give many people reason enough to laugh at him.

"Come in," he said in response to a knock.

Richard and Sally James stood at the door. He invited them in, and Richard said, "We just wanted you to know we saw what you did in that game." Sally nodded in agreement. "And we'd like to tell you we thought it was wonderful."

"Did? I didn't do anything—except lose, of course."

"You gave him the game. You did it purposely, and you did it so that no one who didn't know both your styles perfectly would ever realize."

Francis Baron smiled at them. "There's no need to shout it all over the place," he said. "Anyhow, I've got you to thank for my quixotic behavior. You taught me a great deal about games and other things last night."

"Last night?" James looked blank.

"Yes. At the Copley Club, you know, game number seven."

"I don't get it," Richard James said, "I've never been to the Copley Club in my life."

DESPERATE SCENERY

by WHIT BURNETT

THREE DAYS BEFORE HIS SIXTEENTH BIRTHDAY, CHRISTOpher Neilsen, the shoemaker's apprentice, said goodbye to his father and mother, his master, and to his native village of Ribe. His last recollection of the quiet little Danish town was the view of the old *kirche*. It was twelve o'clock, and the big bells boomed out the hour. In his childhood he had gone up into the belfry. He had looked down on the farms and the neat small houses below him, but he had seemed to notice hardly anything at all then, because he had been listening to the bellringer say that the belfry was big enough to drive a team of horses around in. . . . When the train carried him out of Ribe, on his way to Hamburg, all the simple green beauty of the countryside as it had lain before him that day appeared again. He was not sure whether or not he wanted to go to Hamburg.

When he arrived, at length, in the great German city, with its wide, clean squares and streets, its movement, the many people, the large shops, Christopher Neilsen forgot about Ribe. He thought Hamburg was a fine city, and that he would make his fortune and be somebody—maybe the best shoemaker in the town.

Christopher found work, and made shoes with high tops for fine ladies, and finally succeeded with his moustache. It was a pale blond moustache, as soft as the pale blue of his eyes. His work was interesting, precise and yet with room in it for the fancy. Every piece of leather was cut out just so. Every eyelet was made just so. When he had finished a shoe, he had finished something he could look at, holding it in his hand, admiringly. He liked, best of all, ladies' shoes. And in his best moments he achieved something special by his method of tooling the tops.

When he had completed a really fine pair of shoes, he felt the world was a good place to live in, and after supper he would stroll out along a tree-lined avenue, and perhaps later drop into a beer garden, listen to the cafe concert and drink a glass of lager.

One day, there came to the shop where Christopher was working, a girl, or a woman, he was not sure which, with blue eyes the color of the blue of certain china, and with brown hair and a pink and white complexion. She had, too, a certain bearing, a manner. And yet there was something sad about her. She liked the shoes he finally made. The two became acquainted. She thought him a promising young man. He thought she was a very understanding woman, and when he found out from her that she was ten years his senior, he said, "Well, what is that? Ten years. That makes a man sober. He needs maybe a woman who understands how a man feels."

Mrs. Sarah Schultz and Christopher Neilsen were married in 1875. Mrs. Schultz, the widow of a German sea captain, who had steamed out of Hamburg one day and had never come back, had a little money of her own. She lost her sadness. The ten years difference in their ages seemed nothing. But there was something lacking.

Mrs. Neilsen, who had seen her first husband come back from strange lands rich or nearly so, began to feel that her young husband was not making progress. There had been a war, it was true. Many young men had been killed off, men of her own country. Danes she never quite understood. But why didn't Chris become something? Do something? What was shoe-making?

She bought him a partnership in the shoe shop, but coincidentally the interest in Germany in finely made shoes with scrolls all over the uppers seemed to decline and people wanted cheaper shoes which were made, it didn't matter how, by dies, stamps, machines. Not so many people patronized the shoe shop.

They went back where they had spent their honeymoon, to Schleswig-Holstein, that middle country between the Danes and Germans, which had been shuttled back and forth between two owners for years. There, before they returned again to the shoe shop in Hamburg, they first began to quarrel, and their first baby was born.

"Serves me right," said Mrs. Neilsen, "for marrying a *verdamnte* Dane!"

The first child was a boy. They named him Adolphe. In another year a girl appeared and they named her Ida.

One day two young fellows dropped into the Hamburg shoe shop. Neither spoke good German. But they were lively, earnest young men, and they had a long talk with Chris. They were missionaries, Americans from Utah. They talked about their Church, and about Salt Lake, a city in a land of promise.

Chris, soling a shoe, the fancy instruments of his earlier industry lying dusty in a corner, listened with interest.

The next time the two dropped in they were a shade more direct, and asked him what he thought about going to America, where there was plenty of land, and a cooperative spirit, and people had a real chance in life.

Chris discussed the matter with Sarah. One noontime he brought the two Mormon fellows home to lunch. They were serious young fellows; they paid their own way in the mission field. They were clean, honest, bright-eyed. He liked their looks. And well, they said, it stood to reason. A young man, a fine capable woman like Mrs. Neilsen. . . .

"By Yod," said Christopher, "a new country is a new country!"

He listened to what the Mormon fellows told him. He questioned himself about God. He had never paid much attention to God. He connected God with the Catholic church, or with priests, or with church steeples. To associate God with a pioneer country, where a man could take up land, take up a homestead, as they called it, and live a free life, and raise his own crops, and not spend a whole fortune for a rattle-trap of an old stone house on some land already exhausted . . . that was something else again.

In spite of the missionaries' best advice to travel light, the couple, with their two children, packed up nearly everything they had. This included two cuckoo clocks, one cut-away black swallowtail coat, a silk hat, several fancy hightop ladies' shoes, a set of shoe-maker's tools, a new copy of the Book of Mormon, the *Doctrine and Covenants*, and the Pearl of Great Price, Mrs. Neilsen's hat with the plumes and the bird's nest above which, on a thin wire, hovered a delicately poised stuffed canary, Mr. Neilsen's collection of walking sticks, a pair of pearl-handled opera glasses, a stereopticon outfit with pictures of Venice, Vienna, Jerusalem, Shanghai and Berlin, and steamship and railroad tickets to New York and Salt Lake City.

Chris Neilsen fussed so much losing and finding the steamship tickets that they nearly missed the boat at Hamburg and in New York Sarah became so nervous her imprecations rolled out like a litany. Being older made her assume the full responsibility for everything. In the end, Christopher turned the tickets over to her, and took Adolphe and Ida on his lean lap, leaving her to manage things. She spoke a little more English than he did, at the time. But she never learned much more.

They rode across the continent in slow, jolting chair-cars, days of strange land, and piled off in Great Salt Lake City at the station, around which stood several lop-eared nags in front of spring wagons and rigs. They went to a hotel near the railroad, and Chris, relieved to find at last some folks who understood his language, looked up the Church authorities.

The cooperative spirit came into play at once. Converts from Germany were always arriving in Utah, and the Church had become efficient in settling them and getting them started.

A young man at the Church offices got them lodgings with some Germans who had been in Salt Lake four or five years, and soon afterwards a separate house was found for them. Chris and Sarah and the two children were inscribed on the rolls of one of the church divisions of the city called the Eighteenth Ward.

The churches, one in each Ward district, were small, plain buildings, filled with long benches facing a platform. The windows were frosted glass. None were stained, as in the churches of Hamburg. All the little "meeting houses" seemed strangely new, unhallowed.

"Dey don't grow good yet," Chris observed.

The Bishop of the Ward, a sturdy, smooth-shaven Welshman named Williams, took Chris around to the Zion's Cooperative Mercantile Institution, the Church's own organization, and pointed out the shoe department.

Chris picked up a shoe, skeptically.

"Humph! You call dat a shoe?" He fingered the crude, western, machine-made product.

"We ain't after looks, Brother Neilsen."

They assigned him a machine, where he cut out uppers. He did this for two years, and then, one day when the Spring air got him confused, he went home after lunch instead of going back to the shoe department of the Z.C.M.I., and said:

"Vell, vere is all diss landt undt stuff? Ve go take up a homesteadt. Ve raise our own vegetobles."

"Ya, if it ain't here bad enough already!"

Sarah's china-blue eyes hardened and her square jaw set in a straight, sharp line.

The decision to be a farmer came when most of the land bordering streams had already been taken up. Earlier arrivals and the sons and daughters of good members of the Church had followed Brigham Young's advice and bent their energies to irrigate their fields and till them well. The wall of eastern mountains piled up a barrier against expansion in that direction. Toward the west lay the desert. But in between, from north to south, a chain of cultivated valleys stretched like a string of beads, caught between the jagged purple mountains of the east, and emerald in contrast to the gray, alkaline, sagebrush land to the west, good enough, it was said, only for jack rabbits, Jack-Mormons, and Indians.

Chris and Sarah, with their four children, took the train south to Juab. There they bought a spring wagon.

It was summer.

Heat rolled off the desert in waves, and the red sandstone hills and ridges quivered in the light.

"By Yod," said Chris, "dot's desperate scenery!"

He squatted in the front of the wagon, the reins in his lean hands. Behind him Sarah, blowing the dust from her nose, and scolding the fretting children, rode grimly.

The wagon creaked dryly in the dust of the desert. The children sweated and quarreled. And the earth whined with the heat, dead and desolate, quivering false life from the bare horizon dancing naked in the waves of light, sterile and deceptive.

For hours and hours they rode, until the dawn seemed far back in another land.

Toward night, they reached a little group of lumber houses. In front of one stood three struggling trees, the only touch of green in the vast waste.

Bishop Pratt was in charge of the newly opened dry-farming section. He was an eager man, with a sorrel beard, earnest and honest, and with the best interests at heart of both his neighbors and his Church. He had kept the settlers together and did more than his share by way of example. He believed in the settlement, which they called Dover, and he had planted the trees, the only shade trees within a hundred and fifty miles.

When the Neilsens arrived, he told them to camp in his back yard, and he would look around and see what could be found to settle on.

"The rabbits've been uncommonly ornery this year," Bishop Pratt explained. "But everybody has his trials. They eat the grain, and they raise tarnation. We've shot thousands. We use their skins for blankets and coats. We've run out of ammunition though and things don't look any too prosperous for the community at the present time."

A sluggish river, which shriveled up when it was most needed, wound through red sandstone hills which were barren as marble, and sagebrush grew so thick along the level ground that it took weeks to clear a space for planting.

The settlers, occupying the huddled group of frame shacks,

their fields on the slopes some distance from the "town," helped construct a log shack for the Neilsens. Everybody helped. It was a cooperative little settlement. Everybody had children, some families a dozen. Many of the women were pregnant. As soon as the children could, they worked.

On Sundays, the men and womenfolk and the numerous children, all washed, assembled in a small building deserted on the other days of the week, and once a month, one of the women who baked the best and whitest bread brought a few loaves out in what the children at home called "bricks," and these small cubes were passed around. With bowed heads, the men, women and children partook of the body of the Christ, and a moment later washed down the bits of bread remaining in their mouths with a sip of water from the long blue enamel dipper which held the blood of the Saviour.

Bishop Pratt, who wished his community to thrive and prosper, preached behind his red beard with an earnestness which endeared him to his flock. Everyone knew each other, however, and everyone helped each other. There was little to preach about in the way of practical neighborliness. Accordingly he fell back upon the early doctrines, and frequently ended with the words of the Elders: " 'And I say unto you, be fruitful and multiply and replenish the earth, that you may have joy and rejoicing in your prosperity in the day of the Lord Jesus.' "

After he had seen his wife and four growing children established in Dover, and he had cleared enough land and planted the grain, Chris drove back to the weather-beaten Juab station. There entrusting the wagon to another Brother in the Church who was returning to Dover, he climbed onto the slow, smoky train which was bound for the green valleys of the North.

Every two or three months, with enough savings from the shoe factory to pay the railroad fare, and furnished with fresh provisions from the Z.C.M.I., he rode out of Salt Lake to Juab and thence across the bleak desert he drove the long way to Dover.

"Humph! Dese peoples!" Sarah greeted him. "Tithings! Lieber Gott, if we ain't got small enough money now!"

"Ya, vell . . ." said Chris, a little wearily.

But when he could, conveniently, he went over to see Bishop Pratt, and left a few dollars for the Church. He explained that he had very little money. It went without explaining. None of the settlers had very much money. They brought some necessities from Zion, exchanging occasional wheat; when there was any money left over they sent it to the Church Administration Office to help out foreign missionaries and needy families.

"Dey drive me nearly bugs!" Sarah added. "Undt besides—here diss Pratt comes every week undt says: 'Don't you tink it's time you let Brudder Chris go take annudder vife?' Humph! Dot feller!"

"Hmmmm," said Chris. "Dey got a goot opinion of me, huh?"

With him, on his last trip, Chris had brought what few household things had been left in Salt Lake. He hesitated, however, to tell Sarah that he had quit the shoe factory, hoping to settle down in Dover, with no more train trips back and forth, and to succeed, at last, as a farmer.

That winter he herded sheep to the west where the sunlight played upon the hills longer and steadier than in Dover, and where a little winter pasturage could be found.

When he left Dover for the hills, Ida, Adolphe, Almy and Jack scurried around on the hillsides behind the house, picking up brush to build a big pile. Ida and Adolphe, then ten and twelve years old, were the leaders. Almy and Jack stumbled about idly scuffing at the dry bushes and sagebrush roots with their red-top copper-toed shoes until Sarah Neilsen gave them a slap on the ears.

"If it don't cost enough, you have to kick the toes off, huh?"

Jack resented the slap, but Almy took whatever came without comment.

"Is that high enough, Ma?" asked Ida.

"Humph!" said Ma Neilsen. She had come to disapprove of nearly everything, and seldom expressed approval other than by monosyllabic grunts.

When night came, many hours after Chris and his sheep had left the little band of shacks and his outlying fields, and could no longer be seen from the settlement, Ma and her brood kept going in and out of the house and looking toward the west.

Cold, clear air chilled their hands and faces, and they returned to the warmth of the shack and the sagebrush fire in the monkey stove.

"Can I go out again, Ma?"

Ida ran out into the dark. This time she returned with the news.

"*I seen him, I seen him!*"

"Ya, go oudt den qvick. Raus! De whole caboodle!"

Amid shouts and yells from the three boys, Ida applied the match to the big pile of brush. On a hill top, lost in the western patch of darkness, a tiny signal blaze glowed like a yellow star.

"I seen him first all right that time," Ida said. She took up a blazing twig and touched it to other parts of the bonfire.

Ma Neilsen, watching the daughter whom she bossed like a tyrant, stood for a long time apart from her daughter and the three boys who had forgotten her in the excitement of the crackling fire. She felt queer and old.

"Pa's safe all right," Ida was saying. "Pa's safe all right. That's his fire."

The bonfire blazed with a fearful, glorious rage, shooting up sparks, and bathing the shack with red and yellow flares.

On the hilltop to the west, the signal fire seemed to burn suddenly a little brighter, quivering back its distant response to the family.

Mrs. Neilsen, unnoticed, went into the house, dabbling at her eyes.

While the children were outside yelling and jumping about, she sat down on the bedstead, which seemed suddenly to be crude and ugly. She felt lonesome in a deep and indescribable way. A cockroach crawled across the boards of the floor and lost himself in the shadows. She began to think of her first husband, and the times they'd had in Hamburg when he returned from a voyage. She thought of Chris out on the hillside miles away with his sheep, trying to keep warm by a bonfire and wrapped in blankets, sleeping on the ground.

"Ya, vot . . ."

She jumped up suddenly.

"Ida!"

"All right, Ma!"

"Yack! Almy! Adolphe!"

The children trooped in. They wanted to remain outdoors and poke at the fire embers and yell like Indians and play they were pioneers and shoot at each other with sticks.

"Bedt!"

The children undressed, sulkily but obediently.

Both fires died down to pink coals, and finally went out. In the Neilsens' shack it soon was quiet. The children slept all in one bed, Ma Neilsen in another. Her breathing stirred the silence of the two big rooms; she breathed with difficulty, being subject to hay fever, and in the cold weather she had attacks of asthma, which sometimes woke her up, causing her to cough and fight to catch her breath.

A coyote howled outside, so persistently and plaintively that Sarah woke up, but when she recognized the sound, she turned over and went back to sleep.

It was a cold, spacious night, and the few tiny shacks, lost amid the bleakness of the hills and the desert, were like isolated boulders in the dark.

With some impatience Bishop Pratt sat in the kitchen and waited for the return of Chris Neilsen from the range. He had meant to take the matter up with Brother and Sister Neilsen together. But in his earnestness, while sitting talking with Sarah in the afternoon, he had pointed out with sufficient clarity, he thought, since there were more women in the community than men, especially foreign young women, and that since Brother Chris had been in the Church reasonably long and seemed one of the men entitled to be called exceptional, it was violating the higher-orders to refrain from polygamy.

"We need more and more children, more and more Church

members, more and more people to build up the Church and Zion."

Chris walked into the house. His long neck was bent down with fatigue. He was greeted cordially by Bishop Pratt.

"I was just saying to Sister Neilsen—"

"Yah," broke in Sarah. "Anudder vife, again—he's here."

The sight of Chris, whom she could not have said whether she loved or not, threw her into a rage, directed against the bishop.

"Vell, now, Sarah—" Chris began.

"Maybe *you* vant anudder vife, den, huh?"

Chris was too tired to argue. He had walked since dawn. It was past noon. He sat down.

"Now, Sister Neilsen, let me—"

"Get oudt of my house! Get oudt! OUDT!"

The bishop took his hat and made for the door. Mrs. Neilson followed him, menacingly.

"OUDT!"

Without further discussion, Bishop Pratt left, bewildered.

"Undt not anudder vordt again diss *vife* business!" she yelled from the doorway.

She looked at Chris, who was still sitting, exhausted, on a kitchen chair. He had tried two or three times, by motions, to stop Sarah's outburst. Then he had given up. Sarah prepared him some food.

"Humph! Dot *Schlinkpuss!*"

In the Spring, when what was called the Dover road was sufficiently good to drive on, the Neilsens' spring wagon, loaded with furniture and children, creaked down the hillside, past the Bishop's house.

It was Sunday. Bishop Pratt came out to shake hands with Chris, whom he still called, by habit, "Brother Neilsen," although it was agreed that Chris had better dissociate himself from the Church if he had thought the matter over and was so decided.

He was curious what the family would find to do in Salt Lake, but he had asked once, and he refrained from questioning further.

"Oh, vot!" Chris had said, a little independently, he thought. "Dot comes. Ve see. Ve look aroundt."

The Bishop also shook hands with the children and extended his hand to Sarah, who touched it briefly and turned to tell Ida sharply to sit further back in the wagon if she didn't want to fall off.

"Good luck!"

The Bishop waved after them.

A number of the Scandinavian women stood stolidly at their doors, dressed in their Sunday waists, faded but clean from many washings. Some waved. Others simply looked after the creaking, diminishing rig.

Chris turned and looked back as the tinkle of the bell in the settlement meeting house announced the hour for Sunday services. . . .

That day Bishop Pratt preached a stronger sermon than usual, taking as his text "Apostasy," and calling upon the faithful to remember the trials and tribulations of the first pioneers, who forty years before had encountered Indians, mountain fever, death and despair.

"*And yet we have held together,*" he said. His reddish beard thrust forward, rose and fell like an ensign of his faith. "*No Devil's amount of hell and orneriness kin bust us. Stick to the Lord Jesus, and plough yer fields. Live like a man, and not no cussed weasel.*

"*When the Great Brigham, after takin' up the burden of leadership after our beloved Joseph Smith, prophet, seer and revelator, had been murdered in Illinois—when the Great Leader Brigham come through these snow-capped mountains to the East of Salt Lake Valley, and rose up from a cot in one of the brother's waggins, nearly dead of mountain fever, he was enwrapped in a vision, when he gazed down upon the Promised Land, the New Canaan, the Valley of Zion.*

"*The Spirit of Light rested upon him, and hovered over Dese-*

ret. 'This is the right place.' And thar the Saints settled. And starved. And fought locusts. And lived. And prospered.

"And I say unto you if you think here in Dover you got troubles, you ain't had troubles with either rabbits or coyotes or drought or flood like the troubles of the early elders of the Church. And yet they endured. And we're goin' to edure. And any backslidin' may not be punished in this world here below, but I say unto you that the weak, the undecided, the Jack Mormons, they shall be hot pressed in the Lord's garden, and they shall be lost in aimlessness and idleness and lust and sin, and the might of the righteous shall be as rock against the sea. Let us pray, brothers and sisters.

"Oh, Lord. . . ."

The tinkle of the bell was lost in the distance of the west. The wagon wheels creaked in the new road-bed, a strident singing in the sand, as the reluctant Dane and his family jolted, hour by hour, across the desert eastward to the railroad.

BIOGRAPHICAL NOTES

Evelyn Gustafsson, a native American of Swedish parentage, writes short stories as time out from her work as a designer. She did sets for *The Wizard of Oz*, which played at the City Center Theater, in New York City, and is a designer with the Suzari Marionette Studio.

Liam O'Flaherty, author of *The Informer*, *The Puritan*, *Famine*, *Land* and numerous other novels and short stories laid in Ireland or the Aran Isles where he was born, studied for the priesthood but joined the Irish Guards during the first World War and later was active in the Irish Revolution. He wrote his first short stories while working in a tire factory in Connecticut.

Tennessee Williams was born in Mississippi in 1914. He is the author of *A Street Car Named Desire*, *The Glass Menagerie*, and other distinguished plays. His first short story appeared in *Story* and the one in this volume is quite representative of the mood out of which some of his plays have grown.

Mel Dinelli was born in Albuquerque, New Mexico, in 1912 and sold his first one-act play while a student at the University of Washington. He has done considerable work in radio and as a screen writer in Hollywood.

A. E. Shandeling is the by-line of a young woman writer at present living in San Francisco. She was born in California and *Return of the Griffins* was her first published story.

Dorothy McCleary, whose first stories appeared in *Story*, won a Doubleday Doran-Story Magazine novel contest in the thirties. Since then she has written other novels and one book on creative writing. She lives with her husband in New York.

Norman K. Mailer was born in Long Branch, New Jersey, January 31, 1923. He won first prize in *Story's* eighth nationwide contest conducted among the colleges of the United States when he was a student at Harvard. He wants it understood that this story was printed in 1941 when he was eighteen. He was one of *Story's* youngest contributors. Author of *The Naked and the Dead.*

Stanley Kauffmann is a native New Yorker. His two novels, *The King of Proxy Street* and *This Time Forever,* were published both here and in England. He has worked for the theater and radio.

Hallie Southgate Burnett, co-editor of *Story* since 1942 and wife of Whit Burnett, won an O. Henry prize in 1941 with her first published story, *Eighteenth Summer,* published that year in *Story.* She has appeared in other magazines and is editor, with Eleanor Gilchrist, of the recent anthology, *Welcome to Life,* dedicated to her three children.

Rearden Connor was born in Dublin in 1907. Since 1924 he has lived in London. He is the author of a Literary Guild selection, *Shake Hands With the Devil.* He was an expert on jet aircraft with the Ministry of Supply, Aircraft Division, during the second World War.

Leo Dillon Murtagh is a native of Ballinalack, Ireland. For many years he has lived in New York where he has been a correspondent for Irish newspapers.

J. D. Salinger, a native New Yorker just entering his thirties, was discovered in 1940 by *Story* and has been doing considerable writing since his return from Europe where he was in the Battle of the Bulge and other campaigns. He studied short story writing in Whit Burnett's class at Columbia University and it was during this period that his first story was published.

Ruth Domino is an Austrian born in 1908, who lived for a time in Spain and came to New York seven or eight years ago.

Ferenc Molnar is the famous Hungarian playwright now resident in the United States.

Helen McCune, at one time a waitress and at others a stenographer, writes for the fun of it and says it is no fun.

Erskine Caldwell has appeared off and on in *Story* since shortly after its founding in 1931. He is world-famous for his stories and novels of the South. He has been living for several years in the Far West.

Joan Vatsek is a Hungarian-American discovery of *Story* who lives with her husband at Amenia, New York.

Truman Capote was born in New Orleans in 1924. His first appearance as a story writer was in *Story*. Since then he has appeared in many magazines and is the author of two books published by Random House.

Ivan Bunin, whose little pre-Soviet love story was first translated and printed in *Story* in 1948, is a Nobel Prize winner and the author of several novels and the famous long short story, *The Gentleman From San Francisco.*

William Faulkner has frequently appeared in *Story*. He was born in Mississippi in 1897, served with the Canadian and British Air Forces in the first World War, and is one of the finest novelists of our generation.

Freda Thompson is a native of New Jersey. *Blue Bird* was her first published story although she says she began writing stories at the age of seven. She is married and runs her own bookstore in New York City.

Alice Farnham is a native of Philadelphia, and once edited two small Pennsylvania weeklies. She has been spending some time in the British West Indies.

Richard Coleman, whose story in *Story*, *Fight For Sister Joe*, served as the basis of the boxing nun sequences in the film *The Bells of St. Mary's*, is the author of the novel *Don't You Weep, Don't You Moan* and many articles and short stories. He was born in Washington, D. C., in 1907 but has lived in Charleston, South Carolina, for nearly twenty years.

Wallace Graves is twenty-seven. He was born and raised in Seattle. He served in the Navy in the Philippines, Japan and Alaska.

Mina Lewiton, wife of Howard Simon, book illustrator, has worked in book publishing and she says she once had a brief engagement as a Spanish dancer. She is the mother of a daughter, now eleven.

William March was for many years vice-president of a steamship company. His first story appeared in *Story* many years ago. He was born in Mobile, Alabama, studied law at the University of Alabama, and was in the Marine Corps during the first World War. His stories have been published in a collected edition.

Arthur Foff was born in San Francisco. He is a graduate of the University of California and a Phi Beta Kappa. During the war he was with the OWI. He is married and is the author of a first novel published by The Story Press, *Glorious in Another Day*, which grew out of the story *Sawdust*.

Morley Callaghan is the outstanding short story writer of Canada. He has done several books of fiction.

John Modesto lives in West Reading, Pennsylvania. His first published story was *Patches on My Pants*.

Felicia Gizycka, American-Polish fiction writer, was born in 1905 in an Austrian village. She comes from five generations of newspaper people. She has one daughter, and has been married twice, once to Drew Pearson.

Frederic Prokosch was born in Madison, Wisconsin, in 1908, the son of a teacher of German and philology at Yale and a mother who was a concert pianist who once played for the Emperor Franz Josef. He was educated in Austria, Germany, France and England.

Jesse Stuart, an early discovery of *Story*, is the author of a couple of books of poetry and several novels. He lives in his native Kentucky with his wife and daughter, farming and writing. He was in the Navy during the war.

J. William Archibald has written verses for ballets for Weidman and has taught at Temple University. He has appeared as a dancer and singer in several Broadway shows. He was born in 1918 on the island of Trinidad, B.W.I., of Scottish, German, French, Spanish and Irish descent.

Guido D'Agostino, who was with the OWI in Sicily and is now a dairy farmer in northern Pennsylvania, is a *Story* discovery. He has written three novels and is working on his fourth.

Fred E. Ross, a native of South Carolina of Scottish descent, pitched semi-pro baseball for several years in his home state, and later worked as a clerk for the South Carolina Aluminum Company. *The Unbowed Head* was his first published story from which he made a novel which won him the Houghton Mifflin award of 1949.

Mary Norton is a young English writer whose first appearance was in *Story*.

Langston Hughes has written several books of poetry, one book of short stories and an autobiography. One of his main interests, he says, is the encouragement of literary ability among colored people.

John B. L. Goodwin is a California artist and has exhibited with surrealist groups in New York. He is thirty-four.

Alma Denny is the wife of a heart specialist and lives in New York. *Schmule Saves the Schule* was her first published full-length story.

Fred Urquhart, born in Edinburgh, Scotland, in July 1912, has published three or four novels in England and one collection of short stories. His first appearance in America was in *Story*.

William Fifield, descendant of a family of Congregational ministers, won an O. Henry Memorial Prize award with one of his first published stories in *Story*. He graduated from college *magna cum laude* and has done a great deal of radio work.

John Langdon was born in 1913, is married and lives in San Francisco. He has been a professional actor, side-show barker, houseman, tunnel stiff, C.C.C. boy, and an electrician on a boat.

Donald Vining was born in Pennsylvania in 1917. He studied at the Yale 47 Work Shop and has worked in motion-picture companies as a reader.

Robert Payne was born in 1911. He is the author of several books of poetry and an editor of an anthology of Chinese poetry. He has written several books with Chinese backgrounds. He was born in Cornwall of French-English parentage and for a time was professor of English Literature at Lienta University, Kunming.

John Hewlett was born in Conyers, Georgia, in 1905. He has been a newspaperman, prospector and explorer. He lives in New York and is working on his fifth novel and eighth book, a novel about Hoboken. One of his novels, *Cross on the Moon,* has been translated into six languages; *Wild Grape* into four; and *Thunder Beats the Drum* into three.

Jerome Selman, a veteran of the Battle of the Bulge, was for many months hospitalized at Halloran Hospital, and while there was in charge of a writers' group for patients. He is a graduate of Cooper Union and a chemical engineer. He was machine-gunned in Luxemburg.

Edwin A. Gross's story, *The Return*, appeared in the servicemen's issue of *Story* when he was a sergeant with a combat engineering outfit stationed in the Pacific. As a civilian, he has worked for radio, stage, newspapers and magazines, and is a graduate of the Yale School of Drama.

James Atlee Phillips was born in 1915. He attended Texas University and the University of Missouri and served as operations manager of Hicks Field and later was operational representative in India and China for Consolidated Vultee Aircraft Corporation. He was also in the Marine Corps and on the staff of *The Leatherneck* in Washington.

Rudolph Umland was born on a farm in Nebraska in 1907, attended the University of Nebraska, is married, has two children and lives in New Orleans.

Joseph Cross is the pseudonym of two writers—Howard Nemerov and W. R. Johnson. Nemerov, whose first novel appeared in 1949, was born in New York and educated at Harvard. He was a bomber and fighter pilot with the RCAF. Johnson was born in Colorado and educated at Yale. He served with the Second Infantry Division in Europe during the war.

Whit Burnett, editor of *Story*, was born in Salt Lake City, Utah, in 1899, and was active in newspaper work in San Francisco and New York until 1927 and until 1931 in Europe when *Story* was founded in Vienna. He is the author of one book of short stories, *The Maker of Signs*, a book of literary essays, a short novel about Robert Burns, and editor of about a dozen anthologies including *This Is My Best* and the forthcoming *The World's Best.*